Bolitho

1787

Captain 'TEMPEST' [36]. *Great South Sea. Tahiti. Suffered serious fever (see 'Passage to Mutiny')*

1792

Captain, the Nore. Recruiting

1793

Captain 'HYPERION' [74]. *Mediterranean. Bay of Biscay. West Indies (see 'Form Line of Battle!' and 'Enemy in Sight!')*

1795

Promoted Flag Captain 'EURYALUS' [100]. *Involved in the Great Mutiny. Mediterranean. Promoted Commodore (see 'The Flag Captain')*

1798

Battle of the Nile (see 'Signal-Close Action!')

1800

Promoted Rear Admiral. Battle of Copenhagen. Baltic

1802

Promoted Vice Admiral. West Indies

1805

Battle of Trafalgar

1812

Promoted Admiral. Second American War

1815

Killed in action

Captain Richard Bolitho, RN

Richard Bolitho novels by Alexander Kent

in chronological order

1772 RICHARD BOLITHO – MIDSHIPMAN
1773 MIDSHIPMAN BOLITHO AND THE 'AVENGER'
1777 IN GALLANT COMPANY
1778 SLOOP OF WAR
1782 TO GLORY WE STEER
1784 COMMAND A KING'S SHIP
1789 PASSAGE TO MUTINY
1793 FORM LINE OF BATTLE!
1794 ENEMY IN SIGHT!
1795 THE FLAG CAPTAIN
1798 SIGNAL–CLOSE ACTION!

Alexander Kent

CAPTAIN RICHARD BOLITHO, RN

Three complete and unabridged novels

1778 Sloop of War

1782 To Glory We Steer

1784 Command a King's Ship

Hutchinson of London

Hutchinson & Co. (Publishers) Ltd
3 Fitzroy Square, London W1P 6JD

London Melbourne Sydney Auckland
Wellington Johannesburg and agencies
throughout the world

Sloop of War
First published 1972

To Glory We Steer
First published 1968

Command a King's Ship
First published 1973

This edition first published 1978

Set in Linotype Juliana

Printed in Great Britain by
Cox & Wyman Ltd,
London, Reading and Fakenham

ISBN 0 09 134130 2

Contents

Author's Introduction
vii

Sloop of War
1

To Glory We Steer
227

Command a King's Ship.
459

Author's Introduction

It is a particular pleasure for me to have these three Richard Bolitho stories brought together into one volume. They span only six years in Bolitho's life, but those years were the ones in which he learnt what it meant to carry the responsibilities of command – of command of ships of war at sea for months, and sometimes years, on end with little or no direction from any superior authority. These were times when an ally could become an enemy almost overnight and when the total weight of decisions that might precipitate a major conflict – or even a war – could rest on the shoulders of a young naval captain.

Today it is extraordinary to think of this: to realise that a naval officer in his early twenties would be in command of a thirty-two gun frigate, far from the main fleet, and responsible for a ship's company of about 200 men, many of whom would be seasoned veterans old enough to be his father.

This volume contains the first Bolitho story which was published in 1968. However, this is not the first in the chronological sequence of Bolitho's career. When I conceived Bolitho I felt that the stories would remain fresher – and possibly present a greater challenge to me – if they were written out of order. In this way I hoped to vary the plots and, equally importantly, the backgrounds to the stories; there are now twelve published books dealing with Bolitho's life from 1772, when he was a midshipman on the *Gorgon*, to 1798, when he was promoted commodore.

One of the books in this omnibus is, as I have said, the first Bolitho story to be published: *To Glory We Steer*. The others are *Sloop of War* and *Command a King's Ship*, and the three stories are now chronologically arranged. *Sloop of War* opens in 1778, the year in which Bolitho takes command of the *Sparrow*, a small, fast and well-armed sloop, and has as its climax the Battle of the Chesapeake off the eastern seaboard of North America. *To Glory We Steer* is set during the last years of the American War of Independence, when as a junior captain Bolitho is ordered to take his frigate *Phalarope* to the Caribbean. *Command a King's Ship* again has him in command of a frigate, the *Undine*, but in this book the main setting is the East Indies – at that time a little known area where there is no set line of battle or declared cause to rally a ship's company.

Together the three novels cover the years from 1778, the date of his first independent command, to 1784 – the years in which the young Bolitho is tested to the full and during which he is moulded to achieve the senior ranks of flag captain, squadron commodore, and rear admiral in other stories.

August 1978

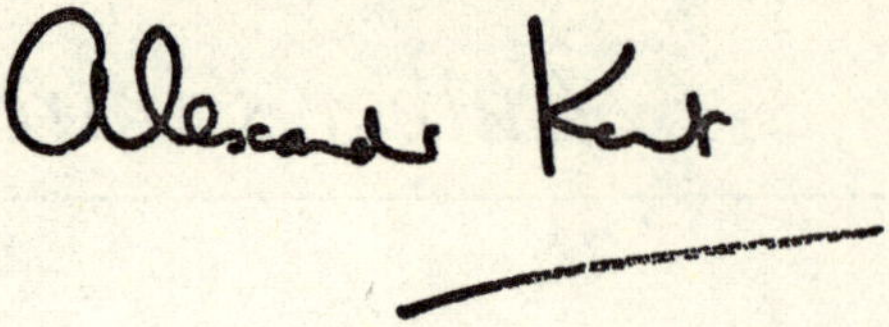

Sloop of War

For Walter J. Minton, with thanks for firing the starting-gun on this series

The author wishes to thank: the U.S. Navy for their help and co-operation during his visit to the Chesapeake in 1970; Captain A. G. Ellis, Director of the U.S. Naval Academy Museum, Annapolis; the Hall of Records, Annapolis; the Mariners Museum, Newport News, Va.; and the Mugar Memorial Library, Boston University.

A. K.

Contents

Part One 1778

1 The Most Coveted Gift 5
2 Freedom 18
3 The Privateer 29
4 A Total Responsibility 44
5 All the luck ... 56
6 Scarlet and Gold 67
7 To Dare or to Die 80
8 A Captain's Decision 91
9 'Boarders Away!' 103

Part Two 1781

10 Sea Change 117
11 Strategy and Spite 128
12 A Twist of Fate 140
13 No Better Epitaph 152
14 Join the Ladies 164
15 A Good Likeness 176
16 One Man's Loss ... 188
17 Mistaken Identity 196
18 Only the Brave 210
Epilogue 223

It seems to be a law inflexible and inexorable
that he who will not risk cannot win.

JOHN PAUL JONES

PART ONE
1778

1

The Most Coveted Gift

It was a little more than a hundred yards' walk from the busy foreshore to the elegant white building at the top of the coast road, but within a minute of leaving the launch Richard Bolitho was damp with sweat. In the broad expanse of English Harbour there had been an illusion of a breeze, but here, as the noon sun stood high above Monk's Hill and bathed the island of Antigua in a shimmering haze, there was no such comfort.

Nevertheless, Bolitho quickened his pace, conscious of his rising excitement and a sense of unreality which had been with him since his arrival just a week earlier. Events had moved so fast that he felt unable to keep a grip on them, as if he was a spectator watching somebody else, a being quite alien to his own resources.

Through wide gates, the sand and dust covering his new shoes with a pale layer, and across some well-tended gardens towards the building itself. But for the flag which hung limply from its staff it could have been the residence of some rich merchant or shipowner. From the number of Negro servants who were working amidst the flowers and shrubs he guessed that the previous occupant had probably been a dealer in African slaves.

Within the deep porch it felt almost cold after the sun's fierce glare, and he found himself confronted by a red-faced sergeant of marines who, after a cursory glance which covered Bolitho from top to toe, said, 'If you will step into this room, sir.' His tone, if not offhand, was that of a man so used to dealing with the comings and goings of sea-officers that he could no longer be excited by anything or anyone.

Bolitho entered the small room and heard the door slam behind him. For the first time since he could recall he was quite alone. Alone, and poised on what might be the most important step in his life.

He made himself walk very slowly to the window and stood looking down at the harbour spread below him like some great painting. English Harbour. The headquarters and linchpin of England's sea power in the Indies and Caribbean. Every type of ship seemed to be here. Stately two-deckers in the deep anchorage, their awnings spread and every gun port open to catch the merest breath of air. Lithe frigates and supply vessels, and a whole collection of smaller craft from brigs to schooners, between which countless oared boats plied back and forth like water-beetles.

Somewhere in the building a man shouted loudly and feet clattered in a passageway. Bolitho tore his eyes from the anchored ships and crossed to a wall mirror, his mind suddenly very aware of what the next minutes might bring or take away.

He still could not get used to his change of appearance. He had never imagined that a uniform would alter a man's outward image so much yet leave him inwardly the same. Just weeks ago he had been second lieutenant in the *Trojan*, an eighty-gun ship-of-the-line. For three years he had lived, worked and nearly died within her crowded hull, rising from his original position of fourth lieutenant by way of one man's death and the promotion of another. He had become used to the *Trojan*, even though he had had to fight off the yearning to free himself from her ponderous authority to find more individual scope for his ideas.

Like everyone aboard he had been kept busy enough. With the rebellion in America every ship-of-war was needed as never before. As the rebellion grew and spread and some real hint of its purpose filtered through to the fleet the *Trojan* was called from one crisis to another.

It seemed incredible that disorganised bands of men could be welded into armies. Armies strong and agile enough to outmanoeuvre some of the best troops from England. But like most of his companions Bolitho had firmly believed that some sort of compromise would still present itself. That was until six months ago in October 1777, when the news of Burgoyne's surrender had burst upon them. Overnight, or so it seemed, the rebellion had developed into a new and bitter conflict. On the one hand the British with their overstretched resources, and on the other the armies of the American Revolution backed as they were by a whole fleet of privateers from France and Spain. No supply ship could sail alone without the real risk of being taken by such privateers. Even troop convoys were not immune from attack.

It was in the middle of this new hit-and-run war that Bolitho's own life had changed. *Trojan* had run down and boarded a prize, a handsome brig, off the coast of Puerto Rico, her holds jammed with contraband goods and powder for the Americans. Caught between two sets of shoals, and confronted by the *Trojan*'s impressive artillery, her master decided to surrender without fuss.

Trojan's first lieutenant was badly needed in his own ship as most of the officers were newly appointed and without much experience. To Bolitho fell the lot of prize-master, with orders to take her to Antigua and await further instructions. It was like the beginning to some impossible dream. Freedom, excitement, the room to move and act without his captain's eye upon him, the little brig seemed to offer unlimited possibilities, even though he knew it would not last.

But fate had other ideas. Within a few days they had sighted another, larger brig, well handled, and displaying a heavier armament than was usual for such a craft. There had been no doubt that she was a privateer and, further, it had seemed likely she was approaching to make a rendezvous with the prize.

There was little time to think, let alone plan. The other ship would outsail and outshoot anything Bolitho's small prizecrew could offer. To fight and die to no purpose was unthinkable, and to surrender without doing so was equally so.

It had turned out to be so simple that looking back it too seemed like part of the dream. Closing the unsuspecting privateer, apparently to pass despatches, they had run alongside and grappled her, both vessels being buried under a mass of fallen spars and canvas in the collision. A volley of musket fire, a wildly yelling rush of boarders, and the other ship was taken, even though her company outnumbered Bolitho's party by four to one. *Trojan*'s seamen were well used to this sort of game. The privateer's crew were not. In fact, it was her captain's first voyage in that capacity.

So instead of one prize Bolitho entered harbour with a pair. With the war going badly on land, and affairs at sea so confused as to be equally disheartening, his arrival under the guns of the harbour's battery was like a tonic. Handshakes from a rear-admiral, smiling greetings from senior captains, Bolitho had been staggered by the welcome.

With the prizes handed over to the dockyard he had been found accommodation in an old hulk called *Octavia*. Originally a two-decker, she had been all but sunk in a hurricane the previous year, and now served as accommodation ship. Junior officers whiled away the time gambling, sleeping or drinking to excess as they awaited their next appointments. Promotion and transfers, courts martial or passage home as a crippled victim of some encounter with the enemy, the old *Octavia* had seen them all.

As the days passed, Bolitho began to imagine he had been forgotten. Soon the *Trojan* would arrive and he would find himself back again in her tight community. Living from day to day. Hoping, yet not daring to hope for too much.

The orders, when they were delivered by an immaculate flag lieutenant, were as brief as they were astounding. By consent of the Commander-in-Chief, Richard Bolitho would take upon himself the appointment of commander with the rank and benefits attached. The appointment would take effect forthwith. He would furnish himself with all necessary vestments and report to the newly acquired headquarters building in two days' time.

He stared at himself in the glass. *Today*.

It seemed that in Antigua you could obtain everything even at such short notice, for a price. And now, instead of his faded lieutenant's uniform, he was looking at the broad blue lapels of commander, the single gold stripe on each sleeve which showed him to be what was to all intent a junior captain. Behind him on the chair a gold-laced cocked hat shone in the filtered sunlight, and like everything else about him, his white waistcoat and breeches, a tight neckcloth and his dusty shoes, even the handsome basket-hilted sword which he had chosen with such care, were so new that they felt like borrowed finery. He had not dared to contemplate the cost, the bribes required to obtain everything within the allotted time. An advance on his well-earned prize money had sufficed for the present.

He touched the lock of black hair which hung rebelliously above his right eye. Beneath it the deep, savage scar which ran to his hairline felt hot, as if it had been a matter of weeks rather than years when he had been struck down by a cutlass.

In spite of his inner tension he grinned at himself. Junior or not, he had taken the first real step. One which would bring him either fame or disgrace, but which like all his family before him he had awaited with both anxiety and eagerness.

More footsteps sounded in the passageway and he adjusted his neckcloth and settled the new sword more comfortably on his hip. Once again his image in the mirror was like a stranger's. The uniform, the tense way he was holding his slim figure as if on parade, displayed more apprehension than he had believed he harboured.

The footsteps halted outside the door, and in one movement Bolitho swept up the cocked hat and jammed it beneath one arm, trying to ignore his heart pounding against his ribs like a hammer. His mouth was bone dry, yet he could feel the sweat running between his shoulder-blades like warm rain.

Richard Bolitho was twenty-two years old and had been in the King's Navy since the age of twelve. But as he stared fixedly at the gilt door handle he felt more like a frightened midshipman than the man who was about to receive the most coveted gift to be bestowed on any living creature. A command of his own.

The marine sergeant stared at him woodenly. 'When you're ready, sir. Cap'n Colquhoun will see you now.'

'I'm ready, thank you.'

The marine eyed him with the merest hint of a smile. 'He'll be glad to know that, I'm sure, sir.'

Bolitho did not hear a word. Following the sergeant he strode out into the passageway, and another world.

Captain Vere Colquhoun rose briefly from behind a large desk, made as if to offer his hand, and then sank back into his chair.

'Pray be seated, Bolitho.'

He had his back to a window and it was impossible to see his expression. But as Bolitho arranged himself into a narrow, high-back chair he was well aware of the other man's scrutiny.

Colquhoun said, 'You have a good report.' He opened a canvas folder and ran his eyes across the attached papers. 'I see that you were commissioned lieutenant in 'seventy-four.' He glanced up sharply. 'Well?'

Bolitho replied, 'Yes, sir. The *Destiny*, frigate.'

He had been long enough in the Navy to realise that interviews with superior officers took time. Each had his own way, but all seemed to result in being kept hanging on a thread of uneasy expectation. He tried to ignore Colquhoun's bowed head and made himself look instead at the room. White walls and a colourful tiled floor. Some pieces of dark, heavy furniture and one table which was almost covered with handsome decanters. Colquhoun, it appeared, enjoyed life. He shifted his gaze to his new superior. At a guess he was about thirty, and from what he could see from the sunlit window he had finely cut features with a small, aggressive chin. He had fair hair, pulled back to the nape of his neck like his own, in the current fashion, and Bolitho noticed that in spite of his service on the station his skin was remarkably pale.

Colquhoun said, 'Your captain speaks well of you.' He rustled his papers. 'Quite well.'

Bolitho tried not to swallow and display the dryness in his throat. Captain Pears of the *Trojan* had sent a report with him aboard the prize. Had he been aware of Bolitho's later luck with the privateer his report might have been even better. It was strange, he thought. In the three years aboard Pears's ship he had never really understood the man. Sometimes he had imagined his captain disliked him, and at best only tolerated his efforts. Yet now, on this desk, under the eyes of a new superior, Pears's words were showing him in a different light.

'Thank you, sir.'

'Hmph.' Colquhoun stood up and walked towards the table and then changed his mind. Instead he moved to the window and stared absently at the anchorage. 'I am commanded to give you your new appointment. It will be up to you to prove your worth, an ability to carry out orders rather than to make play with them for your own advantage.'

Bolitho waited. It was impossible to follow this man.

Colquhoun added, 'Since the military disaster at Saratoga last year we have seen all the signs of the French increasing their aid to the Americans. Originally they sent supplies and military advisers. Then privateers and soldiers-of-fortune, mercenaries.' He spat out the words. 'Now they are more open in their efforts to use the Americans to further their own ends and regain territory lost to us in the Seven Years War.'

Bolitho gripped the hilt of his new sword and tried to remain outwardly calm. Somewhere outside this room was a ship awaiting her new captain. Old or new, large or insignificant as a fighting unit, she was to be all his own. And he had to remain quite still, listening to Captain Colquhoun's observations on the war. Bolitho had been involved in the war since its beginning, and he had already learned from a fellow officer in the *Octavia* that Colquhoun had arrived from England just six months ago.

Colquhoun was saying in the same dry tone, 'But while we command the sea-lanes and supply routes neither the French nor the damned Pope can stop us regaining overall control of the mainland.' He turned slightly, the sun glinting across the gold lace of his coat, 'Don't you agree?'

Bolitho shifted in his chair. 'Up to a point, sir. But . . .'

Colquhoun snapped, '*But* is not a word which appeals to me! Either you agree or you disagree.'

'I think more should be done to seek out the privateers and destroy them in their bases, sir.' He paused, anticipating some caustic remark. Then he continued, 'We have too few ships to spare for convoy work. Any attack on merchantmen, pressed home by two or more vessels at once, can play the devil with a solitary escort.'

'Really. You surprise me.'

Bolitho bit his lip. He had allowed himself to be drawn. Perhaps Colquhoun had been hoping that one of his friends or protégés would be given the new appointment, and saw Bolitho as an intruder. Whatever it was, there seemed to be no doubting his hostility.

'I have, of course, heard of your family, Bolitho. Seafaring stock. None of 'em ever afraid to risk his neck. And out here at this moment we need the best fighting officers we can get.'

He turned abruptly to the window. 'Come over here.'

Bolitho crossed to his side and followed his glance towards the ships at anchor.

'Look impressive, don't they?' Colquhoun gave what might have been a sigh. 'But once at sea, scattered to the winds, they are just a handful. With the Frogs at our backs and threatening England once more we are stretched beyond any safety limit.' He gestured across the harbour. A frigate was being careened, heeled right over on her beam, her bilges covered with busy figures, their naked backs shining in the glare like polished mahogany. Colquhoun said, quietly, '*Bacchante*, thirty-six.' He tightened his jaw. '*My* ship. First time I've been able to get her underwater repairs done since I assumed command.'

Bolitho darted a quick glance at him. He had always dreamed of commanding a frigate since his first and only experience in the little twenty-eight-gun *Destiny*. Freedom to move and hit hard at anything but a ship-of-the-line, with all the dash and agility that any young captain could ask for. But Colquhoun did not seem to fit the role. Slightly built, with the pale, petulant good looks of a true aristocrat. His clothes were beautifully made, and the sword at his hip must be worth two hundred guineas.

Colquhoun raised his arm. 'Look yonder. Beyond my ship you will see the rest of our flotilla. With these and nothing more I am expected to patrol and seek out the enemy, run errands for the fleet, dab away the tears of rich merchantmen whenever they sight an unfamiliar sail. It would need a force five times as large, and even then I would hope for more.'

He turned to watch Bolitho's expression as he stared across the shimmering water.

Bolitho said slowly, 'Three sloops-of-war.' He saw a tiny armed schooner anchored beyond the others. Was she to be his? He swallowed hard. 'And a schooner.'

'Correct.' Colquhoun moved to his table and picked up a heavy decanter. As he held it against the sunlight he said, 'You are being given the *Sparrow*, Bolitho. Eighteen guns and only two years old.' He eyed him flatly. 'Next to my frigate, she is the best under my command.'

Bolitho could only stare at him.

'I do not know what to say, sir.'

The other man grimaced. 'Then say nought.' He poured two glasses of brandy.

'I have no doubt of your ability as a sea-officer, Bolitho. Your past record is proof of that. To obey and carry out orders without question is one thing, however. To lead others, to hold their skills and lives in your hands without ever losing grip, is something else entirely.' He offered him a glass. 'To your first command, Bolitho. I wish you more of the luck which has guided your feet to this year of 'seventy-eight, for I *promise* you will need it!'

The brandy was like fire, but Bolitho's head was still reeling and he hardly noticed it. A new sloop. The best under Colquhoun's command. In a moment he would awake aboard *Octavia* to find today just beginning.

Colquhoun said calmly, 'Your predecessor in *Sparrow* died recently.'

'I am sorry to hear it, sir.'

'Hmm.' Colquhoun studied him thoughtfully. 'Fever. His first lieutenant is too junior even for temporary command.' He shrugged. 'Your timely arrival, the blessing of our devoted admiral, and, of course, Bolitho, your obvious qualities for the appointment, made you an immediate choice, eh?' He was not smiling.

Bolitho looked away. It would be safer to assume from the beginning that Colquhoun had no sense of humour.

He said, 'I will do my best, sir.'

'Be sure of that.' Colquhoun took out his watch and flicked it open. '*Sparrow* is at full complement. For seamen, that is. I will have to send your prize-crew to other vessels in greater need. Unless you have any particular fellow you wish to keep?'

'Yes, sir. Just one. I appreciate that.'

Colquhoun sighed. 'You are a curious mixture. A Cornishman, I believe?'

'Aye, sir.'

'Ah well ...' He did not continue. Instead he said, 'I have made arrangements for a boat to collect you in a half-hour. Your documents will be ready by then.'

Bolitho waited, half expecting some fresh advice

Colquhoun seemed to read his thoughts and said quietly, 'From time to time you will receive written instructions. But you will only be told *what* to do. How you achieve success and carry them out will be your burden alone.' He turned back to the window, his eyes on the careened frigate. 'I have held four different commands. The first was, of course, the most exciting. But also, as I recall, the loneliest. No more could I ask for help from my companions in the wardroom. Nor could I seek freedom outside my hours of duty. In earlier days I always imagined a captain to be a kind of god, put on earth to command and to leave all worry of execution to mere subordinates. Now, I know different, as you will.'

Bolitho picked up his hat. 'I shall try and remember that, sir.'

Colquhoun did not face him. 'You will not. You will think you know better than everyone else, which is as it should be. But somewhere along the way, in the teeth of a gale, or facing an enemy broadside, or becalmed perhaps with the ship's people near mad with thirst, you will know the true meaning of command. When you need help and advice most, and there is none. When all others are looking aft at you, and you have the power of life and death in your fingers. *Then* you will know, believe me.'

He added shortly, 'You may wait in the room by the entrance.'

The interview was ended.

Bolitho crossed to the door, his eyes on the silhouette against the bright window. It was such an important moment that he wanted to hold on to every part of it. Even the furniture and the well-stocked decanters.

Then he closed the door behind him and returned to the waiting room. When he looked at his watch he saw he had been just twenty minutes in the building.

At the window he stood staring at the small ships on the far side of the anchorage, trying to distinguish one from the other, wondering what she would be like. What his company would think of him.

Eventually the door opened and an elderly lieutenant peered into the room.

'*Sparrow*, sir?'

Bolitho saw the sealed envelope in the man's hands and took a deep breath.

He nodded. 'Yes.'

The lieutenant bobbed his head and smiled. 'Your orders, sir. The boat has been sighted approaching the jetty. I will arrange for your gear to be collected from *Trojan* when she reaches here.' He shrugged. 'I am not so sure it will ever catch up with you, however.'

Bolitho grinned, unable to maintain his outward calm.

'Have it sold for me, eh? Put it towards helping some of those wounded seamen awaiting passage to England.'

As he strode towards the sunlight the lieutenant took out a pair of steel-rimmed glasses and peered after him. Then he shook his head very slowly. A remarkable young man, he thought. It was to be hoped he would remain so.

After the shadowy cool of the building Bolitho found the sun's glare harsher than before. As he strode down the coast road, his mind half dwelling on the interview with Colquhoun, he was already wondering what his new command would offer. With, but not *of* the fleet, there should at least be room to move, freedom from the daily flow of signals and requirements which had been his lot in the powerful *Trojan*.

He paused at a curve in the road and shaded his eyes to watch the boat which was already drawing near to the jetty. He shivered in spite of the heat and started to walk more quickly towards the sea. To anybody else it was just one more boat going about its ship's affairs, but to him it represented far more. A first contact. Some of his men. *His* men.

He saw the familiar shape of Stockdale standing beside some of his newly bought belongings and felt a sudden touch of warmth. Even if Colquhoun had said that not one single man of Bolitho's prize-crew could be spared for his first command he felt sure Stockdale would have arrived aboard in his own way. Thickset and muscular, in his broad white trousers and blue jacket, he reminded him of some indestructible oak. He, too, was watching the approaching boat, his eyes slitted against the light with critical interest.

Bolitho had been junior lieutenant in the frigate *Destiny* when their paths had first crossed. Sent ashore on the thankless task of drumming up recruits for the ship, and with little hope of much success, he had arrived at a small inn with his party of seamen to set up headquarters, and, more to the point, to find some peace and a moment to refresh himself for the next attempt to obtain volunteers. Tramping from village to village, inn to inn, the system rarely changed. It usually resulted in a collection of those who were either too young for the harsh demands of a frigate or old sailors who had failed to find fortune or success ashore and merely wanted to return and end their days in surroundings they had originally sworn to forsake forever.

Stockdale had been none of these. He had been a prizefrighter, and stripped to the waist had been standing like a patient ox outside the inn while his sharp-faced barker had called upon all and sundry to risk a battering and win a guinea.

Tired and thirsty, Bolitho had entered the inn, momentarily leaving his small party to their own devices. Exactly what had happened next was not quite clear, but on hearing a string of curses, mingled with the loud laughter of the sailors, he had hurried outside to find one of his men pocketing the guinea and the enraged barker beating Stockdale round the head and shoulders with a length of chain. Whether the victorious seaman, a powerful gunner's mate well used to enforcing authority with brute force, had tripped Stockdale or gained a lucky blow was never discovered. Certainly, Bolitho had never seen Stockdale beaten in any fight, fair or otherwise, since that day. As he had shouted at his men to fall in line again he had realised that Stockdale had been standing as before, taking the unjust punishment, when with one stroke he could have killed the barker who was tormenting him.

Sickened by the spectacle, and angry with himself at the same time, he had asked Stockdale to volunteer for the King's service. The man's dumb gratitude had been almost as embarrassing as the grins on the sailors' faces, but he had found some comfort in the barker's stunned disbelief as without a word Stockdale had picked up his shirt and followed the party away from the inn.

If he had imagined that was the end of the matter he was soon to discover otherwise. Stockdale took to a life at sea in a manner born. As strong as two men, he was gentle and patient, and whenever Bolitho was in danger he always seemed to be there. When a cutlass had hacked Bolitho to the ground and his boat's crew had retreated in panic, it had been Stockdale who had rallied them, had fought off the attackers and carried his unconscious lieutenant to safety. When Bolitho had left the frigate for the *Trojan* Stockdale had somehow contrived to transfer also. Never far away, he had been his servant as well as a gun captain, and when aboard the prize ship he had merely to glare at the captured crew to obtain instant respect. He spoke very little and then only with a husky whisper. His vocal cords had been maimed over the years of fighting for others in booths and fair grounds up and down the country.

But when Bolitho's promotion had been delivered he had said simply, 'You'll be needing a good cox'n, sir.' He had given his lazy, lopsided grin. 'Whatever sort of a ship they gives you.'

And so it was settled. Not that there would have been any doubt in Bolitho's mind either.

He turned as Bolitho strode down the jetty and touched his hat.

'All ready.' He ran his eyes over Bolitho's new uniform and nodded with obvious approval. 'No more'n you deserve, sir.'

Bolitho smiled. 'We shall have to see about that.'

With oars tossed, and a seaman already scrambling ashore with a line, the cutter eased gently against the piles.

Stockdale stooped and steadied the gunwale with his fist, his eyes on the motionless oarsmen as he said hoarsely, 'A fine day for it, sir.'

A slim midshipman leapt from the boat and removed his hat with a flourish. About eighteen, he was a pleasant looking youth, and as tanned as a native.

'I'm Heyward, sir.' He shifted under Bolitho's impassive gaze. 'I – I've been sent to collect you, sir.'

Bolitho nodded. 'Thank you, Mr. Heyward. You can tell me about the ship as we go.'

He waited for the midshipman and Stockdale to follow his sea-chest and bags into the boat and then stepped after them.

'Shove off forrard! Out oars!' Heyward seemed very conscious of Bolitho's nearness. 'Give way all!'

Like pale bones the oars rose and fell in regular precision. Bolitho glanced swiftly at the two lines of oarsmen. Neatly dressed in check shirts and white trousers, they looked fit and healthy enough. A ship could always be judged by her boats, some people contended. Bolitho knew otherwise. Some captains kept their boats as outward showpieces, while within their own ships the people lived little better than animals. Their expressions gave nothing away. The usual, homely faces of British sailors, set in careful masks to avoid his scrutiny. Each man was probably wondering about the new captain. To any seaman his captain was not much junior to God. He could lead, and use his skills on their behalf in battle. He might just as easily turn their lives into a daily hell with no one to whom they could protest or plead their cause.'

The midshipman said haltingly, 'We have been at anchor for three days, sir.'

'Before that?'

'Patrol duty of Guadeloupe. We did sight a French brig but lost her, sir.'

'How long have you been in *Sparrow?*'

'Two years, sir. Since she commissioned on the Thames at Greenwich.'

Stockdale craned round. 'There she is, sir. Fine on the larboard bow.'

Bolitho sat upright in the sternsheets, knowing that as soon as his eyes left the boat every man would be staring at him. He could barely contain his excitement as he peered towards the anchored sloop which was now fully in view beyond a heavy transport. She was riding almost motionless above the twin of her own reflection, her ensign making a scarlet patch of colour against the haze-shrouded hills beyond.

Bolitho had seen sloops in plenty during his service. Like frigates, they were everywhere and always in demand. Maids of all work, the eyes of the fleet, they were familiar in most naval harbours. But right at this moment in time he also knew that the *Sparrow* was going to be different from all those others. From her gently spiralling mastheads to the single line of open gun ports she was a thing of beauty. A thoroughbred, a miniature frigate, a vessel which seemed eager to be free of the land. She was all and none of these things.

He heard himself say, 'Steer round her bows.'

As the tiller went over he was conscious of the silence, broken only by the sluice of water around the cutter's stern and the rhythmic creak of oars. As if he was sharing this moment with nobody. Like a raked black finger the sloop's long jib-boom swept out and over his head, and for a few more moments he stared up at the figurehead below the bowsprit. A man-sized sparrow, beak wide in fury and wings spread as if to fight, its curved claws firmly gripping a gilded cluster of oak leaves and acorns. Bolitho watched until the boat had moved around and under the starboard cathead. He had never thought a mere sparrow could be depicted as being so warlike.

He started with surprise as his eyes fell on a gun muzzle in the first port.

Heyward said respectfully, 'We have a thirty-two-pounder on either bow, sir. The rest of the gun deck is made up of sixteen twelve-pounders.' He flinched as Bolitho turned to look at him. 'I beg your pardon, sir, I did not mean to intrude.'

Bolitho smiled and touched his arm. 'I was merely surprised. She seems to have very heavy artillery for such a small ship.' He shook his head. 'Those two bow-chasers must have brought many an enemy aback with shock. Nine-pounders are more common in sloops, I believe.'

The midshipman nodded, but his eyes were on the ship's side, his lips in an anxious line as he gauged the moment.

'Put her about!'

The cutter swung in a tight arc and headed for the main chains. There were many heads lining the gangway, and Bolitho saw the blue and white of an officer's uniform by the entry port, a press of more figures by the mainmast.

'Toss your oars!'

The boat idled towards the chains where the bowman brought down his boathook with a well-timed slash.

Bolitho stood up in the sternsheets, conscious of all the eyes above and around him. Of Stockdale's hand, half-raised, ready to steady him if he lost his balance. Of the new sword at his hip and not wanting to look down to make sure it would not tangle with his legs as he climbed up the sleek tumblehome.

With a quick breath he reached out and hauled himself from the boat. He had been prepared for almost everything but was still taken totally off guard by the piercing shrill of pipes as his head and shoulders rose through the port. Perhaps, more than anything else, the time-honoured salute from a ship to her captain made him realise just how great was the step from lieutenant's berth to command.

It was all too much to take in and comprehend in this small cameo. The drawn swords, the boatswain's mates with their silver calls to their lips, the bare-backed seamen on the gangways and high in the shrouds. Below his feet he felt the deck lift easily, and once more was aware of the change this ship had brought him. After the *Trojan*'s fat bulk, her massive weight of guns and spars, this sloop even *felt* alive.

One officer stepped forward as Bolitho removed his hat to the quarterdeck and said, 'Welcome aboard, sir. I am Graves, second lieutenant.'

Bolitho regarded him searchingly. The lieutenant was young and alert, but had the controlled caution on his dark features of a man much older.

He half turned and added, 'The others are awaiting your pleasure, sir.'

Bolitho asked, 'And the first lieutenant?'

Graves looked away. 'In the flagship sir. He had an appointment.' He faced him quickly. 'He meant no disrespect, sir, I am quite sure of that.'

Bolitho nodded. Graves's explanation was too swift, too glib. Or that of a man who wished to draw attention to the absent officer's behaviour by excusing it.

Graves hurried on, 'This is Mr. Buckle, the sailing master, sir. Mr. Dalkeith, surgeon.' His voice followed Bolitho down the small line of senior warrant officers.

Bolitho marked each face but checked himself from further contact. That would come soon enough, but now his own impression on them was far more vital.

He stood by the quarterdeck rail and stared down at the gun deck. The *Sparrow* was one hundred and ten feet long on that deck, but had a broad beam of thirty feet, almost that of a frigate. No wonder she could contain such powerful armament for her size.

He said, 'Have the hands lay aft, Mr. Graves.'

As the order was passed and the men came pressing down on those already assembled, he drew his commission from his pocket and spread it on the rail. How hot the wood felt beneath his hands.

Again he darted a glance at the faces beneath him. In so small a ship how did they all manage to exist? There were one hundred and fifteen souls crammed aboard *Sparrow*, and as they jostled together below the quarterdeck there appeared to be twice that number.

Graves touched his hat. 'All present, sir.'

Bolitho replied with equal formality, 'Thank you.' Then in a steady voice he began to read himself in.

He had heard other captains do it often enough, but as he read the beautifully penned words he felt once more like a spectator.

It was addressed to Richard Bolitho, Esquire, and required him forthwith to go on board and take upon him the charge and command of captain in His Britannic Majesty's Sloop-of-War *Sparrow*.

Once or twice as his voice carried along the deck he heard a man cough or move his feet, and aboard another sloop close by he saw an officer watching the proceedings through a telescope.

He put the commission in his coat and said, 'I will go to my quarters, Mr. Graves.'

He replaced his hat and walked slowly towards a covered hatch just forward of the mizzen mast. He noticed that the ship's wheel was completely unsheltered. A bad place in a storm, he thought, or when the balls begin to fly.

At his back he heard the rising murmur of voices as the men were dismissed, and noticed, too, the heavy smell of cooking in the listless air. He was glad he had restrained himself from making a speech. It would have been vanity, and he knew it. All the same, it was so precious a day that he wanted to share it with all of them in some way.

In his excitement he had forgotten about the time. Now as he made his way down a ladder to the gun deck and aft behind Graves's crouched figure he was more than glad he had restricted himself to the formal reading of his appointment. Men kept standing in the sun to hear a pompous speech were one thing. Men kept also from their well-earned meal were something else entirely.

He gasped as his head crashed against a deck beam.

Graves spun round. 'I beg your pardon, sir!' He seemed terrified Bolitho should blame him for the lack of headroom.

'I will remember next time.'

He reached the stern cabin and stepped inside. For an instant he stood motionless, taking in the graceful sloping stern windows which spread from quarter to quarter, displaying the anchorage and the headland like some glistening panorama. The cabin was beautifully painted in pale green, the panels picked out with gold leaf. The deck was concealed with a black and white checked canvas covering, and arranged on either side was a selection of well-made furniture. Gingerly he raised his head and found he could just stand upright between the beams above.

Graves was watching him worriedly. 'I am afraid that after a ship-of-the-line, sir, you'll find this somewhat cramped.'

Bolitho smiled. 'Have the ship's books brought to me after you have dined, Mr. Graves. I will also want to meet the other officers informally sometime today.' He paused, seeing again the caution in his eyes. '*Including* the first lieutenant.'

Graves bowed himself out and Bolitho turned his back to the closed door.

Cramped, after a ship-of-the-line, Graves had said. He hurled his hat across the cabin on to the bench seat below the windows. His sword he unbuckled and dropped in a green velvet chair. He was laughing aloud, and the effort to restrain it was almost painful.

Cramped. He walked, ducking between the beams. It was a *palace* after the *Trojan*'s wardroom.

He sat down beside his hat and stared around the neat, cheerful-looking cabin.

And it was his own.

2

Freedom

It was late afternoon when Bolitho finally decided he had read all that there was available about the ship around him. Muster and punishment books, watch-bills and ledgers of stores and victualling returns, the list seemed endless. But at no time was he bored. With his new coat hanging on a chairback, his neckcloth loosened and shirt unbuttoned, he found each item fascinating.

His predecessor, Captain Ransome, had kept a smart and well-run ship on the face of things. The punishment book had all the usual culprits and awards for minor misdemeanours. A few for drunkenness, even less for insolence and insubordination, and the worst recorded crime was that of a seaman who had struck a petty officer during gun drill.

Ransome had been extremely lucky in one thing. With the ship being commissioned on the Thames he had been able to secure the cream of the press. Men off incoming merchant ships, transfers from vessels laid up in ordinary, he had been in a position to complete his company with far less difficulty than most captains.

Against the apparent taut atmosphere in the ship was a rather negative list of reports in the log books. Only once had *Sparrow* been called to action in the two years since leaving England, and then as secondary reinforcement to a frigate attacking a blockade runner. It was little wonder that Midshipman Heyward had showed some concern at his remarks about the big bow-chasers. He had probably imagined his words to be some sort of criticism at their lack of use.

There were the usual lists of men transferred to other ships because of promotion and the like. Their places had been filled by what Ransome had termed 'local colonist volunteers' in his personal log. Bolitho had lingered a good deal on the previous captain's daily records. His comments were extremely brief and it was impossible to get even a feel of the man. As he paused to glance around the cabin from time to time Bolitho found himself wondering about Ransome. An experienced and competent officer, obviously a man of good breeding and therefore influence, the cabin seemed at odds with his mental portrait. Extremely attractive, comfortable, yet just that too much removed from what you might expect in a ship-of-war.

He sighed and leaned back in the chair as his cabin servant, Fitch, padded into the shafted sunlight to remove the remains of his meal.

Fitch was tiny. A miserable scrap of a man, who had already confessed to having been a petty thief in his unfortunate past. Saved from transportation or worse by the timely arrival of a King's ship as he awaited sentence at the Assizes, he had accepted life at sea more as an extension to his punishment than any love of service. But he seemed a capable servant, and was probably well pleased with his work. It kept him from the heavier tasks on deck, and provided his current master was a humane man he had little to fear.

Bolitho watched him as he collected the crockery on to a tray. It had been an excellent meal. Cold tongue and fresh vegetables from ashore, and the claret which Fitch had mournfully observed was 'the last of Cap'n Ransome's stock' had been a touch of perfection.

'Your late captain.' Bolitho saw the small man stiffen. 'Did he leave any instruction as to his property aboard?'

Fitch dropped his eyes. 'Mr. Tyrrell 'as attended to it, sir. It's been sent to a transport for passage 'ome.'

'He must have been an officer of some consequence.'

Bolitho hated this form of questioning, but he felt he needed some link, no matter how small, with the man who had controlled this ship from the day she had slid into the water.

Fitch bit his lip. ' 'E were a strict cap'n, sir. 'E saw that the 'ands took fairly to their work. If they obeyed, 'e was 'appy. If not . . .' he shrugged his frail shoulders, 'then 'e tended to swear a piece.'

Bolitho nodded. 'You may leave.'

It was useless to proceed with Fitch. His life concerned only the comings and goings. Food and drink, a warm cot, or a swift curse if things were not to his master's liking.

Feet padded overhead and he had to restrain himself from running to the stern windows or standing on a chair to peer through the skylight above the table. He thought of his old companions in the *Trojan*'s wardroom and wondered if they were missing him. Probably not. His promotion would mean a gap, and therefore a step up the ladder for another. He smiled to himself. It would take time to fit himself into this new role. Time and vigilance.

There was a tap at the door and Mathias Buckle, the sailing master, stepped inside.

'Do you have a moment, sir?'

Bolitho gestured to a chair. Again this was so unlike a bigger ship-of-war. There were no marines in the company, and visitors to the captain's quarters seemed free to come and go almost as they pleased. Perhaps Ransome had encouraged such informality.

He watched Buckle fitting himself into the chair. He was a short, square built man, with steady eyes and hair almost as dark as his own. Aged forty, he was the oldest man in the ship.

Buckle said, 'I'd not trouble you, sir, but as the first lieutenant's away, I thought . . .' He shifted in the chair. 'I thought I should settle the matter of promotion for one of the hands.'

Bolitho listened in silence as Buckle ran through the points which concerned a man named Raven. It was an internal matter, but he was conscious of the importance it represented. The very first time as captain he was being confronted with the affairs of one of his own company.

Buckle was saying, 'I thought, begging your pardon, sir, that we might advance him to master's mate for a trial period.'

Bolitho asked, 'How long have you been master?'

'Just in this ship, sir.' Buckle's clear eyes were distant. 'Before that I was master's mate in the old *Warrior*, seventy-four.'

'You've done well, Mr. Buckle.' He was trying to place the dialect. London, or further east. Kent.

'How does she handle?'

Buckle seemed to consider it. 'She's heavy for her size, sir. All of four hundred and thirty tons. But the better the wind, the livelier she goes. You can even get the stunsails and royals on her in anything but a true blow.' He frowned. 'In a calm she can be the devil's daughter.' He gestured vaguely. 'You've probably seen the little port alongside each gun port, sir?'

Bolitho had not. He said slowly, 'I am not too sure.'

Buckle smiled for the first time. 'If you gets becalmed you may run a sweep through each o' those ports, sir. Clear lower deck and get every man-jack on the sweeps and you can still get a knot or two out of her.'

Bolitho looked away. Reading the ship's books and correspondence had not even told him the half of it. He felt vaguely angry that his first lieutenant was still not present. Normally the departing captain would have been aboard to tell him the ship's behaviour and failings, or at least the senior lieutenant.

Buckle said, 'You'll soon get the feel of her, sir. She's the best yet.'

Bolitho eyed him thoughtfully. The master was nobody's fool, and yet, like Graves, he seemed to be holding back. Maybe waiting for him to display his strength or weakness to them.

He made himself reply coldly, 'We shall see about that, Mr. Buckle.'

When he glanced up he saw the man watching him with sudden anxiety. He added, 'Any other matter?'

Buckle rose to his feet. 'No, sir.'

'Good. I anticipate that sailing orders will be arriving shortly. I will expect the ship to be ready.'

Buckle nodded. 'Aye, sir. Have no fear.'

Bolitho relented slightly. It was just possible his own uncertainty was making him unnecessarily harsh towards his sailing master. And it was equally likely he would need Buckle's guiding hand very much until he got the feel of his new command.

He said, 'I have no doubt that I will be as satisfied with your appointment as Captain Ransome was.'

Buckle swallowed hard. 'Yes, sir.' He stared round the low cabin. 'Thank you, sir.'

The door closed behind him and Bolitho ran his fingers through his hair. Just a few hours since he had climbed aboard to the squeal of pipes and already he was beginning to *feel* different.

It was all so alien to his past life when you could argue and compete with your companions, curse your captain behind his back or reveal his weakness which only you really understood. As from today a mere word could bring a shutter across a man's eyes or make him fear for his own safety. Buckle was eighteen years his senior, yet at the first hint of Bolitho's displeasure had almost cringed.

He closed his eyes and tried to fathom out how he should proceed. To try to be too popular was to be a fool. To hold unswervingly to matters of discipline and order was to be a tyrant. He recalled Colquhoun's words and grinned ruefully. Until you reached Colquhoun's lofty post-rank you could never be certain of anything.

Somewhere beyond the bulkhead he heard a challenge and a shouted reply from a boat. Then the squeak of a hull alongside, the patter of feet on a gangway. It seemed unreal and incredible that the ship, his ship, was running her affairs while he just sat here at the table. He sighed again and stared at the pile of papers and books. It would take longer than he had imagined to adjust.

There was another rap at the door and Graves ducked inside, removing his hat and jamming it under his arm as he announced, 'The guardboat has just been alongside, sir.' He held out a heavily sealed canvas envelope. 'From the flag, sir.'

Bolitho took it and laid it carelessly on the table. His sailing orders without doubt, and he had to restrain himself from acting as he truly felt. He wanted to rip them open, to know and understand what was required of him.

He saw Graves looking round the cabin, his eyes passing swiftly over the discarded dress coat, the hat lying on the bench seat, and finally on Bolitho's unbuttoned shirt.

Graves said quickly, 'Will you wish me to stay, sir?'

'No. I will inform you of their content when I have had time to study them.'

Graves nodded. 'I am waiting for the last water-lighter to come out to us, sir. I have sent the cooper ashore to speed them up, but . . .'

Bolitho smiled. 'Then attend to it, if you please.'

Bolitho watched him leave and then slit open the envelope. He was still reading the neatly worded orders when he heard voices in the passageway beyond the door. Graves first, curt and resentful, then another, calm to begin with and then loud with anger. The latter finished with, 'Well, how in God's name was I to know? You could have made a signal, you bloody fool!'

There was a sudden silence and then a further tap on the door.

The lieutenant who stepped into the cabin was not at all what Bolitho had been expecting. Too junior for temporary command, Colquhoun had said, and yet this man was probably two years older than himself. He was tall, broad-shouldered, and deeply tanned. His thick auburn hair brushed the deckhead between the beams so that he seemed to fill the cabin.

Bolitho glanced up at him calmly. 'Mr. Tyrrell?'

The lieutenant nodded briefly. 'Sir.' He took a quick breath. 'I must apologise for my late arrival aboard. I have been in th' flagship.'

Bolitho looked down at the table. Tyrrell had an easy drawl, the mark of a man born and bred in the American colony. He was like a half-tamed animal, and the quickness of his breathing betrayed the anger which he still harboured.

Bolitho added, 'Our sailing orders have just arrived.'

Tyrrell did not seem to hear. 'It was personal business, sir, I hadn't th' time to arrange otherwise.'

'I see.'

He waited, watching the man as he stared restlessly towards the stern windows. He had a strange way of standing, with one arm hanging down his side, the other inclined towards his sword. Relaxed, but wary. Like someone expecting an attack.

He continued, 'I would have preferred to meet my first lieutenant on board when I arrived.'

'I have sent Cap'n Ransome's remains ashore to be conveyed home with his possessions, sir. As you were not yet in command I felt personally free to act as I thought fit.' He looked at Bolitho evenly. 'I was aboard th' flagship to ask, plead if required, for a transfer to another ship. It was refused.'

'You felt that by being passed over for command that your talents would be better suited elsewhere, is that it?'

Tyrrell gave a slow smile. It changed him instantly from an angry man to one of obvious charm, with the inbuilt recklessness of a fighter.

'I really am sorry, sir. But no, it was not that. As you no doubt know, I am what th' late Cap'n Ransome would term a *"local colonist"*.' He added bitterly, 'Although when I came aboard a year back it appeared we were all on th' same side against th' rebels.'

Bolitho stiffened. It was strange he had never considered the feelings of those like Tyrrell before. Good American families, loyal to the Crown, the first to stand together against the sudden revolution in their midst. But as the war had spread, and Britain had fought to retain a grip, then a foothold in the colony, the loyal ones like Tyrrell had all at once become the outsiders.

He asked quietly, 'Where is your home?'

'Virginia. Gloucester County. My father came out from England to found a coastal shipping trade. I was master of one of his schooners when th' war began. I have been in th' King's service since that time.'

'And your family?'

Tyrrell looked away. 'God knows. I have heard nothing of them.'

'And you wished to transfer to a ship nearer home? To take yourself back to what you now consider your own people?' Bolitho did not conceal the bite in his tone.

'No, sir. That ain't it.' He raised one arm and dropped it again, his voice angry. 'I am a King's officer, no matter what Ransome chose to believe, damn his eyes!'

Bolitho stood up. 'I will not have talk of your late captain!'

Tyrrell replied stubbornly, 'Cap'n Ransome is safe now in his cask of spirits in th' hold of a transport. His widow at his great London residence will weep for him, his service which cost him his life.' He laughed shortly. '*Fever*, they said.' He looked round the cabin. 'See all this, sir? A woman's hand. We barely logged a mile in *Sparrow* without him having some damned doxy aboard for company!' He seemed unable to stop himself. 'That's th' sort of *fever* which killed him in th' end, and damned good riddance, if you ask me.'

Bolitho sat down. Once again the ground had been cut from under him. Women, here in this cabin. He had heard of such things in grander ships, but only occasionally. But in *Sparrow*, where there could be little safety if called to do battle, it was unthinkable.

Tyrrell was studying him grimly. 'I had to tell you, sir. It's my way. But I'll say this one thing more. If disease hadn't taken him, I'd have killed him myself.'

Bolitho looked up sharply. 'Then you're a fool! If you have no more strength than in your bare hands then *I* will ask for your transfer, and make no mistake about it!'

Tyrrell stared at a point beyond Bolitho's shoulder.

'Would you behave so calmly, sir, if one of th' women had been *your* sister?'

The door opened a bare inch and Stockdale's battered face peered in at them. In his hand was balanced a small silver tray two glasses and a decanter

He wheezed, 'thought you might want a bit o' refreshment, sir.' He watched the two men and added, 'Sort o' celebration like.'

Bolitho gestured to the table and waited until Stockdale had left. Still without speaking he filled the glasses, conscious of Tyrrell's eyes following every movement. A bad start. For both of them. If there was still time to make amends it was now. This minute. If Tyrrell took advantage of his surrender, there was no saying where it would lead.

He handed him a glass and said gravely, 'I have two sisters, Mr. Tyrrell. In answer to your question, I daresay that I would not.' He smiled, seeing the sudden surprise in the lieutenant's eyes. 'I suggest you propose a toast for the pair of us, eh?'

Tyrrell reached out and held his glass against Bolitho's.

'Then let's drink to a new beginning, sir.'

Bolitho held his glass steady. 'No transfer?'

He shook his head. 'None.'

Bolitho raised the glass. 'Then, to a new beginning.' He took a sip and added quietly, 'Which is well for you, Mr. Tyrrell. We are sailing tomorrow to join the inshore squadron.' He paused, seeing the sudden desperation on the other man's features. 'Not so very far from the coast of Maryland.'

Tyrrell said, 'Thank God. I know I'm being stupid, but just being off that shoreline again will make th' world of difference.'

Bolitho put down his glass. 'Then I will meet our officers informally at the close of the first dog watch.' He was careful to make his tone formal again. Each of them had shown enough of his inner reserves for the present. 'In the meantime you can take me on an inspection around the ship. And I will want to see everything, good and bad.'

Tyrrell nodded. 'So you shall, sir.' A slow grin spread across his face. 'I have a shrewd feeling that *Sparrow* is going to fly like she's never done before.' He stood aside as Bolitho threw on his coat and buttoned his shirt. 'Now if you will follow me, sir.'

Bolitho looked at Tyrrell's broad shoulders as they walked towards the sunlight on the gun deck and held down a sigh. If each day was going to present a battle of wills, it would make the privilege of command a testing experience.

He said, 'We will begin with the starboard battery, Mr. Tyrrell.'

The first lieutenant paused below the break in the quarterdeck. 'As you said, sir. Everything.' He grinned again. 'Good and bad.'

Stockdale picked up Bolitho's shaving bowl and peered at the untouched breakfast on the cabin table. Overhead and throughout the ship the air was alive with noise and bustle. To a landsman the activity of preparing to get under way would appear haphazard and disorganised, but to the practised eye each man had his place, and his reason for being there. The miles of cordage and rigging, each scrap of sail had a vital part to play if a ship was to move and act to perfection.

Bolitho crossed to the stern windows and stared at the nearest strip of land. It was a bright morning, with the sky above the hills very pale, washed-out and clean. He could just see the staff above the headland battery, its flag no longer listless but lifting and curling to a fair north-easterly. It was almost physical pain to stay sealed in the cabin, waiting and fretting for the exact moment to show himself.

Voices pealed along the upper deck and shadows flitted busily across the skylight. Occasionally he could hear the plaintive squeak of a fiddle, the distorted rumble of a shanty as the men tramped around the capstan.

In the past hours and for most of the night he had tossed and turned in his cot, listening to the sea noises, the creak of timbers and rigging, his mind exploring every contingency, his brain bursting to the mental picture of his chart. Every unemployed eye would be watching him this morning. From the flagship's quarterdeck to some unknown lieutenant who probably hated Bolitho for getting the golden chance which he considered should have been his.

'The coffee, sir.' Stockdale hovered by the table. 'While it's still 'ot.'

Bolitho swung round to curse him for breaking his racing thoughts, but the sight of his anxious face was too much for him. As was so often the case.

He sat down at the table and tried to relax. Stockdale was right. If he had forgotten anything it was already too late. You could cram your head just so much. After that the mind became awash and confused beyond reason.

He sipped his coffee and stared at the cold meat. He could not touch that. His stomach was already twisting with apprehension, the lean slices of pork would be just enough to tip the balance.

Stockdale peered through the windows. 'It will be a good passage, sir. Long enough to get the measure of these fellows.'

Bolitho glanced up at him. He must be a mind-reader. In company with another sloop they were to escort two fat transports with supplies for the troops at Philadelphia once a rendezvous with the inshore squadron had been made. Two thousand miles, mostly in open waters, would certainly allow him time to test himself and his company. He had met his officers in the small wardroom the previous evening. With the exception of Tyrrell, all had been aboard since commissioning at Greenwich. He felt vaguely jealous of their obvious familiarity with the *Sparrow*. The two midshipmen, each eighteen years old, had joined as untrained novices. They had grown up in the *Sparrow*, and were now hopefully awaiting promotion. It was a pity they were only midshipmen, he thought. They might vie too much for their captain's approval, where in a larger ship and with more competition amongst the 'young gentlemen' it would be less direct.

Buckle had said little during their informal meeting. Reserved, and no doubt waiting to see how his captain would behave under sail, he had restricted himself to matters of navigation.

Robert Dalkeith, the surgeon, was an odd one. Young, but already too plump for his own good, he was also completely bald, and wore a bright red wig. But he appeared more skilled in his trade than was usual in a King's ship, as well as cultivated, and Bolitho imagined there was more to him than he showed at face value.

Lock, the purser, a bobbing, genial stick of a man, completed the gathering.

Graves had joined them later, making a good deal of noise about his trouble with the water-lighters, the difficulties in obtaining help ashore for loading boats, in fact the list had been formidable.

Tyrrell had interrupted cheerfully, 'It ain't fair, Hector. You being singled out to be a bloody martyr like this!'

Graves had frowned and then forced a smile when the others had joined Tyrrell in the laughter.

Bolitho leaned back and stared at the skylight. He was not sure of Graves either. A hard worker. Ransome's toady? It was hard to see where the latent bad feeling had started between him and Tyrrell. But it *was* there right enough.

'Captain, sir?'

Bolitho started and looked at the door. Midshipman Bethune was standing with his hat under his arm, his free hand grasping the hilt of his dirk. He was a round-faced, sturdy youth, and his face was a mass of dark freckles.

'Well?'

Bethune swallowed. 'Mr. Tyrrell's respects, sir, and the transports have weighed. *Fawn* has her preparative hoisted, sir.' He glanced curiously round the cabin.

Bolitho nodded gravely. 'I will be up directly.'

With elaborate care he forced himself to take another sip of coffee. It almost choked him. *Fawn* was the other sloop for the escort and would be carrying Colquhoun, in addition to her commander, as senior officer.

The midshipman was still inside the cabin. He added awkwardly, 'I am from Cornwall, too, sir.'

Bolitho smiled in spite of his tension. The competition had begun already.

He replied, 'I will try not to hold it against you, Mr. Bethune.' He dropped his eyes as the boy fled from the cabin.

He stood up and took his hat from Stockdale. Then with a brief nod he strode out towards the waiting sunlight.

The gangways and decks seemed more crowded than ever as seamen ran this way and that, pursued by the hoarse shouts of their petty officers. As he reached the quarterdeck he saw two heavy transports idling towards the headland, their tan sails flapping and billowing in the breeze.

Tyrrell touched his hat. 'Anchor's hove short, sir.'

'Thank you.'

Bolitho strode to the larboard side and stared towards the anchored *Fawn*. He could see the muddle of men at her capstan, the scurrying preparations as the cable became bar-taut beneath her beakhead.

He crossed to the opposite side, trying to ignore the seamen who were poised at their stations on every hand. Beyond the nearest headland towards the hard blue horizon he saw a lively pattern of small white horses. Once outside this sheltered anchorage it would be good sailing weather. He glanced at the sluggish swirl of currents around a nearby storeship and bit his lip. He had to get free of all the shipping first.

'*Fawn*'s signal is close up, sir!' Bethune was clinging to the shrouds with his telescope, although Colquhoun's signal was clear enough to be seen without any glass.

'Stand by on the capstan!'

Tyrrell ran to the rail and cupped his big hands. 'Loose th' heads'ls!'

Beside the wheel Buckle stood near the two helmsmen, his eyes watching Bolitho.

'Breeze is freshening a mite, sir.'

'Yes.'

Bolitho walked to the rail and stared along his command. He saw Graves watching over the anchor party, Midshipman Heyward at the foot of the mainmast with his division of seamen.

'Signal, sir! *Up anchor!*'

'Hands aloft and loose tops'ls!'

He stood back to watch the seamen surging up the shrouds and out along the swaying yards, their bodies black against the sky. Tyrrell said very little and Bolitho observed that the topmen were well able to manage without added inducement from the deck. As canvas thundered loosely from the yards and the ship gave a long-drawn shudder, he saw the *Fawn*'s masts already swinging across the stern, her foretopsail filling to the wind as she heeled over.

Bethune called, 'Signal! *Make haste*, sir!' He lowered his glass, trying to avoid Bolitho's eye.

'Man the braces!'

He tried to shut out Colquhoun's last signal. Maybe he was endeavouring to goad him into doing something foolish. Perhaps he was always the same. But nothing must or would spoil this moment.

From forward came the cry, 'Anchor's aweigh, sir!'

Free of the land the *Sparrow* tilted steeply to the wind, the headland sliding across her jib-boom as with more and more canvas thundering and hardening from her yards she paid off into the wind.

Blocks clattered and whined, and high above the decks the seamen sprang about like monkeys.

Bolitho looked at Buckle. 'Lay her on the larboard tack. Then set a course to weather the headland.' He held the master's gaze and added. 'We will get the courses on her directly and see if we can take the edge off *Fawn's* lead.'

Moments later, with her courses and topsails filling to the morning breeze, the *Sparrow* glided swiftly past an anchored two-decker which wore a vice-admiral's flag at the fore.

Bolitho glanced at Tyrrell and saw him give a quick grimace. He might have cause to regret his application for transfer, Bolitho thought. And so, if his trust in Tyrrell proved false, would he.

Between two anchored Indiamen and on down the fairway towards that beckoning headland. Small craft bobbed astern in the frothing wake, and when Bolitho moved from studying the compass he saw they had already cut *Fawn's* lead by half a cable.

Buckle glanced at the surgeon who was clinging to the mizzen shrouds with one hand and holding on to his outrageous wig with the other.

He winked. 'We have a rare one here, Mr. Dalkeith.'

Dalkeith kept his face immobile as Bolitho glanced aft towards him before replying, 'Poor Captain Ransome would never have left port with such dash, eh?' He gave a sly grin. 'But then, at this time o' the morning he would have been somewhat *tired*!'

They both laughed.

Bolitho's voice brought them up with a jerk.

'There is a yawl on the larboard bow, Mr. Buckle. Laugh later with my blessing, but run her down within sight of the flagship and you will laugh to another tune!'

He turned back to the rail as Buckle hurled himself towards his helmsman.

The tip of the headland was already dropping abeam, and he felt the *Sparrow's* stem bite into the first gentle roller, her deck tilting still further under her press of canvas.

Tyrrell shouted, 'Anchor's secured, sir!' Spray had soaked his face and shirt but he was grinning broadly.

Bolitho nodded. 'Good. Now get the forecourse trimmed. It looks like a piece of untidy linen.' But he could not hold his severity. 'By God, she *flies*, does she not?'

He looked aloft at the squared sails and braced yards, the masthead pendant which flicked out like a coachman's whip. He had seen it all before so many times, but now it felt as if it was unique.

Bethune called, 'From *Fawn*, sir. *Take station to wind'rd!*'

Bolitho smiled at him. 'Acknowledge.'

To the quarterdeck at large he added, 'A *fine* morning.'

By the hatchway Stockdale watched Bolitho's pleasure and felt inwardly happy. He ran his eye over the hurrying seamen as they slithered down once more to the deck. Tanned and healthy, what did they know about anything? He picked his uneven teeth with an ivory pin. The captain had seen more action in the past years than they knew about. He watched Bolitho's squared shoulders as he paced restlessly on the weather side. Given time, they'd come to find out, he decided.

3

The Privateer

Bolitho opened his eyes and stared for several seconds at the unlit lantern spiralling above his cot. Despite the weariness in his limbs and the fact he had been on deck repeatedly during the night he found it hard to sleep. Beyond the screen which partitioned his sleeping quarters from the cabin he could see the pale light of dawn, and knew from the lantern's sluggish movement and the uneasy creak of timbers that the wind was little more than a breeze. He tried to relax, wondering how long it would take to break the habit of awakening with each dawn, to enjoy his new-found privacy.

Feet thudded on the quarterdeck above, and he guessed that soon now the seamen would be turning to for another day. It had been two weeks since the little convoy had sailed from Antigua, and in that time they had covered only half their set distance. One thousand miles in open waters, and each mile marked by perverse winds and no winds at all. Barely an hour passed without the need to call the hands to make or shorten sail, to trim yards in the hope of catching a dying breeze, or to reef against one violent and taunting squall.

Buckle's gloomy prediction about *Sparrow*'s sailing qualities in a poor wind had proved only too true. Time and time again she had paid off, her canvas flapping in confusion as yet one more wind had died and left them almost becalmed. Hard work and angry words had eventually brought her back on station again, only to have the whole thing repeated before the end of a watch.

Patrol and scouting duty had been the lot of *Sparrow's* company for most of their commission and they had yet to learn the true misery of convoy over long passages. The two transports had not helped. They appeared totally unwilling to realise the importance of staying in close company, so that if they became scattered by a swift squall it took many hours to urge, threaten and finally drive them back into formation. Colquhoun's curt signals had only succeeded in antagonising the master of one of them, a big transport named *Golden Fleece*. On more than one occasion he had ignored the signals altogether or had caused the *Fawn* to withdraw from her proper station at the head of the convoy in order to commence a verbal exchange which could be heard by everyone else nearby.

Bolitho climbed from the cot and walked slowly into the cabin, feeling the deck lifting gently beneath his bare feet before slipping away in a trough, the motion bringing the usual clatter of blocks, the drawn-out groan of the rudder as the helmsman brought the sloop back under command.

He leaned his hands on the sill of the stern windows and stared out at the empty sea. The two transports, if they were still together, would be somewhere on *Sparrow*'s starboard bow. Bolitho's orders were to stay to windward of the well-laden ships so as to be ready to run down on any suspicious vessel and hold the maximum advantage until she was proved friend or foe.

In fact they had sighted an unknown sail on three separate occasions. Far astern, it had been impossible to know if it was the same on each sighting or three individual vessels. Either way, Colquhoun had refused to be drawn to investigate. Bolitho could sympathise with his unwillingness to leave the valuable transports, especially as the wind might choose the very moment when his sparse forces were scattered to play a new trick or bring some real enemy amongst them. On the other hand, he was very conscious of a sense of uneasiness after each call from the masthead. The strange sail was like a will-o'-the-wisp, and if it was hostile could be methodically following the little convoy, awaiting exactly the right moment to attack.

The door opened and Fitch padded into the cabin carrying two jugs. One was coffee, and the other contained water from the galley for Bolitho's shave. In the pale light from the windows he looked smaller and scrawnier than ever, and as usual kept his eyes averted while he prepared the necessary cup for Bolitho's first coffee of the day.

'How is it on deck?'

Fitch raised his eyes only slightly. 'Mr. Tilby reckons it'll be another roastin' day, sir.'

Tilby was the boatswain, a great untidy hulk of a man who was given to some of the most profane language Bolitho had heard in ten years at sea. But his knowledge of weather, his forecast of what each dawn might bring, had been only too accurate.

And under a blazing sun, with little space to find shade or comfort, the *Sparrow*'s seamen had more torment to face before night found them again. It was amazing how they all managed to survive in such a small hull. What with extra stores and spare spars, powder and shot, and countless other requirements for keeping a ship at sea, some of the men were hard put to find space for a hammock. In addition the *Sparrow* had all the great lengths of anchor cable to be neatly stowed when she was under way. Several hundred fathoms of thirteen-inch hemp for the main anchors and another hundred of eight inch for the kedge took up more space than fifty human beings required for even the most basic needs.

But if this or any other ship was to survive and live from her own resources then such discomforts had to be endured.

He sipped the coffee. If only the wind would freshen and stay with them. It would help drive away the weariness and drudgery of work aloft, and also give him time to drill the guns' crews to better advantage. They had had few such drills during the first days out of harbour, and once more he had been made aware of the strange attitude of acceptance he had originally noticed. Perhaps they had been so long without actually being called to do battle they had taken the drills as merely something to be tolerated, even expected from a new captain. Their timing had been good enough, if somewhat rigid, they had gone through all the motions of running out, traversing and pointing, but again and again he had felt something was badly lacking. As the crews had faced outboard through their open ports he had sensed their indifference. There was nothing to fight, so what was the point of it all, their relaxed bodies seemed to indicate.

He had tackled Tyrrell about it but the first lieutenant had said cheerfully, 'Hell, sir, it don't signify they won't be able to fight if th' time calls for it.'

Bolitho's sharp reply brought a new barrier between them, and for the moment he was prepared to let it remain.

Captain Ransome must have used the sloop like a personal possession, a yacht, he thought. Sometimes during the night when Bolitho had come down to the cabin after a frustrating hour on deck watching the hands shortening sail yet again he had pictured Ransome with some woman or other. Or Tyrrell pacing the quarterdeck, tearing himself apart as he imagined his sister just a few feet below him. He had not mentioned the matter to Tyrrell since his first outburst, but had found himself wondering about the real story, and what had happened to the girl after Ransome's sudden death.

Stockdale came into the cabin with the shaving bowl. He glared at Fitch and wheezed, 'Get the cap'n's breakfast!'

To Bolitho he added, ' 'Nother clear mornin', sir.' He waited until Bolitho was in his chair and then held the razor against the window. He seemed content with its edge. 'Wot we need is a real good blow.' He showed his uneven teeth. 'Make some o' these young puppies jump about!'

Bolitho relaxed as the razor moved precisely over his chin. Stockdale said very little but he always seemed to hit the exact point.

In between strokes he replied, 'In another month we'll be in the hurricane season again, Stockdale. I hope *that* will satisfy you.'

The big coxswain grunted. 'Seen 'em afore. Us'll see 'em again an' live to tell of it.'

Bolitho gave up. Nothing, it seemed, could break the man's supreme confidence in his ability to produce a miracle, even in the face of a hurricane.

Voices rang out overhead, and then he heard feet dashing down the companion ladder from the quarterdeck.

It was Midshipman Heyward, impeccable as ever in spite of being on his feet for much of the night.

'Captain, sir.' He watched Stockdale's razor poised in mid-air. 'Mr. Graves's respects and *Fawn* has just signalled. Sail to the nor'-east.'

Bolitho snatched the towel. 'Very well. I will come up.'

Stockdale laid down the bowl. 'That same one, sir?'

Bolitho shook his head 'Unlikely. She'd never overreach us in one night, even if she was after our blood.' He rubbed his face vigorously. 'But in this empty sea a sight of anything is welcome.'

When he reached the quarterdeck he found Tyrrell and most of the others already there. Below the mainmast the hands had just been mustered in readiness for the morning assault on the decks with holystones and swabs while others were waiting by the pumps or just staring up at the barely filled sails. Graves touched his hat.

'Masthead lookout has not yet sighted anything, sir.'

Bolitho nodded and strode to the compass. North-west by north. It seemed as if it had been riveted in that direction since time began. It was hardly surprising *Fawn* had sighted the newcomer first. In her position ahead and slightly to starboard of the transports she was better placed. All the same, he would have wished otherwise. *Fawn's* signals and execution of Colquhoun's orders always seemed to be that much quicker than his.

Through the criss-cross of rigging and shrouds and slightly to starboard of the rearmost transport he saw the other sloop tacking awkwardly in the gentle westerly breeze. With every stitch of canvas on her braced yards she was barely making headway.

From aloft came the sudden cry, 'Deck there! Sail on the starboard beam!'

Tyrrell crossed to Bolitho's side.

'What d'you think? One of our own?'

Graves said swiftly, 'Or a damned Yankee, eh?'

Bolitho saw the exchange of glances, the sudden hositility between them like something physical.

He said calmly, 'We will know directly, *gentlemen*.'

Midshipman Bethune called, 'From *Fawn*, sir. *Remain on station*.'

Graves said complacently, 'There goes *Fawn*. She's going about to take a soldier's wind under her tail.'

Bolitho said, 'Get aloft, Mr. Graves. I want to know everything you can discover about that sail.'

Graves stared at him. 'I've a good hand aloft, sir.'

Bolitho met his resentment gravely. 'And now I require a good officer there, too, Mr. Graves. An experienced eye and not just a clear one.'

Graves moved stiffly to the weather shrouds and after the merest hesitation began to climb.

Tyrrell said quietly, 'Do him good, that one!'

Bolitho glanced around the crowded quarterdeck.

'Maybe, Mr. Tyrrell. But if you imagine I am using my authority to foster some petty spite between you then I must assure you otherwise.' He lowered his voice. 'It is an enemy we are fighting, not each other!'

Then he took a telescope from the rack and walked to the foot of the mizzen mast. Steadying his legs against the uncomfortable motion he trained the glass on the *Fawn* and then very slowly beyond her. Minutes passed, and then as the distant ship lifted on some large roller he saw her topgallant sails shining in the first sunlight like matched pink shells. She was clawing her way close-hauled on a converging course, her yards braced so tightly they were almost fore-and-aft.

Graves yelled down, 'Frigate, sir!' A pause as every man looked up at his tiny silhouette against the sky. 'English built!'

Bolitho stayed silent. English built perhaps. But who now stood behind her guns? He watched *Fawn* edging round, her masthead pendant lifting and curling listlessly. More flags shot up her yards and Bethune yelled,

'From *Fawn*, sir. Recognition signal.' A further pause as he groped through his grubby book. 'She's the *Miranda*, thirty-two, Captain Selby, sir.'

Buckle said to the deck at large, 'From England most likely.'

The light was already stronger, and as he stared across the brightening water Bolitho could feel the first warm rays against his face. From England. Every man aboard was probably thinking of those words. Except for Tyrrell and the colonists in the company. But all the rest would be picturing his own past way of life. Village or farm, some ale house outside a harbour or fishing port. A woman's face, a child's last grip before the harder hands of the pressgang.

He found himself thinking of his own home in Falmouth. The great stone house below Pendennis Castle where his father would be waiting and wondering about him and his brother Hugh, while he remained in Cornwall. Like all the Bolitho ancestors, his father had been a sea-officer, but having lost an arm and his health was now confined to a landbound existence, always within sight of the ships and the sea which had forsaken him.

'From *Fawn*, sir. *General. Heave to.*'

Colquhoun, it seemed, was quite satisfied with the other ship's identity. For once the two transports needed no extra goading to obey the signal. Perhaps like the rest they, too, were eager for news from that other world.

Bolitho closed the glass and handed it to a boatswain's mate.

'Shorten sail, Mr. Tyrrell, and heave to as ordered.' He waited until the lieutenant had shouted for the topmen to get aloft and then added, 'That frigate has been hard worked so her mission must be important.'

He had watched the newcomer while she had forged towards the uneven cluster of ships, had seen the great scars on her hull where the sea had pared away the paintwork like a giant knife. Her sails, too, looked much repaired, evidence of a rapid voyage.

Bethune shouted, '*Miranda*'s hoisted another signal, sir!' He swayed in the shrouds as he tried to level his big telescope. 'To *Fawn*. *Captain repair on board.*'

Once again *Fawn's* response was swift, her big gig being swayed out within minutes of the signal. Bolitho could imagine Colquhoun hurrying to the other ship and the *Miranda*'s consternation when they discovered that he was senior to their own captain.

Whatever it entailed, the matter was obviously urgent, and not merely an exchange of gossip at this chance encounter in open waters.

Bolitho rubbed his chin and said, 'I'm going below. Call me if anything happens.'

In the cabin he found Stockdale waiting with his coat and sword, his lopsided grin very broad as he muttered, 'Thought you'd be wantin' these, sir.'

Fitch was gripping the table, his legs spread apart as the sloop rolled and staggered in the uncomfortable troughs, the power gone from her sails. He was staring at the breakfast he had just brought, his narrow features resigned.

Bolitho smiled. 'Never fear, I'll find time to eat it later.'

It was strange that the mere sight of another ship, the obscure hint of excitement, had given him an appetite at last. He gulped down some coffee as Stockdale adjusted his sword-belt before handing him the coat.

Perhaps *Miranda* had discovered an enemy and needed help to attack them. Maybe the war was over, or another had broken out elsewhere. The possibilities seemed endless.

He looked up and saw Tyrrell peering through the open skylight.

'Cap'n, sir! The *Fawn*'s gig is shoving off from th' frigate.'

Bolitho replied, 'Thank you.' He forcibly disguised his disappointment. 'That was quick.'

Tyrrell vanished and he added quietly, 'There'll be time for breakfast after all.'

He was mistaken. Even as he began to unfasten his sword-belt Tyrrell's face reappeared at the skylight, his words filling the cabin as he shouted, 'From *Fawn*, sir. *Repair on board forthwith*.'

Stockdale bounded from the cabin, his hoarse voice bellowing for the gig's crew which the boatswain had already thought prudent to muster.

With frantic haste the boat was swung outboard and dropped alongside, where with little thought for dignity or safety, Bolitho hurled himself into the sternsheets, his sword clattering against the gunwale and almost tripping him on top of the oarsmen.

Stockdale bawled, 'Give way all!' In a lower but no less menacing tone he added, 'An' remember, my beauties, if one o' you misses a stroke you'll 'ave me to answer!'

The gig seemed to fly across the water, and when at last Bolitho regained his composure and looked astern he saw the *Sparrow* was already a cable clear. She was pitching steeply in the swell, her sails rippling and flashing in disorder while she lay hove to in the pale sunlight. In spite of his own busy thoughts and anxiety he could still find time to admire her. In the past he had often watched the stern cabin of a passing man-of-war and pondered about her captain, what sort of person, his qualities or lack of them. It was very hard to accept that the *Sparrow*'s cabin was his own and that others might be wondering about him.

He turned and saw *Fawn*'s outline overlapping that of the idling frigate, figures moving round her entry port to receive him with all formality. He smiled to himself. In the face of hell it seemed likely that no captain, no matter how junior, was expected to go without his proper acknowledgement.

Bolitho was met at the entry port by Maulby, *Fawn*'s commander. He was very thin, and but for a pronounced stoop would have stood well over six feet. Life between a sloop's decks must be uncomfortable for such a man, Bolitho thought.

He appeared a few years older than himself and had a drawling, bored manner of speaking. But he seemed pleasant enough and made him welcome.

As they ducked beneath the quarterdeck Maulby said, 'The little admiral is excited, it would seem.'

Bolitho paused and stared at him. 'Who?'

Maulby shrugged loosely. 'In the flotilla we *always* refer to Colquhoun as our little admiral. He had a way of inserting himself in the role without actually holding the necessary rank!' He laughed, his bent shoulders touching a deckhead beam so that he appeared to be supporting it with his own frame. 'You look shocked, my friend?'

Bolitho grinned. Maulby, he decided, was a man you could like and trust on sight. But he had never before heard such comments made about a superior by two subordinates meeting for the first time. In some ships it would be inviting disaster and oblivion.

He replied, 'No, but I am refreshed!'

The stern cabin was much the same size as his own. There was no other similarity. Plain, even spartan, he was reminded of Tyrrell's anger, his bitter attack on the *woman's touch*. He saw Colquhoun sitting at a table, his chin in his hands as he stared at some newly opened despatches.

Without pausing he said, 'Sit down, both of you. I must give this matter my attention.'

Maulby looked gravely at Bolitho and dropped one eyelid in a quick wink.

Bolitho glanced away, Maulby's easy acceptance of their superior was daunting. *The little admiral*. It suited Colquhoun very well.

Maulby seemed well able to remain relaxed, yet he was nobody's fool. Bolitho had noted the smart way his men had moved about the gun deck, the crisp passing and execution of orders. Bolitho had not met the other captains of Colquhoun's flotilla. If they were all such odd birds as Maulby it was hardly surprising that Colquhoun was showing signs of strain. Or maybe in such small ships individual characters were more noticeable. He thought of Pears in the old *Trojan*, his rugged features which had never seemed to alter under any circumstances. In a gale, close to a lee shore, or under enemy fire, witnessing a flogging, or commending some sailor on promotion, he had always seemed remote and beyond personal contact. It was hard to imagine Maulby, he paused, or himself either, with such aloof and godlike powers.

Colquhoun's voice broke across his thoughts, sharp and incisive. '*Miranda*'s captain has brought serious news.' He still did not lift his head. 'France has signed an alliance with the Americans. It means that General Washington will have the full support of French regular troops *and* a powerful fleet.'

Bolitho shifted in his chair, his mind grappling with Colquhoun's announcement. The French had already done much to help their new ally, but this would mean that the war was now firmly in the open. It also implied that the French were showing fresh confidence in the Americans' chance of victory.

Colquhoun stood up quickly and stared through the stern windows. 'The *Miranda* is carrying despatches and intelligence for the Commander-in-Chief at New York. When he left Plymouth he had a brig in company with duplicate information for Antigua. The ships were caught in a storm shortly after clearing the Channel and the brig was not seen again.'

Maulby asked quietly, 'Taken by the French, sir?'

Colquhoun swung on him with unexpected anger. 'What the hell does it matter? Taken or wrecked, dismasted or bloody well eaten by worms, it makes no difference to us, does it!'

Suddenly Bolitho realised the cause of his attack. Had Colquhoun remained at Antigua until his own ship had refitted, Maulby would have been in charge of the convoy's escort. *Miranda*'s captain, desperate to carry his news to New York, and senior to Maulby, would have ordered him to make arrangements for the information to be taken without delay to Antigua. Nobody could rely on the brig's survival as an excuse for doing nothing. By a mere twist of fate, or Colquhoun's determination to keep control of his ships at sea, *Miranda*'s captain had been able to pass on the decision to him.

In a calmer tone Colquhoun continued, 'It has been reported that the French have been preparing ships for months. From Toulon a whole squadron set sail weeks ago and slipped through the Gibraltar patrols without so much as a squeak of news getting out.' He looked at each of them in turn. 'They could be on their way here, to the American coast, anywhere, for all we know, damn their eyes!'

The *Fawn* had swung slightly in the slow procession of troughs, and through the swaying windows Bolitho could see the two transports, huge and ungainly, their yards askew as they awaited the next signal. Each transport was filled to the deck seams with much needed supplies for the army in Philadelphia. In the wrong hands they would represent a tremendous prize, and the realisation must be foremost in Colquhoun's mind.

Colquhoun said, '*Miranda* has agreed to stand by the convoy until we contact the inshore squadron. But in this damned weather it might take weeks.'

Bolitho imagined Colquhoun was picturing the distance like a mental chart. All those miles, with the knowledge that he must eventually make the long passage back to Antigua to resume control of his small force.

Maulby drawled, 'May I suggest that I continue with the transports, sir? With *Miranda* in company we will be safe enough.' He glanced at Bolitho. 'You could then return in *Sparrow* to English Harbour, pass the news to the admiral and prepare our own ships for further work.'

Colquhoun stared at him, his eyes unseeing.

'God damn the complacency of our precious Government! For years this has been brewing, and while the French have been building new ships, ours have been allowed to go rotten for want of money. If the Channel Fleet were to be ordered to sea tomorrow I doubt that more than twenty sail of the line would be capable!' He saw their surprise and nodded vehemently. 'Oh yes, gentlemen, while you have been out here imagining that all would be ready if once the call came, I have been made to stay silent and watch it happening.' He struck the table with his fist. 'Some flag officers are too concerned with political power and gracious living to care for the wants of the fleet!'

He sat down heavily. 'I must decide . . .'

The door opened slightly and a frightened-looking midshipman said, 'From *Miranda*, sir. She requests instructions . . .' He got no further.

'Tell him to mind his manners!' Colquhoun glared at him hotly. 'It is *my* decision!'

Bolitho glanced at Maulby. For the first time in his life he was beginning to realise the meaning of command. Whatever Colquhoun decided could be equally right or wrong. Bolitho had learned one thing well. If you made a right decision, others often received the credit. But make a wrong one and you were in no doubt where the blame would lie.

Colquhoun said suddenly, 'Send for your clerk, Maulby. I will dictate new orders for . . .' he looked at Bolitho, 'for *Sparrow*.'

He seemed to be speaking his thoughts aloud. 'I do not doubt your ability, Bolitho, but you lack experience. I will need Maulby's *Fawn* with me until I know what is to happen next.' He gestured to the table as the ship's clerk entered the cabin. 'You must remain with the transports. *Miranda's* captain will give you guidance, and you will obey him to the best of your skill. Your orders will allow you to return to the flotilla when the transports have been delivered.' He paused and added softly, 'Delivered.'

Bolitho rose to his feet. 'Aye, sir.'

'Now get out and leave me to draft these orders.'

Maulby took Bolitho's elbow and guided him towards the gun deck.

'I think the little admiral is worried, my friend.' He sighed. 'I was hoping to rid my ship of his presence and pass him on to you.' He turned and gave a quick grin. 'There is no justice in this world!'

Bolitho saw his gig falling and rising in the swell, Stockdale shading his eyes as he watched the sloop for a recall.

He said, 'The news is bad, but not unexpected. At least the pretence is done with.'

Maulby nodded gravely. 'No comfort, I fear, to the lamb about to be devoured.'

Bolitho stared at him. 'Not that serious surely?'

'I am not certain. What the Frogs do today the damned Spaniards will copy tomorrow. Soon we will have the whole world at our throats.' He frowned. 'The little admiral is right on one score. It seems that our Government is run by demons, most of whom appear determined to drive the rest of us to madness.'

The first lieutenant hurried into view and proffered a freshly sealed envelope.

Maulby clapped Bolitho on the shoulder and said cheerfully, 'Think of us sometimes. While you enjoy your leisurely voyage, I will be forced to share my table with *him*.' He rubbed his hands. 'But with any luck he may get promotion and vanish forever.'

The lieutenant said urgently, 'Captain Colquhoun's compliments, and will you join him immediately?'

Maulby nodded and held out his hand.

'Until we meet again, Bolitho.' He seemed unwilling to let him leave. Then he said awkwardly, 'Be warned, my friend. You have a fine command, but you also have a large number of colonists in your company.' He tried to smile. 'If the war goes badly, there are some who might be tempted to change allegiance. In their shoes I could perhaps feel the same.'

Bolitho met his gaze and nodded. 'Thank you. I will remember it.'

Maulby did not hide his relief. 'There, I knew you were a good fellow! Not one to treat my clumsy advice as patronage.'

Bolitho grinned. 'You took a risk. I might have gone to Colquhoun and told him of your name for him.'

'I would have denied it!'

'Naturally!'

They both laughed.

Then as the gig hooked on to the chains they became formal again. Even before Bolitho had reached the boat flags were soaring up the *Fawn's* yards, and an acknowledgement appeared above the frigate with equal speed.

Bolitho settled himself in the sternsheets and stared towards his ship. Colquhoun had taken the responsibility and made a decision. His own responsibility was just beginning.

Lieutenant Tyrrell turned as Bolitho's head and shoulders rose through the quarterdeck hatch and waited until he had made his usual inspection of the sails and compass before remarking, 'She's running well, sir.'

Bolitho walked across the tilting deck and rested his hands on the rail, feeling the hull quivering beneath him like a living creature. The noon sun stood high over the ship, but he was able to ignore it, conscious only of the well-filled sails, the leap of spray up and over the bowsprit. It had been five days since *Fawn* had turned back for Antigua, and it seemed as if Colquhoun's disappearance from their midst had brought a change of luck and weather. Perverse as ever, but for once on their side, the wind had backed suddenly to south-south-west and had freshened into a lively blow which had hardly dropped during the whole time. Under bulging canvas the ships had driven on towards the American coast, which according to the most recent calculations now lay some two hundred and fifty miles away. The heavy merchantmen had maintained a good five knots, satisfied perhaps that *Miranda's* captain was content to leave them to their own devices. The frigate's signals had been confined for the most part to *Sparrow*. For within twenty-four hours of leaving *Fawn* the masthead lookout had sighted a solitary sail once again, far astern of the convoy, a tiny white flaw on the horizon.

Bolitho had sent Graves aloft with a telescope, but even he had been unable to identify the mysterious follower. Next he signalled to the frigate, requesting permission to investigate. He had been refused. *Miranda's* captain was probably regretting his meeting with the convoy. But for their dragging weight he would have reached his objective by now and would have borne no blame for failing to pass his news to Antigua. But once in contact with the slower vessels he had no choice but to act as he had. Also, he would be fully aware that once beyond his control *Sparrow* might become too involved with a separate situation to return, and thus leave him with total responsibility for the transports.

The unknown sail had not been sighted again, and Bolitho had accepted that *Miranda's* captain had been right, if over cautious, to restrain his efforts.

He looked at Tyrrell's bronzed features and nodded. 'I am well satisfied.'

He watched some foretopmen sliding down the backstays, racing each other to the deck after their work aloft. Buckle was right. She moved like a bird with any sort of wind. He watched the *Bear*, the transport closest to his own ship, and wished they were free of the convoy. Then he could really put *Sparrow* to the test. Royals, even studding sails could be rigged, if only to find out what she could accomplish under every stitch of canvas.

Most of the unemployed officers were on deck enjoying their usual gossip before the midday meal, careful to stay on the lee side and as much out of his way as possible.

He saw Dalkeith, the surgeon, laughing with Buckle, his head very white in its baldness under the harsh light. The red wig was being vigorously shaken by the wardroom servant, and Bolitho guessed it had been given some sort of a wash. Lock, the purser, was in a more serious conversation with young Heyward, opening and ruffling a big ledger in the wind as he explained some point of victualling which might place the midshipman's knowledge above that of his friend Bethune. The latter, being on watch, stood untidily by the quarterdeck rail, his shirt open to his waist and massaging his stomach with one hand. Bolitho smiled. The boy was no doubt hungry. Midshipmen like Bethune usually were.

Down on the gun deck many of the seamen were lounging beneath the sails' great shadows or passing the time like their officers. The boatswain was with his own friend Yule, the gunner, and together they would have made a frightening pair of highwaymen, Bolitho thought. Whereas Tilby was vast and ungainly, his heavy features seamed with too much drink, Yule was swarthy and lithe, like a stoat, with darting, flinty eyes which were forever on the move.

As he glanced from group to group he was again reminded of his new-found isolation. Privacy which could lead to loneliness. Privilege which might become a burden.

He thrust his hands behind him and began to pace slowly along the weather side, letting the warm wind ruffle his hair and play with his open shirt. Somewhere out there beyond the hammock nettings was the coast of America. It would be strange to drop anchor only to find the war had finished, that blood had proved too strong in the face of France's new challenge. If England were to admit to America's independence then perhaps both nations would unite against France and settle her ambitions once and for all. He glanced at Tyrrell's profile and wondered if he was thinking the same.

He shut Tyrrell's personal problems from his mind and tried to concentrate on the string of affairs which daily needed his attention. The water supply should be replenished as soon as possible. The casks were poor, and water soon became rancid in this climate. And he would purchase fresh fruit whenever they contacted the land or some supply vessel. It was amazing that the ship's company had stayed so healthy when Ransome had failed to take such simple precautions. Aboard the old *Trojan* he had not seen one case of scurvy in the three years he had been in her, evidence of Captain Pears's concern for his men and a valuable lesson to all his subordinates. He had already spoken about it to Lock, and after some hesitation the purser had muttered, 'A *costly* affair, sir.'

'Costlier if our people go down with disease, Mr. Lock. I have known a whole squadron rendered useless because of such skinflint methods.'

Then there was the matter of a flogging, his first as captain. He had always disliked unnecessary use of punishment even though he knew it to be necessary on occasions. In the Navy discipline was harsh and instant, and when a ship was miles from home and other authority, it was a captain's deterrent to insubordination and final confusion. Some captains used it without thought. Brutal and inhuman floggings were commonplace in many ships, and as a young midshipman Bolitho nearly fainted after one such spectacle. Other captains, weak and inefficient, left authority to subordinates and shut their ears to its misuse.

But for the most part the English seaman knew the measure of his service, and if he took chances was prepared to accept the consequences. And if one man thieved or cheated another of his messmates he had no mercy at all. The justice of the lower deck was equally feared to that of a captain.

But this case was different, or could be from what he knew of it. A seaman had defied Lieutenant Graves during a night watch when the hands had been called to reef topsails in an unexpected squall. He had shouted at the officer and called him a 'heartless bugger' within earshot of some twenty other people.

In confidence Tyrrell had asked Bolitho to accept the seaman's explanation. He was a good hand, and Graves had provoked him in a fit of anger when he had failed to reach his station on the mainyard with his companions.

A *dirty Yankee bastard*. They were the words Graves had used. Too lazy to do his proper duty, and no doubt too gutless to fight when the time came.

All this and Tyrrell's heated attack on Graves's handling of the matter were fresh proof of the latent tension amongst the company under his command.

Graves had been adamant. The man had insulted him in front of his watch and must be punished.

He was right in one respect. His authority had to be upheld or he would never be able to retain control again.

Bolitho blamed himself. If he had had more time to consider this unusual situation, or had taken less comfort from his own new position, he could have prevented it. By example or by forcing his will on his officers he might have made them realise that such behaviour would not be tolerated. But that was all too late now. It had happened.

He had compromised by standing the man over, knowing then as at this moment that he was merely postponing the inevitable.

He glanced up towards the mainyard, braced hard round as the ship heeled close-hauled on a larboard tack. He could see the man now, naked but for a scrap of canvas, working with some others on the endless business of re-splicing and repairs high above the deck. Did Tyrrell really think the man was provoked? he wondered. Or was he standing up for him because he imagined Graves was getting at him by punishing another colonist?

'Deck there!' The masthead lookout's cry was muffled by the wind and the lively crack of sails.' '*Miranda*'s signallin'!'

Bolitho swung round. 'Jump to it, Mr. Bethune! You are half asleep today!'

Tyrrell stood aside as the midshipman ran to the lee shrouds with his telescope.

'Thinking of his next meal!' He was smiling at the boy's confusion.

'It seems that the masthead lookout was the only one in *this* watch thinking of his duty, Mr. Tyrrell!'

The edge of his voice brought a flush to the lieutenant's face and he turned away without answering.

Bethune called, 'From *Miranda*, sir! *Sail to the nor'-west!*'

'Acknowledge.'

Bolitho was angry with Tyrrell's careless attitude, angrier still more with his own unfair outburst.

Some two miles ahead of the *Golden Fleece*, her patched sails hard-bellied and drawing well, the *Miranda* was already setting her topgallants in readiness to investigate. The unknown ship, whatever she was, lay somewhere across the larboard bow, and as she had not been seen before it seemed likely she was on a converging course.

'Deck there! Sail in sight! Fine on th' weather bow!'

Bolitho looked round at the intent faces. For an instant he toyed with the idea of making his way to the dizzy mainmast crosstrees himself, in spite of his fear of heights which he had never been able to overcome. The long climb up those shivering, vibrating shrouds might drive his anger away and leave his mind clear once again.

He saw Raven, the newly-appointed master's mate, and said, 'Go aloft. Take a glass and tell me what you see.'

Buckle had told him that the man was an experienced sailor, one who had already served in several King's ships and would not be easily fooled by first appearances.

Before Raven had even reached the mainyard the lookout called again, 'Two ships! Close in company!'

Every eye was on Raven's body as he swarmed out and around the futtock shrouds and up towards the topmast head.

Bethune, still smarting over his failure to see *Miranda*'s signal, suddenly stiffened and called, 'Gunfire, sir!' He had his hands cupped round his ears, giving his round face the appearance of a freckled goblin.

Bolitho looked down at him. Then as his hearing adjusted itself beyond the crack of sails and the plunging sweep of spray around the hull, he, too, heard the deeper, discordant thud of cannon fire. He was almost beside himself with impatience, but he knew if he hurried Raven he might become too confused to make a proper assessment.

'Deck there!' It was Raven at last. 'First ship's a merchantman! She's under attack from a brig!'

Buckle exclaimed thickly, 'Privateer, by God!'

Bolitho snatched a telescope and trained it through the dark mass of rigging and beyond some men who were grouped on the forecastle. A trick of the light. He blinked and tried again. No, there it was, a tiny white speck which seemed to mingle with the unending pattern of crisp wavecrests. The lonely merchantman had been unlucky, but now with any sort of good fortune they might turn the tables on her attacker.

The *Miranda* was already tacking violently, her sails in confusion as she headed away from her original station. Even as her sails refilled and hardened on the new tack Bolitho saw her signal flags breaking to the wind.

Bethune said quickly, 'General signal, sir. Remain on station.'

Buckle swore. 'After the bloody prize money himself, the greedy bugger!'

The gunfire was clearer now, and as he raised the glass again Bolitho saw smoke drifting down-wind from the two ships, the lithe shape of the attacking brig as she endeavoured to close the range still further.

He shut the glass with a snap, aware of the muttering behind him, disappointment which matched his own. *Miranda*'s captain was probably making the attack more to break the frustration of a slow passage than to humiliate the *Sparrow*.

He looked at Tyrrell's broad shoulders and said, 'Signal the *Bear* to make more sail. She's dropping astern badly.'

Then he turned back to watch the frigate. She was moving fast in spite of the wind being almost abeam of her sails, and he could see her port lids opening, the single line of muzzles catching the sunlight as they were run out in readiness to fight.

The brig's captain must have realized what was happening. Even so, he was probably unwilling to lose his prize with victory almost in his grasp.

On the gangways and gun deck his own seamen were chattering and waving their arms about, and he guessed they were discussing how they would have acted had they been given the chance to go for the privateer.

Bolitho recalled Raven to the deck and said. 'You did well.'

The man grinned uncomfortably. 'Thank you, sir. The brig's a Yankee right enough. Seen many like her in me time. T'other one's an Indiaman by her looks, 'though her gunnery ain't so good as some on 'em. There's never a mark on the Yankee's canvas.'

Tyrrell shouted, 'Th' brig's broken off the action! He's going to make a run for it!'

Bolitho sighed. The merchantman was already turning steadily towards the little convoy while the *Miranda* under full sail charged towards her attacker. The brig, if well handled, stood a fair chance against a frigate in matters of speed and manoeuvrability. But this one had waited just that much too long. Converging like prongs of a trap the three vessels would pass beam to beam, the frigate shielding the merchantman and well able to rake the brig from stem to stern as they passed.

Provided the brig was not too badly damaged she might be useful to the fleet. Either way, *Miranda*'s captain would gain a nice purse of prize money.

He tore his eyes away as sounds of angry voices came up the quarterdeck ladder at his side.

It was Tilby, flushed from some secret hoard of rum, his face heavy with rage as he said, 'Beg pardon, sir, but this 'ere man says 'e wants to speak to 'ee.' He glared severely at the seaman in question. 'I told 'im that no man under punishment can speak to an officer without permission.'

Bolitho saw that the seaman behind Tilby was the one waiting to be flogged. He was a young, well-made man and was dragging at the boatswain's arm with frantic determination.

'What is it, Yelverton?' Bolitho nodded to Tilby. 'Is it *so* important?'

The seaman reached the quarterdeck and swallowed hard. 'That ship, sir! She ain't no Indiaman! She's a damned Frenchie! I seen her in Boston some years back!'

Bolitho swung round. 'God in heaven!'

It was at that moment the oncoming merchantman fired a full broadside into the *Miranda*'s unmanned side as she passed, the sound going on and on until it reached the heart of every man in the convoy.

4

A Total Responsibility

Even at two miles' range Bolitho saw the *Miranda* give a violent shiver as the broadside swept across her. It must have been aimed high, for as the smoke fanned away he saw the havoc left by the sudden onslaught, maintopmast gone, and most of her sails ripped and punctured like rags in a gale.

He thrust himself from the nettings and noticed that the men near him were still standing like groups of statues, or people so stricken they were unable to think or respond.

He shouted, 'Mr. Tyrrell! Beat to quarters and clear for action!' He gripped Bethune's arm, seeing his dazed expression as he added, 'Run up the colours!'

A ship's boy seized his drum and began to beat out the staccato tattoo. The men on deck, and poised in the bows where they had waited to watch *Miranda*'s swift victory, came alive and began to run to their stations. But gone was the automatic movement of men at drill, or the grim silence of old hands facing one more battle. They hurried like those already too confused to act for a set purpose. Some cannoned into one another, others stood momentarily at the wrong gun, or groping with unfamiliar equipment until a petty officer kicked them away.

Bolitho looked at Buckle, trying to keep his tone level amidst the din around him. 'Get the courses off her and set the t'gallants. There'll be enough risk of fire without having the canvas burn around our ears.'

Below the quarterdeck he heard the thud and bang of screens being torn down, a patter of feet as the boys dashed from the magazine with powder for each waiting gun.

He made himself face the approaching ships, knowing it was taking far too long to prepare for action. How near they looked. There was more gunfire, and he saw smoke lifting and writhing between the vessels making it impossible to know what was happening.

He held his breath as he saw the *Miranda*'s yards swinging above the smoke, and knew her captain was trying to go about and run parallel with his attacker. Guns roared through the drifting fog, their long orange tongues flashing above the churned water, some of the balls whipping away over open sea, leaving vicious spurts of spray to mark their progress.

Miranda was still edging round, her pockmarked sails flapping weakly as she began to swing past the wind's eye. Her captain was either going to fight the bigger ship gun to gun, or intended to slip past her stern and rake her with a broadside as he did so.

Bolitho heard someone groan as the enemy fired into the smoke. Gun by gun down her hidden side, the balls could almost be felt across the tumbling white-horses.

It was superbly timed, catching the frigate even as she was beginning to pass across the wind. The enemy was using langridge or chain-shot, for as the slow broadside smashed home Bolitho saw the *Miranda*'s fore and mainmasts stagger and then begin to topple sideways into the smoke, the sails jerking to the bombardment. From a lithe and beautiful ship to a crippled wreck, the *Miranda* was still trying to turn, her bow-chaser firing blindly, the ensign showing scarlet from her mizzen.

Tyrrell shouted wildly, 'Cleared for action!'

Bolitho looked at him. 'Load and run out, if you please.'

The lieutenant stayed facing him, his eyes very bright in the sunlight. 'You ain't going to fight *both* of 'em, surely?'

'If necessary.'

Bolitho turned as more shots echoed and murmured across the shortening distance. He saw the brig clawing away from the two larger ships, her maintopgallant leaning at a dangerous angle where *Miranda*'s first balls had found their mark.

The planks vibrated under his shoes, and as the port lids opened the *Sparrow*'s eighteen guns squeaked and rumbled towards the sunlight, the bare-backed seamen slipping on sanded decks as they tried to keep in time to the shouted commands from their captains.

Bolitho stared along the length of his ship with something like despair. In moments now, all would be finished. His ship, his precious *Sparrow*, would be sharing the frigate's fate.

And it had all been so easy. It had happened so often in the past that the sight of a helpless merchantman being harried by a well-armed privateer had not even aroused the faintest suspicion. No wonder the privateer's sails had been unmarked in their carefully staged battle. How the two American captains must have laughed when *Miranda* had swept in to defend her own murderer.

He felt Stockdale breathing noisily beside him, the sudden grip of the swordbelt around his waist.

He said huskily, 'By God, sir, them's bad odds!'

'Deck there!' The masthead lookout had been forgotten in the sight of disaster. *Miranda*'s goin' to grapple!' The unseen lookout gave a cracked cheer. 'She's goin' to close with the bugger!'

Bolitho ran to the rail. The frigate was almost hidden by the heavier shape of the enemy ship, but he could tell from the set of her mizzen that she was indeed lurching towards her attacker. Another crash of gunfire made the smoke spout upwards between them, and the frigate's remaining mast vanished in a welter of rigging and ripped canvas. But Bolitho could see the sudden activity on the enemy's gangways, the surge of figures by her foremast, and pictured the battered frigate heading her bows straight for the forecastle. Muskets cracked feebly across the water, and he saw the telltale flash of steel as the two vessels ground momentarily together and the fight became hand to hand.

He grasped Tyrrell's arm and shouted, '*Miranda*'s given us time!' He saw no understanding in his eyes, only disbelief. 'If she can hold on, we will close with the brig!'

He shaded his face against the glare and watched the brig as she swept down towards the two transports.

'She'll cross *Golden Fleece*'s bows, and rake her as she passes.' He was shouting his thoughts aloud. 'We will wear ship directly, pass between the transports, and return the compliment!'

Tyrrell bit his lip. 'But we might collide with th' privateer, sir!'

Bolitho swung him round, pointing him at the embattled ships.

'Do you want those lads to die for nothing, man?' He pushed him to the rail. 'Now get ready to wear when I give the order!'

The brig was already dead ahead of *Sparrow*'s raked jib-boom, no more than a mile away. Aboard the leading transport Bolitho could see smoke from a solitary gun, although he saw no sign of a ball.

'Signal the transports to keep station, Mr. Bethume!' He repeated the order to break the midshipman from his unmoving stance. '*Lively!*'

If either of the transports' captains lost this head now all would fail. The enemy would destroy or capture at leisure. Even now there was little room for hope of any kind.

And all of it, from the first hint of surprise to this moment, had been merely minutes.

He made himself walk aft towards the taffrail, his eyes passing over the crouching swivel gunners, the two helmsmen at their unprotected wheel, Buckle grim-faced and staring at the sails above. All of them.

He saw Raven, the new master's mate, watching him wretchedly, and paused to say, 'You weren't to know. She *was* an Indiaman after all, but not, I fear, as she was intended.'

Raven shook his head, so concerned with his failure to recognise the enemy that he seemed oblivious to the sporadic crash of cannon fire.

'I should've *seen* 'er, sir. But I saw what I *expected* to see, an' I'm powerful sorry on it after you givin' me a chance to better meself.'

Bolitho smiled, feeling his lips cracking with the effort.

'And I will expect you to do even better this day, Mr. Raven!'

He strode aft, hands behind his back, the new sword flapping against his thigh.

Buckle pursed his lips in a silent whistle. 'He's a calm one. Death coming up the hawse an' he just walks about like he was enjoying himself.'

Behind the fixed smile Bolitho continued to pace the deck, his ears pitched above the gunfire to catch the news that the brig had reached the first transport. If her captain saw through his frail plan it would be pointless to continue with it. He would either have to run away from the fight and carry *Miranda*'s important news to the admiral, or stay and await the final meeting with the converted Indiaman. A few of the *Miranda*'s guns were still firing here and there, their muzzles almost overlapping those of the other ship. Between decks it must be a slaughterhouse, he thought despairingly.

Tyrrell shouted, 'Brig's crossing her bows!'

Sharper explosions echoed over the water, and Bolitho knew the brig was firing her starboard battery as she ran easily across the transport's bowsprit. Before she had vanished beyond *Golden Fleece*'s great bulk he saw the American flag whipping jauntily from her gaff, the sudden stab of musket fire from her low deck as sharpshooters practised their aim.

'*Now!*' Bolitho sliced the air. 'Wear ship!'

As the helm went over and along the *Sparrow*'s crowded decks the men threw themselves on the braces, the hull seemed to stagger violently under the shock. Blocks screamed, and above the decks the great yards creaked round with such speed that Bolitho could feel the whole fabric shaking in protest. But nothing carried away, and as she heeled steeply to take the wind under her stern the sails lifted then filled to its thrust.

Bolitho cupped his hands. 'Mr. Graves! Engage with the larboard guns first! You will point the thirty-two-pounder yourself!' He saw Graves nod before vanishing beneath the forecastle in the direction of the bow-chaser.

How fast she was moving, despite both her courses being brailed up to the yards for fear of fire when the guns started to engage. The main-topgallant seemed to bend forward, the masthead pendant flicking straight out towards the bows as if to point the way.

Already the jib-boom must be crossing the leading transport's quarter, and to starboard Bolitho saw the second one, *Bear*, altering course slightly as if fearful of a collision with the sloop which was dashing across her path. More shots came from beyond the first transport, and he saw smoke funnelling down her hull to mark the brig's progress.

From forward came the cry, 'Thar she be! On th' larboard bow!'

The *Sparrow*'s unexpected appearance between the two transports seemed to have caught the brig's captain totally by surprise. The privateer was passing down the transport's side, about a cable clear, her yards braced round to hold her on a starboard tack.

Bolitho yelled, 'We'll cross the enemy's hawse and rake him as we go!' He saw some of his men staring at him from their guns, faces strained and confused. He drew his sword and held it over his head. 'As you bear, lads! Make each ball strike home!'

The brig was barely half a cable away, her bowsprit pointing at right angles towards *Sparrow*'s figurehead. The distance seemed to be falling away at a tremendous speed, and Bolitho knew that if he had misjudged it, or if the wind chose this instant to drop, the enemy would drive into the sloop's side like a battering ram and split her seams wide open.

The big thirty-two-pounder in the bows broke the spell, the crash of the explosion transmitting itself through the deck until it reached Bolitho's feet. He saw the brig's shrouds slashed open, the whirl of bright wood splinters as the ball ploughed into her tiered boats. Then gun by gun down *Sparrow*'s side the broadside continued, with Graves bursting into the smoky sunlight, waving his sword and yelling orders to each crew in succession.

Frantically the enemy captain tried to wear ship and follow *Sparrow's* onrushing charge. Unable to get her own guns to bear, and with most of the forward shrouds and rigging hanging like black weed above her deck, the brig was staggering drunkenly under the well-aimed barrage.

Then with the helm over and some wind still alive in the torn sails the brig finally came under command. Here and there a gun banged out, but in their haste the privateers were firing haphazardly into the whirling smoke.

'Load and run out!' Tyrrell was yelling above the din. 'Roundly!'

Bolitho shouted, 'Don't wait for a broadside! Let each captain fire whenever he has loaded!' It was useless to expect these men to keep on firing as a team once they, too, were under the enemy's metal.

Graves rasped, 'Sponge out, you stupid bugger!' He had to drag a dazed man to the rear of his gun. 'Are you mad?' He pushed the luckless seaman towards the gun captain. 'I'll put you in irons if I see you . . .'

Bolitho did not hear the rest of it. The brig was slowly edging round until she was lying almost diagonally across the larboard quarter. Smoke fanned down around him and he felt musket balls thudding into the deck planks, the maniac whine as one ricochetted from a swivel gun just feet away.

Stockdale said desperately, 'Keep on the move, sir! Them buggers'll mark you down else!'

Bolitho stared at him, knowing his own face was set in a wild grin. It never failed to amaze him that it was so easy to lose control and reason once a battle had begun. Later perhaps . . . He shook himself. There would be no later when they closed with the bigger ship.

He yelled, 'They are shooting blind, Stockdale!' He waved his sword around the quarterdeck. None of the officers had found time to get their uniform coats or hats and like himself were dressed only in shirts and breeches, and those were already grimy with drifting powder-smoke. 'See? They can take their pick of us today!'

A seaman at the mizzen braces gave a terrible scream and was hurled on to his side by the force of a musket ball. Blood spurted from his chest, and as he rolled about in agony Bolitho called, 'See to that man, Mr. Bethune!' When the midshipman hesitated, his face like chalk under the freckles, he added harshly, 'Your mother is at home, boy, so you can weep alone *after* you have done your duty!'

Bethune dropped to his knees, his breeches spattered with the blood, but his face suddenly determined as the dying sailor groped for his hand.

Buckle yelled, 'The Yankee will try to work across our stern, sir!'

Bolitho nodded. There was nothing else the enemy could do. With most of his sails damaged by cannon fire, and already overreached by *Sparrow's* maddened attack through the transports, the brig's captain must either try to cross astern or tack and risk his own poop coming under fire.

He snapped, 'We will wear ship, Mr. Buckle. Lay her to the larboard tack and follow the brig round, nose to tail!'

He was still grinning, but could feel his mouth raw with tension as once again the men hurled themselves on the braces, their smoke-grimed bodies glistening in the glare as they angled back above the deck, their eyes on the yards above them.

'Helm a'lee!' Buckle was adding his own weight to the wheel.

Bolitho watched the bowsprit swinging, heard the immediate crash of guns as Graves directed his newly loaded battery towards the other ship.

Through the dense gunsmoke Bolitho saw the murky shape of the leading transport, now some two cables away.

'Steady as you go, Mr. Buckle!' A ball whimpered overhead, and when he glanced up he saw a neat hole in the centre of the big spanker. 'Keep station on *Golden Fleece*, she is better than any compass today!'

He winced as the hull jumped once, twice and yet again, as some enemy shots smashed into it. But the brig was in a bad way, and she was drifting stern-first, her complete foremast dragging over the side like a fallen tree. Men were working in the wreckage, axes flashing, while others continued to fire and reload the guns as before.

'Steady, sir! Nor'-west by north!'

Bolitho raised his sword, his eyes narrowed against the reflected sunlight as he watched the brig swinging drunkenly on the tow of fallen spars.

'Easy!' The sword held the sunlight. '*Easy*, lads!' Not a gun fired, and along the deck only at the weapons not yet reloaded was there any sort of movement.

Another ball slammed into the lower hull, and somewhere a man screamed in torment as he was clawed down by flying splinters.

The sun was shining into his eyes now, and through the drifting smoke he saw the outline of the brig's tattered maintopsail, the glint of glass as she helplessly presented her stern.

'Fire as you bear!'

Driven by the wind, the smoke came funnelling inboard through port after port as Graves ran along the gun deck, his voice cracking from the strain of shouting directions.

A shadow passed briefly above the smoke, and through the din Bolitho heard the splintering crash of a complete mast falling, and guessed it had been sheared off between decks by the *Sparrow*'s merciless bombardment.

Then as the *Sparrow* forged ahead once more he heard cheering and knew it was from the *Golden Fleece*. As wind drove the smoke apart he saw the brig very clearly and someone on her splintered deck waving the flag in surrender. Mastless, and with her stern gouged open by the slow broadside, she was little better than a hulk. Within her small hull her company must have been savagely mauled.

Tyrrell was staring at it, his eyes bright with concentration, and by his side Heyward was almost jumping up and down, his voice half choked by smoke.

Then, almost before the *Sparrow*'s dazed company could feel the taste of their conquest, the air was blasted apart with one deafening explosion. Spars, complete sections of timber and deck planking, all whirled above an angry scarlet core, and across the water a shock wave rolled towards the sloop like a miniature typhoon. When the smoke and flying fragments subsided there was nothing to show of the privateer but for a few pieces of charred flotsam and an upended jolly boat which was miraculously undamaged. A sudden spark, an upended lantern, or someone so crazed in the horror between the shattered decks that he had ignited a fuse, the brig's end was terrible in its completeness.

Bolitho said, 'Get the maincourse on her, Mr. Tyrrell! We must make haste to assist *Miranda.*' He waited until Tyrrell had brought the stunned seamen to their senses, his voice hoarse through his speaking trumpet, and then added, 'They will know that we can still sell our lives dearly.'

It took little time to overhaul the *Golden Fleece* and to see the two embattled ships about a mile distant. They had drifted in the fury of combat, their hulls masked in smoke, through which the flash of musket fire, the occasional glare of a swivel, were clear to see.

The frigate was listing against her heavier adversary, like a hulk already dead, and without using a glass Bolitho could see that the fighting had spread down across the fore deck as more boarders hacked their way between the grappled ships.

'We will go about, Mr. Tyrrell. Lay her on the starboard tack once we have gained some room and prepare to engage with the other battery.'

He bit his lip to steady his racing thoughts. A quick glance aloft told him that the masthead pendant was lifting as firmly as ever. The wind was steady from south-south-west.

'Pass the word for Mr. Graves to lay aft.'

When the lieutenant arrived, his face gaunt with fatigue, Bolitho said, 'I want the starboard bow-chaser to keep firing at the enemy. As soon as we have gone about I'll expect it to concentrate on that ship, no matter what.'

Buckle called, 'Ready on th' quarterdeck, sir.'

Bolitho nodded. 'Put the helm down, if you please.'

'Helm a'lee, sir!'

Tyrrell was already bellowing through his trumpet, and forward the seamen were leaping like demons at the headsail sheets, and with canvas flapping the *Sparrow* started to swing into the wind.

'Man the braces!'

Bolitho gripped the rail, his eyes smarting as the sun lanced between the shrouds.

'Heave there! With all your weight!'

Across the wind and still further round, the yards groaning in unison. Then as the sails refilled and laid the deck over in the opposite angle he watched the distant ships edging very slowly between the foremast shrouds as if caught in a giant web.

'Steady, Mr. Buckle! Hold her!'

He paced a few steps this way and that, aware that Tyrrell was urging the men at the braces to trim the yards still further, that the dead seaman had gone from the quarterdeck, and that Ben Garby, the carpenter, with his mates, was slithering through the after hatch to inspect the damage there. Aware of all this and more, yet not a part of it as he had once been.

'Steady, sir! Full an' bye!'

He nodded, his mind busy with the two ships. Close-hauled it would take thirty minutes to reach them, maybe more. *Miranda* was almost overrun by enemy boarders. Outnumbered from the start, she would have lost many good men in that first savage broadside.

'Fire!'

As the muffled cry came from forward he saw the puff of smoke beneath the starboard cathead, felt the sharp convulsion as the thirty-two-pounder crashed inboard on its tackles. He snatched up a glass and saw the ball plunge close to the enemy's hull, throwing up a tall waterspout.

Heyward muttered hoarsely, 'Near!'

Bolitho looked away. The big ex-Indiaman mounted anything up to forty guns, at a guess. She could finish *Sparrow*, if ever she could bring her artillery to bear, with even a badly aimed broadside. Less.

Bang. Another ball crashed away from the bow-chaser, and he watched the feathers of spray lifting from wave to wave until it plunged hard alongside the other ship.

They should hear us and see we are coming. He tried to clear his brain. What should he do? Signal the transports to run? No. They were helplessly overladen and slow. It would merely prolong their agony.

Overhead, the spanker cracked noisily, and Buckle cursed it before allowing the helm to be eased still further.

Bolitho knew without looking that sailing so close to the wind was cutting away his chances of reaching the ships in time to help.

Someone walked past him. It was Bethune, his arms hanging at his sides, his breeches covered with dark blood blotches and a smear where the seaman's fingers had made their last agonised grip on this earth. Bolitho stared at him.

'Mr. Bethune!' He saw the youth jump. 'Come here!'

He walked to the rail and back again. It was worth an attempt. Anything was now. If they arrived alongside after *Miranda* had struck to the enemy, *Sparrow*'s decks would be as red as the flag above his head.

The midshipman waited. 'Sir?'

'Make this signal at once.' He rested his hand on Bethune's plump shoulder. He could feel the skin through his shirt. Like ice, in spite of the sun.

'*Signal*, sir?' He stared up at him as if he had misheard. Or his captain had gone mad.

'Yes. To *Miranda*. Sail in sight to the nor'-east!' He tightened his grip. 'Then *move* yourself!'

Bethune fled, calling shrilly for his assistants, and within a minute the bright signal flags broke to the wind, while Tyrrell stared from them to Bolitho, first with incredulity and then with slow understanding.

Buckle said, 'There's few poor devils'll see that aboard *Miranda*.'

Tyrrell was studying Bolitho. 'No. But th' privateer will. He might just think that a patrol from th' squadron has come to join th' fight!'

Bolitho waited until Graves's bow-chaser had fired yet again and said, 'It is all we can do at present.'

Minutes dragged by like hours, and then as a freak downdraught of wind swept across the two snared ships Bolitho caught his breath. A thin shaft of light where there had been none. Then a glint of water. Wider still, as the ships drifted apart and the big privateer set her foresail and jib to work clear. Then *Miranda* was quite separate, the water between her and the other ship dotted with wreckage and torn canvas, where here and there a man thrashed to stay afloat amidst a litter of bobbing corpses.

A ragged cheer came up from *Sparrow*'s gun deck, and several ran to the gangways to watch while the enemy spread more canvas and lengthened her outline against the wind.

Tyrrell's grin froze as Bolitho snapped, 'Keep those men *silent*!' He realised he was still holding his sword, that his hand was aching with the force of his grip. 'Look yonder, Mr. Tyrrell. There's no call for cheers this day.'

Tyrrell turned to stare at the *Miranda*'s dark shape. The rising clouds of smoke as her remaining hands quenched fires and groped amidst the wreckage of their ship. As *Sparrow* drew closer they could all see the thin tendrils of scarlet which ran from her scuppers, the great pitted holes along every part of her hull.

'Pass the word for Mr. Tilby to prepare boats for lowering. Call the surgeon and send him with them.' Bolitho hardly recognised his own voice. Clipped, dull, inhuman. 'Then shorten sail and get the t'gallants off her. We will stand under *Miranda*'s lee for the present.'

He ignored the rush of feet as Tilby's men dashed to the boat shackles. He saw Graves walking aft towards the quarterdeck, wiping his face and chest with a wet rag. Above the activity the sails were still drawing well, but there were plenty of holes which would need attention before nightfall. A few stays and halyards were broken, and he knew the hull had been hit several times on or near the waterline. But the pumps sounded normal enough. She was taking it like a veteran.

Dalkeith came hurrying up the ladder, his heavy bag gripped against his chest, face streaming with exertion.

'How many, Mr. Dalkeith?' Again he heard his own voice as a stranger's.

The plump surgeon was staring at the frigate, his eyes dull. 'Two killed, sir. Five wounded by splinters.'

Bolitho tried to recall the man who was killed by his side. Manners. That was his name.

He said, 'Manners. Who was the other?'

'Yelverton, sir. He was killed by a ball at the foremast.' He looked down. 'Took his head off.'

Graves was half-way up the ladder but recoiled as Bolitho said, 'Yelverton. Did you hear that, Mr. Graves? The one man who kept his senses when all others were too blind to see the truth. The one you wanted to flog?' He turned away. 'Well, he'll not trouble you further, Mr. Graves. Nor we him.'

Blindly he saw Stockdale watching from the foot of the mizzen mast. 'Call away the gig. I will visit Captain Selby and see what must be done.'

'Aye, sir.'

Stockdale glanced back at him as he hurried to the boat tier. He had never seen Bolitho so stricken or so moved before. And for once he did not know what to do to help.

Bolitho entered his cabin and unbuckled his sword before throwing it on to the bench seat below the windows. Fitch and a young seaman were busy replacing the furniture, and another was mopping away smoke stains from the low deckhead. For in action even the captain's quarters were not spared. With the hasty removal of screens the cabin became an extension of the gun deck, and on either side of it was a squat twelve-pounder, now once again hidden by discreet chintz covers.

He stared at the nearest gun, his eyes blurred with strain. A *woman's touch*. Then he turned abruptly to face Tyrrell and Graves who had followed him into the cabin upon his return from the crippled *Miranda*.

His mind was so filled with questions and suppositions, his brain so wracked by the sights and sounds aboard the frigate, that for a moment he was unable to speak at all.

Beyond the bulkhead he could hear the steady thud of hammers, the rasp of saws as the ship's company continued work on repairs. After a full hour aboard the *Miranda* he had returned to find his own command settling down to the task of making good the damage from their encounter with the privateer with such orderly dedication that he had been unable to compare the scene with what he had just left. The sailmaker and his mates had already replaced the punctured canvas, and with their needles and palms flashing in the sunlight covered every foot of deck space as they patched the others sent down from the yards.

Garby, the carpenter had greeted him at the entry port and had told him that the brig's gunnery had not been too damaging. Two shot holes below the waterline which his men were already plugging, and several others which he would repair before sunset. Garby had spoken quickly, professionally, as if like the rest he was unwilling to think about the *Miranda* and the fate which could have been theirs.

Graves was the first to break the silence.

'All guns secured, sir. No damage to tackles or ports.' He dropped his eyes under Bolitho's unmoving stare. 'Better'n we could have hoped.'

Tyrrell asked quietly, 'How was it, sir?'

Bolitho let himself drop into a chair and thrust out his legs in front of him. The breeches were black with powder stains and from his climb up the frigate's side. *How was it?* Once again he saw the pictures of death and horror, the few uninjured men who were trying even now to put the frigate to rights. Smoke stains and great patches of drying blood, gaping corpses littered amongst the fallen spars and broken planking. It was a miracle that *Miranda* was still able to keep afloat.

He said, 'They hope to get a jury rig hoisted by sometime tomorrow. Provided the wind doesn't get up, or the pumps foul, they will obtain steerage way.' He rubbed his eyes with his knuckles, feeling the weariness enclosing him like a vice. 'Some of the wounded will be transferred to the transports directly. There they will have more room to recover.'

He tried again to shut the agony from his mind. Men so badly mutilated by splinters that they should be dead already. Midshipmen and even seamen in charge of repairs because of the carnage on the quarterdeck. He had found the frigate's first-lieutenant supervising the recovery of the mizzen topmast when he had climbed aboard. The man had had one arm in a sling and his forehead had looked as if it had been laid open by a hot iron.

Graves breathed out very slowly. 'They did well against such odds.'

'Yes.'

Bolitho wanted to get them out of the cabin. Seal the door and shut them away from his uncertainty.

Tyrrell said, 'I've passed th' word around th' ship, sir. I think our people know how satisfied you . . .'

Bolitho's tone made him fall back. '*Satisfied?*' He lurched to his feet. 'If you feel cause for complacency, Mr. Tyrrell, then please contain it!' He moved to the windows and back again. 'I have seen it for myself. Our people are not moved by a sense of victory. They are *relieved*, and nothing deeper than that! Thankful to be spared a similar mauling, and all too eager to overlook their own shortcomings!'

Tyrrell said quickly, 'But that's a mite unfair, surely.'

'You think so?' He sank down at the table, his anger spent. 'Raven had the measure of it. He saw what he expected to see, as did Captain Selby in *Miranda*. And like you, Mr. Tyrrell, our people thought that fighting an enemy was just an extension of drill, a few cuts and a few curses, and all would be well. Perhaps we have been too victorious in the past and have been overreached by this newer kind of warfare.'

There was another silence, so that the hammering somewhere deep in the hull became insistent, and to Bolitho suddenly urgent.

Graves asked, 'What will we do now, sir?' He sounded wary.

Bolitho faced them gravely. 'Captain Selby is dead. Killed in the first broadside'.

He walked to the quarter windows and stared towards the drifting frigate. Without effort he could picture the wounded first lieutenant, the man who had somehow fought his ship alongside the enemy. Knowing it was all he could do despite the crippling losses and damage already suffered. Now, without a single lieutenant, aided by a mere handful of junior warrant officers, he was doing his utmost to repair the ship. To get her to safety before the sea or an enemy found him again.

In the shattered chaos of Selby's cabin he had unlocked the safe and handed Bolitho the despatches without hesitation. Even now that he was back in his own cabin he found it hard to believe. Junior command, and then, almost in the twinkling of an eye, he was to shoulder the total responsibility for them all. Colquhoun and Maulby were beyond reach. And Selby was dead. He had seen his corpse on the splintered quarterdeck, pinned beneath an upended nine-pounder, one hand still clutching his sword like a useless talisman.

Tyrrell's voice made him turn towards them again.

'Then *you* are in command, sir?'

The lieutenants were watching him intently, their faces showing both doubt and apprehension.

Bolitho nodded slowly. 'We will continue with the transports before dusk. After we have ferried the *Miranda*'s wounded across to them and done what we can for their own ship.' He tried not to think of the endless problems which lay ahead. 'When we have made contact with the squadron as ordered we will proceed with the despatches to the Commander-in-Chief.'

He let his eyes stray around the cabin. All at once it was smaller, the sloop more vulnerable.

'And *Miranda*, sir?' Tyrrell's tone was hushed.

Bolitho kept his voice level and without emotion, knowing that if he showed them even for an instant, his true feelings, they would lose what small faith they still retained.

'Her people will do what they must. We cannot stay with her, nor would they wish it.'

Spray pattered against the thick windows. The wind was already freshening slightly.

Tyrrell licked his lips, his eyes distant as he stared towards the dismasted frigate.

Bolitho added, 'That will be all. Keep the hands working until the last minute.'

The two lieutenants, in their filthy shirts and breeches, turned and left the cabin without another word.

Bolitho looked at Fitch and said, 'You may go, too. I wish to think.'

When Fitch and his helpers had gone he rested his head in his hands and allowed his body to sway with the ship's uncomfortable motion.

Tyrrell probably thought him heartless for leaving the other ship without company or aid. Graves, too, would no doubt be finding plenty of fuel for his own personal fires.

He stood up, fighting back the tiredness and strain, knowing he must not heed nor care about their considerations. They were in a war which for too long they had only skirted like spectators. If learn they must, it were better to be done at once.

Then he recalled the *Miranda*'s lieutenant, the bitterness in his voice as he had described the action. He was able to add little to what Bolitho already knew and guessed. But for one thing, the name of the big privateer. *Bonaventure*. It was a name he would not forget.

There was a tap at the door. It was Lock, his face dark with gloom as he began to recount a list of stores damaged in the brief fight with the brig.

Bolitho faced him and said quietly, 'Now let me have a full list, Mr. Lock, and I will give you my opinion.'

It was useless to think of what had passed. He was alone now, and only the future, like the next horizon, had any true meaning for him.

5

All the Luck . . .

'Guardboat approaching, sir!'

Bolitho nodded, 'Very well.'

He had already seen it, but was concentrating instead on the overlapping lines of anchored ships, the nearest of which, a two-decker, wore a rear-admiral's flag at her mizzen.

Then he took a quick glance along the busy gun deck, the preparations to drop anchor for the first time since leaving Antigua. It was ten days since they had watched the *Miranda's* battered outline fall further and further astern until they had lost it altogether. Days of fretting impatience as they repeatedly shortened sail to keep station on the two transports. And when at last they had found a frigate of the inshore squadron they had received not freedom but yet another unexplained leg to the journey. *Sparrow* would not hand over her charge of the transports, nor would she close with the shore to supervise their unloading. Instead she was to proceed with all despatch to New York. The frigate's captain had been impatient to be away and had merely sent a midshipman across to *Sparrow* with his orders. From what little he had discovered, Bolitho gathered the frigate had been waiting and patrolling for three weeks in order that his message could be passed on to the convoy and had no wish to be involved further.

He shifted his gaze to the guardboat, rocking gently in the offshore swell, a large blue flag lifting and curling from her bows to mark where the sloop should anchor.

The wheel creaked as Buckle passed his directions to the helmsmen, and forward on the beakhead, framed against the glittering water, he saw Graves waiting for the command to anchor. He heard someone laugh and saw the two transports idling awkwardly towards another anchorage, their yards alive with men as they shortened sail.

Dalkeith saw him turn and remarked, 'Glad to see the back of 'em, eh, sir?' He mopped his face with a handkerchief. 'They've been with us so long I felt we were towing the beasts.'

The gunner climbed half-way up the ladder and called, 'Permission to begin the salute, sir?'

Bolitho nodded. 'If you please, Mr. Yule.' He turned away, knowing that but for the gunner's request he would have forgotten all about it in his concern for what would happen next.

While the *Sparrow* continued easily towards the guardboat, her canvas clewed up but for topsails and jib, the air shook to the regular bang of cannon fire as she paid her respects to the rear-admiral's flag.

Bolitho wanted to take Bethune's big telescope and study the other ships, but guessed too many glasses would now be on him. His natural curiosity might be seen as uncertainty, or the apprehension of a young commander approaching an unfamiliar anchorage. Instead he made himself walk a few paces along the weather side, noting with satisfaction that the nettings were neatly filled with hammocks and every unused line and halliard was either belayed or flaked down on the decks. Of their clash with the brig there was little or no visible sign. The ten days had been well used to replace woodwork and apply fresh paint.

Tyrrell was standing at the rail, a speaking trumpet under one arm. In his blue coat and cocked hat he seemed unfamiliar again, a stranger, like the day he had come into the cabin after his visit to the flagship.

The last wisp of gunsmoke drifted forward above the anchor party, and he concentrated his attention on the last half cable of distance. The other ships were spread out on either bow and looked impressive, indestructible.

He raised one hand slowly. 'Lee braces, Mr. Tyrrell. Hands wear ship!'

Why then was he so apprehensive? Perhaps the frigate's curt orders had hidden something deeper? He tried to disregard it. After all, he had been sick to death of the slow passage with the transports, so how much worse it must have been for the solitary frigate.

Tyrrell's voice brought a screaming chorus from the circling gulls which had been with them for several days.

'Tops'l sheets!' He was squinting into the sunlight, watching the darting figures high above the deck. 'Tops'l clew lines! Roundly does it, lads!'

Bethune's voice cut across the shouted orders and the flapping crack of canvas.

'From *Flag* to *Sparrow*, sir. *Repair on board.*'

Bolitho nodded. 'Acknowledge.' The admiral did not believe in wasting time.

'Helm a'lee!'

Gently, easily, the *Sparrow* turned her jib-boom into the wind, her sails vanishing as the top men vied with each other to fist the unruly canvas under control.

'Let go!'

From forward came a brief splash as the anchor plunged to the bottom. And before Graves had turned to signal the quarterdeck Tilby, the boatswain, was already urging the boat-lowerers to sway out the gig.

Tyrrell came aft and touched his hat. 'I hope you get good news, sir.'

'Thank you.'

Bolitho wondered what it must be like for Tyrrell. He was back off his own coastline. Sandy Hook. He must have sailed this way many times in his father's schooner. But there was nothing on his features to betray whatever he was thinking. The usual controlled respect which he had shown since the battle.

Tyrrell had not spared himself in his efforts to get the damage repaired. He had a manner which at first glance seemed easy going, even casual, but there was no doubting his ability, or the edge of his tongue if someone was foolish enough to mistake his attitude for weakness.

'I doubt that I will be long in the flagship.' Bolitho watched the gig's crew tumbling down the side.

'Th' admiral may ask you to take lunch, sir.' Tyrrell's eyes crinkled in a rare smile. 'I gather th' old *Parthian* is known for a good table.'

Stockdale called, 'Gig's ready, sir.'

Bolitho looked at Tyrrell. 'Make arrangements for taking in fresh water and casks. I have told Mr. Lock to see what he can do about fruit.'

Tyrrell followed him to the entry port where the side party were assembled.

He hesitated and then asked quietly, 'If you could find out anything about . . .' He shrugged. 'But then I guess you'll be too busy, sir.'

Bolitho ran his eye over the nearby seamen. Had he learned anything about them since he had taken command? Did he even know what they thought of him?

He replied, 'I will do what I can. Perhaps your father has sent some message for you.'

Tyrrell was still staring after him as he clambered into the boat, his ears ringing to the squeal of pipes.

When Bolitho climbed up through the *Parthian*'s gilded entry port and doffed his hat to the quarterdeck he was immediately reminded of the *Trojan*, the life he had so recently left behind. All the old smells and sights came crowding back, and he marvelled that he had forgotten so much in so brief a time.

A lieutenant guided him to the flag captain's cabin and relieved him of the despatches and a bag of letters which *Miranda* had brought from England.

He said, 'The admiral will read these first, sir.' His eyes moved swiftly over Bolitho's new uniform coat. Searching perhaps for the same old answer. *Why him and not me?*

The admiral did not send for him for a full hour, although it felt twice as long. To avoid repeatedly examining his watch he made himself listen to the sounds around and above him. The old, familiar noises of a teeming community encased in one great hull. It took little imagination to hear Captain Pears's harsh voice complaining, 'Mr. Bolitho! Are you aware that the weather forebrace is as slack as a sow's tail? 'Pon my soul, sir, you'll have to do better if you wish to make something of yourself!'

He was smiling ruefully when the lieutenant returned and without further ceremony led him aft to the great cabin.

Sir Evelyn Christie, Rear-Admiral of the Red, and commanding the Inshore Squadron, was fanning his face with a napkin, and after a searching examination of Bolitho's general appearance said, 'A glass of claret, Commander.' He did not wait for an answer but gestured to his servant, a splendid-looking man in scarlet jacket and brilliant yellow breeches.

'I was somewhat surprised to see *your* name affixed to the report.' The admiral's eyes were fastened on the claret, as if daring the servant to spill even a drip. 'You say in it that Ransome died of fever.' He took a glass and examined it critically. 'Damn good job, if you ask me. Young popinjay. Too much money and no damn integrity.' Ransome disposed of, he continued calmly, 'I expect you're concerned about the change of plans, eh?'

Bolitho felt a chair nudge the back of his legs and realised the silent servant had somehow managed to arrange a glass of claret on a small table, fetch a chair, and all without apparently moving or uttering a sound.

The admiral scowled. 'Take no notice. The man's a fool.' He added sharply, '*Well?*'

Bolitho replied, 'I was expecting to . . .'

Rear-Admiral Christie interrupted, 'Yes, I imagine you were.' He paused his head on one side like an irritable bird. 'The claret. Well?'

'Very good, Sir Evelyn.'

'Hmm.' The admiral seated himself carefully on a gilt chair. 'Took it off a blockade runner last month. Palatable.'

Something metallic crashed across a deck beyond the bulkhead and he snapped savagely, 'Go and tell the officer of the watch with my *compliments*, that if I hear one more unseemly sound during this interview I will personally take him to task!'

The servant fled from the cabin and the admiral gave a slow smile.

'Keep them jumping. That's the answer. Don't give 'em too much time to think.'

In the very next breath he changed the tack yet again.

'Fact is, Bolitho, things are not going too well. Thank God you at least are a man who knows how to abide by the letter of his orders. In your place I might have said to hell with waiting around for some damn patrol to find out what was happening. I might even have gone so far as to take those transports direct to the army.'

Bolitho stiffened. It sounded genuine enough, but perhaps the admiral was merely hinting at a criticism. Maybe he thought he should have made straight for the exact rendezvous, used his initiative instead of acting as he had.

The admiral's next words changed that.

'You were not to know, of course, that the army is in the process of evacuating Philadelphia. Falling back.' He looked down at the empty glass. 'Sounds better than a retreat, but it amounts to the same.'

Bolitho was stunned. Reverses he could accept. This war was so extended, the areas so vast and little known, that no plan of battle of the old style could be expected. But to quit Philadelphia, the vital command garrison of the Delaware, was unthinkable. In spite of his caution he said, 'Surely that was unnecessary, sir? I thought we had destroyed all the American forts and outposts on the Delaware last year.'

The admiral eyed him shrewdly. 'That was *last* year, before Burgoyne surrendered at Saratoga. The whole of this area is overrun with bands of raiders and enemy informers.' He threw open the chart. 'With my squadron I must patrol and keep watch over the whole three hundred miles of coastline, from New York down to Cape Henry on Chesapeake Bay. It is a labyrinth. Inlets and rivers, coves and hiding places where you could fail to sight a three-decker at a mile's range. And every day the sea teems with shipping. From the north, and as far south as the Spanish Main and Caribbean. Dutch, Portuguese, Spanish, and most of 'em intent on slipping past my patrols with stores and guns for the enemy.'

He poured two more glasses of claret.

'However, now that you have brought these despatches we are aware of the extent of our dangers. The French are out in the open at last. I have already sent word to the Commander-in-Chief and all senior officers here.'

He smiled. 'You did well, Bolitho. No one could have expected so newly appointed a commander to act as you did.'

'Thank you, sir.'

Bolitho thrust away the opposite side of the picture. If he had sailed with the rich transports into an enemy trap, the admiral would have spoken very differently.

'Pity about *Miranda*. We are cruelly short of frigates.'

'About the *Bonaventure*, sir, I was wondering . . .'

'You are a man who does a lot of wondering.' The admiral continued to smile. 'Not too bad a fault in some. I knew your father. I hope he is well?' He did not wait for or expect an answer. He hurried on, 'I am drafting fresh orders for you. The military, in their haste, unfortunately allowed an headquarters company to become lost.' He added dryly. 'Between ourselves, I, too, have done a certain amount of *wondering*. About some of our military colleagues ashore. Some, or so it would appear, did not obtain the necessary brains to match their appointments.'

He gave an elaborate sigh. 'But then, who am I to judge? We are fortunate. We carry our homes, our manner of existence, around with us like sea-turtles. It is hard to compare that with some wretched infantryman, loaded down with pack and musket, footsore and half starved. He has to contend with living off the land, fighting shadows, being shot at by American woodsmen as well as coming to grips with well-trained troops.'

Bolitho watched him curiously. On the face of it the admiral was nothing out of the ordinary, no more than you would expect of one backed up by his power and authority. But his features certainly hid a razor-sharp mind, the way he could throw it around from one aspect to the next without losing sight of anything.

'What about the *Bonaventure*, by the way?'

'She's big and fast, sir.' Bolitho readjusted his mind again. 'At least forty guns and well handled. I am sure she was the one which followed us, yet was well able to outsail us when the time came.' He waited, but the admiral's face was a mask. 'A match for any frigate.'

'Point taken. I will make inquiries about her pedigree.' He opened his watch. 'I want you to sail today and find that missing company of foot-soldiers before they are captured.'

Bolitho stared at him. 'But, sir, I have my orders.'

'Ah, yes.' He bobbed his head. 'Now you have *mine*, eh?'

Bolitho sank back in the chair, 'Yes, sir.'

'I neglected to mention that the soldiers are transporting gold bullion. God knows the exact amount, I find it difficult on occasions to crack the military mind into precise details. But it is a great deal. Fortunes of war, army pay, booty, whatever it is, you may be sure it is valuable.' He smiled. 'It has a complete general with it!'

Bolitho swallowed the claret in one gulp.

'A general, sir?'

'No less. Take care, he is well connected, and not given to much tolerance.' He continued evenly, 'Your arrival is a god-send. I have only one small brig available, and I was loath to send her.'

Bolitho stayed silent. *Lose* her, was probably what he really meant.

'Arrangements have been made for some army scouts to accompany you, and a small detachment is already trying to make contact with the missing company.' He paused before saying quietly, 'You will be under the instruction of one, Colonel Foley. He knows the area well, so you must abide by his experience.'

'I undersand, sir.'

'Good. I will have your written orders sent to you without delay.' Another glance at the watch. 'I will expect you to be ready to weigh before dusk.'

'May I ask where I am to go, sir.'

'You may not. It will be clear in your orders. I do not want the whole of New York to learn of it yet. General Washington has many friends here, just as we have many who are waiting to change sides if things go badly for us.'

He held out his hand. It was over.

'Take care, Bolitho, England will need all her sons if she is to survive, let alone win this damn war. But if you succeed in this venture you will be more than able to face whatever lies ahead. You can rejoin your own squadron with much more than seniority to your credit.'

In something like a daze Bolitho found his way to the entry port, his mind grappling with the admiral's words.

This time he was greeted by the flag captain in person who asked quickly, 'Has he told you what he wants of you?'

'Yes.'

The captain studied Bolitho thoughtfully. 'The general's brother is a member of the Government. I thought I should tell you.'

Bolitho tugged his hat down on his forehead. 'Thank you, sir. I will try to remember.'

The Captain grinned at his grave expression. 'You youngsters have all the luck!' His laughter was drowned by the trilling pipes as Bolitho climbed once more into his gig.

It was towards the end of the last dog watch when Bolitho's passenger, Colonel Hector Foley, climbed aboard from the guardboat. In his early thirties, he had the dark, even swarthy good looks of a Spaniard, set off with a hooked nose and deepset brown eyes. The appearance seemed totally at odds with the impeccable scarlet coat and close-fitting white breeches of an infantry officer. He glanced around the stern cabin, and accepted Bolitho's offer of the sleeping compartment and cot with little more than a nod, before seating himself in one of the chairs. He was tall and straight-backed and like Bolitho had to be careful when moving between the deckhead beams.

He took out his watch and said calmly, 'I suggest you read your orders, Captain. Given luck, your part of the game should be no more than transport.'

He did not smile or show any emotion which Bolitho could recognise. His contained, aloof manner was vaguely disturbing. Irritating. It made Bolitho feel cut off from the more vital aspects of his strange mission.

The orders took little time to read. He was to proceed with as much despatch as possible, some one hundred and fifty miles southward along the coastline of New Jersey. Under cover of darkness, if considered possible and prudent, he would then enter Delaware Bay to such distance and position as would be directed by Colonel Foley. He re-read the orders more slowly, conscious the whole time of Foley's polished boots tapping gently on the deck beside the table.

If considered possible and prudent. That passage seemed to stand out more than all the rest, and he was again reminded of Colquhoun's prophecy. It meant simply that it was his responsibility. Foley could suggest what he liked, pick any landing place or rendezvous with equal indifference to the problems of sailing the ship close inshore through badly charted channels where in places the sea-bed was visible even to a man nearly blind.

He looked up. 'Can you tell me nothing more, sir?'

Foley shrugged. 'I have twenty scouts aboard. They will have to make the first contact.'

The scouts had arrived some time before the colonel. They were Canadians, and in their buckskin clothing and fur caps, their outward appearance of slovenly ease, gave little hint of being soldiers. Bolitho had seen them sprawled around the gun deck, cleaning their assortment of weapons or idly watching the busy seamen with amused contempt.

Foley seemed to read his mind. 'They are good soldiers, Captain. Well used to this sort of warfare.'

'I should have thought you could have obtained similar assistance locally, sir?'

Foley regarded him coldly. 'An American is an American. I do not choose to trust any of them if I can obtain an alternative.'

'Then there seems little point in continuing the war, sir.'

For the first time Foley smiled. 'I need to have perfect trust in my men. Idealists I do *not* need at present.'

Stockdale opened the door and asked huskily, 'Are you ready for the officers, sir?' He glanced at Foley. 'Eight bells 'ave just struck.'

'Yes.'

Bolitho pulled at his neckcloth, angry that he could rise so easily to Foley's arrogance.

Fitch hurried into the cabin and lit two lanterns, for although it was early evening the sky was unusually overcast and the wind veered to the west with a hint of rain in it. It was also hot and stuffy, and when the other officers had somehow crammed themselves into the cabin it was almost unbearable.

He waited, watching Foley's gently tapping boots as there were more delays while chairs were brought from the ward room and in awkward, shuffling silence they got themselves sorted out.

Then he said, 'We will weigh as soon as this meeting is over. Is everything prepared, Mr. Tyrrell?'

Tyrrell had his eyes fixed on the colonel. 'Aye, sir.'

'Mr. Buckle?'

'Ready, sir.'

Bolitho looked at the carefully worded orders, recalling Tyrrell's astonishment when he had returned from the flagship.

He had blurted out, 'But we ain't had time to take on water, sir.'

The admiral had kept to his word on the matter of secrecy. He was not even going to allow the *Sparrow*'s boats in contact with the shore, no matter for what purpose.

What he would have said if he had learned that Lock had begged a trip ashore in a passing lighter, Bolitho could not imagine. Lock had returned just as secretly with several large casks of lemons, and a more mournful face than usual as he had told of their cost.

He said, 'We will proceed to the south'rd and enter Delaware Bay. There we will act in co-operation with the army and take aboard . . .'

Foley interrupted calmly, 'I think that will suffice for the present, Captain.' Without looking at Bolitho he added, 'So, gentlemen, your duty is to ensure that this vessel is in the right place at the right time, and ready to fight if necessary to complete the mission.'

The others shifted in their seats, and Bolitho saw the two midshipmen staring at him with surprise. To them, Foley's obvious control must seem strange.

Buckle muttered, 'Bad bit o' coast down there, sir. Shoals and sandbars a'plenty.' He sucked his teeth noisily. 'Bad.'

Foley glanced at Bolitho, his deepset eyes showing annoyance. 'We are not here to discuss the competence or otherwise of your officers, surely?'

Bolitho met his gaze steadily, suddenly very calm. 'Indeed not, sir. I will vouch for my people.' He paused. 'Just as I am sure you will vouch for yours when the time comes.'

In the stiff silence Bolitho heard Tilby's booming voice along the upper deck, driving some unfortunate man about his work. Again, he had made a bad start, but he was unrepentant.

Foley nodded slowly. 'We shall see.'

Graves asked, 'May I speak, sir?'

Bolitho nodded.

'Why cannot one of the inshore squadron do this mission, sir?'

Foley stood up, his head lowered between the beams. 'Because your vessel is the more suitable, Lieutenant. Not, I assure you, because you are in any way outstanding in such work.'

Bolitho looked at their faces. Resentment, surprise, even hurt. It was all there.

He said slowly, 'Carry on, gentlemen. Call all hands in ten minutes.'

When they had filed out he said, 'You have said that my duty is to act as your transport. How I do it is my responsibility, and I am not required to remain quiet while you insult my officers.'

When the soldier stayed silent he continued. 'These same men helped to save two transports which are needed so badly for the military. They fought and sank a privateer and helped to drive away another, more powerful ship.'

'For which you will receive the credit, no doubt?'

Bolitho faced him quickly, his voice low with anger. 'Thank you, Colonel. I had no doubt you expected me to say that in front of the others, just so you could make such a suggestion.' He picked up his hat. 'Had I known that the army was already quitting Philadelphia, I might have spent more time in harrying that privateer than dragging my heels with your transports!'

Foley smiled. 'Well said, Captain. I like a man who can still show some feeling.'

Bolitho slammed out of the cabin and strode unseeingly to the companion ladder. He could tell from the way some seamen avoided his eye, the alert manner with which young Bethune was studying the flagship, that they could all recognise his fury.

Had he changed so much? Before he would have laughed or cursed at Foley's rudeness once his back was turned. Now, at the mention of some criticism, the merest hint of an attack on his subordinates, and therefore his ship, was enough to drive away control and reason.

Tyrrell came aft and said quietly, 'I know those waters well enough, sir. Mr. Buckle is a mite bothered, but I can stand by him.'

'I know. Thank you.'

He had seen Tyrrell's expression when Buckle had voiced his concern at the meeting. He had been about to make the same suggestion. Perhaps that was why he had rushed in to defend the master against Foley's sarcasm. Foley had already made it clear what he thought of Americans. Rebels, colonists, or those unwillingly caught between the crossfire of different factions and divided families, any of them.

Tyrrell turned to watch the gig being swayed up and over the starboard gangway.

'Bit of a bastard, that one, sir.' He shrugged. 'I've met 'em before.'

Bolitho bit back the reproof he should have given. But what was the use? Even Bethune must have seen the antagonism between himself and Foley.

'Let us hope he knows what he is doing, Mr. Tyrrell. For all our sakes.'

The boatswain's mates charged along the gun deck and hovered over hatchways as they bawled, 'All hands! All hands! Clear lower deck!'

Bolitho said, 'I did not get time to discover any news of your family.'

'Ah well.' Tyrrell tilted his hat to shade his eyes in a shaft of dying sunlight. 'Maybe later.'

The hatch casing slid open and Foley appeared at the top of the companion.

Bolitho said evenly, 'I must ask you to leave the quarterdeck, sir.' He saw him start angrily and added, 'Or cover your red coat. It will not help if we are seen to be carrying even one soldier with us.'

Foley withdrew and Tyrrell said cheerfully, 'One to you, sir!'

'It was unintended.' Bolitho took a telescope and trained it beyond the anchored shipping. 'Our sailing must be seen as normal. Spies will have reported our arrival and no doubt will think only of our despatches. I don't intend to have the news abroad that we are going on some special mission. The world may soon know of it, but the later the better.'

He walked to the quarterdeck rail, watching the seamen being mustered at their stations by the petty officers, but wondering at the truth of his words. Could a man like Foley really make him so quick to hit back as Tyrrell believed?

'Man the capstan!' Tilby was clinging to the foremast shrouds, his mottled face shining with sweat as he yelled at the scurrying seamen. 'Jump to it, you idle buggers, or I'll be amongst you with my starter!' Caught off guard by the unexpected sailing orders, he was showing signs of a recent drinking bout.

Bolitho looked at Buckle. 'Once we have worked clear of the land we will get the t'gallants on her. The wind seems steady enough, but we'll have rain before nightfall, I'm thinking.'

Buckle tugged his hat. 'Aye, sir.' He hesitated. 'I'm sorry I spoke out as I did I should have known different.'

Bolitho smiled. 'Better to speak your doubts before you meet trouble. It is too late when you are hard aground, eh?' He touched his arm lightly. 'But before we draw that close to land we will see what *Sparrow* can do under full canvas.'

He walked away, hoping Buckle felt less worried. It could not be easy for him either. His first ship as master, and about to plunge into dangerous waters he had never seen before.

'Anchor's hove short, sir!' Graves's voice was loud on the blustery wind.

Bolitho looked at Tyrrell. 'Get the ship under way, if you please.'

He swung round as a chorus of derisive laughter burst from deck below. A seaman had caught his foot on one of the army scout's muskets and gone sprawling into the scuppers. It seemed to amuse the soldiers greatly.

Bolitho added coldly, 'With this fresh wind you'll need plenty of weight on the capstan bars.' He let his eyes rest on the Canadians.

Tyrrell grinned. 'Right away, sir!' He cupped his hands. 'Bosun! Put those men on th' capstan!' He silenced the immediate protests by adding, 'Don't hesitate to start 'em if you find 'em slacking!'

Bolitho thrust his hands beneath his coat tails and walked away from the rail so that he could watch the topmen more easily. He had taken enough insults from Foley. There was no good reason for his own seamen to suffer also.

'Anchor's aweigh, sir!'

He stared up at the thundering pattern of canvas as the ship heeled over, free to the wind.

Once clear of the land's sheltering arm the motion became more violent, the waves shorter and the colour of straw in the dull light. Spray lifted and dashed over the busy seamen and pattered across the quarterdeck like heavy rain. Bolitho felt it on his lips and wet against his shirt, sensing the released power as the courses and then the topgallant sails filled and bellied to the wind.

He watched the jib-boom rise towards the scudding clouds, stagger and then plunge forward and down over the next line of crests, the stays and shrouds gleaming like wet ebony. He pictured the angry sparrow beneath the beakhead clutching its oak leaves and acorns, and wondered if the *Bonaventure's* captain had seen it when he had broken off the action, and would remember it.

Tyrrell lurched aft, his body angled steeply to the deck. He yelled to the mizzen topmen before pausing to check those working at the weather braces. Fitch scrurried past carrying a bucket and Tyrrell called after him.

Bolitho shouted above the thunder of canvas, 'What is it?'

Tyrrell laughed. 'Th' colonel's being sick, sir! A shame, ain't it?'

'Terrible.' Bolitho turned away to hide a grin. 'Especially as it seems to be blowing harder now!'

Buckle clung to the binnacle and yelled, 'Steady she goes, sir! Sou'-east by south!'

'Hold her so!' Bolitho removed his hat and let the wind press the hair against his forehead. 'We will wear ship soon.' He walked up the deck and rapped the half-hour glass beside the compass. 'I am going below to inform the colonel.'

As he swung down the ladder he heard Tyrrell laughing and Buckle's equally cheerful chuckle. It was a small thing. But it was a beginning.

6

Scarlet and Gold

Bolitho entered his cabin and was surprised to see Foley seated at the table studying a chart. He was fully dressed, and his features had regained most of their colour. After leaving Sandy Hook he had spent most of the passage sprawled on the bench seat, unable or unwilling to climb into the cot, eyes half closed and his face like a wax mask.

He glanced up and grimaced. 'The motion feels easier.'

Bolitho nodded. 'We are standing into the bay. Cape May lies about five miles off the starboard beam.'

'I see.' Foley peered at the chart for several seconds, his fingers drumming a little tattoo across Bolitho's calculations and bearings 'What is your opinion, Captain?'

Bolitho looked at his lowered head. It was the first time he had asked him for his views on anything. Under full canvas the *Sparrow* had lived up to her name, so that on the passage southward Bolitho had been able to put aside his apprehensions, if not forget them, while he had enjoyed the sloop's vitality and freedom of movement. Then as they had closed the land to fix their position a great squall had risen, bleating and moaning with such violence that it had taken all hands to reef down and gain more sea room. After the untroubled sailing with even the royals set to catch the wind it was a severe disappointment. They had arrived off Cape May at the entrance to Delaware Bay precisely as Bolitho had planned, one full day after weighing anchor. Yet even as Buckle had been taking his bearings the squall had swept offshore, flattening the wavecrests and cloaking the distant land more effectively than night itself. It had taken another day, beating and clawing round in a great circle, the land hidden to all but the masthead lookout by rainsqualls and low cloud.

He heard himself answer, 'The wind has backed again, sir. To the sou'-west, and it is dropping.'

He listened to the groan of yoke lines as the rudder went over beneath the transom, and thought of Tyrrell and Buckle beside the wheel. He could also imagine the chart, the great bay opening up on either beam as the *Sparrow*, under close-reefed topsails, headed further and further away from the sea. Tyrrell was a tower of strength, and seemed to remember these waters as if every sandbar and current was imprinted on his brain.

Foley looked up, his face grim. 'It has already taken too long. I must know if you think we can proceed.' He laid one finger on the chart. 'Here, directly north of where you say we are now. I estimate it to be about six leagues. There is a cove.' He was speaking quickly and Bolitho could feel his agitation.

Bolitho leaned over the table. 'To the west of Maurice River?' He paused, visualising the set of the yards, the weakening wind across the quarter. 'It will take at least four hours. More if the wind goes.'

He stood back and tugged his neckcloth. With the shutters tightly closed to mask the chance of showing even a glimmer of light, the cabin was like a small oven. On deck, as he had been for much of the passage, he had not felt either fatigue or strain. Now, he was not so sure, and could even pity Foley's misery during the journey. Outside the hull it was pitch-black, and once the ship had slipped past the protective headland he had felt the same sensation as a man striding blindly into an unlit cave.

He asked, 'How long will your scouts need?'

'Six hours maybe.' Foley stretched his arms and yawned. He was giving little away.

Bolitho made up his mind. 'In that case we will have to anchor and wait for tomorrow night before we can leave the bay. There may be enemy ships nearby, and I can't risk a conflict in these confined waters. Especially if your scouts fail to find our missing soldiers and need one more day.'

'Handling the ship is *your* concern.' Foley regarded him evenly. 'Well?'

'The tide is right and if we wait further we might lose the wind altogether.' He nodded. 'I'm ready.'

Foley stood up and massaged his stomach. 'Good. By God, I think I have recovered my appetite.'

'I'm sorry, sir.' Bolitho smiled. 'For the galley fire has been doused.' He added, 'Unless you would care for some salt beef from the cask?'

Foley eyed him ruefully. 'You have a cruel streak. One sight of that muck would render me as weak as a rat.'

Bolitho made for the door. 'In a King's ship the rats are rarely that!'

On deck he had to wait several seconds before he could see further than the rail. Below on the gun deck he could just make out the waiting seamen, their bodies etched against the darker shapes of the nearest guns. He walked aft and held his hand above the shaded compass light.

Buckle said, 'Due north, sir. Full an' bye.'

'Good.' He beckoned to Tyrrell. 'I want our two best leadsmen in the chains.'

'Already done, sir.' Tyrrell shrugged. 'Seemed th' thing to do.'

'When we draw closer to the northern shore we will slip the gig.' Bolitho sought out Stockdale's thick outline by the hammock nettings. 'You will take the gig and a boat's lead and line. The waters hereabouts are so shallow and treacherous that you must keep ahead of the ship, sounding all the while. Understood?'

Stockdale said stubbornly, 'I should be 'ere, sir. Just in case.'

'Your place is where I *say*, Stockdale.' He relented immediately. 'Do as I ask, and keep a shaded lantern with you. You may need to signal us.' He glanced towards Tyrrell. 'If that happens we will drop the kedge anchor and pray.'

The sails flapped loosely above the deck, and Bolitho knew the wind was still dropping, its touch clammy across his face. He pushed the nightmare of *Sparrow* grinding aground from his mind. He was committed. No, he had committed all of them.

'When we reach our destination, Mr. Tyrrell, you may have the starboard cutter lowered. Mr. Heyward will convey our passengers ashore and return when all is well.'

Tyrrell said, 'They'll have to wade th' last few yards, I'm thinking. It's shallow up there.'

'You've guessed the place then?'

He grinned, his teeth white in the gloom. 'There ain't no other suitable for this sort of game, sir.'

From forward, hollow-toned like a lost spirit's, came the leadsman's cry, 'By th' mark five!'

Tyrrell muttered, 'Bring her up a point, Mr. Buckle.' His palm rasped over his chin. 'We must have drifted a piece.'

Bolitho remained silent. They were doing all they could. Thank God *Sparrow* had such shallow draught. Otherwise...

'Deep six!'

Tyrrell grunted. 'Fair enough. In bad times I've seen a tide race turn a schooner round like a bit o' flotsam.'

'Thank you.' Bolitho watched the faint splash beyond the bows as another lead went down. 'That is a comfort.'

'By th' mark five.'

'Trust a soldier to choose such a place.' Tyrrell leaned over the compass. 'To th' west still further and in th' main Delaware channel there's depth to spare for us, even if th' tide's wrong.'

'A quarter less five!'

Buckle whispered, 'Hell's teeth!'

Boots scraped on the planking and Foley asked crisply, 'How are we getting along, Captain?'

'By th' mark three!'

'Is it necessary for that man to make so much noise?' Foley stared round at the figures grouped by the wheel.

Tyrrell drawled calmly, 'It's either that, Colonel, or we rip our keel out.'

Bolitho said, 'A man as tall as yourself, sir, could just about walk twixt the keel and the ground below if he had a mind to.'

Foley did not speak for a full minute. Then he said, 'I'm sorry. It was a foolish thing to say.'

'Deep four!'

Buckle breathed out slowly. 'Better.'

Bolitho felt Tyrrell's fingers on his arm as he said, 'If we can keep her steady we should rest easy, with some room to swing at anchor. The bottom's safe and we might touch without too much danger.'

'Captain!' Foley's tone was as before. Sharp and impatient. He waited by the nettings and then said, 'Tyrrell. Is he an American?'

'A colonist, sir. Like a good many of the hands.'

'God damn!'

Bolitho added, 'He is also a King's officer, sir. I hope you will remember that.'

Foley's white breeches vanished into the hatchway, and Tyrrell said bitterly, 'Thinks I'm running th' ship aground just to spite him, I suppose.'

'That will be enough.' Bolitho stared past him at the dancing phosphorescence below the closed gun ports. Like magic weed, changing shape and vanishing only to reappear elsewhere along the slow-moving hull. 'I do not envy him his work.' Surprisingly, he found that he meant it.

Somewhere out there in the darkness was the great mass of land. Hills and rivers, forest and scrub which could tear out a man's eye if he was careless. There had been many stories of attacks and ambushes in this area, and even allowing for their being magnified in the telling, they were enough to chill even a seasoned fighter. Indians who were used to scout for Washington's army, who moved as silently as foxes and struck with the savagery of tigers. A world of shadows and strange noises, cries which would bring a drowsy sentry wide awake in a cold sweat, if he was lucky. If not, he would be found dead, his weapons gone.

'Deep eight!'

Tyrrell moved restlessly. 'We can leave th' channel now. I suggest we steer nor'-east.'

'Very well. Man the braces and bring her round.'

And so it went on, hour by hour, with the leads going and the reefed topsails being trimmed and re-trimmed to hold the fading wind like something precious. Occasionally Tyrrell would hurry forward to feel the tallow in one of the leads, rubbing particles from it between his fingers or sniffing it like a hunting-dog.

Without his uncanny knowledge of the sea bottom, his complete confidence despite the shallow water beneath the keel, Bolitho knew he would have anchored long ago and waited for the dawn.

Foley came and went several times but said nothing more about Tyrrell. He mustered the Canadian scouts and spoke for several minutes with their sergeant. Later he remarked, 'Good men. If I had a regiment of them I could retake half of America.'

Bolitho let him talk without interruption. It broke the tension of waiting. It also helped to discover the man behind the disciplined arrogance which Foley wore like a shield.

'I have fought the Americans in many places, Captain. They learn quickly and know how to use their knowledge.' He added with sudden bitterness, 'So they should, they have a hard core of English deserters and soldiers-of-fortune. Whereas I have had to manage with dregs. In one battle most of my men spoke only a few words of English. Imagine it, Captain, in the King's uniform, yet their tongues were more used to German dialect than ours!'

'I did not know there were so many English deserters, sir?'

'Some were stationed here before the rebellion. Their families are with them. They have found roots in this country. Others pin their hopes on rich pickings later, land, maybe, or some abandoned farmstead.' Again the harsh bitterness. 'But they will fight dearly, no matter what their conviction. For if they are taken and are found to be deserters, they will leave this world on a noose and with Jack Ketch to speed their passing!'

Tyrrell loomed out of the darkness, his voice hushed. 'Ready to slip th' gig, sir. Th' cove will be fine on th' larboard bow, by my reckoning.'

The tension was momentarily removed as with whispered commands and groping fingers the waiting seamen hoisted the gig over the gangway to tow jerkily alongside.

Midshipman Heyward was standing nearby as the gig idled clear, and Bolitho said quietly, 'Take good care when you land with the cutter. Keep your wits about you, and no heroics.' He gripped his arm, feeling the tension like the spring of a cocked pistol. 'I want to see you leave *Sparrow* as a lieutenant and in one piece.'

Heyward nodded. 'Thank you, sir.'

Graves climbed lightly up the ladder. 'Cutter's hoisted out and ready.' He glanced at the midshipman. 'Send me, sir. He's no match for this sort of thing.'

Bolitho tried to see Graves's expression but it was impossible. Maybe he really cared about the midshipman. Or perhaps he saw the prospect of action as his first chance of quick promotion. Bolitho could sympathise with him on either count.

But he replied, 'When I was his age I was already commissioned lieutenant. It was not easy then, and it will not be so for him until he has learned to accept all that goes with his authority.'

Bethune said quickly, 'Signal from gig, sir! Three flashes!'

Tyrrell snapped, 'Th' bottom has changed, most likely.' He became calm again. 'I suggest you anchor, sir.'

'Very well.' Bolitho saw the black outline of the gig bobbing slowly off the larboard bow. 'Back the mizzen tops'l. Prepare to go about. We will let go the anchor and then take the kedge away in the other cutter. Lively there, or we'll be joining Stockdale in the gig!'

Feet thudded on the gangways, and somewhere above the deck a man yelped with pain as he almost fell headlong. The mizzen topsail was flapping and cracking in spite of the wind's weak pressure, and the noise seemed loud enough to wake the dead. On darkened decks the men ran to braces and halliards, each so familiar that there was hardly any more delay than if they had been in bright sunlight.

Unsteadily, drunkenly, the sloop rode into her cable, the water beneath the stem alive with swirling phosphorescence. Both cutters were already swaying up and over the gangways, their crews tumbling into them, groping for oars and each other in the rush to get clear.

Then, and it all seemed to happen in a matter of minutes, everything was quiet again. Sails furled, and the hull rocking gently to a pair of anchors, while close by the boats moved warily, like predators around a tethered whale.

Foley stood beside the nettings and said, 'Send my scouts ashore, Captain. You have done your part.'

Then he strode to the larboard gangway to watch Heyward's cutter hooking on to the chains where the army scouts were already clinging like so many untidy bundles.

Bolitho asked softly, 'What is this cove like, Mr. Tyrrell? Describe it.'

The lieutenant ran his fingers through his thick hair. 'It's well sheltered, 'less some other vessel comes close by. Inland it's heavily wooded, and as I recall, there's two rivers running down towards us.' He peered over the side. 'Th' cutter's nearly there. If we hear shooting we'll know we're in for a spell of bother.' He forced a grin. 'One thing. We don't need no wind to work clear. We can run out th' sweeps and *pull* her to safety.'

Bolitho nodded. In almost any other vessel this mission would have been madness. Close inshore and with little chance of beating clear into the centre of the bay, they would have been as good as wrecked.

He said, 'Get Tilby to grease the sweeps while we are waiting. If go we must, then I think we had best do it silently.'

Tyrrel strode away, his head jutting forward to seek out the boatswain.

Foley reappeared and remarked, 'I think I will get some sleep. There is nothing more we can do but wait.'

Bolitho watched him go. You will not sleep, Colonel. For now it is your turn to bear the load.

Bethune said excitedly, 'Cutter's returning, sir. All's well.'

Bolitho smiled. 'Pass the word that our people will remain at quarters during the night, but may sleep watch by watch. Then find the cook and see what he can produce without relighting his fires.'

The midshipman hurried away and Graves said sourly, 'He'd eat anything. Even if he cannot see the damn maggots in the dark.'

Bolitho sat down on the hatch casing and loosened his shirt. As his head lolled in a doze he heard a heavy body lower itself to the deck nearby. Stockdale had returned. Waiting. *Just in case*, as he always put it.

The very next instant Bolitho fell into a dreamless sleep.

'Where th' *hell* are they?' Tyrrell trained a glass over the nettings and moved it slowly from side to side.

It was approaching noon, and lying at two anchors the *Sparrow* held the heat like a kiln. The cloud, like the wind, had gone overnight, and beneath an empty sky and dazzling sunlight it was impossible to move without sweating badly.

Bolitho plucked his shirt away from his waist. He had been on deck since awakening at dawn, and like Tyrrell was uneasy about the lack of results. How different it was in daylight. At the first glimmer of sunrise he had watched the nearby land growing from the shadows, the rounded hills and thick green trees beyond. Pleasant crescents of beach, shaded by thick foliage which ran almost to the water's edge. It had all seemed quiet and harmless. Perhaps too quiet.

He made himself walk to the opposite side of the quarterdeck, wincing as the sun burned his shoulders like fire. The bay looked vast. The water was unbroken by crests, and but for a swirling uneasiness of currents it could have been one large lake. It measured about twenty miles across and as much from the headland to the north, where the great Delaware River gave it its substance. Beyond the jutting point which made the cove and protected *Sparrow* from any passing vessel, the rivers curved and twisted in an ever-changing concourse, with a full seventy miles before you could sight the outskirts of Philadelphia.

He looked along the gun deck, seeing the men on watch, some protruding legs to mark where others lay resting beneath the gangways to escape the merciless glare. He let his gaze move upwards, where the yards were now festooned with branches and leaves brought aboard soon after first light. They might help disguise her outline and deceive all but the professional observer.

Between the ship and the nearest beach a cutter pulled slowly and painfully back and forth, Midshipman Bethune squatting in the sternsheets watching the shore. Foolishly he had stripped to the waist, and despite his tan would suffer for it later.

Tyrrel followed him as he returned to the shelter of the hammock nettings.

'I'd like to go ashore, sir.' He waited until Bolitho faced him. 'I could take a small party of men. Try and find out what's happening.' He opened the front of his soiled shirt and sucked in a lungful of air. 'Better'n waiting like bloody cattle for slaughter.'

'I'm not sure.' Bolitho shaded his eyes as a movement made the trees shimmer by the beach. But it was only a large bird.

Tyrrell persisted, 'Look sir, I guess th' orders are supposed to be secret, but th' whole ship knows why we're here. Them scouts spoke freely enough with a tot of rum under their belts.'

Bolitho smiled wryly. 'I thought as much.'

'Yes. And it seems we're expected to rescue a whole crowd of soldiers who've got lost coming overland.' He grimaced. 'I can well believe it too. It ain't no barrack square.'

Bolitho studied his strong profile and pondered over the suggestion. He had not mentioned the gold bullion, so that was obviously a secret which Foley had not even shared with his own men. And it was just as well. Some might be tempted to try for it rather than any kind of rescue.

'Very well. Pick your men quietly and take the gig. You will need arms and provisions, too, otherwise . . .'

Tyrrell smiled. 'Otherwise it might be too bad for us if *Sparrow* sails without waiting, eh?'

'It is a risk. Do you want to reconsider?'

He shook his head. 'I'll start now.'

Bolitho said, 'I'll make a report of this in the log.'

'No need, sir. If I come to grief it'd be best left unwritten.' He smiled sadly. 'I'd not want for you to face a court martial on my account.'

'I will make it, none the less.' Bolitho forced a grin. 'So be off with you.'

The gig had covered less than a cable from the side when Foley burst on deck, his face screwed up in the glare.

'Where is he going?' He clung to the nettings, staring after the small boat which was almost shapeless in a drifting haze. 'Did you give him permission?'

'I did.'

'Then you are a bigger fool than I imagined!' Foley's anxiety was pushing aside his self-control. 'How dare you take it on yourself?'

'Colonel Foley, I have no doubt you are an excellent field officer. Experienced enough to realise that if your scouts have failed to make contact with those landed here earlier they must either be dead or taken.' He kept his voice level. 'You will also appreciate that I am not going to risk my ship and company to comply with a plan already misfired.'

Foley opened his mouth and then shut it again. He said flatly, 'I have my orders. The general must be rescued.'

'And the gold.' Bolitho could not hide the bitterness. 'That, too, surely?'

Foley rubbed his eyes, his face suddenly showing the strain. 'You'd need a regiment to search this area. Even then . . .' His voice trailed away

Bolitho took a glass and swung it over the rail. There was no sign of the gig now.

He said, 'Mr. Tyrrell has my confidence. At least *he* might discover something.'

Foley glanced around the sunlit deck. 'I hope so, Captain. Otherwise you will lose this ship, and that will be the very least of your worries.'

Graves appeared on the ladder, saw them together and walked away. Bolitho frowned. So he had been the one to inform Foley of Tyrrell's expedition.

He asked, 'This general. Who is he, sir?'

Foley dragged himself from his brooding thoughts. 'Sir James Bundell. He came out here on a tour of inspection!' He laughed shortly. 'By the time he reached New York there was less to inspect than he had anticipated. He owned a great deal of property in Pennsylvania, enough to buy a thousand ships like this one.'

Bolitho turned away. He had never heard of the man, but this was more than he wanted to know. Foley would never speak his mind more clearly than he had already done. But it was enough. Blundell had obviously been caught in the middle of retrieving some of his personal wealth by the sudden military evacuation. Worse, he had been using his role of an inspector-general for his own ends and had involved a company of desperately needed soldiers.

Foley looked at him for several seconds. 'The men with him are mine. All that are left from the whole battalion. So you see why I must do this thing.'

Bolitho replied quietly, 'Had you told me that from the beginning, Colonel, it might have been better for both of us.'

Foley did not seem to hear. 'They were the best men I have commanded here and we've seen a dozen skirmishes together. By God, when it comes to the line of battle there is nothing to beat the English foot soldier. Even a small square of them will withstand the cream of French cavalry.' He spread his hands. 'But out here, they are like lost children. They cannot compete with men who have lived all their lives in the woods and plains, who have known times when one musket ball was the margin between survival and starvation!'

Bolitho did not know how to phrase the next question. He said slowly, 'But you were not with your men when it all happened?'

'No.' Foley stared at two gulls diving and screaming around the topgallant yards. 'I had been sent to New York with a convoy. Mostly it consisted of unwanted supplies and the soldiers' women.' He looked hard at him. 'And the general's niece, I should not forget to mention *her*.' He was speaking quickly. 'Even on a safe trail we were dogged by enemy skirmishers, and there was never a day without some poor devil being brought down by one of their long muskets. By God, I think some of them can knock the eye out of a fly at fifty paces!'

The deck moved very slightly, and when he looked aloft Bolitho saw the masthead pendant flicking out feebly before falling lifeless once more. But it was the first hint of a breeze so far.

He said, 'I suggest you get some rest while you can, Colonel. I will inform you when I hear anything.'

Foley said heavily, '*If* your Mr. Tyrrell returns.' In the same breath he added, 'That was unfair. I have been so unbalanced by all this I am not myself.'

Bolitho watched him walk to the hatchway and then seated himself on a bollard. If nothing happened soon Foley would have to make a fresh decision. With Tyrrell out of the ship and a mission a failure, there would be little hope for his own future once they returned to Sandy Hook.

All afternoon and into the evening the *Sparrow* lay pinned down by the unwavering glare. Deck seams were so sticky that they gripped a man's foot, and the gun barrels were as hot as if they had been in action for many hours. The watches changed and sentries came and went, hearing and seeing nothing.

The first rosy glow of sunset had settled over the cove, and the hillside beyond was deep in purple when Foley came on deck again.

He said, 'There is nothing more we can do.'

Bolitho bit his lip. Tyrrell had not returned. Perhaps he was already on his way south overland. Or even now guiding American scouts towards the cove. He shook himself like a dog. His tiredness and disappointment were tearing down his reserves. His trust.

Midshipman Heyward was standing by the starboard gangway, his body limp against the rail like a man half asleep. Suddenly he jerked upright, his voice hoarse as he called, 'Gig, sir! Coming from the point!'

Bolitho ran to his side, caring nothing for what Tyrrell may or may not have discovered. He had come back. That was more than enough.

When the gig ground alongside he saw the oarsmen lolling on the thwarts like puppets, faces and arms raw from the harsh sunlight of the day. Tyrrell climbed to the quarterdeck, his legs and feet filthy, his clothing torn.

He said thickly, 'Your scouts couldn't find th' ones sent on ahead, Colonel. But we did.' He took a mug of water and gulped it down gratefully. 'They're all dead. Up river in a burned-out fort.'

Foley stared at the dark trees beyond the cove. 'So my men are still out searching.'

Tyrrell ignored him. 'We pulled th' gig into th' inlet and tumbled on this old fort by accident.' He looked away. 'An' that ain't all, by a potful.'

Bolitho waited, seeing the tension, the pain of what he had found.

Tyrrell said slowly, 'Just up th' channel, sitting as bold as you please, is a bloody frigate!'

Foley swung round. 'American?'

'No, Colonel, not American.' He looked at Bolitho gravely. 'A Frenchie by th' cut of her. No colours, so I guess she's a privateer.'

Bolitho steadied his racing thoughts. But for their stealthy entry into the bay under Tyrrell's guidance, they would have run under the frigate's guns, or at best been attacked when they had anchored.

Tyrrell was saying, 'So it looks as if your general has been took, Colonel. Not much use in us staying here to follow his example, eh?'

'Did you see what they were doing?' Bolitho tried to picture the great river sweeping around the point. The frigate anchored in the safe knowledge she could fight off an attacker from either direction.

Tyrrell shrugged. 'There were marks on th' beach. I guess they'd had boats ashore getting fresh water. But no sign of prisoners.'

'Then it would appear that the missing soldiers are *still* missing.' Bolitho glanced at the colonel. 'If the wind gets up it is my guess that the frigate will weigh. She'd not risk a night passage, so we're safe here 'til dawn at least. After that . . .' He did not have to explain further.

Heyward called, 'Cutter's signalling, sir!'

They all turned and stared at the darkening beach as the oars came to life and the cutter started towards the shore. A solitary figure was just visible waving his musket back and forth towards Bethune. It was one of Foley's scouts.

Foley snapped, 'I must go ashore at once.' He ran towards the entry port. 'They have found the general!'

Bolitho hurried after him, and with Stockdale on his heels plunged into the waiting gig.

When the boat had grounded in the shallows Bolitho leapt over the gunwale and waded the last yards through clear water, vaguely aware that it was the first time he had been on land, apart from a few occasions in Antigua, for months. He stood beneath a tree as Foley questioned the scout, knowing the man would probably become flustered with both of them present.

Foley walked towards him, his boots squeaking in the sand. 'They found them.' He gestured to the wall of trees. 'The first party will arrive in about an hour.'

'First party?' Bolitho saw the despair in Foley's eyes.

'The general is coming with my scouts and all the fit men.' He took a deep breath. 'But there are some sixty sick and wounded following behind at a slower pace. They've been on the move for days. They ran into an ambush in a gully the night before last but fought their attackers off. The general says they were French.'

'Off that frigate most likely.' Bolitho tried to imagine what it must be like for the sick and injured soldiers. Not knowing where they were. How they would survive.

He said, 'The cat is out of the bag now. That ship will be expecting some rescue attempt. *I* would be in their shoes.'

Foley sighed. 'I agree. What will you do?'

Bolitho did not reply directly. He beckoned to Bethune who was giving the weary scout some water from his flask.

'Return to the ship at once. My compliments to Mr. Tyrrell. Tell him to stand by to receive the first party in an hour. I want one watch of the hands ashore and all the boats. It must be well handled and these men fitted into the ship if we have to jettison the stores to do it.'

He watched the youth running to the cutter, his shoulder glowing like a ripe fruit.

Foley said quietly, 'It'll be a miracle if we can get them off in time.'

Bolitho smiled. 'Miracles do happen, Colonel. Just occasionally.'

He walked towards the gig, his tiredness forgotten. Then he realised that Foley had not followed but was standing with his scout.

The colonel called after him, 'I'm going inland.' He looked away. 'To meet my men. Or what is left of them.'

His scarlet coat faded between the trees and he was gone.

General Sir James Blundell lay back in one of Bolitho's chairs and thrust a leg towards his orderly.

'For God's sake get these damn boots off!' He stared up at a deckhead lantern and added, 'I could relish a glass of something. I am as dry as dust!' He cursed the orderly and pushed him in the shoulder with his boot. '*Easy*, you damn fool!'

Foley turned and looked at Bolitho by the door, his eyes showing anger and embarrassment.

'Could you arrange something for the general?'

Bolitho nodded, and saw Fitch scurrying away for some wine. It was all like a part of a dream. A nightmare.

As the last of the daylight had begun to fade the soldiers who had accompanied the general had appeared along the beach. Even *Sparrow's* seamen, who moments before had been skylarking and chattering while they enjoyed their unusual freedom of dry land, had fallen still and silent.

Torn and bedraggled, red coats filthy from forced marches and sleeping when they could in the undergrowth, they had shuffled into lines like obedient animals. Others had followed with pack mules, so loaded that it was a wonder they had survived.

Bolitho had been on the beach with Dalkeith, explaining the needs and preparations for this mass of passengers, and had watched in silence as Foley had stood with his face like stone while a solitary lieutenant had lurched towards him, the regimental colours across one shoulder, his sword dangling from his wrist on a lanyard. Foley had been unable to speak. He had merely touched the lieutenant's shoulder and nodded towards the dull-eyed soldiers along the edge of the trees before saying to Bolitho, 'For God's sake, do what you can for these fellows.'

As the seamen had hurried forward to help the soldiers into the waiting boats the last reserve had cracked. Along the swaying lines of red coats men had dropped like corpses, while others had merely stared speechlessly at the bronzed sailors, their filthy faces running with tears, hands outstretched like men seeing messengers of salvation itself.

It had been pitiful and moving just to watch while they had lurched into the shallows and the boats. The lieutenant carrying his regiment's colours, as he must have done all the way south from Philadelphia, trying to show some last control but his face reversing the lie, the despair and the disbelief.

Now, as he stood watching the general it was hard to connect the two scenes together. Blundell was a rotund but powerfully built man, and apart from dirt on his boots, his uniform looked as if it had been only recently pressed. His iron-grey hair was neat, and his heavy, florid features must have been shaved within the day.

So far, he had given Bolitho little more than a cursory glance, and was content to make his needs known through Foley.

He touched the glass of wine with his tongue and grimaced. 'I suppose one cannot hope for too much in a craft of this size, what?'

Foley looked again at Bolitho, his expression one of physical pain.

Overhead and deep in the hull the timbers were alive with thudding boots, the occasional bellow of orders and the squeak of tackles above the boats.

The general said, 'You should have put those men to work, Foley. No sense in letting 'em lie about like squires of the manor.'

Bolitho said, 'My people can manage the loading, sir.'

'Hmm.' The general seemed to consider him for the first time. 'Well, make sure that every mule is properly checked. Some careless or greedy fool might be thinking of stealing their loads. There's a king's ransom in those packs. So think on these things when you report you're ready for sea.'

Graves appeared in the door. 'All the soldiers are on board, sir. Some of them are in a poor way.'

Bolitho tore his eyes from the general, the droplets of wine on his lips.

'Have the cook light the galley fire, Mr. Graves. That French frigate will not attempt to weigh in the dark, even if the wind gets up. I want those men to get something hot to eat. Rum, too, while they are waiting. Tell Mr. Lock to arrange it.'

He thought of the staggering men, the fallen redcoats by the trees. And this was the party of *fit* men.

Foley asked quietly, 'When will you be raising anchor, Captain?'

Bolitho saw the anguish in his eyes, the way he lingered on his question.

'An hour after dawn the tide will be right, as will the current hereabouts, according to my information.'

The general's glass hovered in mid-air, so that his orderly allowed the wine to pour from the decanter and across the deck.

'What the hell are you talking about?' He struggled up in the chair. 'You can sail *now*. I heard your men saying the time was as good as any for it.'

Bolitho faced him coldly. 'That is true only up to point, sir. But if I am to wait for the sick and wounded to reach the cove, I must prepare for the next tide.' He hardened his tone. 'I have sent my first lieutenant and forty seamen to aid their passage here. I pray to God we can save them from more suffering.'

The general lurched to his feet, his eyes flashing angrily. 'Tell this young upstart, Foley! There is an enemy ship up-channel and no time to be wasted. I have gone through enough in the last few days, and I command you to ...'

Bolitho said, 'My orders say that I am in command of *transportation* for this mission, sir. They make no distinction between gold bullion or men.' He paused, the anger churning his stomach like brandy. 'Even those too weak and sick to fend for themselves. Is that not so, Colonel?'

Foley was staring at him, his eyes in dark shadow. When he spoke his voice was different, husky. 'It is true, Captain. You are in command.' He swung round and faced his astonished superior. '*We*, Sir James, are just so much cargo.'

Bolitho turned and walked from the cabin. On deck the air seemed cleaner, and he made himself stand quite still by the rail above the nearest twelve-pounders for several minutes.

Below he could see figures moving in all directions, and from the galley funnel he caught the aroma of meat stew. Even Lock must have been too overcome by the tattered, starving soldiers to restrain the cook.

He heard Foley's boots beside him but did not turn.

'Thank you, Captain. From me and my men. And those who will owe their lives to your humanity. And courage.' He held up his hand as Bolitho turned to reply. 'You could risk your very future because of this action, as well you know.'

Bolitho shrugged. 'Rather that than live with a foul memory.'

Someone called in the darkness and a nearby cutter began to pull inshore.

'I'd not leave those men behind.' He walked towards the gangway. 'If needs be, I'll drop the gold overboard first!'

'Yes. I believe you would, Captain.'

But Foley was speaking to the darkness. And when he reached the side he saw the gig already on its way to the beach, Bolitho sitting beside Stockdale at the tiller. He peered down at the gun deck. Where would Bolitho put all these men? He heard the creak of oars as the first boat thrust off from the beach. One thing was certain. He would find the space somehow, if it cost him his commission.

7

To Dare or to Die

Bolitho opened his eyes and stared at the mug of steaming coffee which Stockdale was holding above the side of the cot. He struggled upright, his mind and vision readjusting to the unfamiliar surroundings, the awareness that it must already be dawn. He was in Tyrrell's small screened cabin adjoining the wardroom, and as he held the mug to his lips he realised he could not remember how he came to be there.

Stockdale wheezed, 'You've 'ad a good hour's sleep, sir. I was fair loath to wake you.' He shrugged heavily. 'But your last orders was to rouse all 'ands afore dawn.'

Bolitho's aching mind suddenly cleared. He could feel the uneven motion around him, the creak of stays and shrouds.

'The wind? How is it?' He threw his legs over the side of the cot, feeling crumpled and unclean.

'Risin', sir.' Stockdale sounded unhappy. 'From the west'rd.'

Bolitho looked at him. '*Damn!*'

With the mug still in his hand he hurried from the cabin and almost fell across a line of sleeping soldiers. Despite the need to know what was happening he stood motionless looking at them. Remembering the long night, the stream of sick and wounded men he had watched brought aboard by his sailors. Some would not see another day pass, others were like skeletons, racked with fever or the agony of wounds gone rotten. He still felt that same cold anger and shame which he had endured then. The realisation that most of the men could have been carried on the mules instead of being left to stagger further and still further in the rear of their comrades. And the general.

He stepped over the inert shapes and continued to the quarterdeck.

Tyrrell saw him and said, 'You know about th' wind?'

Bolitho nodded and walked to the nettings, seeing the bay opening up in the pale early light like ruffled steel, the dancing cat's-paws against the hull, pushing it gently but insistently on the taut anchor cables.

Buckle came to his side, his face grey with fatigue.

'We can't set even a scrap o' canvas, sir. We're on a lee shore an' no mistake.'

Bolitho was staring along the larboard gangway and away towards the dark slab of land emerging from the shadows. The point, around which lay the river and the deep channel.

Graves said, 'We will have to stay where we are and hope that Frog has a mind to do likewise.' He sounded doubtful.

Bolitho shook his head, thinking aloud. 'No. The Frenchman will have guessed we are about, even if he does not realise our exact strength. Either way he will up anchor soon and make for open water. If he sees us in passing he will have little difficulty in aiming his broadsides.'

He peered up at the yards where some topmen were casting away the last of their leafy camouflage. Above their heads the masthead pendant was whipping towards the cove, and he saw the beach regaining shape in the light, the marks of many feet, the small humps to show where some of the soldiers had been buried within sight of rescue. *Rescue.* He rubbed his chin and tried to think more logically.

Once out in the bay they could make sail and tack towards the entrance and open sea. The Frenchman, on the other hand, already had the advantage of the wind. Could even anchor if desired and pound *Sparrow* to fragments while she lay helpless in the cove. She would sink with her masts above water. It was a cruel picture.

He said, 'Break out the kedge anchor, Mr. Tyrrell, and then hoist all boats.' He looked at the long racks of sweeps. 'We will have to see what those will achieve this morning.'

Once free of the kedge the hull swung sternwards towards the beach, the current swirling around her stem as if she was already under way.

The gun deck and gangways were crowded with men, and he knew that below every space was filled with exhausted soldiers. He watched the gig rising above the gangway before dropping neatly on its chocks between the cutters, the seamen working in unusual silence, glancing occasionally towards him by the rail as if to see his intentions.

He was able to pick out individual faces in the strengthening light, and realised he now knew most of them by name. The reliable and the lazy, the malcontents and those who were able to accept their calling, enforced or otherwise, with varying degrees of trust. He remembered that first day, the sea of unknown men, with Graves excusing Tyrrell's absence. It seemed so long ago.

Tyrrel reported, 'Boats secured, sir!'

Bolitho walked to the rail and leaned on it. The wood was moist and clammy, but within a few hours would be like a furnace bar. If it was still above water.

He said, 'You all know of that frigate, lads. She's up there now, taking her time, as Frogs do in such matters.' He paused, seeing some of the older men nudging each other and grinning at his feeble wit. 'You can also see that we are unable to loose tops'ls without driving ashore. But if soldiers can march all the way across country to us, I reckon we should be able to get 'em home again, what d'you say?'

For a long moment nobody moved or spoke, and he felt despair rising as if to mock him. Why should they care? After his displeasure following the fight with the privateers they might simply see it as a just rebuff.

Surprisingly, it was the boatswain who was the first to break the silence. Bursting from the larboard gangway, his face glowing like a grotesque heated shot, he bellowed, 'What are we waiting for, my lovelies? A huzza for the cap'n! An' another for *Sparrow*!'

The cheering spread along the decks and up to the topmen on the yards. To the dazed soldiers below and in the cramped holds, and wherever a foot or so had been found for them.

Tilby yelled, 'An' to *'ell* with them bloody Frogs!' He was already cutting the lashings on the nearest sweeps, pushing men towards them while others scampered to open the small ports on either beam.

Bolitho turned away, seeing Tyrrell's great grin and Buckle nodding his head and beaming as if they were already at sea and away under full sail. Even Graves was smiling, his tired face both dazed and pleased by the din.

He said, 'Man the capstan.' He wished they would stop cheering. That Tyrrell would obey and leave him to his thoughts. 'Run out the sweeps, if you please.'

Tyrrell shouted the order, and as the helmsmen stood to the wheel and the capstan took the first slow strain, he turned and said, 'They'll not let you down. Not after what you've done for those poor redcoats. Not now. Not ever, Cap'n.'

Bolitho could not face him. Instead he stared along the larboard side at the wavering line of sweeps poised above the swirling water like the oars of some ancient galley. It would take a great deal of effort to move her into the bay. With the wind against her and the dead weight of all her guns and extra passengers it might prove impossible.

'Stand by!'

The sweeps swung gingerly forward, and the seamen clinging to the long looms and gripping the deck with their bare toes.

'Anchor's aweigh!' Graves came running aft above the seamen and yelled, 'She's paying off, sir!'

'Give way all!' Tilby threw his own weight on the aftermost sweep, his bulging muscles showing evidence of the strain. '*'Eave!* Come on, boyos, 'eave! Again now!'

Rising and falling, the lines of sweeps thrust and slashed at the water to hold the *Sparrow*'s drift towards the beach, and then very slowly, painfully brought her under command and towards the bay.

Bolitho called, 'Mr. Buckle, take the wheel!' To Tyrrell he added, 'Every officer and man on the sweeps! *Everyone!*'

As the anchor was catted home and Graves led his own party to the sweeps others slithered down backstays or ran from their stations elsewhere to give weight to the stroke.

Bolitho tried not to watch the point, green and brown now in the light. It was stationary and the sloop was hardly making headway. Yet already the men were gasping for breath, and only Buckle and himself were not helping. The wind was too strong, the current too insistent.

Tyrrell's voice carried like a trumpet. 'Heave! Heave! An' one more, lads!' But it was no use.

Buckle called softly, 'We'll have to anchor again, sir! They'll be beat in a moment!'

Several seamen missed their grip and almost fell as a voice shouted above the plunge and creak of sweeps.

'Quickly there! Spread yourselves out with the seamen!'

Bolitho stared with disbelief as Foley emerged below the quarterdeck, and following him, two by two, some limping, others blinded by bandages, came the remnants of his company.

Foley looked up. 'The 51st have never been known to fail in showing up the Navy, Captain!' He steadied one of his men who was groping past him before adding, 'You spoke earlier of miracles. But sometimes they, too, need a little help.' He turned away and put himself beside a master's mate on the end of a sweep.

Bolitho gripped the rail, wanting to hide his face from them, but unable to tear his eyes from their combined efforts.

Buckle called huskily, 'I've got steerage way, sir. She's answering now!'

Bolitho said softly, 'The colonel told me he could take half the continent with the right men. With men such as these he could conquer the world.'

When he looked again he saw that the point was slipping across the starboard quarter as with great care Buckle eased the helm over and watched the jib-boom pointing towards deeper water.

Here and there a man fell exhausted from a sweep, but the stroke barely faltered.

When the full rim of sunlight eventually broke above the distant hills, *Sparrow* was well out into the bay.

Bolitho shouted, 'Topmen aloft! Stand by to make sail!'

The jib cracked and flapped angrily, then hardened into a firm crescent, and as the long sweeps were withdrawn from their ports the deck tilted to a small but satisfying angle.

'Lay her on the starboard tack, Mr. Buckle. As close to the wind as you can. We will need all the room possible to weather Cape May.'

Tyrrell came aft and stood beside the compass, his eyes fixed on the hazy shoreline. He looked strangely contented. Reassured.

He saw Bolitho watching him and remarked, 'It was a good feeling to get ashore again. But then I guess you feel th' same about England.'

Bolitho nodded gravely. Maybe Tyrrell had been tempted after all. But he had come back, and that was what counted.

He said, 'You did well, Mr. Tyrrell. You all did.'

Tyrrell gave his lazy grin. 'If you'll pardon th' liberty, sir, you ain't no hoof-dragger yourself.'

'Deck there! Sail on th' starboard quarter!'

Bolitho looked at Buckle. 'The Frenchman is after us sooner than I thought. Get the t'gallants on her, if you please.' He walked up the slanting deck and shaded his eyes. 'We'll give him a run for his money.'

Tyrrell was still grinning. 'For th' *general's* money, you mean!'

Bolitho glanced down at his stained breeches. 'I'm going to shave.' But the mood persisted for him also. 'In case we have visitors this morning, eh?'

Buckle watched him go and then said. 'Nothing ever seems to worry that one.'

Tyrrell was peering up at the topmen, his eyes critical. He recalled Bolitho's face when the wounded soldiers had staggered on deck to help man the sweeps. For just those few moments he had seen beyond the brittle composure, the mantle of command, to the real man beneath.

Half to himself he murmured, 'Don't be too sure of that, Mr. Buckle. He *feels* it right enough. Just like th' rest of us.'

Bolitho closed the telescope with a snap and steadied himself against a belaying-pin rack.

'Alter course two points, Mr. Buckle. Steer due east.'

It had taken another two hours from sighting the French frigate to tacking dangerously close around Cape May. With the nearest spur of that untidy headland barely two cables under the lee side they had surged towards the open sea, close enough to see smoke from some inland fire and the morning sunlight flashing on a hidden window or an unseen watcher's telescope.

It had been harder than he could have imagined to remain in a wardroom chair while Stockdale shaved him and laid out a clean shirt. Now, as he watched the men running to the braces, the lifting, dipping bowsprit beyond the taut rigging, he wondered why he had made himself waste time below. Pride or conceit, the need to relax even for minutes, or a greater need that his seamen should think him so calm he could concentrate on his own comfort?

As the sloop plunged round still further until she had the wind directly astern, he could feel every spar and timber quaking to the motion. Above the quarterdeck rail he saw the mainyard bending like one huge bow, the splayed legs of the topmen denoting the savage vibration aloft, the need for care when one false step could mean instant death. Or the longer agony of watching the ship ploughing away to leave the fallen man to drown alone.

'Steady she be, sir! Due east!'

He walked to the compass and then took a careful glance at the set of the sails. Every inch of canvas was fully drawn, the bellies so rounded and hard they looked about to burst.

He gestured with the telescope. 'Another pull on the larboard forebrace, Mr. Tyrrell, and then belay.'

As the men ran to obey he took one more glance astern. The enemy had gained on them during the dash from the bay, had cut away their early advantage while *Sparrow* had lost valuable time clawing around the last headland. Now, as he steadied the glass across the taffrail he could see their pursuer rising and driving over the lively white-horses, her hull bathed in spray, the gun ports awash as she surged on a starboard tack, showing her sleek hull and full pyramids of canvas. She had set her royals once away from the headland and was heading into deeper water before continuing the chase.

Tyrrell came aft, wiping droplets of salt from his arms and face.

'We're standing well afore th' wind, sir. There's nought else we can do at present.'

Bolitho did not reply. At the quarterdeck rail he leaned over and saw the uneven lines of wounded soldiers, and others less handicapped, helping with food and bandages. Two of Dalkeith's assistants came on deck and hurled a bundle over the gangway and vanished down a hatchway with hardly a glance. Bolitho watched the bundle bobbing away on *Sparrow's* creamy wake and felt his stomach contract violently. Some bloodied bandages, but most likely the amputated limb of one more luckless soldier. Dalkeith was in his makeshift sickbay, as he had been since the sloop had weighed anchor, working in almost total darkness with saw and swabs while the ship yawed and staggered around him.

Graves called above the boom of canvas, 'The Frenchman's wore, sir!'

The frigate was now about eight cables to the starboard quarter. Certainly no more, and steering a parallel course, her royals fully squared and straining at their bolts like pale breastplates.

Bolitho said, 'She's pulling up, Mr. Tyrrell. Not a great deal, but enough to worry about.'

Tyrrell rested at the rail and kept his eyes forward, away from the enemy frigate.

'Will I clear for action?'

He shook his head. 'We cannot. Every bit of space is packed with soldiers. There is barely room on the gun deck for a twelve-pounder to recoil.'

He thought of the big thirty-two-pounders pointing from either bow. With the enemy astern they were impotent. Just so much extra weight. Had the enemy been in their line of fire they might have been able to cripple her, if only temporarily, or until some ship of the inshore squadron could give them support.

Tyrrell looked at him worriedly. 'You have a choice, sir. You close th' shore now and risk losing th' wind altogether. Or you alter course to seaward within th' hour.' He angled his thigh against the rail as *Sparrow* plunged heavily, the spray dashing aft over the decks, rattling against the courses like lead pellets. 'There's a long ridge of sandbars running north to south. You take one side or t'other. But in an hour you'll have to decide which.'

Bolitho nodded. Even with the barest information he had discovered on his charts he knew Tyrrell's estimate was only too true. The sandbars, like uneven humps, ran for over twenty miles across their line of advance. To wear ship north or south to avoid them would mean loss of time, and with the enemy so near, it could represent the measure of disaster.

Tyrrell said, 'We could wait and see what th' Frenchie intends.' He rubbed his chin. 'But it would be too late for us by then.' He shrugged helplessly. 'I'm sorry, sir. I ain't much help.'

Bolitho stared past him towards the land. As the coast turned north-east it was falling away. Ten, fifteen miles, it was hard to gauge in the bright sunlight and low sea haze.

'You have been helpful.'

He walked aft to the compass and saw Buckle watching him grimly. The earlier laughter, the sudden relaxation of clearing the land, had all gone now. From a rumour to the sight of a sail. From a distant ship to real, deadly menace in the frigate's line of gun ports. It had all changed against them so quickly.

'Deck there! Sail fine on th' starboard bow!'

Graves said excitedly, 'The squadron! By God, that's better!'

Moments later, 'Deck! She's a lugger, sir! Headin' away!'

Bolitho clasped his hands behind his back. Some frightened trader, no doubt. If still within sight she might witness a swift one-sided fight within the hour.

'The Frenchman's altered course apiece!' Buckle was peering astern through a telescope. 'His yards are coming back!'

Bolitho waited, counting seconds. The frigate had swung off her original course, her speed and drive taking her away slightly further off *Sparrow's* quarter. He tensed, seeing the telltale puff of brown smoke, driven away instantly by the following wind.

The heavy ball plunged short by a cable, the waterspout rising violently as if to mark a spouting whale.

Bolitho shut the seamen's jeers from his thoughts. No matter what they believed, it was a fair shot. She had fired nearly two miles with what must be a powerful bow-chaser like his own.

Foley appeared at his side. 'I heard the cannon.' He shaded his eyes to peer over the nettings. 'He means to unnerve you.'

Bolitho smiled gravely. 'He intends much more than that, Colonel.'

He heard more footfalls on the quarterdeck and saw Dalkeith blinking in the sunlight, wiping his face on his big handkerchief. He had removed his heavy apron, but there were dark stains on his legs and shoes, not yet dry.

He saw Bolitho and reported, 'That is all for now, sir. Ten have died. More will follow, I fear.'

Foley said admiringly, 'Thank you, Mr. Dalkeith. It is better than I dared hope.'

They all looked round as another dull bang echoed across the cruising white-caps. It was nearer, and level with the starboard quarter.

Dalkeith shrugged. 'On dry land I might have saved more, Colonel.' He walked away towards the taffrail, his brilliant wig askew, his shoulders sagging as if from a great weight.

Bolitho said, 'A good surgeon. Usually the calling attracts the failure or the drunkard. He is neither.'

Foley was studying the frigate with a telescope. 'A woman drove him to sea maybe.' He ducked involuntarily as the other ship fired and the ball whimpered high overhead before throwing up a shark's fin of spray on the opposite side.

Bolitho said, 'Hoist the colours, Mr. Tyrrell. He has the feel of us now.' He watched the scarlet flag break from the gaff. 'Mr. Dalkeith! Have your helpers move those wounded men to the larboard side.' He silenced his unspoken protest with. 'Better now than when we are in real trouble.'

Graves came running aft along a gangway. 'Run out, sir?'

'No.' He looked up as another ball fanned above the deck. 'Load the starboard battery. Double-shotted and with grape for good measure.' He ignored Graves's puzzled expression and added to Foley, 'If we must fire it will have to be the one broadside. You have been below yourself. You know we cannot indulge in close action with the hull filled to its brim with sick men.'

Foley looked away. 'I am sorry, Captain.'

Bolitho studied him gravely. 'Do not be. My orders said little of fighting. Transportation was the ideal arrangement.' He forced a smile. 'Unfortunately, the Frenchman has not read them also!'

He turned to watch the wounded being carried to the opposite side, while Graves and Yule, the gunner, supervised the slow loading of every starboard gun which was not impeded by either passengers or cargo.

Graves came to the ladder eventually and called, 'All but four guns loaded and ready, sir.' He broke off with a gasp as the air overhead came alive with a long-drawn-out shriek, as if a thousand devils had been freed from the sea itself.

Rigging and shrouds jerked savagely, and men ducked holding their hands above them as torn cordage and several severed blocks hurtled amongst them.

Bolitho gripped his hands together behind him still tighter until the pain helped to steady him. Langridge shot, as used by the big *Bonaventure*. It was vicious and very dangerous. Consisting of fragments of iron bound together, it could cut away rigging and tear down spars with ease. But unlike chain-shot, which was more generally used, it could also do terrible damage to men otherwise hidden by gangway or bulwark. The Frenchman obviously wanted to dismast *Sparrow* and take her and cargo intact. The gold would pay for many requirements in the future, and *Sparrow* would make a valuable addition to the enemy's fleet. It had happened before. Within the hour he might see it happen again. To him.

The bow-chaser threw out a spurt of smoke and the *Sparrow's* main course burst open with a searing explosion, the great sail ripping itself to a hundred fragments in the wind even before the enemy's iron had finished falling alongside.

Bolitho could feel the difference instantly, the heavier motion between each lift and plunge, the increase of turns on the wheel as Buckle's helmsmen fought to hold her on course.

Yet again that demoniac scream of whirling fragments, the thud and clatter of falling rope and halliards. Men were working feverishly far above the decks to make good the severed rigging, but the frigate was much nearer, and as Bolitho swung round he saw three of her foremost guns belching fire and smoke, proof that she was overhauling rapidly to bring more of her armament to bear.

Balls shrieked and whimpered overhead and one ripped through the mizzen topsail with the slap of a whip against wood. Men yelled and cursed to control it as once again the wind explored the damage, tearing the shot-hole in an uneven gash from head to foot.

Bolitho gripped the rail hard. If only there was sight of a friendly sail, anything which might make the frigate lose heart or change tack even for a few moments.

He saw a ball skipping across the wave-crests, its progress clearly marked by the leaping feathers of spray; winced as the deck jumped beneath him as the shot slammed into the lower hull.

From below the gun deck he heard muffled cries, and pictured the sick and wounded, some with limbs only just cut away by Dalkeith, enduring the menacing roar of gunfire, the increasing accuracy of each successive shot.

Bethune came running from the ladder. 'Captain, sir! The general wishes to be kept informed . . .' He ducked as a ball burst through the taffrail and hurled two seamen in a tangle of writhing limbs and horrifying spurts of blood.

Bolitho turned from the sight. He had been speaking to one of them just minutes ago. Now he was less than a man. Nothing.

'Tell the general to stay below and . . .'

He broke off as with a splintering crash the maintopgallant canted over, the sail whipping madly in a web of parted rigging, while the yard itself snapped into equal halves before pitching towards the deck. Men ran in confusion until the avalanche of wood and cordage had draped itself over the larboard gangway to trail alongside in a maelstrom of spray. A man, it must have been the lookout, was hurled bodily to the topsail yard, and even above the din Bolitho heard his shrill scream, saw him roll over and fall the rest of the way to the gun deck.

Another ragged burst of cannon fire, and Tilby dashed amongst the struggling seamen, his arms flailing as he pushed and drove them with their axes to free the ship from its torn rigging.

Tyrrell shouted, 'We will have to alter course, sir!' He was yelling to make himself heard as men rushed past him, faces screwed into tight masks, their eyes blind even to the butchered corpses beside the nettings.

Bolitho stared at him. 'How much water is there over those bars?'

Tyrrell seemed to think he had misheard. 'At *this* time? Next to nothing!' He peered wildly at the sails as more jagged iron screamed amongst them.

A topman had slipped and was being suspended by his hands by two of his companions while his legs kicked helplessly in the air. Sweat, fear or a flying splinter cut the contact, and with a brief cry the man fell head over heels, seemingly very slowly, until he hit the sea by the hull. Bolitho saw him passing below the quarterdeck, arms outspread, his eyes very white as the water closed over them.

'I must risk it!' He was shouting aloud without realising it was more than a murmur. 'Tack either way and that frigate will rake us!'

Tyrrell nodded jerkily. 'As you say! I'll get a leadsman in th' chains and . . .'

Bolitho seized his arm. '*No!* Do that, or shorten sail, and that bastard will know what we're about!' He shook him violently. 'If I fall, you must try to take her through.'

A ball crashed into the nettings and sliced behind him. Splinters and fragments filled the air, and he saw Foley throw one hand to his shoulder where the epaulette had been torn cleanly away.

He faced Bolitho and said, 'Warm work, Captain.'

Bolitho stared at him, feeling that same fixed grin on his mouth and jaw like a cruel vice. Like him, the ship was acting like something beyond control, the remaining sails driving her onwards towards the hidden menace of those hard sandbars. He was banking everything on Tyrrell's knowledge, and the hope that the Frenchman was ignorant of his danger, or so blinded by all else but *Sparrow*'s closeness to defeat that he was totally absorbed.

Yet in spite of the intermittent gunfire, the responding crashes and thuds of balls striking home, he was able to see small but important details on every side.

A badly wounded seaman, his shoulder mashed to bloody pulp, was being held in the arms of a wounded soldier. The latter was blinded from some previous fight and his face covered by bandages. But his hands seemed to stand out even in all the confusion around him. Moving and calming, shielding the sailor and groping for a flask of water to ease his suffering. And Dalkeith, his wig screwed into one pocket while he knelt beside another injured man, his fingers like scarlet claws as he felt the extent of the wound, while his eyes rested on the next victim, and the one after that.

And through it all Graves walking behind the loaded guns, chin on chest, pausing only to check a particular crew or to step astride a corpse or fallen rigging.

From forward came the frightened cry, 'I kin see th' bottom!'

Bolitho ran to the nettings and pulled himself above the tightly stowed hammocks. In the bright sunlight he saw the spray bursting from the rounded bilge, trailing ropes and a complete section of a broken cutter dragging alongside. Then he saw the darting, shadowy shapes gliding deeper still, weed and rock clusters, some of which seemed to be rising towards the keel like disturbed monsters.

If she struck now the masts would be ripped out of her, and she would plough forward, grinding and breaking open to the waiting sea.

He turned to seek out the enemy. How near she looked. Less than three cables off the quarter, her complete battery run out in readiness to finish the contest.

Buckle muttered hoarsely, 'By the living God, the Frenchie's in a safe channel!' There was a break in his voice. 'The bastards have done for us!'

Bolitho looked at Tyrrell. 'Get the t'gallants off her.' He could not hide the despair this time.

As the men swarmed aloft to shorten sail, Tyrrell shouted, 'There was nothing else you could do . . .'

He broke off as Buckle and Midshipman Heyward yelled together, *'She's struck!'*

Bolitho pushed between them and stared with sick disbelief at the other ship. She had been changing tack, either because her captain had at last seen his danger or was about to rake the sloop with his first full broadside, and had struck one of the bars at full speed. Across the strip of water they could hear the jarring crashes, the awful rumble of her hull pounding aground. And as she began to slew round, her foremast followed and entangled with her main and mizzen topmasts, came down in one mighty curtain of leaping spray.

Bolitho had to yell several times to stop his men from shouting and cheering, to make them understand that their own danger was just as real.

'Alter course five points to starboard!' He dashed the sweat from his eyes to peer at the compass, his mind dulled by the crash of spars and groaning timbers. 'Steer sou' sou'-east!'

With only her torn course and topsails set, the *Sparrow* came round sluggishly, as if she, too, was beyond reason.

Gear flapped and banged, and men clambered over the scattered debris like dazed animals in their efforts to obey the shouts from aft.

Bolitho cupped his hands and yelled, 'Mr. Graves! Run out!'

The ports squeaked open, and on their trucks the guns which could be manned trundled into the sunlight. With the sloop leaning over on her new tack each cannon moved quickly down the deck until with a shout of, 'All run out!' Graves stared once again towards Bolitho.

Bolitho watched narrowly, his hand lifting while he forced himself to see the other ship as a target and not a once living creature writhing in agony.

'As you bear, Mr. Graves! Full elevation!'

He saw the listing, dismasted frigate falling past *Sparrow's* starboard bow, the churned sand around her beakhead to mark the extent of her charge on to the bar.

His hand came down. '*Fire!*'

The hull jerked and bucked as gun by gun the double-shotted charges ripped over the wave crests to smash into the helpless enemy. A few shots from swivel guns answered the first onslaught, but as the heavy balls, coupled with a full load of grape, swept into her side and decks those, too, fell silent.

Bolitho held up his hand. 'Cease firing! Secure guns!' To Buckle he added, 'We will wear ship directly. Nor'-east by north.' He glanced astern at the smoking wreck. 'She will rest there until someone comes, friend or foe, it makes little difference for her.'

Tyrrell watched him gravely. 'Aye, aye, sir.'

He appeared to be waiting for something more.

Bolitho walked to the rail and studied the men below him. Restoring lashings on the guns, working to repair damage and sort out the tangle of rigging, everywhere something was happening to prepare *Sparrow* for her next challenge. There was no cheering, in fact little sound of voices at all. Just a few grins as seamen discovered good friends still alive. A nod here, a casual thump of the shoulder there. Together they told him more than words.

'They've learned well, Mr. Tyrrell.' He saw Dalkeith coming aft again and steeled himself for the list of dead and dying. 'After this they will be ready for anything.'

He handed his sword to Stockdale, who had been near him the whole time although he could not recall seeing him.

'As *I* will.'

8

A Captain's Decision

The *Sparrow's* stay at New York proved to be the most frustrating and testing time Bolitho could remember. Instead of weeks, as he had hoped, to carry out his repairs and replace stores, he was forced to wait and watch with mounting impatience while every other ship, or so it appeared, took precedence.

As the time dragged into one and then a second month, he found himself ready to plead rather than demand, beg instead of awaiting his rightful aid from the shore authorities, and from what he could gather elsewhere, it seemed that most other junior vessels were in the same situation.

Work aboard continued without pause, and already *Sparrow* had taken on the appearance of a tried veteran. Sails were carefully patched rather than being replaced without thought of cost. Nobody seemed to know when more replenishments were arriving from England, and those already in New York were jealously guarded or, he suspected, hoarded for some suitable bribe. The maintopgallant yard had been fished, and from the deck appeared as good as new. How it would withstand a real storm, or a chase after some blockade runner, was often in Bolitho's mind, along with the endless stream of reports to be made, requisition and victualling lists to be checked and argued over with the supply yard, until he began to think neither he nor his ship would ever move again.

Most of the pride and excitement at running the French frigate aground, of seeing the rescued soldiers safely landed, had given way to resigned gloom. Day after day, the ship's company endured the heat and the work, knowing there was no chance of setting foot on land unless under close supervision and then only on matters of duty. Bolitho knew the reasons for this rule were sound up to a point. Every vessel which came and went from Sandy Hook was shorthanded, and unscrupulous captains had been known to steal seamen from other ships if offered half a chance.

Since assuming command he, too, was short of fifteen men, those killed or so badly injured as to be unfit for further service.

And the news was not encouraging. Everywhere on the mainland the British forces were in trouble. In June a complete army was forced to retreat from General Washington's attacks at the battle of Monmouth, and the reports which filtered to the anchored ships showed little hope of improvement.

To add to the fleet's troubles had come the first hurricane of the season. Sweeping up from the Caribbean like a scythe through corn it had destroyed several ships in its path, and so damaged others they were out of commission when most needed. Bolitho was able to appreciate the admiral's concern for his patrols and prowling frigates, for the whole management of strategy along the American coast depended on their vigilance, their ability to act like his eyes and an extension to his brain.

He was thankful for one thing only. That his ship had not been so seriously damaged below the waterline as he had first feared. As Garby, the carpenter, had said, 'She's like a little fortress, sir.'

On his regular inspections below decks to watch the work's progress Bolitho had understood the carpenter's pride. For *Sparrow* had been built as a sloop of war, quite unlike most of her contemporaries which had been purchased for the Navy from the less demanding tasks of merchant service. Even her stout frames had been grown to the right proportions and not cut with a saw, so that the hull had all the added security of natural strength. The fact that but for a few ragged shot-holes below the quarter which needed the aid and tools of the New York shipwrights his ship could sail and fight as before, made the delay all the more unbearable.

He had been to see Rear-Admiral Christie aboard his flagship, but had gained little idea of when he could complete repairs. The admiral had said wryly, 'If you had been less, er, difficult with General Blundell, things might be different.'

When Bolitho had tried to draw him further he had snapped, 'I know the general was wrong to act as he did. The whole of New York knows it by now. He may even be censured when he returns to England, although knowing his influence in certain regions, I doubt that.' He had shrugged wearily. '*You*, Bolitho, had to be the one to humble him. You did right, and I have already written a report to show my confidence in you. However, the *right* way is not always the most popular.'

One item of news hung over Bolitho like a cloud and seemed to torment him as day by day he tried to prepare his ship for sea. An incoming brig had brought news of the privateer *Bonaventure*. She had fought several actions against supply vessels and ships-of-war alike. She had seized two prizes and destroyed an escorting sloop. Just as he had predicted, as he had feared. But to him the worst part was that the privateer had returned to the same area where they had exchanged shots, and had found the crippled frigate *Miranda*.

A handful of survivors had been discovered drifting in a small boat, some wounded or half-mad with thirst, the rest stunned by the suddenness of their ship's end, when they had done so much to repair and save her.

Over and over again Bolitho searched his mind to examine his actions, to discover what else he might or should have done. By carrying out his orders, by putting duty before the true desire to help the damaged frigate, he had left her like a helpless animal before the tiger.

In his heart he believed he could have made no other decision. But if he had realised that the two transports were no longer so desperately needed, he also knew he would have acted differently. When he had admitted as much to the brig's captain he had replied, 'Then your *Sparrow*, too, would be at the bottom, for *Bonaventure* is more than a match for anything but a ship of the line!'

Apart from matters of duty, errands to use his presence or his purse on shipyard clerks, Bolitho refrained from going ashore. Partly because he thought it unfair when his men were penned in their ship, the size of which seemed to shrink with each passing day, and partly because of what he saw there. The military preparations were usual enough. Artillery wheeling and exercising, the horse-drawn limbers charging at full tilt, to the delight of idlers and yelling children. Foot soldiers drilling and sweating in the grinding heat, he had even seen cavalry on several occasions.

No, it went far deeper. The worsening news from inland seemed to reach just so far and then stop. In the great houses, rarely a night passed without some fine ball or reception being held. Staff officers and rich traders, ladies in full gowns and glittering jewels, it was hard to realise they were so close to a full-scale war. Equally, he knew his disgust came from his own inability to mix in such circles. In his home town of Falmouth his family had always been respected, but more as seafarers than local residents. He had gone to sea at the age of twelve, and his education had been more concerned with navigation and learning the mysteries of every eye and cleat, each foot of cordage required to sail a ship under all conditions, than the art of making small-talk and mingling with some of the bewigged jackadandies he had seen in New York. The women, too, seemed different. Beyond reach. Unlike the outspoken countrywomen in Cornwall or the wives and daughters of fellow sea-officers, they appeared to give off a power all of their own. A boldness, a certain amused contempt which both irritated and confused him whenever he came in contact with their perfumed, privileged world.

He had allowed Tyrrell to go ashore whenever possible, and had been surprised to see the change in him. Instead of showing excitement or relief at being amongst men like himself, places he had often visited in his father's schooner, he withdrew still further, until eventually he avoided leaving the ship unless on some particular duty. Bolitho knew he had been making inquiries about his family's whereabouts, anything which might give him some hint of their safety or otherwise. Also, he believed that Tyrrell would tell him in his own good time, if that was what he wished.

And then, three months almost to the exact day after watching the French frigate pounding herself to fragments on the hidden bar, *Sparrow* was once more ready for sea. When the last shipwright had been escorted ashore, each watched to make certain he took no more than he had brought with him, and the water-lighters and yard hoys had pulled clear of the side, Bolitho wrote his report for the admiral. Another special mission, to carry despatches, or merely to return to Captain Colquhoun's command, he now cared very little which it was to be. Just to be under sail again, free of urbane flag officers and inscrutable clerks, it was all he wanted.

When Tyrrell came aft to report the ship cleared of shore workers Bolitho asked, 'Will you dine with me this evening? We may be too occupied in the near future.'

Tyrrell looked at him dully. 'My pleasure, sir.' He sounded worn out. Spent.

Bolitho stared through the open stern windows towards the anchored ships and the pale houses beyond.

'You may share your worries with me, Mr. Tyrrell, if you wish.' He had not meant to say what he did. But the look of despair on the lieutenant's face had pushed all caution aside.

Tyrrell watched him by the windows, his eyes in shadow. 'I did get news. My father lost his schooners, but that was expected. They went to one side or t'other. Makes no difference. My father also owned a small farmstead. Always said it was like th' one he had once in England.'

Bolitho turned slowly. 'Is that gone, too?'

Tyrrell shrugged. 'Th' war reached th' territory some months back.' His voice became distant, toneless. 'We had a neighbour, called Luke Mason. He an' I grew up together. Like brothers. When th' rebellion began Luke was up north selling cattle an' I was at sea. Luke was always a bit wild, an' I guess he got carried along by all the excitement. Anyway, he joined up to fight th' English. But things got bad for his company, they were almost wiped out in some battle or t'other. Luke decided to go home. He had had enough of war, I guess.'

Bolitho bit his lip. 'He went to your father?'

'Aye. Trouble was, my father was apparently helping th' English soldiers with fodder an' remounts. But he was fond of Luke. He was like family.' He gave a long sigh. 'Th' local colonel heard about it from some goddamn informer. He had my father hanged on a tree and burned th' house down for good measure.'

Bolitho exclaimed, 'My God, I'm sorry!'

Tyrrell did not seem to hear. 'Then th' Americans attacked an' th' red coats retreated.' He looked up at the deckhead and added fiercely, 'But Luke was safe. He got out of th' house before it burned around him. An' you know what? Th' American colonel hanged Luke as a deserter!'

He dropped on a chair and fell against the table. 'In th' name of hell, where's th' goddamn sense in it all?'

'And your mother?' He watched Tyrrell's lowered head. His anguish was breaking him apart.

'She died two years back, so she was spared all this. There's just me now, an' my sister Jane.' He looked up, his eyes reflecting the sunlight like fires. 'After Cap'n Ransome had done with her, she disappeared. Christ alone knows where she is!'

In the sudden silence Bolitho tried to discover how he would feel if, like Tyrrell, he was faced with such an appalling discovery. Ever since he could remember he had been taught to accept the possibility of death and not shirk from it. Most of his ancestors had died at sea in one manner or another. It was an easy thing to do. Quite apart from a brutal end under cannon fire or the plunge of an enemy's sword, there were countless traps for the unwary. A fall from aloft, drowning, fever, men died as much from these as anything fired from a gun. His brother Hugh had been a lieutenant in the Channel Fleet when he had last seen him. He could be commanding a ship against the French, or at this very moment lying many fathoms down with his men. But the roots would still be there. The house in Falmouth, his father and married sisters. What would he be suffering if, like Tyrrell, he knew all that was broken and trodden down in a country where brother fought brother and men cursed each other in the same language as they struggled and died?

Now Tyrrell, and many more besides, had nothing left. Not even a country.

There was a rap on the door and Graves stepped into the cabin.

'This was delivered by the guardboat, sir.' He held out a canvas envelope.

Bolitho walked to the windows again and slit it open with a knife. He hoped Graves would not notice Tyrrell's misery, that the time taken to read the message would give him a moment to recover.

It was very brief

He said quietly, 'We are ordered to weigh at first light tomorrow. We will be carrying important despatches to the admiral in Antigua.'

He had a mental picture of the endless sea miles, the long passage back to English Harbour and Colquhoun. It was a pity they had ever left in the first place.

Graves said, 'I'm not sorry. We'll have something to boast about this time.'

Bolitho studied him gravely. What an unimaginative man he is.

'My compliments to the master. Tell him to make preparations at once.'

When Graves had gone Bolitho added, 'Maybe you'll wish to postpone dining with me?'

Tyrrell stood up, his fingers touching the table as if to test his own balance.

'No, sir. I'd like to come.' He looked round the cabin. 'This was th' last place I saw Jane. It helps a bit now.'

Bolitho watched him leave and heard the slam of a cabin door. Then with a sigh he sat down at the table and began to write in his log.

For seven untroubled days the *Sparrow* pushed her bowsprit southwards, taking full advantage of a fresh wind which hardly varied in bearing or substance throughout that time. The regrets and brooding despondency which most of the company had felt at New York seemed to have blown away on the wind, and their new freedom shone in the straining canvas which gleamed beneath a cloudless sky. Even the memory of the last fight, the faces of those killed or left behind crippled to await passage home had become part of the past, like old scars which took just so much time to heal.

As Bolitho studied his chart and checked the daily sunsights he felt cause for satisfaction in *Sparrow*'s performance. She had already logged over a thousand miles, and like himself seemed eager to leave the land as far away as possible. They had not sighted even a solitary sail, and the last hopeful gulls had left them two days earlier.

The routine aboard such a small ship-of-war was regular and carefully planned, so that the overcrowded conditions could be made as comfortable as possible. When not working aloft on sails and rigging the hands spent their time at gun drill or in harmless contests of wrestling and fighting with staves under Stockdale's professional eye.

On the quarterdeck, too, there was usually some diversion to break the monotony of empty horizons, and Bolitho came to know even more about his officers. Midshipman Heyward had proved himself to be an excellent and skilful swordsman, and spent several of the dog watches instructing Bethune and the master's mates in the art of fencing. The biggest surprise was Robert Dalkeith. The plump surgeon had come on deck with the finest pair of pistols Bolitho had ever seen. Perfectly matched and made by Dodson of London, they must have cost a small fortune. While one of the ship's boys had thrown pieces of wood chippings from a gangway, Dalkeith had waited by the nettings and when they had bobbed past on the wash had despatched them without seeming to take aim. Such marksmanship was rare for any ship's surgeon, and added to the price of the pistols made Bolitho think more deeply about Dalkeith's past.

Towards the end of the seventh day Bolitho received his first warning that the weather was changing. The sky, clear and pale blue for so long, became smeared by long tongues of cloud, and the ship reeled more heavily in a deep swell. The glass was unsteady, but it was more the feel of things which told him they were in for a real blow. The wind had backed to the north-west and showed every sign of strengthening, and as he faced it across the taffrail he could sense the mounting power, its clamminess on his skin.

Buckle observed, 'Another hurricane, I wonder?'

'Maybe.' Bolitho walked to the compass. 'Let her fall off a point.' He left Buckle to his helmsman and joined Tyrrell by the quarterdeck rail. 'The fringe of a storm perhaps. Either way we will have to reef down before dark, maybe much sooner.'

Tyrrell nodded, his eyes on the bulging canvas. 'Th' mainto'gan'sl seems to be drawing well. They did good work aloft while we were in port.' He watched the masthead pendant as it twisted and then flapped out more firmly towards the larboard bow. 'Goddamn th' wind. It backs still further by th' looks of it.'

Buckle smiled glumly. 'Course sou' sou'-east, sir.' He cursed as the deck tilted steeply and a tall spectre of spray burst above the nettings.

Bolitho considered the matter. They had made a good passage so far. There was no point in tearing the sails off her just to spite the wind. He sighed. Perhaps it would ease again soon.

'Get the t'gallants off her, Mr. Tyrrell. It's coming down on us now.'

He stood aside as Tyrrell ran for his trumpet Out from the swaying hull he saw the telltale haze of rain advancing across the uneven swell and blotting out the horizon like a fence of chain-mail.

Within an hour the wind had backed even further and had risen to gale force with the sea and sky joined together in a torment of bursting wave-crests, and torrential rain. It was useless to fight it and as the clouds gathered and entwined above the swooping mastheads *Sparrow* turned and ran before it her topmen fighting and fisting the sodden canvas as yet another reef was made fast. Half-blinded by rain and spray, their feet groping for toeholds, while with curses and yells they used brute strength to bring the sails under control.

Night came prematurely, and under close-reefed topsails they drove on into the darkness, their world surrounded by huge wave-crests, their lives menaced at every step by the sea as it surged over the gangways and boiled along the decks like a river in flood. Even when the hands were dismissed in watches to find a moment of rest and shelter below there was little to sustain them. Everything was dripping or damp, and the cook had long since given up any idea of producing a hot meal.

Bolitho remained on the quarterdeck, his tarpaulin coat plastered to his body like a shroud while the wind howled and screamed around him. Shrouds and rigging whined like the strings of some mad orchestra, and above the deck, hidden in darkness, the crack and boom of canvas told its own story. In brief lulls the wind seemed to drop, holding its breath as if to consider its efforts against the embattled sloop. In those small moments Bolitho could feel the salt warming on his face, raw to the touch. He could hear the clank of pumps, the muffled shouts from below and on the hidden forecastle as unseen men fought to make fast lashings, seek out severed cordage, or merely to reassure each other they were alive.

All night the wind battered against them, driving them further and still further to the south-east. Hour by hour, as Bolitho peered at the compass or reeled below to examine his chart, there was neither rest nor relief from its pounding. Bolitho felt bruised and sick, as if he had been fighting a physical battle, or dragged half-drowned from the sea itself. Despite his reeling mind he thanked God he had not tried to lie to and ride out the storm under a solitary reefed topsail. With this strength of wind and sea *Sparrow* would never have recovered, could have been all aback and dismasted before anyone had realised what they were truly against.

He could even find a moment to marvel at *Sparrow*'s behaviour. Uncomfortable she was to every man aboard. Fighting the jerking canvas or working on the pumps with sea and bilge water swirling amongst them like rats in a sewer, their lives were made worse by the motion. Up, higher still, and then down with the sound of thunder across a great crest, every spar and timber shaking as if to rip free of the hull. Food, a few precious possessions, clothing, all surged about the decks in wild abandon, but not a gun tore away from its lashings, not a bolt snapped, nor was any hatch stove in by the attacking sea. *Sparrow* took it all, rode each assault with the unsteady belligerence of a drunken marine.

By the time they sighted a first hint of grey in the sky the sea had begun to ease, and when the sun peeped languidly above the horizon it was hard to believe they were in the same ocean.

The wind had veered again to the north-west and as they stared with salt-caked eyes at the patches of blue between the clouds they knew they were being left in comparative peace.

Bolitho realised that if he allowed the hands to rest now they would not be able to move again for hours. He looked down at the gun deck and gangways, seeing their tired faces and torn clothing, the way the topmen's tarred hands were held like claws after their repeated journeys to those treacherous yards to battle with the sails.

He said, 'Pass the word for the galley fire to be lit. We must get some hot food into them directly.' He looked up as a shaft of sunlight touched the upper yards so that they shone above the retreating darkness like a triple crucifix. 'It will be warm enough soon, Mr. Tyrrell. Rig wind-sails above each hatch and open the weather gun ports.' He let his salt-stiffened lips crack into a smile. 'I suggest you forget your usual concern for the ship's looks and have the hands run their spare clothing aloft to dry out.'

Graves came aft and touched his hat. 'Able Seaman Marsh is missing.' He swayed and added wearily, 'Foretopman, sir.'

Bolitho let his eyes stray over the starboard quarter. The seaman must have been hurled overboard during the night, and they had not even heard a cry. Which was just as well. They could have done nothing to save him.

'Thank you, Mr. Graves. Note it in the log, if you please.'

He was still watching the sea, the way the night appeared to withdraw itself before the first gold rays, like some retreating assassin. The seaman was out there somewhere, dead and remembered by just a few. His shipmates, and those at home he had left so long ago.

He shook himself and turned to the master. 'Mr. Buckle, I hope we can fix our position today. Somewhere to the sou-west of the Bermudas, I have no doubt.' He smiled gently at Buckle's gloomy expression. 'But fifty miles or five hundred, I am not sure.'

Bolitho waited another hour until the ship had been laid on a new tack, her jib-boom prodding towards the southern horizon, her decks and upperworks steaming in the early sunlight as if she was smouldering.

Then he nodded to Tyrrell. 'I will take some breakfast.' He sniffed the greasy aroma from the galley funnel. 'Even that smell has given me an appetite.'

With the cabin door firmly closed and Stockdale padding around the table with fresh coffee and a pewter plate of fried pork, Bolitho was able to relax, to weigh the value and cost of the night's work. He had faced his first storm in command. A man had died, but many others had stayed alive. And the *Sparrow* was once again dipping and creaking around him as if nothing out of the ordinary had happened at all.

Stockdale put a plate with half a loaf of stale bread on it beside a crock of yellow butter. The bread was the last of that brought aboard at New York, the butter probably rancid from the cask. But as Bolitho leaned back in his chair he felt like a king, and the meagre breakfast seemed no less than a banquet.

He stared idly around the cabin. He had survived much in so short a time. It was luck, more than he deserved.

He asked, 'Where is Fitch?'

Stockdale showed his teeth. 'Dryin' your sleepin' gear, sir.' He rarely spoke when Bolitho was eating and thinking. He had learned all about Bolitho's odd habits long back. He added, 'Woman's work.'

Bolitho laughed, the sound carrying up through the open skylight where Tyrrell had the watch and Buckle was scribbling on his slate beside the binnacle.

Buckle shook his head. 'What did I tell you? No worries, that one!'

'Deck there!' Tyrrell stared up at the masthead as the cry came. 'Sail! Fine on th' starboard quarter!'

Feet clattered on the ladder and Bolitho appeared beside him, his jaw still working on some buttered bread.

He said, 'I have a feeling about this morning.' He saw a master's mate by the mainmast trunk and called, 'Mr. Raven! Aloft with you!' He held up his hand, halting the man as he ran to the shrouds. 'Remember your lesson, as I will.'

Graves had also come on deck, partly shaved and naked to the waist. Bolitho looked around the waiting men, studying each in turn if only to contain his impatience while Raven clawed his way to the masthead. Changed. They were all different in some way. Toughened, more confident perhaps. Like bronzed pirates, held together by their trade – he hesitated – their loyalty.

'Deck there!' Another maddening wait and then Raven yelled down, 'It's her right enough! The *Bonaventure*!'

Something like a growl came from the watching seamen.

One man shouted, 'The bloody *Bonaventure*, is it? Us'll give that bugger a quiltin' today an' that's for sure!'

Several others cheered, and even Bethune called excitedly, 'Huzza, lads!'

Bolitho turned to look at them again, his his heart suddenly heavy, the promise of the morning sour and spoiled.

'Get the t'gallants on her, Mr. Tyrrell. The royals, too, if the wind stays friendly.'

He saw Tyrrell's eyes, worried, even sad, and snapped, 'We have orders. To carry despatches to our admiral.' He gestured angrily towards the taffrail. 'Do you want to match guns with her?' He turned away, adding vehemently, 'But God, I'd like nothing better than to see her strike!'

Tyrrell took his trumpet and shouted, 'Call th' hands! All hands make sail!'

He glanced quickly at Bolitho who was staring astern. The privateer was not visible from anywhere but the masthead. Nor would she be now. But Bolitho was staring fixedly, as if he could see every gun, each gaping muzzle, like the day she had swept *Miranda*'s defences aside like so much rubbish.

Graves moved to his side, his eyes on the seamen as they hurried to their various stations, some still puzzled by their orders.

Tyrrell said quietly, 'It ain't easy to run before an enemy.'

Graves shrugged. 'How about you? I'd have thought you should be somewhat comforted by the fact.' He fell back before Tyrrell's cold stare but added smoothly, 'It would have been less easy for you to fight a Yankee, eh?' Then he hurried down the ladder towards his men at the foremast.

Tyrrell followed him with his eyes. 'Bastard.' He spoke only to himself and was surprised to find he was so calm. '*Bastard*.'

When he turned his head he saw that Bolitho had left the deck.

Buckle dipped his thumb to the skylight. 'He's not laughing now, Mr. Tyrrell.' He sounded grim. 'I'd not have his rank for all the whores in Plymouth!'

Tyrrell tapped the half-hour glass and said nothing.

How different from Captain Ransome, he thought. He would have shared neither hopes nor fears with any of them. And these same seamen who were already swarming up the ratlines on either beam would have shown no surprise if he made a similar decision as Bolitho. It was because they seemed to think Bolitho could lead them anywhere, and with all odds against them, that they were puzzled by his action. The sudden realisation troubled him. Partly because Bolitho did not understand, but mainly because he should have been the one to make Bolitho realise how they all felt for him.

Ransome had always used and never led them. Instead of example he had laid down rules. Whereas he ... Tyrrell glanced at the cabin skylight now shut, and imagined he could hear a girl's voice again.

Graves strode aft and touched his hat, his tone formal in front of the watching eyes.

'Permission to dismiss the watch below, sir?'

'Aye. Carry on, Mr. Graves.' They held each other's gaze then Tyrrell turned his back.

He walked to the rail and stared up at the freshly trimmed sails, the seamen on the upper yards, their skins brown in the sunlight.

The privateer would never catch them now, even if she so intended. It would be another ship, a fat merchantman, or some unsuspecting trader from the Bahamas.

He saw the captain's coxswain beside the nettings and asked, 'How is he, Stockdale?'

Stockdale regarded him warily, like a watchdog examining a possible intruder.

Then he relaxed slightly, his big hands loose at his sides. ' 'E's in irons at th' moment, sir.' He stared angrily at the blue water. 'But we've come through worse afore. A whole lot worse.'

Tyrrell nodded, seeing the certainty in Stockdale's eyes like something written.

'He has a good friend in you, Stockdale.'

The coxswain turned his broken face away. 'Aye. I could tell you things I seen 'im do that'd make some of these Jacks run to their mothers and pray.'

Tyrrell kept quiet and very still, watching the man's profile as he relived some memory, an incident so vivid it was like yesterday.

Stockdale said in his wheezing voice, 'I've carried 'im like a child, seen 'im so beside hisself with anger there's not a man-jack'd draw near. Other times I've seen 'im 'old a man in 'is arms until 'e died, even though there was nought anyone could do for th' poor bugger.' He swung round, his eyes fierce. 'I ain't got the words for it, else I'd make 'em all listen.'

Tyrrell reached out and touched his massive arm.

'You're wrong. You've got th' words right enough. And thanks for telling *me*.'

Stockdale grunted and walked heavily towards the hatch. He had never spoken like that before, but somehow he trusted Tyrrell. Like Bolitho, he was a man, not just an officer, and for him that was more than enough.

All that day the *Sparrow* ran freely towards an empty horizon. The watches changed, drills were carried out, and one man was flogged for drawing his knife against a messmate after an argument. But there were no contests on deck, and when Heyward appeared with his swords to begin another period of instruction he found no takers, nor did Dalkeith leave his sickbay for a pistol shoot.

In his cabin Bolitho remained with his thoughts, wondering why a simple action was so hard to bear, merely because he had been the one to dictate it. Command, leadership, authority, they were mere words. At no time could they explain his true feelings, or wipe away inner misgivings.

As Rear-Admiral Christie had said, the right way was not always the most popular, or the easiest to accept.

When the bell chimed out for the first dog watch he heard another cry from the masthead.

'Deck there! Sail on the lee bow!'

He made himself remain seated at the table until Midshipman Bethune came down to report that the sail was barely moving and was perhaps hove-to.

Even then he delayed before going on deck. Another disappointment, a fresh need to take avoiding action from one more enemy, only time and distance would tell him these things.

Graves, who had the watch, said, 'if it's one of our frigates we could turn and close with the *Bonaventure*, sir.'

Heyward added, 'Maybe we could take her as a prize.'

Bolitho faced them coldly. 'And if she's a *French* frigate, what then?' He saw them stiffen under his stare. 'I suggest you hold your suppositions until later.'

But it was neither privateer nor patrolling ship-of-war. As *Sparrow* sped down towards her Bolitho watched the stranger through his glass, seeing the gap in her outline where her main topmast had been torn away like a branch from a tree, and the huge scars along her tumblehome to show the battering she had received from sea and wind.

Buckle said quietly, 'By God, she must have taken the storm full on herself. She's in a poor way, I'm thinking.'

Tyrrell, who had climbed to the main topmast yard, shinned down a back-stay and reported, 'I know her, sir. She's th' *Royal Anne*, West Indiaman.'

Buckle agreed. 'Aye, that's so. She set sail from Sandy Hook three days afore us. Bound for Bristol, I heard.'

'Run up the colours.'

Bolitho shifted the glass carefully, watching the tiny figures swarming along the other ship's decks, the broken gangway where a great sea had thundered inboard like a falling cliff. She made a pitiful sight. Spars missing, sails in ribbons. She must have ridden out the same storm which they had skirted just a night ago.

Bethune exclaimed, 'I have her here in my book, sir. She is under warrant to the Commander-in-Chief.'

But Bolitho barely heard him. He saw the figures along the vessel's upper deck pausing to stare at the approaching sloop, while here and there a man was waving, perhaps cheering to see a friendly flag.

He stiffened and then said, 'There are women aboard that ship.' He lowered the glass and looked at Tyrrell questioningly. 'Under warrant, is she?'

Tyrrell nodded slowly. 'Indiamen do take a government charter when it suits sir.' He glanced away. 'Th' *Royal Anne*'ll be carrying folk from New York to England. And away from th' war, no doubt.'

Bolitho raised the glass again, his mind working on Tyrrell's words.

He said, 'We will close her now, Mr. Tyrrell, and keep her under our lee. Have the starboard cutter cleared for lowering. The surgeon will accompany me on board.' He glanced at Bethune. 'Signal her to that effect. If she fails to understand, then hail her when we draw nearer.'

He walked away from the rail as the flags soared aloft on their halliards.

Tyrrell followed him and said gravely, 'She'll not be able to outsail th' *Bonaventure*, sir. Even if she was without damage.'

Bolitho faced him. 'I know.'

He tried to sound composed even though his mind was screaming. Turn after all and face the big privateer. The facts had not altered. *Sparrow* would still be outgunned and sunk without too much difficulty. The *Royal Anne* was so badly damaged that a respite brought about by sacrificing this ship and all her company would make no difference. But to run once more. Leave her helpless and allow the enemy to take her at leisure was too cruel even to contemplate.

He *must* contemplate it. It was his decision. *His.*

Buckle called, 'She's standing by, sir! We'd best take the way off us.'

'Very well.' Bolitho walked slowly along the side. 'Get the royals and t'gallants off her, Mr. Tyrrell. We will heave-to directly.'

He saw Stockdale hurrying towards him with his coat and sword. It would be dark in five hours. If they were to do anything, they would need haste and luck. Especially the latter.

He slipped into his coat and said, 'Mr. Tyrrell, you will come with me.'

Then as the boat was hoisted over the gangway and lowered alongside he looked astern, almost expecting to see a sliver of sail, or hear the masthead's call.

'Cutter alongside, sir!'

He nodded and strode towards the gangway.

'Let us be about it then.'

And without a glance at the others he followed Tyrrell down into the boat.

9

'Boarders Away'

As he pulled himself up a dangling rope ladder to the *Royal Anne's* thick bulwark Bolitho was conscious of the tension which awaited him. There were many people on the upper and poop decks, passengers and sailors, singly and in large groups, but all joined together in some way as they stared at him, then at the seamen who followed him up from the cutter.

Bolitho paused to collect his thoughts, and while he adjusted the sword on his hip and Tyrrell mustered the boarding party into line, he took a slow appraisal of the ship around him. Fallen rigging and broken spars, whole strips of torn canvas and cordage littered the decks in profusion, and he could tell by the heavy motion that she had taken a good deal of water in the bilges.

A tall, gangling man in a blue coat stepped forward and touched his forehead.

'I'm Jennis, sir.' He swallowed hard. 'Mate and senior officer.'

'Where is the Master?'

Jennis gestured wearily towards the rail. 'He went overboard in the storm. Him and twenty more besides.'

Boots thudded on a companion ladder and Bolitho stiffened as a familiar figure thrust the others aside and strode towards him. It was General Blundell, impeccable as ever, but with two pistols at his belt.

Bolitho touched his hat. 'I am surprised to see you, Sir James.' He tried to mask his dislike. 'You appear to be in some trouble.'

The general glared around him then across at the *Sparrow* as she swayed easily in the swell, her sails flapping loosely as if resting.

He barked, 'And about time, too! This damn ship should never have been allowed out of harbour!' He pointed at the mate. 'That fool cannot even keep order!'

Bolitho looked at Tyrrell. 'Take your men and examine the hull and other damage. Quick as you can.' He glanced narrowly at a group of sailors lolling by the forward hatch, noticing how they swayed out of time with the deck, their eyes devoid of interest in his arrival or the disorder which lay on every hand.

The mate explained hurriedly, 'We've had to use pistols, sir. Some men ran wild when the storm broke. We've a full cargo of rum and other spirits, as well as molasses and coffee. While the rest of us were working the ship they and a few passengers broached holds and began drinking.' He shuddered. 'What with women crying an' screaming, the ship falling about us, an' Cap'n Harper lost overboard, I was hard put to watch everything at once.'

Blundell snapped, 'You're bloody useless! I'd have you shot for your incompetence!'

As the first of *Sparrow*'s seamen approached the fore hatch the drunken figures seemed to come to life. With jeers and taunts they blocked the way across the deck, and from right forward an unseen hand hurled a bottle which shattered against a ring bolt, bringing bright droplets of blood down a sailor's chest.

Bolitho said sharply, 'Carry on, Mr. Tyrrell!'

The lieutenant nodded. 'Party! Draw cutlasses!' He took his pistol and pointed it at the line of swaying figures. 'Kill anyone who interferes! Bosun's mate, take 'em below and put 'em on the pumps!'

One made as if to run amongst the small party, but fell senseless as the boatswain's mate brought the flat of his blade hard down on the side of his head.

Bolitho said, 'There is much to do. Mr. Jennis, turn the hands to and replace your fores'l. Have all this clutter cut adrift so that the injured may be laid on deck where my surgeon can attend them.' He waited until the mate had shouted his instructions before adding, 'How are you armed?'

Jennis waved vaguely around him. 'Not much, sir. Twenty six-pounders and some swivels. We aim to steer clear of trouble. These guns are all we need for fighting off the *boucanier* or would-be pirate.' He looked up, startled. 'Why do you ask?'

General Blundell interrupted, 'Hell's teeth, must I stand here while you people discuss the fittings of this wretched ship? I have had all I can tolerate and . . .'

Bolitho said abruptly, 'Sir James, there is an enemy privateer to the north. She is probably still following us. The *fittings*, as you call them, will be very useful if that enemy comes our way.'

He turned, cocking his head, as the clank of pumps told him Tyrrell had the mutinous seamen in hand.

To Stockdale he said, 'Go aft, see what you can discover.'

Blundell sounded less confident. 'Privateer? Attack us?'

Bolitho replied, 'The *Sparrow* is very small, sir. The enemy more than twice our strength.'

The general grunted. 'Well, better than nothing. If fight you must, it will be for the finest reasons.'

Bolitho ignored him as Tyrrell came on deck again.

'I have sounded th' well. Th' hull is taking water steadily, but th' pumps seem to be containing it. Its all hell below. Cabins broken open, drunks, and two dead from knife wounds.' He frowned towards the mate who was urging his men to clear away fallen spars. 'He must have been mad with worry.' He saw Bolitho's expression. 'What'll we do?'

Blundell said, 'Your captain will do his duty. If we are attacked he will defend this ship and passengers. Do you need telling, man?'

Tyrrell eyed him coolly. 'Not by *you*, General.'

Bolitho snapped, 'How many women are there?' He was watching Stockdale ushering them from the poop, his voice barely audible as he tried to placate them.

There were children, too. More than he had realised.

'For God's sake, how much longer are you going to stand like this?' The general was shouting, his face almost as red as his tunic. 'What does it matter how many this or that we have on board, or what colour their eyes are?' He got no further.

Tyrrell stepped between them, his head lowered so that their faces were nearly touching.

'Look here, General, what th' cap'n says is right. Th' enemy can outshoot anything we have to offer, an' this Indiaman is a damn sight worse off.'

'Not my concern, and I'll tell you once more to mind your manners!'

'Warn me, General?' Tyrrell laughed silently. 'But for you meddling with us at Sandy Hook th' *Sparrow* would have completed repairs an' been away at sea a month back. So but for that you would be alone out here, sitting like a fat duck waiting to be shot for the' pot.' His tone hardened. 'So mind *your* damn manners, *sir*!'

Bolitho was standing apart from them, only half listening to their hushed anger. Once again Blundell's interference was to put him and the ship in real jeopardy. But the facts were unchanged. He turned to conceal his despair. All he had was the hope that *Bonaventure* would not find them. That he could set sail on the battered Indiaman and leave the area with all possible haste.

The mate, Jennis, came after again. 'I've got the hands behind on a new fores'l, sir. Apart from that we've little spare canvas aboard, not made up that is. This is a Company ship, and we were expecting to have a complete overhaul once we reached Bristol. That's why we sailed short-handed and one officer under strength.' He wiped his hand across his lined face. 'If you hadn't found us I think more of the men might have gone mad and mutinied. We've a fair sprinkling of rogues amongst the passengers as well as honest ones.'

Bolitho looked up as a block swayed and clattered against the mizzen topmast. He saw the torn sails stirring like ragged banners, the sudden movement in the bright Company flag. He frowned. The wind was freshening. Very slightly, but it made things harder if he was to face the decision which had to be made.

And yet, there was still a chance he might be wrong. If so, all this would do nothing but harm and cause more suffering to the passengers.

He pulled out his watch and flipped open the cover. Less than four hours of visibility left.

'Mr. Tyrrell, have the *Royal Anne*'s boats lowered at once. Send a message to Graves and tell him I want our boats and fifty seamen here without delay. We must work like the devil if we are to get this ship fit to make sail again.' He waited until Tyrrell and the Indiaman's mate had hurried away before saying, 'Well, Sir James, I must see what needs to be done.'

The general called after him, 'And if as you fear the enemy appears, do you intend to steal away and leave us?' He sounded hoarse with suppressed anger. 'Will written orders save your disgrace after taking such a course?'

Bolitho stopped and faced him again. 'No, Sir James, to both questions. If we are allowed time I will transfer all *Royal Anne's* passengers and additional hands to my own ship.'

The general's eyes were bulging. '*What?* Leave the cargo and sail away without it?' He seemed stunned in disbelief.

Bolitho shifted his gaze outboard, watching the boats alongside, the slow return of order as his own men took control.

Of course, he should have realised. The general's booty was on board, too. Surprisingly, the thought helped to steady him. He could even smile as he said, 'You can appreciate the need for haste, sir. For both our reasons!'

Tyrrell fell in step beside him. 'That took th' wind from his sails!'

Bolitho said, 'It is no joke. If we can get under way in company at dawn we will have a fair chance. It may be that the *Bonaventure* changed tack altogether when we lost her. She could be many leagues away by now.'

Tyrrell glanced at him. 'But you don't think so?'

'No.' He stepped aside as broken rigging was dragged like black snakes from an upended boat. 'It is the *when* rather than the *if* which troubles me.'

Tyrrell pointed across the bulwark. 'Graves is sending th' first of th' men over.' He grimaced. 'It'll leave him shorthanded in *Sparrow*. Barely enough to work ship.'

Bolitho shrugged. 'If the company was halved by fever the rest would *have* to manage.'

He added, 'Now let us meet the ladies. They will be more worried than the general, I should imagine.'

There were about fifty of them. Crowded together below the high poop, but separated by their rank and station in that other world outside the ship. Old and young, plain and beautiful, they watched Bolitho in silence, as if he had risen from the sea like a messenger from Neptune.

'Ladies.' He licked his lips as a strikingly beautiful girl in a gown of yellow silk smiled at him. He tried again. 'I must regret the inconvenience, but there is much to do before we can see you safely on your voyage.' She was still smiling. Direct. Amused. Just the way which always reduced him to confusion 'If anyone is injured my surgeon will do his best for her. A meal is being prepared, and my own men will stand guard over your quarters.'

The girl asked, 'Do you think the enemy will come, Captain?' She had a cool, confident voice which spoke of education and breeding.

He hesitated. 'It is always possible.'

She showed her even teeth. 'There now. What profound words from so young a King's officer!' Several of the others smiled. Some even laughed aloud.

Bolitho said stiffly, 'If you will excuse me, ladies.' He shot the girl a fierce stare. 'I have work to do.'

Tyrrell hid a smile as he strode past him, recalling Stockdale's words. *So angry that not a man-jack would draw near.* He was angry now. Blazing. It was good, Tyrrell concluded. It might take his mind off the real danger.

A servant girl touched his arm. 'Beggin' yer pardon, sir, but there's a lady below in a poor way. Very feverish.'

Bolitho stopped and looked at them. 'Fetch the surgeon.'

He tensed as the other girl came towards him, her face suddenly grave.

'I am sorry I made you angry, Captain. It was unforgivable.'

'Angry?' Bolitho plucked at his swordbelt. 'I do not recollect . . .'

She touched his hand. 'Now that is beneath you, Captain. Unsure maybe, but never pompous. I see you quite differently.'

'When you have *quite* finished . . .'

Again she stopped him without even raising her voice. 'The other women were close on hysteria, Captain. One minute the storm was throwing us about like rag dolls, the very next instant there is the cry of mutiny and riot. Men fighting each other, for the drink and for what they might take from us when they were too crazed to know otherwise.' She dropped her eyes. 'It was horrible. Terrifying.' The eyes came up again and levelled on his face. They were the colour of violets. 'Then all at once there was a shout. Someone called, "A ship! A King's ship!", and we ran on deck despite the dangers.'

She turned to look across the bulwark. 'And there you were. Little *Sparrow*. It was almost too much for most of us. Had I not made that jest at your expense, I think some might have broken down.'

Bolitho's defences wavered. 'Er, yes. Quite so.' He toyed with his swordhilt, seeing Dalkeith hurry past and giving him a curious glance as he went. 'You thought quickly, ma'am.'

'I know about some things, Captain. I saw your eyes when you spoke to your lieutenant and Sir James. There is worse to come, is there not?'

Bolitho shrugged. 'In truth I do not know.'

He heard the general shouting angrily at a seaman and said, 'That man is bad enough for me!'

She gave a mock curtsy, smiling again. 'Sir James? He can be difficult, I agree.'

'You know him?'

She moved back towards the other women. 'My uncle, Captain.' She laughed. 'Really you must try to hide your emotions better! Or else you will never be an admiral!'

Tyrrell came on deck and said, 'That woman in th' cabin is ill. But Dalkeith is managing well enough.' He frowned. 'Are you all right, sir?'

Bolitho rasped, 'In God's name stop asking me stupid questions!'

'Aye, sir.' He grinned, seeing the girl by the rail and far more beside. 'I understand, sir.'

There was a dull bang, and as they all turned Bolitho saw a puff of smoke drifting from one of *Sparrow*'s larboard batteries.

The general came panting up a ladder and shouted, 'What was that?'

Bolitho replied quietly, 'The signal, sir. My lookout has sighted the enemy.'

He ignored the general and those near him as his mind accepted the one important fact. In a way it was almost a relief to meet it. Recognise what must be done.

'Mr Tyrrell, *Bonaventure* will take several hours to show her intentions.

By then it will be too dark for her captain to attack. Why should he? He merely has to await the dawn and then pounce.'

Tyrrell watched him, fascinated by his even tone.

Bolitho continued, 'If the wind does not act against us, we will be able to transfer the passengers to *Sparrow*. I want every boat working, and all who are neither sick nor injured to take fairly to their tasks.'

'I understand.' Tyrrell studied him impassively. 'There's nothing else you could do. Many would leave 'em to their own devices.'

Bolitho shook his head. 'You have *not* understood. I am not going to abandon the *Royal Anne* or scuttle her to avoid capture as a prize.' He saw Tyrrell's jaw tighten, the quick anxiety in his eyes. 'I intend to stay in her with sixty volunteers. What happens later will depend very much on *Bonaventure*'s captain.'

He had not noticed that the others had crowded round him, but turned as the general exclaimed, 'You cannot! You dare not risk this ship and cargo! I'll see you damned first!'

Silk rustled against Bolitho's arm and he heard the girl say calmly, 'Be still, Uncle. The captain intends to do more than dare.' She did not turn her face. 'He intends to *die* for us. Is that not enough, even for you?'

Bolitho nodded curtly and strode aft, hearing Stockdale's voice as he hurried to cover his retreat. He had to think. Plan every last moment until the actual second of death. He paused and leaned against the ornate taffrail. Death. Was it so soon upon him?

He turned angrily and said, 'Pass the word for those boats to begin loading immediately! Women and children, then the injured.' He glanced past the ship's mate and saw the girl staring after him. 'And no arguments from anyone!'

He walked to the opposite side and looked at his own command. How beautiful she was as she edged carefully across the Indiaman's quarter. Soon now he would be able to see the enemy's sails on the horizon. Closing, like the hunter, for his kill. There was so much to do. Orders for *Sparrow* to carry to Antigua. Perhaps even a quick letter to his father. But not just yet. He must stand quite still a little longer to watch his ship. Hold her in his memory before she was taken from him.

Bolitho was still staring across the water when Tyrrell came aft to report that all available boats were working, carrying the passengers and Indiaman's company over to the waiting sloop.

He added, 'She'll be a mite more crowded than when we rescued th' redcoats.' He hesitated and then said, 'I'd like to stay with you, sir.'

Bolitho did not look at him. 'You realise what you are saying? There is more at stake than your life.'

Tyrrell tried to grin. 'Hector Graves will make a better commander, sir.'

Bolitho faced him. 'You will be called on to fight some of your own people.'

Tyrrell smiled. 'I knew that was what you were thinking.' He gestured towards some of *Sparrow*'s seamen as they carried an elderly woman towards the boat tackles. 'These are my people.' Then, 'Can I stay?'

Bolitho nodded. 'Gladly.' He removed his hat and ran his fingers through his hair. 'Now I'll go and write Graves's orders.'

'Deck there! Sail on th' larboard quarter!'

They looked at each other and then Bolitho said quietly, 'Hurry our people along. I do not want the enemy to see what we are about.'

As he strode away Tyrrell stared after him and then murmured, 'So be it, Cap'n.'

He heard a sudden cry and saw the girl who had made Bolitho angry struggling to push her way through a cordon of seamen.

A boatswain's mate bellowed, 'She don't want to go, sir!'

The girl punched the sailor's arm but he did not seem to feel it.

Then she shouted at Tyrrell, 'Let me stay! I want to be here!'

He grinned down at her and then pointed at the boat alongside. Kicking and protesting she was picked up bodily and carried to the rail, where with little ceremony she was passed down the side like a bright silk parcel.

The sky was much darker when Bolitho came on deck with a sealed envelope for the boat still hooked on to the chains. All other boats were hoisted, and the ship around him seemed very quiet and empty.

He raised a telescope and trained it over the quarter. The *Bonaventure* was visible now, some six miles distant. But she had already shortened sail, waiting, as he had expected, for the new day.

Tyrrell touched his hat. 'Our men are aboard, sir.' He gestured to the main deck where Midshipman Heyward was speaking to a petty officer. 'I picked 'em myself, but you could have had volunteers a'plenty.'

Bolitho handed the envelope to a seaman. 'Pass this to the boat.' To Tyrrell he added slowly, 'Go and take some rest. I shall think awhile.'

Later as Tyrrell lay in an abandoned cabin, the deck of which was littered with open chests and discarded clothing, he heard Bolitho's shoes on the planking overhead. Back and forth, up and down. Thinking. Eventually the sound of his pacing made his eyelids droop, and he fell into a dreamless sleep.

Bolitho stood straddle-legged on the *Royal Anne's* poop, seeing his own shadow for the first time across the taffrail. How long the night had been, but at the hint of dawn everything seemed to begin at once, like the start of some ill-rehearsed drama. Away on the larboard quarter he saw the hardening pyramid of sails where the big privateer moved purposefully before the wind. Strangely, her hull was still lost in shadow, with only a bone of white around her stem to reveal her growing speed. About three miles distant. He turned his glass to the opposite quarter, to the little sloop. *Sparrow* was much closer, yet in spite of this seemed even smaller.

Tyrrell joined him and said, 'Th' wind seems steady enough, sir. Nor'-west by north, by my reckoning.' He was speaking in a hushed voice, as if afraid to disturb the ships and their deliberate preparations to fight.

Bolitho nodded. 'We will steer sou'-east. It is what the enemy will expect.'

He tore his eyes from the privateer and turned to look along the Indiaman's deck. The new foresail was drawing well, as were spanker and jib. The rest were little better than shreds, and to try to tack more than a point or so would be a waste of time.

Tyrrell sighed. 'I've checked th' guns myself. Loaded as ordered.' He scratched his stomach. 'Some of 'em look so old they'd split if we double-shotted 'em.'

Bolitho faced aft again to watch the other ships. Raising his glass he moved it slowly over *Sparrow*'s deck, seeing the figures on the gangways, a solitary seaman at her mainmast crosstrees. Then aft, as a freak gust lifted the foot of the maincourse like a miller's apron, he saw Graves. He was standing beside the wheel, arms folded, looking every inch a captain. Bolitho breathed out very slowly. So much depended on Graves. If he lost his head, or misinterpreted his carefully worded instructions, the enemy would still catch two for the price of one. But Graves had got the first part right. He was wearing Bolitho's new uniform, the gold lace showing clearly in spite of the feeble light. The enemy captain would be wary; watchful. Nothing must go wrong at the beginning. Heaven alone knew how all the extra passengers had been crammed below and out of sight. It would be like a sealed tomb, a nightmare for the women and children once the gunfire began.

Midshipman Heyward came to the poop and said, 'All our boarding party are ready, sir.' Like Bolitho and Tyrrell he had discarded his uniform and looked even younger in his open shirt and breeches.

'Thank you.' Bolitho noticed that instead of a midshipman's dirk Heyward had thought fit to wear one of his precious swords.

There was a bang, and he saw a ball ricocheting across the lively wave crests before throwing up a quill of spray between him and the *Sparrow*'s bows. A sighting shot, a declaration of intent, probably both, he thought grimly.

Over the water, and audible above the rustle of torn canvas, he heard the staccato beat of drums, and pictured the scene aboard *Sparrow* as her men ran to quarters. Phase two. He saw the patch of scarlet as the ensign broke jauntily from her gaff, felt a catch in his throat as the ports opened to reveal her line of guns. With less than half a company available, Graves must have pressed some of the Indiaman's crew into service to get the guns out so smartly. But it had to look exactly right. As if the sloop was preparing to show defiance and trying to defend her heavy consort.

Another bang, and the ball ploughed into the sea about a cable clear of *Sparrow*'s stem.

Bolitho clenched his jaw. Graves was cutting it fine. If the wind chose this moment to veer he would be unable to go about, would be in irons if he tried to fall back and try again.

Tyrrell said hoarsely, 'There she goes!'

The sloop's yards were swinging and as her lee gangway dipped heavily into the swell she began to tack close-hauled to larboard, crossing *Royal Anne*'s stern like a small protective terrier. Flags broke from her yards, and Bolitho imagined Bethune yelling at his party and to make haste and hoist the meaningless signal. The enemy would think *Sparrow* was preparing to fight to the death and was ordering the Indiaman to make a run for it.

Cannon fire ripped along the *Bonaventure*'s foremost battery and more splashes leapt closer to the heeling sloop. Graves was shortening sail, clearing away the hampering canvas from his guns, even though it was unlikely he had more than a quarter of them manned.

Tyrrell spoke between his teeth. 'That's close enough, Hector! For God's sake don't make a meal of it!'

One heavy bang rolled across the shark-blue water, and even though the flash was hidden by *Sparrow*'s hull, Bolitho knew it was one of her bow-chasers. He saw the ball slap hard into the spray by the other ship's forecastle, the immediate spurt of orange tongues as she fired back in earnest.

The *Sparrow*'s foretopgallant mast quivered and then seemed to curtsy downwards into the swirling brown smoke, the furled sail marking its progress as it caught and swung in the criss-cross of rigging before plunging into the sea alongside. Holes appeared in several of her sails, and Bolitho caught his breath as the hammock nettings below the quarterdeck bucked and burst apart from a direct hit.

The enemy was much nearer now, her foretopsail bulging as she stood before the wind, charging down on the sloop which was now less than two cables from her starboard bow.

Tyrrell exclaimed, 'He's done it! Blast th' man, he's going about!'

The *Sparrow* was wearing, her masts swinging upright as she came round violently, the growing light making her sails shine as they flapped and puckered to the strain.

The gunfire had stopped, for with her stern towards the enemy *Sparrow* presented no target at all. The forecourse was already being unleashed, and as she gathered way through the water Bolitho saw the topmen running out along the yards like black insects until more and still more canvas bellied to the wind. He could see Buckle by the quarterdeck rail, too intent on his work even to watch the labouring Indiaman as she surged past. *Sparrow* was abeam, and then in minutes was well beyond the Indiaman's bows, heading towards the first rays of sunlight from the placid horizon.

Bolitho felt suddenly dry, his limbs very loose, as if belonging to someone else. He watched the *Bonaventure*'s forecourse being brailed up to reveal her great span of poop, the men on her gangways who were waving and gesturing after the retreating sloop. Jeering no doubt. All the madness of intended battle now lost in the confused actions of an unfought victory.

Bolitho walked to the rail and said quietly, 'Remember, Mr. Tyrrell, and remember it well. We have to cripple her if we can. Then if a patrolling frigate finds her she can finish what we started.' He gripped his wrist. 'But make sure our people play their parts. If *Bonaventure* hauls off now, she can pound us to pieces without losing a breath!'

The privateer had edged closer, running down towards the quarter so that she would eventually overhaul *Royal Anne* along her larboard side. Her captain was a superb seaman. With all but his topsails clewed up he was handling the heavy vessel with both confidence and skill, and would certainly hold the wind-gage no matter what Bolitho tried to do.

A gun flashed out its long tongue, and Bolitho felt the ball smack into the lower hull, jerking the planks at his feet with savage violence.

He saw bunched figures on the other ship's poop, the wink of sunlight on raised telescopes, and guessed they were examining their victim. It looked much as it had when he had come aboard. Damaged bulwarks and broken rigging. One hatch had been purposefully left open, and several of his men were running about in apparent confusion while Heyward directed their performance from beneath the forecastle.

'Now!' Bolitho waved his hand, and from the main deck one then another of the six-pounders hurled its challenge across the narrow strip of water.

From aft a swivel banged sharply, the canister probably falling harmlessly long before it reached the enemy's side.

The response was immediate. Gun by gun, the *Bonaventure*'s broadside sent ball after ball crashing into the hull. Bolitho was thankful he had sent most of his men below, otherwise they would have been cut down by the fierceness of the onslaught. Timber and planks flew in all directions, and he saw a seaman hurled like a bloody rag to the opposite side, his limbs kicking as he died.

Stockdale looked at Bolitho and saw him nod. With a grunt he dashed along the deck waving a cutlass, while Bolitho drew his pistol and yelled after him. When Stockdale ran on towards the halliards he fired, praying that his hand was steady as the shot whined clear above the coxswain's head. Stockdale reached his goal, and with one slash severed the halliards, bringing the big Company flag tumbling down like some bright shroud across the weather rail.

In a lull of noise and gunfire Bolitho heard a voice across the water, magnified and unreal in a speaking trumpet.

'Heave to or I'll sink you!'

From forward he heard Heyward urging his men to obey the call, the sudden groan of timber as the ship lurched drunkenly into the wind, her remaining sails flapping and banging in disorder.

Tyrrell said, 'He's going to grapple!'

There were men on the *Bonaventure*'s yards, and as the big hull surged carefully and then more insistently against the side Bolitho saw grapnels flying from a dozen points at once. The men on the yards were busily making fast their lines to *Royal Anne*'s shrouds and spars, so that as both ships lifted and swayed together Bolitho knew the moment to act had arrived.

'Now! Boarders away!'

With a wild chorus of yells the hidden seamen surged up from both hatches and on to the bulwarks, their cutlasses and boarding pikes marking down several enemy hands before they realised what was happening. Moments, seconds earlier, they had seen *Royal Anne* as one more helpless prize, a ship which had struck to them, her flag hacked down by one of her own crew. Then, as if from nowhere, the bulk of Bolitho's seamen came surging up and over the side, their steel bright in the sun, their voices hoarse and wild with the madness of combat.

Bolitho ran to the rail and jerked the lanyard of another swivel, seeing the packed canister scything through a bunch of men on *Bonaventure's* gangway and blasting them aside in its murderous hail.

Then he was running with the second party and pulling himself on to the shrouds, slashing with his sword at a man's arm on the chains below. Screams and curses, the bang of pistols and raps of steel, he was dazed by the noise. A man plummeted past him to be held like a tortured animal between the two grinding hulls, his blood running pink in the leaping feathers of foam.

He was on the enemy's deck, his arm jarring as he struck down a man's guard and drove the hilt against his jaw, throwing him back into the struggling figures beyond. Another charged forward with a levelled bayonet, slipped on a smear of blood and took Stockdale's blade across his neck. It sounded like an axe biting into a log.

He yelled wildly, 'Cut the rigging, lads! Cripple the bastard!'

He felt a ball fan hotly past his face, and ducked as another smacked into a seaman's chest right beside him, his cry lost in the other din of battle.

Now he was on a ladder, shoes sliding in blood, his fingers feeling up a rail, conscious of the torn wood where one of the swivels had made its mark. Two officers were parrying aside pikes and swords as they tried to rally their men from the opposite side. Bolitho saw one of them drive his sword into a boatswain's mate, saw the eyes roll with agony as he pitched to the deck below, then he was up and facing the privateer's officer, their swords clashing as they struck and explored their strength and weakness.

'Damn you!' The man ducked and thrust up at Bolitho's throat. 'Strike while you are still alive, you mad bugger!'

Bolitho caught the blade across his basket hilt and levered the man clear, feeling the warmth of his body, the fierceness of his breathing.

He yelled back, 'Strike be damned!'

A pistol exploded and the officer dropped his arm, staring blankly at the blood which pumped through his shirt in a bright red stain.

Tyrrell strode past and fired a second pistol into the man's chest. When he turned Bolitho saw that Tyrrell's face was like stone.

He shouted, 'I knew that bastard, Cap'n! A bloody slaver afore th' war!'

Then with a gasp he dropped on one knee, blood running from his thigh. Bolitho dragged him aside, cutting down a screaming seaman and thrusting the blade through his chest in two swift movements.

'*Easy!*'

He stared desperately above the nearest men. Much of the enemy's rigging had been slashed, but the attack had made little impression after all. And his men were falling back around him, the lust to fight and win dwindling to match their numbers.

On every hand, or so it appeared, muskets and pistols were firing down into the retreating English seamen, and he saw Heyward standing astride a wounded man and screaming like a madman as he fought off two attackers at once.

As if from a great distance he saw the American captain watching from his poop, a tall, handsome man who was standing quite motionless, either so confident in his men's efforts or so appalled by his attackers' sacrifice that he was unable to tear his eyes away.

Bolitho hacked a cutlass aside and sobbed aloud as his blade broke within inches of the hilt. He hurled the remains at the man's head and saw him fall kicking, impaled on a pike. In a half daze he recalled the glib trader at English Harbour who had sold him the sword. He would not get his money now, damn his eyes.

To Stockdale he croaked, 'You know what to do!' He had to push him away, and even as he ran from the fighting he was still peering back, his eyes filled with anxiety.

Then there was the distorted voice again, and when he looked up he saw the American captain using his trumpet.

'Strike now! You have done more than enough! Strike or die!'

Bolitho swung round, his heart bursting, his mind sick as he saw a young seaman fall to the deck, his face opened by a cutlass from ear to chin.

Tyrrell was struggling on his injured knee and pointing wildly, 'Look! Stockdale's done it!'

From the main hatch on the Indiaman's deck came a growing plume of dark smoke, spreading and thickening until it seemed to spurt up through the seams like steam under pressure.

Bolitho yelled, 'Fall back, lads! *Back!*'

Then they were limping and staggering across the bulwarks, dragging their wounded, carrying others too crippled to move. There were not many of them, wounded or otherwise.

Bolitho wiped his streaming eyes, hearing Tyrrell gasp with agony as he half carried, half dragged him to the opposite bulwark. Behind him he could hear frenzied shouts, the sudden click of steel as the *Bonaventure's* men tried to cut away the lashings which they themselves had so skilfully used to hold both ships together. But it was too late. It had been from the instant Stockdale had begun the last and most dangerous act. A short fuse, and then the fire had burst amongst the cargo of rum and the massive barrels of spirits, spreading through the hull at a terrible rate.

Flames licked out of open ports and ran along the *Bonaventure's* tarred rigging like angry tongues, sails vanished into ashes, and then with a bellow one great sheet of flame leapt between the two hulls, joining them finally in a single pyre.

Bolitho peered down at the one remaining boat tethered to the ship's quarter, riding where it had been since taking his orders across to Graves.

'Abandon ship, lads!'

Some clambered down, while others fell headlong, splashing and yelling until they were helped inboard by their companions. Blazing canvas, ashes and gusts of sparks rained across their heads, but as a seaman severed the bow rope and they groped half blinded for the oars Bolitho heard another great explosion, as if from the sea itself.

The Indiaman began to settle down immediately, her masts and spars interlocking with her attacker's to throw flames and sparks hundreds of feet into the air.

He watched his small handful of fit men pulling at the oars, feeling the heat searing his back as he steered the boat away from the blazing ships. Exploding powder and toppling masts, a ship's hold splitting wide open in an inferno of noise and shooting flames, and later the engulfing sounds of inrushing water. He heard it all, even pictured the general's gold bullion, which someone might discover one day on the sea bottom.

But it was all beyond him now. They had done the impossible. *Miranda* was avenged.

He looked sadly at his men, at their faces which now meant so much to him. At young Heyward, filthy and exhausted, a wounded seaman propped across his lap. Tyrrel, a bloody bandage around his thigh, eyes closed with pain, but holding back his head as if to seek the first yellow bars of warmth from the sun. And Stockdale, who was everywhere. Bandaging and baling, lending weight to an oar, or helping to heave a dead man over the gunwale. He was tireless. Indestructible.

He held out his hand and studied it. It was quite steady, even though every nerve and muscle seemed to be quivering. He glanced at his empty scabbard and gave a rueful smile. No matter. Nothing mattered now.

How long they pulled at the oars, the time it took for the two blazing hulks finally to sink, Bolitho did not remember. The sun beat down on their aching, exhausted limbs, the stroke became slower and more hesitant. Once, when Bolitho peered astern he saw the sea's face covered by a great spread of drifting remains from the ships and the men who had fought across them. But the privateer had managed to launch at least one boat, and before it was blotted out in haze he saw it was crammed with survivors. Perhaps they, too, would know the same despair as *Miranda*'s men.

Then a shadow flitted across his face and he stared round, caught off guard as *Sparrow*'s topsails flashed gaily across the sun's path.

The men in the boat watched silently, unable to speak even to each other. Unable yet to realise they had survived.

Bolitho stood by the tiller, his eyes stinging as he watched her careful approach, the lines of heads along her decks and gangways. She had come for him. Despite the danger, the unlikelihood of his plan succeeding, she had returned to make sure.

Across the water a voice hailed, 'Boat ahoy?'

It sounded like Buckle, anxious maybe to know who had survived.

Stockdale looked at him, his battered face questioning. When Bolitho said nothing he stood up and cupped his big hands.

'*Sparrow!* Stand by for th' captain!'

Bolitho sank down, the last reserve draining from him. He was back.

PART TWO
1781

10

Sea Change

Captain Richard Bolitho stared at the partly written letter he had been composing to his father, and then with a sigh carried his chair to the opposite end of the table. It was stifling hot, and as the *Sparrow* idled sluggishly on a flat calm she swung her stern very slightly allowing the hard sunlight to reach him and require him to move still further away from the windows.

Becalmed. How used he had grown to this situation. He rubbed his eyes and held his pen above the paper again. It was difficult to know what to write, especially as he never knew when this or any letter might find its way aboard a home-bound vessel. It was harder still to feel involved with that other world in England which he had left in *Trojan* nearly six years back. And yet . . . the pen hovered uncertainly, his own world, so close and so vital in colour and smell in the bright sunlight, and that word *becalmed* would still be too painful, too harsh a reminder for his father of the Navy which he had been forced to leave.

But Bolitho wanted to tell him so desperately, put his thoughts and memories into perspective, to share his own life and thereby fill the one remaining gap in it.

Overhead, blocks clattered and feet thudded on the quarterdeck. Someone laughed, and he heard a faint splash as one of the hands cast a fishing line outboard to try his luck.

His eyes moved from the letter to his open log which lay across the chart nearby. The log had changed as much as himself. Worn around the edges, matured perhaps. He stared at the date on the open page. April 10th, 1781. Three years, almost to the day, since he had first stepped aboard this ship in English Harbour to assume command. Without moving it was possible to glance back through the bulky log book, and even though he did not even touch a page he could recall so many of the things which had happened, faces and events, the demands made upon him and his varying successes in dealing with them.

Often, during moments of quiet in the cabin, he had tried to fathom out some set thread in his life beyond the narrower explanations of luck or circumstance. So far it had defied him. And now as he sat in the familiar cabin where so much had happened he could accept that fate had had much to do with his being here. If, when he had left the *Trojan* he had failed to take a prize *en route* for Antigua, or upon arrival there had been no opportunity for immediate promotion, he might still be a lieutenant in the old ship-of-the-line. And on that very first convoy, if Colquhoun had sent him back to English Harbour instead of going himself, would he have ever succeeded in proving to be more than average in either skill or luck?

Perhaps Colquhoun's fateful decision on that far-off day had been the chance, the offering which had set his feet on the final path.

Bolitho had returned to Antigua not merely as just one more officer rejoining his rightful squadron, but to his astonishment, as some sort of hero. In his absence the stories of his rescuing the soldiers from Delaware Bay, his running a frigate aground, had been well spread. Then, with the news of *Bonaventure*'s end and his arrival with the rescued passengers, it seemed that every man wanted to see him and shake his hand.

The *Bonaventure* had been even more deadly than Bolitho had realised at the time, and her successes formidable. Her loss to the enemy might mean little, but to the British it was a tremendous lift to their battered pride and morale.

The admiral had received him in Antigua with controlled pleasure, and had made no bones about his hopes for the future. Colquhoun, on the other hand, had been the one man to offer Bolitho neither encouragement nor praise for his achievements in so short a time.

Whenever Bolitho recalled their first meeting, Colquhoun's warnings about the lot of any sea captain, he was reminded of the thinness of margin between fame and oblivion. Had Colquhoun stayed with that first convoy it was unlikely he would have shared *Miranda*'s fate, for he was too shrewd and cautious to take anything for granted. Had he been lucky enough to meet and destroy *Bonaventure* he would have gained the one thing he cared about, just as Commander Maulby had suggested, the unshakable power of flag rank, or at very least the coveted broad-pendant of commodore. Instead he had stayed where he was, frigate captain, and, with the war changing so rapidly, now likely to lose even his control of the small flotilla. Maulby no longer called him *little admiral*. Today it seemed too cruel, too unjust even for him.

Eight bells chimed out from the forecastle, and without effort he pictured the hands preparing for the midday meal, the welcome ration of rum. Above his head Tyrrell and the master would be taking their noon sights, comparing their findings before bringing them down to the chart.

The year after Bolitho's destruction of the big privateer he had received his next surprise. The admiral had sent for him and had calmly announced that their lordships of Admiralty, like himself, believed in offering *Sparrow*'s commander a chance of exploiting his experience and skill. Promotion to full captain. Even now, after eighteen months of it, he found it hard to accept and believe.

Within the flotilla the unexpected rise up the ladder had caused a great stir. Genuine pleasure from some, open resentment from others. Maulby had taken the news better than Bolitho had dared to hope, for he had come to like the *Fawn*'s laconic commander too much to have their friendship broken. Maulby was senior to him, but had merely remarked, 'I'd like to see the rank go to no other man, so let's drink to it!'

Aboard *Sparrow* the news had had no division at all. They all seemed to share the same pride, the same sense of achievement, which could not have come at a better time for them. For the war had changed greatly even in the past year. No longer was it a matter of patrol or convoy for the army. The great powers had taken their stand, and Spain and Holland had joined France against England in their support of the American Revolution. The French had mustered a well-matched and powerful fleet in the West Indies under the Compte de Grasse, the most effective and talented admiral available. Admiral Rodney commanded the British squadrons, but with the pressures mounting daily he was hard put to spread his resources where they were most needed.

And the Americans were not content to leave affairs to their seasoned allies. They continued to use privateers whenever possible, and a year after *Bonaventure*'s destruction yet another challenger emerged to shake British morale to its foundation. The privateer and ex-slaver Paul Jones, in his *Bonhomme Richard*, defeated the frigate *Seraphis* off the coast of England itself. The fact that the privateer, like the *Seraphis*, was reduced to a battered wreck in the hotly contested battle made no difference. British captains were expected to take on odds and win, and the defeat so close to home did more than many Americans believed possible to take the war and its reasons into English homes as well as their own.

In the West Indies and along the American coast the work of patrolling took on new importance. As Bolitho had always thought, it was far better for the eyes of the fleet to be left unhampered by close authority. True to his word, the admiral had offered him almost total independence, and had given him scope to patrol and seek out the enemy in his own way, provided, of course, his efforts were rewarded with some success.

Bolitho leaned back in his chair and stared at the deckhead. Again the word luck seemed to hover in his mind.

Maulby had scoffed at the explanation. He had once said, 'You are successful because you have trained yourself to think like the enemy! God damn it, Dick, I caught a lugger loaded with contraband which had come from as far south as Trinidad, and even that wretched fellow had heard of you and *Sparrow*!'

It was certainly true about one thing, Bolitho decided, they had been successful. In the past eighteen months alone they had taken twelve prizes and despatched two small privateers with the loss of twenty killed and wounded and very little damage to the ship.

He let his eyes wander round the cabin, less elegantly painted now, even shabby after ceaseless service in all weathers. It was strange to realise that apart from the unexpected promotion, symbolised by the dress coat with white lapels and bright gold facings which swung gently inside the sleeping compartment, there was outwardly little to show for it. And yet he was a rich man, and, for the first time in his life, independent of the home and estate in Falmouth. He smiled ruefully. It seemed almost shameful to become moderately wealthy merely because he was doing the one thing he enjoyed.

He frowned, trying to think of something to purchase if and when they were allowed a stay in port. And they were well overdue for that. Despite her coppered hull, Sparrow's speed had been reduced by a full knot in otherwise perfect sailing conditions by long clinging weed which defied the copper and their efforts to move it. He would buy some wine perhaps. Good wine, not the bitter-tasting muck which was normally used as the only alternative for foul drinking water. A dozen shirts or more. His mind played with the idea of such luxury. At the present moment he had only two shirts which would bear close inspection.

It might be possible to find a good sword somewhere. Not like the one which had shattered aboard the privateer, nor the curved hanger which he had used since, but something better. Lasting.

He heard footsteps beyond the door and knew it was Tyrrell. He would have known it even if it had been another time, a different watch. For since being wounded Tyrrell had been unable to rid himself of a limp and not a little pain.

The first lieutenant had otherwise not changed very much, he thought. Or maybe the three years had drawn them so close he had not noticed it. Unlike Graves, who seemed to have withdrawn even further and had grown noticeably more nervous after each action or skirmish. Upon his promotion to captain, Bolitho had become entitled to an extra lieutenant, and the appointment fell vacant on the very day the two midshipmen went aboard the flagship to sit for their commissions. Heyward had passed with flying colours, and now, looking back, it was hard to recall him as a midshipman at all. Bethune had unfortunately failed his exams, not once, but three times, and Bolitho repeatedly wondered how best to get rid of him. He had grown very fond of Bethune, but knew that being retained in *Sparrow*'s confined community was only acting against his remaining, if dwindling, chances. His navigation was hopeless, his ability to take charge of the quarterdeck and set the hands to making or shortening sail was dismal to behold. As a marine officer, or even a foot soldier, he would have been adequate. He could obey orders, even if he found them hard to formulate. Under fire he had shown plenty of courage, and a boyish stoicism which was rarely matched even by a seasoned sailor. Now, aged twenty, and with no hope of gaining the commission he so obviously desired, he stood out like a sore thumb. Heyward had tried to help him, more so than Bolitho had imagined he would. But it was no use. The ship's company treated him with cheerful acceptance, as they would a child. His burden had not been eased by the appointment of a new midshipman to take Heyward's place.

Roger Augustus Fowler, sixteen years of age, and with the pouting features of a petulant pig, had soon learned to add to rather than detract from Bethune's misery.

Fowler's arrival had further enlarged the rift between Bolitho and Colquhoun. The boy was the son of the admiral's best friend, and so his appointment to this or any ship was very close to a royal command. The offspring of some influential person could be a great handicap to a young and busy captain, but equally he could open doors otherwise denied by the chain of command. Colquhoun had probably seen the boy's arrival from England as an opportunity in the latter category, and had been outraged when the admiral had chosen *Sparrow* rather than his frigate *Bacchante*.

Fowler had been aboard for eight months and was not popular. It was nothing you could put a name to. Obedient and attentive in the presence of his superiors, he could be equally sharp and sarcastic with seamen old enough to be his father. He had a way of shutting off his expressions, using his pale eyes and pouting lips like the extensions of a mask. If he ever reached command rank he would be a tyrant to serve, Bolitho thought.

There was a tap at the door and Bolitho swept his musings into the background.

Tyrrell limped into the cabin and sat down at the table. Against his open shirt his skin was burned almost to mahogany, and his hair had become a shade lighter under forgotten suns. He pushed the calculations across the chart and together they looked at *Sparrow*'s approximate position.

To the south lay the nearest extensions of the Bahama Islands, the countless spans of cays and reefs, treacherous sandbars and islets. Some eighty miles to the west lay the coast of Florida, and to the east the main routes used by ships going to and fro from the Indies and New York. It was a veritable warren of islands and narrow channels, although to the untried eye of a landsman the sea might appear at peace, broken here and there by restful purple humps of land shrouded in low haze. But to the mariner the chart showed much more, and that was less than he required to know the true margin of safety. The occasional dab of white betrayed a reef, the duller patch on the sea's face might represent a cloak of weed across some vast pinnacle lurking beneath the surface, the spines of which could tear the keel from a ship like the string from an orange.

Tyrrell said at length, 'I reckon we've lost th' bugger.'

'Maybe.' Bolitho opened a drawer in the table and took out two long clay pipes. Handing one to Tyrrell he groped for a tobacco bowl and then said, 'Is *Fawn* still in sight?'

Tyrrell grinned. 'Sure enough. 'Bout three miles to th' east'rd.' He tamped down the tobacco in his pipe and added, 'Our masthead lookout thought he saw breakers to th' sou'-west. If so, that would be the Matanilla Shoal, which fixes our calculations, so to speak.'

Bolitho lit his pipe from the hanging smoking-lantern and then walked restlessly to the windows. Once near the sill he felt the slow breeze across his face and chest like air fanned from a blacksmith's forge. When eventually the wind returned to give life to the sails it was to be hoped it came from the south-east as before. It was no time to be driven closer to those deadly shoals. But they had to stay near enough to be able to watch at least three channels while *Fawn* patrolled further to the east. For six weeks, in company with the other sloop, they had been searching for a big blockade runner, a French *flute* which had been reported out of Martinique and heading north, most likely for the enemy base of naval operations in Newport, Rhode Island. The information from spies, or those merely after recognition or reward, was always open to doubt. But a *flute*, which was a large man-of-war with some of her armament removed to facilitate the fast passage of men or stores, was too important to be ignored.

The flotilla's third sloop, *Heron*, was sweeping somewhere to the south, off the Andros Islands, and Colquhoun's *Bacchante* had, as far as he knew, remained in more open waters to the west, between the Bahamas and the American mainland.

Once away from Colquhoun's supervision, Bolitho had taken the sloops to their present position. On the chart the chance of making contact with a solitary enemy seemed impossible, but he knew by now that if the sea appeared empty, it was in fact divided into channels by sprawling reefs and cays, and was just as much a hazard to enemy as to friend.

'If we take her, it'll be another feather for us.' Tyrrell watched his pipe-smoke drifting through the skylight above him. 'I often wonder if it makes all that difference to th' war.'

'It *all* helps, Jethro.'

Bolitho studied him gravely. How close they had become. Like the use of first names, the ritual pipe-smoking for as long as the tobacco stock lasted, it all seemed to symbolise what the ship had made them.

Time and distance, hours and days spent in every sort of condition, they had all left their mark on *Sparrow*'s company. Even the necessary changes brought about by death and injury, transfer and discharge had seemed unable to break the little ship's hold on their destiny. Over a third of the company were replacements made since he had taken command, and apart from colonists, included a sprinkling of Negroes, some merchant seamen pressed from a home-bound ship, a solitary Greek who had deserted his own vessel only to be taken aboard a French brig as a captive. The brig, seized as a prize by *Sparrow*, had yielded several new hands, and the Greek had proved to be an excellent assistant cook.

'How long will you give her?'

Bolitho considered the question. 'Another week maybe. If she doesn't show herself, I think we can assume she's slipped past us, or turned back somewhere. She might have run into one of the patrols further south.'

'Aye.' Tyrrell yawned. 'An' then *we* can get some time in port.'

Feet pounded overhead and they heard Buckle shout, 'Call all hands! Th' wind's a'coming back!'

Then there was a rap on the door and Bethune peered in at them, his round face sweating badly.

'Mr. Buckle's respects, sir. The wind is freshening from the sou'east. *Fawn*'s tops'ls are already filling.'

'I'll come up.' Bolitho waited until the midshipman had withdrawn before asking quietly, 'What am I to do about him?'

Tyrrell shrugged. 'He'll not get promoted unless by a miracle. Maybe if we put him in charge of our next prize?' He shook his head before Bolitho could comment. 'Almighty God, the lad'd lose his way *an'* th' prize!'

On deck they found the hands already being mustered while overhead the sails were stirring uneasily, the masthead pendant lifting as the first breeze reached it.

'Man th' braces!' Tyrrell strode to the rail and squinted into the glare. 'It'll be up to us soon, lads.'

Bolitho shaded his eyes to stare at the other sloop as her sails suddenly filled and brought her round in a slow pirouette. Across the sea's glittering face he saw the first ruffle of wind, then felt the sun-dried planking lift under his shoes, the immediate response of blocks and halliards.

The *Sparrow*'s decks were like tinder and it made no difference how many times they were doused down. Paintwork was blistered by the heat, and as he turned to watch the busy seaman he realised it was hard to tell the Negroes from his original company. Lean and sun-dried maybe, he thought, but they looked healthy and bright-eyed, ready for anything.

Tyrrell called, 'Shall I have th' larboard cutter towed astern now, sir?'

Bolitho nodded. Only by towing them alternately could they hope to keep them from drying out and opening their seams. Even half filling them with water on board seemed to have small effect.

'Yes. Tell Mr. Tilby to . .' He checked himself and added, 'Pass the word to the boatswain, if you please'

After six months, it was still difficult not to speak his name, or expect to see his sweating features peering aft at the quarterdeck.

They had run down a Spanish schooner off the Great Bahama Bank, but had been forced to fire on her when she refused to yield. Then, with grapnels flying like snakes, *Sparrow* had surged alongside in the manner so well practised that it was accepted without comment even by the new men. A few pistol shots, the sight of the half-naked boarders with drawn cutlasses had been enough to quench the Spaniard's resistance and it was all over almost before it had begun. Sometime in the middle of it, while men had dashed to shorten sail and prepare for boarding, as Bolitho had waved his arm to signal the Spanish master to strike and avoid bloodshed, Tilby had died.

Not in the heat and terror of close action or under an enemy broadside, but quietly and without fuss while he had stood at the foot of the foremast, his favourite place where he usually kept an eye on the workings of his ship. Dalkeith had examined him and reported the boatswain's heart had given out, like a clock which had run its course and could take no more.

His death made a deep impression on everyone who had known him. To die in such a way was unthinkable. Tilby, who had survived battles at sea and countless drunken brawls in taverns the world over, had gone without a man seeing his passing.

When Tyrrell had collected his possessions Bolitho had been dismayed to see that there was hardly anything to barter amongst the company and thereby raise money for dependants he might have in England. Two small wood carvings of ships he had onced served, and one of them was broken, a collection of foreign coins, and his silver call which had been presented to him by no less a person than Captain Oliver of the *Menelaus* where he had served as a bosun's mate. Poor Tilby, he had not even learned to write his own name, and his language was limited to the profane for much of the time. But he knew ships, and he knew *Sparrow* like his own body.

Harry Glass, the senior boatswain's mate, had been promoted in his place, but like most of the others seemed unable to accept that he was now independent of Tilby's booming voice and ever-vigilant eye.

As he watched the cutter rising from its chocks on the gun deck Bolitho wondered if indeed Tilby had anyone ashore to grieve for him. He touched the sun-heated taffrail and shuddered. He was a captain now, the realisation of a dream which had been with him since he could remember. If the war suddenly ended, or other circumstances forced him to leave the Navy, he would drop from his present foothold like a falling stone. Not being confirmed to post-rank, he would end up as a mere lieutenant on half-pay, and all this would just be a mocking memory. But how much worse for those like Tilby. He ran his eyes quickly across the men nearest to him as they worked at the braves to set *Sparrow* before the wind again. They had nothing. A little prize money if they were fortunate, some bounty maybe from a charitable captain, otherwise they would be thrown on the beach less able to face the demands of the outside world than when they had volunteered or been pressed into service. It was unjust. Worse, it was dishonourable to treat men so shabbily, when without their sacrifice and courage their country would have fallen to an enemy years ago.

He began to pace the deck, his chin sunk on his chest. Perhaps one day they could change it. Make the Navy a Service where men from all walks of life would be as glad as he was to serve in reasonable security.

'Deck thar! Breakers on the larboard bow!'

He came out of his thoughts and said, 'Bring her round two points, Mr. Buckle. We will give those reefs a wide berth until we are clear.'

'Aye, sir.'

He turned his attention to the other sloop, noting that Maulby had managed to repaint his hull in spite of the heat. *Fawn* was exactly the same colour as *Sparrow*, and to any uncertain eye would appear a twin. It was another part of Bolitho's hard-won experience. When sailing separately, the fact they looked so similar helped to keep the enemy or his spies guessing. Like the flag locker, which he had stocked with almost every foreign flag in the book. Deception and surprise had been the enemy's game. Bolitho was reaping the benefit of their past success and turning the tables against them.

'West nor'-west, sir! Steady as she goes!'

'Very well.' He glanced at the compass and at the set of the main topsails. 'Not much of a wind, Mr. Buckle, but it suffices for the present.'

All afternoon and into early evening the two sloops continued on the same tack, with the wind showing no sign of changing in strength or bearing.

The first dog watch was just drawing to its close and Bolitho was making another attempt to complete his letter when a sail was reported to the south-west. Signalling *Fawn* to remain in company, Bolitho altered course to investigate, but as the newcomer showed no sign of running he guessed it was a friendly ship. The masthead soon confirmed that she was in fact the flotilla's little schooner *Lucifer*, a vessel kept as busy if not busier than any of them, carrying despatches and poking into coves and bays where even sloops found little room to move in safety.

In the dull bronze sunlight she made a pretty sight, with her big fore-and-aft sails spread like wings across her narrow hull as she tacked towards the sloops, her signal flags soaring aloft to break in brightly coloured squares.

Bethune called, '*Have despatches on board*, sir!'

Bolitho looked at Tyrrell. 'Heave to, if you please.' To Bethune he added, 'Make to *Fawn*. *Remain in close company*.' He crossed to the rail as Tyrrell lowered his speaking trumpet. 'You can never be sure. She might have good news for us.'

Tyrrell gripped the rail, grimacing with pain as, with sails slapping fussily, *Sparrow* came up into the wind.

'Damn this leg!' In a calmer tone he said, 'Good or bad, it's grand to see a friend. I was beginning to think we had th' bloody sea to ourselves.'

A jolly boat was already on its way, and Bolitho saw that Lieutenant Odell, the schooner's captain, was coming in person, and felt a sudden twinge of hopeful excitement.

Odell clambered up the side and doffed his hat to the quarterdeck. He was a quick, darting young man, and was said to be slightly mad. But he seemed calm enough, and when he reached the cabin handed Bolitho his bulky envelope before saying, 'I have just come from Captain Colquhoun.' He took a glass of wine from Fitch and stared at it. 'He is much excited.'

Bolitho slit open the envelope and ran his eyes quickly over the scrawling hand of Colquhoun's personal clerk.

Tyrrell stood just inside the door, and Bolitho was well aware of Buckle's shadow across the skylight above the table. Not actually eavesdropping, but if he happened to hear anything, well . . .

He looked up and said, 'Captain Colquhoun took a fishing boat and questioned the crew.' He flattened the damp paper on the table. 'That was a week ago.'

Odell held the empty glass in front of him and waited until Fitch had refilled it before saying dryly, 'Actually, *I* caught the boat, sir,' he shrugged disdainfully, 'but the good Captain Colquhoun seemed to take it over, as it were.'

Bolitho eyed him gravely. 'It also states here that the crew provided valuable information about the Frenchman.' He beckoned to Tyrrell and pushed the unfinished letter from his chart. 'The *flute* was sighted here, close inshore,' his finger rested on the western end of Grand Bahama Island, 'right amongst the islets. She was carrying out repairs according to the fishermen.'

Tyrrell nodded slowly. 'It sounds likely. If th' Frenchman knew a hunt was mounted, he would take th' most hazardous passage amongst th' islands to throw us off. It don't signify he's still there of course.'

Bolitho nodded. 'A week back. Allow another few days before that for the fishing boat to reach the place where *Lucifer* sighted her.' He snatched up his dividers and bent over the chart. 'Thirty leagues from our present position. We could be off the island by noon tomorrow if the wind holds.'

Odell said wearily, 'But I understand that Captain Colquhoun wishes you to flush her out and nothing more, sir?' He smiled. 'Or did I not comprehend the good captain's desires?'

Bolitho sat down and opened the despatches again '*Bacchante* is to approach by the North West Providence Channel, while we remain to north'rd and harry the Frenchman if he tries to run for it.'

Odell nodded, satisfied. '*Bacchante* can be barely twenty miles from her attacking position by now, sir. I am to find her again and report that I have met you and that you *understand* the instructions.'

Bolitho glanced at him quickly. 'Thank you. I do understand.'

The lieutenant stood up and reached for his hat. 'Then I will return to my ship. I have no wish to be caught in these waters after dark.'

Together they watched the lieutenant being rowed back to his schooner.

Then Tyrrell said heavily, 'Seems clear enough to me. Cap'n Colquhoun is set on taking th' Frog as a prize, all to himself, while we just act as beaters.'

'There is something which bothers me far more.' Bolitho rubbed his chin. 'The fishing boat was a small one, according to the despatches. Too frail to be out in deep water where she might *expect* to find *Bacchante* or some other frigate. It was a mere fluke that she met with *Lucifer*, for as we know, Jethro, schooners in the King's service are rare out here.'

Tyrrell's eyes glistened in the dying sunlight. 'You mean that th' fishermen were looking for *another* ship?'

Bolitho met his gaze. 'Aye.'

'But there's only us an' the *Fawn* between here an' th' inshore squadron, an' their nearest patrol must be four hundred miles away.'

'Exactly.' Bolitho stared astern at the other sloop, her topsails already painted in deepening shadows. 'And who would know that better than some island fisherman, eh?'

Tyrrell breathed out slow. 'Hell, you're saying *we* was meant to get the information, but once Colquhoun got his hands on 'em they acted for their own safety.'

'I don't know.' Bolitho walked to the nettings and back to the compass, seeing neither. 'But *Fawn*'s captain said something to me a while ago. That our exploits were getting well known, which is another way of saying they have been hurting the enemy.'

Tyrrell nodded. 'A trap. Is it likely?' He waved one hand towards the sea. 'Surely we're not that important!'

'It depends what the enemy intends.'

Bolitho turned away, feeling a chill on his spine. It was a new sensation, uncanny. To think that someone might be discussing him, planning and scheming like runners after a wanted criminal.

But it was certainly how it appeared, how he must anticipate it if he was to prepare himself. Fleets and valuable convoys stayed to the east or west of the Bahama Islands, so it was much more likely that the enemy was out after one particular prize.

He said, 'We will show a stern lantern for *Fawn's* benefit tonight. At dawn I will tell Commander Maulby what I think.' He grinned, suddenly amused by his unusual caution. 'Or maybe by that time I will have driven my ghosts away.'

Tyrrell watched him doubtfully. 'To our enemy, th' Frogs in particular, you're like a thorn.' He frowned. 'There's only one way to deal with thorns, you tear 'em out and stamp on 'em!'

Bolitho nodded. 'I agree. We will continue with our new course, but be prepared to treat every event as a trick and a ruse until proved otherwise.'

He looked abeam for the *Lucifer*, but she was little more than a blur in the evening haze. He cursed Colquhoun for not supplying more information about the fishing boat, where it came from, or the reliability of its crew. Yet he could almost feel sorry for him. He was obviously beset with anxiety about his own future, and now there was the chance of catching a rich prize, and probably military information as well, he could think of little else.

He went below to his cabin and stared at the chart beneath a gently spiralling lantern. Between his hands the islands, the countless tentacles of reefs and shallows were like the neck of some gigantic bag, around which Colquhoun's flotilla, accidentally or otherwise, were converging to close with the finality of a noose.

Bolitho sighed and turned to lean from one of the windows. In the shaded stern lantern's beam the small frothing wake glowed like blue wool, and beyond it the horizon had faded to mingle with the first pale stars.

Then he touched the scar beneath the lock of hair, noting that it was hurting, throbbing in time with his heart. He knew he was uneasy, more so because he could not find a proper reason for it.

Overhead he heard Graves murmuring as he took over the watch, and Tyrrell's limping step as he walked towards the companion ladder. Normal, regular sounds which usually gave him a sense of pleasure. Now, perhaps because they represented people he had come to know, and not merely extensions of the ship's efficiency, he was suddenly afraid. Not of an enemy or the ever-present shadow of death, but of his responsibility which their trust had given him.

11

Strategy and Spite

Bolitho was hastily tying his neckcloth when Tyrrell thrust his head through the cabin skylight and called, '*Bacchante*'s just signalled, sir! *Capn's to repair aboard!*'

'I will come up directly.'

He threw on his coat and took a quick glance round the cabin. He did not see Colquhoun very often, but he had learned it best to forget nothing.

On deck he found the gig being swayed over the gangway, and when he glanced abeam he saw *Fawn*'s boat already in the water and Maulby hurrying down into it with his usual agility.

It was early afternoon and the deck burning hot through his shoes. All night, with *Fawn* keeping as close as safety allowed, they had driven south, with the sprawling barrier of sandbars and shallows some ten miles off the larboard beam. But it had taken longer than he had hoped to find Colquhoun's *Bacchante*, and almost as soon as the masthead had sighted her topsails the wind had fallen away to a mere breath, allowing the sun to tighten its grip over them like a furnace.

As he waited for the gig's crew to man their boat he turned to stare across the opposite beam, towards the distorted hump of blue and purple which he knew of be the western tip of Grand Bahama. Colquhoun was taking no chances. He was standing well clear of the land, either to give himself sea-room, or to prevent the enemy from seeing his intentions.

'Ready, sir.'

He ran down to the entry port and said to Tyrrell, 'Keep a sharp lookout for inquisitive craft of any kind. Send a cutter after 'em if they draw near. Don't wait for my orders.'

Then he was in the gig and settling himself on a hot thwart as Stockdale swung the tiller and sent the boat dipping and swaying towards the frigate. *Bacchante* was hove-to, her sails flapping loosely, showing her copper as she rolled unsteadily in the swell. She was a fine ship, he thought. Clean-cut and designed by a craftsman. Thirty-six guns and the ability to live off her own resources for many months, she was, or should be, every young captain's ambition. It did not seem to fit Colquhoun at all.

Stockdale was muttering under his breath, and Bolitho knew he was cursing his opposite number in *Fawn*, who always seemed to manage to get his boat anywhere just that bit faster. The gig turned swiftly, oars backing in close unison, the bowman hooking on to the frigate's main chains as *Bacchante*'s shadow gave them brief respite from the glare.

Bolitho clambered up the side, doffing his hat and regaining his composure while the calls shrilled in salute and a squad of red-coated marines slapped their muskets to the present.

The first lieutenant, a gaunt, harassed-looking man, bobbed his head in welcome.

'The captain is aft, sir. He is preparing his strategy, otherwise . . .'

Maulby stepped from the shade of the gangway and took his arm. '*Otherwise*, my friend, he would have had the good grace to meet us at the entry port, eh?' He laughed at the lieutenant's embarrassment. 'You, sir, deserve rich recognition for your penance aboard this ship.'

Together they strode beneath the poop, automatically ducking their heads despite the ample room above.

A marine stamped his boots together and threw open the cabin door, his eyes never blinking or shifting until both officers had stepped over the coaming.

Colquhoun was standing by the stern windows, studying his watch with obvious impatience.

'So you have arrived, gentlemen.' He sat down at his table. 'Eventually.'

Bolitho relaxed slightly. So it was to be this way

He replied, 'We had adverse winds overnight, sir.'

Maulby added calmly, 'And I thought you might be closer inshore, sir. We seem to be somewhat, er, out of touch with affairs at present.' He glanced towards his own ship as she rolled uneasily about a cable from *Bacchante*'s quarter. 'But I expect you have a reason for that, sir.'

Colquhoun stared at him fixedly, as if to seek out the truth of his words. Fortunately he seemed quite oblivious to Maulby's sarcasm.

He snapped, 'Look at my chart.' They gathered round and he tapped it with some brass dividers. 'The Frenchman is here. I sent a cutter under sail before dawn to investigate.' He looked up, his eyes triumphant. 'So there's an end to speculation.'

Bolitho leaned closer. What a formidable place. From the western tip of the main island the chain of reefs and bars ran northward for about forty miles to link with the notorius Matanilla Shoal. The latter then turned eastward, enclosing the great span of open water known as the Little Bahama Bank like one monstrous snare. In places the water was only feet deep, and the fathoms were few and far between.

According to Colquhoun's marks on the chart, the French ship had passed through or around one of the cays to rest up on the other side of the island. It was perfect for anyone trying to avoid a skirmish. For on this side and elsewhere in the channel the sea bottom was over two hundred fathoms, and any hope of a close attack was foiled by the steepness of the island's face. Whereas on the other side, within the Little Bahama Bank, the water was very shallow and sandy, ideal for a master who wished to careen his ship and carry out temporary repairs.

'Was your cutter seen, sir?' Maulby did not look up.

'Of course not!' Colquhoun seemed angry even at the simple suggestion. 'My first lieutenant was in charge. He knows what would happen to him if he allowed such carelessness.' He calmed himself with an effort. 'He saw many lights on the water. The cutter pulled through the surf and between two sandbars and watched the enemy at work. She's big, probably a forty-gun frigate with some armament removed. Must have touched bottom and sustained damage sometime after entering the islands.'

Bolitho glanced at his profile. Colquhoun was very excited, there was no doubt about it, despite his efforts to conceal his true emotions. There was a strong smell of brandy, and he guessed he had been celebrating privately the victory already in his pocket.

He asked quietly, 'What do you intend, sir?

Colquhoun looked at him searchingly. 'I am working on the assumption that the enemy is near finished repairs. Now, he will either continue on passage, or make for Martinique again if he is badly holed and needing greater help. Either way, we must act at once and avoid another chase.'

'I would suggest a boat action, sir. We could cross the bar from two directions and cut her out before they know what is happening. With men and boats from all three ships we can swamp her defences with darkness on our side.'

Colquhoun said mildly, 'With *you* in overall command of the boats, no doubt?'

Bolitho flushed angrily. 'Your frigate is too large by half to be of use in those confined waters, sir! If the Frenchman makes a run for it, or decides to show fight, you will be needed to present your ship to him and without delay.'

'Easy, Bolitho.' Colquhoun was smiling gently. 'You rise quickly to my words. Such haste to speak tends to show guilt more than conviction.'

He turned swiftly before Bolitho could reply. 'You, Maulby, will take *Fawn* across the bar tonight, under sweeps if required, but I want you in position *at dawn tomorrow*.' He leaned over the chart again. 'If the enemy is repaired enough to make sail he will no doubt hope for one of three possible channels. To the north his passage could be adversely affected by wind and tide. South is more likely in which case *Bacchante* will be well placed to take him as he tacks around the point. But if he is still laid up or careened, you will be able to rake him there and then. He will see no use in firing back at you. Just a few more holes will be sufficient to render him immovable, or long enough for us to present more drastic measures.' He wagged one finger. 'But I know these Frogs. They'll not fight if the odds are so well laid.'

Across his bowed shoulders Maulby looked at Bolitho and shrugged.

Bolitho said nothing, knowing Colquhoun was waiting for him to protest. *Sparrow* was better suited to the task as defined by Colquhoun. Her armament was heavier, and her thirty-two pounders were far more accurate and deadly than *Fawn*'s lesser battery of nine-pounders. He knew that any such suggestion, however, would only bear out Colquhoun's earlier hint that he was greedy for more success and fame, or that he was a better man than Maulby for the mission.

Maulby asked slowly, 'Will you send men overland, sir?'

Colquhoun still did not look at them. 'God in heaven! Where is all this stuff of combat I have been reading in the *Gazette*? I am beginning to wonder at its substance!'

Bolitho said, 'It is a sensible suggestion, sir. I would prefer a boat action by night, but in daylight a force of men, including your marines, would be able to . . .' He got no further.

Colquhoun straightened like a steel spring. 'Enough of this! My plan leaves no room for nervous fumbling about the rocks like a lot of damn lizards! That Frenchman is as good as taken, and I intend to sail her into port intact and with her cargo or whatever ready for closer inspection!'

He walked from the table and stared at a half-filled decanter on his desk. As he reached out for it Bolitho saw his hand was shaking with anger or agitation. His voice was equally unsteady as he continued, 'And *you*, Bolitho, will close from the north. Stay out of sight until the time of attack and then make contact with me for further orders.' His fingers closed around the decanter like claws. 'That is all. My clerk will give you written details of attack as you leave.'

They left the cabin and walked in silence to the quarterdeck.

Maulby spoke first. 'It should be *your* doing, Dick. I agree with you about trying to cut the enemy out, but either way, it is your right to lead if Colquhoun intends to stand offshore.'

Bolitho touched his shoulder. 'I wish you all success, but you know that. You are more than due for promotion, and I hope this will bring it for you.'

Maulby grimaced. 'I'll not deny that I'd relish the chance. But I would wish it done with less bitterness.' He glanced aft. 'That man will be the death of me with his bloody moods.'

Bolitho bit his lip, trying to find the right words.

'Look, John, take good care. I know Colquhoun is desperate for this victory, but I do not share his scorn for Frenchmen. They fight well, they fight with courage. They are not given to empty gestures, even in the cannon's mouth.'

Maulby nodded, his eyes grave. 'Have no fear. If that Frenchman decides to match gun for gun with me I will haul off and await support.'

Bolitho forced a smile. Maulby was lying to ease his troubled mind. Lying as he would probably do under similar conditions. Before and after a fight at sea there was always room for recriminations and counter-proposals, but once joined in battle there was usually only one thought. To fight, to keep on firing until the enemy broke or the tide turned against you.

'Boats alongside!' The first lieutenant greeted them with a tired smile. 'Is it done, sir?'

Maulby held up his written orders. 'Aye. Done.'

The lieutenant sighed. 'I have made a small sketch which may be of some help for you, sir. The tide-race is bad there, and the surf no better. But if the French could enter, then you should have less hardship.'

The two gigs were hooked on to the chains, and Bolitho said with sudden urgency, 'I will be making sail directly if I am to take station by dawn.' He held out his hand. 'I wish I was coming with you.'

Maulby returned the clasp. 'I, too.' He grinned. 'But at least you will be spared the sight of *Fawn* as she makes Colquhoun both rich and famous in one blow.'

Stockdale stood up in the gig as Bolitho descended the frigate's side, his eyes puzzled.

As the boat shoved off and the oars picked up the stroke, he hissed, 'Then we're not fightin', sir?'

Bolitho sighed. Secret orders, plans of battle, meant nothing to the lower deck. Stockdale had not left the gig, but he and probably every Jack in the flotilla knew what was happening.

'Not this time, Stockdale.'

He had already forgotten Colquhoun's snub, the calculated attempt to drive a rift between him and Maulby. He was thinking of *Fawn*'s task, the chances of success without prolonging the attack so that Colquhoun could blame Maulby for the delay.

'It ain't right, sir.' Stockdale was muttering from the tiller.

Bolitho glared at him. 'Just attend to your work! I have had a bellyful of strategy for one day!'

Stockdale studied the captain's squared shoulders, the way he was gripping his hanger so that the fingers showed white through his tan. *It ain't no use you blowin' off at me, my lad, it still ain't right, an' wot's more, you knows it!*

With his secret rebuff held firmly in his mind Stockdale eased the tiller bar and headed straight for the *Sparrow*.

As the bowman hooked on to the chains Bolitho turned abruptly and said, 'But thank you for your concern.'

Stockdale stood and removed his hat while while Bolitho reached for the sloop's side.

He grinned broadly at his back. 'Thankee, sir!'

Tyrrell was no less ready to speak out. 'But that's a strange choice! Commander Maulby's a fine officer, but . . .'

Bolitho swung round. 'Prepare to get the ship under way. Rig the royal yards as soon as we are under command, for I want to make all speed with what wind there is!' He relented again. 'Just do as I *ask*, Mr. Tyrrell, and let us have no more of it.'

Buckle ambled across the deck as Bolitho hurried below to rid himself of his heavy dress coat.

'What d'you make of it, Mr. Tyrrell?'

Tyrrell frowned. 'That damn Colquhoun! I never took to th' man. Like bloody Ransome, his eyes are slits for the Devil to peer through!'

Buckle shook his head. 'Cap'n's worried, there's no doubt on that.'

'Not for himself.' Tyrrell watched the men hauling at the boat tackles as the gig bobbed above the gangway. 'That is equally certain.'

Bolitho's voice rose sharply through the skylight. 'When you have *finished*, gentlemen, I would be obliged if you would attend to my orders!'

Buckle looked at Tyrrell and grinned sheepishly.

'That's more like it! Our Dick's not the one to brood too long!'

Within the hour *Sparrow* was ghosting slowly to the northwest, her yards alive with canvas, as with all sail set she left her consorts further and still further astern.

The wind rose very slightly, and by the time the first stars appeared above the raked masts they had logged nearly fifty miles. Back along the same course they had used to join Colquhoun with such haste the previous night.

But there was nothing anyone could do about it, and there were some who were inwardly pleased to be spared *Fawn*'s uncomfortable passage through the shoals.

On the quarterdeck Lieutenant Graves leaned against the rail, half watching the loosely flapping sails, partly listening to the creak of the wheel, an occasional voice from his seamen on watch. He was thinking about his home in Chatham and the news he had received in a rare letter from England. His was not a seafaring family, and his father had owned a small but flourishing grocer's shop where Graves and his sister had been born and had grown up together. His mother, a sickly woman, had died a year before *Sparrow* had sailed from the Thames, and in the past years his father had apparently taken to drink. The business had fallen into debt, and his sister, probably out of desperation, had married an impoverished lieutenant in the army garrison.

She had written asking for money, for herself and to try to keep their father from a debtors' prison. Graves had sent all he had, which had been little enough. His share of *Sparrow*'s prize money would help considerably, but until he received more news from home he was unwilling to sign it over when it had been so hard to come by. If only he had been better moulded to dealing with the ways of the Navy. Like the captain, whose seafaring background and famous ancestors put him apart from men like himself. Or even Tyrrell, who seemed indifferent to all authority, although God knew he could ill afford to be so. He remembered exactly when Tyrrell's sister had come aboard. They had been in Kingston, Jamaica, where she had been living with friends, waiting until the *troubles*, as she called them, in America were over. A vivacious, lively girl, with none of Tyrrell's casual attitudes. To Graves she had appeared like some sort of angel, an answer to everything he had ever dreamed. She came from a settled, prosperous family, and as a wife would have given him the chance to better himself, find his rightful place in the world instead of remaining unsure and cautious. Tyrrell had seen his intentions clearly enough, but had neither encouraged nor come out directly against him. Then, the fool had had an argument with Captain Ransome over a man being punished. Graves could no longer remember if the punishment was just or not, nor did he care. All that remained clear was that Ransome had acted swiftly and had used all his charm, which was considerable, and his obvious skill on the girl's defences to break his own chances as well as alienating her brother completely. But Graves still blamed Tyrrell, hated him whenever he thought of her and the way she had looked when Ransome had finally put her ashore in Antigua.

He gripped the rail until the pain steadied him. Where was she now? Someone said she had sailed for America again, others mentioned a passing Indiaman which had gone south to Trinidad. Would she ever think of him? He turned away, angry with himself for daring to hope after so long. Why could he never be confident when it was most needed? Perhaps he had been too long in that damned grocer's shop, hearing his father grovelling to the *quality*, bowing and scraping to customers who ran up bills far greater than his own debts.

The worry about his sister, the uncertainty about himself, had taken their toll in other ways, too. He had sensed it after the fight with the *Bonaventure*, even though he had been aboard *Sparrow* with the rescued passengers. Suppose the captain had failed to grapple her long enough to carry out his wild plan? Would he have had the strength to turn *Sparrow* against orders and attempt to rescue Bolitho and his men? But for Buckle and some of the others he doubted if he would have done so even when both grappled ships had burst into flames. They had seen the great pall of smoke from the horizon itself.

And later, when they had closed with the other prizes and had exchanged shots with privateers, he had felt the fear spreading inside him like some loathsome disease. Nobody had noticed. Yet. He shook himself and crossed to the weather side, trying to clear his mind in the cool breeze.

The two midshipmen were standing by the lee nettings, and Bethune said quietly, 'Mr. Graves seems worried.'

The new midshipman, Fowler, ignored the comment. 'Now look here.' He had a lisp, which became more evident whenever he was trying to appear innocent before his superiors. Now it was barely noticeable. 'I have to supervise swabbing the cable tier tomorrow.'

Bethune was watching lieutenant. 'I know. It's your turn.'

Fowler showed his small teeth. 'You do it for me. When we rejoin the fleet I will speak with the admiral.'

Bethune gaped at him. 'For *me?*'

'Perhaps.'

Bethune's gratitude was pathetic. 'Oh, if only . . .' He nodded firmly. 'Yes, I will take charge of the cable party. Anything else I can to . . .'

The youth regarded him coolly. 'I will let you know.'

Throughout the ship the company lived out their hopes and dreams in their own way.

In his tiny cabin Tyrrell was sitting on his sea-chest massaging his wounded thigh, while on the other side of the bulkhead Bolitho finished his letter to his father.

In the dimly lit wardroom Dalkeith was drowsing over a glass of rum, hearing Buckle re-telling a yarn about some woman or other in Bristol, while young Heyward listened to him with his eyes closed.

Right forward above the plunging beakhead, his hair blown by wind and drifting spray, Yule, the gunner, squatted with his back against a stanchion, a bottle between his knees, his blurred mind thinking of Tilby, the good times they had shared together.

Deep in the hold, a lantern above his narrow head, Lock, the purser, inspected a cask of lemons, examining each one like some robber with his booty, while he made notes in a ledger.

And below her pale canvas *Sparrow* held them all. Oblivious to their various troubles and pleasures, indifferent even to the sea. For she needed none of them, and seemed content.

As soon as Bolitho reached the quarterdeck, he knew the wind was changing against them, and rapidly. He had been in a deep sleep when a master's mate had groped into the cabin to tell him that Lieutenant Heyward was requesting advice.

It was only half-way through the middle watch, and the stars still very bright above the mastheads, but as he hurried across the deck, his bare feet soundless on the damp planking, he heard the topsails shaking violently, the responding chorus from stays and shrouds.

Buckle was beside the wheel, and like himself was wearing only his breeches, evidence, if it was still needed, of Heyward's unwillingness to call for help until it was almost too late.

'Well?' He peered at the slanting compass bowl, seeing the helmsmen's eyes glowing faintly in the binnacle light. 'I'm waiting, Mr. Heyward.'

He did not wish to fluster the young lieutenant, and at another time could appreciate his wishing to control his own watch without showing uncertainty. But this was not the time, and in such dangerous waters they would have to act fast.

Heyward explained, 'The wind backed a point or so, and I had my watch trim the yards.' He gestured vaguely above his head. 'But now it has backed at a faster rate, I fear maybe from the north-east.'

Buckle muttered, 'We'll never be able to change tack in time to reach the head o' the shoals, sir.' He glared at the compass. '*Never!*'

Bolitho rubbed his chin, feeling the wind playing across his bare shoulders. Heyward had been foolish to let *Sparrow* have her head like this. Maybe he expected the wind to veer again, as it often did hereabouts, but whatever he thought or hoped, the ship's bow was now pointing almost north-west by north, and she was not holding that course very well either. Every minute was taking them further from the chain of shoals, and it would waste hours of wearing and tacking to fight round again towards their station as Colquhoun had directed.

Heyward said miserably, 'I'm sorry about this, sir. I – I thought I could hold her.'

Bolitho was thinking busily. 'You cannot help the wind. But in future you must learn to call me the moment you are unsure of anything. I'll not think worse of you.' He looked at Buckle. 'What is your opinion? We have four hours before dawn.'

Buckle was adamant. 'Impossible,' he sighed. 'I'm afraid we must remain close-hauled and try to wear ship in perhaps three hours or so.'

Bolitho pictured the chart in his mind, recalling vividly the nearest sandbars, the set of the tide.

'Call all hands, Mr. Heyward. We will wear ship directly.'

'But, *sir!*' Buckle sounded anxious. 'We'll never be able to take up our proper course! With the wind staying steady from the nor-east it's not possible.'

Bolitho heard the shrill of calls below decks, the sudden stampede of feet on gangways and ladders. 'I agree, Mr. Buckle.' He paused as Tyrrell came out of the gloom, dragging his leg badly as he tried to buckle his belt. 'I intend to pass *through* the bars.' He looked at Tyrrell. 'If we stay as we are we will be unable to offer assistance if it is needed when daylight comes.

Once inside the bank we will at least be able to use the wind if an opportunity presents itself.'

Graves ran to the quarterdeck, his feet very loud above the hushed voices. He had evidently found time to put on his shoes.

Bolitho said, 'Very well. Leadsmen in the chains, and then get the royals and t'gallants off her.' He was speaking fast in time with his thoughts, 'Tell the bosun to unleash the sweeps in case the wind drops altogether.'

Tyrrell nodded. 'Aye, aye, sir. I reckon we stand a fair chance of getting through. Th' set of th'tide is in our favour.' He hesitated. 'When it drops a piece we may find it bothersome.'

Bolitho smiled in spite of his thoughts. 'Well spoken!'

Shouts came along the gun deck where petty officers completed their count of topmen and hands for the braces. So well did most of them know the ship that darkness made little or no difference to them.

Bolitho nodded. 'Shorten sail, Mr. Tyrell.' He lowered his voice. 'Quick as you can.'

Within minutes all canvas had vanished from the upper yards, and with her topsails and courses thrusting noisily to the wind *Sparrow* lifted and staggered in an uncomfortable swell.

Bolitho gripped the weather nettings, watching the thin slivers of spray darting across the gangway, the extreme angle of the yards as with sail and helm Buckle tried to hold her as close to the wind as he dared.

And all the while he was thinking rapidly. Once the ship had gone about the nearest strip of sandbar and shoal would lie some ten miles across the bows. A false estimate of speed and distance, a wrong or careless description on the chart, and he might drive her hard aground. But in his heart he knew the risk was worthwhile. No one could blame him for keeping to his original orders and thereby allow the wind to carry him away from the area. Colquhoun would probably be pleased to have him as far off as possible if only to deny *Sparrow* even the role of spectator for the final act. By ignoring the rigid span of his orders he might lay himself open to reprimand, but with luck he would be better placed to give *Fawn* assistance if the Frenchman decided to fight. With the wind backed to the north-east, Colquhoun would be hard put to remain in his own sector when the time came, and that in itself would offer some excuse for Bolitho's action.

'Ready, sir!'

He tightened his jaw. 'Put the helm down!'

He tensed, feeling the sea dragging against the weeded keel in a strong undertow.

'Helm's a'lee, sir!'

Through the darkness he saw the headsails shaking wildly, heard the tramp of feet as the men hauled steadily at the braces to get the yards round.

'Off tacks and sheets!' Graves's voice was hoarse above the din of canvas and blocks.

'Mainsail haul!'

A man fell in the darkness and a voice yelled harshly to restore calm on the gun deck.

Bolitho gripped the nettings, his body tilting with the hull as *Sparrow* lifted her jib-boom, hesitated and then sliced heavily across the wind.

'Braces there!' Tyrrell was leaning over the rail as if to seek out individual seamen in the gloom. 'Heave, lads! *Harder!*'

Sparrow resisted awhile longer, then with sails filling and booming again she heeled over on the opposite tack, the spray sluicing up over the gangways and drenching the men beneath.

Bolitho had to shout to make himself heard above the noise. 'Close as you can, Mr. Buckle!'

'Aye, sir.' He sounded breathless. 'Full an' bye!'

More uncomfortable minutes while men scampered above and along the gangways. A pull here and belay. Men hauling busily at halliards, while in the bows the selected hands took their leads and lines to the forechains in readiness to begin sounding.

Eventually even Buckle seemed satisfied. 'Sou' by east, sir!'

'Very good.'

Bolitho peered up at the hard-braced yards. Not even a frigate could sail this close to the wind. Nothing could.

Tyrrell staggered towards him, his shirt plastered to his body. 'You wanted this, didn't you, sir?' He was shouting, but his voice matched by the surge of water alongside. 'You were worried about *Fawn*?' He cursed as his foot slipped and then clapped his hands to his thigh.

Bolitho supported him and waited for the hull to sway upright again.

'Easy, Jethro! Is it painful?'

Tyrrell showed his teeth. 'Dalkeith said there might be some small splinters left in th' bone. Them pistol balls can split open when they cut into a man.' He stood up gingerly and grimaced. 'Not too bad.'

Bolitho watched the topmen slithering down stays and shrouds and then said, 'Yes. I suppose I did want it. I cannot explain my fears.' He shrugged and added, 'So I will not try.'

He pushed his uncertainties away. 'Now, Jethro, I want our people to have breakfast and a tot of blackstrap. No sense in waiting for daylight, and I imagine they are too well drenched to sleep just now.' He ticked off the points on his fingers. 'Then have the fires doused, and muster the hands at quarters. We will not clear for action, but I intend that every available man is on deck when we cross the bar.'

Tyrrell was watching him intently. 'What about Heyward? Are you going to log him?'

Bolitho shook his head. 'He's learned his lesson, so there's no harm done. When I was a junior lieutenant I once fell asleep on watch.' His teeth showed white in the darkness. 'I'm not proud of the fact, but by God I never did it again!'

He moved to the hatch cover and paused. 'I will go below and get into some clothes. It'll never do for our people to see their captain like this in daylight.' He laughed, the sound carrying up to a solitary man working on the mainyard. 'I may live like a savage, but I see no cause to look like one!'

Tyrrell turned back to the rail, easing his leg as the pain lanced through it. He had just seen yet another Bolitho. Naked to the waist, his black hair plastered over his forehead, he had looked as young, if not younger than Heyward. In such a moment Tyrrell had been touched by his concern for the hands as he had been impressed by his cheerful recklessness over the approaching sandbars.

Heyward came from the gun deck and waited to resume his duty.

Tyrrell said, 'Dismiss th' watch below. Then have th' petty officers lay aft for instructions.'

Heyward asked glumly, 'Will this go badly for me?'

Tyrrell clapped him on the arm. 'God, boy, *no*!' He laughed at his astonishment. 'You did th' cap'n a favour! If you *had* called him earlier he'd have been forced to change tack. Your *mistake* allowed him to take another course of action.' He strolled away whistling to himself, his bare feet slapping on the the spray-drenched planking.

Heyward walked up the tilting deck and joined Buckle by the wheel.

'I don't think I understand.'

Buckle studied him dubiously. 'Well, don't you try, that's my advice.' He shuffled towards the hatch and added, 'An' next time you feels like playing God with my ship, I'd be obliged if you'd pass the word *first*.'

Heyward glanced at the compass and crossed to the weather side. There was more to being lieutenant of the watch than holding a commission, he decided wearily. He looked at the taut mainsail and grimaced. It had been a near thing, and at one time he had felt stricken by the swift change of events, so that he had imagined the ship was running wild, carrying him and all aboard like some uncontrollable juggernaut. Now, in these moments, he had learned something. If it all happened again he would know what to do. Of that he was quite certain.

Stockdale was waiting in the cabin with Bolitho's shirt, and after handing him a towel asked, 'Did you *really* fall asleep on watch, sir?'

Bolitho rubbed his chest and arms, feeling the salt drying on his lips like another skin.

'Almost.' Was nothing secret from Stockdale? 'But we have to embroider things a little sometimes.'

He stepped out of his sodden breeches and threw them across the cabin. As he continued to towel his naked body he listened to Heyward's measured tread across the deck above.

Then he added quietly, 'I once knew of a lieutenant who beat a man for giving a false report from the masthead. After that the seaman was too frightened to say anything, and when there *was* danger he held his tongue for fear he would get another beating. As a result, the ship was driven ashore and the lieutenant drowned.'

Stockdale watched him warily. 'Serve 'im right.'

Bolitho sighed. Moralising was wasted on Stockdale.

The big coxswain shook out a clean pair of breeches and handed them across. For another minute or so he did not speak, but his forehead was wrinkled in thought.

Then he asked, 'An' wot 'appened to the seaman, sir?'

Bolitho stared at him. 'I am afraid he was flogged for neglect of duty.'

Stockdale's battered face lit up in a broad grin.

'Proves me point then, don't it, sir? There ain't no justice in th' world for any on us!'

Bolitho sat down, one leg still tangled in the breeches. As was often the case, Stockdale had had the last word.

12

A Twist of Fate

Lieutenant Tyrrell gripped the quarterdeck rail and peered fixedly along the starboard gangway.

'God damn this mist!' He leaned across the rail, straining his eyes forward in an effort to see beyond the forecastle. 'And God damn our luck!'

Bolitho said nothing but moved to the opposite side of the deck. Since before dawn, when with leads going and every ear and eye pitched to the shouted depths, the sounds of distant surf and the occasional feather of warning spray in the darkness, he had been aware of the thickening sea mist. It was not unusual in these waters at the time of year, but he had expected it to pass quickly, to clear with the first hint of morning sunlight.

Now, as he stared abeam, he knew it was thicker than ever. Moving steadily with the wind, it wreathed between the shrouds and seemed to cling to the rigging like pale weed. Above the topsail yards he could see nothing, and apart from a clear patch of water below the quarterdeck, the sea was equally hidden. Keeping pace with the ship's cautious progress, the mist cut away all impression of movement, so that it felt as if *Sparrow* was suspended in cloud like some phantom vessel.

A voice below the quartedeck called, 'By th' mark five!'

The seaman's call was hushed as the sounding was passed from mouth to mouth from the leadsmen in the forechains. Once over the bar, Bolitho had ordered the ship to be cleared for action, and with the enfolding mist shutting out both sight and sound, it was necessary to take every precaution.

He glanced at the maintopsail again. It was drawing quite well, taking the sloop steadily across the shallows, the flapping canvas shining with moisture in the grey light to show that somewhere above the mist there was a sun and maybe a sight of land, too.

'Deep four!'

Bolitho walked aft to the wheel where Buckle stood with his men, the mist moving through his splayed legs and making him appear like a spectre.

He stiffened as Bolitho approached and reported, 'She's holding well, sir, sou' by east as afore.'

From the gun deck came a scrape of wood, and when he turned Bolitho saw one of the long sweeps swaying above the water before coming into line with the rest. He had ordered the sweeps to be run out an hour earlier, for if the wind dropped or they came upon some shoal, they would be the only means of working clear.

'Deck there!' The masthead's voice seemed to come from the mist itself. 'Ship on th' starboard quarter!'

Bolitho stared upwards, aware for the first time the mist was tinged yellow like a North Sea fog. Sunlight at last. Far above the deck, isolated by a layer of mist, the lookout had sighted another vessel.

He saw Tyrrell and the others watching him, caught in their various attitudes by the lookout's sharp call.

Bolitho said, 'I shall go aloft, Mr. Tyrrell.' He unbuckled his sword and handed it to Stockdale. 'Keep good watch and ensure that the anchor can be dropped instantly if need be.'

He hurried to the gangway, his mind torn between the unexpected sighting of a strange ship and his rising nausea at the prospect of a climb to the lookout.

Then he swung himself out on to the main shrouds and gripped the gently quivering ratlines with as much force as if the ship had been in a full gale. Through the ratlines he saw Graves below on the gun deck, shoulders hunched his eyes looking neither right nor left.

Bethune was close by him, one hand resting on a twelve-pounder, the other shading his eyes as he peered up at the mist. All along the ship men stood like crude statuary, bare backs shining with moisture which dripped ceaselessly from the sails and rigging so that they appeared to be sweating, as if they had just been in battle.

Here and there a checked shirt, or the darker blue and white of a gunner's mate, stood out from the rest, as if the artist had found more time to complete their postures before passing on to some other part of the picture.

'By th' mark five.' The chant came aft from the forecastle like a dirge.

In his mind Bolitho pictured the chart. The tide was on the turn now. Soon even the so-called safe channels between the shoals and sandbars would be drawn closer together, like great jaws closing around a capture.

He gritted his teeth and started to climb. When he paused to draw breath the ship had lost her outline in the mist. Only the guns and oblong hatchways stood out with any clarity, and aft by the taffrail Buckle and the others seemed to be cut in halves by the following tendrils of haze.

Up and up. At the maintop he swarmed quickly through the lubber's hole rather than tackle the additional agony of hanging by fingers and toes from the futtock shrouds. A seaman gaped at him as he passed and was still staring as Bolitho increased his rate of climb until he, too, was lost from view.

A few moments later Bolitho stared up at the main topgallant yard witn something like awe. For there, above it, clean and empty of cloud, the sky was bright blue, and as he started up the last ratlines he saw the taut stays and shrouds shining like copper in the early sunlight.

The lookout, legs swinging carelessly from the crosstrees, moved over to allow his captain to climb up beside him.

Bolitho gripped a stay with one hand and tried to control his rapid breathing.

'Ah, Taylor, you have a good perch up here.'

The maintopman gave a slow grin. 'Aye, sir.' He had a soft North Country burr, and his homely voice did more than he would have dreamed possible to steady Bolitho's sickness.

He raised a bronzed arm. 'There she be, sir!'

Bolitho twisted round, trying not to look at the vibrating mast as it vanished below into the mist. For a moment longer he could see nothing. Then, as the sluggish wind stirred the mist into movement he saw the raked topmasts and flapping pendant of a frigate some three miles away on the starboard quarter.

He forgot his precarious position, the nausea of the dizzy climb, everything in fact but the other ship.

The lookout said, 'There be breakers yonder, too, sir. I reckon that frigate's on t'other side o' the bar.'

Bolitho looked at him gravely. 'You know her, don't you?'

The man nodded. 'Aye, sir. She's *Bacchante*, Cap'n Colquhoun's command flag is at the fore.' He watched Bolitho's impassive face. 'Anyway, I was in 'er once, two years back.'

Bolitho nodded. He had known it was *Bacchante*, too. Perhaps he had been hoping he was mistaken, that the mist and light were playing tricks.

But there was no doubting Taylor's conviction. It was typical of such seamen as he. Once they had served with or aboard a ship they seemed to know her under any condition. Taylor had only seen the frigate's upper yards, but he had recognised her instantly.

Bolitho touched his arm. 'Keep a good watch on her, Taylor.' He slung his leg over the edge. 'You've done well.'

Then he was climbing and slipping downwards, his mind grappling with this new encounter. Once, when he peered over his shoulder he thought he saw hazed sunlight on the water, further away from the hull. So the mist was thinning after all. But it was too late now, if things went wrong.

Tyrrell was waiting for him by the quarterdeck rail, his eyes anxious as Bolitho jumped down from the shrouds and hurried towards him.

'It's *Bacchante*!'

Bolitho stared past him at the upturned faces on the gun deck, the faint leap of spray as the leadsman made yet another cast.

'Quarter less five!'

He turned to Tyrrell. 'Colquhoun must have stood well clear of land during the night. When the wind backed it caught him out, as it did us. He must have been driven miles along the Channel.' He turned away, his voice suddenly bitter. 'The damn fool should have stayed closer inshore! Now he's useless out there beyond the shoals! It'd take him near half a day to beat back into an attacking position!'

Tyrrell's hand rasped over his chin. 'What'll we do? With the tide on th' turn we'll have to look sharp if we're to close with th' Frogs.' He glanced at Buckle. 'My guess is we should stand away and try again later.'

Buckle nodded slowly. 'Mine, too. If Cap'n Colquhoun's plan has gone off at half-cock then we can't be expected to do better.'

Bolitho ignored him. 'Pass the word, Mr. Tyrrell. Withdraw sweeps and have the guns loaded and run out. Gun by gun, if you please, with as little noise as possible.' He studied Buckle's dubious expression and added quietly, 'I *know* the risk. So brail up the courses and have the bosun prepare a stream anchor in case we have to take the way off her directly.' He thrust his hands behind his back. 'You can think me mad, Mr. Buckle.' He heard the sweeps thumping inboard on to their racks and the slow rumble of trucks as the first cannon were hauled towards the open ports. 'And maybe I am. But somewhere out there is a British sloop like ourselves. Thanks to others she is quite alone now, and God knows, if I am *not* mad then *Fawn* is going to need every bit of help she can get!'

The big main course rose billowing and protesting to its yard as men worked busily to bring it under control and lay bare the decks from bow to quarterdeck.

A gunner's mate called huskily, 'Loaded an' run out, sir!'

Tyrrell strode aft, his speaking trumpet jammed beneath his arm.

Bolitho met his gaze and smiled briefly. 'You were faster this time.'

Then together, with their backs to the helmsmen and an apprehensive Buckle, they leaned on the rail and stared directly ahead. The mist was still all around them, but thinner, and as he watched Bolitho knew it was at last outpacing the ship, moving stealthily through the shrouds and away across the lee bow. There was sunlight, too. Not much, but he saw it reflecting faintly from the ship's bell and playing on a black twelve pounder ball which one gun captain had removed from a shot garland and was changing from hand to hand, testing its perfection or otherwise.

Bolitho asked softly, 'How far now, in your opinion?'

Tyrrell raised his injured leg and winced. 'Th' wind stays regular from th' nor'-east. Our course is sou' by east.' He was thinking aloud. 'Th' soundings have found no lie in th' chart.' He made up his mind. 'I reckon we're about six mile from th' place where *Fawn* crossed through th' shoals.' He turned and added firmly. 'You'll have to put about soon, sir. You'll be hard aground if you keep on this tack much longer.'

The chant seemed to float aft to mock him. 'By th' mark three!'

Lieutenant Heyward, who was standing very still by the quarterdeck ladder, murmured, 'Holy God!'

Bolitho said, 'If the Frenchman is still there, then there must be ample room for him to work clear.'

Tyrrell eyed him sadly. 'Aye. But by th' time we reach that far we'll be in no position to go about. Th' Frog can thumb his nose at us.'

Bolitho pictured the disembodied masts and yards of Colquhoun's frigate and gripped his hands together to steady his nerves and restrain his rising anger. That fool Colquhoun. So eager to keep the spoils to himself he had failed to anticipate a change of wind. So keen to keep *Sparrow* out of the victory that he had now left the gate open for the enemy to run free if he so desired. *Fawn* could not bring her to battle even if she could catch her.

'An' a quarter less three!'

He grasped the nettings and tried not to imagine the sea's bottom rising slowly and steadily towards the keel.

It was no use. He swung away from the nettings, his sudden movement making Midshipman Fowler start back in alarm. He was risking the ship and the life of everyone aboard. *Fawn* was probably anchored, or had already found the enemy gone. His apprehensions, his personal doubts would cut little cloth with the relatives of those drowned by his risking *Sparrow* for a whim.

He said harshly, 'We will wear ship. I intend to cross the bar and rejoin *Bacchante* as soon as the mist clears.' He saw Buckle nod with relief and Tyrrell watching him with grave understanding. 'Convey my compliments to Mr. Graves and have the guns ...' He swung round as several voices shouted at once.

Tyrrell said tersely, 'Gunfire, by God!'

Bolitho froze, listening intently to the intermittent cracks and the heavier crash of larger weapons.

'Belay that last order, Mr. Tyrrell!' He watched as a shaft of sunlight ran down the trunk of the mainmast like molten gold. 'We will not be blind for long!'

More minutes dragged by, with every man aboard listening to the distant gunfire.

Bolitho found that he could see beyond the tapering jib-boom, and when he glanced abeam he saw a writhing necklace of surf to mark the nearest prongs of reef. Perhaps it was the mist, or back echoes from the hidden land, but the gunfire did not sound right. He could pick out the sharper bark of *Fawn*'s nine-pounders from the enemy's heavier artillery, but there were other explosions from varying bearings which seemed totally at odds with the circumstances.

Sunlight swept down across the damp planking and raised more haze from the dripping shrouds and hammock nettings, and then, like some fantastic curtain, the mist was drawn aside, laying bare the drama with each detail sharp in the morning light.

There was the tip of the island, hard blue against an empty sky, and the intermingled patterns of surf and swirling currents to show the nearness of the bar. And dead ahead of *Sparrow*'s slow approach, her hull seemingly pinioned on the jib-boom, was Maulby's *Fawn*.

Further away, with masts and furled sails still shrouded in departing mist, lay the Frenchman, half hidden in shadow, the outline blurred into the landmass beyond. She was firing rapidly, her battery flashing long orange tongues, her flag clearly visible above the gunsmoke.

It was only then Bolitho realised that *Fawn* was still anchored. Sickened, he watched the sharp waterspouts bursting all around her, the occasional fountain of spray as a ball smashed hard alongside.

Buckle called hoarsely, 'He's cut his cable, sir!'

Maulby's men were already running out the long sweeps to try to work clear of the murderous barrage, while from her own deck the guns maintained a brisk fire towards the enemy.

Bolitho gripped the rail as *Fawn*'s foretopmast staggered and then reeled down in a great welter of spray and smoke. He heard Tyrrell's voice as if in a dream, saw him pointing wildly, as more flashes sparkled, not from the Frenchman but from the headland and low down as well, probably on some small beach.

What a perfect trap. Maulby must have been caught by the mist, and after making sure the enemy was still apparently moored close inshore, had anchored to await Colquhoun's support. No wonder *Bacchante*'s first lieutenant had reported so much activity. The French captain had taken time to land artillery so that any attacker would be caught in one devastating arc of fire from which there was small chance of escape.

The sweeps were out now, rising and falling like wings, bringing the little sloop round until she was pointing away from the enemy and towards the bar and the open sea.

A chorus of cries and groans came from the gun deck as the larboard bank of sweeps flew in wild confusion, the splintered blades whirling high into the air before splashing around the ship in fragments.

Bolitho raised a telescope and held it trained on *Fawn*'s quarterdeck. He saw running figures, faces magnified in the lens and made more terrible by distance and silence. Open mouths, gesturing arms as men ran to hack away the wreckage and keep at least some of the guns firing. A spar fell across his small encircled world, so that he flinched as if expecting to feel the shock of its impact on the deck. A seaman was running and stumbling along one gangway, his face apparently shot away, his terror agonising to watch as he fell and was mercifully lost alongside.

Someone had kept his head, and high above the deck Bolitho saw the maintopsail billowing free to the wind, the sudden response beneath *Fawn*'s gilded figurehead as she began to gather way.

He felt Buckle shaking his arm and turned as he shouted desperately, 'We *must* go about, sir!' He pointed frantically towards the glittering water and at a mass of brown weed which glided so close to its surface. 'We'll be ashore this instant!'

Bolitho looked past him. 'Prepare to anchor, Mr. Tyrrell!'

He did not recognise his voice. It was like steel against steel. 'Have the cutters swayed out and prepare to lay a kedge anchor directly.' He waited until Tyrrell had run to the rail and the first dazed men had swarmed out along the yards. 'We will remain *here*.'

Moving more slowly, *Sparrow* edged into the shallows, and when she passed above one sandbar it was possible to see her own shadow before the water deepened once more.

Bolitho continued to pass his orders, making each one separate and detached from the next while he forced himself to concentrate, to shut his ears to the gunfire, to shield his eyes from *Fawn*'s slow and methodical destruction.

The cutters were lowered, and as ordered, Glass, the boatswain, took one of them to lay out a small kedge. With sails brailed up, and loosely anchored from bow and stern, *Sparrow* finally came to rest.

Then and only then did Bolitho raise his glass again and turn it on the *Fawn*. Listing badly, and all but her mizzen shot away, she was still trying to work clear of the bombardment. It was hopeless, for although her rudder seemed intact, and the spanker and crossjack were giving her some sort of steerage way, she was badly hampered by a mass of dragging spars and canvas, and appeared to have few men left who were able to cut it adrift. She was hit again and again, the splintered sections of timber and planking plummeting in the shallows, floating with and astern of her like blood from a wounded beast.

She gave a violent lurch, and as her mizzen came down to join the rest of her spars, Bolitho knew she had driven aground. She was broaching to, her deck tilting towards him as the first savage spines ground into her bilges and keel. It was finished.

He closed the glass and handed it to someone nearby. He saw no individual faces, heard no voices he could recognise. His own was as strange and unnatural as before.

'The Frenchman lies on our larboard bow.' How quiet it was now. The enemy had ceased fire, for as *Fawn* lay gripped on a shoal she was at last out of reach from those guns. Smoke drifted above the headland, and Bolitho pictured the French artillerymen sponging out the muzzles, watching perhaps the unexpected arrival of another sloop. One more victim. 'The range is less than a mile. He is well moored to present a perfect deception.' He knew Tyrrell and the rest were watching him. Transfixed. 'Equally, he cannot hurt us. We on the other hand . . .' He turned despite his guard to see *Fawn*'s beakhead and bowsprit tear away and drop into the swirling current beneath her stem. He continued tonelessly, 'We can hit him, and *hard!*'

Graves was on the ladder, his face pale from shock or at seeing the other ship destroyed so cruelly.

Bolitho looked at him. 'Get the larboard bow-chaser to work. You will open fire when ready. Pass your requirements to the bosun. By using the anchor cables you will be able to traverse at will.' He turned to Tyrrell. 'Have the capstan manned at once.'

Graves was half-way along the deck when Bolitho's voice brought him stockstill in his tracks.

'Fetch Mr. Yule! Tell him I want him to build a small furnace where he can heat shot for your gun. Take good care that it is done right and well.' He shifted his eyes to the enemy ship. 'We have time now. Plenty of it.'

Then he walked to the nettings and waited for Tyrrell to come aft again.

Tyrrell said quietly, 'You were right after all, sir. It was *us* they were after. Good God Almighty, it was *us* we just watched being destroyed!'

Bolitho studied him gravely. 'Aye, Jethro.' He recalled with stark clarity Maulby's words to him at their last meeting. Of Colquhoun. *That man will be the death of me. . . .*

He swung round, his voice harsh again. 'What the hell is the delay?'

He was answered by a loud bang from forward, and was in time to see the fall of shot some half a cable from the enemy.

An order was passed down the deck and the men at the capstan bars took the strain, tautening the cable very slightly so that *Sparrow*'s bows edged round to give Graves's crew a better traverse.

Bang! The ball shrieked away, this time slapping down in line with the enemy's poop.

Bolitho had to grip his hands to steady himself. The next ball would strike. He knew it would. From then on . . . He beckoned to Stockdale.

'Away gig. Pipe for the second cutter to head for *Fawn*. We may yet pick up some of her people.'

He saw Dalkeith below the ladder, already dressed in his long, stained apron.

Another bang came from the bow-chaser, and he saw the brown smoke billowing through the beakhead, hiding the actual fall of shot. But a voice yelled, 'Got 'er! Fine on th' quarter!'

He said, half to himself, 'Not pop-guns this time, Mr. Frenchman! *Not this time!*'

'Gig's ready, sir!' Even Stockdale sounded shocked.

'Take charge until I return, Mr. Tyrrell.' He waited for him to drag his leg down to the entry port. 'We will work out of here on the next tide.'

He heard dull hammering as Yule and his mates constructed a crude furnace. It was dangerous, even foolhardy under normal circumstances to consider heating shot aboard ship, a tinder-dry hull, cordage and canvas, tar and gunpowder. But this was not normal. *Sparrow* was anchored in sheltered waters. A floating gun-platform. It was merely a matter of accuracy and patience.

Tyrrell asked awkwardly, 'How long do we keep firing, sir?'

Bolitho swung himself out above the gently slapping cat's-paws and green reflections.

'Until the enemy is destroyed.' He looked away. '*Completely.*'

'Aye, sir.'

Tyrrell watched Bolitho climb into the gig, the quick flurry of oars as Stockdale guided it towards the hulk which had once been *Fawn*.

Then he walked slowly to the quarterdeck rail and shaded his eyes to watch the enemy ship. There was little sign of damage, but the balls were hitting her regularly now. Shortly, the heated shot would be cradled from Yule's furnace, and then . . . he shivered despite the growing sunlight. Like most sailors he feared fire more than anything.

Heyward joined him and asked quietly, 'Did he mean it?'

Tyrrell thought of Bolitho's eyes, the despair and hurt when *Fawn* had been taken by the trap. 'Aye, he did.'

He flinched as a gun fired from the Frenchman's deck, and saw the ball throw up a thin column almost a cable short. Seamen not employed on the capstan or boats were watching from the gangways and shrouds, some even made wagers as to the next shot. As each French ball fell short they cheered or jeered, spectators only and as yet unaware that but for a twist of fate they and not *Fawn*'s people would have died under those cannon.

Tyrrell continued, 'Colquhoun brought us to this. If our cap'n had been given his rightful position to attack we'd have got clear.' He banged his palms together. 'Arrogant bastard! An' he just sits out there like some sort of god while we finish his mess for him!'

Another bang echoed acrosss the water and he saw a spar fall from the enemy mainmast. Very slowly, or so it appeared, like a leaf from a tree in autumn.

Midshipman Fowler called, 'Our boats are standing off the wreck, sir!'

He was pale, but as he raised his telescope his hand was as steady as a gun.

Tyrrell looked at him coldly. And there's another one. Like Ransome, like Colquhoun. Without humanity or feelings.

Wreck was how he had described *Fawn*. Yet moments ago she had been a living, vital creature. A way of life for her people and those who would have come after.

Savagely he said, 'Get aloft, Mr. Fowler, and take your glass with you! Keep an eye open for *Bacchante* beyond th' reef and watch for her signals.'

If any.

Then as the gun banged out again he made himself walk to the opposite side leaving Heyward to his thoughts.

Bolitho heard the gun's regular bombardment even as the gig hooked on to *Fawn's* listing side, and with some of his men he climbed aboard.

'The cutter first!' He gestured to Bethune who was staring at the bloody shambles like a man in a trance. 'Full load, and then the gig.'

Stockdale followed him up the slanting deck, over smashed boats and tangled rigging. Once as they passed a hatchway Bolitho saw a green glow, and when he peered below he saw the sea surging jubilantly through a great gash in the hull, the reflected sunlight playing on two bobbing corpses. Huge patches of blood, upended guns around which the dazed survivors staggered down towards the waiting boats. There seemed very few of them.

Bolitho wiped his face with his shirt-sleeve. *Us*, Tyrrell had said. It was not difficult to understand.

He paused on the quarterdeck ladder and looked down at Maulby. He had been crushed by a fallen spar, his features frozen in the agony of the moment. There was a small smudge of blood on his cheek, and there were flies crawling on his face.

He said hoarsely, 'Take him, Stockdale.'

Stockdale bent down and then muttered, 'Can't be done, sir. 'E's 'eld fast.'

Bolitho knelt over the spar and cover his face with a scrap of canvas. Rest easy, old friend. Stay with your ship. You are in the best of company today.

The deck gave a quick shiver. She was beginning to break up. The sea, the tide and the unlashed guns would soon finish what the enemy had begun.

Bethune's voice came up from alongside where the cutter rose and plunged in a dangerous swell. 'All off sir!'

'Thank you.'

Bolitho heard the sea crashing through the deck below swamping the wardroom and on into the stern cabin. One like his own. There was no time to retrieve anything now. He bent down and unclipped Maulby's sword.

He handed it to Stockdale. 'Someone in England might like it.'

He made himself take one long glance around him. Remembering every detail. Holding it.

Then he followed Stockdale into the gig. He did not look back, nor did he hear the sounds of *Fawn's* final misery. He was thinking of Maulby. His drawling voice. Feeling his last handshake.

Tyrrell met him and then said, 'Mr. Yule has th' furnace ready, sir.'

Bolitho looked at him emptily. 'Douse it, if you please.'

'Sir?'

'I'll not burn men for doing their duty. The Frenchman is too badly holed now to get away. We will send a boat across under a flag of truce. I don't think he'll wish to prolong senseless killing.'

Tyrrell breathed out slowly. 'Aye, sir. I'll attend to it.'

When he turned back from passing the order to cease fire he found that Bolitho had left the deck.

He saw Stockdale carrying the sword and wiping it with a scrap of waste, his battered face totally engrossed in the task. He thought of Tilby's two model ships. Like Maulby's sword. Was that all that was left of a man?

He was still pondering about it when *Bacchante*'s topmasts hove in sight and she hoisted her first signal.

It was evening before *Sparrow* was able to close with the frigate. For almost as soon as she had worked clear of the bar the wind veered and gained considerably in strength, so that it was necessary to use every effort to beat clear of those treacherous breakers. In open waters again, with the darkening slab of Grand Bahama some five miles abeam, *Sparrow* reduced sail and hove to within a cable of Colquhoun's ship.

As he sat in the crazily tossing gig Bolitho watched the frigate and the last signal for him to repair on board being hauled down to the deck. It had been hoisted for some time, but like Colquhoun's previous ones, he had ignored it. Had not even made an acknowledgement.

Spray lanced back from the oars and dashed across his face. It helped to calm him, if only slightly. His sorrow was matched by anger, his self-control by an eagerness to confront Colquhoun.

The gig turned and rose dizzily on a steep swell, the bowman almost pitching overboard as he hooked on to the chains and made fast.

Bolitho clambered up the frigate's tumblehome, for once ignoring the sea which swirled along the hull as if to pluck him away.

Colquhoun was not at the entry port, and the first lieutenant said quickly, 'By God, sir, I am sorry for what happened.'

Bolitho eyed him gravely. 'Thank you. The fault was not of your making.'

Then without another word or a glance at the swaying side party he strode aft to the cabin.

Colquhoun was standing by the windows, as if he had not moved since their last encounter. In the lanterns' yellow glare his face looked stiff and unsmiling, and when he spoke his tone was like that of a much older man.

'It took you long enough! How dare you ignore my signals!'

Bolitho faced him coldly. The anger in Colquhoun's voice was as false as his composure, and he saw one hand twitching badly against his white breeches.

'Your earlier signals were made to *Fawn*, sir.' He saw him start and continued slowly, 'But she was already in pieces and her people mostly killed in battle or drowned when she struck.'

Colquhoun nodded jerkily, his brows tightening as if he was trying to keep a grip on his emotions.

'That is beside the point. You disobeyed my orders. You crossed the bar without permission. You . . .'

Bolitho said, 'I did what I considered to be my duty.' It was no use. He could feel his control slipping away like an icy yard beneath a topman. 'But for your lust after glory we would have taken the Frenchman together, without loss. We had all the advantage, for the enemy knew nothing of your full strength. She was after one prize only. *Sparrow*.' He turned away, trying to hide his grief. 'Because of you, Maulby and his men were killed, his ship lost. Because of your senseless rigidity, your failure to see beyond prize money, you could not help when the time came.' He swung round again, his voice harsh. 'Well, the Frenchman is taken! What d'you want now, a bloody knighthood?'

Surprisingly, Colquhoun's voice was very low, and as he spoke he kept his eyes on some point away from Bolitho.

'I will ignore your outburst.' He paused. 'Ah, I remember now, you have young Fowler aboard. It would have done no good to lose him in battle.' He was speaking more quickly, the disjointed sentences falling from his lips in time with his thoughts. 'The admiral will expect a full report. I shall . . .'

Bolitho watched him, sickened. 'I have the written orders you originally gave me. The ones which were to send me as far from the point of attack as you could invent.' Despite Colquhoun's pathetic explanations and excuses he forced himself to go on. 'If I had obeyed them, or the wind had remained constant, *Fawn* would still have perished. What would you have done then? Sent the little *Lucifer* maybe?'

Colquhoun walked to his desk and pulled a decanter from its rack. Some of the brandy slopped over his hand but he did not seem to notice it.

'I received orders some while back. When we had run the French *flute* to ground, or given up the search, we are ordered to proceed to New York. The flotilla is to be reduced.' He swallowed half a glass of brandy and had to fight to regain his breath. '*Bacchante* will be returned to fleet duties.'

Bolitho stared at him. Any compassion or pity he might have harboured behind his anger was gone with that admission.

In a low tone he asked, 'All this while, and you *knew* we were to go to New York?' He listened to his own voice, wondering how he could sound so calm. 'You thought it was a last chance to prove yourself. A great show of victory, with you entering port, a fine fat prize under your colours! Yet because of your greed you could not see the real danger, and *Fawn* has paid dearly for your ignorance!'

Colquhoun lifted his eyes and watched him desperately.

'In New York things might seem different. Remember, I was the one who helped you . . .' He broke off and swallowed another drink. 'I needed that prize! I've *earned* it!'

Bolitho moved towards the door, keeping his eyes on Colquhoun's quivering shoulders.

He said, 'I sent *Fawn*'s remaining lieutenant to take charge of the *flute*. Surrender was arranged by Lieutenant Heyward.' He made himself keep to the details, if only to stop Colquhoun from pleading. 'The French ship'll not be much use again. I suggest you send your marines to take charge and await the military, who'll wish to escort the prisoners elsewhere.'

Colquhoun leaned against the stern window, his voice muffled by the sounds of sea and rudder.

'It will mean a court martial.' His shoulders stiffened. 'You will be ordered to attend.'

Bolitho nodded. 'It would seem so.'

Colquhoun waved one hand towards the cabin without turning.

'All this gone. In just a moment of bad circumstances. Fate.'

'Maulby probably thought that, too.' Bolitho rested his fingers on the door.

Colquhoun pushed himself from the windows and lurched across the cabin.

'So you've won in the end, eh?' His voice cracked. 'You and your bloody *Sparrow*!'

Bolitho saw the man's anguish and answered, 'Three years ago when I was given *Sparrow* I thought command was everything, all a man could desire. Then maybe I would have agreed with your decisions, no matter what they entailed. Now I know better, perhaps after all, thanks to you. Command is one thing. But responsibility, the duty to those who depend on you, is the greater burden. We must share the guilt for Maulby's death.' He saw Colquhoun staring at him incredulously but continued, 'Your folly blinded you to everything but future advancement. My crime was pride. A pride which goaded the enemy into laying a snare for me, and one which cost *Fawn*'s people dearly.' He opened the door. 'I hope I never forget it. Nor you.'

He walked quickly to the quarterdeck and heard the door slam behind him, the slap of a musket as the sentry returned to a more relaxed stance.

By the gangway he found the first lieutenant waiting for him. Across the heaving water, its crests and troughs already painted with shadows, he saw *Sparrow* swaying unsteadily against the first pale stars. A lantern gleamed from her taffrail, and he thought he saw the splash of oars to mark where Stockdale held the gig in readiness. He could have waited in vain. Colquhoun might have made one last gesture by throwing him under arrest for his outburst. That he had not was proof enough of his true guilt. More, that Colquhoun was well aware of what he had done.

He said, 'We are to rejoin the Flag at New York.'

The lieutenant watched the gig bobbing towards the side and replied sadly, 'I'll not be sorry to quit this place.'

Bolitho sighed. 'Aye. A defeat is a bad business. But a victory can often bring the greater pain.'

The lieutenant watched him climb into the gig and pull clear.

So young, yet with so much responsibility. Not for me. Even as the thought crossed his mind he knew it was a lie, and upon looking round the darkening deck he wondered if Colquhoun's error had brought him any nearer to his own promotion.

13

No Better Epitaph

Almost immediately after dropping anchor at Sandy Hook, *Sparrow* and her company were thrown into the urgent work of a short but well-deserved overhaul. Under the wintry eye of a senior dockyard officer the ship was careened and the thick growth of weed cut and cleaned from her hull. Bolitho was able to send Lock ashore, and with more careful bribes obtained fresh provisions as well as replacements for some of the fouler casks of beef and pork.

In the midst of all this activity, which continued from dawn to dusk, he was occasionally visited by a scholarly lieutenant of the Commander-in-Chief's staff. He took statements from Bolitho and Tyrrell and compared them with notations in the log at the time of *Fawn*'s destruction, as well as those leading up to the actual attack. Buckle was required to display and explain each section of the charts used, and was instantly reduced to mumbling confusion under the lieutenant's skilful examination. But as one day followed the next, and *Sparrow* regained her original trim appearance, the bitter memories of *Fawn*'s loss, even the display of hot anger in Colquhoun's cabin, became blurred, if not erased from Bolitho's mind.

He had been kept continuously busy with the affairs of his ship, never knowing for sure when his next orders would arrive, and had spent any spare moments studying the wider aspects of the war on land. When the summons to appear at a court martial was delivered to him, it came as something like a shock. Three weeks had gone by since he had confronted Colquhoun in *Bacchante*'s cabin and almost every day had been occupied with incident and activity.

Only certain details still stood out with stark clarity in his mind. The picture of slaughter and desolation on *Fawn*'s shattered deck. Maulby's face, the flies crawling over his contorted features. Young Heyward's obvious pride at being given the task of receiving the Frenchman's surrender, and the *Fawn*'s one surviving officer who had gone to take charge of the enemy until the marines arrived. Maulby's lieutenant had been like a man coming out of the shadow of death itself. His movements disjointed, his face stricken from the sights and sounds he had endured.

On the morning of the court martial Bolitho stood on *Sparrow*'s quarterdeck with Tyrrell and Buckle, aware of the many watching eyes, of his men, and those on nearby ships at anchor.

Tyrrell shifted his leg and muttered, 'I may be called as witness, but by God I feel like a guilty man!'

Bolitho watched the gig moving towards the entry port, and noticed that Stockdale and the oarsmen were dressed in their best clothes. Conscious, too, of this moment perhaps.

As well they might, he thought grimly. It was Colquhoun's day, but it was not unknown for a drowning man to drag others down with him.

He shifted his gaze to the old seventy-four which lay some three cables distant. The *Parthian*, where he had been given his instructions for rescuing the soldiers and General Blundell's bullion from the Delaware. How long ago it seemed now. An eternity.

The gig made fast and Tyrrell said abruptly, 'That bastard deserves to hang!'

Bolitho followed the others to the entry port, trying once again to find his true feelings. It was difficult to go on hating Colquhoun. His weakness had perhaps been too human, which made it harder to condemn after the first anger had passed.

As eight o'clock came and the bells chimed from each anchored ship-of-war, a solitary gun crashed out from the *Parthian*'s side, and the court martial Jack broke simultaneously from her gaff. It was time.

Graves stood with the rigid side party, his face expressionless as they climbed into the gig. He was not implicated, and Bolitho wondered if he saw his chances of promotion reflected in the court martial flag.

Once through *Parthian*'s gilded entry port and past the marine guard and assembled band, Bolitho felt a rising sense of disgust. The two-decker's quarterdeck was thronged with visitors. Senior officers, some of them military, several prosperous-looking civilians and a solitary artist gave the impression of a carefree outing rather than a trial. The artist, a bearded, intent little man, busied himself from every angle, making quick sketches, dotting in detail of uniform or title, hardly pausing between each capture.

He saw Bolitho and hurried between the chattering throng, his pad already poised in readiness.

'Ah, good sir! Captain Bolitho?' The pencil hovered and then darted down. 'I am so glad to see you at last. I have heard much of your exploits.' He paused and smiled shyly. 'I wish I could have been aboard your ship to take sketches. The people at home need to be told . . .'

Tyrrell murmured, 'For Christ's sake!'

A master-at-arms opened a door and the visitors began to filter aft towards the great cabin. Left isolated and ill at ease in their best uniforms, the witnesses remained on the quarterdeck.

Bolitho said quietly, 'At some other time maybe.'

He turned his head to watch a marine captain with drawn sword marching aft to the cabin. Just the sight of it made him feel sick. The grim array. Like the crowds at Tyburn, or the jeering fools who stood for hours to watch some wretch choking out his life on a village gibbet.

The artist's smile faded. 'I understand. I thought . . .'

Bolitho replied, 'I know what you thought. That I'd be pleased to see a man fall from office!' He did not hide his contempt.

'That, too.' The artist's eyes flickered in the sunlight as he made a quick alteration to his sketch. 'I also imagined you might see your future made stronger by this man's disgrace.' He shrugged as Bolitho turned on him angrily. 'That I am wrong on both counts makes me a fool, and you an even better man than they say you are.'

Bolitho looked at him sadly. 'What *they* say will count for little today.'

A lieutenant called, 'This way, gentlemen.'

They followed him in order of seniority and filed into the ship's wardroom.

The artist passed quickly and vanished towards the great cabin as Tyrrell growled, 'God, what is happening to us? Will they make pictures of th' Day of Judgement, too?'

All morning the wearing business went on. Witnesses were called and evidence mounted. Factual and hearsay, technical or just plain imagination, it seemed to take an eternity to get it down in writing. There were occasional pauses for refreshment and to allow the visitors to stretch their legs on the quarterdeck.

Throughout the whole morning Bolitho hardly spoke. Around him, their faces displaying either confidence or uncertainty, the rest of the witnesses waited their turn. Odell off the schooner *Lucifer*, his quick, agitated movements only adding to the tension. *Bacchante*'s first lieutenant and sailing master. *Fawn's* surviving lieutenant and a blinded seaman who had stood beside Maulby when he had been struck down.

In seniority, or as their value directed, the witnesses dwindled until only Bolitho and Tyrrell remained. Through the open ports Bolitho saw boats plying between the ships and the shore, the haze of smoke from a nearby spit of sand where a man was burning driftwood.

It was stiflingly hot. The first day of May. He pictured what it would be like at home. In Falmouth. Sometimes he thought he would never see it again. Tiny pale dots of sheep on the hills and headland. Noisy cows in the lane below the house, always inquisitive as they passed the gates, as if they had never seen them before. And in the town square, where the coaches loaded up for Plymouth or the horses were changed for another route to the west there would be plenty of laughter and good cheer. For if the war was a threat, so, too, was winter, and that was well behind them until the next time. Now, the fishermen could put to sea in safety, and the fields and markets would show the evidence and rewards of their labours.

'Mr. Tyrrell.' The lieutenant held the door open. 'This way.'

Tyrrell picked up his hat and looked at him. 'Soon now, sir.' Then Bolitho was alone.

It did not take very long. Tyrrell's evidence was purely factual and concerned the times of crossing the bar and commencing the attack. In all events, he was obeying orders. He was safe.

When his call came Bolitho followed the lieutenant into the cabin without remembering hearing his name announced.

It was packed with seated figures, and right aft, behind a table which reached almost from side to side, he saw the officers of the court. In the centre, as President, was Sir Evelyn Christie, flanked by ten captains of varying status and seniority, none of whom was known to Bolitho.

Rear-Admiral Christie eyed him bleakly. 'Your sworn statement has been read and submitted in evidence.'

He sounded clipped and formal, so that Bolitho was suddenly reminded of their last meeting. The difference almost amounted to hostility.

'We have heard of the plan to take the *flute,* of the events leading to her discovery, including evidence given by *Lucifer's* captain and that of your own officers.' He paused and ruffled through some papers. 'In your statement you said that you had advised your senior officer against a cutting-out expedition of the kind which was eventually employed?'

Bolitho cleared his throat. 'I thought that under the circumstances...'

The nearest captain snapped, 'Yes or no!'

'Yes.' Bolitho kept his eyes on the admiral. 'I gave my opinion.'

The admiral leaned back slowly. 'The accused has already stated that is *not* the case. He gave you your orders only after you had insisted that your ship would be better placed to the north of the Bank.'

In the sudden silence Bolitho could feel his heart pounding like a hammer. He wanted to turn his head and look at Colquhoun, but knew that any such attempt would be immediately seen as guilt.

The senior captain at the table said abruptly, 'Were there any witnesses as to what occurred when these decisions were reached?'

Bolitho faced him. 'Only Commander Maulby, sir.'

'I see.'

Bolitho felt the cabin closing in around him, saw the nearest faces watching him like a row of greedy birds.

The admiral sighed. 'I will continue. After leaving the other vessels you proceeded towards your allotted station.'

'Yes, sir.'

The admiral looked up with a jerk. 'Then why did you cross the bar?' He slapped one hand on the papers, bringing a mingled gasp from the spectators. '*Was it guilt?* Did you at last realise that Captain Colquhoun was right and that he needed your support in the south?'

'No, sir.' He could feel his hands shaking, the sweat like ice-rime between his shoulders. 'I have stated my reasons. We lost the wind, I had no option but to tack when I did.' Pictures flashed through his mind like parts of a nightmare. Heyward, ashamed at losing control of the ship. Buckle, doubtful and anxious for her safety as he had told him his intentions. He heard himself add quietly, 'Commander Maulby was my friend.'

The senior member of the court regarded him flatly. 'Really?'

Bolitho turned his head and saw Colquhoun for the first time. He was shocked to see the change in him. He was very pale, and in the reflected light his skin was the texture of wax. He was standing with his arms limp at his sides, his body moving only slightly to the gentle tilt of the deck. But his eyes were the worst part. They were fixed on Bolitho's face, on his mouth when he spoke, and shone with such incredible hatred that Bolitho exclaimed, 'Tell them the truth!'

Colquhoun made as if to step forward, but his escort, the marine captain, touched his arm and he relaxed again.

The admiral snapped, 'That will do, Captain Bolitho! I'll have no exchanges in this court!'

The senior captain coughed discreetly and continued, 'The rest we know. The French deception, and your destruction of their *flute*, all of which is above criticism. Despite obvious dangers you managed to rescue some of *Fawn*'s company and several of her wounded are now alive and recovering, thanks to your efforts.'

Bolitho watched him emptily. He had done his duty, but the lies already told by Colquhoun about his character, and his statement which only Maulby could confirm, made a mockery of it. He looked down at Colquhoun's sword on the table. His own might lie there soon. He found he cared little about that, but the slur on his name he could not bear.

The admiral looked around the crowded cabin. 'I think we have heard enough before we withdraw, gentlemen?'

Bolitho swayed. A long lunch. More delays. It was torture.

Like most of those present he jerked round as a chair at the rear of the court went over with a loud clatter.

A husky voice shouted, 'No, dammee, I won't keep still! In God's name, I've given me eyes for the King! Ain't I allowed to speak the truth?'

The admiral rasped, 'Keep silent there! Or I will call the officer of the guard!'

But it was no use. Most of the visitors were on their feet, all talking and shouting at once. Bolitho saw that some had even climbed on to their chairs to see what was happening behind them.

The admiral sat speechless, while the rest of the court waited for him to carry out his threat.

The voices died away, and the crowded figures parted to allow the small artist to come aft to the table. He was leading the seaman who had been blinded aboard *Fawn* and who had already stated briefly what he knew of the preparations to cut the cable and escape the French artillery.

Now, in his ragged trousers and borrowed blue coat, with his head tilted as if to sniff out those nearest him, he approached the table.

The admiral said gravely, 'Very well, Richards.' He waited for the people to sit down again. 'What is this you wish to say?'

The seaman reached out and gripped the edge of the table, his bandaged eyes trained above the admiral's head.

'I were *there*, sir. Right there on th' quarterdeck with Cap'n Maulby!'

Nobody moved or spoke except the blind seaman named Richards.

Bolitho watched his hand as it moved vaguely in the air, saw his chest heaving as he relived those last terrible moments.

He said huskily, 'The Frogs had our measure, sir. We was all but dismasted an' with more'n half our brave lads cut down.'

The senior captain made as if to interrupt but the admiral's gold-laced cuff froze him to stillness.

'Th' sweeps was shot away, but all th' time Cap'n Maulby was shoutin' and cussin' in his same old style.' Beneath the stiff bandage the man's mouth twisted in a smile. 'An' he could cuss when given occasion, sir.' The smiled faded. 'I were quartermaster an' alone at th' wheel. The master was down an' so was my mate, both killed. The first lieutenant were below havin' his arm off, an' it was then that th' cap'n turns to me an' cries, *"God damn that Colquhoun, Richards! He's done for us this day!"* ' His head drooped and his fingers slipped from the table as he repeated brokenly, 'That's what he said. *He's done for us this day.*'

The admiral asked quietly, 'And then what happened?'

Richards waited for a few moments to compose himself. Still nobody moved or even whispered. Beyond the stern windows the wheeling gulls seemed too loud to be real.

Then he said, 'Mr. Fox, th' second lieutenant, had just gone forrard, I think to seek some men for th' pumps. Several balls from th' Frog guns ashore came inboard an' killed Mr. Midshipman Vasey. He were only fourteen but a good lad when he put his mind to it. When he fell, th' cap'n shouts to me, *"If Richard Bolitho was with us today as he wanted to be, then by God we'd show 'em, artillery or no"!*'

The admiral snapped. 'Are you absolutely certain? He said those very words?'

Richards nodded his head. 'Aye, sir. I'm not likely to forget 'em. For it was then that we was hit again and th' cro'jack yard came down to th' deck. It took Cap'n Maulby with it. He never even cried out.' He nodded again, very slowly. 'He were a good cap'n, even if he did cuss more'n most.'

'I see.' The admiral glanced at his senior captain. Then he asked, 'Do you recall anything more?'

'We struck th' reef, sir. Th' mizzen come down an' a bloody swivel, beggin' your pardon, sir, exploded on th' rail and took away me sight. I don't remember much else till I come-to aboard th' *Sparrow*.'

'Thank you.' The admiral gestured to a marine orderly. 'I will see that you are taken care of.'

Richards groped up to knuckle his forehead and then said, 'Thankee, sir. I hopes you'll forgive me, but I had to speak me piece.'

He was guided between the watching faces, and as the cabin door closed a slow murmur began to grow like combined anger.

The admiral snapped, 'I will not order you to be silent again!'

'Surely you're not going to believe that lying hound?' Colquhoun's voice was shrill. 'That . . . that . . *half-wit*!'

The marine captain stepped forward to restrain him but faltered as the admiral said calmly, 'Pray continue, Captain Colquhoun.'

'Oh, I knew about Bolitho and Maulby all right! As thick as thieves!' Colquhoun had turned slightly, his arms outstretched as if to embrace the court. 'And I was well aware that Bolitho wanted all the glory for himself. That was why I sent him to the north and gave Maulby the chance to prove himself.' He was speaking very rapidly, and his face was shining with sweat. 'I saw through Bolitho's little game from the start, which was why he tried to condemn me. I knew he wanted to take the Frenchman for himself without giving me time to take up my proper attacking station. An attack overland and with boats indeed!' He stopped, his jaw hanging open with astonishment.

The admiral said coldly, 'So he did *not* agree with your plan of attack, Captain Colquhoun? Your testimony was a lie?'

Colquhoun turned and stared at him, his mouth still open, as if he had just been struck by a pistol ball and was beginning to feel its first searing agony.

'I – I . . .' He reeled away from the table. 'I only wanted . . .' he could not go on.

'March the accused out, Captain Reece!'

Bolitho watched Colquhoun as he lurched past the assembled officers, his gait less steady than the blind seaman's had been. It was incredible. Yet despite what had just happened he could sense neither release nor satisfaction. Shame, pity, he did not know what he really felt.

'You may stand down, Captain Bolitho.' The admiral eyed him calmly. 'It will be placed on record that you and your people acted and behaved in the best traditions of the Service.' He turned to the cabin at large. 'Court will reassemble in two hours. That is all.'

Outside the stuffy cabin it felt like a different world. Faces swam around him, hands gripped him, and many voices called greetings and congratulations.

Tyrrell and Odell, with Buckle bringing up the rear, managed to guide him to a quieter part of the upper deck to await their respective boats. Bolitho saw the small artist and strode across to him.

'Thank you for what you did.' He held out his hand. 'I was hard on you earlier.' He looked round. 'Where is that man Richards? I would like to thank him, too. It took true courage to act as he did.'

'He's already gone across to a transport, Captain. I asked him to wait, but . . .' He shrugged sadly.

Bolitho nodded. 'I understand. Here we all are, congratulating ourselves, while he has nothing to look forward to and no eyes to see what awaits him either.'

The little man smiled, his gaze on Bolitho's face, as if seeking to discover something.

'My name is Majendie. I would like to speak with you again.'

Bolitho clapped him on the shoulder, forcing a smile.

'Then join me in my ship. If we must wait two hours, then I'd rather do it where I have a sense of freedom.'

The court assembled at the exact moment prescribed, and Bolitho found he was barely able to take his eyes from Colquhoun's sword. It was pointed towards him, the hilt on the opposite side of the table.

The senior captain's voice was lost, too, in his confused thoughts and memories. He heard fragments like 'hazarding the lives of men under your command, the ships used at your direction'. And later: '. . . did lay false evidence to smear the name of a King's officer and thereby bring discredit on this court'. There was a lot more, but Bolitho heard other voices intermingled with the cold summing-up. Maulby, Tyrrell, even Bethune, they were all in it. And above all, the blind seaman, Richards. *He were a good cap'n.* Surely there was no better epitaph for any man?

He jerked from his thoughts as the admiral said, 'The sentence is that you be dismissed your ship and be confined under close arrest until such time you may be transported to England.'

Colquhoun stared at the grave-faced officers and then at his sword.

Dismissed his ship. Bolitho looked away. They should have hanged him. It would have been kinder.

A voice broke the silence, 'Prisoner and escort, quick *march*!'

It was over.

As the orderlies ushered the chattering spectators towards the quarter-deck, Rear-Admiral Christie came round the table and held out his hand.

'Well *done*, Bolitho.' He shook Bolitho's hand warmly. 'I have great hopes for young officers of your cut.' He saw Bolitho's uncertainty and smiled. 'It grieved me to treat you as I did. But I had to have your name cleared of that slur. Right or wrong, it would have marked you for the rest of your service.' He sighed wearily. 'Only Colquhoun could do it, and it took poor Richards to spark the flint.'

'Yes, sir. I see that now.'

The admiral picked up his hat and studied it.

'Come ashore with me tonight. The Governor is holding a reception. A ghastly business, but it does no harm to see 'em enjoying themselves.' He seemed to sense Bolitho's mood. 'Take it as an order!'

'Thank you, Sir Evelyn.'

Bolitho watched him as he walked to his adjoining cabin. An invitation ashore. The admiral could just as easily have sentenced him to ignominy, if fate had not stepped in to aid him.

He let out a long breath. When did you ever cease to learn about such complex matters?

Then he strode out to look for his gig amongst the many boats alongside.

The reception that evening proved to be even more breathtaking and unnerving than Bolitho had imagined it could be. As he handed his hat to a bewigged Negro footman and waited for Rear-Admiral Christie to exchange a few words with another flag officer, he stared up and around the great pillared hall, at the teeming throng of colourful figures who seemed to fill every inch of floor space and a handsome balcony as well. The scarlet coats of the military were very much in the majority, interspersed with velvets and brocades of their ladies, the familiar blue of sea-officers, although Bolitho noted with some alarm that most of the latter appeared to be admirals of one sort or another. Marine officers, too, their white facings and silver buttons distinguishing them from the soldiers, and so many civilians it was a wonder that New York had not come to a standstill. Along one side there were alcoves where Negro footmen and servants were kept busy at long tables, the contents of which were enough to make Bolitho think he was dreaming. The nation was at war, yet those tables were groaning under the weight of food and delicacies of every kind. Meats and huge portions of pie, tempting fruits and a glittering array of silver punch-bowls which were being refilled even as he watched.

Christie rejoined him and murmured, 'Take a good look at 'em, Bolitho. A man needs to know whom he is serving, as well as his cause!'

A footman in green livery met them at the top of the marble stairs, and after a cursory glance addressed the assembled guests in a voice which would have fitted a foretopman in a gale. 'Sir Evelyn Christie, Knight of the

Bath, Rear-Admiral of the Red.' He did not bother to announce Bolitho, probably taking him as a mere aide, or some dependent relative.

Not that it mattered. There was no break in the tide of laughter and conversation, and hardly anybody turned to examine the newcomers.

Christie moved nimbly through the fringe of the crowd, nodding to a face here, pausing to pat a sleeve or bow to a lady there. It was hard to see him in his role that morning. President of the court. Answerable to nobody when he passed his sentence.

Bolitho followed the admiral's slight figure until they reached a table at the far end of the hall. Beyond it and the perspiring footmen a doorway opened on to a great lawn, where he could see a fountain shining in the reflected glow of lanterns.

'Well?' Christie waited until each had a heavy goblet in his hand. 'What do you make of 'em?'

Bolitho turned to study the press of figures by the alcove, hearing the strings of some invisible orchestra as they joined in a lively quadrille. How anyone could find room to dance he could not imagine.

'It's like a fairyland, sir.'

Christie regarded him with amusement. 'Fools' paradise is a better description!'

Bolitho tasted the wine. Like the goblet, it was perfect. He relaxed slightly. The question had put him on guard, but the admiral's comment had shown that he had no intention of testing him.

Christie added, 'A town under siege, and we must accept that is the true position here, is always unreal. It is crammed with refugees and tricksters, merchants out for quick profit who care little for which side they trade with. And as always in a campaign of any size, there are two armies.'

Bolitho watched him, momentarily forgetting the noise and bustle around him, the despair and anxiety of the morning. As he had believed from the first, Christie's austere appearance hid a rapier-sharp mind. A brain which could sift and examine each challenge and problem, discarding everything that was superfluous.

'Two armies, sir?'

The admiral signalled for fresh goblets. 'Drink your fill. You'll not find wine like this elsewhere. Yes, we have the military who daily face the enemy, search out his weakness or try to contain his attacks. Soldiers who live on their feet. Know nothing of clean beds or good food.' He smiled sadly. 'Like those you saved in Delaware Bay. *Real* soldiers.'

'And the others?'

Christie grimaced. 'Behind every great army there is the *organisation*.' He gestured towards the crowd. 'The military government, the secretariat, and the traders who live off the fighting like leeches.'

Bolitho eyed the swaying figures outside the alcove with growing uncertainty. He had always mistrusted people of the sort described, but it seemed impossible that it was all so blatant, so dishonest as the admiral had said. And yet ... he thought of the cheerful, chattering visitors at the court martial. Spectators to a man's disgrace, but seeing it only as something to break the boredom of their own world.

Christie watched him thoughtfully. 'God alone knows how this war will end. We are fighting too many enemies, over too vast a span of the world to hope for some spectacular victory. But you, and those like you, must be warned if we are to have any chance of honour, let alone mastery over our adversaries.'

The wine was very strong, and the heat of the hall helped to break Bolitho's caution.

'But, Sir Evelyn, surely here in New York, after all that has happened since the rebellion, they must be aware of the true facts?'

He shrugged, a weary gesture. 'The general staff is too busy with its own affairs to retain much concern for what is happening here. And the Governor, if we may call him so, spends so much time in chasing giddy young girls and enjoying his mounting riches, that he has no wish to alter matters. He was once an army quartermaster, therefore an accomplished thief, and is ably supported by a Lieutenant Governor who was originally a customs officer in a city which was renowned only for its smuggling!' He chuckled. 'So between them they have tied this place into a bag for their own booty. No merchant or shipmaster can enter or leave without permits, from which our *leaders* reap a rich profit. New York is crammed with refugees, and the Governor decided that city, church and college moneys should be gathered into a fund for their relief.'

Bolitho frowned. 'Surely *that* was in good faith?'

'Maybe. But most of it has been squandered away. Balls and dances, receptions such as this, misses and whores, hangers-on and favourites. It all takes a great deal of money and support.'

'I see.'

In fact he did not. When he thought of his ship, the daily risk of injury and death with little comfort or relief, the manner in which every fighting man was facing a determined enemy, he was appalled.

Christie said, 'To me duty stands before all else. I would hang anyone who acted otherwise. But these . . .' he did not hide his contempt, 'These maggots deserve no loyalty. If we must fight a war, we should also ensure they have no gain from our sacrifice!'

Then he smiled, the sudden relaxing of the lines around his eyes and mouth altering him yet again.

'There, Bolitho, you have learned the next lesson, eh? First you command respect, then a ship. Next you achieve control of more and larger vessels. That is the way of ambition, without which no officer is worth a wet fuse to me.'

He yawned. 'Now I must be off.' He held up one hand. 'But you remain and continue your education.'

'Will you not stay to meet the Governor, sir?'

Something like panic at the thought of being left abandoned made him show his inner feelings.

Christie smiled cheerfully. 'Nobody will meet him tonight. He merely holds these affairs to pay off old debts and to keep his pot a'boiling.' He beckoned to a footman. 'So enjoy yourself. You have earned it, although I daresay you'd wish rather for London, eh?'

Bolitho grinned. 'Not London, sir.'

'Ah, of course.' The admiral watched the footman approaching with his hat and boatcloak. 'A son of the soil. I forgot.' Then with a nod he moved through the door to merge quickly with the deep shadows on the lawn.

Bolitho found an empty corner at the end of the table and tried to decide what he should eat. He had to have something, for the wine was doing its work well. He felt unusualy lightheaded, although he knew that drink was not entirely to blame. By leaving him to fend for himself the admiral had momentarily cut the strings of control. He had given him his head to act and think as he wanted. He could not recall it ever happening like this before.

A thickset post-captain, his face blotchy with heat and good wine, thrust past him and carved a huge piece of pie, adding several other sorts of cold meat to his plate before any footman could assist him. Bolitho thought of Bethune. The plate would have satisfied even his appetite for several days.

The senior captain turned and focused his eyes on him.

'Ah. What ship?'

'*Sparrow*, sir.' Bolitho watched him squinting as if to clear his vision.

'Never heard of her.' He frowned. 'What's yer name, eh?'

'Richard Bolitho, sir.'

The captain shook his head. 'Never heard of *you* either.' He ambled back into the crowd, brushing some of the meat against a pillar without even pausing.

Bolitho smiled. In these surroundings you soon found a proper awareness of your status.

'Why, *Captain*!' The voice made him swing round. 'It is! I just *knew* it was you!'

Bolitho stared at the girl for several seconds without recognition. She was dressed in a beautiful, low-cut gown, the colour of tawny port wine, and her hair, which hung in ringlets across her bare shoulders, shone beneath the chandeliers like silk.

He exclaimed, 'Miss Hardwicke! I did not know you were here, in America.'

He felt as foolish as he sounded, but her sudden appearance had caught him entirely aback. She was lovely, more so than he remembered since that far-off day. When she had defied her uncle, General Blundell, had shouted and kicked as his seamen had carried her bodily from the Indiaman before his fight with the *Bonaventure*.

And yet she was exactly the same. The smile, half amused, partly mocking. The violet eyes which seemed to strip away his defences and leave him like some inarticulate ploughman.

She turned to the tall officer at her side, wearing a frogged jacket of the dragoons, and said, 'He was so young, so *serious*, I think all the ladies on board fell in love with the poor man.'

The dragoon eyed Bolitho coldly. 'I think we must hurry, Susannah. I would wish you to meet the general.'

She reached out and laid a white-gloved hand on Bolitho's sleeve.

'It is good to see you again! I have often thought about you and your little ship.' Her smile faded and she became suddenly serious. 'You look well, Captain. Very well. A little older perhaps. A little less ...' the smile crept back again, 'of the boy dressed as a man?'

He flushed, but was conscious of pleasure to match his confusion.

'Well, I suppose . . .'

But she was already turning away as two more escorts pushed from the jostling crowd to join her.

Then she seemed to make up her mind.

'Will you dine with me, Captain?' She studied him thoughtfully. 'I will send a servant with the invitation.'

'Yes.' The words came out in a rush. 'I would like that very much. Thank you.'

She gave a mock curtsy, bringing back the memory of their first meeting like a stab in the heart.

'Then it is settled.'

The crowd eddied and swayed and seemed to swallow her up completely.

Bolitho took another goblet and walked unsteadily towards the lawn. Susannah, the dragoon had called her. It was perfect for her.

He stopped beside the tinkling fountain and stared at it for several minutes. The reception had turned out to be a success after all, and made the morning seem just a blurred memory.

14

Join the Ladies

Three days after the Governor's reception the *Sparrow* was to all intents ready for sea again. Bolitho had carried out a careful inspection, and under Lock's anxious scrutiny had signed the final manifest for stores and supplies. The last days had been uneventful, almost lazy, and Bolitho found it easier to understand, if not share, New York's apparent lethargy. It was an unreal existence, with the war seen only at the end of a marching column of soldiers, or in some colourful account on the news-sheets.

The flotilla's other surviving sloop, *Heron*, had recently dropped anchor at Sandy Hook, and was now waiting hopefully for a similar overhaul.

On this particular forenoon Bolitho sat in his cabin enjoying a glass of good claret with *Heron*'s commander, Thomas Farr. The latter had been a lieutenant at their last meeting, but Maulby's death had given him a well-deserved promotion. He was elderly for his rank, probably ten years or so older than himself, Bolitho decided. A big, broad-shouldered man, uncouth, and with a ripe turn of phrase which reminded him vaguely of Tilby. He had come to his present appointment by a roundabout route. Sent to sea as a boy of eight years old, he had been in merchant service for most of his life. Coasters and mail-packets, Indiamen and humbler craft, he had eventually risen to command a collier brig out of Cardiff. With England embroiled in war he had offered his services to the Navy and been gratefully accepted. For if his manners and background marked him apart from many of his brother officers, his experience and skill in sail put him well ahead of them. Paradoxically, *Heron* was smaller than *Sparrow*, and like her commander had begun life as a merchantman. Consequently, her armament of fourteen guns was of lesser size. She had already gathered several good prizes, nonetheless.

Farr sprawled untidily on the stern bench and raised his glass to the sunlight.

'Bloody fine stuff! Though give me a tankard of English ale an' you can spit this against a wall!' He laughed and allowed Bolitho to pour another glass.

Bolitho smiled. How things had changed for all of them. Looking back to that moment at Antigua when he had gone to meet Colquhoun it was hard to recall just how the years and weeks had affected them as individuals. Then, as he had looked from Colquhoun's window in the headquarters building, he had seen the flotilla as a whole, had wondered what his new command would be like. So many other doubts and fears had plagued him on that morning.

Now, *Fawn* was gone, and *Bacchante* had sailed only the previous day to rejoin the fleet under Rodney. Her captain had been appointed from the flagship, and Bolitho wondered if Colquhoun had been able to watch her clear the anchorage from wherever he was being held in custody.

Only *Sparrow* and *Heron* remained now. Apart from the little schooner *Lucifer* of course, and she was almost a rule unto herself. She would stay on her stop-and-search patrols of small coasting craft, or continue probing into coves and creeks in search for enemy blockade-runners.

Farr watched him comfortably and remarked, 'Well, you are doing famously, I hear. Reception with the mighty, wine with the admiral! By the living Jesus, there'll be no saying where you'll end up. Probably on some ambassador's staff, with a dozen little girls to dance to your tune, eh?' He laughed loudly.

Bolitho shrugged. 'Not for me, I have seen enough.'

He thought quickly of the girl. She had not written to him. Nor had he seen her, although he had made it his business to pass by way of her residence when he had been ashore on ship's affairs.

It was a fine house, not much smaller than where he had attended the reception. There had been soldiers at the gates, and he guessed that its owner held some sort of government appointment. He had tried to tell himself not to be foolish, so naïve as to expect someone of her background to remember him beyond a momentary meeting. In Falmouth the Bolitho family was much respected, its land and property giving work and substance to many. Bolitho's own recent gains in prize money had made him feel independent for the first time in his life, so that he had lost sight of reality when it came to people like Susannah Hardwicke. Her family probably spent more in a week than he had earned since taking command of *Sparrow*. She was accustomed to travel, even when others were held still by war or lack of means. She would know the best people, and her name would be accepted in any of the great houses from London to Scotland. He sighed. He could not see her as the lady of the house in Falmouth. Entertaining ruddy-faced farmers and their wives, attending local fairs and the rough and tumble of a community which lived so close to nature.

Farr seemed to sense his mood and asked, 'What about the war, Bolitho? Where is it getting us?' He waved his glass. 'Sometimes I get to thinking we will go on patrolling an' running after bloody smugglers till we die of old age.'

Bolitho stood up and moved restlessly to the windows. There was plenty of evidence of power nearby. Ships-of-the-line, frigates and all the rest. And yet they gave an appearance of waiting. But for what?

He said, 'Cornwallis seems intent on retaking Virginia. His soldiers are doing well, I hear.'

'You don't sound too damn confident!'

Bolitho looked at him. 'The army is pinched back to its lines. They can no longer rely on supplies or support by land. Everything must move by sea. It is no way for an army to fight.'

Farr grunted. 'Not our concern. You worry too much. Anyway, I think we should leave 'em all to their own games. We should go home an' smash hell out of the Frogs. The bloody Dons would soon call for peace, an' the Dutch have no liking for their so-called allies anyway. *Then* we can come back to America an' have another go at 'em.'

Bolitho smiled. 'I fear we *would* die of old age if we followed that course.'

He heard a shouted challenge, the scrape of a boat alongside. He realised that his mind had recorded it, but that he felt at ease, even remote. When he had first come aboard there had been neither sound nor event which had not caught his immediate attention. Perhaps at last he was accepting his true role.

Graves appeared in the cabin door with a familiar sealed envelope.

'Guardboat, sir.' He darted a glance at *Heron*'s commander. 'Sailing orders, I expect.'

Bolitho nodded. 'Carry on, Mr. Graves. I will inform you directly.'

The lieutenant hesitated. 'This letter was delivered also, sir.'

It was small, and the handwriting was almost hidden by a seal. *Office of the Military Government.*

As the door closed Farr asked thickly, '*Graves?* No bloody relative of our admiral, I trust!'

Bolitho grinned. With Rodney in the West Indies, and further restricted by bad health, the command of American waters came under the flag of Rear-Admiral Thomas Graves. Lacking the wisdom of Rodney, the hard-won respect of Hood, he was looked upon by most of the fleet's officers as a fair but cautious commander. He believed utterly in the rigid rules of fighting, and had never been known to change one jot of their interpretation. Several senior captains had put down suggestions for improving the system of signalling between ships engaged in close action. Graves had said icily, according to the many stories circulating amongst the fleet, 'My captains know their function. That should be enough for any man.'

Bolitho replied, 'No. Perhaps it would be better if he were. We might know more of what is happening.'

Farr stood up and belched. 'Good wine. Better company. I'll leave you to yer sealed orders. If all the written despatches from all the admirals in the world was laced together we'd have enough to cover the Equator, an' that's a fact! God's teeth, I sometimes think we choke on paper!'

He shambled out of the cabin, refusing Bolitho's offer to see him over the side by saying, 'If I can't manage on me own by now, then it's time I was weighted with a pair of round-shot and dropped overboard!'

Bolitho settled down at the table and slit open the canvas envelope, although his eyes rested mainly on the smaller one.

The orders were briefer than usual. Being in all respects ready for sea, His Britannic Majesty's Sloop-of-War *Sparrow* would weigh and proceed at the earliest convenience the following day, she would carry out an independent patrol, eastward to Montauk Point at the top of Long Island and thence via Block Island to the approaches of Newport itself.

He contained his rising excitement with some difficulty and made himself concentrate on the sparse requirements of the patrol. He was not to become involved with enemy forces other than at his own discretion. His eye rested on the last words. How they reminded him of Colquhoun. So brief, yet concealing the very precariousness of his own position should he act wrongly.

But here at last was something direct to carry out. Not merely harrying blockade-runners or seeking some sly privateer. This was French territory. The fringe of the second greatest sea-power on earth. Beneath the flag captain's scrawling signature he saw that Rear-Admiral Christie had added his own. How typical of the man. A sign of his trust, and the extent of his arm.

He stood up and rapped on the skylight.

'Midshipman of the watch!'

He saw Bethune's face above him and called, 'My compliments to the first lieutenant. I would like to see him at once.' He paused. 'I thought you were on watch earlier?'

Bethune dropped his eyes. 'Aye, sir. That is true. But . . .'

Bolitho said quietly, 'In future you will take your watches as laid down. I suppose Mr. Fowler should have been on duty?'

'I promised him, sir.' Bethune looked uneasy. 'I owed him a relief.'

'Very well. But remember my orders. I'll have no *retired* officers in this ship!'

He sat down again. He should have noticed what was happening. Poor Bethune was no match for the Fowlers of this world. He smiled in spite of his concern. He was a fine one to talk.

He slit open the second envelope and came up with a jerk against the table.

> *My dear Captain. I would be so pleased if you could dine with us this evening. I feel wretched at this inexcusable delay and hope for instant forgiveness. As you read this letter I am watching your ship through my uncle's telescope. So that I shall not be held in suspense, please show yourself.*

It was signed, *Susannah Hardwicke.*

Bolitho stood up and winced as his skull collided with a deck beam. Pausing only to lock his orders in the cabin strongbox, he hurried out of the door and up the companion ladder. Her uncle's telescope. So General Blundell was here, too. It would explain the sentries at the gates.

But even this fact did not depress him. He almost collided with Tyrrell as he came limping aft, his arms spattered with grease.

'Sorry I was adrift when you called for me, sir. I was in th' cable tier.'

Bolitho smiled. 'Taking the opportunity of an empty tier to look for rot, eh?'

Tyrrell rubbed his thigh. 'Aye. But she's fine. Sound as a bell.'

Bolitho walked to the nettings and shaded his eyes against the fierce glare. The distant houses were almost lost in haze, their outlines quivering and intermingling as if they were melting in the heat.

Tyrrell watched him questioningly. 'Something wrong, sir?'

Bolitho beckoned to Bethune and took his telescope. It was no better. The one trained upon *Sparrow* was probably a huge affair. Very slowly he raised his arm and waved it from side to side.

Behind him Tyrrell and Bethune stood stockstill, each as puzzled as the other by the captain's strange behaviour.

Bolitho turned and saw Tyrrell's face. 'Er, I was just waving to someone.'

Tyrrell looked past him at the anchored ships and busy harbour craft. 'I see, sir.'

'No you don't, Jethro, but no matter.' He clapped his shoulder. 'Come below and I will tell you what we are about. You will be in charge of the ship this evening, for I am dining ashore.'

A slow grin spread across the lieutenant's face. 'Oh, I *see*, sir!'

They were examining a chart and discussing the sailing orders when they heard Bethune yell, 'Avast there! Stand still, that man!' Then there was a splash and more shouts along the gun deck.

Bolitho and Tyrrell hurried to the quarterdeck again to find Bethune and most of the unemployed hands lining the larboard gangway or clinging to the shrouds.

A man was in the water, arms striking out strongly, his dark hair glossy in the spray and sunlight.

Bethune panted, 'It was Lockhart, sir! He dived overboard before I could stop him!'

Tyrrel murmured, 'A good seaman. Never any trouble. I know him well.'

Bolitho kept his eyes on the swimmer. 'A colonist?'

'Aye. Came from Newhaven some years back. He's done it now, poor devil.' There was no anger in Tyrrell's voice. If anything it was pity.

Bolitho heard the men near him exchanging guesses at the swimmer's success of getting ashore. It was a long way to go.

He had known many deserters during his life at sea. Often he had found room for sympathy, although he had thought their actions to be wrong. Few men would volunteer for the harsh demands of service in a King's ship, especially as nobody ever knew for sure if he would regain his home in safety. Seaports were full of those who had returned. Cripples and men made old before their time in many cases. But as yet, no one had found a better way of crewing the fleet. Once pressed, most men accepted it, could even be relied upon to take others by similar methods. The sailor's old rule, 'If I'm here, why not him?' carried a lot of weight in ships-of-war.

But this was different. The seaman, Lockhart, had seemed nothing out of the ordinary. A good worker and rarely adrift for his watch or station. Yet all the while he must have been brooding over his proper homeland, and the stay in New York had done the rest. Even now, as he thrashed steadily past an anchored two-decker, he was no doubt thinking only of his goal. Some vague mental picture of house and family, or parents who had almost forgotten what he looked like.

A faint crack came from the two-decker's beakhead, and Bolitho saw a red-coated marine already ramming another ball into his musket for a further shot at the lone swimmer.

A growl of anger came from *Sparrow*'s seamen. Whatever they thought of the man's desertion, or of the man himself, had nothing to do with their reaction. He was one of their own, and the marine sentry was momentarily an enemy.

Yule, the gunner, muttered, 'That damn bullock should be shot down hisself, the bloody bastard!'

The marine did not fire again, but sauntered to the end of his little platform to watch the swimmer, like a wildfowler who has given his quarry best for the time being. Or so it appeared. Then as a guardboat swept round the stern of another two-decker, Bolitho knew why he had not bothered to shoot.

The longboat was moving swiftly, the oars sending it through the glittering water like a blue fish. In the sternsheets he saw several marines, a midshipman with a raised telescope trained on the seaman.

Yule observed dourly, ' 'E'll not escape now.'

Tyrrell said, 'It's out of our hands.'

'Aye.'

Bolitho felt suddenly heavy, the pleasure of the letter spoiled by this man's despair. Nobody who had *run* from a King's ship could expect mercy. It was to be hoped he was hanged rather than face the horror of flogging round the fleet. He chilled. If he was to be hanged ... He stared up at *Sparrow*'s mainyard, his eyes desperate. There was no doubt where the execution would be carried out. Even Christie would make sure of that. An example. A warning clear to all aboard and throughout the nearby ships. He tried not to watch the guardboat as it swept down on the tiny, bobbing head.

His own friends, *Sparrow*'s loyal seamen, would be forced to witness the halter being set around his neck before they, and they alone, were ordered to run him up to the yard. After all they had endured together, this sickening act might drive a wedge between officers and men and destroy what they had achieved.

Tyrrell gasped, 'Look, sir!'

Bolitho snatched a glass and trained it beyond the guardboat. He was just in time to see the man, Lockhart, treading water, turning to stare either at the boat or perhaps at *Sparrow* herself. Then, even as the boat's oars backed water and a marine groped over the stemhead for the man's hair, he threw up his hands and disappeared beneath the surface.

Nobody spoke, and Bolitho found himself holding his breath, perhaps like the man who had vanished so suddenly. Sailors were usually poor swimmers. Perhaps he had got cramp. In a moment he would break surface nearby and the guardboat would haul him on board. Seconds, minutes passed, and then at a shouted command the guardboat resumed its leisurely patrol between the anchored ships.

Bolitho said quietly, 'I thank God for that. If he had to suffer, I am glad it was gently done.'

Tyrrell watched him dully. 'That's true.' He turned with sudden anger on the gunner. 'Mr. Yule! Clear these idlers off th' gangway or I'll find em some harder work for their wits to dwell on!'

He was unusually disturbed, and Bolitho wondered if he was comparing his own fate with that of the drowned seaman.

He said, 'Make an entry in the log, Mr. Tyrrell.'

'Sir?' Tyrrell faced him grimly. 'As a deserter?'

Bolitho looked past him at the seamen as they wandered towards the gun deck again.

'We do not *know* for certain he was deserting. Mark him as *Discharged – Dead.*' He walked to the hatch. 'His relatives will have enough to bear without the weight of shame also.'

Tyrrell watched him go, his breathing returning slowly to normal. It would not help Lockhart. He was beyond reach. But Bolitho's order would ensure that his name carried no stigma, and his loss would be recorded with those who had fallen in battle, in fights which he had also suffered without complaint. It was a small distinction. But even so, he knew that only Bolitho would have thought of it.

When Bolitho climbed from his gig he was astonished to find a smartly painted carriage waiting for him on the jetty. A liveried Negro doffed his tricorn hat and beamed hugely.

'Good evenin', Sah.' He opened the carriage door with a flourish while Stockdale and the gig's crew watched in silent admiration.

Bolitho paused. 'Er, do not wait, Stockdale. I will return to the ship in a local boat.'

He was strangely elated, and conscious of watching townsfolk on the road above the jetty, an envious glance from a passing marine major.

Stockdale touched his hat. 'If you says so, sir. I *could* come along with you . . .'

'No. I'll have full need of you tomorrow.' He felt suddenly reckless and pulled a coin from his pocket. 'Here, buy some grog for the gig's crew. But not too much for safety's sake, eh?'

He climbed into the coach and sank back against the blue cushions as with a jerk the horses took the first strain at their harness.

With his hat on his knees he watched the passing houses and people, Stockdale, even the ship, temporarily forgotten. Once, when the coach reined to a halt to allow a heavy wagon to cross ahead of it, he heard a faraway murmur of cannon fire. It was a fine evening, and the steady westerly wind was dry and warm. Sounds carried easily in such conditions. Even so, it was hard to connect the distant gunfire with the brightly lit houses, the occasional snatches of music and song from taverns along the road. Some army battery testing its guns perhaps. But more likely a nervous duel between opposing pickets where the two armies lay in watchful readiness.

It did not take long to reach the house, and as he stepped down from the coach he realised there were other guests arriving, too. Again he called himself a fool for imagining he alone would be entertained this evening.

Servants glided from the shadows, and like magic his hat and boatcloak were spirited away.

A footman opened some doors and announced, 'Captain Richard Bolitho of His Brittanic Majesty's Ship *Sparrow*.'

How different from the reception, he thought. As he walked into a fine, high-ceilinged room he was conscious of comfort and luxury mixed with an air of intimacy which had been lacking before.

At the end of the room General Sir James Blundell watched his approach in silence, and then called gruffly, 'You are an unexpected guest, Bolitho.' His heavy features yielded slightly. 'My niece told me of your arrival.' He thrust out his hand. 'You are welcome here.'

The general had changed very little. Heavier perhaps, but otherwise the same man. In one hand he was holding a brandy glass, and Bolitho was reminded of his stay aboard *Sparrow*, of his obvious contempt for the men who had carried him to safety.

Something of their first meeting must have circulated amongst his friends, for upon Blundell's show of greeting the room came alive again with laughter and noisy conversation. It was as if they had all been waiting to see how Blundell would react. Bolitho's own feelings were of course unimportant. He could always be told to leave.

Bolitho felt the girl's hand on his arm and turned to find her smiling up at him. With a nod to her uncle she steered him towards the other side of the room, the guests moving aside for her as if she were royalty.

She said, 'I saw you today. Thank you for coming.' She patted his cuff. 'I thought you were splendid just now. Uncle can be rather troublesome.'

Bolitho returned her smile. 'I think I can appreciate that. After all, he lost a great deal of bullion because of me.'

She wrinkled her nose. 'I have no doubt he will have recovered it by insurance elsewhere.' She gestured to a servant. 'Some wine before dinner.'

'Thank you.'

He saw several officers, mostly military, watching him intently. Envy, resentment, curiosity, it was all there.

She said, 'Sir James is Adjutant General now. I came out here with him after our return to England.' She watched his face as he sipped the wine. 'I am glad I came. England is full of woe because of the war.'

Bolitho tore his mind from what she had just said of her uncle. Christie had already spoken scathingly about the Governor and his assistant. With Blundell involved in controlling the city, there seemed little hope of improvement.

As the girl turned to curtsy to a white-haired man and his lady he let his eyes devour her as if seeing her for the last time. The curve of her neck as she bowed to her guests, the way her hair seemed to float across her bared shoulders. It was beautiful hair. Golden brown, like the wing of a young thrush.

He smiled awkwardly as she looked up at him.

'*Really*, Captain! You make a girl feel indecent the way you stare so!' She laughed. 'I suppose you sailors are so long away from civilisation you cannot control your ways!' She clutched his arm, her mouth quivering with amusement. 'Do not fret! There is no need to be so serious about it. I really must teach you to accept what is there, to enjoy what is yours by right.'

'I am sorry. You are most likely right about me.' He looked at the marble floor and grinned. 'At sea I can stand upright. Here, I feel as if the deck is moving!'

She stepped back and regarded him searchingly. 'Well, I shall have to see what can be done about that.' She tapped her lips with a slim fan. 'Everyone is talking about you, what you have done, how you faced that awful court martial and made fools of them.'

'It was not exactly like that ...'

She ignored him. 'Of course *they* will not mention any of this. Some are probably afraid you will turn into a wild, bloodthirsty sea-dog!' She laughed gaily. 'Others see in your success something of their own failure.'

A footman was whispering to the general and she added quickly, 'I will have to leave you to your own devices for dinner. I am hostess tonight.'

He said, 'Oh, I thought ...' To cover his confusion he asked, 'Is Lady Blundell not here, too?'

'She stays in England. My uncle's habits are those of a soldier. I think she is content to keep them well away from her.' She held his arm again. 'But do not look so sad. I will see you later. We must talk of your future. I know people who can help you. Put you where you deserve, instead of ...' She did not finish.

A gong boomed and the footman intoned, 'My lords, ladies and gentlemen. Dinner is now served.'

They followed the general and his niece into an even greater room, and Bolitho found himself paired off with a dark-haired little woman who was apparently the wife of a staff officer. He was not present, and with something like gloom Bolitho thought he would be saddled with her for the rest of the evening.

The dinner matched the room. Every course larger, more extravagantly prepared than the one before. His stomach had long become used to the sparse fare aboard ship and the varying efforts of many sea-cooks. No one else seemed to find difficulty, however, and he could only marvel at the way the plates emptied without any apparent break in conversation.

There were many toasts, with the wines as varied as their reasons for drinking them.

After the loyal toast to King George there were all the usual ones. *Death to the French. Confusion to our enemies. A curse on Washington.* As the wine flowed they became as meaningless as they were incoherent.

The lady at Bolitho's side dropped her fan, but as he bent to collect it she reached below the tablecloth and seized his wrist, holding it against her thigh for several seconds. It seemed like an hour, and he thought every eye at the table must be on him. But she was the only one, and her face was filled with such desire that he could almost feel her control slipping away.

He returned the fan and said, 'Easy, ma'am, there are quite a few courses yet.'

She stared at him, open-mouthed, and then gave a secret smile.

'God what it is to find a real man!'

Bolitho forced himself to take another portion of chicken, if only to regain his wits. He could feel her knee pressing into his leg, and was very aware that whenever she required something from the table she seemed to need it from across his arm. Each time she lingered over the motion, letting her shoulder or breast touch for just a few moments more every time.

He glanced desperately along the table and saw the girl watching him. It was hard to understand her expression when she was so far away. Part amused, part watchful.

His companion was saying casually, 'My husband is much older than I. He cares more for his damned office than for me.'

She reached for some butter, allowing her breast to touch his sleeve while she kept her eyes on his.

'I expect you have been many places, Captain. How I *wish* I could take a ship somewhere. Away from this place. And *him*.'

At last the meal was over, and with a scraping of chairs the men rose to allow their ladies to withdraw. Even at the last moment Bolitho's companion persisted with her campaign, like a frigate cutting out a ship which was totally outmatched from the start.

She whispered, 'I have a room here. I will send a servant to guide you.'

As she moved from the table he saw her stagger but recover instantly. It would take more than wine to break her, he thought anxiously.

The doors closed again and the men moved their seats closer to the head of the table.

More brandy, and some black cheroots which Blundell said had come from *some damned rascal who tried to avoid his dues*.

'I hear you are now on our local patrols, Bolitho.' Blundell's harsh voice reduced the other guests to attentive silence.

'Yes, Sir James.'

Bolitho eyed him evenly. Blundell was well informed, considering he had only received his orders that forenoon.

'Good. We need a few captains with the will to guard our lifelines, what!' Blundell's features were crimson from the extent of his dinner. 'These damn Yankees have had too much their own way, I say!'

There was a growl of approval, and someone called tipsily, 'thash th' bloody truth, shir!' He shrank under Blundell's withering gaze.

Bolitho asked quickly, 'Colonel Foley, sir. Is he still in America?'

'He has a battalion under Cornwallis.' Blundell seemed disinterested. 'Best bloody place for him, too.'

Bolitho allowed the conversation to flow around him like a protective cloak. He heard little about the war. Horse breeding and the cost of keeping house in New York. The affair of some unfortunate artillery captain who had been found in bed with a dragoon's wife. The growing difficulty of obtaining good brandy, even at smugglers' prices.

Bolitho thought of Christie's summing up. *Two armies*, he had said. How true it now seemed. Colonel Foley, whether he was a likeable man or not, was one of those fighting for his country's cause, and his life. Around this table sat a goodly proportion of the other sort. Spoiled, cosseted and completely selfish, he wished he could be rid of them.

Blundell heaved himself upright. 'We will join the ladies, God help us!'

When Bolitho glanced at the ornate French clock he saw it was almost midnight. It seemed incredible that time could pass so swiftly. But despite the hour there was no lessening in the pace. A small string orchestra struck up a lively dance, and laughing noisily the guests pushed and jostled towards the sounds of music.

Bolitho walked slowly through the connecting rooms, watching for Susannah Hardwicke and keeping a wary eye open for his earlier companion.

As he passed a book-lined study he saw Blundell speaking with a group of men, most of whom were prosperous-looking civilians. One, very tall and broad-shouldered, stood partly in shadow, but the side of his face which was visible in the candlelight made Bolitho start with shock, then pity. It had been scoured away, the skin burned almost to the bone from hairline to chin, so that it had the appearance of some grotesque mask. He seemed to feel Bolitho's eyes on him, and after a quick glance turned his back, hiding himself in shadow.

No wonder he had not joined the others at dinner. It was easy to imagine the agony of that disfigurement, the torment which had left him so scarred.

'Ah, there you are!' She came out of another room and rested her hand on his arm. 'Take me into the garden.'

They walked in silence, and he felt her dress swishing against his legs, the warmth of her body.

'You were absolutely splendid, Captain.' She paused and looked at him, her eyes very bright. 'That poor woman. I thought for an instant you would fall to her.'

'Oh, you saw.' Bolitho felt uneasy. 'She has gone, it seems.'

'Yes.' She led him into the garden. 'I sent her off.' She laughed, the sound carrying through the shrubs like an echo. 'I cannot have her interfering with *my* captain, now can I?'

'I hope you were easy with her?'

'Actually, she burst into tears. It was all rather pathetic.'

She turned inside his arm, her full dress spreading out behind her like pale gold.

'I must leave you now, Captain.'

'But . . . but I thought we were going to talk?'

'Later.' She studied him gravely. 'I have plans for your future, as I told you earlier, did I not?'

'I weigh anchor tomorrow.' He felt wretched. Helpless.

'I *know* that, silly!' She reached up and touched his lips. 'Do not frown. I cannot allow it. When you come back I will introduce you to some friends of mine. You will not regret it.' Her gloved fingers moved gently to his cheek. 'And neither, I trust, shall I.'

A servant appeared through the gloom. 'Carriage ready, Missy.'

She nodded. To Bolitho she said, 'After you have left I will try and clear these dreary people from the house.' She tilted her head and faced him calmly. 'You may kiss my shoulder, if you wish.'

Her skin was surprisingly cool, and as soft as a peach.

She twisted away from him and called, 'Be good, Captain, and take care of yourself. When you return I will be here.' Then she laughed and ran lightly up the terrace into the house.

The coach was waiting for him as he walked dazedly through the shadowed garden and on to the carriageway. His hat and cloak were on the seat, and strapped to the boot was a large wooden box.

The footman's teeth shone in a white crescent. 'Missy Susannah had the kitchen pack some food for you, Sah.' He chuckled. 'Nothin' but the best, she said.'

Bolitho climbed into the coach and sank against the cushions. He could still feel her skin against his mouth, smell the perfume from her hair. A girl who could drive a man mad, even if he was not half-way there already.

At the end of the jetty he found a waterman nodding over his oars, and had to call several times to attract his attention.

'Wot ship, sir?'

'*Sparrow*.'

Just saying the name helped to steady his racing thoughts. Before he stepped down into the dory he turned to look at the coach, but it had already disappeared. Like one more part of the dream

The waterman was grumbling to himself as he hauled the heavy box down the steps. Not enough to offend a ship's captain, but enough to add slightly to his fare.

Bolitho wrapped his cloak around him and felt the sea-breeze cold against his face. Still westerly. It would be good to get away again. If only to find time to collect himself and examine his hopes for the future.

15

A Good Likeness

Sparrow's mission to investigate the strength of French shipping at Newport proved to be more difficult than Bolitho had expected. The passage from Sandy Hook to the eastern extremes of Long Island showed nothing but promise for a quick completion and an equally swift return. But the weather decided otherwise, and in a savage westerly gale the little sloop was driven and battered continuously, so that Bolitho had to run with it rather than risk damage to spars and canvas.

Even when the wind moderated it took many more days to beat back again, and hardly an hour passed without the need to shorten sail or lay the ship on a tack which would take her away rather than towards her goal.

New York's entertainment seemed a long way behind, and Bolitho found the reality of driving his ship against wind and tide more than enough to occupy his energy. Even so, he found plenty of time to think about Susannah Hardwicke. Pacing the deck, hair whipping in the wind, his shirt often drenched with spray, he remembered their parting, the hint of an embrace which he could recall as clearly as if it had just occurred.

He suspected that his officers knew or guessed what had happened in New York, if only because of their careful silence.

The drudgery of fighting against the wind, and constant demands on every man aboard, were eased in part by the presence of their passenger. Rupert Majendie, true to his word, had arrived within minutes of weighing, complete with sketching and painting materials, and a repertoire of stories which did more than pay for his keep on board. When the sea and wind calmed he would be seen with his pad, sketching seamen at their daily task or catching them at their relaxation off watch, dancing or making small models and scrimshaw work. If the weather was less friendly he would disappear below to find fresh scope for his busy hands with only a swinging lantern to guide his pencil or brush. He and Dalkeith had become firm friends, which was hardly surprising. Each came from another sphere of culture and high intellect, with far more to discuss than the average sailor.

At the end of three long weeks, and with each day adding to his frustration, Bolitho decided to wait no more. He called Tyrrell to the cabin and unrolled his chart.

'We will close with the shore at daylight tomorrow, Jethro. The wind is still strong, but I see no other choice.'

Tyrrell let his eyes move across the chart. The approaches to Rhode Island were always a problem with a prevailing westerly wind. To be caught in a full gale might mean being driven eastwards again, and once within the jaws of the mainland and Newport itself there would be little room for manoeuvre. Under normal conditions it required patience and understanding. But with the French in control of the area it was something else entirely.

As if reading his thoughts, Bolitho said quietly, 'I'd not wish to be caught on a lee shore. But if we stay out here in open water, we might as well admit failure.'

'Aye.' Tyrrell straightened his back. 'I doubt th' Frogs'll have much in the' way of ships anyway. They depend on their batteries to defend themselves.'

Bolitho smiled, some of the strain slipping from his face. 'Good. Pass the word. I'll want the very best eyes at the mastheads tomorrow'.

But true to Buckle's gloomy prediction, the next morning was something of a disappointment. The sky was clouded over and the wind which made the topsails bluster and crack despite their trim, told there was rain nearby. And yet the air felt sultry and oppressive, affecting the hands as they went to their stations for changing tack. The welcome stay in harbour, followed by the nervous uncertainty of thrashing this way and that at the wind's discretion, had taken their toll. There were plenty of curses and not a few blows from boatswain's mates before *Sparrow* laid herself over on the larboard tack, her plunging beakhead pointing towards the shore once again.

A grey day. Bolitho gripped the weather nettings and mopped his forehead with his shirt-sleeve. His skin and clothing were wringing wet, as much from sweat as from flying spray.

Only Majendie seemed content to remain on deck willingly, his pencil busy, his thin body and jutting beard dripping with moisture.

'Land ho! Fine on the weather bow!'

Bolitho tried not to show his satisfaction and relief. With the dull visibility and blustery wind you could not be too secure with mere calculations. He looked up at the masthead pendant. The wind had backed slightly. He stared at the pendant until his eyes watered. There was no doubt about it. Good for a steady approach. Not so comforting if they had to turn and run. 'Bring her up a point, Mr. Buckle.'

'Aye, aye, sir.'

Buckle dabbed his face with a handkerchief before passing his orders. He would be well aware of the difficulties, Bolitho thought. There was no sanity in worrying him further.

To Majendie he said, 'I hope you are getting it all down. You will make your fortune when you return to England.'

Buckle yelled, 'Nor' nor'-east, sir! Full an' bye!'

'Very good. Hold her so.'

Bolitho walked a couple of paces and thought of the girl in New York. What would she think of him now? Crumpled and soaked to the skin, his shirt more patches than original cloth. He smiled to himself, not seeing Majendie's pencil as it recorded his mood.

Tyrrell limped up the deck and joined him by the nettings.

'I reckon that Newport is 'bout five miles off th 'starboard bow, sir.' He looked up with surprise as a shaft of watery sunlight played across the bucking hull like a lantern beam. 'Hell, you can never tell in these waters.'

'Deck thar! Ships at anchor to the nor'-east!'

Tyrrell rubbed his hands. 'Frogs may be assembling a convoy. Our in-shore squadron'll catch 'em if we carry th' word fast enough.'

The lookout yelled again. 'Six, no, *eight* sail-o'-the-line, sir!'

Graves staggered from the rail as *Sparrow* lurched sickeningly into a deep trough.

'The man's mad!' He spluttered as spray burst above the nettings and cascaded over him like hail. 'A couple of frigates at most, if you ask me!'

Bolitho tried to ignore the buzz of speculation and doubt around him. De Grasse had a powerful fleet in the West Indies, that was well known. His subordinate, de Barras, who commanded at Newport, had no such strength. His usefulness was placed in frigates and smaller craft and in quick forays against British coastal trade. De Barras had made one attempt to challenge the New York forces off Cape Henry earlier in the year, but the action had been desultory and ineffective. He had retired to his defences and had re-mained there.

He said, 'Aloft with you, Mr. Graves. Tell me what you see.'

Graves hurried to the shrouds muttering, 'That fool. Can't be ships-of-the-line. Can't be.'

Bolitho stared after him. Graves was acting very strangely. It was as if he dreaded what he might discover. Afraid? No. That seemed unlikely. He had been aboard long enough to know the risks and rewards of the game.

'Deck there!' It was another seaman clinging high above the mizzen yard. 'Sail on the larboard quarter!'

'Damn!' Tyrrell snatched a telescope and hurried with it to the taffrail.

Mist and spray, the distance made worse by *Sparrow*'s drunken motion, it took time to find the newcomer.

Tyrrell snapped, 'Frigate. No doubt, sir.'

Bolitho nodded. The other ship was clawing close inshore, coming around the jutting headland with every available sail set to the wind.

Buckle cupped his hands. 'Stand by to come about!'

'*Belay that!*' Bolitho's voice held the master motionless. 'We have got this far. Let us see what there is to see and *then* run.'

Graves came lurching from the gangway, his shirt torn from his rapid descent.

He gasped, 'He was right, sir. Eight of the line. Maybe two frigates, and a whole clutter of supply ships anchored closer in.'

Bolitho thought of his talk with Farr at Sandy Hook, his own reaction at seeing the British two-deckers nearby. Waiting, he had thought, but for what? And were these Frenchmen doing likewise?

Tyrrell said, 'Can't be none of de Grasse's ships, sir. Our patrols, even blind ones, would've seen 'em!'

Bolitho met his stare. 'I agree. It's a gathering for something. We must inform the admiral directly.'

Buckle shouted, 'Frigate closing fast, sir. Less than three miles, by my reckoning.'

Bolitho nodded. 'Very well, run up French colours, and prepare to come about.'

The flag rose swiftly to the gaff, to be greeted by an immediate blast of cannon from the frigate's forecastle.

Bolitho smiled grimly. 'He is not deceived. So hoist our own, if you please.'

Buckle crossed to Bolitho's side, his features screwed tight with worry.

'I think maybe we should wear ship, sir. That Frenchman'll be up to us afore we knows it otherwise.'

Bolitho shook his head. 'We would lose too much time. The frigate might chase us all the way to Nantucket or run us aground.' He swung on Graves. 'Clear away the bow-chasers. Load but do not run out.' He clapped him on the forearm, seeing him start with alarm. 'Lively, man! Or Mr. Frenchman'll be aboard for grog!'

Men scampered wildly to their stations, some pausing only to peer over the hammock nettings at the other ship which was driving purposefully towards the larboard quarter. She was much nearer, but in the bursting spray her hull was almost lost to view. Only her bulging courses and topsails displayed her captain's eagerness to do battle.

'Ready about!' Bolitho had his hands on his hips as he peered aloft at the slashing pendant. 'Stand by on the quarterdeck!'

'Put the helm down!' He felt the deck stagger, and wondered how *Sparrow* would appear to the enemy. Running? Preparing to fight?

He almost fell as the ship heeled and tilted still further to the thrust of sail and rudder.

'Helm a'lee, sir!' Buckle added his own weight to the wheel.

Headsails flailing about like mad things, yards bending to the contest between braces and booming canvas, it was a picture of confusion as *Sparrow* heeled sickeningly round into the wind. The sea surged up and over the beakhead, and men fell cursing and sprawling, some being washed into the gun deck scuppers like corpses.

Majendie clung to the nettings, his pad already sodden with spray as he stared transfixed at the sloop's wild turn across the wind.

Tyrrell's voice rose above the pandemonium like a trumpet. 'Braces there! Heave, my lads! Bosun, drive 'em hard today!'

Bolitho tried not to watch his ship's torment, but concentrated instead on the frigate. As *Sparrow* swung and plunged round on to her new tack, the wet sails thrusting her over until the lee gangway was awash, he saw the enemy's topmasts appear suddenly above the starboard bow. Barely a mile between them, but the violent turn had had the desired effect. Instead of closing comfortably on *Sparrow*'s larboard quarter, she now lay across the opposite bow and on a dangerously converging tack.

'Starboard chaser!' Bolitho had to repeat the order before young Fowler heard him and scurried forward to find Graves.

He yelled at Tyrrell, 'He must be made to think we are going to fight!'

Faintly from forward he heard the squeal of chocks as the gun crew hauled the thirty-two-pounder to its port. It would not be easy for them. With the ship lying hard over it would be like dragging it uphill.

'Fire!'

The smoke whipped inboard above the forecastle as the bow-chaser roared its challenge at the enemy.

Nobody reported a fall of shot, and at such an angle it was likely the ball had passed clean above the other ship.

Bolitho felt his jaw tighten into a grin. The enemy's forecourse was being brailed up, her topgallants disappearing as if by remote hand as they shortened sail to fight the impudent *Sparrow*.

'Fire!'

Again the gun hurled its heavy ball into the murky confusion of sea and drifting spume.

Bolitho looked at Buckle. 'Stand by!' He strode to the rail and touched Tyrrell's arm. 'Get the forecourse on her! Hands aloft and loose t'gallants! 'Tis time for a little prudence!'

As the great foresail billowed and then hardened to the wind Bolitho felt the hull steady and hold firm to its thrust. Right above the deck the topmen were busy releasing the topgallant sails, so that as he peered aloft the mainmast seemed to be bending forward like a tree in a storm.

When he turned towards the French frigate again he saw that his plan had worked well. She was trying to reset her foresail, but the momentary pause to present her broadside had cost her dearly. She was plunging past the *Sparrow*'s quarter a full three cables clear.

By the time she had regained her control of wind and tack she would be well astern. Also, *Sparrow*'s sudden manoeuvre had now given her the wind-gage.

A ripple of flashes spouted from the frigate's side. Balls plunged into the sea nearby, although with so many white-horses on each beam it was hard to tell shot from spray.

Overhead a ball whined between the masts, and a seaman fell from the mainyard, hitting the sea alongside without surfacing until he was far astern.

Majendie said hoarsely, 'The poor fellow! God rest his soul!'

Bolitho nodded. 'Aye. That was bad luck.'

He stared along the gun deck where his men worked like demons to retrim the yards and secure halliards which were swollen with damp. Hardly one of them had looked up as the man had fallen. Later perhaps they would mourn. But maybe, like himself, they were thanking God that *Sparrow* had answered their call, had not scorned their efforts to drag her into the wind and risk demasting or crippling her to lie an easy prize under the enemy's guns.

'Steer due south, Mr. Buckle. We will gain some room before we attempt to wear.'

Buckle gazed astern. The frigate was going about, the heart gone from her original challenge.

'There he goes, God rot him!' Buckle grinned at his helmsmen. 'Thought we were going to surrender without a fight, did he?'

Majendie watched Bolitho's strained face. 'Many would have done, Captain. Even I, a landsman, know you were badly matched.'

Bolitho forced a smile. 'But we did *not* fight, my friend.' He glanced briefly astern. 'Not *this* time.'

He shut the picture of the falling topman from his mind. It was to be hoped he died instantly. To see his ship sailing on without him would make his last moments on earth worse than death itself.

'Now, fetch Mr. Graves and the lookouts. We will put all our information together.' He caught Majendie's arm as a deep plunge all but threw him down the quarterdeck ladder. 'Steady there! I may want you to make some sketches for the admiral. It seems the fashionable thing to do these days.'

When at last he was satisfied with *Sparrow*'s course and trim he walked aft and looked for the land. But it was lost from view, and he guessed that rain covered the headland and the frigate which had so nearly caught them in a trap.

He stripped off his shirt and mopped his neck and chest with it. Majendie watched him and then peered glumly at his sodden pad. That, he decided would have been the best sketch of all.

Bolitho read carefully through his prepared report and then thrust it into an envelope. Stockdale stood beside the table, a candle and wax ready to seal it, now that it seemed there was nothing more to add.

Bolitho leaned back and stretched his arms. For two whole days they had fought their way south-west, losing sight of land and intent only on gaining advantage over the wind. Tacking back and forth for hours at a time to record but a few miles in actual progress. It had been hard work for everyone, but now that the wind had decided to back still further *Sparrow* had at last been able to turn towards the mainland. With luck they would anchor at Sandy Hook tomorrow. He glanced at the open log book and smiled. It was sobering to realise that in the time it had taken to reach Newport, fight the adverse weather and return to Sandy Hook by this frustrating and delaying method, he could have sailed his ship clear across the Atlantic to Falmouth with days to spare.

'Will I seal it now, sir?' Stockdale watched him patiently.

'I think so.'

He closed his eyes, memorising the statements he had obtained from Graves and the lookouts. They differed in small details, but one thing was clear. It seemed more than likely to expect a combined Franco/American attack on New York, and soon. He found some satisfaction in the fact that if the weather had delayed his swift return, then it would equally hamper the enemy.

'Deck there! Sail on th' weather bow!'

Bolitho pushed Stockdale's candle aside. 'Later.' Then he hurried from the cabin.

Because of the *Sparrow*'s need to gain advantage from the wind they had driven far to the south-west. Now, having at last found the wind's favour, the compass pointed north-west by north, with Sandy Hook some ninety miles ahead. The afternoon was hot but clear, and even from the deck it was possible to see the small pyramid of canvas to show that the other vessel was standing on a converging tack.

'Bring her up a point. Steer nor'-west.'

He took a glass from Bethune and steadied it above the nettings.

The masthead called 'Brigantine, sir!'

He looked at Tyrrell. 'Ours probably.'

It was the only sail they had sighted since narrowly avoiding action with the French frigate. It was always good to meet a friendly ship, and he would pass some of his news across to her, in case she was making for the north and might pass too close to the enemy's squadron at Newport.

With the wind blowing keenly it did not take long for both ships to draw near one another.

'He intends to pass to lee'rd.' Bolitho raised the glass again.

Brigantines were untidy looking ships. Square-rigged on the foremast, and with a schooner's fore-and-aft sail on the main, they appeared ill-designed, but were known capable of outdistancing even a frigate under good conditions.

Bolitho said, 'Signal her to heave to. I will speak with her master.'

Tyrrell said, 'Anyway, she's English. No doubt about that.'

Flags soared up the newcomer's yards and broke to the wind.

Bethune shouted, 'She's the *Five Sisters*, sir!' He fumbled with his book while Fowler stood a little apart, his mouth set in an expression of disdain. 'Shown here as under warrant to the Governor at New York.'

'Thought as much.' Tyrrell frowned. 'Law unto themselves, and crewed by some real rascals, I can tell you.' He sighed. 'Still, a warrant keeps 'em safe from th' press and risking their precious necks.'

The brigantine had crossed *Sparrow*'s bows and was moving steadily on the starboard tack. Bolitho could see the red and gold flag at her fore, the trim semblance of order usually found in a government sponsored vessel. She was drawing closer, and would eventually pass less than half a cable clear.

Bolitho saw Majendie and Dalkeith by the nettings. The former scribbling frantically, the surgeon peering over his shoulder with obvious interest.

'She's heaving to, sir.'

The brigantine was coming up into the wind, her canvas aback and the big mainsail diminishing steadily as the seamen took charge of it.

Bolitho nodded approvingly. It had been well executed.

'Luff, Mr. Tyrrell. I will hail her while she rides under our lee.'

The crash and boom of flapping canvas made any sort of conversation difficult, for as *Sparrow* turned closer into the wind and her way was reduced to a crawl, every sail and shroud seemed intent on drowning Bolitho's voice.

He held the speaking trumpet in both hands and shouted, '*Where are you bound?*'

Across the short wave-crests he heard the reply.

'Montego Bay! Jamaica!'

Tyrrell remarked, 'Bit off course, I'd say.'

The voice came again. 'We were chased by a Spanish frigate yesterday.

Gave him the slip during the night, but you might report him for me.'

The brigantine was falling downwind and her yards were moving restlessly to show her master was eager to be on his way.

Bolitho lowered the trumpet. There was no point in detaining her longer. And he would get precious little thanks for so doing by the New York authorities. It was odd to realise that she probably came under the control of men like Blundell, who knew nothing and cared less for the sea.

He heard Dalkeith murmur, 'By God, that captain's face! I've never seen such cruel burns and know a man to live!'

Bolitho snapped, 'Give me that glass!' He snatched it from the astonished surgeon and levelled it on the other ship's poop.

Through the black rigging and loosely flapping sails he saw him. His coat collar was turned up to his ears despite the heat, and his hat was drawn firmly almost to eye-level. Bolitho realised that the brigantine's captain had not only lost half his face, but an eye as well, and he was holding his head at a stiff, unnatural angle as he trained the remaining one on the sloop.

So the brigantine had something to do with Blundell. He could picture them murmuring together in the study, the scarred face half hidden in shadow.

Buckle called worriedly, 'Permission to get the ship under way, sir? We're riding a bit close.'

'Very well.'

Bolitho waved to the men on the brigantine's deck and turned to watch Majendie again. He was hanging on the nettings, scribbling and shading, smoothing out and adding detail even as the *Five Sisters* reset her foresail and began to gather way downwind.

Dalkeith grinned. 'Not bad, Rupert! I daresay some of our naval companions will assist you with detail of rigging, eh?'

Tyrrell limped over to him and peered across his narrow shoulder. He seized the pad and exclaimed, 'Holy God! If I didn't know for sure . . .'

Bolitho strode to his side. The picture was of the brigantine's poop, with officers and seamen caught in realistic attitudes, even if, as Dalkeith had hinted, the details of rigging were imperfect.

He felt himself go cold as he saw Majendie's drawing of the ship's captain. Distance and scale had wiped away the terrible scars, so that he stood out like a figure from the past. He looked at Tyrrell, who was still watching his face.

Tyrrell said quietly, 'You remember, sir? You were too busy fighting and guarding me from attack.' He turned to stare at the other ship. 'But after I took that ball in my thigh I had plenty of time to watch *that* bugger.'

Bolitho tried to clear the dryness from his throat. With stark clarity he saw the fury and hatred of battle as if it had been yesterday. The *Sparrow's* seamen being cut down and driven from *Bonaventure's* decks. And the privateer's captain, standing like some detached onlooker, calling on him to strike and surrender.

He snapped, 'Put the ship about! Hands aloft and set t'gallants!'

To Majendie he added softly, 'Thanks to you, I think we may solve a mystery today.'

The instant *Sparrow* showed her intentions, and even as the fore topgallant sail bellied from its yard, the brigantine also increased her canvas and headed away.

'Clear for action, sir?'

He watched the jib-boom edging round until it fastened on the brigantine's starboard quarter like a bridge. In fact she was two cables clear and showed no sign of losing her lead.

'It must be quickly done. We will go alongside and grapple. Tell Mr. Graves to loose off a ball from the larboard bow-chaser. Lively now!'

Buckle said grimly, 'We're overhauling him, sir.'

Bolitho nodded. Tyrrell understood what was happening, but so far nobody else had even hinted surprise at his actions. To all intents he was chasing a government vessel with which, minutes earlier, he had been exchanging pleasantries.

Bang. The bow-chaser's black muzzle lurched inboard on its tackles, and Bolitho saw the waterspout shoot upwards within a boat's length of the brigantine's side.

'She's shortening sail now!' Buckle sounded satisfied.

'Pass the word for Mr. Graves to muster a boarding party!' Bolitho watched narrowly as the other ship began to yaw heavily in a procession of troughs. 'Mr. Heyward, take charge of the gun deck! Mr. Bethune, accompany the second lieutenant!'

Men scampered to the larboard gangway, cutlasses bared, and some carrying muskets above their heads to avoid misfiring into their companions.

'Steady, Mr. Buckle!' Bolitho held out his hand and looked up at the yards. Sails were vanishing briskly, and as the forecourse rose booming and writhing to its yard he saw the brigantine slipping under the larboard bow, as if both ships were being drawn together by hawsers. '*Steady!*'

Along the gangway picked seamen swung their grapnels, while others scurried forward to fend off the first contact.

Across the shortening range Bolitho heard, 'Stand away there! I command you to keep clear! I will have the law on your head!'

Bolitho felt his tension easing. If he had harboured doubts they were gone now. There was no mistaking that voice. Two many of *Sparrow*'s seamen had died that day aboard *Bonaventure* for him ever to forget.

He raised the trumpet. 'Take in your sails and bring to *instantly*!'

He heard the grumble of chocks and guessed the brigantine's crew were well able to see the big thirty-two-pounder as it was run out again.

Warily, and with great skill, both vessels slowly edged round, their progress through the choppy water falling almost to nothing, their seamen taking in canvas and trimming yards in harmony with the change of rudder. It was perfectly done, and with little more than a shudder *Sparrow* nudged against the brigantine's hull and ground forward before coming to rest with her bowsprit level with the other's foremast. Grapnels flew from the gangway, and Bolitho saw Graves waving his men forward, and Bethune swinging out on the fore shrouds, his dirk seeming too small for so heavy a midshipman.

Tyrrell rested his hands on the rail and said, 'She carries a deck cargo as well.' He pointed to a large canvas hump below the forecastle. 'Booty for th' master, no doubt!'

Even as he finished speaking, and as the first seaman jumped out and down on to the brigantine's bulwark, the deck cargo revealed itself. Hands tore the canvas away to uncover a sturdy twelve-pounder which was rigged in the centre of the deck, its bulk controlled by tackles and ring-bolts.

The crash of its explosion was matched only by the shriek of grape-shot as it burst with terrifying impact along *Sparrow*'s gangway. Men and pieces of flesh flew in bloody profusion, and through the rolling bank of brown smoke Bolitho saw some of them smashed to the opposite side of the deck.

Then came the shouting, and from the brigantine's poop and main hatch he saw some fifty men charging to the attack.

He groped for his hanger, but realised he had forgotten to bring it from the cabin. Everywhere men were shouting and screaming and above it all came an increasing rasp of steel, the bang and whine of musket fire.

A seaman fell bodily from the nettings and knocked Tyrrell against the rail. His leg doubled under him and his face contorted with pain.

Bolitho yelled, 'Take charge, Mr. Buckle!'

He snatched a cutlass from the dead seaman's belt and ran to the gangway. His eyes smarted in smoke, and he felt several balls fan past him, one severing a netting like an invisible knife.

The brigantine stood no chance against *Sparrow*'s cannon. But, grappled together like this, the fight could easily turn against them. He had done this very thing himself and knew the odds.

He vaulted wildly on to the main shrouds and then saw with astonishment that Graves was still below him on the gun deck. He was yelling at his men, but seemed unable to follow them. Of Bethune there was no sign, and he realised that Heyward had gone forward to meet a rush of boarders who were trying to climb across the beakhead.

He slipped and almost dropped between the hulls, and then with a gasp he was on the brigantine's deck. A pistol exploded beside his face, nearly blinding him, but he slashed out with the heavy cutlass, felt a brief impact and heard someone scream.

'The poop!' He thrust his way between some of his men and saw Bethune using a musket like a club, his hair blowing wildly as he tried to rally what remained of his boarding party. 'Take the poop, lads!'

Somebody raised a cracked cheer, and with fresh heart the seamen lunged aft. Feet and legs kicked and swayed above groaning wounded and corpses alike. There was no time to reload muskets, and it was blade to blade at close quarters.

Through the struggling, interlocked figures Bolitho saw the ship's wheel, a master's mate standing alone beside it, while others lay in various attitudes of death around him to show that aboard *Sparrow* someone had mustered a few sharpshooters in the maintop.

Then, all at once, they were face to face. Bolitho, with his shirt torn almost to his waist, his hair plastered across his forehead and the cutlass outstretched towards his enemy.

The other captain stood quite motionless, his sword held easily and angled across his front. Close to, his face was even more terrible, but there was no doubting his agility as he suddenly darted forward.

The blades came together with a sharp clang. Sparks flew as they ground inwards until both hilts locked and each man tested the weight of his adversary's arm.

Bolitho looked into the unwinking eye, felt the heat of his breath, the quivering tension in his shoulder as with a curse he thrust Bolitho back against the wheel, withdrawing his sword and striking forward in two swift movements. Again and again, strike, parry, guard. The cutlass felt like a lead weight, and each movement became an agony. Bolitho saw the other man's mouth set in a grim smile. He knew he was winning.

Beyond the rail the fighting continued as before, but above it he heard Tyrrell yell from the quarterdeck. 'Help th' cap'n! For Christ's sake, *help him*!'

As they circled each other like jungle cats, Bolitho saw Stockdale slashing and hacking to try to reach him. But he was fighting at least three men, and his bellows were those of an anguished bull.

Bolitho lifted his cutlass and levelled it at the other man's waist. He could raise it no further. His muscles seemed to be cracking. If only he could change hands. But he would die if he attempted it.

The sword flicked out, its point cutting through his sleeve and touching his skin like a white-hot iron. He could feel blood running down his arm, saw the man's single eye gleaming through a mist of pain like some glowing stone.

The brigantine's captain shouted, 'Now, Cap'n! This is the moment! For *you*!'

He moved so quickly that Bolitho hardly saw the blade coming. It caught the cutlass within inches of the hilt, turned it from his fingers like something plucked from a child, and sent it flying over the rail.

There was a loud crack, and Bolitho felt the ball pass his shoulder, the heat so fierce it must have missed him by an inch. It struck the other man in the throat, hurling him aside even as the sword made its final lunge. For a moment longer he kicked and convulsed in his blood and then lay still.

Bolitho saw Dalkeith throw one leg over the bulwark and climb up beside him, a pistol smoking in his hand.

Throughout the two ships there was stricken silence, and the brigantine's crew stood or lay to await quarter from their attackers.

Bolitho said, 'Thank you. That was close.'

Dalkeith did not seem to hear him. He said brokenly, 'They killed Majendie. Shot him down like a dog as he tried to save a wounded man.'

Bolitho felt the surgeon's fingers on his arm as he ripped his shirt into a deft bandage.

Majendie gone, and so many others, too. He looked down at the dead man by the bulwark. If he had kept his head he might have got away with the deception. But for Majendie he certainly would have done. Perhaps, like himself, he had never forgotten that day aboard the privateer, and once more fate had decided to end the memory in its own way.

He turned to survey the two vessels. There was much to be done, a lot to be discovered before they reached Sandy Hook.

Some of his men gave a hoarse cheer as he walked to the bulwark, but most were too spent even to move.

Anger, disgust, as well as a sense of loss, flooded through him as he walked amongst his gasping seamen. To think men had died because of treachery and to gain riches for others who remained aloof from blame.

'But not *this* time!' He spoke aloud without realising it. 'Somebody will pay dearly for today's grief!'

Then he thought of the girl in New York and wondered how he could protect her when the truth became known.

16

One Man's Loss . . .

Rear-Admiral Sir Evelyn Christie rose from behind a table crammed with documents and leaned forward to offer his hand.

'Welcome.' He gestured to a chair. 'Good to meet you again.'

Bolitho sat down and watched the admiral as he moved towards the stern gallery It was stiflingly hot, and even though there was a regular breeze across Sandy Hook the air in the flagship's great cabin was lifeless.

Christie added abruptly, 'I am sorry to have kept you so long. But the politics of high command are no area for a young captain.' He smiled. 'Your courage is beyond doubt, but here in New York they would eat you alive.'

Bolitho tried to relax. For three days after dropping anchor he had been to all intents confined to his ship. Once his report had been spirited to the flagship and his wounded landed for care ashore, he had been left in little doubt as to his own position. No actual command had been issued but the Officer-of-the-Guard had told him that his presence aboard would be in everyone's best interests until word from the admiral.

He began, 'If I have done wrong, sir, then . . .'

Christie looked at him sternly. '*Wrong?* Quite the reverse. But you have certainly set a fox amongst the geese this time.' He shrugged. 'But you did not come aboard to hear what you already know. Your action in capturing the brigantine *Five Sisters*, the seizure of certain documents before her master could dispose of them, far outweigh individual discomfort elsewhere.'

'Thank you, sir.' He was still uncertain where Christie's comments were leading.

'It now seems evident that the brigantine's master, one Matthew Crozier, intended to pass information either to an enemy vessel or to some spy along the coast. That would explain his being so far off course, his excuse of avoiding a Spanish frigate. But there can be no doubt as to his main mission. Whilst on passage for Jamaica he was to deliver a message for the Compte de Grasse at Martinique. My people have examined the despatch most throughly.' He eyed Bolitho steadily. 'In it they found full details of our defences and all available ships-of-war. Deployments, both sea and military, even to the extent of our strength under Cornwallis.' He picked up a document and studied it for several seconds. 'One way or t'other, this will be a year to remember.'

Bolitho shifted in his chair. 'How could a privateersman like Crozier obtain a warrant to work for the British?'

Christie smiled wryly. 'He owned the brigantine. It was no doubt purchased by his own side. The crew were hand-picked. The sweepings of a dozen ports and almost as many countries. With small vessels in such demand his deception was not so very difficult. Even on his official voyages he was apparently smuggling.' He turned away, his shoulders suddenly rigid. 'Mostly for those in power in New York!'

'May I ask if they are to be punished?'

Christie turned and shrugged. 'If you mean General Blundell, then you may be assured he will be leaving America very soon. After that I am equally certain he will be saved by influence and powerful friends at home. Distance and time are great healers where the guilty are concerned. But others will certainly go to the wall, and I have been told that the Military Command intends to use your discovery to rid itself, in part at least, of the parasites who have lived too long off its back.'

He smiled at Bolitho's grave features. 'Pour some madeira. It will do us both good.' He continued in the same unruffled tone, 'Admiral Graves is well pleased with you. He has sent the schooner *Lucifer* to Antigua to inform Admiral Rodney of the situation here. Patrols have been ordered to Newport to watch de Barras's squadron, although, as you well know, it is hard to see what is happening there. In fact, everything is being done with the forces available to watch over local waters to see which way the tiger will pounce.'

He took a glass from Bolitho's hand and asked, '*Sparrow*, is she in good repair?'

Bolitho nodded. It was still difficult to keep pace with the small admiral 'My carpenter has almost completed repairs to the gangway and ...'

Christie nodded briskly. 'In any case, *that* can be finished at sea. I want you to take on full supplies, for three months at least. My flag captain has it in hand. He might even find you some seamen to replace those lost in battle. I have sent *Heron* to the south'rd again, but my other inshore patrols are too well spread for comfort. I need every available ship, especially yours.' He smiled. 'And you.'

'Thank you, sir.' He put down the glass. 'Newport again?'

The admiral shook his head. 'You will join Farr and his *Heron*.'

Bolitho stared at him. 'But sir, I thought you needed ships to watch de Barras?'

Christie picked up the decanter and examined it thoughtfully. 'I may do so later. But for the present I want you out of Sandy Hook. Away from those who will try to bring you down. You have made enemies by your actions. As I said just now, you are no match for the devious ways of politics.'

'I am prepared to take that risk, sir.'

'*I am not!*' Christie's voice was hard. Like it had been at the court martial in this very cabin. 'To you, your ship and her affairs are paramount. But I must think on a wider scope, and my superiors wider still. If it is thought best for you to lead my whole squadron against de Barras, then that is how it will be. And if your ship must be sacrificed like a tethered animal in a snare, then that, too, will be ordered!' He relented. 'Forgive me. That was unpardonable.' He waved one hand above his charts. 'The enemy is powerful, but not so that he can attack everywhere at once. He can strike against New York, for deprived of it we have no pretence at government in America. Or he can turn his iron on General Cornwallis's army in the field, for without that we are just as pointless. Either way there will be a battle, and I believe that a sea fight will decide our course and that of history for years to come.'

Feet pounded overhead and Bolitho heard the bark of commands, the scrape of tackles and blocks. Even the old *Parthian* was preparing to sail, to show her readiness for whatever the enemy intended.

Bolitho stood up. 'When can I expect my orders, sir?'

'Before sunset. I would advise you to contain your, er, other interests, until some later date.' He proffered his hand. 'The heart is a fine thing, but I would prefer you to rest your judgements on the brain.'

Bolitho walked out to the sunlight, his mind buzzing with all Christie had said and the greater part which he had left unspoken. It was all so unfair. A sailor stood to his gun in battle until told otherwise. Or he struggled aloft in a shrieking gale, frozen with icy spray, and scared half to death. But he obeyed. It was the way of things, or had been in Bolitho's experience. Until now.

Yet Blundell's kind ignored such distinctions, could and did use their personal authority for gain, even when the country was fighting for its life. No wonder those like Crozier could prosper and achieve more results than an army of paid spies. Crozier had been doing his duty in the only way he knew. By ignoring the dangers, Blundell had committed little better than treason.

He stopped by the entry port and stared at the waiting gig with sudden anxiety. So why had he not told Christie of Crozier's presence in Blundell's house? There would have been no hiding from conspiracy had that piece of news been released. He swore under his breath and signalled to Stockdale.

Fool, fool! Perhaps he should have told her first. To allow her time to disassociate herself from her uncle's affairs.

The flag captain joined him by the port. 'I have had the water hoys sent over to *Sparrow*. Another lighter will be alongside within the hour. If your people turn to with a will, you should have all the stores aboard before dusk.'

Bolitho eyed him curiously. Such calm assurance, yet this captain had not only his own ship and the whims of an admiral to consider, he must concern himself with the needs of every officer and man in the squadron. He was jolted by his discovery. It was like seeing Christie's charts on the cabin table. To all but himself, *Sparrow* and her company were just a tiny part of the whole.

He doffed his hat to the shrill calls and shining bayonets and clambered down to the gig. He said nothing as the boat pulled lustily across the anchorage, and Stockdale for once seemed content to leave him in peace.

He was in his cabin with Lock studying the latest return of ship's stores when Graves entered to announce the arrival of another hoy carrying fresh water.

As the purser scuttled away to watch over the casks before they were lowered into the hold, Bolitho said, 'I was meaning to have a word with you, Mr. Graves.' He saw the lieutenant stiffen, the way his fingers locked into his coat. Poor Graves. He looked like an old man, and even his tan could not hide the shadows under his eyes, the pinched lines at each side of his mouth. How did you begin to ask an officer if he was a coward? He added, 'Are you troubled about something?'

Graves swallowed hard. 'My father is dead, sir. Some weeks back. I just received a letter.'

'I am sorry to hear that, Mr. Graves.' Bolitho watched his face with sudden compassion. 'It is harder to bear when you are out of reach, as we are.'

'Yes.' Graves did not even blink. 'He had been, er, ill for some while.'

The door swung open and Tyrrell limped noisily into the cabin. He did not appear to see Graves as he exclaimed, 'By God, Cap'n! I've had news!' He leaned on the table, all his excitement and pleasure welling out of him in an uncontrollable flood. 'My sister. She's safe an' well! I met a man who was a trapper in th' country. He said she's living with our uncle. That's about twenty mile to th' north of our old farmstead.' He grinned widely. 'Safe! I still can't believe I'm awake.' He turned and saw Graves for the first time. 'Oh hell! I'm sorry. I forgot myself with th' fair excitement of it all.'

Graves was staring at him glassily, and his fingers had screwed his coat into two tight balls.

Tyrrell asked, 'What's wrong? You sick or something?'

Graves muttered, 'I must go. If you'll excuse me, sir.' He almost ran from the cabin.

Bolitho stood up. 'It *was* good news, Jethro.' He looked at the open door. 'I am afraid Graves just brought some of a sadder note. His father.'

Tyrrell sighed. 'I'm sorry. I thought maybe it was something I said . . .'

'In what way?'

Tyrrell shrugged. 'No matter. He was once in hopes of courting my sister.' He smiled at some secret memory. 'It all seems a long way back now.'

Bolitho tried not to think about Graves's stunned expression.

'One day you'll be able to join your sister again. I am very glad for you.'

Tyrrell nodded, his eyes dreamy. 'Aye. One day.' He nodded more firmly. 'I don't feel quite so lost any more.'

Midshipman Fowler stepped neatly over the coaming and removed his hat. 'The lighterman brought you a letter, sir.' His lisp was very pronounced. 'He insisted I give it to you myself.'

'Thank you.'

Bolitho held it in his fingers. Like the other one which he had locked in his strong-box. Her own hand.

He opened it quickly and then said, 'I'll be ashore for an hour. Maybe longer. Call away my gig.'

Fowler ran from the cabin, his sharp voice calling for the boat's crew.

Tyrrell asked quietly, 'Is it wise, sir?'

'What the hell do you mean by that?' Bolitho swung towards him, caught off guard by his question.

Tyrrell frowned. 'I met several people when I was ordering some new cordage, sir. It's well known all over New York what you've done. Most are laughing fit to burst that your action has unmasked these bloody scabs and traitors. But some think you'll be in real danger while you're here. There'll be plenty more quaking in their beds. Wondering what you discovered, an' when th' soldiers are going to bang on *their* door.'

Bolitho dropped his eyes. 'I'm sorry about my anger. But have no fear. I've no intention of parading my back for the benefit of that sort.'

Tyrrell watched him as he snatched up his hat and fretted impatiently for Fitch to adjust his swordbelt.

Then he said, 'I'll rest easier when we're at sea again.'

Bolitho hurried past him. 'And that will be tonight, my cautious friend. So stir yourself and watch over the provisions!' He smiled at Tyrell's concern. 'But beware. There may be an assassin hiding in the salt beef!'

Tyrrell saw him over the side but remained by the rail for a long while, despite the sun and the pain in his thigh.

There was a small carriage waiting for Bolitho at the end of the jetty. It was a shabby affair and not in the least like the one which had carried him to the general's residence. But the driver was the same Negro, and as soon as Bolitho was inside he cracked his whip and urged the horses into a brisk trot.

They rattled through several narrow streets and then out into a quiet road which was lined by sturdy houses, most of which seemed to be occupied by some of the city's refugees. The buildings had lost their façade of well-being, and where there had been gardens there were piles of discarded boxes and sorry-looking vehicles. At many of the windows he saw women and children staring out at the road below. They had the lost look of uprooted people with little to do but wait and hope.

The coach wheeled through a pair of sagging gates and towards another such house. Except that this one was empty, its windows bare in the sunlight like blind eyes.

For an instant he recalled Tyrrell's warning, but as the coach slid to a halt he saw the girl beside the house, her gown reflected in a partly overgrown pond.

He hurried towards her, his heart pounding in time with his shoes.

'I came as fast as I could!' He took her hands in his and studied her warmly. 'But why must we meet here?'

She tossed her head, throwing the hair from her shoulder in the way he had remembered in the weeks he had been away.

'It is better so. I cannot bear the watching eyes. The sneers behind my back.' There was little emotion in her voice. 'But we will go inside now. I must speak with you.

Their shoes rang hollowly on the bare boards. It had been a fine house, but now the plaster was flaking and the walls were heavy with cobwebs.

She walked to a window and said, 'My uncle is in serious trouble, but I expect you know. He was perhaps foolish, but no more than many here.'

Bolitho slipped his hand beneath her arm. 'I do not want you to be involved, Susannah.'

His insistence, or the use of her name, made her turn and face him.

'But I *am* involved, as you put it.'

'No. The smuggling and other offences could have had nothing to do with you. Nobody would ever believe it.'

She stared at him calmly. 'Nor does it matter. But one hint of treason would ruin my uncle and all connected with him.' She gripped his arm. 'That man, Crozier, have you spoken of his presence at our house? Please, I must know. For if you remain silent, all may yet be well.'

Bolitho turned away. 'Believe me, I can save you from that. Your uncle will be sent to England. There is no reason why you cannot remain here.'

'*Here?*' She stood back from him. 'What use is that?'

'I – I thought, given time you might see your way to becoming my wife.' In the empty room his words seemed to come back to mock him.

'Marry you?' She brushed her hair from her forehead. 'Is that what you thought?'

'Yes. I had cause to hope.' He watched her despairingly. 'You hinted that . . .'

She replied sharply, 'I hinted no such proposal, Captain! If things had gone as I had planned, well then maybe . . .'

He tried again. 'But nothing *need* change for us.'

She continued as if he had not spoken. 'I did think that with some help from my friends you might one day amount to something. A position in London, perhaps even a seat in Parliament. All is possible if the will is there.' She lifted her eyes to his face again. 'Did you really expect me to marry a sea-officer? Live from day to day waiting for one ship after the other to drop anchor? There are other lives beyond your miserable Service, *Captain*!'

'It is my life.' He felt the walls closing in on him. The air forced from his lungs as if he was drowning.

'The path of duty.' She walked to the window and looked down at the carriage. 'You were a fool to think of my sharing such an existence. An even bigger one if you continue to do so!' She turned easily, her eyes flashing. 'There's more to living than catching some poor smuggler in the King's name!'

Bolitho said, 'I did not tell of Crozier being with your uncle. But it is certain to come out when the authorities have finished their inquiries.' He added bitterly, 'Rats always turn on one another when the pickings are few.'

She breathed out slowly, one hand resting lightly below her heart. 'Stay a few minutes while I go to my carriage. I have no wish to be seen here.'

Bolitho reached out his arms and then let them drop to his sides. He was defeated. Had been so for longer than he had understood.

Yet in the dusty sunlight, as she stood watching him, her violet eyes holding him at a distance, he knew that if there was anything he could do or say to keep her he would use it.

She moved to the door. 'You are a strange man. But I can see no future for you.' Then she was gone, her shoes fading on the staircase until he was quite alone.

He did not remember how long he stood in that empty room. Minutes? An hour? When at last he walked down the stairs and into the overgrown garden he realised that even the shabby carriage had gone. He crossed to the pond and stared at his own reflection.

If she had been angry, or frightened, anything he could have recognised, he might still have known what to do. There had not even been contempt. She had dismissed him with no more thought than if she had been rejecting a useless servant.

A foot scraped on stone and he swung round, seeing in those seconds four dark figures lined against the ragged bushes.

'*Easy*, Cap'n!' One of them had a drawn sword, and he saw the others were also well armed. 'There's no sense in strugglin'!'

Another of the men chuckled. 'Aye, that's right, Cap'n. Somewhere for us'n to hide yer corpse when we've done with you. Most considerate, eh, lads?'

Bolitho remained quite still. He knew it was useless to bargain with any of them. They had the looks of professional criminals, men who worked for a fee, no matter what the final cost might be to them. He was suddenly very calm, as if their arrival had driven away his other despair like a cold wind.

'Then I'll take a couple with me!'

He snatched out his hanger and waited for them to attack. Two carried pistols, but there were probably military patrols nearby and a shot might bring them running.

Steel clashed with steel, and he saw the leader's grin fade to an intent frown as they locked blades together. He ducked as one man struck at his neck, twisted his hanger and slashed him across the face, hearing him scream as he tumbled back into the bushes.

'Damn you, you bloody bastard!' Another dived forward, his sword sweeping under Bolitho's guard. But it glanced from his belt buckle and he was able to thrust him aside with the hilt, catching him on the jaw with such force it almost tore the hanger from his grip.

The garden swam in a mist of pain as something struck him savagely on the forehead, and he realised that one of them had hurled a stone. He hit out with the hanger but felt it pass through air. Someone laughed, and another called hoarsely, '*Now*,' Arry! In the guts!'

Feet pounded through the shrubs, and Bolitho was pushed aside by someone in a blue coat who shouted, 'At 'em, lads! Cut 'em down!'

Swords grated and sparked, and a body rolled thrashing into the pond, the blood staining the surface like red weed.

Bolitho lurched to his feet, realising that Heyward and Tyrrell were driving the two attackers against the house, while Dalkeith stood watchfully nearby, his beautiful pistols shining in the sunlight.

Heyward brought his man to his knees and jumped back to let him roll silently on to his face and stay there.

The sole survivor threw down his heavy sword and yelled, 'Quarter! Quarter!'

Tyrrell swayed awkwardly on his crippled leg and said harshly, 'Quarter be damned!'

The sword took him in the chest, holding him to the wall for an endless moment before allowing him to slide beside his companion.

Tyrrell sheathed his blade and limped to Bolitho's side.

'All well, Cap'n?' He reached out to steady him. 'Just in time it seems.'

Heyward stepped over one of the corpses. 'Someone wanted you dead, sir.'

Bolitho looked from one to the next, the emotion rising to mingle with his understanding.

Tyrrell grinned. 'You see, I was right.'

Bolitho nodded heavily. *Someone wanted you dead.* But the worst part was knowing that she had realised his peril, and had done nothing. He glanced at the corpse sprawled in the pond.

'What can I say? How can I find words?'

Dalkeith murmured, 'Let's say it was for Rupert Majendie, too.'

Tyrrell slipped his arm over Heyward's slim shoulder for support.

'Aye, that'll do.' He glanced at Bolitho and held his gaze. 'You've done plenty for us. An' in *Sparrow* we look after our own!'

Then together they walked out to the road and towards the sea.

17

Mistaken Identity

Bolitho leaned back in his chair and stared wearily at the open log. He was stripped to the waist, but could feel no benefit in the overheated cabin. He touched his mouth with the pen, wondering what he should write, when there was nothing to report. Around and above him the ship swayed and dipped in a gentle south-easterly breeze, and he pitied the watch on deck, sweating out another day of relentless glare and fierce sunlight. Even the *Sparrow* seemed to be voicing her protest. The timbers groaned and trembled to the motion, dried out by salt and heat, and through the open windows he saw the carved scrollwork by the sill splitting open, the paint flaking away to reveal bare wood.

Once on station north of the Little Bahama Bank he had anticipated being recalled to more active duty within a matter of weeks. But like most of his men, he had long since given up hope. Week followed week, with *Sparrow* and her attendant sloop, *Heron*, dragging their wearying patrol through July, each dawn bringing an empty horizon, and every hour tightening its grip on their small, isolated existence.

And now it was August. Perhaps Christie had insisted on three months' supplies because he had had no intention of recalling *Sparrow* until the end of that time. Maybe they had all been forgotten, or the war was over. It was as if the whole patrol area had been drained of movement. Unlike their last visit to the Bahama Banks, when they had taken prizes or had gossiped with lawful merchantmen, they had seen nothing. Their routine varied little. Usually they kept *Heron's* topsails just within sight below the horizon, and on a parallel tack swept back and forth well clear of reefs and shoals. With the masthead lookouts of both sloops able to see one another it was possible to sweep an area some sixty miles wide, unless the weather changed against them. Even a real storm would be welcome. But the agonising discomfort was getting everyone down, not least himself.

There was a tap on the door and Dalkeith entered, his round face shining with sweat. The forenoon watch had half run its course, and Bolitho had found it necessary to meet the surgeon at this time every day when he had completed his inspection of the sick.

He gestured to a chair. 'Well?'

Dalkeith groaned and shifted his bulk carefully to avoid the glare from the open skylight.

'Two more down today, sir. I've got them below. A few days' rest might revive 'em for a while.'

Bolitho nodded. It was getting serious. Too much heat and not enough fresh food or fruit. Lock had already opened the last barrel of lemons. After that ..

Dalkeith had been carrying a glass of water which he now stood on the table. It was the colour of tobacco juice. Without comment he took a flat bottle from his pocket and looked at Bolitho for permission to pour himself a stiff glass of rum.

Again, it was one of their little routines. Although how the plump surgeon could stomach rum in this heat was beyond Bolitho.

Dalkeith smacked his lips. 'Better'n this water.' He frowned. 'If we can't get a fresh supply of drinking water I'll not answer for the consequences, sir.'

'I'll do what I can. Maybe we can close with some small island and find a stream. But I am not too hopeful hereabouts. Was that all?'

Dalkeith hesitated. 'I'm supposed to hold my peace, but friendship and duty rarely go hand in hand. It's the first lieutenant.'

'Mr. Tyrrell?' Bolitho tensed. 'What about him?'

'His leg. He tries to pretend it's all right, but I'm not happy about it.' He dropped his eyes. 'Worse, I'm getting anxious.'

'I see.' He had noticed Tyrrell's limp getting more pronounced, but whenever he had mentioned it he had replied, 'It'll pass. Nothin' to bite on!'

'What d'you advise?'

Dalkeith sighed. 'I can probe for more splinters. But if that fails ...' He took another swallow of neat rum. 'I might have to cut it off.'

'Oh God.'

Bolitho walked to the windows and leaned out over the transom. Below, the sea looked very clear, and he could see small darting fish in the rudder's frothing wake.

Behind him he heard Dalkeith add firmly, 'I could do it, of course. But it would have to be while he is still strong. Before the pain and this damn heat gets him down like some of the others.'

Bolitho turned, feeling the sun across his bared back.

'I was not doubting your ability. You've proved that more than enough.'

Dalkeith said grimly, 'I was at a fine hospital in London before I left England.' He grimaced. 'We practised on the poor and worked for the wealthy. It was a hard training ground, but very useful.'

'Will you return when the war is over?' He tried not to think of Tyrrell being held on a table, the saw poised above his leg.

Dalkeith shook his head. 'No. I'll settle out here somewhere. Maybe in America, who can tell?' He gave a wry smile. 'I'm afraid that I had to leave England in somewhat of a hurry. A matter of honour over a lady.'

'I have wondered these three years where you found your skill with pistols.'

Dalkeith nodded. 'Unfortunately, I shot the wrong man. His death was considered a greater loss than mine, so I caught the packet from Dover, and eventually, two years later, I arrived in the Indies.'

'Thank you for telling me.' Bolitho massaged his stomach with the palm of one hand. 'I will see what I can do to obtain a berth in another ship, if and when we are ordered home.'

The surgeon lurched to his feet. 'I would appreciate that.' He watched Bolitho doubtfully. 'And Tyrrell?'

'I'll speak with him.' He turned away. 'In God's name, what do I say? How would I feel if it were me?'

Dalkeith rested his hand on the bulkhead until *Sparrow* had completed a slow uproll.

'I can't answer. I'm just a surgeon.'

'Aye.' Bolitho looked at him gravely. 'And I'm just a captain.'

Midshipman Bethune clattered through the wardroom and paused outside the cabin.

'Mr. Graves's respects, sir. *Heron* has signalled she has sighted an unknown sail to the east'rd.'

'Very well. I'll come up.'

Dalkeith waited for Bethune to go. 'Recall to New York, sir? If so, I could take Tyrrell to a hospital. They have facilities, proper care.'

Bolitho shook his head. 'I fear not. That sail will be from the south'rd to be on such a bearing. Friend or foe, we have yet to see.'

He heard Dalkeith sigh as he left him and hurried up the ladder to the quarterdeck.

He glanced quickly at the helmsman who called hoarsely, 'Nor' nor'-west, sir!' His lips were cracked in the heat.

Graves reported, 'Our masthead has not sighted her yet, sir.' His mouth jerked at one corner and he added quickly, 'Could be anything.'

It was an empty comment, but Bolitho knew it was merely to cover his embarrassment. He had seen the growing strain on Graves perhaps worst of all. Now the twitch in his jaw laid bare his inner torment like the mark of some disease.

'Very well. Call the hands and prepare to run down on *Heron*. Get the t'gallants on her and lay her on the starboard tack.' He saw Buckle climbing wearily through the hatchway and called, 'A sail, Mr. Buckle! Maybe it'll bring us luck today!'

The master pouted. ' 'Bout time, sir.'

Bolitho heard the familiar limping step and turned to see Tyrrell walking from the larboard gangway.

Tyrrell grinned. 'A sail, did I hear, sir?' He shaded his eyes as he watched the men mustering at their stations. 'Now there's a thing indeed!'

Bolitho bit his lip. It made it more painful to see Tyrrell's new contentment. To know what must be done. That was if Dalkeith knew his trade. And he did.

On the horizon he could see *Heron*'s sails glinting brightly, and knew Farr would wait for him to join him. To break the monotony if nothing else.

Within the hour the stranger had identified herself. It was the *Lucifer*, her great schooner sails spread like wings as she ran before the wind, the spray bursting above her jib-boom in a lively silver pattern.

Fowler was in the lee shrouds with a telescope, his small, piggy face glowing with heat.

'From *Lucifer*. *Have despatches on board*.' He looked down at the quarter-deck as if proud of his revelation.

'Heave to, Mr. Tyrrell.'

Bolitho watched the mad dash aboard *Lucifer* to shorten sail and put her about before running down beneath *Sparrow*'s lee. A fine little vessel. Had she been his instead of *Sparrow*, he wondered if his life would have been changed to the same extent.

He saw the haste with which the schooner's boat was being hoisted out above the water. Something acted like a small warning in his mind, and he said, 'Signal *Heron*. Captain repair on board.'

'Aye, aye, sir!' Fowler snapped his fingers and continued to do so until the flags had broken from *Sparrow*'s yard.

Farr's gig hooked on the chains within minutes of *Lucifer*'s jolly boat.

Odell had come aboard in person, and as he removed his hat to the quarterdeck and darted a sharp glance at Bolitho's bare torso, Farr climbed up beside him and said cheerfully, 'By God, what brings you here, man? Were you pining for us in Antigua?'

Odell walked a few paces clear and then faced them.

'The French are out, sir.'

For a moment nobody spoke. Bolitho held the words in his mind, yet was also aware of those about him. Stockdale by the hatchway, slightly stooped as if to hear better. Buckle and Tyrrell, their faces showing astonishment and more. Relief perhaps that the guessing was over.

'Come below.'

Bolitho led them to his cabin, the heat and the drudgery of patrol forgotten.

Odell sat on the edge of a chair, his features giving little hint of strain at driving his command all those miles from Antigua.

Bolitho said quietly, 'Now, tell us.'

'I carried the despatches to the fleet as ordered.'

Odell had a quick, erratic manner of speaking, nodding his head in time with his words. It was not hard to see how he got his reputation for being slightly mad. A man on a knife-edge, Bolitho suspected. But there was no doubting the accuracy of his report.

'Admiral Rodney despatched a fleet of fourteen ships-of-the-line to assist our forces at New York.'

Farr muttered, 'By God, that's more like it. I've no stomach for our Admiral Graves.'

Odell's eyes flashed dangerously at the interruption.

He snapped, 'Rodney has sailed for England. He is a sick man. Hood commands the reinforcements.'

Farr was unabashed. 'Ah well, even better, I've served Admiral Hood and respect him.'

Bolitho said, 'Let us hear all of it. I suspect there is more.'

Odell nodded. 'The Compte de Grasse set sail with some twenty sail-of-the-line. The patrols reported that he was escorting the season's convoy clear of the islands.'

Bolitho said, 'That is quite usual, I believe.'

'Yes. But de Grasse has not been seen since.' The words fell into the cabin like round-shot.

Farr exclaimed, 'A whole fleet! Disappeared? It's bloody impossible!'

'But fact.' Odell glared at him. 'Admiral Hood's ships must have passed this area well to the east'rd. And there are several frigates searching elsewhere.' He spread his hands. 'But of de Grasse there is no sign'

'God!' Farr looked at Bolitho. 'What d'you make of that?'

Odell said testily, 'I could relish a glass, sir. I am as dry as a pauper's loaf.'

Bolitho opened his cupboard and handed him a decanter.

He said, 'Hood will join with Graves at Sandy Hook. They will still be outnumbered, but can give good account if de Grasse chooses to head their way.'

Farr said less firmly, 'And Hood will show the damn Frogs, eh?'

Bolitho replied, 'His fleet is larger than Admiral Graves's. But Graves is senior now that Rodney has gone home.' He looked at Farr's anxious face. 'I am afraid Graves will lead our forces if and when the time comes.'

He turned to Odell, who was drinking his second glass of wine.

'Do you know anything else?'

He shrugged. 'I understood that Admiral Hood will examine Chesapeake Bay while on passage to New York. Some believe the French may strike at Cornwallis's army from the sea. If not, then New York is to be the melting pot.'

Bolitho made himself sit down. It was strange to be so moved by Odell's information. For months, even years, they had expected some great confrontation at sea. There had been skirmishes and bitter ship-to-ship actions in plenty. But this was what they had all known would happen sooner or later. Who commanded the waters around America controlled the destiny of those who fought within its boundaries.

He said, 'One thing is certain, we are doing no good here.'

Farr asked, 'Are you saying *we* should join the fleet?'

'Something like that.'

He tried to clear his mind, put Odell's brief facts into perspective. De Grasse could be anywhere, but it was ridiculous to imagine he had sailed back to France, his mission left incomplete. Without his presence in the Indies, the British would be able to throw every ship and man into the fight for America, and de Grasse was astute enough to know his own value.

He moved to the table and pulled a chart from its rack. It was close on seven hundred miles to Cape Henry at the mouth of Chesapeake Bay. With the wind remaining friendly they could make landfall in five days. If Admiral Hood's ships were lying there he could request further orders. Sloops would be more than useful for searching close inshore or relaying signals in a fleet action.

Bolitho said slowly, 'I intend to head north. To the Chesapeake.'

Farr stood up and exclaimed, 'Good! I'm with you.'

Odell asked, 'Are you taking full responsibility, sir?' His eyes were opaque.

'Yes. I would wish you to remain here in case any ships come this way. If they do, you can come after us with all haste.'

'Very well, sir.' Odell added calmly, 'I would like it in writing.'

'Damn your eyes, you impudent puppy!' Farr thumped the table with his fist. 'Where's your bloody trust?'

Odell shrugged. 'I trust Captain Bolitho, have no doubts, *sir*.' He gave a quick smile. 'But if he and you are both killed, who is to say I only obeyed orders?'

Bolitho nodded. 'That is fair. I will do it directly.' He saw the two men watching each other with open hostility. 'Easy now. Right or wrong, it will be good to move again. So let's not start with disharmony, eh?'

Odell showed his teeth. 'I meant no offence, sir.'

Farr swallowed hard. 'In that case, I suppose . . .' He grinned broadly, 'But by God, Odell, you push me to the limit!'

'A glass together.'

Bolitho wanted to go on deck, to share his news with Tyrrell and the others. But he knew this moment was equally vital. Just a few seconds, which each would remember when the other ships were mere silhouettes.

He raised his glass. 'What shall it be, my friends?'

Farr met his eye and smiled. He at least understood. 'To *us*, Dick. That will do fine for me.'

Bolitho placed his empty glass on the table. A simple toast. But, King, Cause, even Country were too remote, the future too uncertain. They had only each other and their three little ships to sustain them.

With legs braced against *Sparrow*'s uncomfortable, corkscrewing motion, Bolitho levelled a telescope across the nettings and waited for the shoreline to settle in the lens. It was close on sunset, and as the dull orange glow withdrew beyond the nearest shoulder of land he forced himself to concentrate on what he saw, rather than what he had anticipated from his charts. Around him other glasses were also trained, and he heard Tyrrell's heavy breathing at his side, the squeak of a pencil on Buckle's slate by the wheel.

Within a few miles of Cape Henry, the southernmost cape at the entrance of Chesapeake Bay, the wind had backed sharply, and backed again. A full day had been added to their previously fast passage, and as they had clawed desperately from a lee shore, had fought to obtain sea room, Bolitho had watched the bay fading across the quarter with something like anger. And now, after their long beat back towards the entrance, he was faced by a new decision. To lie offshore until dawn, or take his chance and thrust between Cape Henry and the northern headland in what would certainly be total darkness.

Tyrrell lowered his glass. 'I know this entrance well. There's a great middle-ground which reaches into th' bay. With care you can pass either side, but with th' wind under our coat-tails I'd suggest trying th' southern channel. If you stay to lee'rd of th' middle-ground you can hold mebbe three miles clear of Cape Henry.' He rubbed his chin. 'If you misjudge and tack too far to south'rd. You'll have to move lively. There are shoals off th' cape, an' bad ones at that'

Bolitho shifted the telescope to watch some dancing red flashes far inland.

Tyrrell remarked, 'Cannon. Good way off.'

Bolitho nodded. If Tyrrell was feeling the strain of drawing so near to his home territory he did not show it.

Tyrrell continued, 'Up beyond York River, I reckon. Heavy artillery, by th' looks of it.'

Heyward, who was standing nearby, said, 'No sign of any ships, sir.'

'There wouldn't be.' Tyrrell was watching Bolitho. 'Just around Cape Henry lies Lynnhaven Bay. Good shelter where big ships anchor sometimes when there's foul weather around. No, you'd not even see a fleet from out here.' He paused. 'You'd have to go inside th' old Chesapeake.'

Bolitho handed the glass to Fowler. 'I agree. If we wait longer the wind might veer. We'd be on a lee shore again and lose more time fighting clear from it.'

He turned to look for *Heron*. Her reefed topsails were still holding the fast fading sunlight, but beyond her the sea was in deep shadow.

'Show the signal lantern to *Heron*. Captain Farr knows what to do.'

He turned to Tyrrell. 'The place is badly charted.'

Tyrrell grinned, his eyes glowing in the dull light. 'Unless things have changed, I reckon I can take us through.'

Fowler called, 'Signal passed, sir!'

Bolitho made up his mind. 'Alter course two points to starboard.' To Tyrrell he added slowly, 'I hate entering any bay like this one. I feel more secure in open sea.'

The lieutenant sighed. 'Aye. Th' Chesapeake is a brute in many ways. North to south it measures close on a hundred an' forty miles. You can sail a fair-sized craft right up to Baltimore without too much hardship. But it measures lessn' thirty across, an' that's only where the Patowmack flows into it.'

Buckle called, 'Course sou'-west, sir.'

'Very well.'

Bolitho watched the nearest headland of Cape Charles losing its bronze crest as the sun finally dipped behind a line of hills.

'You may clear for action, Mr. Tyrrell. Better safe than sorry.'

He wondered briefly what Farr was thinking as he tacked to follow *Sparrow*'s shadow towards the dark mass of land. Doubt, regret, even mistrust. You could hardly blame him. It was like groping for coal in a shuttered cellar.

Under his shoes he felt the planks quiver to the hurrying seamen, the thud of screens being torn down and mess tables dragged clear of tackles and guns. That was another difference he had found in *Sparrow*. Even clearing for action had a sort of intimacy which was lacking in a ship-of-the-line. In *Trojan* the hands had scurried to quarters, urged on by the drums' staccato beat and the blare of a marine's bugle. Sometimes you never knew men who did not serve in your own watch or division. But here it was entirely different. Men nodded to each other as they dashed to their stations, a grin here, a brief touch of hands there. In many ways it made death harder to accept, a man's cries too personal to ignore.

'Cleared for action, sir.'

'Good.' Bolitho gripped the nettings and watched the tiny feathers of surf far abeam. 'Alter course another point.'

'Aye, sir.' Buckle was muttering to his helmsmen. Then, 'Sou'-west by south, sir.'

'Hold her steady.'

He moved restlessly below the great spanker, seeing a faint glow on the boom from the compass bowl.

There were already plenty of stars in the velvet sky, and there would be a moon on the water in a few hours. But by then he must be inside the bay.

Tyrrell joined him by the wheel. 'It's a strange feeling. My sister'll be no more than fifty miles from where I'm standing. I can still remember it clearly. Th' York River, th' place in th' woods where we used to get together as kids . . .' He turned and said sharply, 'Let her fall off a point, Mr. Buckle! Mr. Bethune, take some men forrard and trim the foreyard again!' He waited until he was satisfied with the ship's head and the bearing of the nearest cape and continued, 'It's a funny business all round'.

Bolitho agreed. After the first few weeks he had not thought much about Susannah Hardwicke. Now, as he pictured an unknown girl out there in the darkness beyond the occasional flash of gunfire, he realised how their lives had become merged. Tyrrell's sister, and Graves's secret longings for her. Dalkeith's affair of honour which had cost him his career and almost his life. And himself? He was surprised he could still not examine her memory without regret and a sense of loss.

When he looked again he realised that Cape Charles had merged with the shadows. A quick glance at Tyrrell reassured him. He seemed relaxed, even cheerful, as he stood where he could watch the compass and the set of the spanker overhead. But for the treacherous span of middle-ground, they could have sailed boldly between the capes with a comfortable four miles or more on either beam.

Tyrrell said, 'We will alter course again, with your permission, sir.'

'She's in your hands.'

Tyrrell grinned. 'Aye, aye, sir.' To Buckle he called, 'Steer west by north, full an' bye!'

Then he cupped his hands and yelled, 'Pipe th' hands to th' braces!'

With the helm down and the seamen hauling at the braces, *Sparrow* turned her bows towards the land. Voices called in the gloom, and above the decks the paler shapes of arms and legs moved busily about the yards.

'West by north, sir!' Buckle peered at the flapping sails as the ship heeled still further, close-hauled on the starboard tack.

Tyrrell limped from side to side, his arm darting out to catch a man's attention, or his voice sending another to pass his orders right forward where Graves was equally busy.

'Right, lads! Belay there!' He cocked his head as if to listen to the chorus of shrouds and vibrating halliards. 'She's loving it!'

Bolitho walked up to the weather side and felt the cold spray across his face. Tyrrell had come and gone through these capes many times in his father's schooner. Perhaps that memory, and the realisation that his sister was now safe and close at hand, made him forget the purpose of their mission, the chance of danger with each passing minute.

'Breakers on the weather bow!' The lookout sounded nervous.

But Tyrrell called, 'Breakers be damned! That'll be th' middle-ground.' His teeth gleamed in the darkness. 'True as a bloody arrow, if I do say so myself!'

Bolitho smiled at his excitement. *Breakers be damned!* He had used much the same phrase and tone when he had driven his sword through the man who had almost killed him beside the pond.

The massive, looming shoulder of Cape Henry hardened from the darkness on the larboard beam, and for a brief instant Bolitho imagined they were too close, that the wind had thrust them further downwind than Tyrrell had allowed.

He dragged his eyes to the opposite side, and through the spray and across the deep inshore swell he saw a revolving patch of white. The middle-ground was clearly marked by the swirl of broken water, but if Tyrrell had misjudged his approach it would have been too late to avoid it.

Tyrrell shouted, 'Once saw a damn fine Dutchman aground there! She broke her back!'

Buckle muttered, 'That's bloody encouraging!'

Bolitho peered astern. 'I hope *Heron*'s seen our entrance.'

'She'll be fine.' Tyrrell hurried to the side and studied the darker wedge of land. 'She draws less and is better to handle close-hauled.' He patted the rail. 'But *Sparrow*'ll do for me!'

'Take in the forecourse, if you please.' Bolitho pitched his ear to the sea's changing sounds. The hollow boom of surf against rocks, the deeper note of water exploring a cave or some narrow gully below the headland. 'Then the spanker.'

Under topsails and jib *Sparrow* crept deeper into the bay, her stem rising and plunging across tiderace and swell alike, her helmsmen tensed at the wheel, fingers sensing her will almost as soon as she did.

Minutes dragged by, then an half-hour. With eyes straining into the darkness, and other men poised at gun-port tackles and braces, the sloop tacked delicately below the cape.

Then Tyrrell said, 'No ships here, sir. Lynnhaven lies abeam now. Any squadron at anchor, ours or th' Frogs, would be showing some sort of light. To deter an enemy, if for no other reason.'

'That makes good sense.'

Bolitho walked away to hide his disappointment. Odell had been right to ask for written orders, for if Bolitho had misjudged Hood's whereabouts this badly he could be equally at fault for quitting his proper station in the south.

A series of dull explosions echoed across the water, and one bright stab of flame, as if some powder had been accidentally fired.

He ran his fingers through his hair, wondering what he should do next. Sail on for New York? It seemed the only solution.

Tyrrell said quietly, 'If we are to beat clear of th' cape, then I suggest we wear ship now.' He paused. 'Or anchor.'

Bolitho joined him by the compass. 'Then we anchor. We must make contact with the army. They at least should know what is happening'.

Tyrrell sighed. 'It's hard to think that there's a damn great army out there across our bows. Poor bastards. If they are in Yorktown as Odell was led to believe, then they are well placed. But it'll be no comfort if they come under siege.'

'Let's waste no more time.' Bolitho beckoned to Fowler. 'Show the lantern again. Captain Farr will anchor when he sees the signal.'

The topsails stirred noisily as *Sparrow* turned obediently into the wind, her anchor throwing up a sheet of spray like some disturbed water-spirit.

Buckle called, 'Easy with that light, Mr. Fowler! Enough is enough!'

Tyrrell dropped his voice. 'No matter. We'll have been sighted from th' moment we weathered th' cape.'

Bolitho looked at him. It was not difficult to picture some scurrying messenger or a mounted man riding through the darkness to warn of their arrival. He felt much as he had done in Delaware Bay. Cut off and restricted, with only the vaguest idea of what was happening.

Tyrrell said, 'I can take a boat, sir. If th' army is encamped in th' town, then they'll be well shielded around th' next spit of land along York River.' He sounded suddenly on edge. 'God, this quiet disturbs me more'n gunfire! My grandfather was a soldier. Used to make my flesh creep with his yarns of night fighting.'

Bolitho watched the topmen sliding down to the deck, seemingly indifferent to the closeness of land or a possible enemy.

'Rig boarding nets and have half the twelve-pounders loaded with grape.'

Tyrrell nodded. 'Aye. An' I'll put some good hands on th' swivels, too. No sense in being rushed by some crazy boat attack.' He waited and then asked, 'Shall I go?'

'Very well. Take both cutters. Mr. Graves can command the second one. Mr. Fowler will go with you in case we need any signals made.'

A voice called, '*Heron*'s anchored, sir!

But when Bolitho looked across the nettings he could see nothing. The lookout must have caught a brief glimpse of her reefed topsails as she edged around the cape, or the splash of her anchor when she let go.

Tackles creaked and jerked as both cutters were swayed over the gangways before the decks were sealed off in a web of nets. That could be left safely to the boatswain. Not too taut to afford a grip to some daring boarder, just slack enough to confuse him, to allow a pike or bayonet to catch him before he could slip free.

Men shuffled across the deck, and he heard an occasional clink of steel, the thud of oars being released from their lashings.

Graves came aft, his breeches white in the darkness.

'You know what to do?' Bolitho looked at each in turn. 'Mr. Tyrrell will lead. Muffle your oars, and watch out for enemy pickets.'

Graves sounded breathless. 'How will we recognise our own soldiers?'

Bolitho could imagine his mouth jerking uncontrollably and was tempted to keep him on board. But Tyrrell was all important. He knew the lay of the land like his own cabin. It needed an experienced officer to back him if things went wrong.

He heard Tyrrell reply calmly, 'Easy. Th' Frogs speak French!'

Graves swung round and then controlled himself with an effort.

'I – I didn't ask for your sarcasm! It's all right for you. This is your country.'

'That will do!' Bolitho stepped closer. 'Remember, our people are depending on you. So let's have none of this bickering.'

Tyrrell eased his sword in its sheath. 'I'm sorry, sir. It was my fault.' He rested his hand on Graves's shoulder. 'Forget I spoke, eh?'

Fowler's voice came up from the boats. 'All ready, sir!'

Bolitho walked to the gangway. 'Be back by dawn.' He touched Tyrrell's arm. 'How is the pain now?'

'Hardly feel a thing, sir.' Tyrrell stood back to allow his men to clamber into the cutters. 'A bit of exercise will do me good.'

The boats shoved off and pulled steadily into the darkness. Within minutes they had vanished, and a watchful silence settled over those who stood at the loaded guns on either beam.

Bolitho sought out Stockdale and said, 'Have the gig lowered. I may want word carried to *Heron*.' He saw Bethune's plump outline by the rail and added, 'You take the gig and pull round the ship. I will signal if I need a message passed.'

Bethune hesitated. 'I would have willingly gone with the first lieutenant, sir.'

'I know that.' It was hard to believe that in the midst of all this confusion Bethune had managed to see his choice of Fowler as a personal slur. 'He is very young. I need all the *men* I can get to manage the ship.' It was a lame explanation, but it seemed to suffice.

It was cool under the stars, and after the heat of the day, a gentle relief. Bolitho kept the seamen in short watches, so that those not on lookout or standing at the guns might snatch a few moments' rest.

Likewise, the officers stood watch and watch, and when he was relieved by Heyward, Bolitho squatted against the mainmast trunk and rested his head in his hands.

He felt someone gripping his wrist and knew he must have fallen asleep.

Heyward was crouching beside him, his voice a fierce whisper. 'Boat approaching, sir, maybe two.'

Bolitho scrambled to his feet, his mind grappling with Heyward's words. Surely they were not returning already. They could not even have reached the first part of their destination.

Heyward said, 'It's not the gig. She's away on the starboard quarter.'

Bolitho cupped his hands round his ears. Above the slap of water alongside he heard oars and the squeak of a tiller.

A boatswain's mate asked, 'Shall I call a challenge, sir?'

'No.' Why had he said that? 'Not yet.'

He strained his eyes and tried to pick out the splash of oars amidst the lapping cat's-paws of the bay. It had to be Tyrrell returning for he was coming straight for the ship without caution or hesitation.

A thin shaft of moonlight had made a small rippling pattern across the water, and as he watched a longboat glided into it, the oars moving unhurriedly.

Before it slid once more into shadows Bolitho saw the gleam of crossbelts, some soldiers wearing shakos crowded in the sternsheets.

Heyward gasped hoarsely, 'Holy God, they're French!'

The boatswain's mate whispered, 'There's another one astern of 'er!'

Thoughts and wild ideas flooded through Bolitho's mind as he watched the boats' slow approach. Tyrrell and his men captured and being returned for parley. The French coming to announce that Yorktown was theirs and to demand *Sparrow*'s surrender.

He moved quickly to the gangway and cupped his hands. *'Ohé! du canot! Qui va la?'*

There was a babble of voices from the boat and he heard someone laughing.

To Heyward he snapped. 'Quick, recall the gig! We'll catch these beauties with any luck!'

The first boat was already grinding alongside, and Bolitho held his breath, half expecting one of his own men to fire.

From a corner of his eye he saw a cream of spray, and thanked God that the gig's crew had kept their wits. It was sweeping around the stern, and he could imagine Stockdale willing his men to pull with all their strength.

Heyward came back, the signal lantern still in his hand.

Bolitho shouted, *'Now!'*

Even as the first men appeared on the chains and clung uncertainly to the nets, a line of armed seamen leapt on to the gangway with levelled muskets, while Glass, the boatswain, swung a swivel gun and trained it threateningly.

There was a chorus of shouts and a musket stabbed fire through the night. The ball slammed into the rail and brought a savage fusilade of shots from Heyward's marksmen.

Glass depressed the swivel and jerked the lanyard, changing the crowded boat into a screaming, bloody shambles.

It was more than enough for the second boat. The crash of musket fire, the devastating hail of canister from Glass's swivel were sufficient to render the oars motionless. Hardly a man moved as the gig tore alongside and made fast, and across the choppy water Stockdale bawled, 'Got 'er, sir!' A pause and he called again, 'There's a dozen English prisoners in this 'un!'

Bolitho turned away, feeling sick. He saw Dalkeith and his mates climbing down to the boat alongside and pictured the whimpering carnage he would find there. It could just as easily have been the second boat and the canister would have carved its bloody path amongst their own people.

He said harshly, 'Get those men aboard, Mr. Heyward. Then send the gig to *Heron*. Farr will be wondering what the hell we are about.'

He waited beside the entry port, as with boarding nets lifted the first dazed men were pushed or hauled aboard. The second boatload, French and English alike, came with obvious relief. The French glad to have been spared their companion's slaughter. The English redcoats had different reasons, but their stunned disbelief was pitiful to watch.

Bedraggled and filthy, they were more like scarecrows than trained soldiers.

Bolitho said, 'Take the prisoners below, Mr. Glass.' To the redcoats he added, 'Have no fear. This is a King's ship.'

One, a young ensign, stepped forward and exclaimed, 'I thank you, Captain. We all do.'

Bolitho gripped his hand. 'You will get all the rest and help I can offer. But first I must know what is happening here.'

The officer rubbed his eyes with his knuckles. 'We were taken several days back. It was a skirmish with one of their patrols. Most of my men were killed.' He rocked on his feet. 'I still cannot believe we are saved ...'

Bolitho persisted, 'Is General Cornwallis holding Yorktown?'

'Yes. But as I expect you know, sir, Washington and the French general, Rochambeau, crossed the Hudson some weeks back to the head of Chesapeake Bay. They have a great army massed around Yorktown. A musket behind every tree. But when we heard that an English squadron had looked into the bay we thought we were relieved. I understand a little French and heard the guards speaking of their arrival.'

Heyward said, 'Hood's ships.'

Bolitho nodded. 'When was this?'

The ensign shrugged. 'Three days back. I have lost count of time.'

Bolitho tried to shut out the pitiful cries alongside. He knew little French. Little more than he had used to deceive the boat, but sufficient to recognise pleading. A man being held while Dalkeith got busy with his knife.

Three days back. That fitted what Odell had reported. Hood must have taken a quick look into the bay, and finding no sign of de Grasse had pushed on for New York.

The ensign added weakly. 'The French are expecting their own fleet. That was why, when someone hailed them in their own language, they ...'

What?' Bolitho seized his arm, his voice harsh despite the man's condition. 'Expecting their own fleet?'

The ensign stared at him. 'But I thought ... I imagined our ships had gone to fight them off, sir!'

'No.' He released his arm. 'I fear that when they reach New York and discover their mistake it will be too late.'

'Then the army is done for, sir.' The ensign walked unsteadily to the rail. 'All this.' He shouted across the dark water. 'All for *bloody nothing*!'

Dalkeith appeared on deck and with a brief nod took the officer's arm.

Bolitho said, 'Take care of them for me.'

He turned away. They would be prisoners again very soon unless he could decide what to do.

Buckle was watching him anxiously. 'What about Mr. Tyrrell, sir?'

'D'you imagine I've not thought about him?' He saw Buckle recoil. 'We will pass the word to Heron immediately. If she can work clear tonight Farr must carry the news to Admiral Graves. There might still be time.' He saw the purser hovering by the hatch. 'Fetch some paper and I will write a note for Farr.'

To Buckle he added, 'I'm sorry I abused you. It was a fair question'.

He looked towards the land. 'We will weigh at first light and move closer inshore. Have the sweeps ready in case the wind loses us. I'll not throw Tyrrell and his men away without a fight.' He remembered the lieutenant's words in that far off garden. *In* Sparrow *we look after our own.* He added quietly, 'We've all come too far together for that.'

Dalkeith crossed the deck as Bolitho walked to the taffrail. To Buckle he whispered, 'What's the captain going to do?'

Buckle shrugged. 'Something crazy, I expect.'

The surgeon wiped his hands on a piece of waste. 'But you approve, nonetheless?'

Buckle grinned. 'Don't make much difference what I think, does it? But I s'pect he'll think of something.' He added vehemently, 'I bloody well hope so, for all our sakes!'

18

Only the Brave

Stockdale padded across the quarterdeck and held out a pewter mug.

' 'Ere, sir. Some coffee.'

Bolitho took it and held it to his lips. It was barely hot, but cleared the dryness from his throat.

Stockdale added thickly, 'The galley fire was doused, so I 'ad to warm it on a lantern in the shot locker.'

Bolitho looked at him. Was it imagination, or were Stockdale's features growing more distinct in the gloom? He shivered. More likely he had been too long on deck, waiting and wondering. Yet he could do no good by pacing the deck and going over his ideas again and again.

'It was a kind thought.' He handed him the mug. 'I feel awake now.'

He peered up at the rigging and furled sails. The stars were still there, but paler. That was no illusion.

'Where is the wind?'

Stockdale considered the question. 'As afore, sir. Nor' nor'-east, if I'm not mistook.'

Bolitho bit his lip. He had already decided it was so. Stockdale was usually right, but his confirmation did little to help.

He said, 'Rouse the master. He is by the hatchway.'

Buckle sprang to his feet, wide awake at Stockdale's first touch.

'What is it? An attack?'

'Easy, Mr. Buckle.' Bolitho beckoned him to the rail. 'The wind has dropped, but still too far north'rd to help us.'

The master said nothing and waited to see what the captain had in mind.

'If we are to be of any use, we must drive higher into the bay. It would take hours of tacking back and forth, with little to show for our pains. But if we stay here at anchor we can help neither the first lieutenant nor ourselves if an enemy arrives.'

Buckle yawned. 'That's true enough.'

'So call all hands and run out the sweeps. We will get under way and not wait for the dawn.'

Buckle pulled out his watch and held it against the compass light.

'Hmm. It'll be a hard pull, sir. But the current will not be too much against us.'

He walked to the nettings and kicked a shadowy figure who was sleeping soundly on the bare planks.

'Up, boy! Tell Mr. Glass to call the hands. Jump to it!'

Bolitho went quickly to his cabin and concentrated for several minutes on his chart. Recalling what Tyrrell had told him, and adding the information to what he knew already, he settled on his plan of action. Beyond the cabin he could hear the tramp of feet at the capstan, the regular clink of a pawl as the cable came inboard.

He put on his coat and adjusted his swordbelt. How strange the cabin looked in the solitary lantern's light. Cleared for action like the rest of his ship, the guns creaking gently behind their sealed ports, powder and shot, rammers and sponges, all within easy reach. But no one stood near them, for like the remainder of the gun deck, every hand would be needed to raise anchor and man the long sweeps. The latter had got them out of trouble before. This time they might do the same for Tyrrell and his men.

He left the cabin and ran swiftly up the ladder.

It was lighter. There could be no doubt about it. A sort of greyness above Cape Henry, and he could see the swirl of currents well clear of the hull.

He saw the long sweeps swaying above the water on either beam, the men hunched around them, chattering quietly while they awaited an order from aft.

Heyward touched his hat. 'Anchor's hove short, sir.' He sounded tense and very alert.

Bolitho strode from side to side, watching the ship's swing towards the shore, the ripple of water below the gangways.

'How does it feel? From midshipman to first lieutenant with barely a pause?'

He did not hear Heyward's reply, and knew he had only asked the question to cover his own anxiety. If the men lost control of the sweeps he would have to anchor immediately. Even then he might be driven too close inshore for comfort.

From forward he heard Bethune's cry, 'Anchor's aweigh, sir!' The patter of feet as men ran from the capstan bars to add their weight on the sweeps.

Then Glass's voice, 'Steady! *Stand by!*'

Bolitho gripped his hands together until the fingers almost cracked. Why the hell was he leaving it so late? In a moment the ship would be aground.

'Give way all!'

The sweeps swayed forward, dipped and then came steadily aft.

Behind him Bolitho heard the wheel easing gently, and Buckle's quiet cursing as he endured the tension in his own style. He tried to relax his muscles. Glass had been right to make sure of that first stroke. But it was one thing to know it, another to remain aloof in the face of danger to his ship.

Up and down, forward to aft, the sweeps creaked busily but without undue haste, until Buckle called, 'Steerage way, sir!'

Good. Hold her due north, if you please.'

Heyward removed his coat. 'I'll go and lend a hand, sir.'

'Yes. Make sure we have every available man working. Those redcoats as well, if they have the strength.' He checked him as he ran for the ladder. 'There is no need to tell the soldiers we are heading *towards* the enemy, Mr. Heyward!' He saw him grin. 'They'll find out soon enough.'

Buckle and a solitary seaman stood at the wheel, and Bolitho walked right aft to the taffrail without speaking. He saw the nearest cape more clearly now, the pattern of white-caps at its base to mark some small cove. An empty place. When daylight came, and *Heron* was seen to be gone, his men might question his action, and rightly. But if their presence was to be of any use to the admiral, then they must learn everything possible. The released soldiers had told them much. But a lot could have changed since they had been taken. He smiled grimly. He was deluding himself. But for Tyrrell and the others, would he really have remained here in the bay?

He heard shouts on deck and someone speaking in French. Heyward was more than a good companion, he was proving to be an excellent officer. Without further consultation, and at the risk of his captain's displeasure, he had released the French prisoners and put them to work. All strong, beefy soldiers who had led a fairly comfortable life guarding prisoners, they would make a small but significant difference to the heavy sweeps.

Some gulls rose screaming angrily from the water where they had been sleeping as the *Sparrow* moved amongst them at a slow but steady crawl. Time dragged by, and Bolitho saw that the soldiers' coats were red again instead of black as they had appeared in the darkness. Faces regained personality, and he was able to see those who were standing the strain and others who were being relieved at more frequent intervals to regain their breath.

A blacker shadow loomed and held firm across the starboard bow. That must be the inner side of Cape Charles, he decided, with Tyrrell's middle-ground some distance below it.

'Bring her up a point, Mr. Buckle.' He heard the helm squeak. 'We must pass the cape with the mainland to larboard. There'll not be too much water in the channel, so hold her steady.'

'Aye, sir. Nor' by east it is!'

The ship was heading almost directly into the wind, and he could feel it on his face, smell the land and its freshness in the dawn air. But it was more sheltered, and he was relieved to see the sweeps were still moving in unison, although the actual progress was probably less than a knot.

He sought out the young ensign and called him aft. He arrived panting on the quarterdeck, and Bolitho said, 'Look abeam. How near are your outposts?'

The soldier peered across the larboard nettings and raised one arm.

'That bit of land, sir. That'll be the turning point. A lot of sand there. We lost some barges a few weeks back when they ran ashore. A mile or so further and you'll be able to see the mouth of York River just beyond a pair of small islands."

Bolitho smiled. 'I expect you're surprised we're heading this way.'

The ensign shrugged. 'I am past surprise, sir.' He stiffened. 'I heard a bugle. That'll be our lads.' He tapped the rail with his fingers, his face engrossed. Then there was a long-drawn-out trumpet call, which sent a cloud of gulls flapping and squeaking from the land. He said, 'The Frogs. Always a minute behind our reveille.'

Bolitho tried to break him from his mood. 'What of the Americans?'

The ensign sighed. 'They have artillery over the river. They'll start firing at first light. More effective than any damn bugle!'

Bolitho turned towards Buckle. 'We will keep on this course as long as our people have strength for it. The wind will favour us when we finally go about, but I want to get as far above York River as I can.'

He looked aloft and saw the masthead pendant for the first time. It was flapping gently astern, but showed no warning of a strengthening wind. If it got up now, his men would be unable to hold the stroke. Even with Tyrrell's boat crews it would have been hard. Without them, impossible.

When he glanced abeam he saw the over hanging spur of Cape Charles, and far beyond it, like a thin gold thread, the horizon. Showing its face to the sun which was easing into view, parting sea from sky, night from day.

There was a muffled bang, and seconds later he saw the telltale white fin of spray to mark where a ball had ploughed into the bay.

The ensign remarked indifferently, 'They'll never reach you at this range. You've a good half a mile to play with.'

'Where is the battery?'

The soldier studied him curiously. 'Everywhere, sir. There are guns right round this sector. Yorktown and its approaches are hemmed in a ring of iron. Our army has the sea at its back.' He suddenly looked very young and vulnerable. 'Only the fleet can being relief.'

Bolitho pictured Farr's *Heron* making all haste towards New York. Even there he might find Hood gone, perhaps further still to Newport to contain de Barras.

He thought, too, of Odell's solitary vigil in his *Lucifer*. If the French did come by way of the little used Bahama Channel, he would need no encouragement to make sail and run.

He blinked as a shaft of sunlight played across the distant cape and coloured the yards and stays like honey. He pulled out his watch. Tyrrell should have made his contact with Cornwallis's pickets and be on his way back to Lynnhaven by now. By weighing and putting the men to the sweeps, their meeting should have been brought forward by an hour at least.

Glass ran up the ladder, his chest heaving from exertion.

'Can't hold 'em much longer, sir!' He peered down at the sweeps, at their sluggish rise and fall. 'Shall I put the rope's end to 'em, sir?'

'You will not.' Bolitho looked away. There was no malice in Glass, nor was he prone to unnecessary force. It was just that he did not know what else to do. 'Tell them. Another half hour. Then we make sail, or anchor.'

Glass shifted awkwardly. 'It'd be better from you, sir.'

Bolitho walked to the rail and called, 'One more turn of the glass, lads!' He heard groans, the mingled curses and gasps from those still hidden in shadow. 'It's that or leave our people out there to fend for themselves! Remember, it might have been you!'

He turned away, not knowing if his words had achieved anything but resentment.

Glass watched critically and then spat on his hands. 'That done it, sir! Better already!'

Bolitho sighed. The stroke looked as weary as before, but if the boatswain was satisfied, then ...

He swung round as a voice called, 'Boat, sir! Fine on the larboard bow!'

Bolitho gripped the rail. 'Just the one?'

'Aye, sir.'

'Bring her round two points to larboard.'

Bolitho tried not to think about the missing boat. He felt the hull yaw, the stroke failing as the helm went over.

The soldier said quietly, 'No closer, I pray you. You'll be in cannon-shot before long.'

Bolitho ignored him. '*Pull*, lads! Come on, do your damndest!'

One man fell exhausted from a loom and was dragged away by Dalkeith.

The lookout yelled, 'It's the second cutter, sir! Mr. Graves!'

Dalkeith heaved himself up the ladder and stood at the rail.

'I *know* what you're thinking, sir.' He did not flinch under Bolitho's cold stare. 'He'd not leave you. Not for anything.'

Bolitho looked past his shoulder at a patch of land. In the strengthening light he saw tall trees and a round hill beyond. They were motionless. The sweeps were only keeping *Sparrow* steady against wind and current. In a minute she would start to pay-off and drift inshore. They had done their best. It was not enough.

He snapped, 'Damn your eyes, Mr. Dalkeith! I'll not be lectured by you!' He leaned over the rail. 'Mr. Heyward! Stand by to let go the anchor!'

Bolitho waited while men ran to the call and Glass sent others to bear down on the flagging sweeps where exhausted sailors had fallen to the deck. He heard a bang and saw a ball ricochet across the water to throw up a plume of spray very close to the approaching cutter. The boat was moving rapidly towards him, and he could see Graves by the tiller, his hat awry as he beat out the time to his oarsmen.

'Ready, sir!'

He chopped with his arm. 'Let go!'

Even as the anchor took grip and the hull swung carelessly to the cable, he yelled, 'Withdraw sweeps! Mr. Glass, *get those men on their feet!*'

Dalkeith stood his ground. 'You can't blame yourself, sir.' He met Bolitho's gaze stubbornly. 'Curse me if you will, but I'll not stand by and see you torment yourself.'

The cutter was hooking on to the main chains, and he heard Graves shouting at the men on deck to make fast his lines.

He said quietly, 'Thank you for your concern. But there is no one else to blame.'

He made himself wait by the rail until Graves had scrabbled aboard, and then called sharply, 'Lay aft, if you please! The boatswain can deal with the cutter.'

Graves hurried towards him, his face twitching violently.

Bolitho asked, 'Where are the others?' He kept his voice very calm, but was conscious of his whole being screaming at Graves's stricken face.

'We grounded in some shallows, sir. Both boats separated. It was the first lieutenant's idea. A patrol of soldiers had signalled where we should secure the boats, but there was some shooting. Enemy marksmen, I believe.'

'And then?' He could feel others standing nearby, see Heyward's frozen expression as he listened to Graves's quick, erratic account.

'In the darkness we were all trying to take cover. I lost a man, and Tyrrell sent word for us to stay hidden in a creek.' He shook his head vaguely. 'The balls were flying everywhere. Tyrrell was going to meet one of the officers. They knew we were coming, apparently. Their scouts had seen us.' His mouth jerked uncontrollably. 'We stayed there waiting, and then there was more firing, and I heard men charging through the brush, there must have been a platoon or more!'

'Did you not think of going to assist Mr. Tyrrell!?'

Graves stared at him, his eyes blank. 'We were in mortal danger! I sent Fowler to find the others, but...'

'You did *what?*' Bolitho reached out and gripped his coat. 'You sent that boy on his own?'

'He – he volunteered, sir.' Graves looked down at Bolitho's hand on his coat. 'When he failed to return I decided to' – he raised his eyes, suddenly composed – 'to obey your orders and withdraw to the ship.'

Bolitho released his hold and turned away. He felt sick and appalled with what Graves had done. The lieutenant's pathetic defiance made it worse, if that were possible. He had obeyed orders. So his crime was acceptable.

A puff of smoke rose above the nearest spit of land, and he saw the ball drop within half a cable of the ship. Even now, some officer might be ordering up a heavier gun. One which would make short work of so promising a target.

He heard himself say, 'Tell Mr. Yule to run out the larboard bow chaser and lay it on that gunsmoke. He will fire with grape until I order otherwise. It might cool their eagerness.'

He walked past Graves without a glance.

'Have the cutter manned at once.' He looked down at the silent seamen on the gun deck. 'I want volunteers for...' He swallowed as the assembled men moved towards the side as if drawn by wires. 'Thank you. But just a boat's crew. Mr. Glass, see to it at once!'

To Heyward he added, 'You will remain here.' He did not look at Graves. 'If I fall, *you* will assist the master in getting the ship under way, understood?'

Heyward nodded, his eyes filling his face.

Dalkeith touched his arm. '*Look*, sir!'

It was the other cutter, or what was left of it. Even in the poor light it was possible to see the splintered gunwale, the few remaining oars which moved it so very slowly on the uneasy water.

There was a bang and another waterspout shot skyward just beyond it. The hidden gun had shifted to a smaller but closer target.

Bolitho flinched as Yule's crew fired their first shot from forward, saw the trees quiver as if in a freak gust as the packed grape scythed towards the drifting smoke.

'A glass!'

He hardly dared to raise it to his eye. Then he saw the cutter, the scars in its side left by musket balls, the lolling corpses still propped between the remaining oarsmen. Then he saw Tyrell. He was sitting on the gunwale right aft, someone draped across his knees as he steered the boat past the white patch left by the enemy's ball.

He said quietly, 'Thank God.'

The bow-chaser hurled itself inboard again, dragging him from his thoughts, his overwhelming relief.

He shouted, 'Mr. Bethune, take the cutter and assist Mr. Tyrrell!' He looked for Buckle. 'Get the hands aloft and prepare to loose tops'ls!'

All exhaustion and dread at Graves's report seemed to be fading as men tore to their stations. The cutter was pulling from the side, Bethune standing upright as he urged his crew to greater efforts.

Dalkeith said, 'Well, sir . . .' He got no further.

One of the topmen who had reached the uppermost yard before his companions yelled, 'Deck there! Sail comin' around th' 'eadland!'

Bolitho snatched a glass and trained it above the nettings. She was standing well out from the bay, but was already tacking frantically towards Cape Henry. It was the *Lucifer*.

Odell would be shocked to find no fleet, nor even *Heron* at anchor. He tensed. There was damage to the schooner's mizzen, and she was handling sluggishly as she tried to beat closer to the entrance. She must have been caught unprepared by another ship, perhaps under cover of darkness. There was no mistaking the flapping rents in her great foresail, the uneven spread of rigging.

He saw flags breaking to the wind, and held the glass motionless while his lips spelled out the brief signal.

He turned to Buckle. '*Enemy in sight.*'

'God A'mighty.'

'Mr. Heyward!' He saw him swing round from the capstan.

'Stand by to cut the cable! We will not recover the boats, but make sail as soon as our people are aboard!'

He heard a chorus of shouts, and when he turned aft he saw *Lucifer* folding her great sails like the wings of a dying bird. She must have risked everything to reach him with her news, even to make that one vital signal. She had driven too close and had struck the shoals which Tyrrell had described so vividly.

He made himself walk to the rail and look for the boats. Tyrrell's cutter was almost awash, but Bethune was there, and he saw the wounded being hauled across, a patch of scarlet to mark at least one soldier in the party.

Several more guns were firing now, and balls threw up tall splashes in the pale sunlight like a line of leaping dolphins.

Some of the topmen gave a ragged cheer as Bethune cast the waterlogged cutter adrift and headed back towards *Sparrow*.

Bolitho turned towards Graves who was standing much as before. 'Take charge of your guns.' He kept his voice formal without understanding why or how. He could picture *Lucifer*'s frail hull breaking up on the rocks and Tyrrell's shattered boat trying to reach *Sparrow*. He could even see young

Fowler, a mere child, running through some unknown woods while shots shrieked all about him. 'Do your duty. That is all I ask of you.' He looked away. 'All I will ever ask of you again.'

He heard the boat grind alongside and saw Tyrrell and the others being dragged through the entry port, being clapped on the shoulders and bombarded with questions and cheers.

Bolitho strode towards him and saw with sudden despair that Tyrell was carrying Midshipman Fowler. It must have been his body across his legs in the boat.

Tyrrell looked at him steadily and gave a tired grin. 'He's all right, sir. He was crying fit to break his heart, an' then fell asleep in th' boat.' He handed the midshipman to some seamen. 'Worn out, poor little bugger.' He saw Graves and added flatly, 'But he's got guts. Plenty of 'em.' Then he strode forward and gripped Bolitho's hands. 'He's not th' only one, it seems.'

A new voice drawled, ''Pon my *word*, I knew we'd meet again!'

It was Colonel Foley. A bandage round his throat, his uniform in tatters, but somehow remaining as impeccable as Bolitho remembered him.

Bolitho said, 'I, too.' He looked at Tyrrell. 'We are in for some warm work today, I fear. *Lucifer's* done for, and we must leave quickly if we are to avoid her fate.'

'Aye.' Tyrrell limped towards the wheel. 'I'd guessed as much.'

A cry from aloft brought every eye towards the headland. Very slowly, their yards braced round in the sunlight, a frigate and a deep hulled transport were passing level with the wrecked schooner.

Bolitho said simply, 'Sooner than I thought.' He looked at Heyward. 'We will cut the cable.' To Tyrrell he added, 'Then you may pass the word to load and run out.'

The cutter and its dead oarsmen drifted away from the side, a discarded reminder of their sacrifice.

Bethune hurried aft, his face glowing with excitement.

Bolitho said, 'Well done. I'll see you a lieutenant yet, despite what *you* do to the contrary.'

He felt suddenly composed, even relaxed. 'Run up the colours! We'll show the army we're not leaving them to no purpose!'

The cable cut, and with her topsails bellying to the wind, *Sparrow* tilted round in a tight arc, the thunder of her canvas drowning the gunfire from the trees, her seamen too busy even to think beyond their work and the need to reach the open sea.

By the time *Sparrow* had gone about and settled on her course towards the capes, there could be no doubt in anyone's mind as to the enemy's intentions. Even as Tyrrell reported all guns loaded and run out, Bolitho raised his glass to examine yet another ship as she rounded the southern headland. One more heavy transport, and beyond her he could see the billowing topsails of a protective frigate.

Tyrrell said, 'God's teeth, a fleet and nothing less!'

Buckle called, 'Steady as she goes, sir! Sou' by west!'

The first transport had already dropped anchor, and through his glass Bolitho saw her boats being lowered with swift precision, the glint of sunlight on weapons and uniforms as soldiers clambered down ladders and nets in a manner which spoke of much practice. He shifted his glass to the second large vessel. She, too, was crammed with soldiers, and there were limbers on her upper deck, and her yards were festooned with heavy tackles, the kind used for lowering horses into boats or lighters.

Colonel Foley drawled, 'We heard Rochambeau was expecting reinforcements. It would appear they have arrived.'

Bolitho glanced at him. 'What is your mission now?'

'If you can get to New York I have despatches for General Clinton. They may not help Cornwallis, but he will be glad to know what is happening here.' He gave a brief smile. 'I heard that you dealt severely with our old friend Blundell? Not before time.' He raised one eyebrow. 'You met his niece again, I understand?'

Bolitho watched the jib-boom swing very slightly and settle on the outthrust wedge of headland. How could they speak so calmly and detachedly when death lay so close at hand? He replied, 'Yes. She will be in England now.'

Foley gave a sigh. 'I am relieved. I recognise all the signs, Captain. She wanted you to quit the Service and join her train of admirers, eh?' He held up one hand. 'Do not bother to reply! It is plain on your face, as it must have been on mine.'

Bolitho smiled gravely. 'Something of the sort.'

'When she tired of me I was sent to serve under Cornwallis. A favour as it turned out. And you?'

Tyrrell stepped back from the rail. 'She almost had him killed!'

Foley shook his head. 'A formidable woman indeed.'

'Deck there! Ship-o'-the-line roundin' the cape!'

Bolitho felt a chill on his spine as he thought of Odell's dash from the south. Day by day and at each dawn he would look astern at the pursuing ships. It must have been a nightmare for every man aboard.

The boats from the two transports were pulling towards the land now, and he could see the hulls deep in the water as testimony of the numbers they carried.

'Set the t'gallants, Mr. Tyrrell. We will need all our wind today.'

Foley drew his sabre and turned it over in his hands. 'You are not merely running away, I take it?'

Bolitho shook his head. 'Those two frigates are shortening sail, Colonel. They intend to rake us when we attempt to clear the middle-ground.' He pointed towards the anchored transports. 'There is our course. Close inshore, where we'll be least expected.'

Foley grimaced. 'Or welcome, I suspect.'

Bolitho looked at Buckle. 'When we go about you must lay her as close as you can to Cape Henry.'

'Aye, sir.' Buckle was peering through shrouds and stays, his eyes fixed on the ships.

Bolitho raised his glass again. The two frigates were under minimum canvas standing before the wind with some difficulty as they waited for the small sloop to dash past them. Less than a mile now. He watched them narrowly, noting their drift, the sun gleaming on their broadsides and on the raised telescopes of their officers.

He snapped, 'How many boats in the water?'

Bethune called, 'At least thirty!'

'Good.'

Bolitho imagined the packed soldiers who would be watching *Sparrow's* apparent dash for safety. A spectacle to drive away their own doubts and fears of what lay ahead on the American mainland.

Bolitho drew his hanger and held it above his head. Along the gun deck he saw the crews crouching at the tackles, each captain peering aft, a slow-match held ready. In the maintop two swivels were training this way and that, a seaman squatting on the barricade with fresh canister cradled to his chest. Curiously, as he ran his eyes quickly over his command, he was reminded of Colquhoun's words so long ago. *When all others are looking aft at you.*

He heard a sharp bang, and seconds later the high-pitched whine of a ball whipping overhead. One of the frigates had fired a ranging shot. But he kept his eyes on the nearest transport as she swung to her cable, her high poop towards the beach. Aboard the frigates the gun crews would be betting with each other. How many balls would they get off before the *Sparrow* was overwhelmed by their cross-fire or she struck her colours?

He brought down his hanger with a flourish. '*Now!*'

The wheel creaked noisily, and as men hauled at the braces to retrim the yards, *Sparrow's* stem began to turn. Bolitho held his breath, watching the frigates slipping further and further down the larboard bow, while the nearest transport and then the great spread of oared boats swam across the jib-boom, and beyond them the land opened up as if to receive their onrushing charge.

'Hold her!'

Bolitho ran to the nettings, his mind hanging on to Tyrrell's words of Lynnhaven Bay, the depths and currents, the dangers and margin of survival.

Buckle's helmsmen cursed and spun the wheel against the opposite thrust of wind and sea, and as spray leapt above the beakhead Bolitho saw the nearest boats careering off course, the realisation and horror of his intentions at last only too clear.

Gunfire thudded across the bay, and the balls whimpered and splashed very near to the hull. But the two frigates had been taken by surprise, and as *Sparrow* lunged towards the shore, Bolitho knew that within minutes she would be screened from their fire by the first transport.

He could feel the madness surging through him like fever, and as he yelled down at the gun deck he knew it was infectious, saw the men poised at their open ports like half-naked demons.

'*Stand by!*' The hanger was above his head again. 'Full depression!'

He saw the nearest muzzles dipping towards the creaming water, the gun captains dancing from side to side while their men stood ready with charges and fresh shot for the next barrage, and the one after that.

'As you bear!' The hanger hovered, holding the fresh sunlight like gold. '*Fire!*'

The air was blasted apart by the ragged broadsides from either beam. As the dense smoke swirled inboard, and the gun crews yelled and cheered above the squeak of trucks, the clatter of handspikes and rammers, Bolitho saw the next spitting tongues from forward, the double shotted charges smashing into boats and soldiers, the whirl of splinters and spray. Above the decks the braced topsails quivered to each explosion, the smoke fanning out on either side in a choking fog while the guns roared out again and again.

Sharper cracks from muskets, the metallic bangs of swivels, made words impossible. It was a nightmare, a world in torment. Boats lurched into the hull and Bolitho felt the deck shake as *Sparrow's* stem smashed into a launch, breaking it in two and spilling out the overloaded soldiers in a kicking, screaming profusion.

A transport was firing now, her upper tier cutting over the scattered boats and slapping through *Sparrow*'s canvas like great fists.

A ball burst through the nettings, and Bolitho heard shrill screams as two seamen were pulped against the opposite side. He noticed that he was snapping his fingers.

The hull gave another great lurch, and below his feet he felt the enemy's iron smashing through the gun deck, the attendant rumble of a twelve-pounder being overturned.

Another longboat lurched down the starboard side, some men firing with their muskets, others scrambling over the frantic sailors at the oars. Balls thudded into the rail and bulwark, and a seaman fell choking on blood as one took him in the throat.

Bolitho ran to the side and wiped his streaming eyes to peer astern. The surface was littered with smashed boats and drifting woodwork. Men, too, some swimming, others fading beneath the water under their weight of weapons and equipment.

Foley was reloading a musket and shouting, 'A few less for our boys to fight!' He leaned over the nettings and shot down a soldier even as he stood to fire at the sloop.

Bolitho strained his eyes towards the shore. It was near enough. Almost too close.

'Bring her about!' He had to repeat the order before Buckle understood.

With blocks screaming and her yards braced round once more, *Sparrow* heeled dangerously on the larboard tack, her bows seemingly pointed straight at the land.

And there was the second transport, swinging drunkenly across the bow, her gun-ports already flashing and tearing the air apart with shot.

A ball ripped through the quarterdeck rail, splitting it apart like match-wood, and cutting down a master's mate who was yelling to the hands at the mizzen braces. Blood splashed across Bolitho's breeches, and he saw other men falling on the gun deck, the protective nets above it jerking with fallen cordage and torn canvas.

A quick glance aloft told him the masthead pendant was streaming almost abeam. They were as close to the wind as they could be. Enough or too little made no difference now. There was no room to go about, nor time to change tack.

Tyrrell yelled, 'Rake that bastard's poop!' He gestured to the nearest gun captains. 'Grape! Bring them down!'

He stared at Bolitho, his eyes glazed with fatigue, the fury of battle.

'She's coming round!' He caught a seaman as he dropped from the nettings, his face a mask of blood. 'Another for th' surgeon!' He turned to Bolitho again and then gave a short cry, his hands to his thigh as he fell.

Bolitho knelt beside him, holding his shoulders as more balls blasted splinters from the deck. Tyrrell stared up at him, his eyes dark with pain.

' 'S'all right.' He gritted his teeth. 'It's th' same bloody leg!'

Bolitho saw Dalkeith stooping and running across the deck, some of his men at his back.

Tyrrell added weakly, 'I knew it had to come off. Now there's no excuse, eh?' Then he fainted.

From the littered gun deck Graves watched him fall, although his mind was cringing to the noise and the stench of death.

He screamed, 'Run out!' He thrust at a wild-eyed seaman. 'Point! *Ready!*' He stared fixedly at the towering sails of the transport as it rose ponderously abeam. '*Fire!*'

The deck lurched beneath his feet, and he saw two men blasted into crimson fragments, their screams cut short before they reached the stained planking. But somewhere in his reeling mind he was thinking of Tyrrell. He must be dead, *God rot him*. His sister would be all alone now. One day, maybe sooner than the others realised, he would find her. *Take her for himself*.

A gunner's mate gaped up at him, his mouth like a black hole as he bellowed, 'Look out, sir! For Christ's sake . . .' His words were lost in the grating crash of timber as the main topgallant yard plunged through the nets like a great tree. It gouged into the planking and further still to the deck below. As its trailing rigging and severed halliards thundered between the blazing guns Graves died, his body impaled under the broken spar.

At the quarterdeck rail Bolitho saw him die, and knew that the months of patrol duty, the storms and the fights, had at last broken the yard which they had once fished so carefully after another battle, a thousand years ago.

But Heyward was there, his voice rallying the gun crews as the anchored transport faded into the smoke, her hull pitted with holes from the bow-chaser's merciless bombardment.

The wind fanned the smoke aside, and with something like disbelief he saw the sheer of Cape Henry pulling back like a huge door, the horizon glittering beyond it in welcome.

Fowler slipped and fell on some blood and sobbed. 'It's no use! I can't . . .'

Bethune strode towards him. 'You can and you damn well will!'

The young midshipman turned and blinked at him. '*What?*'

Bethune grinned, his face black with powder smoke. 'You heard me! So jump to it, *boy!*'

'Mr. Buckle!' Bolitho winced as some stray shots shrieked through the shrouds and brought down more lengths of cordage. 'I want you to . . .'

But the master took no notice. He was sitting with his back to the hatchway, hands to his chest as if in prayer. His eyes were open, but the spreading pattern of blood around him told its own story.

Glass and a solitary seaman stood at the unprotected wheel, their eyes wild, their legs straddled amidst dead and dying.

Bolitho snapped, 'As close as you can. *Lucifer*'s remains will guide you clear of the shoal.'

As sunlight enveloped the sloop from stem to stern, and her yards swung yet again to take her out of the bay, Bolitho saw the great array of ships coming down from the southern horizon and filling the sea. It was a fantastic spectacle. Squadron by squadron, the ships-of-the-line appearing to overlap as they headed purposefully towards the Chesapeake.

Foley murmured, 'De Grasse. I have never seen such a fleet.'

Bolitho tore his eyes away and hurried to the taffrail. There was no sign of pursuit from the bay, nor had he expected one. The two frigates would be guarding their new anchorage and trying to rescue some of the soldiers who had escaped *Sparrow's* fury. He turned towards the wheel where Heyward and Bethune stood watching him.

'We will wear ship directly.' He saw Dalkeith and called, 'Tell me!'

Dalkeith eyed him sadly. 'It's done. He's sleeping now. But I am confident.'

Bolitho wiped his face and felt Stockdale steady his arm as the ship pitched heavily to the freshening wind.

So much still to do. Repairs to be carried out even as they avoided the oncoming might of France. To find Admiral Graves and tell him of the enemy's arrival. To bury their dead. His mind felt numb.

Yule, the gunner, clattered up a sagging ladder and barked, 'Any spare hands, sir? I need 'em for the pumps!'

Bolitho faced him. 'Get them elsewhere.'

He looked around at the sprawled bodies caught in their various attitudes of death.

'Only the brave lie here.'

He looked up, startled, as from high above the deck he heard someone singing. Beyond the pitted canvas and dangling rigging, to where the topgallant yard had splintered apart before falling to kill Graves, he saw a solitary seaman working in the sunlight, his marlin-spike glinting as he spliced a broken stay. The sounds of sea and booming sails were too loud for him to hear the words, but the tune seemed familiar and strangely sad.

Foley joined him and said quietly, 'If they can sing like that, after what they've done.' He turned away, unable to watch Bolitho's face. 'Then, by God, I *envy* you!'

Epilogue

Two days after fighting out of the bay, *Sparrow*'s lookouts sighted the van of Admiral Graves's fleet bearing down the coast of Maryland. The occasion was both exciting and bitter, for with many of her company wounded or killed it was hard not to feel emotion. Well ahead of the fleet, her signal flags rippling in the sunlight, *Heron* stood before the wind, a small symbol of what they had endured and achieved together.

Bolitho could remember the moment exactly, as with his men he had waited on the splintered quarterdeck while his signals were passed to *Heron* and repeated to the flagship.

When the reply had been received, Bethune had turned, his face suddenly matured.

'*Flag* to *Sparrow*, sir. *You will lead. Yours is the honour.*'

For an admiral who disliked superfluous signalling, Admiral Graves had done them proudly.

Once again, *Sparrow* had gone about, her torn sails and battered hull acting like a pointer to the great ships-of-the-line which followed obediently in her wake.

Once in sight of the bay, and with the knowledge that the French were still there, *Sparrow*'s role had become that of a mere spectator to a battle which was to leave its mark on all who took part. A warning to young officers like Bolitho, a grim lesson to the hidebound who had for so long fought by the book, a book which had become outdated by hard experience.

Perhaps Admiral Graves had expected, even hoped, up to the last moment that the French had quit the Chesapeake or at worst de Barras's smaller squadron would be there, having slipped past his patrols and escaped from Newport some days earlier. *Sparrow*'s signal had put paid to any such belief, and the sight of such a grand array must have filled him with misgivings. But if his fleet was inferior to de Grasse's in both ships and guns, he had much in his favour. The wind gave him the advantage, and as Tyrrell had so often predicted, the treacherous middle-ground between the Chesapeake's capes was soon to show its impartiality to those who braved it.

With the British bearing down on the bay, and de Barras's reinforcements not yet in close company, de Grasse decided to weigh and meet them in open water. An adverse wind and tide, the dangerous spit of middle ground, soon told him he was unable to leave his protective anchorage as a complete fleet. Squadron by squadron, his ships fought their way around Cape Henry, with *Lucifer's* skeleton close by as a warning to the foolhardy or the careless.

This should have been Graves's great opportunity. To signal *General Chase* and allow his captains to fall on the enemy before he could re-assemble and proclaim his superiority. Had there been a Hawke or a Keppel in command there was little doubt in anyone's mind that the effect would have been devastating.

But once again Graves faltered, his mind grasping the written word of the 'Fighting Instructions' and seeing no other alternative.

His flagship hoisted the rigid signal to form line of battle, and it remained flying throughout the action. The delay allowed de Grasse to assemble his fleet and when the two adversaries finally drove together it was impossible for the rearmost British ships even to engage. By evening, failing light forced the fleets to disengage, and driven by a strong north-easterly both soon lost contact.

When at last Graves was able to re-form his squadrons, the French had beaten back into the Chesapeake. They did not leave it again, and after further hesitation Graves ordered his frustrated captains to sail for New York.

Helpless and beyond reach of the action itself, Bolitho had watched much of the tactics and guessed far more of what was happening. He left the deck at regular intervals to speak with Tyrrell in the sickbay, holding his hand as he tried to describe the sequence of events.

He could recall each visit exactly. Tyrrell's face very pale in the lanternlight, his mouth clenched against the agony. And around him, groaning or sobbing quietly, the others who had suffered, and some who were beyond pain.

Tyrrell had said hoarsely, 'That's th' army finished.' He had gripped Bolitho's hand with some of his old vigour. 'But *we* did what we could!'

Later at Sandy Hook, as *Sparrow* had carried out repairs and Bolitho had received orders to sail for England with the admiral's despatches and news of the battle, the blow had fallen.

Cut off from the sea, his ammunition and supplies exhausted, Cornwallis and his whole Army had capitulated.

True to his reputation, General Washington had allowed the British to surrender with both honour and dignity, but it was a crushing defeat, nevertheless.

Couriers who had brought the news of the surrender told of the British military band which led their soldiers into Washington's camp. They had been playing 'The World Turned Upside Down', which gave some hint of what they thought about their situation if nothing else.

Under low cloud and a steady drizzle *Sparrow* weighed and turned her stern to Sandy Hook for the last time. Her company reacted to their sailing orders with mixed feelings. Some mourned old friends whom they had buried at sea or left crippled to await more comfortable transport. Others were almost afraid of what they might find in England after so long. And there were plenty who turned their backs on America and dreamed only of that moment when they would step ashore in their own country, thankful at being spared the pain and despair, grateful even to see the leaden sky above the mastheads.

When not required on deck Bolitho spent much of the voyage alone in his cabin. It made contact less painful, the losses of familiar faces easier to bear.

He could remember his last handshake with Tyrrell as he had said his farewells at a New York hospital. Dalkeith had been there, too, and it had been a sad parting. It was still hard to think of Tyrrell with one leg, nor did he want to. One thing seemed certain, Tyrrell was without despair.

'After this, I'm going home.' He had said it several times. 'I don't know how or when, but by th' Lord I'll get there!'

Dalkeith had been appointed to an accommodation ship off Sandy Hook, and had added quietly, 'Reckon they'll need a good doctor, too, eh, Jethro?' He had given his deep chuckle. 'So here's me hand on it!'

Bolitho shivered and pulled his coat more closely across his body. It was cold and very damp, and the bulkhead was dripping with condensation. He glanced at the open log book. It was the first day of January 1782, another year for all of them. He stood up and walked slowly from the cabin, his legs taking the pitch and plunge without conscious thought or effort. Over three and a half years since he had stepped into this ship which had become so much a part of him.

He climbed the ladder and saw Heyward at the weather nettings. It would be worse for him. He had been aboard since she had commissioned five years back. He walked across to him, seeing the grey mist swirling through the dripping shrouds, the spray bursting high above the gangway.

'Well, Mr. Heyward, the English Channel. Yonder, with any sort of luck, lies the Isle of Wight. We will anchor at Spithead before dark.'

Heyward looked at him steadily. 'It's a strange feeling, sir.' He shrugged. 'I'm not sure if I want to leave the ship now.'

Bolitho nodded. 'It is often the case. *Sparrow* is no different from the rest of us. She needs a proper overhaul in the yard, and she is to be fitted with these new carronades we keep hearing about. She'll not be the same after this.' He saw Bethune climbing from the gun deck, his jaw working on a stale biscuit. 'I doubt if any of us will.'

'Land ho! Fine on th' starboard bow!'

Bolitho took a glass. 'Wight. You'd better let her fall off a point.' He watched Heyward hurry to the rail with his speaking trumpet. It could have been Tyrrell.

Then he looked around the rain-soaked deck at the seamen by the mizzen braces, their faces and arms even darker in the hostile grey light.

A tan-sailed yawl bobbed past, a bearded man waving from the tiller. On the other beam he saw a smudge of land through the drizzle and mist. England. He gripped the rail hard. After so long and so much.

'Steady as she goes, sir!' Heyward joined him again.

Bethune stood on his opposite side and murmured, 'I feel as if I've grown up in *Sparrow*.'

Bolitho thrust his arms around their shoulders.

'We *all* did.'

Then he turned away and said formally, 'Muster your anchor party and tell the gunner to prepare a salute.'

He began to pace slowly up and down the weather side, seeing the busy seamen around him, and many more. Buckle and Tilby, Graves and the artist Majendie.

He paused and touched the rail, the scars where balls had cut down so many of his men.

A frigate loomed through the mist on an opposite tack, her flags very bright against the murky backcloth.

Fowler called, '*What ship?*, sir.'

Bolitho nodded. 'Hoist our number.'

Sparrow, sloop-of-war, had come home.

To Glory We Steer

Contents

1	The *Phalarope*	231
2	Beware, the Press!	245
3	Beef for the Purser	257
4	The Signal	270
5	Rum and Recriminations	282
6	A Sight of Land	294
7	A Spanish Lugger	307
8	The Raid	320
9	Defeat	332
10	The Red Baize Bag	346
11	Fortune of War	359
12	'Confusion to Our Enemies!'	370
13	Danger from Within	383
14	Blood and Fresh Water	394
15	The Storm Breaks	407
16	A Special Sort of Man	421
17	Form Line of Battle!	431
18	A Tradition of Victory	442
	Epilogue	454

'To be sure I lose the fruits of the earth,
But then I am gathering the flowers of the Sea.

ADMIRAL BOSCAWEN, 1756

1

The Phalarope

The New Year of 1782 was only three days old but already the weather had made a decided change for the worse. Steady drizzle, pushed by a freshening southerly wind, explored the narrow streets of Portsmouth Point and made the stout walls of the old fortifications gleam like polished metal. Moving threateningly above the huddled buildings the cloud was unbroken and the colour of lead, so that although it was all but midday the light was feeble and depressing.

Only the sea was really alive. Across the normally sheltered expanse of the Solent the surface quivered and broke with each eager gust, but in the distorted light the wave crests held a strange yellow hue in contrast with the dull grey hump of the Isle of Wight and the rain-shrouded Channel beyond.

Captain Richard Bolitho pushed open the door of the George Inn and stood for a few moments to allow the drowsy heat to enfold him like a blanket. Without a word he handed his cloak to a servant and tucked his cocked hat beneath his arm. Through a door to his right he could see a welcoming fire in the coffee room, where a noisy throng of naval officers, interspersed with a few bright scarlet uniforms of the military, were taking their ease and keeping their worries and demands of duty beyond the low, rain-slashed windows.

In another room, grouped in contemplative silence around several small tables, other officers studied their playing cards and the faces of their opponents. Few even glanced up at Bolitho's entrance. In Portsmouth, and at the George Inn in particular, after years of war and unrest, only a man out of uniform might have warranted attention.

Bolitho sighed and took a quick glance at himself in a wall mirror. His blue coat and gold lace fitted his tall figure well, and against the white shirt and waistcoat his face looked unusually tanned. Even allowing for a slow voyage back from the West Indies, his body was still unprepared for an English winter, and he forced himself to stand a little longer to clear the aching cold from his limbs.

A servant coughed politely at his elbow. 'Beg pardon, sir. The admiral is waitin' on you in his room.' He made a small gesture towards the stairway.

'Thank you.' He waited until the man had hurried away to answer some noisy demand from the coffee room and then took a final glance at the mirror. It was neither vanity nor personal interest. It was more of a cold scrutiny which he might offer to a subordinate.

Bolitho was twenty-six years old, but his impassive features and the deep lines on either side of his mouth made him appear older, and for a brief instant he found himself wondering how the change had come about. Almost irritably he pushed the black hair away from his forehead, pausing only to allow one rebellious lock to stay in place above his right eye.

Neither was that action one of vanity. More perhaps one of embarrassment.

Barely an inch above his eye, and running deep into his hair-line, was a savage diagonal scar. He allowed his fingers to touch it momentarily, as a man will let his mind explore an old memory, and then with a final shrug he walked briskly up the stairs.

Vice-Admiral Sir Henry Langford was standing, feet well apart, directly in front of the highest log fire Bolitho had ever seen. His glittering uniform shone in the dancing flames, and his thick shadow seemed to reach out across the spacious room to greet Bolitho's quiet entrance.

For several seconds the two men stood looking at each other. The admiral, in his sixties, and running to bulkiness, his heavy face dominated by a large beaked nose above which his keen blue eyes shone like two polished stones, and the slim, tanned captain.

Then the admiral stirred into life and stepped away from the fire, his hand outstretched. Bolitho felt the heat from the fire released across the room, as if a furnace door had been flung open.

'I am glad to see you, Bolitho!' The admiral's booming voice filled the room, sweeping away the years and replacing the image of an overweight old man with that of Bolitho's first captain.

As if reading his thoughts the admiral added ruefully, 'Fourteen years, isn't it? My God, it doesn't seem possible!' He stood back and studied Bolitho critically like a plump bird. 'You were a scraggy midshipman, twelve years old, if I remember correctly. Hardly an ounce of flesh on you. I only took you aboard because of your father.' He smiled. 'You still look as if a good meal would not come amiss!'

Bolitho waited patiently. Those fourteen years of service had taught him one thing at least. Senior officers had their own ways of getting round to the reasons for their actions. And it usually took time.

The admiral moved ponderously to a table and poured two generous glasses of brandy. 'With most of the world against us, Bolitho, brandy has become somewhat of a luxury.' He shrugged. 'However, as I am more troubled by rheumatism than gout, I look upon it as a last remaining necessity.'

Bolitho sipped carefully and studied his superior over the rim of the glass. He had arrived back from the West Indies just three days earlier, as one year faded and gave way to the next. His ship, his beloved *Sparrow*, had been handed over to the dockyard for a well-earned refit, while her less fortunate company were scattered through the ever-hungry fleet to replace the growing gaps left by death and mutilation. Most of the sloop's crew had been away from their homeland for six years, and with a little well-earned prize money they had been hoping to see their loved ones again, if only for a short while. It was not to be, but Bolitho knew that his feeling of resentment and pity would be as useless as a ship without sails.

The pale eyes fixed suddenly on Bolitho's face. 'I'm giving you the *Phalarope*, Bolitho.' He watched the brief shaft of emotion play across the young captain's features. 'She's lying out at Spithead right now, rigging set up, yards crossed, a finer frigate never floated.'

Bolitho placed the glass slowly on the table to give his mind time to deal with the admiral's words. The *Phalarope*, a thirty-two-gun frigate, and less than six years old. He had seen her through his glass as he had rounded the Spit Sand three days ago. She was certainly a beautiful ship, all that he could ever have hoped for. No, more than he could have dreamed of.

He pushed the *Sparrow* to the back of his thoughts. It was part of yesterday, along with his own hopes of taking a rest at his home in Cornwall, and getting to know the firm feel of the countryside, of so many half-remembered things.

He said quietly, 'You do me a great honour, sir.'

'Nonsense, you've more than earned it!' The admiral seemed strangely relieved. As if he had been rehearsing this little speech for some time. 'I've followed your career, Bolitho. You are a great credit to the Navy, and the country.'

'I had an excellent teacher, sir.'

The admiral nodded soberly. 'They were great days, eh? Great days.' He shook himself and poured another brandy. 'I have told you the good news. Now I will tell you the other part.' He watched Bolitho thoughtfully. 'The *Phalarope* has been attached to the Channel Fleet, mostly on blockade duty outside Brest.'

Bolitho pricked up his ears. Being on blockade duty was no news at all. The hard-pressed fleet needed every frigate like gold in its constant efforts to keep the French ships bottled up in their Channel ports. Frigates were maids of all work. Powerful enough to trounce any other vessel but a ship of the line in open combat, and fast enough to out-manoeuvre the latter, they were in permanent demand. What caught his immediate attention was the way the admiral had stressed *has been attached* to the Channel Fleet. So there were new orders. Maybe south to help relieve the beleaguered garrison in Gibraltar.

The admiral continued harshly, 'Most ships go rotten from without. Wind and sea are cruel masters, even to the best timbers.' He stared at the rain splattering across the windows. '*Phalarope* has received her rot from within!' He began to pace angrily, his shadow crossing and recrossing the room like a spectre. 'There was almost a mutiny a month back, and then when her squadron was engaged in battle with some blockade runners she avoided action!' He halted and glared at Bolitho with something like shock. 'Can you believe that? A King's ship, and she failed to engage!'

Bolitho bit his lip. Mutiny was always a threat. Men pressed from life ashore, a handful of troublemakers, even one stupid officer, could turn a well-drilled ship into a living hell. But it rarely occurred with other ships in company. Usually this sort of madness broke out in a ship becalmed under a relentless tropical sun, with fever and disease the main instigators. Or during a long voyage out of sight of land, when a ship seemed to shrink in size with each dragging day, as if to force the men at each others' throats.

Sir Henry Langford added sharply, 'I've relieved her captain of his command, of course.'

Bolitho felt a strange warmth for this tired, irritable old man, whose flagship, a massive three-decker, was even now taking on stores in the harbour and preparing to carry her master back to his squadron off the hostile French coast. He had said '*of course*'. Yet Bolitho knew that many admirals would have backed up their captains even knowing them to be both guilty and incompetent.

The admiral gave a small smile. 'I am afraid your honour is double-edged! It is never easy to take over an unhappy ship, especially in time of war.' He pointed at a sealed envelope on his desk. Its seals glittered in the firelight like fresh blood. 'Your orders. They require you to take command forthwith and proceed to sea.' He weighed his words carefully. 'You will seek out Sir Samuel Hood's squadron and place yourself under his orders.'

Bolitho felt dazed. Hood was still in the West Indies whence he had just returned. He had a brief picture of the same thousands of miles of empty sea, in command of a strange ship, with a crew still seething in discontent.

'So you see, Bolitho, I am still a hard taskmaster!' The admiral shuddered as a squall hit the window. 'I am afraid you are nearly one hundred men under strength. I had to remove many of the troublemakers, and replacements are hard to come by. Some I will have to hang, as soon as a court martial can be convened. You have barely enough men to work the ship under way, let alone in action.' He rubbed his chin, his eyes glittering. 'I suggest you make sail at once and head for the West Country. I understand that the fishing fleets are mostly in port in Devon and Cornwall. The weather it seems is not to their liking.' His smile broadened. 'I see no objection to your visiting Falmouth, Bolitho. While your officers are ashore pressing some of these fishermen into the King's service, you might well find the time to call upon your father. You will give him my kind regards, I hope.'

Bolitho nodded. 'Thank you, sir. I will do that.' All at once he wanted to get away. There was so much to attend to. Stores and cordage to be checked, food and provisions for the long voyage. Above all, there was the *Phalarope*, waiting for him, ready to judge or condemn him.

The admiral picked up the canvas envelope and weighed it in his hands. 'I will not advise you, Bolitho. You are young, but have more than proved yourself. Just remember this. There are bad men and good aboard your ship. Be firm, but not too hard. Do not regard lack of knowledge as insubordination, like your predecessor.' There was a bite to his tone. 'If you have difficulty in remembering all this, try and recall what you were like when you came to serve me as midshipman.' He was no longer smiling. 'You can give the ship back her rightful place by returning her pride. But if you fail, even I cannot help you.'

'I would not expect you to, sir.' Bolitho's eyes were hard grey, like the sea beyond the harbour.

'I know. That is why I held the command for you.' There was a murmur of voices beyond the door and Bolitho knew the audience was nearly over. The admiral added, 'I have a nephew aboard the *Phalarope*, he is one of your young gentlemen. His name is Charles Farquhar, and he might yet make a good officer. But do him no favours for my sake, Bolitho.' He sighed and handed over the envelope. 'The ship is ready to sail, so take advantage of this southerly wind.' He held Bolitho's hand and studied his face intently, 'We may not meet again, Bolitho, for I fear my days are numbered.' He waved down the other man's protest. 'I have a responsibility, and I have certain rewards for my duty. But youth I cannot have.'

Bolitho hitched up his sword and tucked his hat under his arm once more. 'Then I will take my leave, sir.' There was nothing more he could say.

Almost blindly he walked through the door and past the little group of whispering officers awaiting their admiral's pleasure.

One officer stood apart, a captain of about his own age. There the similarity ended. He had pale, protruding eyes and a small, petulant mouth. He was tapping his fingers on his sword and staring at the door, and Bolitho guessed him to be the man who had been taken from the *Phalarope*. But he seemed unworried, merely irritated. He probably had influence at Court, or in Parliament, Bolitho thought grimly. Even so, he would need more than that to face Sir Henry.

As he crossed to the stairway the other captain met his stare. The pale eyes were empty of expression yet vaguely hostile. Then he looked away, and Bolitho reached the foot of the stairs where a marine orderly waited with his cloak.

Outside the inn the wind howled in his face and the rain dashed across his skin like ice rime. But as he walked slowly towards the Sally Port he noticed neither.

When he reached the Hard, Bolitho noticed that the high-water garland of slime and weed was all but covered by the angry, hissing wavelets, and he knew that the tide was nearing the flood. With luck he could get his new ship under way on the ebb. Nothing made a ship's company settle down to a fresh master more quickly than routine and work.

As he left the shelter of the last line of buildings he caught sight of the boat which waited to carry him away from the land. The oars were tossed, and swayed like twin lines of bare trees as the small craft rocked uneasily in the swell, and he guessed that each man in the boat was watching his slow approach. At the top of the stone ramp, his thick body framed against the cruising wavelets, was the familiar shape of Stockdale, his personal coxswain. Aboard the *Phalarope* there would be one friend at least, he thought grimly.

Stockdale had followed him from ship to ship. More like a trusting dog than a man. Bolitho often found time to wonder at the bond which had held them together, a link which was beyond explanation in words.

As a young and very junior lieutenant Bolitho had been sent ashore with a recruiting party during the uneasy peace, when he had considered himself more than fortunate to be spared the indignity of so many of his fellows, that of being beached and unwanted on half-pay. Volunteers had been few, but when about to return to his ship to face the wrath of his captain

Bolitho had seen Stockdale standing miserably outside a local inn. Stripped to the waist he had made a truly imposing figure, his thickset body a mass of muscle and power. A loud-mouthed barker at his side had called to the small naval recruiting party that Stockdale was a prize fighter of great repute, and that a golden guinea would be immediately awarded to any one of Bolitho's men who could lay him low. Bolitho had been weary, and the thought of a cool drink at the inn while his men tried their luck overcame his normal objections to what he thought to be a degrading spectacle.

As it happened, he had had in his party a gunner's mate who was not only a very proficient fist-fighter but a man quite used to maintaining discipline by that and any other means which came his way. He had thrown aside his jacket, and encouraged by the other sailors had gone to the attack.

Exactly what had happened next Bolitho was not quite sure. It was said that one of the sailors had managed to trip Stockdale, and that seemed likely, as Bolitho had never seen him beaten since that day, but the next instant, even as Bolitho had been reaching for his ale, there had been a scream of rage from the barker and a great bellow of laughter from the sailors.

Bolitho had found the gunner's mate pocketing his guinea while the infuriated barker had proceeded to beat Stockdale with a length of chain, interspersed with threats and curses.

It was then that Bolitho had discovered that Stockdale accepted loyalty like a manacle. He never flinched from the unjust beating, although he could have killed his tormentor with one blow.

Pity or disgust drove Bolitho to stop the beating, and the look of dumb gratitude on Stockdale's battered face only helped to make things worse. Watched by the grinning sailors and the flint-eyed barker he had asked Stockdale to volunteer for the King's service. The barker had raised a storm of protest at the thought of his living being removed for all time.

Stockdale had given a brief nod and picked up his shirt without a word. Even now he hardly ever spoke, his vocal cords having been damaged over the years of fighting in one town after another.

Bolitho had imagined that his angry gesture had ended the matter. But it was not so. Stockdale had settled down aboard ship in a manner born. For all his strength he was gentle and patient, and only one real object seemed to alter his placid way of life. Wherever Bolitho went, so did he.

At first Bolitho decided to ignore this fact, but when at length he had his own command and required a personal coxswain, Stockdale just seemed to be there, ready. As he was now.

He was staring emptily at the sea, his body motionless in the wind, his wide white trousers and blue jacket flapping around his limbs like pennants on a heavy ship of the line. He turned at Bolitho's approach and knuckled his forehead, his deep brown eyes watching his captain with silent concern.

Bolitho gave a tight smile. 'Is everything ready, Stockdale?'

The man nodded slowly. 'I've stowed your boxes in the boat, sir.' He glared at the waiting boat's crew. 'I've had a word with this lot about how things should be done from now on!'

Bolitho stepped down into the boat and gathered his cloak tightly around him. Stockdale grunted an order and the boat idled clear of the stonework.

'Out oars! Give way together!' Stockdale swung the tiller and squinted between the oarsmen as the boat turned and bit into the first angry swell.

Bolitho watched the oarsmen through narrowed eyes. Each man was careful to avoid his scrutiny. The new captain, any captain, was second only to God. He could promote and flog, reward and hang any man aboard, and when a ship was out of company, alone on the high seas, the powers were exercised according to a particular captain's temperament, as Bolitho well knew.

As the boat pushed into open water he forgot the straining seamen and concentrated his full attention on the distant frigate. Now that he was closer he could see the steady pitch and roll of the graceful hull as she strained at the taut cable in the freshening wind. He could even see the flash of bright copper as she showed her bilges, and then as she canted to the opposite side he could make out the busy activity on the maindeck below her tall, tapering masts and furled sails. Aft by the entry port there was a neat scarlet rectangle of marines already drawn up to greet him, and momentarily in the wind he caught the sound of twittering pipes and the hoarse bellow of orders.

She was a fine ship, he thought. One hundred and forty feet of power and living grace. From the high gilt figurehead, a strange bird mounted on the back of a dolphin, to her carved poop with the rippling ensign above she was the proof of a shipbuilder's art.

Now he could see the group of officers waiting on the quarterdeck, more than one with his glass raised and trained on the tossing boat. He set his face in an impassive mask, forcibly dampening down the excitement and the sense of challenge which the ship had given him.

'Boat ahoy!' The hail was caught by the wind and tossed to the screaming gulls above.

Stockdale cupped his hands and yelled, '*Phalarope!*' There was no doubt now for the waiting officers. No doubt at all that their new overlord was approaching.

Bolitho opened his cloak and threw it back across his shoulders, the feeble light glinting on his gold lace and the hilt of his sword. Still the frigate grew bigger and bigger, until at last she towered above the boat, blotting out all else.

As the oarsmen manoeuvred towards the entry port Bolitho ran his eye slowly along the masts and yards and the taut black rigging. There was no sign of slackness, everything was as it should be. The hull was well painted, and the amount of gold leaf around the figurehead as well as the broad-windowed stern was proof that her last captain had spent a good deal of his own money to make her so.

The thought of money well spent made him glance briefly at his boxes in the sternsheets. He had brought over a thousand pounds of prize money back from the Indies, yet apart from the new uniforms and a few small luxuries he had little to show for it. And now he was off to sea again, where a mutineer's knife might end his life as quickly as a French cannon ball, unless he was constantly vigilant. He suddenly recalled the admiral's warning, 'If you fail, even I cannot help you!'

The boat lurched alongside and almost threw him from his feet as he jumped clear of the gunwale and began to climb up the spray-dashed side.

He tried to shut his ears to the crash of sound which greeted him. The trilling pipes from the side party, and the slap of muskets as the marines presented arms; it was too easy and too dangerous to let his guard slip even for an instant. Even to allow himself to enjoy this moment to the full, for which he had been waiting for so long.

A tall, heavily built lieutenant stepped forward and removed his hat. 'Lieutenant Vibart, sir. I am the senior here.' He had a thick, rasping tone, and his face was unsmiling.

'Thank you, Mr. Vibart.' Bolitho stared past him along the full length of his ship. The gangways on either side of the hull which connected the forecastle with the quarterdeck were crowded with silent men, and others had climbed into the shrouds so that they could see their captain better. His eye moved on, across the neat lines of guns, firmly lashed behind closed ports, the spotless decks and well-flaked lines. Lieutenant Vibart was a good first lieutenant as far as smartness and outward appearance was concerned, he thought.

Vibart was saying gruffly, 'Mr. Okes and Mr. Herrick, the second and third lieutenants, sir.'

Bolitho nodded, keeping his expression non-committal. He had a quick impression of two young officers, nothing more. Later the men would emerge from behind the strange faces. Right now it was more important that his own impression on them was made quite clear.

'Have the hands lay aft, Mr. Vibart.' He drew his commission from inside his coat and unrolled it as the men were urged towards him. They looked healthy enough, but their bodies were clad in rags, and some of them seemed to be dressed in the remains of what they had been wearing when pressed into service. He bit his lip. That would have to be changed, and at once. Uniformity was all important. It killed envy amongst the men, if only for poor remnants of clothing.

He began to read himself in, his voice carrying crisply above the sigh of wind and the steady thrumming of stays and rigging.

It was addressed to Richard Bolitho, Esquire, and required him forthwith to go on board and take upon him the charge and command of captain in His Britannic Majesty's frigate *Phalarope*. He finished reading and rolled the scroll in his hands as he looked down at the assembled faces. What were they thinking and hoping at this moment?

He said: 'I will address the men further, Mr. Vibart.' He thought he saw a gleam of resentment in Vibart's deepset eyes, but ignored it. The man looked old for his rank, maybe seven or eight years older than himself. It could not be pleasant to see a chance of command moved back another pace by his sudden arrival. 'Are you in all respects ready to proceed to sea?'

Vibart nodded. 'Yes, sir.' He sounded as if he meant to say '*of course*'. 'We were warped out here a week ago, and the fresh water came aboard this forenoon by lighter. We are fully provisioned in accordance with the admiral's orders.'

'Very good.' Bolitho turned back to the crew. Sir Henry Langford had taken no chance, he thought dryly. With the ship fully provisioned and safely anchored away from the shore there was little chance of contaminating the fleet with her unhappiness. He longed for a few minutes alone so that he could read fully the extent of his orders. They might give him a further clue to the puzzle.

He cleared his throat. 'Now, men, I just want to tell you of our destination.' They would know he had had no time to inform his officers, and this immediate show of confidence might well help to bridge the gulf between quarterdeck and forecastle.

'England is fighting for her life! Even as we lie here, anchored and impotent, our country is at war with France and Spain, with the Dutch and the rebellious colonialists in the Americas. Every single ship is needed to win the day, each man amongst you is vital to our just cause!' He paused and waited a few seconds. In the *Sparrow* his men would have cheered, would have shown some animation. Suddenly, as he stared along the packed, expressionless faces he felt a pang of longing and loneliness. In his mind's eye he could see the little sloop's cheerful, tanned company, like a lot of carefree pirates. The healthy faces, the feeling of oneness which was totally absent here. He saw Stockdale standing by the lee rail and wondered what he thought about his new shipmates.

He allowed a note of hardness to creep into his voice. 'Today we sail for Falmouth.' He steeled himself. 'And from thence to the West Indies to join Sir Samuel Hood against the French and their allies!'

No indvidual called out, but something like a moan of pain transmitted itself through the packed figures below him. A petty officer snarled, 'Silence on deck! Keep quiet, you scum!'

Bolitho added flatly, 'I ask nothing but your loyalty. I will do my duty, and I would wish you to do the same!' He turned on his heel. 'Carry on, Mr. Vibart. We will make sail in one hour. See that all boats are secured, and then be so good as to have the anchor hove short.' His tone was cold and final, but the lieutenant blocked his way, his mouth working angrily.

'But, sir! The West Indies!' He struggled for words. 'God, we've been on the blockade for two years!'

Bolitho let his voice carry to the other officers. 'And I have been away for *six*, Mr. Vibart!' He walked aft where Stockdale soundlessly marked the cabin hatch for his retreat. 'I want all officers and senior warrant officers in my cabin in ten minutes!'

He ran lightly down the ladder, his head automatically bowed beneath the low deck beams. Right aft, below a spiralling lantern, a red-coated marine snapped to attention outside his cabin door. Beyond it would be his haven, the only place aboard a crowded ship where he could think and dream alone.

Stockdale held open the door and stood aside as Bolitho entered the cabin, which after *Sparrow's* cramped and spartan quarters seemed almost spacious.

The sloping stern windows ran the whole width of the main cabin, and the thick glass gave a wide, panoramic picture of tossing water and the hostile, grey sky. The air was heavy and damp, and once again he was conscious of the cold in his limbs. It would be good to get back to the sun, he thought. To see blue and gold through those windows, and know again the peace of a friendly sea.

A partition hid his sleeping quarters, and another concealed the small chart room. The main cabin itself contained a good table and matching chairs, as well as a bulkhead desk and a hanging wardrobe for his uniforms which even now Stockdale was unpacking from the boxes.

The previous captain had done well for himself, Bolitho thought. On either side of the cabin, discreetly hidden in a canvas cover, was a big twelve-pounder, lashed down like some leashed beast, so that even here, in the captain's own domain, the air would be filled with smoke and death when action found the frigate.

He made himself sit quietly on the padded bench below the windows, and ignoring Stockdale's furtive movements and the shipboard noises above and beyond the door began to read his orders.

But apart from the usual directions the orders told him nothing. There were extra marines aboard, with a full captain in charge of them instead of the original sergeant. That was interesting. Sir Henry Langford obviously considered that if all else failed Bolitho could defend himself with the afterguard.

He slammed the thick papers on the table and frowned. He did not want protection. He had meant what he had said. He wanted loyalty. No, he *needed* loyalty!

The deck canted beneath him and he heard the patter of bare feet overhead. In spite of everything he was glad to be leaving the land. At sea you had room to think, and space to act. Only time was at a premium.

Exactly ten minutes after Bolitho had left the quarterdeck the officers filed through the door into his cabin.

Vibart, his head lowered beneath the deck beams, introduced each one in order of seniority in the same rasping tone.

Okes and Herrick, the two other lieutenants, and Daniel Proby, the master. The latter was old and weathered like carved wood, his body round-shouldered beneath his well-worn coat. He had a lugubrious, heavy-jowled face, and the most mournful eyes Bolitho had ever seen. Then there was Captain Rennie of the marines, a slim and languid young man with deceptively lazy eyes. Bolitho thought that he at least would guess that there might still be trouble in the offing.

The three midshipmen stood quietly in the background. Farquhar was the most senior, and Bolitho felt a small pang of uneasiness as he studied the youth's tight lips and haughty expression. The admiral's nephew might be an ally. He could equally be the admiral's spy. The other young gentlemen, Neale and Maynard, seemed pleasant enough, with the usual crumpled cheekiness which most midshipmen reserved as their defence against officers and seamen alike. Neale was minute and chubby, and could not be more than thirteen, Bolitho thought. Maynard, on the other hand, was keen-eyed and as skinny as a pike, and watched his captain with a fixed and intent expression which might mean anything.

Then there were the senior warrant offivers. The professional men. Evans, the pursuer, a small ferret in a plain dark coat, dwarfed by Ellice, the surgeon, brick-red and perspiring, with anxious rheumy eyes.

Bolitho stood wit hhis back to the windows, his hands clasped behind him. He waited until Vibart had finished speaking and then said, 'We shall get to know each other better very soon, gentlemen. For the moment let me say that I shall expect all of you to do your best to pull the ship's people together into one efficient company. When I left the Indies things were not going well for England. It is likely, indeed it is more than probable, that the French will take full advantage of our military commitments in that area for their own ends. Action will certainly seek us out, and when that happens I want this ship to give a good account of herself.' He watched their faces, trying to pierce their guarded expressions. His gaze fell on Herrick, the third lieutenant. He was a round-faced, competent looking officer, but there was an air of assumed attentiveness about him, like one who had been betrayed in the past and no longer trusted a first impression.

He dropped his eyes to the deck as Vibart said, 'May I ask if we're being despatched to the Indies because of the trouble we had aboard, sir?' He stared unflinchingly at Bolitho's grey eyes, his voice challenging.

'You may ask.' Bolitho watched him narrowly. There was something dominant about Vibart. A sense of inner force which seemed to cow all the others into mere spectators. He said calmly, 'I have studied the reports and the logs. I consider that the near-mutiny,' he let his voice hang on the last word, 'was caused as much by negligence as anything else.'

Vibart replied hotly, 'Captain Pomfret trusted his officers, sir!' He pointed to the books on the table. 'You can see from the log books that the ship did all which could be expected of her!'

Bolitho pulled a book from beneath the others and saw Vibart look momentarily off guard.

'I often find that this, the punishment book, is a better gauge of a ship's efficiency.' He turned the pages idly, forcibly hiding the disgust he had felt when he had first examined it. 'In the past six months over a thousand lashes were awarded to the crew.' His voice was cold. 'Some men received four dozen at a time. One apparently died after punishment.'

Vibart said thickly, 'You can't win men by weakness, sir!'

'Nor by senseless cruelty, Mr. Vibart!' His tone was like a whip. 'In future I will have more attention to leadership than to brutality in my ship!' He controlled his voice with an effort. 'Also, I want every man fitted out with proper clothing from the slop chest before we reach Falmouth. This is a King's ship and not a Spanish slaver!'

There was a sudden heavy silence, so that ship and sea intruded into the cabin. The clatter of deck gear, the sluice of the tide around the rudder, and the distant bark of commands added to Bolitho's sense of isolation.

He continued evenly, 'At Falmouth we will make efforts to increase our company to full strength. I will send parties of trusted hands ashore to press suitable men for service. Not cripples and young boys, but *men*. Do I make myself clear?'

Most of them nodded. Lieutenant Okes said carefully, 'I have often read of your exploits in the *Gazette*, sir.' He swallowed painfully and glanced quickly at Herrick. 'I think the whole ship will be happy to have you as captain.' His voice trailed away miserably and he fidgeted with his sword.

Bolitho nodded. 'Thank you, Mr. Okes.' He could not afford to add anything else. Okes might be seeking favouritism, or making haste to cover up some old misdemeanour. But still, it was a beginning.

He added, 'I cannot alter what Captain Pomfret did or did not do. I have my own ways, and I expect them to be considered at all times.' From the corner of his eye he saw the master shaking his head doubtfully. 'Do you wish to say anything, Mr. Proby?'

The old man looked up with a jerk, his jowls shaking. 'Er, no, sir! I was just thinking it will make a change to navigate in some deep water instead o' all these shoals an' mudbanks!' He smiled, the effort only adding to his mournful appearance. 'The young gentlemen will benefit from a long voyage, no doubt?'

It was meant in all seriousness, but the midshipman Neale nudged his companion Maynard and they both tittered. Then Neale saw Vibart's frown and hurriedly looked at his feet.

Bolitho nodded. 'Very well, gentlemen, prepare to get under way. I will come on deck in ten minutes.' He met Vibart's eye. 'I shall be interested to see the men at their stations, Mr. Vibart. A bit of sail drill might take their minds off their troubles for a while!'

The officers filed away and Stockdale firmly closed the door. Bolitho sat down and stared at the piles of books and papers. He had tried to find an opening and had failed. There was a barrier, a shield of resentment, or was it fear? He had to find out himself. He could trust no one, confide in nobody until he was sure of his ground.

He looked at Stockdale and asked quietly. 'Well, how do *you* like the *Phalarope*?'

The ex-fighter swallowed hard, as he always did to clear his maimed cords. 'She's a good craft, Captain.' He nodded slowly. 'But I don't care much for the meat inside the bones!' He placed Bolitho's sword carefully beside the pistol rack and added meaningly, 'I should keep these by you, Captain. Just in case!'

Richard Bolitho climbed the ladder to the quarterdeck and made himself walk slowly to the weather rail. The frigate was alive with fresh activity, and he could see men standing at the capstan bars, while others waited below the masts with their petty officers. He gauged the wind against his cheek and glanced quickly aloft at the masthead pendant. The ship tugged at her cable eagerly and fretfully, as if she too wanted to be free of the land once again, and Bolitho curbed his own impatience as he watched and waited the final preparations for sea.

The decks gleamed with blown spray and drizzle, and he realised with a start that he was already soaked to the skin. But perhaps it was just as well that his seamen should see him unshrouded in watchcoat and unprotected from the weather as indeed they were themselves.

He caught sight of the midshipman Maynard hovering by the lee rail, and again thanked God for his ability to remember names after hearing or reading them but once.

'You are in charge of signals, Mr. Maynard?' The youth nodded, his thin body looking like a scarecrow against the angry water alongside. 'Very well. Make a signal to the Flag. "Ready to proceed".'

He saw the flags soaring aloft and immediately forgot them as Vibart strode aft his face set in a grim frown.

'Anchor's hove short, sir!' He touched his hat. 'All stores secured!'

'Very well.' Bolitho lifted his glass and watched the flags blowing out from the shore signal tower. Maybe, just to the right, from his warm room at the inn, the admiral would be watching.

Maynard yelled, 'Reply, sir! "God speed and good luck"!'

Bolitho handed his glass to Stockdale and thrust his hands beneath the tails of his coat. 'Get the ship under way if you please. Lay a course to weather the headland.' He would take no part in it. He would watch each man. And every man would know it.

The boatswain's mates took up the cry, 'Hands aloft! Loose tops'ls!'

The rigging and shrouds were suddenly alive with swarming figures as the topmen ran aloft as surefooted as cats, the laggards urged on mercilessly by the petty officers with fists and ropes ends alike.

'Break out the anchor!' Mr. Quintal, the barrel-chested boatswain, swung his cane over the straining forecastle hands. 'Heave! Put yer backs into it, you whimperin' old women!' His cane whacked down and a man cried out. 'Heave! Heave!' The capstan jerked and then cranked steadily as the dripping cable came inboard.

'Loose heads'ls!' The cry was passed along the deck like a chant. High above, the released canvas flapped and banged in the wind, and the men strung out along the swaying yards like ants kicked and grappled with each growing area of rebellious sail.

Bolitho ignored the flying spray and watched the men dashing from one job to the next. The shorthandedness was all the more apparent now with the topmen aloft.

Herrick called from the bows, 'Anchor's aweigh, sir!'

Like a released animal the frigate paid off into the wind, her deck heeling sharply as the gust found and held her.

Vibart grated, 'Man the braces there! Look alive!'

The men at the braces laid back heaving and panting until the great yards began to squeak round. Then the wind filled the sails and the billowing canvas thundered out hard and full as the *Phalarope* went about and gathered way.

By the time the anchor was catted and made fast the land was already drawing away on the starboard quarter, the Isle of Wight quite invisible in a curtain of drizzle and spray.

Everything creaked and banged as the ship continued to swing on course, with shrouds and rigging whining like the strings of some mad orchestra.

Bolitho watched the unwanted men sliding down the stays and adding their weight to the men at the braces. 'Lay her on the port tack, Mr. Vibart.' He looked back across the taffrail and tried to recall what was so terrible about Captain Pomfret. He remembered the man's cold eyes, and the cowed faces of his men.

Proby was standing hump-backed beside the quartermaster, his battered old hat over his ears like a candle-snuffer. Bolitho said, 'Let her run freely, Mr. Proby. There may be need for reefing down later, but I want to reach Falmouth as soon as possible.'

The master watched the captain's slim figure beside the rail and sucked his teeth. Pomfret had never let the frigate have her head. Now she was flying like a mad thing as more and more canvas crept along her yards and exploded, full-bellied before the wind. When he looked at the spiralling mastheads he could almost imagine they were bending. But his eyesight was not so good now, so he made no comment.

Vibart stood at the quarterdeck rail one foot on a carronade slide, his eyes slitted as he watched the men at their stations. Once he looked back too, towards Portsmouth, where Pomfret had left the ship under orders. Where Bolitho had come aboard to replace him, and by so doing had killed Vibart's own chance of promotion.

He watched Bolitho's profile and felt the anger running through him like fire. It was five thousand miles to Hood's squadron. A lot could happen before that.

He awoke with a start as Bolitho said crisply, 'Dismiss the watch below, Mr. Vibart, and double the lookouts.' He gestured towards the open channel. 'Here, everyone is an enemy.' He gave Vibart a meaning glance and went below.

2

Beware, the Press!

The gig's crew pulled steadily towards the stone jetty and then gratefully tossed their oars as Stockdale growled an order and the bowman jabbed at a ringbolt with his boathook.

Bolitho turned his head to look back at the frigate and smiled slightly to himself. The *Phalarope* was anchored well out in Falmouth Bay, her sleek shape black and stark against the sea and watery sunlight which had at last managed to break through the scudding clouds. The ship had made a slow approach towards the headland, and he had no doubt that her presence had long since been reported, and every able-bodied man in the town would have taken full advantage of the warning to make himself scarce from the dreaded press.

By his side, huddled in his boat cloak, Lieutenant Thomas Herrick sat in silence, his eyes watching the rain-soaked hills beyond the town and the grey, timeless bulk of the castle above Carrick Roads. There were several small craft moored in the safety of the Roads, coasters and tubby fishing boats enjoying the shelter and the protection of the anchorage.

Bolitho said, 'A brisk walk will do us good, Mr. Herrick. It may be the last chance we get for a while.' He stepped stiffly from the boat and waited until Herrick had followed him up the worn steps. An ancient sailor with a grey beard called, 'Welcome, Captain! It is a fine ship you have out there!'

Bolitho nodded. A Cornishman himself, and a native of Falmouth, he knew well enough that it was unlikely any younger men would dare to stay and pass idle remarks to a King's officer. Frigates were too busy to enter port unless for one thing. To gather men.

Vibart had voiced that very thing as the *Phalarope* had swooped through the night, her sails thundering to the wind, her bow throwing back the spray in an unbroken white wake. But when Bolitho had outlined his plan even he had lapsed into silence.

As a boy Bolitho had often seen the approach of a ship of war, and had heard the news shouted down the narrow streets, the cry carried from house to house like a distress signal. Young men had dropped their work, bid hasty farewells to their friends and families, and made for the safety of the hills, where they could watch and wait until the ship had made sail and dipped towards the horizon. There was a rough coast road above the cliffs which led north-east away from Falmouth towards Gerrans Bay and St. Austell. No press gang would take the time and trouble to follow them. Hampered by weapons and the short breath left by lack of exercise, they would know such efforts to be wasted. No, there were few who were slow or stupid enough to allow the King's men an easy catch.

In pitch darkness Bolitho had turned the ship inshore and heaved to, the deck canting savagely to the stiff wind and the swift offshore currents. Old Proby had been at first doubtful, and then had openly showed his admiration. There were no beacons, and apart from a dull shadow of land there was nothing to show that Bolitho had found the exact point below Gerrans Bay where the chart displayed a tiny crescent of beach.

A landing party had been detailed soon after leaving Portsmouth, and below the quarterdeck, their faces pale in a shaded lantern, the selected men had listened to Bolitho's instructions.

'I am putting you ashore here in the two cutters. You will be in two parties. Mr. Vibart and Mr. Maynard with one, and Mr. Farquhar with the second.' He had sought out the severe face of Brock, the gunner. 'Mr. Brock will also accompany the second party.' Farquhar might be too eager if left alone, he thought. Brock's experience and self-contained efficiency would make a nice balance.

'If I know Falmouth, as soon as the ship appears in the Bay at first light the sort of men we are after will make their way along the coast road as fast as they can go. If your parties keep up a steady march along that road as soon as you leave Pendower Beach, they should run right into your arms. It saves selection, I believe.' He had seen Brock nod his narrow head approvingly. 'The boats will return to the ship and you can march straight on to Falmouth.' A few of the men sighed, and he had added calmly, 'It is only five miles. It is better than tramping around the town for nothing.'

With Herrick at his side he walked briskly up the sloping road towards the neat houses, his shoes slipping on the well-remembered cobbles. By now Vibart must have made some catches, he thought. If not, if he had made his first misjudgement, it would only help to add to the tension in the *Phalarope*.

Lieutenant Okes was still aboard in charge of the ship until his return, and Captain Rennie's marines would be able to deter anyone who still hoped to desert. Even a desperate man would find it hard to swim the long stretch of tossing water from the anchored frigate.

He glanced sideways at Herrick and said abruptly, 'You have been aboard for two years, I believe?' He watched the guard drop behind the lieutenant's eyes. He had an open, homely face, yet there was this reserve, this caution, which seemed to symbolise for Bolitho the attitude of the whole ship. It was as if they were all cowed to a point where they neither trusted nor hoped. He added, 'According to the log you were officer of the watch when the trouble started?'

Herrick bit his lip. 'Yes, sir. We were beating up from Lorient. It was during the middle watch and quiet for the time of year.'

Bolitho watched the uncertainty crossing the man's face and felt a touch of pity. It was never easy to be the junior lieutenant in a ship of war.

Promotion was slow and hard without either luck or influence. He thought of his own first chance, how easily it might have gone against him. One piece of luck had followed hard upon another. As a lieutenant in a ship of the line, at the very time of the American rebellion, he had been sent away in charge of a prize crew in a captured brig. While heading towards Antigua he had fallen upon a privateer and had fooled her captain into believing that his brig was still an ally. A rush of boarders, a swift and savage clash of steel, and the second ship had been his. Upon arrival at Antigua he had been welcomed by the Commander-in-Chief like a hero. Victories had been scarce, and reverses only too many.

So at the age of twenty-two he had been given command of the *Sparrow*. Again luck had guided his footsteps. The sloop's original commander had died of fever, and her first lieutenant was too junior for the coveted post.

He forced the sympathy to the back of his mind. 'How many men were in the mutiny?'

Herrick replied bitterly, 'No more than ten. They were trying to release a seaman called Fisher. Captain Pomfret had had him flogged for insubordination the previous day. He had been complaining about the foul food.'

Bolitho nodded. 'That is not uncommon.'

'But Captain Pomfret was not satisfied!' The words burst from his lips in an angry flood. 'He had him lashed to the bowsprit, without allowing the surgeon even to treat his back!' He shuddered. 'In the Bay of Biscay, with frost on the rigging, and he left him lashed there like so much meat!' He controlled himself with an effort and muttered, 'I am sorry, sir. I keep thinking about it.'

Bolitho thought back to Pomfret's neat, matter-of-fact recording in the log. The protesting seamen had rushed the quarterdeck and overpowered the quartermaster and master's mate at pistol point. Only Herrick, a man who obviously agreed with everything the seamen had offered as a grievance, stood between them and a full-scale mutiny. Somehow or other he had cowed them with words. He had ordered them back to the forecastle and they had obeyed because they trusted him. The next day Pomfret's vengeance had broken over the ship in a wave of ferocity. Twenty floggings, and two men hanged. He would not wait until the *Phalarope* rejoined the fleet, nor would he wait for higher authority to gauge his actions. Herrick's bitterness was well founded, or was it? On the face of it, Pomfret was within his rights. Perhaps Herrick should have shot down the mutineers, or even have foreseen the coming danger. He could have summoned the afterguard, given his life if necessary. Bolitho chilled at the thought of what might have happened if Herrick too had been overcome while he tried to reason with the desperate seamen. The sleeping officers would have been slaughtered, the ship thrown into chaos in enemy waters. It did not bear thinking about.

He persisted, 'And then later, when you rejoined the fleet off Brest and came to action with those French ships. Why was the *Phalarope* not engaged?' Again he saw the wretched emotions, the uncertainty and anger.

Then it dawned on him. Herrick feared him almost as much as Pomfret. He was captain. He had taken over the ship where Herrick's own misery and shame moved like a ghost between decks. Gently he added, 'I take it that the crew were making their own protest?'

Herrick sunk his chin into his neckcloth. 'Yes, sir. There was nothing you could put a name to. Sails were badly set. Gun crews slow in responding.' He laughed sharply. 'But it was wasted. Quite wasted!' He looked sideways at Bolitho, a brief spark of defiance in his eyes. 'Pomfret usually avoided action if possible!'

Bolitho looked away. You fool, he thought angrily. You have allowed this man to act as a conspirator. You should silence him now, before everyone aboard knows you have accepted an open criticism of Pomfret, a selected captain, without a murmur.

He said slowly, 'When you have a command of your own, Herrick, you may feel otherwise. The right course of action is not usually the easiest.' He thought of Vibart's hostility and wondered what *he* had been doing during the mutiny. 'I know that every officer must *earn* his men's loyalty.' He hardened his tone. 'But a captain has the loyalty of his officers as a right, do I make myself clear?'

Herrick looked straight ahead along the street. 'Aye, aye, sir!' The guard was restored. His expression wooden and controlled.

Bolitho halted below the church wall and looked up the familiar street which ran beside the churchyard. At the top of the road was the house, its square, uncompromising shape, the familiar grey stonework as enduring as his memory of it.

He stood looking up at it, suddenly apprehensive, like an intruder. He said, 'Carry on, Mr. Herrick. Go and see the garrison victualling officer and arrange to have as many fresh eggs and butter sent over to the ship as you can manage.'

Herrick was looking past him towards the big house, his eyes suddenly wistful. 'Your home, sir?'

'Yes.' Bolitho began to see Herrick in a different light again. Away from the order and discipline of the frigate and framed by the rain-washed building behind him he looked vaguely defenceless. Bolitho knew from his own methodical study of the ship's papers that Herrick came of a poor, middle-class Kentish family, his father being a clerk. For that reason he would be without influence when he most needed it, and unless he was very fortunate in battle his chances of advancement were slight.

The sight of his home, the confusion of judgement and ideas angered him, and he said sharply, 'After you have dealt with the Army perhaps you would care to join me for a glass of wine before we sail, Mr. Herrick?' He gestured up the road. 'My father will welcome you.'

Herrick opened his mouth, an unspoken refusal caught in mid-air. He tugged at his cross-belt and said awkwardly, 'Thank you, sir.' He touched his hat as Bolitho turned away towards the house.

Herrick stood quite still, the wind tugging at his boatcloak, until Bolitho reached the gates. Then, chin sunk on chest, he walked slowly towards the castle, his brow creased in a deep frown.

Lieutenant Giles Vibart cursed as his feet skidded on loose stones and a seaman cannoned into his back. The grey morning light showed the extent of the previous night's wind, and the long grass and gorse was flattened and glittering with rain. He pulled his watch from inside his coat and then held up his hand.

'We'll stop here for a bit!' He saw his order passing down the small party of men, and waited until they had squatted beside the crude track before he crossed to the two midshipmen and the gunner.

'We'll give these idlers ten minutes and them move off again.' He looked round as a shaft of frail sunlight touched his cheek. 'Then you can take a party further inland, Mr. Farquhar, in case of stragglers.'

Farquhar shrugged and kicked at a pebble. 'Suppose nobody comes, sir?'

Vibart snapped, 'Just do as you're told!'

Maynard, the other midshipman, readjusted his dirk and looked anxiously towards the resting seamen. 'I hope none of 'em try and desert. The captain would be very displeased!'

The gunner gave a lazy grin. 'I picked them myself. They're all old hands.' He picked up a piece of grass and pulled it between his uneven teeth. 'All pressed men, too. Much better than volunteers for this job!'

Vibart nodded. 'Quite right, Mr. Brock. There's nothing better to give an edge to the press. No sailor likes to think others are getting away with it!'

Brock frowned. 'An' why should they? It's not right that the fleet is expected to fight bloody battles and keep the country free of the Frogs without help from these lazy, pampered civilians! They make money and live happily with their wives while we do all the hard work!' He spat out the grass. 'To hell with 'em, I say!'

Vibart walked away from them and stared down at the rocky beach below the cliff. What did it matter what anybody said? They needed men, and the sooner the better.

He watched the wind hissing through the tangled grass and thought again of the frigate's dash through the night. How unlike Pomfret, he thought. He had always liked and expected a smart ship. But to him it had been more like a possession than a weapon of war. He lorded it in his fine cabin, enjoying his choice wines and well-stocked food store while he, Vibart, ran the ship and did all the things of which he was totally incapable. He moved restlessly on his thick legs as the old fire of resentment and injustice explored his mind like a drug.

Pomfret had been full of promises. A word in the right quarter and his first lieutenant would receive recognition and promotion when the time was right. All Vibart had to do was take care of the ship and her discipline and he would do the rest.

The captain had no interest in prize money. He was rich beyond Vibart's imagination. He was equally indifferent to glory. He was as inefficient as he was cowardly.

Vibart would have been able to manage Pomfret's indulgences but for the captain's real weakness. Like many cowards he was a bully and a sadist. To Vibart harsh discipline was a necessity, but senseless cruelty seemed to be pointless. It weakened or maimed men who would be better employed on duty, it damaged the blind trust of men required to obey without question.

But Vibart was only a lieutenant, and was thirty-three years old. Unlike most of the other officers he had not entered the Navy as a boy, but had come the hard way, having served in merchant vessels the length and breadth of the world. His last three years at sea, prior to entering the Navy as a master's mate, had been aboard an African slaver where he had soon learned that senseless brutality had meant loss of profit at the end of a voyage, with stinking holds as full of useless carcasses as prime, saleable bodies.

He turned angrily and shouted, 'Right! We'll move off now!' He watched with brooding eyes as the men picked up their weapons and shambled down the track, while that arrogant young monkey Farquhar strode up the hill-side to head inland. He was typical, Vibart thought viciously. Eighteen years old, pampered and well bred, with a powerful admiral to watch over his progress like a nurse. He glared at the lanky Maynard: 'Don't stand there gaping. Go ahead of the party!'

Well, in spite of their advantages of breeding and influence he, Giles Vibart, had shown them. He allowed the knowledge to stir his insides like rum. He had realised that Pomfret's weakness could not be changed, just as he had soon understood that to oppose him would have finished any hope he might have had left for personal reward. He had managed to overcome his own objections. After all, did it really matter that men were unjustly flogged? They might be flogged later for real cause, so where was the difference?

He had had one ally aboard the unhappy frigate. David Evans, the purser, had kept him fully informed of what was going on between decks. Evans was an evil man even by the standards of his trade. Whenever his ship touched land he would be ashore negotiating for stores and food, using his keen brain and ready tongue to purchase the very worst, the most rancid stock available, and adjusting the price to his own pocket. Vibart, as first lieutenant, was well aware of this trick, but used his knowledge to his own advantage. Evans had useful toadies on the lower deck, reliable men who would inform readily on their messmates for small reward.

Carefully and methodically Vibart had put ruthless pressure on the crew. But floggings were all in the captain's name, never in his own. He was always careful to show off his own seamanship and prowess at navigation whenever Pomfret was not there to see it. Whatever happened when the pressure broke through the men's resistance, Vibart had to be sure that he was ready and blameless at any inquiry.

Evans had told him about the proposed mutiny, and Vibart had known that the moment had at last arrived. When he had suggested to Pomfret that the flogged seaman, Fisher, should be lashed to the bowsprit like some flayed figurehead, he had known that it was the last thing needed to fan alive the flame of anger and mutiny.

The ringleaders had chosen their time well, he conceded. If Okes had been officer-of-the-watch he might have panicked and raised an almighty row which even Pomfret, half sodden with drink in his bunk, would have heard. But Herrick was a different matter. He was a thinker. He would be bound to reason with the men, to prevent an uprising rather than to crush it by brute force.

Knowing all these things, even to the chosen time, Vibart had waited breathlessly in his cabin. Squeezed in the wardroom had been the ship's full complement of marines, their sergeant another of Vibart's willing helpers. It was such a straightforward plan that Vibart had wanted to laugh at its simplicity.

The mutineers would rush the quarterdeck and overpower the watch. Herrick, rather than raise the alarm and drive Pomfret to another bloody frenzy, would try to quieten them, to listen to their complaints. But the men would kill him, and then Vibart would rush on deck and blanket the quarterdeck with musket fire.

At the court of inquiry even the most biased admiral would not fail to see that Vibart had saved the ship, when one officer lay dead with his watch and the captain slept in a drunken stupor.

Even now on the wet hillside Vibart could remember the sound of his own breathing in that sealed cabin. Then the stealthy approach of the mutineers even as two bells pealed out from forward. But there were no shots, and no cries. No rasp of steel, or the sound of Herrick's last gasp for life.

When at last, unable to control his anxiety, he had crept on deck he had found Herrick at his post, the maindeck deserted.

The young lieutenant had reported the incident as a 'deputation' concerned with the welfare of the dying Fisher. That was all. When Vibart had pushed him further, Herrick had still stood his ground, his anger giving way to contempt as his eyes had fallen on Vibart's loaded pistols and the marine sergeant at the cabin hatch.

The next morning Pomfret had been almost as beside himself as if an actual mutiny had broken out. 'Complaints?' He had screamed at Vibart across the wide cabin. 'They *dare* to complain?' Even without much prompting he had seen the men's actions as a real challenge to his own authority.

When at last the frigate had been ordered to Portsmouth to face an inquiry, Vibart had known fresh hope. Things had moved fast. The ship had been stripped of known troublemakers and had been fitted out for another long spell of service. Pomfret had stayed in his cabin, sulky and brooding up to the time he was ordered from the ship. But no new commission had arrived for Vibart. No command of either the *Phalarope* or any other ship.

He was back exactly as he had been when he had first joined the frigate under Pomfret, except that the new captain, Bolitho, was another kind of person entirely.

He jerked from his thoughts as Maynard called breathlessly, 'Sir! One of the men is signalling from the hillside!'

Vibart drew his sword and slashed sharply at a small bush. 'So the captain guessed right, did he?' He waved his arm in a half circle. 'Right, you men! Get to either side of the road and wait for Mr. Farquhar's party to work round behind them. I don't want anyone to escape!' He saw the men nod and shuffle to the bushes, swinging their clubs and readjusting their cutlass belts.

When the moment of contact actually came, even Vibart was taken off guard.

It was more like a carefree procession than a party of men avoiding the press gangs. Some fifty or more men tightly bunched on the narrow track, talking, some even singing as they strolled aimlessly away from Falmouth and the sea.

Vibart saw Farquhar's slim silhouette break the skyline and stepped out from the bushes. His appearance could not have affected them more deeply had he been something from another world. He held up his sword as his men stepped out across the road behind him.

'In the King's name! I charge you all to line up and be examined!' His voice broke the spell. Some of the men turned and tried to run back along the road, only to halt gasping at the sight of Farquhar's men and the levelled muskets. One figure bolted up the hillside, his feet kicking the grass like some terrified rabbit.

Josling, a bosun's mate, lashed out with his cudgel. The man screamed and rolled down the slope and lay in a puddle clutching his shin. Josling turned him over with his foot and felt the man's bleeding leg. Then he looked at Vibart and said offhandedly, 'No eggs broken, sir!'

Shocked and dazed the men allowed themselves to be pushed into line on the road. Vibart stood watching and calculating. It had been so easy that he wanted to grin.

Brock said, 'Fifty-two men, sir. All sound in wind and limb!'

One of the uneven rank dropped on to his knees and whimpered, 'Please, *please*, sir! Not me!'

There were tears on his cheeks, and Vibart asked harshly, 'What is so special about you?'

'My wife, sir! She's *ill*! She needs me at home!' He rocked on his knees. 'She'll die without my support, sir, in God's name she will!'

Vibart said wearily, 'Stand that man on his feet. He makes me sick!'

Another at the end of the rank said in a tight voice, 'I am a shepherd, I'm excused from the press!' He stared round challengingly until his eye fell on Brock. 'Ask him, sir. The gunner will bear me out!'

Brock sauntered across to him and held up his cane. 'Roll up your sleeve.' He sounded bored, even indifferent, and several of the watching men forgot their shocked misery to lean from the rank and watch.

The man in question took a half-pace away, but not quickly enough. Like a steel claw Brock's hand fastened on his rough shirt and tore it from his arm to display an intervwoven tattoo of crossed flags and cannon.

Brock stepped back and swayed on his heels. He looked along the rank. 'No man has a tattoo like that unless he is a seaman.' His voice was slow and patient, like a schoolmaster with a new class. 'No man would recognise me as a gunner unless he had served in a King's ship!'

Without warning his cane flashed in the weak sunlight. When it returned to his side the other man had blood on his face where it had cut almost to the bone.

The gunner looked at him levelly. 'Most of all, I dislike being taken for a fool!' He turned his back, dismissing the man from his mind.

A seaman yelled, 'Another signal, sir! One more group comin' down the road!'

Vibart sheathed his sword. 'Very well.' He looked coldly at the shivering line of men. 'You are entering an honourable service. You have just learned the first lesson. Don't make me teach you another!'

Maynard fell into step beside him his face troubled. 'It seems a pity that there is no other way, sir?'

Vibart did not reply. Like the man who had begged for his wife, such statements lacked both purpose and meaning.

Only aboard the ship did anything count for any of them.

Bolitho sipped at his port and waited until the servant girl had cleared away the table. His stomach had long grown used to meagre and poorly cooked shipboard food, so that the excellent meal of good Cornish lamb left him feeling glutted and uncomfortable.

Across the table his father, James Bolitho, drummed impatiently on the polished wood with his one remaining hand and then took a long swallow of port. He seemed ill at ease, even nervous, as he had been from the moment of his son's arrival.

Bolitho watched him quietly and waited. There was such a change in his father. From his own boyhood days to the present time Bolitho had seen his father only on rarely spaced occasions when he had returned here to the family home. From foreign wars and far-off countries, from exploits which children could only guess at. He could remember him as tall and grave in his naval uniform, shedding his service self-discipline like a cloak as he had come through that familiar doorway beside the portraits of the Bolitho family. Men like himself, like his son, sailors first and foremost.

When Bolitho had been a midshipman under Sir Henry Langford he had learned of his father's wounds whilst he had been engaged in fighting for the fast-advancing colonies in India, and when he had seen him again he had found him suddenly old and embittered. He had been a man of boundless energy and ideas, and to be removed from the Navy List, no matter how honourably, was more than the loss of an arm, it was like having his life cut from within him.

Locally in Falmouth he was respected as a firm and just magistrate, but Bolitho knew in his heart that his father's very being still lay with the sea, and the ships which came and went on the tide. Even his old friends and comrades had stopped coming to visit him, perhaps unable to bear what their very presence represented. Interest changed so easily into envy. Contact could harm rather than soothe.

Bolitho had a brother and two sisters. The latter had now both married, one to a farmer, the other to an officer of the garrison. Of Hugh, his older brother, nothing had yet been said, and Bolitho made himself wait for what he guessed was uppermost in his father's mind.

'I watched your ship come in, Richard.' The hand drummed busily on the table. 'She's a fine vessel, and when you get to the West Indies again I have no doubt you will bring more honour to the family.' He shook his head sadly. 'England needs all her sons now. It seems as if the world must be our enemy before we can find the right solution.'

It was very quiet in the house. After the pitch of a deck, the creak of spars, it was like another world. Even the smells were different. The packed humanity, and the varied aromas of tar and salt, of cooking and damp, all were alien here.

It felt lonely, too. In his mind's eye he could still picture his mother, young and vivacious as he remembered her. Again, he had been at sea when she had died of some brief but final illness. Now there was no companion for James Bolitho, and nobody to sit enraptured or amused by stories of the family's past exploits.

Bolitho glanced at the great clock. 'My men will have found new people for the crew by now or not at all,' he said quietly. 'It is a sad necessity that we have to get seamen like this.'

His father's face came alive from his inner thoughts. 'I believe that their duty is more important than their passing comfort! Every week I have to sign deportation orders for the colonies, or hang useless thieves. Life in a King's ship would have spared them the indignity of life ashore, would have saved them from petty greed and temptation!'

Bolitho studied his father's face and remembered himself as he had appeared in the mirror of the George Inn at Portsmouth. It was there in his father, as it was in the portraits along the walls. The same calm face and dark hair, the same slightly hooked nose. But his father had lost his old fire, and his hair was grey now, like that of a man much older.

His father stood up and walked to the fire. Over his shoulder he said gruffly, 'You have not yet heard about your brother?'

Bolitho tensed. 'No. I thought he was still at sea.'

'At sea?' The older man shook his head vaguely. 'Of course, I kept it from you. I suppose I should have written to you, but in my heart I still hoped he might change his ways and nobody would have known about it.'

Bolitho waited. His brother had always been the apple of his father's eye. When last he had seen him he had been a lieutenant in the Channel Fleet, the next in line for this house and for the family inheritance. Bolitho had never felt particularly close to Hugh, but put it down to a natural family jealousy. Now, he was not so sure.

'I had great hopes for Hugh.' His father was talking to the fire. To himself. 'I am only glad his mother is not alive to know of what he became!'

'Is there something I can do?' Bolitho watched the shoulders quiver as his father sought to control his voice.

'Nothing. Hugh is no longer in the Navy. He got into debt gambling. He always had an eye for the tables, as I think you know. But he got into *deep* trouble, and to end it all he fought a duel with a brother officer, and killed him!'

Bolitho's mind began to clear. That explained the few servants, and the fact that over half the land belonging to the house had been sold to a local farmer.

'You covered his debts then?' He kept his voice calm. 'I have some prize money if . . .'

The other man held up his hand 'That is not necessary. It was my fault for being so blind. I was stupid about that boy. I must pay for my misjudgement!' He seemed to become more weary. 'He deserted the Navy, turned his back on it, even knowing how his act would hurt me. Now he has gone.'

Bolitho started. 'Gone?'

'He went to America. I have not heard of him for two years, nor do I want to.' When he turned Bolitho saw the lie shining in his eyes. 'Not content with bringing disgrace on the family name, he has done this thing. Betrayed his country!'

Bolitho thought of the chaos and death at the disaster of Philadelphia and answered slowly, 'He may have been prevented from returning by the rebellion.'

'You know your brother, Richard. Do you really think it likely? He always had to be right, to hold the winning cards. No, I cannot see him pining away in a prison camp!'

The servant girl entered the room and bobbed in a clumsy curtsy. 'Beggin' pardon, zur. There's an officer to zee you.'

'That'll be Herrick, my third lieutenant,' said Bolitho hurriedly. 'I asked him to take a glass with us. I'll tell him to go if you wish?'

His father stood up straight and flicked his coat into position again. 'No, boy. Have him come in. I will not let my shame interfere with the real pride I have in my *remaining* son.'

Bolitho said gently, 'I am very sorry, Father. You must know that.'

'Thank you. Yes, I do know. And you were the one I thought would never make your way in the Navy. You were always the dreamer, the unpredictable one. I am afraid I neglected you for Hugh.' He sighed. 'Now it is too late.' There was a step in the hallway and he said with sudden urgency, 'In case I never see you again, my boy, there is something you must have.' He swallowed. 'I wanted Hugh to have it when he became a captain.' He reached into a cupboard and held out his sword. It was old and well tarnished, but Bolitho knew it was of greater value than steel and gilt.

He hesitated. 'Your father's sword. You always wore it!'

James Bolitho nodded and turned it over carefully in his hands. 'Yes, I always wore it. It was a good friend.' He held it out. 'Take it! I *want* you to wear it for me!'

His father suddenly smiled. 'Well then, let us greet your junior officer together, eh?'

When Herrick walked uncertainly into the wide room he saw only his smiling host and his new captain, one the living mould of the other.

Only Bolitho saw the pain in his father's eyes and was deeply moved.

It was strange how he had come to the house, as he had always done in the past, seeking comfort and advice. Yet he had mentioned nothing about the difficulties and danger of his new command, or the double-edged responsibility which hung over his head like an axe.

For once, he had been the one who was needed, and he was ashamed because he did not know the answer.

At dawn the following day the frigate *Phalarope* unfurled her sails and broke out her anchor. There were no cheers to speed her parting, but there were many tears and curses from the women and old men who watcher from the jetties.

The air was keen and fresh, and as the yards creaked round and the ship heeled away from the land Bolitho stood aft by the taffrail, his glass moving slowly across the green sloping hills and the huddled town below.

He had his ship, and all but a full complement. With time the new men would soon be moulded into sailors, and given patience and understanding they might make their country proud of them.

St. Anthony's Light moved astern, the ancient beacon which was the returning sailor's first sight of home. Bolitho wondered when or if he would see it again. He thought too of his father, alone in the old house, alone with his memories and shattered hopes. He thought of the sword and all that it represented.

He turned away from the rail and stared down at one of the ship's boys, a mere infant of about twelve years old. The boy was weeping uncontrollably and waving vaguely at the land as it cruised away into the haze. Bolitho asked, 'Do you know that I was your age when I first went to sea, boy?'

The lad rubbed his nose with a grubby fist and gazed at the captain with something like wonder.

Bolitho added, 'You'll see England again. Never you fear!' He turned away quickly lest the boy should see the uncertainty in his eye.

By the wheel old Proby intoned, 'South-west by south. Full and by, quartermaster.'

Then, as if to cut short the agony of sailing, he walked to the lee rail and spat into the sea.

3

Beef for the Purser

Twenty days after weighing anchor the frigate *Phalarope* crossed the thirtieth parallel and heeled sickeningly to a blustering north-west gale. Falmouth lay three thousand miles astern, but the wind with all its tricks and cunning cruelties stayed resolutely with the ship.

As one bell struck briefly from the forecastle and the dull copper sun moved towards the horizon the frigate ploughed across each successive bank of white-crested rollers with neither care nor concern for the men who served her day by day, hour by hour. No sooner was one watch dismissed below than the boatswain's mates would run from hatch to hatch, their calls twittering, their voices hoarse in the thunder of canvas and the never ending hiss of spray.

'All hands! All hands! Shorten sail!'

Later, stiff and dazed from their dizzy climb aloft, the seamen would creep below, their bodies aching, their fingers stiff and bleeding from their fight with the rebellious canvas.

Now, the men off watch crouched in the semi-darkness of the berth deck groping for handholds and listening to the crash of water against the hull even as they tried to finish their evening meal. From the deck beams the swinging lanterns threw strange shadows across their bowed heads, picking out individual faces and actions like scenes from a partially cleaned oil painting.

Below the sealed hatches the air was thick with smells. That of bilge water mixing with sweat and the sour odour of seasickness, and the whole area was filled with sound as the ship fought her own battle with the Atlantic. The steady crash of waves followed by the jubilant surge of water along the deck above, the continuous groaning of timbers and the humming of taut stays, all defied the men to sleep and relax even for a moment.

John Allday sat astride one of the long, scrubbed benches and gnawed carefully at a tough piece of salt beef. Between his strong teeth it felt like leather, but he made himself eat it, and closed his mind to the rancid cask from which it had come. The deep cut on his cheek where Brock's cane had found its mark had healed in an ugly scar, and as his jaws moved steadily on the meat he could feel the skin tightening painfully where blown salt and cold winds had drawn the edges together like crude stitching.

Across the table, and watching him with an unwinking stare, sat Pochin, a giant seaman with shoulders like a cliff. He said at last, 'You've settled in right enough, mate.' He smiled bleakly. 'All that squit when you was pressed came to nothin'!'

Allday threw a meat bone on to his tin plate and wiped his fingers on a piece of hemp. He regarded the other man with his steady, calm eyes for several seconds and then replied, 'I can wait.'

Pochin glared through the gloom, his head cocked to listen to some of the men retching. 'Lot of bloody women!' He looked back at Allday. 'I was forgettin', you are an old hand at this.'

Allday shrugged and looked down at his palms. 'You never get rid of the tar, do you?' He leaned back against the timbers and sighed. 'My last ship was the *Resolution*, seventy-four. I was a foretopman.' He allowed his eyes to close. 'A good enough ship. We paid off just a few months before the American Revolution, and I was clean away before the press could lay a finger on me!'

An old, grey-haired man with washed-out blue eyes said huskily, 'Was you really a shepherd like you told 'em?'

Allday nodded. 'That, and other things. I had to stay out in the open. To keep away from the towns. I would choke to death under a roof!' He gave a small smile. 'Just an occasional run into Falmouth was enough for me. Just enough for a woman, and a glass or two!'

The old seaman, Strachan, pursed his lips and rocked against the table as the ship heeled steeply and sent the plates skittering across the deck. 'It sounds like a fair life, mate.' He seemed neither wistful nor envious. It was just a statement. Old Ben Strachan had been in the Navy for forty years, since he had first trod deck as a powder-monkey. Life ashore was a mystery to him, and in his regimented world appeared even more dangerous than the privations afloat.

Allday looked round as a hunched figure rose over the table's edge and threw himself across his arms amongst the litter of food. Bryan Ferguson had been in a continuous torment of seasickness and fear from the very moment Vibart's figure had appeared on that coast road. In Falmouth he had been a clerk working at a local boatyard. Physically he was not a strong man, and now in the swinging lantern's feeble light his face looked as grey as death itself.

His thin body was bruised in many places, both from falling against unfamiliar shipboard objects and not least from the angry canes of the bosun's mates and petty officers as the latter sought to drive the new men into the mysteries of seamanship and sail drill.

Day after day it had continued. Harried and chased from one part of the ship to the next with neither let-up nor mercy. Quivering with terror Ferguson had dragged his way up the swooping shrouds and out along the yards, until he could see the creaming water leaping below him as if to claw at his very feet. The first time he had clung sobbing to the mast, incapable of either moving out along the yard or even down towards the safety of the deck.

Josling, a bosun's mate, had screamed up at him, 'Move out, you bugger, or I'll have the hide off you!'

At that particular moment Ferguson's tortured mind had almost broken. With each eager thrust of the frigate's stem, and with every passing hour, Ferguson's home fell further and further astern. And with it went his wife, sinking into the wave-tossed distance like a memory.

Over and over again he had pictured her pale, anxious face as he had last seen her. When the *Phalarope* had been sighted heading for Falmouth Bay most of the young townsmen had headed for the hills. Ferguson's wife had been ill for three years, and he had seen her get more frail and delicate, and on that day she had been more than unwell and he had begged to stay with her. But gravely she had insisted.

'You go with the others, Bryan. I'll be all right. And I'm not wanting the press to find you here!'

The nightmare became worse when he considered that if he had stayed with her he would still be safe and able to protect and help her.

Allday said quietly, 'Here, take some food.' He pushed a plate of dark meat across the boards. 'You've not eaten for days, man.'

Ferguson dragged his head from his forearms and stared glassily at the relaxed looking seaman. Unbeknown to Allday, Ferguson had almost jumped from the swaying mainyard rather than face another hour of torture. But Allday had run inboard along the yard, his feet splayed and balanced, one hand held out towards the gasping Ferguson. 'Here, mate! Just follow me an' don't look down.' There had been a quiet force in his tone, like that of a man who expected to be obeyed. He had added harshly, 'Don't give that bugger Josling a chance to beat you. The bastard enjoys making you jump!'

He stared now at the man's dark features, at the scar on his cheek, and at his calm, level eyes. Allday had been accepted immediately by the frigate's seamen, whereas the other newly pressed men were still kept at arm's length, as if on trial, until their merits or shortcomings could be properly measured. Perhaps it was because Allday was already hardened to a life at sea. Or maybe it came from the fact he never showed his bitterness at being pressed, or boasted about his life ashore like some of the others.

Ferguson swallowed hard to bite back the rising nausea. 'I can't eat it!' He peered wretchedly at the meat. 'It's swill!'

Allday grinned. 'You'll get used to it!'

Pochin sneered. 'You make me spew! I suppose you used to take your wife up to the 'eadland and go moist-eyed at the sight of a King's ship! I'll bet you used to feel so holy, so almighty proud as the ships sailed safely past'!

Ferguson stared at the man's angry face, mesmerised by his hate.

Pochin glared across the canting deck where the other crowded seamen had fallen silent at his outburst. 'You never had a thought for the poor buggers who manned 'em, nor what they was doin'!' He turned back to Ferguson with sudden malice. 'Well, your precious woman'll be out on the 'eadland now with some other pretty boy, I shouldn't wonder.' He made an obscene gesture. 'Let's 'ope she finds the time to be proud of *you*!'

Ferguson staggered to his feet, his eyes wide with a kind of madness. 'I'll kill you for that!'

He swung his fist, but Allday caught his wrist in mid-air. 'Save it!' Allday glared at Pochin's grinning face. 'His wife is sick, Pochin! Give him some rest!'

Old Ben Strachan said vaguely, 'I 'ad a wife once.' He scratched his shaggy grey head. 'Blessed if I can remember 'er name now!'

Some of the men laughed, and Allday hissed fiercely, 'Get a grip, Bryan! You can't beat men like Pochin. He envies you, that's all!'

Ferguson hardly heard the friendly warning in Allday's voice. Pochin's goading tone had opened the misery in his heart with renewed force, so that he could see his wife propped in her bed by the window as clearly as if he had just entered the room. That day, when the press gang had pushed him down the hillside, she would have been sitting there, waiting for his return. Now he was never going back. Would never see her again.

He staggered to his feet and threw the plate of meat down on the deck. 'I can't!' He was screaming. 'I *won't*!'

A horse-faced fo'c's'leman named Betts jumped to his feet as if shaken from a deep sleep. 'Don't jeer at 'im, mates!' He stood swaying below one of the lanterns. 'He's 'ad enough for a bit.'

Pochin groaned. 'Lord save us!' He rolled his eyes in mock concern.

Betts snarled, 'Jesus Christ! What do you have to suffer before you understand? This man is sick with fear for his wife, and others here have equal troubles. Yet all some of you can do is scoff at 'em!'

Allday shifted in his seat. Ferguson's sudden despair had touched some hidden spring in the men's emotions. Weeks, and in some cases years at sea without ever putting a foot on dry land were beginning to take a cruel toll. But this was dangerous and blind. He held up his hand and said calmly, 'Easy, lads. *Easy*.'

Betts glared down at him, his salt-reddened eyes only half focusing on Allday's face. 'How can you interfere?' His voice was slurred. 'We live like animals, on food that was rotten even *afore* it was put in casks!' He pulled his knife from his belt and drove it into the table. 'While those pigs down aft live like kings!' He peered round for support. 'Well, ain't I right? That bastard Evans is as sleek as a churchyard rat on what he stole from *our* food!'

'Well, now. Did I hear my name mentioned?'

The berth deck froze into silence as Evans, the purser, moved into a patch of lamplight.

With his long coat buttoned to his throat and his hair pulled back severely above his narrow face he looked for all the world like a ferret on the attack. He put his head on one side. 'Well, I'm waiting!'

Allday watched him narrowly. There was something evil and frightening about the little Welsh purser. All the more so because any one of the men grouped around him could have ended his life with a single blow.

Then Evans' eye fell on the meat beside the table. He sucked his teeth and asked sadly, 'And who did this, then?'

No one spoke, and once more the angry roar of the sea and wind enclosed the staggering berth deck with noise.

Ferguson looked up, his eyes bright and feverish. 'I did it.'

Evans leaned his narrow shoulders against the massive trunk of the foremast which ran right through both decks and said, '"I did it, *sir*."'

Ferguson mumbled something and then added, 'I am sorry, sir.'

Allday said coldly, 'It was an accident, Mr. Evans. Just an accident.'

'Food is food.' Evans's Welsh accent became more pronounced as his face became angrier. 'I cannot hope to keep you men in good health if you waste such excellent meat, now can I?'

Those grouped around the table stared down at the shapeless hunk of rancid beef as it lay gleaming in a patch of lamplight.

Evans added sharply, 'Now, you, whatever your bloody name is, *eat it!*'

Ferguson stared down at the meat, his mind swimming in nausea. The deck was discoloured with water and stained with droppings from the tilting table. There was vomit too, perhaps his own.

Evans said gently, 'I am waiting, boyo. One more minute and I'll take you aft. A touch of the cat might teach you some appreciation!'

Ferguson dropped to his knees and picked up the meat. As he lifted it to his mouth Betts pushed forward and tore it from his hands and threw it straight at Evans. 'Take it yourself, you bloody devil! Leave him alone!'

For a moment Evans showed the fear in his dark eyes. The men had crowded around him, their bodies rising and falling like a human tide with each roll of the ship. He could feel the menace, the sudden ice touch of terror.

Another voice cut through the shadows. 'Stand aside!' Midshipman Farquhar had to stoop beneath the low beams, but his eyes were steady and bright as they settled on the frozen tableau around the end table. Farquhar's approach had been so stealthy and quiet that not even the men at the opposite end of the deck had noticed him. He snapped, 'I am waiting. What is going on here?'

Evans thrust the nearest men aside and threw himself to Farquhar's side. With his hand shaking in both fear and fury he pointed at Betts. 'He struck me! *Me*, a warrant officer!'

Farquhar was expressionless. His tight lips and cold stare might have meant either amusement or anger. 'Very well, Mr. Evans. Kindly lay aft for the master-at-arms.'

As the purser scurried away Farquhar looked round the circle of faces with open contempt. 'You never seem to learn, do you?' He turned to Betts, who still stood staring at the meat, his chest heaving as if from tremendous exertion. 'You are a fool, Betts! Now you will pay for it!'

Allday pressed his shoulders against the frigate's cold, wet timbers and closed his eyes. It was all happening just as he knew it would. He listened to Bett's uneven breathing and Ferguson's quiet whimpers and felt sick. He thought suddenly of the quiet hillsides and the grey bunches of sheep. The space and the solitude.

Then Farquhar barked, 'Take him away, Mr. Thain.'

The master-at-arms pushed Betts towards the hatch ladder adding softly, 'Not a single flogging since we left Falmouth. I knew such gentleness was a bad mistake!'

Richard Bolitho leaned his palms on the sill of one of the big stern windows and stared out along the ship's frothing wake. Although the cabin itself was already in semi-darkness as the frigate followed the sun towards the horizon, the sea still looked alive, with only a hint of purple as a warning of the approaching night.

Reflected in the salt-speckled glass he could see Vibart's tall shape in the centre of the cabin, his face shadowed beneath the corkscrewing lantern, and behind him against the screen the slim figure of Midshipman Farquhar.

It took most of his self-control to keep himself immobile and calm as he considered what Farquhar had burst in to tell him. Bolitho had been going through the ship's books again trying to draw out Vibart's wooden reserve, to feel his way into the man's mind.

Like everything else during the past twenty days, it had been a hard and seemingly fruitless task. Vibart was too careful to show his hostility in the open and confined himself to short, empty answers, as if he hoarded his knowledge of the ship and her company like a personal possession.

Then Farquhar had entered the cabin with this story of Betts's assault on the purser. It was just one more thing to distract his thoughts from what lay ahead, from the real task of working the frigate into a single fighting unit.

He made himself turn and face the two officers.

'Sentry! Pass the word for Mr. Evans!' He heard the cry passed along the passageway and then added, 'It seems to me as if this seaman was provoked.'

Vibart swayed with the ship, his eyes fixed on a point above the captain's shoulder. He said thickly, 'Betts is no recruit, sir. He knew what he was doing!'

Bolitho turned to watch the open, empty sea. If only this had not happened just yet, he thought bitterly. A few more days and the damp, wind-buffeted ship would be in the sun, where men soon learned to forget their surroundings and started to look outboard instead of watching each other.

He listened to the hiss and gurgle of water around the rudder, the distant clank of pumps as the duty watch dealt with the inevitable seepage into the bilges. He felt tired and strained to the limit. From the moment the *Phalarope* had weighed anchor he had not spared himself or his efforts to maintain his hold over the ship. He had made a point of speaking to most of the new men, and of establishing contact with the regular crew. He had watched his officers, and had driven the ship to her utmost. It should have been a proud moment for him. The frigate handled well, lively and ready to respond to helm and sail like a thoroughbred.

Most of the new men had been sorted into their most suitable stations, and the sail drill had advanced beyond even his expectations. At the first suitable moment he intended to exercise the guns crews, but up to this time he had been prevented from much more than allocations of hands to the various divisions by the unceasing wind.

Now this, he fumed inwardly. No wonder the admiral had asked him to watch young Farquhar's behaviour.

There was a tap at the door and Evans stepped gingerly into the cabin, his eyes flickering like beads in the lamplight.

Bolitho gestured impatiently. 'Now then, Mr. Evans. Let me have the full story.'

He turned to stare at the water again as Evans launched into his account. To start with he seemed nervous, even frightened, but when Bolitho allowed him to continue without interruption or comment his voice grew sharper and more outraged.

Bolitho said at length. 'The meat that Betts threw at you. What cask did it come from?'

Evans was caught off guard. 'Number twelve, sir. I saw it stowed myself.' He added in a wheedling tone, 'I do my best, sir. They are ungrateful dogs for the most part!'

Bolitho turned and tapped the papers on his table. 'I checked the stowage myself, too, Mr. Evans. Two days ago when the hands were at drill!' He saw a flicker of alarm show itself on Evans' dark face and knew that his lie had gone home. A feeling of sudden anger swept through him like fire. All the things he had told his officers had been for nothing. Even the near-mutiny seemed to have made no impression on the minds of men like Evans and Farquhar.

He snapped, 'That cask was in the low stowage, was it not? And how many others were down there, do you think?'

Evans peered nervously around the cabin. 'Five or six, sir. They were some of the original stores which I . . .'

Bolitho slammed his fist on the table 'You make me sick, Evans! That cask and those others you have suddenly remembered were probably stowed two years ago before you began the Brest Blockade! They most likely leak, and in any case are quite rotten!'

Evans looked at his feet. 'I – I did not know, sir.'

Bolitho said harshly. 'If I could prove otherwise, Mr. Evans, I would have you stripped of your rank and flogged!'

Vibart stirred into life. 'I must protest, sir! Mr. Evans was acting as he thought fit! Betts struck him. There is no way of avoiding that fact.'

'So it appears, Mr. Vibart.' Bolitho stared at him coldly until the other man looked away. 'I will certainly back my officers in their efforts to carry out my orders. But senseless punishment at this time will do more harm than good.' He felt suddenly too tired to think clearly, but Vibart's anger seemed to drive him on. 'In another two weeks or so we will join the fleet under Sir Samuel Hood, and then there will be more than enough to keep us all occupied.'

He continued more calmly, 'Until then, each and every one of you will translate my standing orders into daily fact. Give the men your leadership and try to understand them. No good will ever come of useless brutality. If a man still persists in disobedience, then flogged he will be. But in this particular case I would suggest a more lenient experiment.' He saw Vibart's lower lip quivering with barely controlled anger. 'Betts can be awarded extra duties for seven days. The sooner the matter is forgotten, the sooner we can mend the damage!' He gestured briefly, 'Carry on with your watch, Mr. Farquhar.'

As Evans turned to follow the midshipman Bolitho added flatly. 'Oh, Mr. Evans, I see no reason for me to mention your neglect in the log.' He saw Evans watching him half gratefully, half fearfully. He finished, 'Provided I can show that you purchased the meat for your own purposes, your own mess perhaps?'

Evans blinked at Vibart and then back to Bolitho's impassive face. 'Purchase, sir? Me, sir?'

'Yes, Evans, *you*! You can make the payment to my clerk in the forenoon tomorrow. That is all.'

Vibart picked up his hat and waited until the door had closed behind the other man. 'Do you require me any more, sir?'

'I just want to tell you one thing more, Mr. Vibart. I have taken fully into consideration that you were under considerable strain during your duty with Captain Pomfret. Maybe some of the things you had to do were not to your liking.' He waited, but Vibart stared woodenly across his shoulder. 'I am not interested in the past, except as a lesson to everyone of what can happen in a badly run ship! As first lieutenant you are the key officer, the most experienced one aboard who can implement my orders, do you understand?'

'If you say so, sir.'

Bolitho dropped his eyes in case Vibart should see the rising anger there. He had offered Vibart his due share of responsibility, even his confidence, and yet the lieutenant seemed to accept it like a sign of weakness, of some faltering uncertainty. The contempt was as plain in his brevity as if he had shouted it to the ship at large.

It could not be easy for Vibart to take orders from a captain so junior in age and service. Bolitho tried once more to soften his feelings towards Vibart's hostility.

The latter said suddenly, 'When you have been aboard the *Phalarope* a little longer, sir, then maybe you will see it different.' He rocked back on his heels and watched Bolitho's face with a flat stare.

Bolitho relaxed his taut muscles. It was almost a relief that Vibart had shown him the only way to finish the matter. He eyed him coldly. 'I have read every log and report aboard this ship, Mr. Vibart. In all my limited *experience* I have never known a ship so apparently unwilling to fight the enemy or so incapable of performing her duty.' He watched the expression on Vibart's heavy features altering to shocked surprise. 'Well, we are going back to war, Mr. Vibart, and I intend to seek out and engage the enemy, *any* enemy, at every opportunity!' He dropped his voice. 'And when that happens I will expect to see every man acting as one. There will be no room for petty jealousy and cowardice then!'

A deep flush rose to Vibart's cheeks, but he remained silent.

Bolitho said, 'You are dealing with men, Mr. Vibart, not *things*! Authority is invested with your commission. Respect comes later, when you have earned it!'

He dismissed the first lieutenant with a curt nod and then turned back to stare at the creaming wake below the windows. As the door closed the tension tore at his body like a whip, and he gripped his hands together to prevent their shaking until the pain made him wince. He had made an enemy of Vibart, but there was too much at stake to do otherwise.

He slumped down on the bench seat as Stockdale pattered into the cabin and began to spread a cloth across the table.

The coxswain said, 'I've told your servant to bring your supper, Captain.' There was mistrust in his tone. He disliked Atwell, the cabin steward, and watched him like a dog with a rabbit. 'I don't suppose you'll be havin' any officer to dine with you, sir?'

Bolitho glanced at Stockdale, battered and homely like an old piece of furniture, and thought of Vibart's seething bitterness. 'No, Stockdale. I will be alone.'

He leaned back and closed his eyes. Alone and vulnerable, he thought.

Lieutenant Thomas Herrick tightened the spray-soaked muffler about his neck and shrugged his shoulders deeper into his watchcoat. Above the black, spiralling masts the stars were small and pale, and even in the keen air he could sense that the dawn was not far away.

The labouring ship herself was in darkness, so that the shapes around the deserted decks were unreal and totally unlike they appeared in daylight. The lashed guns were mere shadows, and the humming shrouds and stays seemed to go straight up to the sky, unattached and endless.

But as Herrick paced the quarterdeck deep in thought, he was able to ignore such things. He had seen them all too often before, and was able to pass each watch with only his mind for company. Once he paused beside the ship's big double wheel where the two helmsmen stood like dark statues, their faces partly lit in the shaded binnacle lamp as they watched the swinging compass or stared aloft at the trimmed sails.

Three bells struck tinnily from forward, and he saw a ship's boy stir at the rail and then creep, rubbing his eyes, to trim the compass lamp and adjust the hour-glass.

Time and again he found his eyes drawn to the black rectangle of the cabin hatch, and he wondered whether Bolitho had at last fallen asleep. Three times already during the morning watch, three times in an hour and a half the captain had appeared momentarily on deck, soundless and without warning. With neither coat nor hat, and his white shirt and breeches framed against the tumbling black water, he had seemed ghostlike and without true form, with the restlessness of a tortured spirit. On each occasion he had paused only long enough to peer at the compass or to look at the watchslate beside the wheel. Then a couple of turns up and down the weather side of the deck and he had vanish below.

At any other time Herrick would have felt both irritated and resentful. It might have implied that the captain was too unsure of his third lieutenant to leave him to take a watch alone. But when Herrick had relieved Lieutenant Okes at four o'clock Okes had whispered quickly that Bolitho had been on deck for most of the night.

Herrick frowned. Deep down he had the feeling that Bolitho had acted more by instinct than design. As if he was driven like the ship, by mood rather than inclination. He seemed unable to stand still, as if it took physical force to hold himself in one place for more than minutes at a time.

A figure moved darkly at the quarterdeck rail and he heard Midshipman Neale's familiar treble in the darkness.

'Able Seaman Betts has just reported, sir.' He stood staring up at Herrick, gauging his mood.

Herrick had to tear his thoughts back to the present with a jerk. Betts, the man who had apparently escaped a flogging or worse only at Bolitho's intervention, had been ordered to report at three bells for the first part of his punishment. Vibart had made it more than clear what would happen if he failed to execute the orders.

He saw Betts hovering behind the small midshipman and called, 'Here, Betts. Look lively!'

The man moved up to the rail and knuckled his forehead. 'Sir?'

Herrick gestured upwards towards the invisible topmast. 'Up you go then!' He kept the harshness from his tone. He liked Betts, a quiet but competent man, whose sudden flare of anger had surprised him more than he cared to admit. 'Get up to the main topmast, Betts. You will stand lookout until the first liutenant orders otherwise.' He felt a touch of pity. One hundred and ten feet above the deck, unsheltered from the cold wind, Betts would be numb within minutes. Herrick had already decided to send Neale up after him with something warm to eat as soon as the galley fire was lit for breakfast.

Betts spat on his hands and replied flatly, 'Aye, aye, sir. Seems a fair mornin'?' He could have been remarking on something quite normal and unimportant.

Herrick nodded. 'Aye. The wind is dropping and the air is much drier.' It was true. Betts' instinct had grasped the change as soon as he had emerged from the packed, airless berth deck where eighteen inches per man was the accepted hammock space.

Herrick added quietly, 'You were lucky, Betts. You could have been dancing at the gratings by eight bells.'

Betts stood staring at him, unmoved and calm. 'I'm not sorry for what 'appened, sir. I'd do it again.'

Herrick felt suddenly annoyed with himself for mentioning the matter. That was his trouble, he thought angrily. He always wanted to know and understand the reason for everything. He could not leave matters alone.

He snapped, 'Get aloft! And mind you keep a good lookout. The dawn'll be awake soon.' He watched the man's shadow merge with the main shrouds and followed him with his eye until he was lost in the criss-cross of rigging against the stars.

Again he found himself wondering why Bolitho had acted as he had over a man like Betts. Neither Vibart nor Evans had mentioned the matter, which seemed to add rather than detract from the importance of the affair. Perhaps Vibart had overstepped his authority again, he pondered. Under Pomfret the first lieutenant's presence had moved over the ship, controlling every action and day-to-day happening. Now he seemed hampered by Bolithos' calm authority, but the very fact that their disagreement was close to showing itself openly only made things worse. The ship seemed split in two, divided between the captain and Vibart. Pomfret had remained a frightening force in the background, and Herrick had found his work cut out to stay impartial and out of trouble. Now it appeared as if such neutrality was impossible.

He thought back to the moment he had gone to the big house in Falmouth. Before he had imagined he would find only envy there. His own poor beginnings were hard to shake free. He recalled Bolitho's father, the great pictures along the walls, the air of permanence and tradition, as if the present occupants were merely part of a pattern. Compared with his own small home in Rochester, the house had seemed a veritable palace.

Herrick's father had been a clerk in Rochester, working for the Kentish fruit trade. But Herrick, even as a small child, had watched the ships stealing up the Medway, and had allowed his impressionable mind to build his own future accordingly. For him it was the Navy. Nothing else would do. It was odd because there was no precedent in his family, all of whom had been tradesmen, sprinkled with the occasional soldier.

His father had pleaded in vain. He had warned him of the pitfalls, which were many. Lack of personal standing and financial security made him see only too clearly what his son was attempting to challenge. He even compromised by suggesting a safe berth aboard an Indiaman, but Herrick was quietly adamant.

Quite by chance a visiting warship had been laid up near Rochester while repairs had been carried out to her hull. Her captain had been a friend of the man who employed Herrick's father, a grave senior captain who showed neither resentment nor open scorn when the eleven years old boy had waylaid him and told him of his desire to go to sea in a King's ship.

Faced by the captain and his employer, Herrick's father had given in. To do him full justice he had made the best of it by using his meagre savings to send his son on his way, outwardly at least, a young gentleman as good as any of his fellows.

Herrick was now twenty-five. It had been a long and arduous journey from that time. He had learned humiliation and embarrassment for the first time. He had faced unequal opposition of breeding and influence. The starry-eyed boy had been whittled away and hardened like the good Kentish oak beneath his feet. But one thing had not changed. His love of the sea and the Navy stayed over him like a protecting cloak or some strange religion which he only partly understood.

This timeless thing was the same to all men, he decided. It was far above them. It controlled and used everyone alike, no matter what his ambition might be.

He smiled at himself as he continued his endless pacing. He wondered what young Neale, yawning hugely by the rail, would think of his grave faced senior. Or the helmsmen who watched the swinging needle and gauged the pull of the sails. Or Betts, high overhead on his precarious perch, his own thoughts no doubt full of what he had done and what might lie in store for him behind Evans' vengeance.

Maybe it was better to be unimaginative, he thought. To be completely absorbed in day-to-day worries, like Lieutenant Okes for instance. He was a married man, and that was obstacle enough for any young officer. Okes spent his time either fretting about his distant wife or treading warily to avoid Vibart's eye. He was a strange, shallow man, Herrick thought, unsure of himself and afraid to unbend even with his own kind. It seemed as if he was afraid of becoming too friendly, and nervous of expressing an opinion outside the necessities of duty. As if by so doing he might awake suspicion elsewhere or give a hint of misplaced loyalty.

Herrick moved his stiff shoulders inside his coat and pushed Okes from his thoughts. He might after all be right. Aboard the *Phalarope* it often seemed safer to say nothing, to do nothing which might be wrongly interpreted later.

He stared at the weather rail and noticed with a start that he could see the carved dolphin above the starboard ladder and the fat, ugly carronade nearby. His thoughts had carried him through another half-hour, and soon the dawn would show him an horizon once more. Would bring another day.

Harsh and clear above the hiss of spray he suddenly heard Betts' voice from the masthead. 'Deck there! Sail on the starboard bow! Hull down, but it's a ship!'

Snatching his glass from the rack Herrick scrambled up into the mizzen shrouds, his mind working on the unexpected report. The sea was already gathering shape and personality, and there was a finger of grey along where the horizon should be. Up there, high above the swaying deck, Betts would just be able to see the other ship in the dawn's cautious approach.

He snapped, 'Mr. Neale! Up you go and see what you can discover. If you give me a false report you'll kiss the gunner's daughter before you're much older!'

Neale's face split into a grin, and without a word he scampered like a monkey towards the main shrouds.

Herrick tried to stay calm, to return to his pacing as he had seen Bolitho do. But the newcomer, if there was indeed a ship, filled him with uncertainty, so that he stared at the dark sea as if willing it to appear.

Betts called again. 'She's a frigate, sir! No doubt about it. Steerin' south-east!'

Neale's shrill voice took up the call. 'She's running before the wind like a bird, sir! Under all plain sail!'

Herrick breathed out noisily. For one brief instant he had imagined it might be a Frenchman. Even out here, alone and unaided, it was not impossible. But the French rarely sailed fast or far by night. Usually they lay to and rode out the darkness. This was no enemy.

As if to open his thoughts Betts yelled, 'I know that rig, sir! She's an English ship right enough!'

'Very well, keep on reporting!' Herrick lowered the speaking trumpet and peered back along the quarterdeck. Even in minutes the place had taken more shape and reality. The deck was pale and grey, and he could see the helmsmen again as familiar faces.

There might be new orders in the other frigate. Maybe the American war was already over and they would return to Brest or England. In his heart Herrick felt a sudden twinge of disappointment. At first the prospect of another long commission in the unhappy *Phalarope* had appalled him. Now, with the thought that he might never see the West Indies at all, he was not so sure.

Neale slithered straight down a backstay, disdaining shrouds and ratlines, and ran panting to the quarterdeck.

Herrick made up his mind. 'My respects to the captain, Mr. Neale, and tell him we have sighted a King's ship. She will be up to us in an hour, maybe much less. He will wish to prepare himself.'

Neale hurried down the hatchway and Herrick stared across the tumbling waste of water. Bolitho would be even more concerned, he thought. If the *Phalarope* was ordered home now, all his plans and promises would be without meaning. He would have lost his private battle before he had had time to begin.

There was a soft step beside him and Bolitho said, 'Now, Mr. Herrick, what about this ship?'

4

The Signal

Bolitho steadied his glasses against the weather rigging and waited for the other ship to leap into focus. In the time it had taken him to walk from his cabin to the quarterdeck and listen to Herrick's excited report, the dawn sun had slowly clawed its way over the horizon so that already the endless waste of tossing whitecaps was touched with pale gold, the shadows gone from the short, steep waves.

The other vessel made a fine sight in the strengthening light, he thought, with her tall pyramids of full sails and the unbroken curtain of spray bursting around the high bow. She was moving fast, her topmasts glittering in the weak sunlight like crucifixes.

Over his shoulder he called, 'You have a good lookout, Mr Herrick! He is to be complimented for such an early sighting.'

Even for a trained seaman it was not easy to pick out a ship from the shadows of night and dawn and identify her. She was English right enough, and there was a certain familiarity about her.

Vaguely in the background he could hear the boatswain's mates calling the hands, the shrill twitter of pipes.

'All hands! All hands! Show a leg!'

He could imagine the sleep-dazed men tumbling from their hammocks groaning and protesting, while from forward came the usual mixture of smells from the galley. Another day, but this time it would be different. The sea was no longer empty and hostile. The other ship might make the men remember that they were part of something real and important.

He saw the frigate's big yards begin to change shape and heard Herrick say, 'She going about, sir. She'll be up to us shortly!'

Bolitho nodded absently. The stranger would swing round to run parallel, keeping the *Phalarope* down to leeward. As Herrick had suggested, it might mean new orders.

He climbed down from the rigging suddenly chilled and tired. The keen spray had moulded his shirt to his body and his hair felt wet against his cheek. He noticed that his ship had changed yet again. The quarterdeck seemed thronged with figures, the officers keeping to the lee side, but with their glasses raised and watching the other frigate.

Midshipman Maynard looked anxiously towards the stranger and strained his eye through his big telescope. As he was in charge of signals he knew that Bolitho would be watching him.

The maindeck was also alive with newly awakened seamen, and the bosun's mates had to use their ropes ends more than usual to drive them away from the bulwark as they peered across the water at the frigate's approach. Chattering and excited they stowed their hammocks in the nettings and still staring abeam moved reluctantly towards the galley hatch.

Bolitho lifted his glass again as tiny black balls soared to the other ship's yards and broke out to the wind.

Vibart leaned against the binnacle and growled at Maynard, 'Come on then! Read it out!'

Maynard blinked the spray from his wet eyes and flicked rapidly through his book. 'She's made her number, sir! She's the *Andiron*, thirty-eight, Cap'n Masterman.'

Bolitho closed his glass with a snap. Of course. He should have known her immediately. When in *Sparrow* he had often seen her on patrol off the American coast. Masterman was an old hand at the game. A senior captain, he had chalked up many successes against the enemy.

The *Andiron* had completed her manoeuvre and was settling down on the same course as the *Phalarope*. Her sudden wide turn had taken her across the *Phalarope*'s beam, but as her sails bellied and filled once more she began to overhaul to windward.

Bolitho watched Maynard's signal party hoisting the *Phalarope's* number and wondered what Masterman would say when he eventually discovered that he was now in command. The signal books would still show Pomfret as captain.

Maynard shouted, 'Signal, sir! *Andiron* to *Phalarope*. Heave to, have despatches on board.'

The sunlight glittered along the *Andiron's* closed ports as she swung slightly down on the other ship.

Herrick said, 'She'll not need to lower a boat, sir. She could drift a raft across.' He rubbed his hands. 'I wonder if she has any fresh vegetables aboard?'

Bolitho smiled. This was just what he had hoped for. A distraction to take their minds off themselves if only for a passing moment.

'Carry on, Mr. Vibart. Heave to, if you please!'

Vibart lifted his speaking trumpet. 'Main tops'l braces! Look alive there!'

Stockdale appeared at Bolitho's side holding his captain's blue coat and cocked hat. He squinted at the other ship and grinned. 'Like old times, Captain.' He peered forward as Quintal, the boatswain, let loose a stream of curses and obscenities. The men had been slow to respond to the sudden orders, and already there was chaos on the crowded deck where off-duty idlers collided with others who were struggling with spray-swollen braces.

Maynard said hoarsely, 'Signal, sir!' His lips moved slowly as he spelled out the message. 'Have you news of Hood's squadron?'

Quintal had at last got his men sorted out, and with sails flapping and thundering the *Phalarope* began to swing heavily into the wind.

Bolitho had half slipped his arms into his coat, but pushed Stockdale aside as Maynard's words chilled his mind like ice. Masterman would never ask such a question. Even if he had lost his squadron he would certainly know that *Phalarope* was a stranger and had never served in these waters before. His mind rebelled, and he stared mesmerised as his ship continued to swing until the *Andiron*'s bowsprit seemed to point at right-angles across his own.

Vibart turned startled and confused as Bolitho yelled, 'Belay that order, Mr. Vibart! Stand by to go about!'

He ignored the surprised gasps and the fresh clamour of orders and concentrated his reeling thoughts on the other ship. Suppose he had made a mistake? It was too late now. Perhaps it had been too late from the moment the *Andiron* had appeared.

Then he saw the other frigate's bows beginning to swing round still further. With her yards turning as one she altered course and charged down towards the helpless *Phalarope*. A few more seconds and the way would have been lost from the *Phalarope*'s sails, and the *Andiron* would have crossed her unprotected stern, unchallenged and overwhelming.

Bolitho felt his ship labouring round, his ears deaf to the cries and curses from officers and men alike. The weeks of sail drill in all weathers were taking charge, and like puppets the seamen tugged at sheets and braces, their minds too dazed by their captain's behaviour to understand what was happening.

Vibart yelled, 'My God, sir! We'll collide!' He stared past Bolitho's tense figure towards the onrushing frigate. Still the *Phalarope* wallowed round, her bowsprit following the other ship like a compass needle.

Bolitho snapped, 'Steer south-east! Out second reefs!' He did not listen to his repeated orders but walked briskly towards the scarlet-coated marine drummer boy beside the cabin hatch.

'Beat to quarters!'

He saw the boy's dull expression giving way to something like horror. But again training and discipline took charge, and as the drum began to stutter its warning tattoo the tide of men on the maindeck swayed, faltered and then surged in opposite directions as gun crews rushed madly to their weapons.

Vibart gasped, 'Her ports are opening! My God, she's running up her colours!'

Bolitho saw the striped flag breaking to the crosswind and followed Vibart's shocked stare as the frigate's ports opened and the concealed guns trundled outwards like a row of shining teeth.

He said harshly, 'Clear for action, Mr. Vibart! Have the guns loaded and run out immediately!' He checked Vibart as he ran to the rail. 'It will take all of ten minutes. I will try to give you that amount of time!'

The deck canted as the ship steadied on her new course around and away from the other frigate. But the *Andiron* was already turning on the same circle, her sails flapping as she headed into the wind in an effort to close the range. From her peak the new American flag made a patch of bright colour against the tan sails, and Bolitho had to tear his mind back to the present to stop himself thinking of what would have happened but for that one stupid signal.

Andiron would have crossed the *Phalarope's* unprotected stern and her gunners, hitherto concealed behind the bulwark and sealed ports, would have poured shot after shot through the big cabin windows. The balls would have screamed and torn the full length of his command, and with half the men still below, helpless and unprepared, the disaster would have been over within minutes.

Even now it might be too late. *Andiron* was a bigger ship, and her deep keel was better for this sort of handling. Already she was cutting across the *Phalarope's* stern and beating rapidly up to windward to regain her first advantage. In another fifteen minutes she would try the same manoeuvre again, or she could be content to close the range from the larboard quarter. With the wind in her favour action could not be avoided.

He made himself walk to the taffrail and stare back at the other ship. The pretence had gone now, and he could see the crouching gunners, the clusters of officers on the canting quarterdeck. What had happened to Masterman? He wondered. He were better dead than know his proud ship to be a privateer.

He turned his back on the *Andiron's* dark hull and looked along his own command. The chaos had gone, and to the unpractised eye the ship looked ready and eager for battle.

On both sides the guns had been run out and the gun captains were testing their trigger lines and passing hoarse orders to their men. Boys ran the length of the deck throwing down sand to give the gunners a firm grip when the time came, while others scuttled from gun to gun with water buckets for the swabs and to damp down any sudden fire.

Vibart stood below the quarterdeck rail and yelled, 'Cleared for action, sir! All guns loaded with double shot and grape!'

'Very well, Mr. Vibart.' Bolitho walked slowly towards the rail and ran his eye along the larboard side guns. They would be the first to engage. His heart sank as he picked out faults in the pattern like flaws in a painting.

At one gun a captain was even having to put a rope fall into the hands of one of his men, as the poor wretch stared at it without comprehension. His mind was too full of fear, his eyes too mesmerised by the overtaking frigate with her long row of guns to heed what the petty officer was saying. At each gun there were men like this. With so many new hands, pressed from unwarlike jobs ashore, this danger was inevitable.

Given time, he could have trained each and every one of them. Bolitho banged his fist slowly on the rail. Well, there *was* no more time. *Andiron* not only had more guns, but they were eighteen-pounders against *Phalarope's* twelve-pounders. Most of her crew would no doubt be made up of English deserters and seasoned sailors who were no strangers to battle. Any crew which could take the *Andiron* from Captain Masterman was a force to be feared.

At his back Captain Rennie stood nonchalantly by the hammock nettings, his sword looped to his wrist with a gold lanyard, as he watched Sergeant Garwood dressing his men into neat scarlet ranks. There was something very reassuring about the marines, Bolitho thought grimly, but their muskets would not be much use against eighteen-pounders!

All at once the remorse and despair he had been enduring since the

Andiron's first treachery had shown with her flag gave way to something like blind rage. It was too late for the 'if onlys' and the 'maybes'. He had brought his ship and his men to this. His was the sole responsibility. He had recognised the American's trap just in time to save them all from the first blow, but he should have seen it earlier.

He walked to the rail and shouted along the deck, 'Now listen to me, men! In a few moments we are going to give battle to that ship!' He saw every face turned towards him, but already they had lost meaning and personality. They were a crew. Good or bad, only time would show. But that they should all trust him was essential.

'Just take your time and obey orders, no matter what is happening around you! Each gun is fitted with the new flintlock, but make sure there is a slow-match at hand in case of failure!'

He saw Okes look across from the starboard battery to where Herrick waited by his own guns. A quick exchange of glances which might have meant anything.

He felt Stockdale slipping the coat over his shoulders and then the firm clasp of the swordbelt around his waist. He watched the powerful frigate plunging over towards the larboard quarter, his eyes gauging the speed and the distance.

'One more thing!' He leaned forward as if to will them to listen. 'This is a King's ship! There will be no surrender!'

He thrust his hands beneath the tails of his coat and walked slowly to the weather rail. It would not be long now. He looked across to Proby's shabby outline beside the wheel. 'In a moment we will beat to windward, Mr. Proby.' He heard a mumbled assent and wondered what the master would make of his order.

The American captain would no doubt expect the smaller ship to turn again and try to slip downwind, and as soon as she turned he would pour a full broadside into the *Phalarope*'s stern, as he had first intended. Bolitho's manoeuvre would bring the *Phalarope* round towards the other ship, and with luck Herrick might be able to get in the first blood.

He saw the flash of sunlight on a telescope from the *Andiron*'s quarter-deck and knew the other captain was watching him.

'Stand by, Mr. Proby!' He lifted his hat and yelled along the maindeck, 'Right, lads! A broadside for old England!'

With a protesting groan the yards came round, while overhead the canvas thundered like a miniature battle. Bolitho found that his mouth was as dry as sand, and his face felt chilled into a tight mask.

This was the moment.

John Allday crouched beside the second gun of the larboard battery and stared fixedly through the open port. In spite of the cool morning breeze he was already sweating and his heart pumped against his ribs like the beating of a drum.

It was like being a helpless victim of a nightmare, with every detail clear and stark even before it happened. Somehow he imagined it would be different this time, but nothing had changed. He could have been sailing into battle for the first time, new and untried, with the agony of suspense tearing him apart.

He tore his eyes from the open square of water and glanced back across his shoulder. The same men who had jeered Ferguson or ringed Evans in menacing silence now stood or crouched like himself, slaves to their guns, their faces naked and fearful.

Standing a little apart from the battery, his back to the foremast, Lieutenant Herrick was watching the quarterdeck, his fingers resting on his sword, his bright blue eyes unwinking and devoid of expression.

Allday followed the officer's stare and saw the captain at the quarterdeck rail, his palms resting on the smooth wood, his head jutting slightly as he watched the other ship. The latter was almost hidden from Allday by the high bulwark and gangway and the other guns, but he could see her topmasts and straining sails as she bore down on the larboard quarter, until she seemed to hang over the *Phalarope* like a cliff.

Pryce, the gun captain, slung the powder horn over his hip and squatted carefully behind the breech, the trigger line in his hands. Through his teeth his voice sounded strange and taut. 'Now, lads, listen to me! We'll be firing a broadside first.'

He looked at each man in turn, ignoring the other gunners at the next port. 'After that it will all depend on how quickly we load and run out. So move sharply, and as the cap'n said, take no notice of the din about you, got it?'

Ferguson clung to the rope tackle at the side of the gun and gasped, 'I can't take it! God, I can't stand this waiting!'

Pochin on the opposite side of the breech sneered, 'Just as I said! It takes more than pretty clothing to make men of the likes o' you!' He jerked savagely at the tackle. 'If you'd seen what I've seen you'd *die* of fear, man.' He looked around at the others. 'I've seen whole fleets at each others' throats.' He let his words sink in. 'The sea covered in masts, like a forest!'

Pryce snapped, 'Hold your noise!'

He cocked his head as Herrick called, 'Gun captains! As soon as we engage on the larboard side send your best men to back up the other battery under Mr. Okes!'

The captains held up their hands and then turned back to watch the empty sea.

Allday looked across at Okes and saw the officer's face gleaming with sweat. He looked white. Like a corpse already, he thought.

Vibart's voice rang hollowly through his speaking trumpet. 'Braces there! Stand by to wear ship!'

Allday ran his fingers along the cold breech, and whispered fervently, 'Come *on*! Get it over with!'

The *Phalarope* was outclassed and outgunned, even he could see that. With half her men already too terrified to think it was just a matter of how soon her colours would fall.

He glanced down at his legs and felt a chill of terror. It never left him, and the years on the quiet Cornish hillside amongst the sheep had done nothing to dispel it. The fear of mutilation, and the horror of what followed.

Old Strachan called softly from the next gun, ' 'Ere, you lads!' He waited until his words had penetrated the minds of the new men. 'Wrap a neckscarf around yer ears afore we start to blow! You'll 'ave no eardrums else!'

Allday nodded. He had forgotten that lesson. If only they had been prepared and ready. Instead they had stumbled out from their hammocks and almost at once the nightmare had begun. First the excitement of a friendly ship, fading instantly in the drummer's roll as the men ran gasping and wide-eyed to quarters. He could just see the same little drummer boy beside one rank of marines. He was staring across at the captain as if to read his own fate.

Pryce muttered, 'Never bin in a fight like this afore.' He looked up at the billowing sails. 'Too much wind. It'll be hit hard an' run, you mark my words!'

There was a rasp of steel as Herrick drew his sword. He lifted it above his head, the blade holding the sun like firelight.

'Stand by in the larboard battery!'

Ferguson moaned softly, 'Oh, Grace! Where are you, Grace?'

From aft Vibart bellowed, 'Put the helm down! Hard down there!'

They all felt the deck begin to cant further as the seamen forward let go the headsail sheets and allowed the plunging frigate to swing wildly across the wind.

Allday swallowed hard as the gunport suddenly darkened and the other ship's raked bow pushed across his vision. She filled the port, her guns and spray-soaked hull leaning at an angle as if to reach out and smash the *Phalarope* as she swung impudently towards her.

Herrick dropped his sword. '*Fire!*'

The captains jerked their lines and the whole world fell apart in the staggering, uneven broadside. Choking smoke billowed back through the ports, rasping the lungs and filling every eye as the guns lurched angrily back on their tackles. It was like hell, too terrible to understand.

But already the gun captains were yelling like fiends, urging and hitting at their stunned gunners as the powder monkeys ran forward with fresh cartridges and new, gleaming balls were lifted from the racks.

Pryce knocked down a man's arm and screamed, 'Sponge out, you bastard! Remember what I taught you! You'll blow us all up if you drop a charge into a burning gun!' The man mumbled dazedly and obeyed him as if in a trance.

Herrick shouted, 'Reload there! Lively, lads!'

Allday waited a few more minutes and then threw his weight on the tackles. Squealing like angry pigs the gun trucks rumbled forward again, the muzzles racing each other to be first through the ports.

But the *Phalarope* was almost into the *Andiron*'s bow. A few more feet and it seemed as if both ships would smash into each other, to die together in locked combat.

'Fire!'

Again the savage roar of a broadside, the deck yawing away beneath them with its force. But this time more ragged, less well aimed. Through the din of shouts and groaning spars Allday heard some of the balls strike home, and saw Maynard, one of the midshipmen, waving his hat in the streaming smoke and yelling to the sky, his words lost in the guns' roar.

The *Andiron* must have fired simultaneously with the *Phalarope*, her gunfire lost in the general thunder of noise. There was more of a feeling than a sound, like a hot wind, or sand blasted across a parched desert.

Allday looked up as the sails jerked and twisted as if in agony. Holes were appearing everywhere, and from high aloft came a falling tangle of severed halyards and ropes. A block dropped on to the breech with a loud clang, and Pryce said without looking up from his priming, 'The bastards fired too soon! The Broadside went right over our 'eads!'

Allday peered through the port, still dazed, but understanding at last what Bolitho had done. The *Phalarope* had not turned away, had not offered her stern for punishment. Her sudden swing to attack had caught the enemy off balance, and rather than risk a senseless collision he had hauled off so that his first broadside had failed to make real contact.

He heard Herrick call across to Lieutenant Okes, 'By God, Matthew, that was a close thing!' Then in a wilder tone, 'Look at the masthead pendant! The wind's veering!'

There was bedlam as the enemy ship swung rapidly clear of the charging *Phalarope*. But so sudden or so unexpected was the attack that the *Andiron*'s captain had failed to notice what Bolitho must already have seen even as he steered towards possible disaster.

Instead of beating back to windward the *Andiron* met the full wind hard across her larboard bow. For a moment it looked as if she would rally and at worst come crashing back alongside.

Herrick was jumping with excitement. 'My God, she's *in* irons! She's in irons!'

Men were standing beside their guns calling the news along the deck while across the water, framed in a rolling bank of gunsmoke, the *Andiron* rolled helplessly up wind, unable to pay off on either tack. Already men were running along her yards, and across the shadowed water they could hear the blare of commands through a speaking trumpet.

Herrick controlled himself. 'Over to the starboad battery. Jump to it!'

Pryce touched the men he needed and scampered across the deck.

From aft came the call, 'Stand by to go about! Man the braces!'

Allday threw himself down beside the opposite gun and showed his teeth to the crouching men.

Old Strachan croaked, 'The cap'n can certainly 'andle the ship well enough.'

Okes shouted, 'Silence there! Watch your front!'

Herrick walked to the centre of the deck and watched the carpenter and the boatswain hurrying to repair the brief damage. Men were already climbing aloft to splice the severed lines, and others were at last rigging nets above the maindeck to give some protection from falling blocks or spars.

Round came the yards once more, sails thundering, braces screaming through the blocks as the men ran like goats to obey the constant demands from the quarterdeck.

It did not seem possible. Caught and surprised one instant, and the next moment they were not only attacking, but hitting the enemy again and again.

Bolitho must have thought it all out. Must have planned and schemed during his lonely walks up and down the night-darkened deck, waiting for just an eventuality.

He could see him now, calm-eyed and stiff-backed behind the rail, his hands behind his back as he watched the other ship. Once during the waiting Herrick had seen him wipe his forehead, momentarily brushing away the lock of dark hair and displaying the deep, savage scar. He had seen Herrick watching him and had jammed on his hat with something like anger.

Herrick ran his eye along his own guns, now manned by depleted crews and blind to the enemy as the *Phalarope* tacked round to close the range. He had heard Pochin's bitter remarks and had seen the way Allday had rallied to help the new men. It was strange how they all forgot their other worries when real danger was close and terrible.

It was true that the ship was different under Bolitho. And it went deeper than the uniform clothing now worn by all hands, issued on Bolitho's order to replace the stained rags which had been commonplace in Pomfret's time. There was this violent uncertainty instead of sullen acceptance, as if the men wanted to draw together to match the young captain's enthusiasm, yet had forgotten how to go about it.

Okes said sharply, 'She's under way again! She's swinging round!'

The *Andiron's* sails were flapping and banging in apparent confusion, but Herrick could see the difference in her outline and the new angle of her yards.

Bolitho's voice cut through their speculations. 'Another salvo, lads! Before she completes her turn!'

Herrick breathed out sharply. 'He's going to try and cross her stern! He'll never make it. We'll be broadside to broadside in minutes!'

The wild confidence which their successful attack had brought him changed to the chill of uncertainty as the *Phalarope* gathered way, her masts and spars quivering under the press of sail. He gripped his sword more tightly and gritted his teeth as once more the enemy topsails showed above the hammock nettings. The masts were no longer in line, she was swinging fast and well. There was nothing else for it but to take what had to come.

Okes could only stare at the oncoming ship, his jaw open as the distance was swallowed up in the gap of tossing water between them. He held up his sword. 'Stand by starboard battery!' But his voice was lost in a savage ripple of gunfire from the other ship as gun after gun belched fire and smoke from aft to forward as each one came to bear.

This time there was no mistake.

Herrick felt the hull shudder beneath his feet and reeled against the foremast as smoke blotted out the deck and the air became full of splintering woodwork and falling rigging. Above and around him the air quivered and shook with the crash of guns, and the nerve jarring scream of cannon balls as they whipped through the smoke like things from hell.

The scream of passing shots mingled with closer, more unearthly sounds as flying splinters ripped into the packed gunners and bathed the smooth decks with scarlet. Herrick had to bite his lip to retain control of himself. He had seen men bleed before. In an occasional skirmish, and under the cat. From a fall or a shipboard accident. But this was different. It was all around him, as if the ship was being painted by a madman. He could see specks of blood and gristle across his white breeches, and when he looked across at the nearest gun he saw that it had been upended and one of its crew had been pulped into a scarlet and purple mass. Another man lay legless, a handspike still gripped and ready, and two of his companions were clinging together screaming and tearing at each other's wounds in the insane torment.

The enemy frigate must have reloaded almost at once, and another ragged volley thundered and crashed in the *Phalarope*'s side.

Men cried and yelled, cursed and fumbled blindly in the choking smoke, while above their heads the nets jerked and danced madly to the onslaught of falling gear from aloft.

A powder monkey ran weeping towards the magazine hatch, only to be pushed away by one of the marine sentries. He had dropped his cartridge carrier and was running below, to the safety of darkness. But the sentry yelled at him and then struck at him with his musket. The boy reeled back and then seemed to come to his senses. With a sniff he picked up his carrier and made for the nearest gun.

There was a scream of shot, and Herrick turned biting back vomit as the eighteen-pound shot cut the boy in half. The head and shoulders remained upright on the planking for several seconds, and before he turned away Herrick saw that the boy's eyes were still open and staring.

He cannoned into Okes who still stood with upraised sword, his eyes fixed and glassy as he gaped at the remains of his battery.

Herrick shouted, 'Fire, Matthew! Give the order!'

Okes dropped his sword and here and there a gun lurched back adding its voice to the dreadful symphony.

Okes said, 'We're done for! We'll have to strike!'

'Strike?' Herrick stared at him. All at once the reality was cruel and personal again. Death and surrender had always been words, a necessary but unlikely alternative to victory. He looked towards the quarterdeck at Bolitho's tall figure and the marines beyond. The latter must have been firing their muskets for some while, yet Herrick had not even noticed. He saw Sergeant Garwood with his half-pike dressing one rank where two red-coated bodies had left gaps in the line, while he called out the time and numbers to his men as they reloaded and fired another volley into the smoke. Captain Rennie had his back to the enemy and was staring across the other rail as if seeing the sea for the first time.

Pryce, the gun captain, gave one long scream and fell backwards at Herrick's feet. A long splinter had been torn from the deck and had embedded itself in the man's shoulder. Through the blood Herrick could see the thick stump of jagged timber sticking out like a tooth, and knew that the other end would be deep inside. The splinters were always the most dangerous and had to be cut out from the flesh in one piece.

Herrick gestured towards the men by the main hatch. 'Take this one below to the surgeon!' They had been staring at a pulped corpse beside the hatch, its teeth white against the flayed flesh, and Herrick's harsh tone seemed to give them strength to break the spell.

Pryce began to scream. 'No! Leave me here by the gun! For God's sake, don't take me below!'

One of the men whispered, ''E's a brave 'un! 'E don't want to leave 'is station!'

Pochin spat on the gun and watched the spittle hissing on the barrel. 'Squit! 'E'd rather die up 'ere than face the butcher's knife.'

There was a splintering crack, like that of a coach whip, high overhead, and as Herrick squinted up through the drifting smoke he saw the main-topgallant quiver, and then as the wind tore jubilantly at the released canvas it began to slide forward.

Herrick cupped his hands. 'Look alive, you men! Get aloft and cut those shrouds! It'll foul the foremast otherwise!'

He saw Quintal and some seamen running up the shrouds and then winced as another cannon ball ploughed along the deck by his feet and smashed into two wounded gunners beside the lee bulwark. He looked away, sickened, and heard Vibart yell, 'Heads below! The t'gallant is falling!'

With a jarring crash the long spar pitched over the bulwark and remained trapped and tangled in a mass of rigging, the torn sail ballooning in the water alongside and dragging at the ship like a sea anchor.

To add to the horror, Herrick could see the man, Betts, the one who had first sighted the other frigate, pinned in the trailing rigging like an insect in a web.

Vibart yelled, 'Axes there! Cut that wreckage adrift!'

Betts stared up at the frigate with glazed eyes, his voice short and painful between his teeth. 'Help me! Don't let me go to the bottom, lads!'

But already the axes were at work, the men driven half mad by the din, too dazed to care for the suffering of one more seaman.

Okes seized Herricks' arm. 'Why doesn't he strike? For Christ's sake *look* what he's doing to us!'

Herrick's mind was dulled and refused to work clearly any more. But he could see what Okes was trying to show him. The heart had gone out of the men, what heart there had been. They crouched and whimpered as the enemy balls thundered all around them, and only occasionally did a single gun reply. Then it was usually a small handful of men led by one seasoned and dedicated gun captain which kept up a one-sided exchange with the enemy.

Herrick shut his ears to the screaming wounded as they were dragged below and closed his eyes to everything but the small open patch of quarter-deck where Bolitho stood alone by the rail. His hat had gone and his coat was stained with powder and blown spray. Even as he watched Herrick saw a messenger run towards the captain, only to be cut down by musket fire from the other vessel as she loomed sideways out of the smoke. Musket balls were thudding against the hammock nettings and biting across the deck, yet Bolitho never budged, nor did he alter his expression of detached determination.

Only once did he look up, and then to glance at the large scarlet ensign which streamed from the gaff, as if to reassure himself that it still flew.

Herrick shook his head. 'He'll not strike! He'll see us all dead first!'

5

Rum and Recriminations

The deck slewed over as the *Phalarope*'s helm went hard down and she swung blindly on to her new course. Bolitho had lost count of the number of times his ship had changed direction, or even how long they had been fighting.

Of one thing he was sure. The *Andiron* was outmanoeuvring him, was still holding to windward and keeping up a steady barrage. His own gunners were hampered by yet another hazard. The wind was falling away, and his men were now firing blindly into an unbroken bank of thick smoke which rolled down from the other ship and mingled with their own intermittent firing. The smoke seemed to writhe with many colours as the American privateer continued the attack. Once, when a freak wind had blown the smoke skywards like a curtain Bolitho had seen the *Andiron*'s battery belching long orange flames as each gun was trained and fired singly across the bare quarter mile between the two frigates. They were firing high, the balls screaming through the rigging and slashing the remaining sails to ribbons. Ropes and stays hung from above like weed, and every so often heavy blocks and long slivers of wood would fall amongst the labouring gunners or splash in the clear water alongside.

She intended to dismast and cripple the *Phalarope*. Maybe her captain had plans for using another captured ship, just as he had the *Andiron*.

The long nine-pounders on the quarterdeck recoiled as one, their sharp, barking detonations penetrating the innermost membranes of Bolitho's ears as he stared through the smoke and then back at his own command. Only on the quarterdeck was there still some semblance of unity and order. Midshipman Farquhar stood by the taffrail, his eyes bright but determined as he passed his orders to the gun captains. Rennie's marines were standing fast, too. From their smoke-blinded positions behind the hammock nettings they kept up a steady musket fire whenever the other ship showed herself through the choking fog of powder smoke.

But the maindeck was different. Bolitho let his eyes move slowly over the chaos of scarred planking and grisly remains which marked every foot of deck space. The guns were still firing, but the intervals were longer, the aim less certain.

At first Bolitho had been amazed at the success of that opening broadside. He had known that later the lack of training would slow down the barrage, but he had not dared to hope for such a good opening. The double-shotted guns had fired almost as one, the ship staggering from the combined recoil. He had seen the bulwarks jump apart on the other frigate, had watched the balls tear through the packed gunners and gouge into her spray-dashed hull. It had seemed momentarily that the battle might still be contained.

Through the streaming smoke he saw Herrick moving slowly aft along the starboard battery checking the gunners and aiming each weapon himself before allowing the gun captain to jerk his trigger line. It should have been Okes on the starboard side, but perhaps he was already dead, like so many of the others.

Bolitho made himself examine each part of the agonising panorama which the *Phalarope* now represented. His body felt sick and numb from the constant battering, but his eye and mind worked in cold unison, so that the pain and suffering was all the more apparent.

Small pictures stood out from the whole, so that wherever he looked there was a pitiful reminder of the cost and the price still to be paid.

Many had died. How many he had no way of knowing. Some had died bravely, serving their guns and yelling encouragement and curses up to the moment of death. Some died slowly and horribly, their mutilated and broken bodies writhing in the blood and flesh which covered the deck as in a slaughterhouse.

Others were less brave, and more than once he had seen men shamming death, even cowering in the stench and horror of the discarded corpses until dragged and kicked back to their stations by the petty officers.

Some had escaped below in spite of Rennie's sentries, and would now be covering their ears and whimpering in the bilges to face drowning rather than the onslaught from the *Andiron*'s guns.

He had seen the little powder monkey cut in half, and even above the roar of battle he had heard his own words to that same boy just three weeks ago:

'You'll see England again! Never you fear!'

Now he was wiped away. As if he had never been.

And there had been the seaman Betts, trapped and writhing on the severed topgallant. The man he had used to try to prove his authority. The axes had cut the spar away, and with a sigh it had bobbed clear of the ship before moving away in the smoke in a trial of rigging. The spar had idled past the quarterdeck, and for a brief instant he had seen Betts staring up at him. The man's mouth had been open like a black hole, and he had shaken his fist. It was a pitiful gesture, but it felt like a curse from the whole world. Then the spar had rolled over, and before he had faded astern Bolitho had seen Betts' feet sticking out of the water, kicking in a futile dance.

He tore his eyes from the carnage as more balls slapped through the main course and whined away over the water. It could not last much longer. The *Andiron* had hauled off slightly to windward. He could see her upper yards and punctured sails moving above the smoke bank as if detached from the hidden ship beneath, and guessed she was drawing clear to pound the *Phalarope* into submission with slow, carefully aimed shots.

He did not recognise his own voice as he gave his orders automatically and without pause. 'Tell the carpenter to sound the well! And pass the word for the boatswain to send more men aloft to splice the mizzen shrouds!' There was little point any more, but the game had to be played out. He knew no other way.

His eye fell on an old gun captain at the nearest twelve-pounder below the quarterdeck. The man showed fatigue and strain, but his hoarse voice was unhurried, even patient as he coaxed his crew through the drill of reloading. 'That's right, my boys!' He peered through the haze as one of his men rammed home the cartridge and another cradled the gleaming ball into the gaping muzzle. A splinter flew from the gunport and laid open his arm, but he merely winced and tied a filthy rag around his biceps before adding, 'Ram that wad well home, bucko! We don't want the bugger to fall out agin!' He saw Bolitho watching him and showed his stained teeth in what might have been either pain or pride. Then he bawled, 'Right then! Run out!' The trucks squeaked as the gun lumbered up the canting deck and then roared back again as the old man pulled the trigger.

Vibart loomed across the rail, his figure like a massive blue and white rock. He looked grim but unflinching, and waited for the nine-pounders to fire and recoil before he shouted, 'No water in the well, sir! She's not hit below the water line!'

Bolitho nodded. The American obviously felt sure of a capture. It would not take long to refit a ship in one of the dockyards left by the British retreating from the American colonies.

The realisation brought a fresh flood of despairing anger to his aching mind. The *Phalarope* was fighting for her life. But her men were failing her. *He* was failing her. He had brought the ship and every man aboard to this. All the hopes and promises were without meaning now. There was only disgrace and failure as an alternative to death.

Even if he had contemplated flying from the *Andiron's* attack it was too late now. The wind was falling away more and more, and the sails were almost useless, torn like nets by the screaming cannon balls.

A marine threw up his hands, clawing at the gaping scarlet hole in his forehead before pitching back into his comrades.

Captain Rennie drawled, 'Fill that space. What the hell do you think you're doing?' To Sergeant Garwood he added petulantly, 'Take the name of the next man who dies without permission!'

Surprisingly, some of the marines laughed, and when Rennie saw Bolitho looking at him he merely shrugged, as if he too understood it was all part of one hideous game.

The ship staggered, and overhead the sails boomed in protest as the fading wind sighed against the flapping canvas. Bolitho snapped, 'Watch your helm, quartermaster! Steady as you go!'

But one of the helmsmen had fallen, a pattern of scarlet pouring from his mouth and across the smooth planking. From somewhere another seaman took his place, his jaw working steadily on a wad of tobacco.

Vibart growled, 'The starboard battery is a shambles! If we could engage the opposite side it would give us time to reorganise!'

Bolitho eyed him steadily. 'The *Andiron* has the advantage. But I intend to try and cross her stern directly.'

Vibart peered abeam, his eyes cold and calculating. 'She'll never allow it. She'll pound us to shavings before we get a cable's length!' He looked back at Bolitho. 'We will have to strike.' His voice shook. 'We can't take much more.'

Bolitho replied quietly, 'I did not hear that, Mr. Vibart. Now go forrard and try and get the full battery into action again!' His tone was cold and final. 'When two ships fight, only one can be the victor. I will decide on the course of action!'

Vibart seemed to shrug. As if it was not his concern. 'As you say, sir!' He strode to the ladder adding harshly, 'I *said* that they did not respect weakness!'

Bolitho felt Proby shaking his arm and turned to see the anxiety etched on his mournful face. 'The wheel, Captain! It don't answer! The yoke lines have parted!'

Bolitho stared dully over Proby's rounded shoulders to where the helmsmen pulled vaguely at the wheel, the squeaking spokes responding in empty mockery as the ship paid off and began to sidle sluggishly downwind.

The sudden movement brought more cries from the maindeck as the frigate rolled her gunports skyward in a dizzy, uncontrollable elevation.

Bolitho ran his fingers through his hair, realising for the first time that his hat had been knocked from his head. The masthead pendant was barely flapping now, and without power in her sails the ship would drift at the mercy of the sea until her surrender or destruction. It would take all of an hour to re-rig the rudder lines. By then ... he felt a cold shudder moving across his spine.

He cupped his hands. 'Cease firing!'

The sudden silence was almost more frightening than the gunfire. He could hear the chafe and creak of spars, the gurgle of water below the counter, and the swaying clatter of loose rigging. Even the wounded seemed quelled, and lay gasping and staring at the captain's still figure at the quarterdeck rail.

Then across the water, drifting with the smoke like a final insult, he heard a wild cheering. It was more like a baying, he thought bitterly. Like hounds closing for the kill.

A V-shaped cleft broke in the smoke, and through it came the *Andiron's* raked bow and the long finger of her bowsprit. Filtered sunlight played across her figurehead and glinted on raised cutlasses and boarding pikes. As more and more of the other ship glided into view Bolitho saw the press of men running forward to the point where both ships would touch. Others were crawling out along the yards with grapnels, ready to lash the two enemies together in a final embrace. It was nearly finished.

He heard Stockdale mutter at his elbow, 'The bastards! The *bastards!*'

Bolitho saw that there were small tears in the man's eyes, and knew that the battered coxswain was sharing his own misery.

Above his head the flag whipped suddenly in a small breeze, and he knew that he dare not look at it. A defiant patch of scarlet. Like the red coats of the marines and the great glittering pools of blood which seeped through the scuppers as if the ship herself was bleeding before his eyes.

A new wildness moved through his mind, so that he had to lock his fingers around his swordbelt to prevent his hands from shaking.

'Get Mr. Brock! At the double!'

He saw Midshipman Maynard lope forward, and then forgot him as his glance strayed again to the watching men. They were exhausted and smashed down with the fury of battle. There was hardly a spark amongst them. His fingers settled on the hilt of his sword and he felt the painful prick of despair behind his eyes. He could see his father, and so many others of his family, ranked with his crew, and watching in silence.

Proby said hoarsely, 'I've sent a party to splice the yoke lines, Captain.' He waited, plucking the buttons of his shabby coat. 'It were not your fault, sir.' He shifted beneath Bolitho's unwavering stare. 'Don't you give in, sir. Not now!'

The gunner reached the quarterdeck and touched his hat. 'Sir!' He was still wearing the felt, spark-proof slippers he always wore in the dark magazine, and he seemed dazed by the sudden silence and the litter of destruction about him.

'Mr. Brock, there is a task for you.' Bolitho listened to his own voice and felt the strange wildness stirring him like brandy. 'I want every starboard gun loaded with chain shot.' He watched the *Andiron*'s slow, threatening approach. 'You have about ten minutes, unless the wind returns.'

The man nodded and hurried away without another word. His was not to question a meaningless order. A command from the captain was all he required.

Bolitho looked down at the maindeck, at the dead and wounded, and the remaining gunners. He said slowly, 'There will be one final broadside, men.' The words swept away his own illusion of making a last empty gesture. He continued, 'Every gun will have chain shot, and I want each weapon at full elevation.' They began to stir, their movements brittle and vague like old men, but Bolitho's voice seemed to hold them as he added sharply, 'Load, but do not run out until the word!' He saw the gunner's party carrying the unwieldy chain shot to each gun in turn. Two balls per gun, and each ball linked together with thick chain.

Captain Rennie said quietly, 'They're getting close, sir. They'll be boarding us very soon now.' He sounded tense.

Bolitho looked away. All at once he wanted to share the enormity of his decision, but at the same instant he knew the extent of his own loneliness.

His last effort might fail completely. At best it would only drive the enemy to a madness which only the death of the whole of his crew would placate.

Herrick looked aft, his eyes steady. 'All guns loaded, sir!' He seemed to square his shoulders, as if to project some strange confidence over his battered men.

Bolitho pulled out his sword. Behind him he heard the marines fixing their bayonets and shuffling their booted feet on the stained planking.

He called, 'Stand by the starboard carronade, Mr. Farquhar! Is it ready?' He watched narrowly as the other ship's bowsprit swung over the *Phal-*

arope's bulwark, her forechains and rigging alive with shouting men. Her captain must have stripped his guns to get such a large boarding party. Once aboard, they would swamp the *Phalarope*, no matter how desperate the resistance.

Farquhar swallowed hard. 'Loaded, sir. Canister, and a full charge!'

'Very good.' The *Andiron* was barely twenty feet clear now, the triangular patch of trapped water between them frothing in a mad dance. 'If I fall, you will take your orders from Mr. Vibart.' He saw the young officer's eyes seeking out the first lieutenant. 'If not, then watch for my signal!'

The *Andiron*'s bow nudged the main shrouds and a great yell of derision broke from the waiting boarders.

Bolitho ran down the ladder and leaped on to the starboard gangway, his sword above his bare head. A few pistols banged across the gap and he felt a ball pluck at his sleeve like an invisible hand.

'Repel boarders!' He saw the gunners staring up at him, uncertain and shocked, their guns still inboard and impotent.

Herrick jumped up beside him, his eyes flashing as he shouted, 'Come on, lads! We'll give the buggers a lesson!'

Somebody voiced a faint cheer, and the men not employed at the guns surged up to the gangway, their cutlasses and pikes puny against the great press of boarders.

Bolitho felt a man drop screaming at his side, and another pitched forward to be ground between the hulls like so much butcher's meat. He could see the privateer's officers urging their men on and pointing him out to their marksmen. Shots banged and whistled around him, and the cries and jeers had risen to one, terrifying roar.

The hulls shuddered once more and the gap began to disappear. Bolitho peered back at Farquhar. The quarterdeck with its dead marines seemed a long way away, but as he waved his sword in a swift chopping motion he saw the midshipman jerk the lanyard and felt the gun's savage blast pass his face like a hot wind.

The canister shot contained five hundred closely packed musket balls, and like a scythe the miniature bombardment swept through the cheering boarders, cutting them down into a bloody tangle of screams and curses. The boarders faltered, and a young lieutenant who had climbed up on the *Andiron*'s bowsprit dropped unsupported on to the *Phalarope*'s gangway. His scream was cut short as a big seaman lashed out and down with an axe and then his body was pinned between the hulls and forgotten.

Bolitho shouted wildly, 'Come on, you gunners! Run out! *Run out!*'

He held out his sword like a barrier in front of his men. 'Back there! Get back!'

His small party fell back, confused by this turn of events. They had faced certain annihilation, and had accepted it. Now their captain had changed his mind. Or so it seemed.

But Herrick understood. Almost choking with excitement he yelled, '*All guns run out!*'

Bolitho saw the survivors from the carronade's single blast falling back towards their guns, shocked and dismayed as the *Phalarope*'s muzzles trundled forward and upwards towards them.

'Fire!' Bolitho almost fell overboard, but felt Stockdale catch his arm as the whole battery exploded beneath his feet.

The air seemed to come alive with inhuman screams as the whirling chain shot cut through sails and rigging alike in an overwhelming tempest of metal. Foremast and maintopmast fell together, the great weight of spars and canvas smashing down the remaining boarders and covering the gun-ports in a whirling mass of canvas.

The recoil of *Phalarope*'s broadside seemed to drive the two ships apart, leaving a trail of wreckage and corpses floating between them.

Bolitho leaned against the nettings, his breath sharp and painful. 'Reload! Carry on firing!' Whatever happened next, the *Phalarope* had spoken with authority, and had hit hard.

The frigate's proud outline was broken and confused in tangled shrouds and sails. Where her foremast had been minutes before there was only a bright-toothed stump, and the resonant cheers had given way to screams and confusion.

But she pushed forward across the *Phalarope*'s bows, followed by a further ragged salvo and a single angry bark from a forecastle nine-pounder. Then she was clear, gathering her tattered sails like garments to cover her scars, and pushing downwind into the rolling bank of smoke.

Bolitho stood watching her, his heart thumping, his eyes watering from strain and emotion.

The minutes dragged by, and then the insane realisation came to him. The *Andiron* was not putting about. She had taken enough.

Half stumbling he returned to the quarterdeck where Rennie's marines were grinning at him and Farquhar was leaning on the smoking carronade as if he no longer trusted what he saw.

Then they started to cheer. It was not much at first. Then it gathered strength and power until it moved above and below decks in an unbroken tide.

It was part pride and part relief. Some men were sobbing uncontrollably, others capered on the bloodstained decks like madmen.

Herrick ran aft, his hat awry, his blue eyes shining with excitement. 'You did for them, sir! My God, you scuppered 'em!' He clasped Bolitho's hand, unable to stop himself. Even old Proby was grinning.

Bolitho controlled his voice with one last effort. 'Thank you, gentlemen.' He looked along the littered decks, feeling the pain and the blind exultation. 'Next time we will do better!'

He swung round and pushed through the whooping marines towards the dark sanctuary of the cabin hatch.

Behind him, as if through a fog, he heard Herrick shout, 'I don't know about *next* time, lads! This will do me for a bit!'

Bolitho stood breathing hard in the narrow passageway listening to their excitement and laughter. They were grateful, even happy, he realised dully. Perhaps the bill would not be too high after all.

There was so much to do. So many things to prepare and restore before the ship would be ready to fight again. He fingered the worn sword hilt and stared wearily at the deck beams. But it would wait a moment longer. Just a short moment.

Herrick leaned heavily on the forecastle rail and wiped his forehead with the back of his hand. Only the slightest breeze ruffled the calm sea ahead of the gently pitching bows, and as he watched he saw the sun dipping towards the horizon, its glowing reflection already waiting to receive it and allow night to hide the *Phalarope*'s scars.

Herrick could feel his legs shaking, and again he tried to tell himself it was due to fatigue and the strain of a continuous day's working. Within an hour of the privateer's disappearance Bolitho had returned to the quarterdeck, his dark hair once more gathered neatly to the nape of his neck, his face freshly shaved, and the dust of battle brushed from his uniform. Only the lines at the corners of his mouth, the grave restlessness in his eyes betrayed any inner feelings as he passed his orders and began the work of repairing the damage to his ship and crew.

At first Herrick had imagined the task impossible. The men's relief had given way to delayed shock, so that individual sailors lay aimlessly about the stained decks like marionettes with severed strings, or just stood and stared listlessly at the aftermath of the nightmare.

Bolitho's sudden appearance had started a train of events which nobody could really explain. Every officer and man was too spent, too dulled by the brief and savage encounter to spare any strength for protest. The dead had been gathered at the lee rail and sewn into pathetic anonymous bundles. Lines of kneeling men had moved from forward to aft working with heavy holystones to scrub away the dark stains to the accompaniment of clanking pumps and the indifferent gurgle of sea-water.

The tattered and useless sails were sent down and replaced with fresh canvas, while Tozer, the sailmaker, and his mates squatted on every available deck space, needles and palms moving like lightning as they patched and repaired anything which could be salvaged and used again.

Ledward, the carpenter, moved slowly around the splintered gun battery, making a note here, taking a measurement there, until at length he was ready to play his part in restoring the frigate to her original readiness. Even now, as Herrick relived the fury of the bombardment and heard the screams and moans of wounded men, the hammers and saws were busy, and the whole new areas of planking were being tamped neatly into place to await the pitch and paint of the following morning.

He shivered again and cursed as his knees nearly gave under him. It was shock rather than mere fatigue. He knew that now.

He thought back to his impressions of the battle, to his own stupid relief and loud-voiced humour when the enemy had hauled away. It had been like listening to another, uncontrollable being who had been incapable of either silence or composure. Just to be alive and unharmed had meant more than anything.

Now as the sky grew darker astern of the slow moving ship he examined his true feelings and tried to put his recollections into some semblance of order.

He had even tried to regain some of the brief contact he had made with Bolitho. He had crossed the quarterdeck where the captain had been staring down at the labouring sailors and had said, 'You saved us all that time, sir. Another minute and she'd have been into us with a full broadside! It was a clever ruse to ask us to heave to. That privateer was a cunning one and no mistake!'

Bolitho had not lifted his gaze from the maindeck. When he had replied it had been as if he was speaking to himself. '*Andiron* is an old ship. She has been out here for ten years.' He had made a brief gesture towards the maindeck. '*Phalarope* is new. Every gun is fitted with the new flintlock and the carronades are almost unknown except in the Channel Fleet. No, Mr. Herrick, there is little room for congratulations!'

Herrick had studied Bolitho's brooding profile, aware perhaps for the first time of the man's constant inner battle. 'All the same, sir, she outgunned us!' He had watched for some sign of the Bolitho he had seen waving his sword on the starboard gangway while shots had hammered down around him like hail. But there had been nothing. He had ended lamely, 'You'll see, sir, things will be different after this.'

Bolitho had straightened his back, as if throwing off some invisible weight. When he had turned his grey eyes had been cold and unfeeling. 'I hope you are right, Mr. Herrick! For my part I was disgusted with such a shambles! I dread to contemplate what might have happened in a fight to the finish!'

Herrick had felt himself flushing. 'I was only thinking . . .'

Bolitho had snapped. 'When I require an opinion from my third lieutenant I will let him know! Until that moment, Mr. Herrick, perhaps you would be good enough to make your people get to work! There will be time later for suppositions and self-adulation!' He had swung on his heel and recommenced his pacing.

Herrick watched the surgeon's party carry another limp corpse from the main hatch and lay it beside the others. Again, another picture of Bolitho sprang to his mind.

Herrick had been between decks on a tour of inspection with the carpenter. There were no shot holes beneath the water-line, but it had been his duty to make sure for his own satisfaction. Still dulled by the noise of battle he had followed Ledward beneath the massive, curved beams, his tired eyes half mesmerised by the man's shaded lantern. Together they had stepped through a screen and entered a scene from hell itself.

Lanterns ringed the deck space, to allow none of the horror to escape his eyes, and in the centre of the yellow glare, strapped and writhing like a sacrifice on an altar, was a badly wounded seaman, his leg already half amputated by Tobias Ellice, the surgeon. The latter's fat, brick-red face was devoid of expression as his bloody fingers worked busily with the glittering saw, his chins bouncing in time against the top of his scarlet-daubed apron. His assistants were using all their strength to restrain the struggling victim and pin his spreadeagled body on top of the platform of sea chests, which sufficed as an operating table. The man had rolled his eyes with each nerve-searing thrust of the saw, had bitten into the leather strap between his teeth until the blood had spurted from his lips, and Ellice had carried on with his amputation.

Around the circle of light the other wretched wounded had awaited their turn, some propped on their elbows as if unable to tear their eyes from the gruesome spectacle. Others lay moaning and sobbing in the shadows, their lives ebbing away and thereby spared the agony of knife and saw. The air had been thick with the stench of blood and rum, the latter being the only true way of killing the victims' senses before their turn came.

Ellice had looked up as the man had kicked out wildly and then fallen lifeless even as the severed limb had dropped into a waiting trough. He had seen Herrick's face stiff with shock and had remarked in his thick, tipsy voice, 'A day indeed, Mr. 'Errick! I sew an' I stitch, I saws an' I probes, but still they rushes to join their mates aloft!' He had rolled his rheumy eyes towards heaven and had reached for a squat leather bottle. 'Maybe a little nip for yerself, Mr. 'Errick?' He had lifted it against the light. 'No? Ah well then, a little sustenance for meself!'

He had given the merest nod to his loblolly boy, who in turn had pointed out another man by the ship's rounded side. The latter had been immediately seized and hauled screaming across the chests, his cries unheeded as Ellice wiped his mouth and had then ripped away the shirt from the man's lacerated arm.

Herrick had turned away, his face sweating as the man's scream had probed deeper into his eardrums. He had stopped in his tracks, suddenly aware that Bolitho was standing slightly behind him.

Bolitho had moved slowly around the pain-racked figures, his voice soothing but too soft for Herrick to comprehend. Here he had reached to touch a man's hand as it groped blindly for comfort or reassurance. There he had stopped to close the eyes of a man already dead. At one instant he had paused beneath a spiralling lantern and had asked quietly, 'How many, Mr. Ellice? What is the bill?'

Ellice had grunted and gestured to his men that he had completed his ministrations with the limp figure across the sheets. 'Twenty killed, Cap'n! Twenty more badly wounded, an' another thirty 'alf an' 'alf!'

It was then that Herrick had seen Bolitho's mask momentarily drop away. There had been pain on his face. Pain and despair.

Herrick had immediately forgotten his anger and resentment at the captain's remarks earlier on the quarterdeck. The Bolitho he had seen on the ship's side waving his sword had been real. So, too, was this one.

He stared down at the canvas-shrouded corpses and tried to remember the faces to fit against the names scrawled on each lolling bundle. But already they were fading, lost in memory like the smoke of the battle which had struck them down.

Herrick started as he caught sight of Lieutenant Okes's thin figure moving slowly along the shadowed maindeck. He had hardly seen Okes at all since the action. It was as if the man had been waiting for the hard-driven sailors to finish their work so that he could have the deck to himself.

There had been that moment immediately after the sound of the last shot had rolled away in the smoke. Okes had staggered up through a hatchway, his eyes wild and uncontrolled. He had seemed shocked beyond understanding as he had looked around him, as if expecting to see the enemy ship alongside. Okes had seen Herrick watching him, and his eyes had strayed past to the smoking guns in the battery which he had left to fend for themselves.

He had clutched Herrick's arm, his voice unrestrained and desperate.

'Had to go below, Thomas! Had to find those fellows who ran away!' He had swayed and added wildly, 'You believe me, don't you?'

Herrick's contempt and anger had faded with the discovery that Okes was terrified almost to a point of madness. The realisation filled him with a mixture of pity and shame.

'Keep your voice down, man!' Herrick had looked round for Vibart. 'You damn fool! Try and keep your head!'

He watched Okes now as the man skirted the corpses and then retraced his steps to the stern. He too was reliving his own misery. Destroying himself with the knowledge of his cowardice and disgrace.

Herrick found time to wonder if the captain had noticed Okes's disappearance during the battle. Perhaps not. Maybe Okes would recover after this, he thought grimly. If not, his escape might be less easy the next time.

He saw Midshipman Neale's small figure scampering along the maindeck and felt a touch of warmth. The boy had not faltered throughout the fight. He had seen him on several occasions, running with messages, yelling shrilly to the men of his division, or just standing wide-eyed at his station. Neale's loss would have been felt throughout the ship, of that Herrick was quite sure.

He hid a smile as the boy skidded to a halt and touched his hat. 'Mr. Herrick, sir! Captain's compliments and would you lay aft to supervise burial party!' He gulped for breath. 'There's thirty altogether, sir!'

'Herrick adjusted his hat and nodded gravely. 'And how are you feeling?'

The boy shrugged. 'Hungry, sir!'

Herrick grinned. 'Try fattening a ship's rat with biscuit, Mr. Neale. As good as rabbit any day!' He strode aft, leaving Neale staring after him, his forehead creased in a frown.

Neale walked slowly past the bow-chasers, deep in thought. Then he nodded very slowly. 'Yes, I might try it,' he said softly.

Bolitho felt his head loll and he jerked himself back against his chair and stared at the pile of reports on his table. All but completed. He rubbed his sore eyes and then stood up.

Astern, through the great windows he could see moonlight on the black water and could hear the gentle sluice and creak of the rudder below him. His mind was still fogged by the countless orders he had given, the requests and demands he had answered.

Sails and cordage to be repaired, a new spar broken out to replace the missing topgallant. Several of the boats had been damaged and one of the cutters smashed to fragments. In a week, driving the men hard, there would be little outward sign of the battle, he thought wearily. But the scars would be there, deep and constant inside each man's heart.

He recalled the empty deck in the fading light as he had stood over the dead men and had read the well-tried words of the burial service. Midshipman Farquhar had held a light above the book, and he had noticed that his hand had been steady and unwavering.

He still did not like Farquhar, he decided. But he had proved a first-class officer in combat. That made up for many things.

As the last corpse had splashed alongside to begin its journey two thousand fathoms deep he had turned, only to stop in surprise as he had realised that the deck had filled silently with men from below decks. Nobody spoke, but here and there a man coughed quietly, and once he had heard a youngster sobbing uncontrollably.

He had wanted to say something to them. To make them understand. He had seen Herrick beside the marine guard, and Vibart's massive figure outlined against the sky at the quarterdeck rail. For a brief moment they had all been together, bound by the bonds of suffering and loss. Words would have soiled the moment. A speech would have sounded cheap. He had walked aft to the ladder and paused beside the wheel.

The helmsman had stiffened. 'Course south-west by south, sir! Full an' by!'

He had returned here. To this one safe, defended place where there was no need for words of any sort.

He looked up angrily as Stockdale padded through the door. The man studied him gravely. 'I've told that servant o' yours to bring your supper, Captain.' Stockdale peered disapprovingly at the litter of charts and written reports. 'Pork, sir. Nicely sliced and fried, just as you like it.' He held out a bottle. 'I took the liberty of breaking out one o' your clarets, sir.'

The tension gripped Bolitho's voice in a vice. 'What the hell are you jabbering about?'

Stockdale was undaunted. 'You can flog me for sayin' it, sir, but today was a victory! You done us all proudly. I think you deserve a drink!'

Bolitho stared at him lost for words.

Stockdale began to gather up the papers. 'An' further, Captain, I think you deserves a lot more!'

As Bolitho sat in silence watching the big coxswain laying the table for his solitary meal, the *Phalarope* plucked at the light airs and pushed quietly beneath the stars.

From dawn to sunset she had given much. But there would be other days ahead, thanks to her captain.

6

A Sight of Land

Bolitho walked to the starboard side of the quarterdeck and rested his hands on the sun-warmed hammock netting. He did not need either chart or telescope now. It was like a homecoming.

The small island of Antigua had crept up over the horizon in the dawn's light, and now sprawled abeam shimmering in the forenoon sunlight.

Bolitho felt the old excitement of a perfect landfall coursing through his limbs, and he had to make himself continue in his interrupted pacing, if only to control it. Five weeks to a day since the *Phalarope* had showed her stern to the mist and rain of Cornwall. Two weeks since the clash with the privateer, and as he looked quickly along his ship he felt a quick upsurge of pride. All repairs had been completed, and the remaining wounded were well on the mend. The death roll had risen to thirty-five, but the sudden entry into warmer air, with sun and fresh breezes instead of damp and blustering wind, had worked wonders.

The frigate was gliding gently on the port tack, making a perfect pair above her own reflection in the deep blue water. Above her tapering masts the sky was cloudless and full of welcome, and already the eager gulls swooped and screamed around the yards with noisy expectancy.

Antigua, headquarters and main base of the West Indies squadron, a link in the ragged chain of islands which protected the eastern side of the Caribbean. Bolitho felt strangely glad to be back. He half expected to see the crew and deck of the *Sparrow* when he looked across the quarterdeck rail, but already the *Phalarope*'s company had grown in focus to overshadow the old memories.

'Deck there! Ship of the line anchored around the headland!'

Okes was officer of the watch and he looked quickly towards Bolitho.

'That will be the flagship most likely, Mr. Okes.' Bolitho glanced up to the new topgallant where the keen-eyed lookout had already seen the tall masts of the other vessel.

The frigate slowly rounded Cape Shirley with its lush green hills and the tumbled mass of rocky headland, and Bolitho watched his men as they thronged the weather side, clinging to shrouds and chains as they drank in the sight of the land. To all but a few of them it was a new experience. Here everything was different, larger than life. The sun was brighter, the thick green vegetation above the gleaming white beaches was like nothing they had ever seen. They shouted to one another, pointing out landmarks, chattering like excited children as the headland slipped past to reveal the bay and the landlocked waters of English Harbour beyond.

Proby called, 'Ready to wear ship, sir!'

Bolitho nodded. The *Phalarope* had every sail clewed up except topsails and jib, and on the forecastle he could see Herrick watching him as he stood beside the anchor party.

He snapped his fingers. 'My glass, please.'

He took the telescope from Midshipman Maynard and stared fixedly at the two-decker anchored in the centre of the bay. Her gunports were open to collect the offshore breeze, and there were awnings across her wide quarterdeck. His eye fastened on the rear-admiral's flag at her masthead, the gleam of blue and scarlet from watching figures at her poop.

'Mr. Brock! Stand by to fire salute! Eleven guns, if you please!' He closed the glass with a snap. If he could see them, they could see him. There was no point in appearing curious.

He watched the nearest point of land falling away and then added, 'Carry on, Mr. Proby!'

Proby touched his hat. 'Lee braces there! Hands wear ship!'

Bolitho glanced quickly at Okes and waited patiently. At length he said evenly, 'Clear those idlers off the side, Mr. Okes. That is a flagship yonder. I don't want the admiral to think I've brought a lot of bumpkins with me!' He smiled as Okes stuttered out his orders and the petty officers yelled at the unemployed men by the rail.

The salute began to pound and re-echo around the hills as the frigate swung slowly towards the other ship, and more than one man bit his lips as the saluting guns brought back other more terrifying memories.

'Tops'l sheets!' Proby mopped the sweat from his streaming face as he gauged the slow approach to the anchorage. 'Tops'l clew lines!' He looked aft. 'Ready, Sir!'

Bolitho nodded, only half listening to the salutes and the staccato bark of orders.

'Helm a' lee!' He watched the quartermaster pulling steadily at the polished spokes and saw the nearest hillside begin to swing across the bows as the *Phalarope* turned into the wind and began to lose way.

Now there was no sound but for the gentle lap of water as the ship glided slowly towards the shore.

Bolitho called, 'Let go!'

There was a splash from forward followed by the jubilant roar of cable as the anchor plunged into the clear water.

Maynard said excitedly, 'Signal, sir! From *Cassius* to *Phalarope*. Captain to repair on board.'

Bolitho nodded. He had been expecting it and was already changed into his best uniform. 'Call away the gig, Mr. Okes, and see that its crew is properly turned out!' He saw the harassed lieutenant hurry away and wondered momentarily what was worrying him. He seemed strained. His mind only half on his duty.

Vibart came aft and touched his hat. 'Any orders, sir?'

Bolitho watched the boat being swayed out, the petty officer in charge using his cane more than usual, as if he too was well aware of the watching flagship.

'You can stand by to take on fresh water, Mr. Vibart. We will no doubt be warping through into English Harbour directly, and the men can go ashore and stretch their legs. They've earned it.'

Vibart looked as if he was going to argue but merely replied, 'Aye, aye, sir. I'll see to it.'

Bolitho looked across at the two-decker. The *Cassius*, seventy-four, flagship of Rear-Admiral Sir Robert Napier. He was said to be a stickler for promptness and smartness, although Bolitho had never actually met him before.

He climbed down the ladder and walked slowly towards the entry port. It was a strange to realise that he had been in command for only five weeks. It seemed as if he had been aboard for months. The faces of the side party were familiar now, and already he was able to pick out the personalities and the weaknesses.

Captain Rennie saluted with his sword and the guard presented arms.

Bolitho removed his hat and then replaced it as the gig idled alongside with Stockdale glaring from the tiller. The pipes twittered and shrilled, and as he stepped into the gig he looked up at the ship's side, at the fresh paint and neat repairs which hid the clawing scars of battle. Things might have been a lot worse, he thought, as he settled himself in the sternsheets.

The oars sent the little boat scudding across the calm water, and when Bolitho looked astern he saw that his men were still staring after him. He held their lives in his hands. He had always known that. But before the short battle some might have doubted his ability. They might even have thought him to be like Pomfret.

He thrust the thought to the back of his mind as the flagship grew and towered above him. They did not have to like him, he decided. But trust him they must.

Rear-Admiral Sir Robert Napier did not rise from his desk but waved Bolitho towards a chair by the broad stern gallery. He was a small, irritable-looking man wth stooping shoulders and sparse grey hair. He seemed bowed down by the weight of his dress coat, and his thin mouth was fixed in an expression of pernickety disapproval.

'I have been reading your reports, Bolitho.' His eyes flickered across the younger man's face and then returned to the desk. 'I am still not quite clear about your action with the *Andiron*.'

Bolitho tried to relax in the hard chair, but something in the admiral's querulous tone sparked off a small warning.

Bolitho had been met at the flagship's entry port with due ceremony and greeted courteously by the *Cassius*'s captain. The latter had appeared uneasy and worried, as well he might with a man like Sir Robert aboard, Bolitho thought dryly. The first sign that all was not well had been when he had been ushered into a cabin adjoining the admiral's quarters and told to wait for an audience. His log and reports had been whisked away, and he had stayed fretting in the airless cabin for the best part of an hour.

He said carefully, 'We made a good voyage, in spite of the engagement, sir. All repairs were carried out without loss of sailing time.'

The admiral eyed him coldly. 'Is that a boast?'

'No, sir,' Bolitho replied patiently. 'But I imagined that the need for frigates is still acute out here.'

The other man ruffled the documents with a wizened hand. 'Hmm, quite so. But the *Andiron*, Bolitho? How did she manage to escape?'

Bolitho stared at him, caught off guard. 'Escape, sir? She nearly laid us by the heels, as I have stated in my report.'

'I read that, dammit!' The eyes glowed dangerously. 'Are you trying to tell me that she ran away?' He looked aft through a window to where the *Phalarope* swung at her anchor like a carved model. 'I see little sign of combat or damage, Bolitho?'

'We were well supplied with spare spars and canvas, sir. The dockyard foresaw such an eventuality when they fitted her out.' The admiral's tone was getting under his skin and he could feel his anger smouldering, ignoring the warning in the man's eyes.

'I see. Captain Masterman lost *Andiron* after engaging two French frigates four months back, Bolitho. The French gave the captured ship to their new allies, the Americans.' The contempt was clear in his voice. 'And you state that although your ship was disabled and outgunned she made off without attempting to press home her advantage?' There was anger in his voice. 'Well, *are* you?'

'Exactly, sir.' Bolitho controlled his answer with an effort. 'My men fought well. I think the enemy had had enough. If I had been able to give chase I would have done so.'

'So you say, Bolitho!' The admiral put his head on one side, like a small, spiteful bird. 'I know all about your ship. I have read Admiral Longford's letter and all that he had to say about the trouble there was aboard when with the Channel Fleet. I am not impressed to say the least!'

Bolitho felt the colour rising to his cheeks. The admiral's insinuation was obvious. In his view the *Phalarope* was a marked ship and unacceptable, no matter what she achieved.

He said coldly, 'I did not run away, sir. It happened just as I stated in the report. In my opinion the privateer was unwilling to sustain more damage.' He had a sudden picture of the crashing broadside, the chain shot ripping away the enemy's sails and rigging like cobwebs. Then another picture of the silent dead being dropped overboard. He added, 'My men did as well as I had hoped, sir. They had little time to defend themselves.'

'Please don't take that tone with me, Bolitho!' The admiral stared at him hotly. 'I will decide what standards your people have reached.'

'Yes, sir.' Bolitho felt drained. There was no point in arguing with this man.

'See that you remember it in future.' He dropped his eyes to the papers and said, 'Sir George Rodney has sailed to reorganise his fleet. He will be returning from England at any time. Sir Samuel Hood is away at St. Kitts defending it from the French.'

Bolitho said quietly, 'St. Kitts sir?' It was barely one hundred miles to the west of his chair aboard the flagship, yet the admiral spoke as if it was the other side of the world.

'Yes. The French landed troops on the island and tried to drive our garrison into the sea. But Admiral Hood's squadron retook the anchorage, and even now is holding all the main positions, including Basseterre, the chief town.' He glared at Bolitho's thoughtful face. 'But that is not your concern. I am in command here until either the Commander-in-Chief returns or Admiral Hood sees fit to relieve me. You will take your orders from *me*!'

Bolitho's mind only half attended to the other man's irritable voice. In his mind he could see the tiny island of St. Kitts and knew exactly what its safety meant to the harassed British. The French were strong in these waters, and had been more than instrumental to the British defeats at the Chesapeake the previous year. Driven from the American mainland, the British squadrons would depend more and more on their chain of island bases for supplies and repairs. If they fell, there would be nothing to prevent the French or their allies from swallowing up every last possession in the Caribbean.

The French fleet in the West Indies was well trained and battle hardened. Their admiral, Count de Grasse, had more than once out-guessed and out-fought the hard-pressed ships of the British. It had been de Grasse who had driven a wedge between Admiral Graves and the beleaguered Cornwallis, who had assisted the rebel general, Washington, and had organised the American privateers into useful and deadly opponents.

Now de Grasse was testing the strength of individual British bases with the same sure strategy which had made him his country's most valuable commander. Using Martinique to the south as his main base, he could attack every island at will or, the thought brought a chill to Bolitho's mind, he could speed to the west and fall upon Jamaica. After that there would be nothing to sustain the British. They would have the Atlantic behind them, and nothing to keep them from complete destruction.

The admiral was saying smoothly, 'I will require you to carry out patrols to the westward, Bolitho. I will draft my orders immediately. The enemy may try and transport more troops down from the American mainland to the Leeward Islands, or even further south to the Windward Islands. You will keep contact with the rest of my squadron, and with Admiral Hood at St. Kitts *only if absolutely necessary*!'

Bolitho felt the cabin closing in on him. The admiral had no intention of trusting *Phalarope* with the fleet. Once again the frigate seemed doomed to isolation and suspicion.

He said, 'The French will be reinforced by privateers, sir. My ship would be well employed closer inshore, I would have thought.'

The admiral smiled gently. 'Of course, Bolitho, I had almost forgotten. You are no stranger out here. I think I read somewhere of your little exploits.' His smile vanished. 'I am sick and tired of hearing stories of privateers! They are nothing but scavengers and pirates, and no match for one of *my* ships! You will do well to remember that, too! *Andiron's* capture was a disgrace which should have been forestalled! If you meet her again, I would suggest you summon help to avoid another lamentable failure to capture or destroy her!'

Bolitho stood up, his eyes flashing. 'That is unfair, sir!'

The admiral studied him bleakly. 'Hold your tongue! I am tired of young, hot-headed officers who cannot understand strategy and discipline!'

Bolitho waited for his breathing to return to normal.

'Privateers are just one part of the pattern. The French are the real danger!'

There was a long silence, and Bolitho heard the distant thud of marines' boots and the muted blare of a bugle. The two-decker was like a small town after a frigate, but Bolitho could not wait to get away from it and the admiral's insulting remarks.

The latter said offhandedly, 'Keep a close watch on your patrol, Bolitho. And I would suggest you watch your fresh water and supplies very closely. I cannot say exactly when you will be relieved.'

'My men are tired, sir.' Bolitho tried once more to get through the admiral's cold rudeness. 'Some of them have not been ashore for years'. He thought of the way they had watched the green hills and gasped at the sight of the smooth deserted beaches.

'And I am tired of this interview, Bolitho.' He rang a small bell on the desk. 'Just do your allotted duty, and remember that I will brook no deviation from it at any time. Foolhardy schemes are useless to me. See that you do not allow your apparent sense of self-importance to mar your judgement.' He waved his hand and the door opened silently behind Bolitho.

He stood outside in the passageway, his hands shaking with suppressed anger and resentment. By the time he had reached the entry port his face was again an impassive mask, but he hardly trusted himself to reply to the quiet words of the *Cassius's* captain as the latter saw him over the side.

The older man said softly, 'Watch your step, Bolitho! Sir Robert lost his son aboard the *Andiron*. He will never forgive you for letting her get away, *whatever* the reason, so you must try and ignore his words, if not his warning!'

Bolitho touched his hat to the guard. 'I have had a lot of warnings of late, sir. But in an emergency they are rarely of any use!'

The flagship's captain watched Bolitho step into the gig and move clear of the *Cassius's* long shadow. In spite of his youth, Bolitho looked as if he might make trouble for others as well as himself, he thought grimly.

'Deck there! The cap'n's returnin'!'

Herrick moved out of the shade of the mizzen mast and hurried towards the entry port. He brushed some crumbs from his neckcloth and hastily tugged his cross-belt into position. He had always been able to tolerate the dull and badly prepared food aboard ship in the past, but with the *Phalarope* riding at her anchor and the ample provisions of English Harbour lying within cannon shot, it had been all that he could do to swallow his lunch. He squinted across the glittering water, his keen eyes immediately picking out the returning gig, its small crew clean and bright in their check shirts, the oars rising and falling like gulls' wings. Herrick stiffened as Vibart joined him by the rail.

The first lieutenant said, 'Well, now we shall see!'

'I'll wager the admiral was delighted to see our captain.' Herrick darted a hasty glance to make sure that the side party was properly fallen in. 'It will do a power of good for our people.'

Vibart shrugged. 'What do admirals know about anything?' He seemed unwilling to talk and unable to drag his eyes from the approaching gig.

Herrick could see Bolitho's square shoulders in the sternsheets, the glitter of sunlight on his gold lace.

A master's mate said suddenly, 'Two water lighters shovin' off from the shore, sir. Deep laden by the looks of 'em!'

Herrick glanced in the direction of the man's arm and saw the two ugly craft moving clear of the land. They crawled ponderously towards the frigate, their great sweeps making heavy work of the journey.

Herrick muttered, 'I thought we would wait until we warped through into the harbour?'

Vibart slammed his hands together. 'By God, I knew this would happen! I just *knew* it!' He moved his heavy body violently and pointed towards the blue sea. 'That's for us, Mr. Herrick. No cream for the *Phalarope*, either now or ever!' He added angrily, 'Not until the ship is used as she was meant to be used!'

A boatswain's mate called, 'Stand by!'

Again the pipes shrilled their salute and the sweating guard slapped their muskets to the present.

Herrick touched his hat and watched Bolitho's face as he climbed up through the port. His features were calm and empty of expression, but his eyes as he glanced briefly along the maindeck were cold and bleak, like the North Atlantic.

Vibart said stiffly, 'Water lighters making for us, sir.'

'So I see.' Bolitho did not look round, but stared instead at the newly scrubbed decks, the quiet atmosphere of order and readiness. He added after a moment, 'Carry on with immediate loading, and tell the cooper to prepare extra casks.'

Herrick asked cautiously, 'Are we to sea again, sir?'

The grey eyes fixed him with a flat stare. 'It would appear so!'

Vibart stepped forward, his eyes hidden in shadow. 'It's damned unfair, sir!'

Bolitho did not answer, but seemed entirely preoccupied in his thoughts. Then he said sharply, 'We will be making sail within two hours, Mr. Vibart. The wind seems light, but good enough for my purpose.' He looked round as Stockdale padded on to the quarterdeck. 'Oh, tell my servant I will require some food as soon as possible. Anything will do.'

Herrick stared at him. Bolitho had been away for the best part of two hours, yet the admiral had not even bothered to entertain him or offer him lunch. What the hell could he be thinking of? A young, courageous captain, fresh from England with news, as well as a fine addition to the fleet, should have been welcomed like a brother!

He thought of his own feelings while he had eaten his meagre meal in the wardroom. Each mouthful had nearly choked him as he had imagined Bolitho dining with the admiral and enjoying the full fare which a flagship could provide in harbour. Poultry, fresh lean pork, even roast potatoes perhaps! The climate was unimportant to Herrick where good, familiar food was concerned.

Now he realised that Bolitho had received nothing. The same feeling of shame and pity moved through him that he had earlier felt for Okes. A slur on Bolitho was an insult to every man aboard, yet the captain carried the full brunt of it. It was so unfair, so calculated in its cruelty that Herrick could not contain himself.

'But, sir! Did the admiral not congratulate you?' He fumbled for words as Bolitho shifted to watch him. 'After all you have done for this ship?'

'Thank you for your concern, Herrick.' For a brief moment Bolitho's expression softened. 'Things are not always what they first appear. We must be patient.' There was not a trace of bitterness in his answer, nor was there any warmth either. 'But in war there is little time for personal understanding.' He turned on his heel adding, 'We will have gun drill as soon as we get under way.' He disappeared down the cabin hatch and Herrick looked round in dull amazement.

So Vibart had been right. *Phalarope* was a marked ship, and would remain one.

The master's mate came aft. 'Boat shovin' off from the *Cassius*, sir!'

Herrick felt suddenly angry. It was all so pointless, so stupid. 'Very well. It will be bringing despatches. Man the side, if you please.'

He was still angry when a debonair lieutenant climbed up through the port and after removing his hat stood and stared curiously around the deck, as if expecting to see some sort of spectacle.

'Well?' Herrick scowled at the visitor. 'Have you had a good look?'

The officer blushed and then said, 'My apologies, sir. I was expecting something rather different.' He held out a bulky canvas envelope. 'Orders for Captain Bolitho from Sir Robert Napier, Rear-Admiral of the Red.'

It sounded so formal after their first exchange that Herrick could not help smiling. 'Thank you. I'll take 'em aft in a moment.' He studied the officer's tanned face. 'How goes the war out here?'

He shrugged. 'A hopeless muddle. Too much sea and too few ships to cover it!' He became serious. 'St. Kitts is under siege, and the rebels are consolidating up in the north. Everything will depend on how much the French can bring to bear.'

Herrick turned the heavy envelope over in his hands and wondered if he would ever be opening his own orders. In command of his own ship.

'If the privateers are as good as the one we fought then the battle will be a hard one.' Herrick studied the man's face intently, just waiting for some sign of doubt or amusement.

But the lieutenant said quietly, 'We heard about the *Andiron*. A bad business to lose her so. I hope you get a chance to even the score. What with that renegade John Paul Jones playing hell with our communications, it is only to be expected that others will follow his example.'

Herrick nodded. 'I don't see why it should be a disgrace for Captain Masterman to lose his ship in combat.'

'You have not heard?' The officer dropped his voice. 'She fought two French frigates at once. At the height of the battle the *Andiron* was hailed by some American officer aboard one of the enemy ships. He called on the *Andiron's* people to go over to his side!'

Herrick's jaw dropped. 'And you mean that is what happened?'

He nodded. 'Exactly! They would never surrender to Frogs, but this American made it sound like a new life, so what did they have to lose? And of course they will fight all the better *against us*! Every man-jack knows it will be flogging round the fleet and the gibbet if they are caught now.'

Herrick felt sick. 'How long had *Andiron* been in commission?'

'I'm not sure. About ten years, I believe.' He saw Herrick's mind working and added grimly, 'So *watch* your own people. Out here, thousands of miles from home and surrounded by the King's enemies, emotions play a big part in a man's loyalty.' He added meaningly, 'Especially in a ship where trouble has already felt its way!'

He broke off as Vibart strode back from the maindeck. He touched his hat to the first lieutenant and said formally, 'I have twenty-five men for you in my cutter, sir. The admiral requested they be used as replacements for the ones killed in battle.' He watched as Vibart climbed down to the port where the marines were already mustering a growing rank of lean-looking sailors.

The officer said quickly, 'I have already spoken enough, my friend. But these men are outcasts. Nearly all have been in serious trouble of one kind or another. I think Sir Robert is more concerned in ridding his flagship of their influence than he is of helping your captain.' With a hurried glance at the distant two-decker he made towards his waiting boat. He whispered finally, 'Sir Robert watches everything. No doubt it will soon be common knowledge that I have spent ten minutes in conversation with *you*!' Then he was gone.

Vibart clumped aft, his face wrinkled in a scowl. 'We will read in those men immediately, Mr. Herrick. I suppose the captain will want them dressed like the rest of the precious company?' He sniffed. 'In my opinion they look more at home in rags!'

Herrick followed his angry glance and felt his spirits drop even further. These replacements were not men raw from the press. They were hardened and professional, and at any other time would have been worth their weight in gold. But now they stood idly and insolently watching with all the arrogance of wild animals as the master's mate and Midshipman Maynard sorted them into order and seniority. Curses and beatings would not impress their sort. Even floggings had changed them little, Herrick thought.

Vibart muttered, 'We'll see how the captain deals with this pretty bunch!'

Herrick did not speak. He could imagine the difficulties which seemed to be piling up hour by hour. If the captain tried to separate these troublemakers from the rest of the crew he would lose any respect he had gained. If he did not, their influence could wreak havoc on the crowded berth deck.

On patrol, out of touch with help, the *Phalarope* would need all her resources and skill to stay intact and vigilant.

Herrick had a sudden picture of the *Andiron* as she must have been when Masterman's crew had surrendered. He stared round the sunny quarterdeck and felt chilled in spite of the glare. He imagined himself, suddenly alone, in a ship where disciplined and loyal seamen had become strangers and mutineers.

Midshipman Maynard was watching him anxiously. 'Signal, sir. Flag to *Phalarope*. Complete lightering and proceed to sea with all despatch.'

Herrick said wearily, 'Acknowledge, Mr. Maynard.'

Herrick stared over the rail where the seamen toiled with the fresh-water casks and then across at the tall-masted flagship. Almost to himself he muttered, 'You bastard! You just can't wait, can you.'

Grumbling and cursing, the duty watch climbed down the various ladders and into the already crowded berth deck. Both air and lighting came through the central hatchways, and in addition several canvas chutes had been rigged to help ventilate the overpopulated living spaces. At each scrubbed mess table men sat and made use of their time to their own best advantage. Some repaired clothing, heads bent to catch the filtered sunlight on their needles and coarse thread. Some worked on small model ships, and others merely sprawled yarning with their companions.

There was a brief lull in the buzz of speculation and rumour as some of the new men pattered down a ladder followed by Belsey, the duty master's mate. All of the men had been read in, had taken the regulation shower under the deck pump, and now stood blinking in the shadows, their bodies pale and naked against the ship's dark sides. Each man carried a new shirt and a rolled pair of trousers, as well as his own small possessions.

Belsey spun his cane and pointed to the corner mess table where Allday and old Strachan watched the procession in silence. He barked, 'You two! You'll be in this mess, got it?' He glared into the dark corner of the berth deck. 'You've been given your watch and action stations, so just get settled in, and look sharp about it!' He raised his voice. 'Show these replacements where to sling their hammocks, and then get this deck cleared up!' He wrinkled his thick nose. 'It's like a bloody pigsty down here.'

One of the men detailed dropped his bundle on the table and looked down at Strachan and the others. He was tall and well muscled, and his broad chest was covered in a deep mat of dark hair. He seemed quite unconcerned about his nakedness and the rasp in Belsey's introduction.

He said calmly, 'Harry Onslow is the name, mates.' He looked over his shoulder. 'An' this is Pook, another good topman from the *Cassius*!' He spat out the name of the flagship, and Belsey who was hovering nearby strode across to the crowded table.

'Pay attention!' He stared round the watching faces. 'Don't you start thinking that you've got a real fine fellow here, my friends!' He gave a short grin. 'Turn round, Onslow!' He moved his cane menacingly. 'Just get a bit o' sunlight over you!'

Onslow turned his body obediently so that the light played across his back. Something like a hollow groan came from the packed sailors, and Belsey added coldly, 'Take a good look, afore you start listening to the like o' this scum!'

Allday tightened his lips as he saw the savagely mutilated skin on Onslow's body. He could not imagine how many times the man had been flogged, but that he had survived was surely a miracle.

The whole of his back, from the nape of the neck to the top of his buttocks was ugly with broken and uneven weals, pale and obscene against his tanned arms and legs.

Ferguson looked away, his mouth quivering.

Even Pochin, a hard spectator at many floggings, said thickly, ' 'Ere, mate, put yer shirt on!'

The other man, Pook, was thin and wiry, and although his back also displayed the clawing embrace of the cat, it was nothing compared with Onslow's.

Belsey sauntered away followed by the other new seamen.

Onslow pulled the shirt over his head and shook out the clean new trousers. Calmly he remarked, 'What is so different about your captain? Does he like his men to look pretty?' He had a lazy Norfolk accent, and seemed quite unmoved by the horror his scars had unleashed.

Ferguson said quickly, 'He's different. He stopped Betts being flogged.' He tried to smile. 'You'll be all right aboard this ship, Onslow!'

Onslow looked him over without expression. 'Who asked *you* then?'

'All captains are swine!' Pook was tugging on his trousers, and then strapped a wicked-looking knife around his waist. 'We've had a bellyful in the *Cassius*!'

Onslow said, 'Betts, did you say? What happened to him?'

'He attacked the purser.' Pochin looked thoughtful. 'Cap'n Bolitho refused to 'ave 'im flogged.'

'Where is he now?' The man's eyes were dark and unwinking.

'Dead. Went over the side with the main t'gallant!'

'Well, then.' Onslow pushed Ferguson off the bench and squatted in his place. 'It didn't do him much good, did it?'

Old Strachan folded his carving in a piece of sailcloth and said vaguely, 'But the lad's right. Cap'n Bolitho promised that he would see us fair if we pulled our weight. We'll be taking a run ashore soon.' He squinted towards the hatch. 'Just think of it! A walk through them hills, and maybe a drop o' somethin' from a friendly native!'

Ferguson tried again. As if he had to believe in somebody to retain his own sanity. 'And Mr. Herrick said he would try and get a letter put aboard the next homebound ship for me. Just to tell my wife I'm alive and well.' His expression was pitiful.

'You can read and write, can you, little man?' Onslow studied him calmly. 'You could be very useful to me.'

Allday smiled to himself. Already the noise and rumble of voices was returning to the messes. Maybe Ferguson was right. Things might be better from now on. He hoped so, if only for Ferguson's peace of mind.

Pochin asked sourly, 'How did you get the lash, Onslow?'

'Oh, the usual.' Onslow was still watching Ferguson, his face deep in thought.

Pook said ingratiatingly, ' 'E kicked a bosun's mate! An' afore that he . . .'

Onslow's mouth opened and shut like a trap. 'Stow it! It's what happens from now on that counts!' Then he became calm again. 'I was a boy when I came out here ten years back. For years I've been waiting for that last voyage home, but it never comes. I've been shipped from one captain to the next. I've stood my watches, and I've faced broadsides more times than I can remember. No, mates, there's no let-up for our sort. The only way out is sewn up in a hammock, or take our own course like the lads in the *Andiron*.'

He had every man's attention now. He stood up, his face set and brooding. 'They chose to leave the King's service. To make a new life for themselves out here, or in the Americas!'

Strachan shook his grey head. 'That's piracy!'

'You're too old to matter!' There was a bite in Onslow's voice. 'I've yet to find a fair captain, or one who thought beyond prize money and glory for himself!'

At that moment shadows darted across the hatches and the air was filled with twittering pipes.

Pochin groaned. 'Blasted Spithead nightingales! Do they never get tired of blowin' 'em?'

The voices of the bosun's mates echoed round the berth deck. 'All hands! All hands! Stand by to make sail! Anchor party muster on the fo'c'sle!'

Ferguson stared blankly at the sunlight on the ladder, his mouth hanging open. 'He promised! He promised me I could get a letter home!'

Onslow clapped him on the shoulder. 'And he'll promise a lot more, I shouldn't wonder, lad!' He faced the others, unsmiling. 'Well, mates! Do you understand now what I was saying?'

Josling, a bosun's mate, appeared on the ladder, his face running with sweat. 'Are yew deaf? Jump to it there! A taste of my little rope for the last on deck!'

There was a stampede of running feet as the men came to their senses and surged up to the sunlight.

'Stand by the capstan!' The orders clouted their ears. 'Hands aloft! Loose tops'ls!'

Allday saw Ferguson staring wildly at the green, inviting island with its low, undulating hills. He felt a lump in his own throat now. It was not unlike Cornwall in the summertime, he thought.

Then he touched Ferguson's arm and said kindly, 'Come on, lad. I'll race you aloft!'

Vibart's booming voice filled the air. 'Loose heads'ls! Man the braces!'

Allday reached the mainyard and ran quickly along the footrope to join the others lying across the thick spar. Below him he could see the busy deck, and over his shoulder he could identify Bolitho's tall figure by the taffrail.

From forward Herrick yelled, 'Anchor's aweigh, sir!'

Allday dug his toes into the footrope as the sail billowed and filled beneath him and the great yard moved ponderously to catch the wind. Already the land was sliding away, and by the time the sails were set and trimmed it would be lost in the haze. Perhaps for ever, he thought.

7

A Spanish Lugger

Herrick moved slightly around the mizzen mast in an effort to remain in the shadow cast by its thick trunk. He found that his eyes were constantly slitted against the harsh glare, his tongue continually moving across his parched lips as the forenoon watch dragged slowly to its conclusion.

Above his head the sails hung limp and lifeless, and there was not a breath of wind to ruffle the flat, empty expanse of sea, upon which the becalmed frigate lay motionless and hushed.

He plucked at his grubby shirt, immediately irritated by the futility of his action. It felt sodden with sweat, yet his whole being seemed to cry out for moisture. He could feel the deck seams gripping stickily at his shoes, and once when he had inadvertently rested his hand on one of the quarterdeck nine-pounders he had almost cried out with pain. The barrel had been as hot as if it had been firing without pause. His lip curled bitterly at the thought. There had been no action, nor was there likely to be under these impossible conditions.

After leaving Antigua the *Phalarope* had sailed directly to her allotted station, but apart from sighting another patrolling frigate and then later the bulky shape of the *Cassius*, she had kept the sea to herself.

And now, to top it all, the frigate was becalmed. For twenty-four hours she had idled aimlessly above her reflection, carried at will by the sluggish currents, the lookouts worn and weary from staring hopefully for a squall to break the spell. Seven long days since they had sailed with such haste from Antigua, seven days of watching the burnished horizons and waiting.

Herrick glanced forward where the duty watch lay like dead men below the dark shadow of the bulwark. Their half-naked bodies had already lost their pallor, and more than one unseasoned sailor bore savage burns on his skin from the sun's relentless glare.

Midshipman Neale leaned against the nettings, his round face for once devoid of mischief or interest. Like the rest, he seemed crushed and defeated by the inactivity and heat.

It was hard to believe that anything else existed outside their own enclosed world. St. Kitts lay some fifty miles to the south-east, and the Anegada Passage which separated the Virgin Islands from the disputed

Leewards was spread in an eye-searing haze across the motionless bowsprit.

Of Hood's efforts to hold St. Kitts they had heard nothing, and for all Herrick could guess even the war might have ended. When they had met the flagship, Bolitho had made a signal requesting the latest information, but the reply had been unhelpful to say the least. The *Phalarope* had been carrying out gunnery practice, using several old and useless casks as targets. Herrick knew that Bolitho had done it more to break the monotony than with any hope of improving the standards of marksmanship by such methods.

Cassius's flags had soared angrily to her yards, and soon Maynard had reported warily that the admiral was demanding an immediate cease-fire. 'Conserve powder and shot', the signal had ordered curtly. So that was that.

Bolitho had made no comment, but Herrick knew his captain well enough now to understand the sudden anger in his grey eyes. It was as if the admiral had gone out of his way to isolate the *Phalarope*, as a doctor would separate a leper from his fellow humans.

He jerked from his thoughts as Bolitho's head and shoulders appeared through the cabin hatch. Like the other officers, he was dressed in shirt and white breeches, and his dark hair was clinging to his forehead with sweat. He looked strained and edgy, and Herrick could almost feel the restlessness which was making Bolitho fret at the inaction around him.

Herrick said, 'Still no wind, sir.'

Bolitho shot him an angry glance and then seemed to control himself. 'Thank you, Mr. Herrick. So I see.' He walked to the compass and glanced at the two listless helmsmen. Then he moved to the starboard rail, and Herrick saw him wince as the sun smote his shoulders like a furnace.

Bolitho said quietly, 'How are the men?'

Herrick replied vaguely, 'Not happy, sir. It is bad enough out here, without short water rations!'

'Quite so.' Bolitho nodded without turning. 'But it is necessary. God knows how long we will be pinned down like this.'

His hand moved vaguely to the scar beneath the rebellious forelock of hair. Herrick had seen him touch the livid mark on several previous occasions, usually when he appeared to be entirely wrapped in his own thoughts. Once Herrick had questioned Stockdale about it, and learned that it had happened when Bolitho, as a junior lieutenant, had been sent ashore to an island with a small party of seamen to refill water casks.

Unknown to the captain or anyone else, the island had not been uninhabited, and almost as soon as the launch had grated up the beach the party had been ambushed by a horde of yelling natives. One had snatched up a cutlass from a dying sailor and attacked Bolitho as he had tried to rally his outnumbered men. In his thick, jolting voice Stockdale had described the scene around the launch, with half the sailors butchered or dying and the others falling back desperately in a frantic effort to regain the safety of the sea. Bolitho had fallen, separated from his men, his face masked in blood from the cutlass slash which should have killed him. The sailors who survived were all for leaving their officer, whom they supposed to be dead anyway, but at the last minute they rallied, and as more boats pulled to their aid Bolitho was dragged to safety.

Herrick knew there was a lot more to it than that. Just as he guessed that it had been Stockdale's massive right arm which had held the men from panic and had saved the man he now served like a devoted dog.

Bolitho walked forward to the quarterdeck rail and stared towards the bows. 'The haze, Mr. Herrick. It looks not unlike a Channel mist.'

Herrick's dry lips cracked into a rueful smile. 'I never thought I would miss the Channel Fleet, sir. But how I would like to hear the wind and feel the cold spray again.'

'Maybe.' Bolitho seemed lost in his thoughts. 'But I have a feeling the wind will return soon.'

Herrick stared at him. It was not a boast or an empty statement of hope. It was like another small picture of the man's quiet confidence, he thought.

There was a step on the deck behind them and Vibart said harshly, 'A word, Captain.'

Bolitho replied, 'What is it?'

'Your clerk, Mathias, sir.' Vibart watched Bolitho's impassive face as he continued, 'He's had a bad fall in the hold, sir.'

'How bad?'

Vibart shook his head. 'He'll not see another day, I'm thinking.' There was no pity in his voice.

Bolitho bit his lip. 'I sent him down there myself to check some stores.' He looked up suddenly, his face clouded with concern. 'Are you sure nothing can be done for him?'

'The surgeon says not.' Vibart sounded indifferent. 'Apart from his ribs, which are badly stove in, he's got a split in his skull you could put a marline-spike through!'

'I see.' Bolitho stared down at his hands on the rail. 'I hardly knew the man, but he was a hard worker and tried to do his best.' He shook his head. 'To die in action is one thing, but this . . .'

Herrick said quickly, 'I will get another clerk, sir. There is a new man, Ferguson, one of those pressed in Falmouth. He can read and write, and is more used to that sort of work.' Herrick recalled Ferguson's wretched expression as the ship had left Antigua. He had promised to help him get a letter away to his wife. Perhaps this release from the heavy duties of seamanship and the harsh control of the petty officers would make up for the omission in some way.

Herrick watched Bolitho's grave face and wondered how the captain could find the time to grieve over one man when he himself was burdened with such bitter responsibility.

Bolitho said, 'Very well. Detail Ferguson and tell him his duties.'

A yell came from the maintopmast. 'Deck there! Squall comin' from the starboard bow!'

Herrick ran to the rail, one hand shading his eyes. Incredulously he saw the gentle ripple pushing down towards the becalmed ship and heard the rigging stirring itself as the inert sails moved slowly into life.

Bolitho stood upright and clasped his hands behind him. 'What are you all staring at? Stir those men, Mr. Herrick, and get the ship under way!'

Herrick nodded. He had seen the excitement beneath Bolitho's outburst.

As the sails filled and flapped overhead Bolitho's expression was almost boyish with pleasure.

It was not much of a wind, but sufficient to get the *Phalarope* moving once more. The water gurgled around her rudder, and as the braces squeaked in the blocks the sails swung to embrace every last ounce of air, eager for the life it had given them.

Bolitho said at length, 'Keep her north-west by north, Mr. Herrick. We will remain on this leg until sunset.'

'Aye, aye, sir.' Herrick watched him walk back to the taffrail and peer down at the small wake. There was no sign of the anxiety he must be feeling, he thought. The wind was a small respite and no way a recompense for the endless, meaningless patrol, yet Bolitho acted as if everything was normal, outwardly at least.

Again the masthead lookout was to prove that nothing could be taken for granted.

'Deck there! Sail fine on the starboard bow!'

Herrick lifted his glass but Bolitho snapped, 'You'll not see anything from here! The haze is like a blanket to the north of us!'

Vibart muttered, 'Mr. Neale, get aloft!'

'Belay that!' Bolitho sounded dangerously calm. 'You go, Mr. Herrick. I want an experienced eye at this moment!'

Herrick ran to the main shrouds and began to climb. He quickled realised how out of condition his body had become, and by the time he had reached the topmast trestle and crosstrees his heart was pounding like a drum. The bearded lookout moved over for him and pointed with a tarry hand.

'Over yonder, sir! Can't make her out yet!'

Herrick ignored the ship swinging like a toy beneath his legs and opened his glass. At first he could see nothing but bright sunlight across the low-lying haze with the million glittering mirrors of the sea beneath. Then he saw the sail and felt a tinge of disappointment. The hull was well shrouded in mist, but from the sail's strange dorsal shape he guessed it was small, probably a coasting lugger of some sort. Not worth taking as a prize, and hardly worth sinking, he decided angrily. He yelled the information to the deck and saw Bolitho staring up at him.

'A lugger, you say?' Bolitho sounded interested. 'Keep watching her!'

'She's not seen us.' The lookout squinted towards the sail. 'Reckon us'll be up to 'er afore she spots us.'

Herrick nodded and then looked down as Vibart called, 'Pipe all hands! Stand by to wear ship!'

So Bolitho was going to close her anyway. Herrick watched the sudden burst of activity on the decks below. He had not seen such a sight since he was a midshipman. The scampering, apparently aimless figures, which surged from between decks and then merged as if by magic into recognisable patterns of discipline and purpose. He could see the petty officers checking their watch bills as they bawled names and orders. Here and there the officers and warrant officers stood like little isolated rocks amidst the surging tide of running seamen.

Again the yards moved round, flapping indignantly as the frigate altered course two points to starboard. Herrick felt the mast tremble, and tried not to think of the time it would take to fall to the deck.

But the breeze which had found the *Phalarope* had reached the other sail, and as the mist glided away in its path the lugger gathered way and heeled jauntily, another tan sail already creeping up her stumpy mainmast.

The lookout champed on a wad of tobacco and said calmly, 'Her's a Spaniard! Oi'd know that rig anywhere.'

Bolitho's voice cut through his speculation. 'You may come down now. Mr. Herrick! Lively there!'

Herrick reached the deck gasping and sweating to find Bolitho waiting for him, his face deep in concentration.

'She'll have the edge on us, Mr. Herrick. She can make better use of these light airs than we can.' He gestured impatiently towards the forecastle. 'Clear away the two chasers and fire across her bows!'

Herrick got his breath and gasped, 'Aye, aye, sir! It would only take one ball to shatter her timbers!'

He saw something like amusement in the grey eyes as Bolitho replied, 'She may have the most precious cargo of all time, Mr. Herrick!'

Herrick stared at him dazedly. 'Sir?'

Bolitho had turned to watch the gunners scampering forward towards the two long ninepounders on the forecastle. '*Information*, Mr. Herrick! Out here, the lack of it could lose a war!'

One shot was enough. As the tall waterspout fell in a splatter of spray beyond the lugger's bows, first one sail and then the other crumpled and fell, leaving the boat rocking dejectedly to await the *Phalarope*'s pleasure.

Bolitho's wide cabin seemed almost cold after the furnace heat of the quarterdeck, and he had to force himself to stand quite still by the stern windows to steady his racing thoughts and plan the next move. With real effort he closed his ears to the muffled shipboard noises and distant shouts as a boat was dropped alongside to take a boarding party to the lugger, which now rode uneasily under the frigate's lee. It had been all Bolitho could do to remain outwardly unruffled as his orders were passed and carried out, so that in the end he could no longer face the watchful glances of his officers or avoid the buzzing speculation of the upperdeck idlers.

His casual guess about the coming of a wind had seemed like a miracle, and when the lookout had reported the lugger in the haze he had felt his pent up emotions churning around like raw alcohol. The waiting and petty irritations were momentarily put to one side, even the shame he felt for the admiral's attitude to *Phalarope* could be overlooked, if not forgotten.

There was a tap at the door, and he swung round, caught off guard. 'Enter!'

He stared for a few seconds at the pale-faced seaman who hovered uncertainly in the doorway. He wrenched his mind away from the lugger and nodded towards the desk by the bulkhead.

'You must be Ferguson? You will be working here when I require you.' His tone was terse, his thoughts still following the invisible boarding party.

Ferguson stared round the cabin and blinked. 'Yes, sir. I mean – aye, aye, sir.' He seemed confused and nervous.

Bolitho studied him kindly. 'I will tell you more of your duties later. At the moment I am rather busy.' He looked round with a jerk as little Neale panted up to the door.

'Captain, sir!' He fought for breath. 'Mr. Okes has taken the lugger!'

'So I should hope!' Bolitho added dryly, 'Her skipper has a whole broadside staring down his throat.'

Neale considered the point. 'Er, yes, sir.' He stared up at Bolitho's calm face, obviously wondering how the captain could bear to leave the upperdeck when something was at last happening. He added, 'The boat is returning now, sir.'

'That was what I wanted to hear, Mr. Neale.' Bolitho looked through the stern windows towards the empty sea, its surface still ruffled by a small but steady breeze. 'When the boat comes alongside tell Captain Rennie with my compliments to keep the lugger's officers apart until I can question them. Mr. Okes can carry on with his search of the lugger and report when he finds anything.'

'The lugger's *officers*, sir?' Neale's eyes were like saucers.

'They may be dressed in rags, boy, but they are still officers!' Bolitho watched the midshipman patiently. 'And make no mistake, they will know these waters like their own faces.'

The midshipman nodded and scurried away. Bolitho paced restlessly around the cabin and then paused by his table where his personal chart of the Caribbean lay in readiness. The complex mass of islands and soundings, the vague surveys and doubtful descriptions were like the clues of a giant puzzle. He frowned and tugged at his chin. Somewhere amongst the tangle of scattered islands lay the key to the whole campaign. The first to find it would win the day. The loser would be driven from the Caribbean for ever.

With the points of his brass dividers he traced the *Phalarope's* course and halted at the small pencilled cross. Out here he was doing no good. Fifty miles away St. Kitts might still be fighting a siege, whilst just over the horizon Count de Grasse's great fleet could be mustering for a final attack on the scattered British naval units. With the British driven from these islands, the French and their allies would unroll the South Americas like a chart. Would command the North and South Atlantic and reach for the rich rewards of Africa and beyond.

He pushed the apprehension from his mind as he heard the clatter of feet above and the thuds of muskets on the deck planks.

Vibart appeared in the doorway. 'Prisoners aboard, sir.' He glared at Ferguson who seemed to be trying to curl into a ball beside the desk. 'The lugger is Spanish well enough. Twenty men aboard all told, but no resistance. I have the master and two mates under guard outside, sir.'

'Good.' Bolitho stared at the chart. 'Twenty men, you say? That is a large crew for such a small craft. The Spaniards are usually more sparing when they man a vessel of any kind!'

Vibart shrugged. 'Mr. Farquhar says that the lugger has been used for coastal trading. Not much use for us.'

'I'll see the master first. You can go on deck and keep an eye on Mr. Okes's progress in the lugger. Let me know if he has found anything.'

The lugger's skipper was small and swarthy, dressed in a tattered shirt and wide canvas trousers. Two gold ear-rings bobbed from beneath his lank hair, and his dirty, bare feet completed the picture of neglect and poverty.

Beside him, Midshipman Farquhar seemed elegant and unreal.

Bolitho kept his eyes on the chart, conscious of the Spaniard's uneven breathing and the shuffling movements of his bare feet on the deck. He said at length, 'Does he speak English?'

'No, sir.' Farquhar sounded impatient. 'He just gabbles.'

Still Bolitho kept his eyes on the chart. Almost offhandedly he said, 'Then take him on deck and tell the master-at-arms to run a halter up to the mainyard.'

Farquhar fell back startled. 'Halter, sir? Do you mean to hang him?'

'Of course I do!' Bolitho put a rasp in his tone. 'He is no further use to me!'

The Spaniard's legs buckled and he pitched forward at Bolitho's feet. Sobbing and weeping he pulled at Bolitho's legs, the words flooding from his lips in a wild torrent.

'Please, Captain! No hang, *please*! I am a good man, sir, I have wife and many poor children!' His cheeks were running with tears. 'Please, sir, no *hang*!' The last word was almost a shriek.

Bolitho stepped from the man's grasp and said calmly. 'I had an idea that your knowledge of English might return.' To Farquhar he added crisply, 'You may try that ruse on the two mates. See what you can find out!' He turned back to the whimpering man on the deck. 'Now stand up and answer my questions, or indeed I *will* hang you!'

He waited a few more moments, his mind half dwelling on what might have happened if the Spaniard really had been unable to speak English. Then he asked, 'Where were you heading and with what cargo?'

The man stood swaying from side to side, his grubby hands clasped as if in prayer. 'I go to Puerto Rico, Captain. I take small cargo of timber, a little sugar.' He wrung his hands. 'But you can take it all, excellency! Just spare my life!'

'Hold your tongue!' Bolitho peered at the chart. The story was possible. These small trading boats were as common as fleas in the Caribbean. He asked sharply, 'From where did you come?'

The man smiled ingratiatingly. 'I go all around, Captain.' He waved his hands vaguely. 'I carry only small cargoes. I reap a living where I can. It is a hard, hard life, excellency!'

'I will ask you once more!' Bolitho fixed him with a hard stare.

The man shifted wretchedly. 'Martinique, Captain. I has small work there. But I *hate* the French, you understand?'

Bolitho dropped his eyes to hide the excitement he now felt. Martinique, the headquarters of all French naval operations, the most heavily protected fortress in the whole Caribbean.

'You hate the French? Your gallant allies?' Bolitho's sarcasm was not lost on the Spaniard. 'Well, never mind that. Just tell me how many ships were there in the anchorage.' He saw the man's eyes glitter with fright and guessed that he understood which anchorage he meant.

'Many ships, excellency!' He rolled his eyes. 'Many *big* ships!'

'And who commands these many big ships?' Bolitho could hardly keep the anxiety from his voice now.

'The French admiral, excellency!' The Spaniard puffed out his cheeks as if to spit on the deck, but caught sight of the marine sentry watching from the doorway and swallowed noisily. 'He is a French pig, that one!'

'The Count de Grasse?'

The man nodded violently. 'But you know everything, Captain! You are blessed by the Almighty!'

Bolitho looked up as Farquhar entered the cabin. 'Well?'

'Only a little English between them, sir.' He seemed angry with himself. 'But I gather they were heading for Puerto Rico.'

Bolitho gestured at the sentry. 'Take this prisoner out and keep him closely guarded.' Then he said absently, 'He was lying. He sailed from Martinique. The French would never allow him to carry on trading when they too might be under siege at any time!' He tapped the chart. 'No, Mr. Farquhar, he was at Martinique well enough, but his destination is elsewhere!'

Vibart entered and bowed his head beneath the deck beams. 'Mr. Okes reports that the cargo is much as you already know, sir. But there are new ship's spars and casks of salt meat stowed beneath the main load.' He sounded doubtful. 'There is also a great deal of spare canvas and cordage.'

'As I thought!' Bolitho felt strangely relieved. 'The lugger was taking supplies from Martinique' – his finger moved along the charted islands – 'to where?' He looked from Vibart's brooding face to Farquhar's baffled one. 'Get that Spanish skipper back here at once!'

Bolitho walked slowly to the stern windows and leaned out over the water as if to clear his brain. The Spaniard had seemed pleased to tell him about the French ships at Martinique, when he must have known that patrolling British ships would already know this information. He must have imagined that Bolitho had missed the main item.

He swung round as the man was pushed through the door. 'Now listen to me!' His voice was still controlled, but the harshness made the lugger's master start to quiver uncontrollably. 'You lied to me! I warned you what would happen, did I not?' He dropped his voice still further. 'Now just once more. Where were you bound?'

The man swayed. 'Please, excellency! They will kill me if they know!'

'And I will kill you if you keep me waiting!' He saw Herrick's face watching him from the doorway with fixed fascination.

'We sail for Mola Island, Captain.' The man seemed to have shrunk in size. 'The cargo was for ship there!'

Herrick and Farquhar exchanged mystified glances.

Bolitho bent over his chart. 'Mola Island is Dutch.' He measured the distance with his dividers. 'Thirty miles to the nor'east of our present position.' He looked up, his eyes hard and devoid of pity. 'How many such voyages have you made?'

'Many, excellency.' The Spaniard looked as if he wanted to be sick. 'There are soldiers there. French soldiers. They come from the north. They have ships also.'

Bolitho breathed out slowly. 'Of course! De Grasse would never attempt to move his ships against Jamaica or anywhere else unless he could be sure of a diversion elsewhere and full support from the military!' He stared at the others. 'Our fleet watches Martinique to the south and waits for the French to move, and all the time they are filtering down from the American mainland, gathering for a big, final assault!'

Vibart said bleakly, 'We must inform the *Cassius*, sir.'

Herrick spoke from the doorway, his voice eager. 'We could send the lugger to find the flagship, sir, and stay here in readiness!'

Bolitho did not seem to hear them. 'Sentry, take this prisoner and lock him up with the others. My compliments to the boatswain, and tell him to select any of the lugger's crew he thinks could be sworn into our company. I would imagine that even the *Phalarope* would seem better than a prison hulk!'

The marine grinned. 'Aye, aye, sir!' He jabbed the Spaniard with his musket and hustled the man away.

'It will be two days before we meet up with the *Cassius* again.' Bolitho was thinking aloud. 'By then it may be too late. That Spaniard has told us a good deal, but he cannot know the whole truth. If the French have been gathering a force of men and ships in this small island they must be expecting to move, and soon. I consider it our duty to investigate, and do our utmost to stop them.'

Vibart swallowed hard. 'Do you intend to leave the patrol area, sir?'

'Do you have any objections, Mr. Vibart?' Bolitho eyed him calmly.

'It is not *my* responsibility, sir.' Vibart dropped his gaze before Bolitho's cool stare.

Herrick said quickly, 'It is a great risk, if I may say so, sir.'

'As is everything worthwhile, Mr. Herrick.' Bolitho straightened his back and added briskly, 'My compliments to Mr. Proby. Tell him to wear ship and steer north-east. We will be sailing close to the wind so it will be nightfall before we reach Mola Island. Before that time there is much to be arranged, gentlemen!'

He looked around their faces and continued, 'Put a prize crew aboard the lugger, and ask Mr. Okes to search for the recognition signals. It is my guess that this island will be heavily guarded. The lugger will be too useful to spare for finding the admiral.'

Vibart said sulkily, 'The admiral will not be pleased by your acting like this, sir.'

'And my conscience would never rest if I allowed my own prestige to come before this obvious duty, Mr. Vibart!'

His eyes moved to Herrick and Farquhar. 'This will be a good opportunity for each of you.' He paused and looked around the cabin. 'For the ship, too.'

He waited until the cabin had emptied and then walked to the windows again. For one more minute he allowed the nagging doubts to play havoc with his thoughts. He had acted impetuously and without pausing to consider the possible consequences. Skill and ability were only half the battle. There always had to be a good amount of luck. And if he was mistaken now, there would not be that amount of luck in the whole world.

He saw Ferguson watching from the desk like a mesmerised rabbit and realised that he had forgotten all about his being there. But the story he might repeat on the berth deck might do good for the ship's dwindling morale, he thought vaguely. If the *Phalarope* was lucky this time it would make all the difference.

And if not? He shrugged. There would be few survivors to dispute the matter.

Above his head he heard the afterguard tramping with the braces and felt the deck canting slightly as the frigate went about. Momentarily framed in the stern windows he saw the small lugger swinging round to keep station on the quarter, and wondered how many men had already cursed the keen-eyed lookout for sighting her.

Aloud he remarked, 'You will have something to tell your wife now, Ferguson. She will be proud of you perhaps?'

Bolitho heaved himself from the cutter's sternsheets and allowed groping hands to pull him unceremoniously up and over the lugger's low bulwark. For several seconds he stood swaying on the unfamiliar deck to allow his eyes to get accustomed to the gloom and the packed figures around him.

Already the cutter had shoved off, and apart from the gleam of white spray around the oars it was lost in the enfolding darkness. Bolitho tried to see where the *Phalarope* now lay, but she, too, was well hidden, with not one glimmer of light to betray her presence. He tried to hold on to the mental picture of the chart and of the island which now lay somewhere across the lugger's blunt bows.

Captain Rennie loomed out of the darkness and said in an unnecessary whisper, 'I've packed the marines below, sir. Sergeant Garwood will keep 'em quiet until they are required.'

Bolitho nodded and tried to remember once again if he had left anything to chance. 'You have made sure that all muskets and pistols are unloaded?'

Rennie nodded. 'Yes, sir.' He sounded as if he meant, 'Of course, sir.' A primed musket exploding at the wrong moment, a trigger pulled by an over-excited marine, and their lives would be worth even less than they were now.

'Good.' Bolitho groped his way aft where Stockdale stood straddle-legged beside the crude tiller bar, his head cocked towards the loose flapping sails. Midshipman Farquhar squatted by a shapeless bundle on the deck which Bolitho managed to recognise as the luckless Spanish skipper. He had been brought along as both guide and surety.

Rennie asked flatly, 'Do you think we will get inshore without trouble?'

Bolitho glanced up at the high, bright stars. There was the merest sliver of silver for a moon floating above its reflection in the flat water. The night was dark enough to hide anything. Maybe too dark.

He said, 'We shall see. Now get under way, and make sure the compass light is well shaded.' He walked clear of Rennie and his questions and brushed past the crouching sailors whose eyes gleamed like marbles as they watched him pass. Occasionally he heard the rasp of cutlass or a dull clink from the bows where McIntosh, a gunner's mate, was making a last-minute examination of his hastily rigged swivel gun. It was loaded with canister and at close range would be quite deadly. It had to be perfect, Bolitho thought grimly. There might be no time for a second shot.

He wondered what Vibart was thinking, left in charge of the frigate, with hours to wait before he could play his part in the raid. He thought, too, of Herrick's face when he had told him he was taking Lieutenant Okes with him in the lugger. Herrick had known there was no other choice in the matter. Okes was his senior, and it was only fair that he should get the chance of making a name for himself. Or dying before Herrick, Bolitho thought dryly. Vibart's position and seniority made him the obvious choice for taking charge of the *Phalarope*, and if both Bolitho and Vibart were killed, Herrick could still move his way up the chain of command.

Bolitho scowled in the darkness and cursed himself for his morbid thoughts. Perhaps he was already too tired, too worn out by planning and preparation to think any more. All day long, while the frigate had beaten her way towards Mola Island, things had moved at a swift pace. Men and weapons had been transferred to the lugger, and the latter's cargo had been either dropped overboard or rowed across to the *Phalarope* for their own use. The lugger's cramped hold was now packed with marines, each man too busy fighting back the nausea thrown up by the stench of fish oil and sour vegetables to care much about what might lie ahead.

Mathias, Bolitho's clerk, had died and had been dropped overboard with a brief prayer, his death and passing hardly making a break in the frantic preparations. Looking back, it was hard even to recall his face.

Lieutenant Okes stumbled along the side deck, his shoulders hunched as if he expected to be struck by some unseen object. He peered at Bolitho's watchful shape and muttered. 'All – all the men are ready, sir.' He sounded taut and nervous.

Bolitho grunted. Okes's behaviour had been worrying him for some time. He had even offered to stay aboard the frigate in Herrick's place, which was odd, in spite of the danger. Okes, he knew, was not a rich man, and any extra promotion, a glowing report in the *Gazette*, would make all the difference to his career. He was probably frightened. Well, so was anyone but a raving maniac, Bolitho thought.

He replied, 'We shall see the headland soon. There should be plenty of surf to show its position.' He screwed up his eyes to will himself to see the picture he had built of the island in his mind.

It was shaped something like a rough horseshoe, with the deep anchorage lying snugly between the two curved headlands. But the village was on the seaward side of the nearest headland, that being the only beach on the whole island. According to the chart and what he had wrung from the lugger's skipper, the village was connected to the anchorage by a rough road which crossed a steep ravine by way of a wooden bridge. The tip of the headland was therefore isolated by the ravine, and on its highest point there was said to be a powerful battery of guns, probably twenty-four-pounders, which could easily defend the whole anchorage. A sandbar and several isolated reefs completed the hazardous approach. In fact, the approach was impossible without consent from both battery and good daylight. No wonder the French had chosen this place as their strongpoint.

' 'Eadland, sir!' A seaman pointed abeam. 'There, sir!'

Bolitho nodded and walked aft again. 'Steer close, Stockdale. There is a beach about a quarter of a mile ahead, and a wooden pier, if this Spaniard's word is worth anything!'

From the bow a seaman dropped his leadline overboard and then said hoarsely, 'By the mark two, sir!'

Two fathoms under the keel, and still a long way to go. There was no chance of a surprise attack here either, except by craft as small as the lugger. The only thing in their favour was surprise. Nobody in his right mind would expect a single small boat to approach a heavily guarded island in total darkness.

Belsey, the master's mate, said gruffly, 'I can see th' pier, sir. Look, over yonder!'

Bolitho swallowed hard, conscious of a prickling in his spine. He re-adjusted his sword and made sure that his pistol was ready at his waist.

'Get the Spaniard up here!' The tension was making his voice harsh, and he heard the prisoner's teeth chattering like dice.

He gripped the man's arm, smelling his fear. Now was the time to make the Spaniard more afraid of *him* than of anything the enemy could do. 'Listen to me!' He shook the man slowly with each word. 'When we are challenged, you know what to do?'

The Spaniard nodded violently. 'Show lantern. Give the signal, excellency!'

'And if they ask why you are coming in at night tell them you have despatches for the garrison commander.'

'But, excellency! I never get despatches!'

'Hold your tongue! *Just tell them!* If I know anything about sentries, they'll be satisfied for long enough!'

The pier crept out of the darkness like a black finger, and as the sails were lowered swiftly and the lugger glided gently towards the tall piles a lantern flickered into life and a voice yelled, '*Qui va la?*'

The Spaniard opened the shutter of his own lantern. Two long flashes and two short ones. In a quavering voice he began to stutter his message, his words broken up by great gulps for breath. He was shaking so badly that Farquhar had to hold him upright against the mast like a corpse.

The sentry called something to another man, as yet hidden by a small hut in the middle of the pier, and Bolitho heard him laugh. There was a click of metal and then another as the sentries uncocked their muskets.

The bow swung against the pier, and Bolitho saw the sentry leaning forward to watch the lugger bump alongside. He had slung his musket over his shoulder, and his tall shako shone briefly in the glow from a long clay pipe. Bolitho held his breath. This was the time to see if he had chosen his men correctly.

He saw a sailor, moving with elaborate calm, climb nimbly up the nearest wooden ladder, the mooring rope in his hand. The sentry called after him, his voice muffled as he turned his back to watch the man looping the rope's eye over a bollard.

The next sailor, who had been crouching on the stem, leapt straight upwards like a cat. For a moment the two figures swayed together in a macabre dance, but there was hardly any sound. Only when the sailor released his grip and lowered the dead sentry carefully on the pier did Bolitho realise it was time to act.

He snapped, 'Next man up!'

Belsey, the master's mate, slipped over the bows, and followed by the other seaman who was wiping his knife blade on his trousers, disappeared around the side of the hut.

This time there was a little more noise. A clatter of a falling musket, and something like a gurgle. But nothing more.

Bolitho scrambled up to the pier, his body shaking with suppressed excitement. 'Right, Mr. Okes, get your party ashore and up to the end of the pier at the double!' He stopped an onrushing seaman with the back of his hand and snarled, 'Quietly there! There's a guardhouse at the far end!'

Rennie's marines were already pouring gratefully from the hold, their white crossbelts bright and eerie against their uniforms. Rennie had not forgotten his part, and within minutes he had split his men into two parties, and with a single command had both files trotting briskly along the pier towards the silent village.

Stockdale was the last to leave the lugger, his cutlass swinging from his hand like a toy.

Bolitho took a last look round and checked his bearings. 'Very well, Stockdale, let us go and take a look!'

8

The Raid

Bolitho lifted his hand, and behind him the file of sailors shuffled to a standstill. 'We will wait here for ten minutes! Pass the word down the line!'

He waited until silence had again fallen over the steep roadway and then added quietly to Lieutenant Okes, 'We'll push on a bit further and have a look at the bridge. We can't help Rennie's marines by standing here worrying, and it's already near two o'clock. There is a lot to do before dawn finds us.'

He walked on without waiting for Okes to comment. He could feel the loose stones crunching beneath his shoes, and was conscious of a new sense of light-headedness. Everything had gone so well that the strain was all the more telling. Surely the luck could not last?

It had been less than an hour since the lugger had tied up to the pier. After killing the two luckless sentries, Captain Rennie's marines had gone on to capture the small guardhouse at the end of the coast road with hardly a scuffle. The sleeping soldiers, all ten of them, had been gleefully clubbed into deeper slumber, or worse, and the duty N.C.O. had been seized and trussed like a terrified chicken.

Bolitho had left Rennie to spread his men along the roadside and occupy the high ground above the village. From there they should be able to withstand anything but a really heavy assault until the raiding party had completed its work.

Bolitho dropped on one knee and strained his eyes into the darkness. He could just see the spidery outline of a high wooden bridge and the isolated headland beyond, where the sleeping gun battery lay as yet unaware of what was happening. It was quite a solid bridge, Bolitho thought. Wide and heavy enough for guns and stores, for shot, and all the materials for building breastworks and embrasures. It would take a long time to replace once destroyed.

A boot crunched at his side and Sergeant Garwood peered down at him. 'Cap'n Rennie's respects, sir. The marines is all in position. We've 'ad the lugger warped to the end o' the pier so that we can cover our withdrawal with the swivel gun.' He stared towards the bridge. 'I'd like to 'ave a crack at that lot, sir!' He sounded envious.

'You get back to Captain Rennie and tell him to hold the road until we fall back.' Bolitho smiled in the darkness. 'Don't worry, Sergeant, you'll get your pennyworth of fighting before the night's done!'

He saw the man's white crossbelt fading in the shadows and then said sharply, 'Right, Mr. Okes, call up the rest of the party and keep them quiet! A flogging for the first man to make a sound!' He turned back to the bridge. There was probably a sentry at one end, if not both. It would all have to be very quick.

Okes returned breathing heavily. 'All here, sir.'

Farquhar was close behind him, his face pale in the faint moonlight. He said, 'I have picked Glover for the job, sir.'

Bolitho nodded. He recalled that the seaman in question was the one who had so neatly killed the first sentry.

'Very well. Send him forward.' He watched the man slide over the rim of stones and bushes and fade immediately into the deep patch of shadow before the bridge. Then he added slowly, 'Now remember, men, if Glover fails to find that sentry and the alarm is given, we will have to make a rush for it.' He drew his sword and saw the lethal glitter of cutlasses along the roadside.

To Okes he whispered, 'Mr. Farquhar will take five men to deal with the guns and magazine. McIntosh, the gunner's mate, will lay a good charge to blow the bridge when we fall back, understood?'

Okes nodded. 'I – I think so, sir!'

'You must be *sure*, Mr. Okes!' Bolitho eyed him keenly. Suddenly he wished it was Herrick at his side. Should he be killed before the raid was finished, how would Okes manage? He continued evenly, 'According to our captive Spaniard, there is a rough track down from the battery to the inside of the anchorage. I intend to go down there as soon as the battery is taken and see what can be done about the ships in the harbour. I will try and set fire to one or more of them, and *Phalarope* can deal with any which make a dash for it!' He swung round as Stockdale, dragging the whimpering Spaniard behind him, strode through the bushes, his teeth white in his face.

'Sir! Glover's just whistled! 'E's done for the sentry!'

Bolitho stood up. If only he had a thousand men instead of sixty, he thought vaguely. They could take and hold the whole island intact until help arrived. He tugged his hat down firmly over his eyes and glanced back at his men. He was thankful that every one of them was hand-picked. There had not been a single incident so far to warrant either punishment or anger.

'Now then, lads! Quickly and quietly, and no fuss!' He waved his sword, aware suddenly that his face was fixed in a wild grin. 'Follow me!'

In two files the sailors padded towards the bridge. Bolitho kept just ahead of the nearest men, his eyes straining ahead towards the deserted bridge, which all at once seemed a long way off and vulnerable.

Pad, pad, pad went the feet, and Bolitho knew without turning his head that the orderly approach was already changing into a charge. Then his shoes were booming hollowly on the wooden boards of the bridge, and from the corner of his eye he saw the angry swirl of surf, and heard the roar of a tide-race between the steep walls of the ravine. He almost fell over the spread-eagled corpse of a uniformed sentry, and saw Glover waiting to greet him, a captured musket in his hands.

Bolitho did not pause but gasped, 'Well done, Glover! Now follow me!'

A semi-circular wall pitted with square gunports ran around the far side of the headland, and as his feet slipped on the stubble of gorse and dried grass Bolitho counted seven or eight large guns facing seaward. A high mound was built well behind the guns, and he guessed that these earthworks had been thrown up to protect the magazine.

There was a startled cry from the shadows below the wall and a soldier seemed to rise out of the ground at Bolitho's feet. He saw the bared teeth and heard the man's quick intake of breath as he lunged forward and upward with his bayonet.

Glover, who was pressing close on Bolitho's heels, gave a terrible scream and fell back pinioned on the blade like a slaughtered pig. Bolitho slashed out wildly and felt the shock jar up the sword blade and along his arm like a blow. The soldier seemed to crumple, his arm almost severed from his body by the force of the stroke.

He was lost and forgotten underfoot as the sailors surged wildly along the flattened ground, their eyes staring like madmen as they looked for further victims.

There were only six more French soldiers sleeping in a small stone hut beside a great earth furnace, which even now glowed malevolently and cast an eerie light across the garlands of bright round shot and the cutlasses of the jubilant sailors.

One soldier sat up gaping, as if he no longer trusted what he saw. A cutlass cut him down before he could even cry out, and two more died screaming even as they struggled for their weapons.

Bolitho ignored the gruesome sounds from the hut and leaned across the breastworks to stare down at the great shimmering mirror of the anchorage. There were two big ships anchored well out in the centre and two smaller ones near the foot of the cliffs. He could see the riding lights like fireflies on the still water. There was no alarm. Nothing to break the quiet night watch. Bolitho felt the sweat cold on his brow and realised that his body was shaking uncontrollably.

Farquhar climbed up beside him, his dirk glinting faintly against his dark coat. 'The battery is ours, sir.' He sounded less controlled than usual, and Bolitho knew that he was suffering the same insane wildness as the rest of them.

Farquhar added in a calmer tone, 'Eight guns, sir. Two of them are thirty-two-pounders!' He sounded impressed. 'If they heated the shot in the furnace the Frogs would be able to sink any attacker with ease. A ship would be ablaze in no time from that sort of hammering!'

Bolitho nodded and pointed at the anchored ships. 'I'd like to use the guns on them! But the din would bring the whole island down on us!' He gestured towards the two large craft. 'They'll be troopships, but the soldiers will be sleeping under canvas ashore somewhere. The French would have no use for soldiers too cramped and seasick to march when the time came!'

Okes ran up to him, his sword held across his body like a shield. 'What now, sir?'

Bolitho glanced at the stars. 'It will be getting light in two hours. By that time I want every gun either spiked or pushed over the edge of the cliff. The latter if at all possible. The last thing will be to blow the magazine.'

Farquhar nodded. 'I have put my men to work with hand-spikes already. I think all the guns will go over the edge well enough, sir.'

'Very well.' Bolitho watched Okes's quick breathing. 'You take charge of the bridge and deal with that, Mr. Okes. Seize anyone who comes down the road, although I imagine it would take an eager spy to get past Rennie's pickets!'

Belsey, the master's mate, said, 'I've found the cliff path, sir. It leads right down to the sea. There are two longboats moored at the foot.' He waited. 'Shall I carry on, sir? I got my men ready.'

Bolitho nodded and watched the man lope away. Belsey had already shown he was well able to manage his part in the proceedings.

He walked back past the hut and then said sharply, 'Get those men out of there. There's a lot to be done yet!' The sharpness in his tone was more to cover his disgust than his anger. He had seen three of his men gleefully stripping the butchered corpses and crowing together like ghouls at a sacrifice.

He continued quietly, 'Get everything ready, Mr. Okes, but do not pull back until I give the signal. If I fall, then you must take command and use your own discretion.' He tapped the ground with his sword. 'But the guns must be destroyed and the battery blown, no matter what else is happening. Have a good fuse put on the bridge, and make sure the men know what they are doing.' He clapped Okes across the shoulder, and the man all but fell to his knees. 'It has been well worth our visit, Mr. Okes! Those two troopships alone could carry enough men to storm Antigua itself if necessary!'

Bolitho walked quickly towards the edge of the cliff where Stockdale waited for him, leaning on his cutlass. He paused and looked back. He felt a sudden surge of pride at the way things had gone so far. Men were working busily in the darkness, and already one of the giant guns had been trundled clear of its mounting. He could see Farquhar and McIntosh stooping over the box of fuses, entirely absorbed in their work of destruction, and other men loading their muskets and watching the captured bridge.

He turned on his heel and followed Stockdale down the steep, roughly hewn steps. If only he could enlarge this feeling of pride and purpose to the rest of the *Phalarope*'s company, he thought. It could be done. He had shown these men *how* it could be done.

It was dark and very cold at the foot of the steps, and he saw the small group of armed seamen already squatting in one of the longboats. He said to Belsey, 'Mark how the nearest ship swings at her anchor, Belsey!' He pointed at the small sloop which was riding less than two cables from the crude jetty below the cliff. Her stern was pointing towards the centre of the anchorage, her bowsprit towards the narrow span of water between the headlands.

Belsey nodded and rubbed his chin. 'Aye, sir! The tide's a-comin' in!' He stooped and dipped his arm underwater along the edge of the steps. 'I can feel no weed 'ere, sir. It must be well on the make.'

'It is.' Bolitho squinted his eyes in concentration. 'We'll go for the sloop there. There'll not be much of a watch kept. They'll think themselves safe enough below the battery. I know *I* would!'

Belsey nodded doubtfully. 'An' *then*, sir?' He sounded as if he would accept anything now.

'We'll set fire to her and let her drift into the nearest troop transport. She'll burn like dry grass!'

The master's mate bared his teeth. 'That'll raise the alarm well enough, sir!'

Bolitho laughed shortly. 'You can't get *everything* without payment!'

He clambered over his men and into the sternsheets. 'Get those oars muffled and be sharp about it! Use your shirts, anything!' He glanced quickly at the stars. Was it imagination, or were they paler than the last time he had looked? He snapped, 'Shove off! And pull handsomely!'

The oars rose and fell, the men holding their breaths as the boat sidled clear of the cliffs. The current gurgled impatiently around the counter and sent the hull swinging crazily into the mainstream.

Bolitho laid his hand on Stockdale's arm. 'Let her run. The tide is an ally tonight.'

He could see the sloop clear across the longboat's bow now, her slender bowsprit pointing directly above his head. He whispered, 'Easy, lads! *Easy!*' He could see a lantern aft by the taffrail and another small glow beside the foremast. That was probably the crew's hatch left open because of the warm night.

'Boat your oars!' He gritted his teeth as the heavy oars were laid carefully across the thwarts. Every sound seemed like a thunderclap. 'Steer with the current, Stockdale.' He leaned forward. 'You, in the bow! Have a grapnel ready!' To himself he added, 'The noise won't matter once we get aboard!'

'*Sir!*' The stroke oar was pointing wildly. 'Look, sir! a guardboat!'

Bolitho cursed himself for his over-confidence. When he swung his head he saw the white splash of oars and heard the creak of rowlocks barely twenty yards away.

There were gasps of surprise from some of his men, but Bolitho said harshly. 'Now, bowman! The grapnel!'

The longboat swung clumsily across the sloop's stem even as the pronged grapnel soared up and bit into the bulwark.

Everything seemed to be happening at once. There were shouts and cries from the prowling guardboat, followed by a ragged volley of musket shots. The stroke oarsman beside Bolitho screamed and fell writhing over the gunwale, his arms thrashing as he vanished below the dark water. Bullets thudded into the boat and into the sloop's side beyond.

The men faltered as a face appeared overhead and the longboat was briefly lit in the angry flash of a pistol. Belsey ducked and swore savagely, and another man fell whimpering, blood gushing from his shoulder.

Bolitho ran along the slewing boat and leapt for the sloop's rail. For a moment his feet kicked above the water and then he was up and over, the breath knocked out of him as a seaman followed him across the bulwark and fell on top of him.

He struggled to his feet as the rest of his depleted party scrambled up beside him. The sloop's one misguided defender lay open mouthed and staring in a widening pool of blood, and a second man who suddenly appeared naked at the open hatch gave a shriek of terror and fled below, slamming the hatch behind him.

Bolitho sheathed his sword and said calmly, 'It will save us the trouble of seeking them out.' Then as a further volley banged out from the guardboat he shouted, 'You know what to do, Belsey! Cut the cable, and put a hand at the wheel!'

His men were yelling and shouting like madmen as they scampered about the darkened deck as if it was an everyday occurrence. From astern Bolitho heard the raucous blare of a trumpet and then the strident rattle of a drum. He could imagine the panic and pandemonium as the sleep-fuddled crews tumbled from their hammocks in response to the call to arms.

'Cable's cut, sir!' A voice yelled from the bows.

'Very well, let the current take her!' Bolitho ran to the rail and peered through the gloom towards the nearest transport. There were more lights now, and he thought he could see the gunports being raised along the upperdeck. Their anger will give way to prudence in a moment, he thought wildly.

'Fire the ship, Belsey!' He pointed at the foremast. 'Start from there!'

Fascinated he watched Belsey's busy seamen as they upended the riding light across a deadly mixture of oil, loose cordage and spare canvas. The result was as swift as it was frightening. With a savage roar the flames soared up the shrouds and engulfed the whole forepart of the deck. Great tongues of fire lit up the whole anchorage, so that the other ships stood out stark and tall in the inferno. Rigging and cordage flamed and crackled as the fire reached through the tarred ropes and found the neatly furled sails. Spars and planking, sun-dried and well painted, flared like tinder, so that the roaring heat reached still further, consuming the sloop greedily as the men fell back, stunned by the extent of their destruction.

Bolitho clawed his way aft through the choking smoke and away from the searing heat. He was glad that Belsey had remembered to open the hatch, and noticed that most of the sloop's crew had already jumped over the side and were either swimming or drowning while their world burned about them.

He leaned coughing on the taffrail and stared across at the big transport. Gone was the belligerence and awakened anger. Her decks seemed to be swarming with stampeding figures as officers and men dashed wildly to their stations, colliding with each other as they stared in horror at the approaching fireship.

The second transport was already slipping her cable, but the nearest ship stood no chance at all. Some of her men must have realised the inevitability of the collision, and Bolitho saw several small white splashes alongside as they jumped overboard. There were pistol shots too, and he guessed that the French officers were busy trying to restore calm and order to the last.

Belsey led his choking, wheezing men to the poop and yelled, 'Time to go, sir!' He was grinning, and his eyes were streaming from the smoke.

Bolitho pointed down. 'The quarter boat is tied under the counter! Down you go, lads, and sharp about it! The magazine will blow before long!'

One by one the sailors slithered down the rope and into the small boat below the poop. Bolitho went last, his lungs seared from the advancing fire, his eyes all but blinded.

Stockdale bawled, 'Out oars! Give way together!'

The boat pulled clear, each man's eyes white in the cruel glare as the burning sloop drifted past. Several French sailors were swimming nearby, and one tried to pull himself aboard the overcrowded boat. But Stockdale pushed him away, and Bolitho heard the man's cries fading piteously astern.

A seaman yelled, 'They've struck, by God!'

Sure enough, the sloop had reached the other vessel, and already the flames were racing up the transport's tall masts where the half-loosed sails vanished like ashes in a strong wind.

'Keep pulling, lads!' Bolitho turned to watch, satisfied but awed by the terrible success of his attack.

The sloop's magazine exploded, the shockwave making the little boat jump beneath Bolitho's chattering seamen. The little ship, which thirty minutes earlier had been riding quietly at her anchor, folded amidships and dipped spluttering and hissing below the surface. But the work was done. The transport was ablaze from stem to stern and with fore and main-masts already down in a welter of flame and dense smoke.

Of the second transport nothing was visible through the pall. But Bolitho knew that she had only two choices. To try to warp clear and risk the fate of her sister, or drift ashore to be left a useless ruin when the tide retreated.

Belsey said, 'There are lights at the end of the bay, sir! That must be where the troops are camped!'

Bolitho wiped his smoke-blackened face and nodded. 'There will be a hornet's nest about our ears shortly!' With their ships destroyed and no battery to protect them, the French soldiers would be all the more willing to die to avenge their disgrace, he thought grimly.

But it was done. And done far better than he had hoped. In future, people might remember this when they spoke the name of the *Phalarope*.

Lieutenant Matthew Okes stared down from the gun battery shocked and dazed by the raging holocaust and the echoing thunder of exploding powder. He could feel the hot breath of the burning ship across his sweating face, and his nostrils rebelled against the stench of charred timbers and other horrors he could only guess at.

Farquhar said sharply, 'Time to send the guns over!'

Okes nodded dumbly, his eyes still fixed on the blazing transport as it rolled slowly on to one side. Men were swimming and floating amongst the great mass of fragments and charred flotsam, and the glittering water was constantly pock-marked by falling wreckage from muffled explosions within the shattered hull. Faintly through the drifting smoke he could see the second transport already hard aground, her masts leaning at a dangerous angle.

Behind him he heard the rumble of chocks and then a ragged cheer as the sailors sent the first gun careering over the cliff edge and on to the rocks below. A second and then a third gun crashed after it, and he heard McIntosh yelling at his men to throw their weight against the others.

Okes could feel the strength draining from his limbs, and wanted to run from the scene of hell and destruction which lit the whole anchorage in a panorama of red flames and spark-dappled smoke. It was all sheer madness, something which none of them could control.

There was no sign of Bolitho, and even if he had succeeded in escaping from his drifting fireship he would have a much longer passage to make back to the headland.

Farquhar said, 'Look, sir! There are troops coming over the hill!'

As Okes tore his eyes away the transport took a final roll and plunged beneath the surface. Immediately the fierce light was extinguished like a candle and the anchorage was once more plunged into deep shadow. Okes blinked through the smoke and realised for the first time that the sky was already brighter and there was a tinge of grey along the ridge of hills beyond the anchorage. The fierceness of the blazing ships had hidden the dawn's stealthy approach, and now as he followed the direction of Farquhar's arm he saw with rising panic the faint glint of bayonets and the bright colours of a raised standard moving inexorably over the rim of the nearest hill like a mechanical caterpillar.

His eyes darted from the marching troops to the bridge. From his own position on the battery to the end of the coast road. In a voice he no longer recognised he shouted, 'Prepare to blow the magazine, Mr. Farquhar!' He stared round like a trapped animal. 'I must see Rennie at once. You carry on here!'

He started to walk quickly away from the battery, ignoring the curious stares of the seamen and Farquhar's look of questioning contempt. His racing thoughts seemed to take over his feet, so that all at once he was running, his breath gasping painfully, his shoes skidding across stones and gorse alike as he ran blindly across the bridge, past the armed sailors on the far side and out along the open road. Here and there he could see the scarlet patches of crouching marines amongst the hillside bracken, and he was horrified to realise that he could already see the beach below and the jumble of houses beyond the pier. The growing daylight added to his sense of nakedness, and in his imagination he thought he heard the tramp of French soldiers as they marched steadily to cut his escape to the sea.

He rounded a bend in the road and almost fell on top of Captain Rennie, who was sitting comfortably on a small mound of grass, his cocked hat and sword lying neatly beside him. Cradled on his knees was a half-eaten pie, and even as Okes staggered to a halt Rennie glanced up at him and dabbed at his mouth with a handkerchief.

'Delicious.' He looked curiously past Okes. 'They sound busy back there.'

Okes stared round wildly. This was almost too much. He wanted to scream, to shake Rennie, to make him realise the enormity of the danger.

Rennie's eyes narrowed, but he said calmly, 'A chicken pie? I had almost forgotten what it was like.' He gestured over his shoulder, but kept his eyes on Okes's stricken face. 'Some Dutch folk from the village brought it for me during the night, y'know. Damn nice people really. It's a pity we're at war, isn't it.' He stood up and wrapped the remainder of the pie carefully in his handkerchief. Then he said quietly, 'You'd better tell me what is happening.'

Okes controlled his breathing with a savage effort. 'The French are coming! Over there, behind the hill.'

'I know. My men have already spotted them.' Rennie regarded him calmly. 'What did you expect them to do?'

The marine's obvious indifference gave Okes the little extra strength he still needed. 'You can start falling back. I've given orders to fire the magazine.' He dropped his eyes. 'I'm blowing the bridge as soon as McIntosh is ready!'

Rennie stared at him. 'But the captain! How in hell's name can he get back to us without the bridge?' He clapped on his hat and reached for his sword. 'I'd better go and have a look back there.'

Okes blocked his way, his eyes blazing. 'You know the orders! I'm in charge if anything happens to the captain! Your duty is to cover the withdrawal!'

Sergeant Garwood trotted round the bend, his half-pike glittering in the growing light. 'Sir.' He ignored Okes. 'The Frogs is comin'! There's best part of a company movin' down on our flank. I think the rest will try and work round the village and take us from the rear.'

Rennie nodded, his face suddenly grave. 'Very well. I'll come at once.'

He turned back to Okes and said slowly, 'You'll wait a bit longer surely? It takes time to get a boat back to the headland!'

Okes swung on his heel as a ragged volley of musket fire echoed around the hills. 'Get back to your men, Captain Rennie. I hope I know *my* duty!'

Rennie shrugged and walked quickly up the sloping hillside towards the firing. When he looked back he could see the smoke from the anchorage drifting across the headland in a solid wall, and tried to picture the devastation beyond.

Against the hillside and the glittering water below the cliff Okes's running figure looked frail and lost. 'I hope you *do*, Mr. Okes!' Rennie spoke aloud to the empty hillside. Then he turned and began to run to his prepared positions and his men.

Okes found McIntosh already squatting on one side of the bridge, craning his head to peer down at one of the massive wooden trestles.

'Ready?' Okes could hardly stop himself from shouting. 'Well, are you?'

McIntosh nodded. 'Aye, aye, sir. A two-minute fuse. And a four-minute fuse to the magazine.' He rubbed his hard hands. 'Mr. Farquhar is waiting atop the battery to light it as soon as the cap'n gets back.'

Okes swayed and then controlled himself. 'Wait here!' He started to run again, and as soon as he had reached the outskirts of the battery he blew his whistle and yelled, 'Clear the headland! Fall back there!'

Startled, the seamen gathered up their weapons and began to hurry towards the bridge. Most of them had seen the approaching soldiers and needed no second order.

A petty officer, his face stained with dirt and smoke, strode across to the panting lieutenant. 'Beggin' yer pardon, sir! The cap'n ain't come yet!'

'Yes, yes, I know that!' Okes glared at him glassily. 'You go with the others and get them across the bridge. Wait for me there, and be ready to move!' He peered through the smoke. 'Where is Mr. Farquhar?'

The man shrugged. 'Gone down the steps, sir. He said he'd get a better chance of seeing through the smoke from there.'

Okes strode to the battery wall and leaned against it for support. With the sailors gone and the gunports unoccupied and empty the place seemed strangely dead. He made himself walk to the top of the steps. There was no sign of Farquhar, of anybody in fact.

There was a fresh burst of firing, intermingled with wild cheering, and his limbs started to move as if he had already lost control of them. He walked to the open door of the magazine and stared for several seconds at the waiting fuse and the smouldering slow match beside it. It was not his fault, he told himself. There was nothing else he could do. He sank to his knees, his eyes filled with the fuse and the mental picture of Bolitho hurrying away towards the anchored sloop.

Damn them! Damn them all! He had to steady his wrist with his other hand as he took the match and held it against the fuse.

He felt the nausea hard in his throat as he staggered to his feet and ran quickly towards the bridge.

McIntosh stared up at him, his eyes uncomprehending.

'Light it, you fool!' Okes was already half-way across the bridge. 'Or stay there and go up with the magazine!'

McIntosh fired the fuse and scrambled on to the bridge. He caught Okes up around the curve in the road and gasped, 'Where's Mr. Farquhar, sir? An' what happened to the captain?'

Okes snarled, 'Back to the beach! All of you!' To McIntosh he added, 'All dead! Like you'll be if the French catch you!'

There was a thunderous roar, followed almost immediately by a second, sharper explosion. The force of the detonations seemed to quell the musket fire and distant shouts, so that the whole island appeared to be stunned by the noise.

The growling rumble went on, and Okes heard a splintering crash as the bridge fell into the ravine like so much kindling wood.

Strangely, he found that he could walk now, his feet moving almost steadily as he followed his men down the road towards the pier and safety. He had acted in the only way possible. He kept his eyes fixed on the pier. The *only* way. Others would soon see that, too. He pictured his wife's face when she read the announcement in the *Gazette*.

'Lieutenant Matthew Okes, who carried the brunt of the responsibility of this daring raid after the death of his commanding officer, is to be congratulated on his valour and his keenness to press home an attack against impossible odds!'

He slowed to a halt as a group of marines burst through the gorse and took up position on the road itself.

A marine yelled, 'Here they come, lads!'

Sergeant Garwood's voice boomed from beyond the hilltop. 'Hold your fire, my darlings! Ready, now! *Fire!*'

His last order came as a charging line of blue uniformed soldiers rose above the skyline and started to run down towards the beach. As the musket smoke drifted clear Okes saw the soldiers falling back, leaving others screaming and kicking in the low gorse.

'Reload! Take yer time!' Garwood sounded calm. 'Aim low, lads!'

Another sharp volley, but this time there were more soldiers, and they came on with fresh determination in spite of losses. And here and there a marine lay dead, and several others crawled slowly down the hillside after their comrades.

Okes could see Rennie standing imperturbably on a hillock, ignoring the sharpshooters as he controlled his thin line of retreating men. He felt his envy giving way to hatred. Rennie would never have acted as *he* had done! He would have waited for Bolitho and allowed everyone to die for nothing!

Okes shouted, 'To the lugger! Lively there!'

The sailors ran wildly to the pier, carrying their wounded companions and yelling encouragement to the marines. It seemed to Okes that another age passed before all his men were aboard and the last of the marines were falling back along the pier. There was a fresh morning breeze to fill the lugger's sails, and as the last marine scrambled gasping over the bulwark the boat idled clear.

With a maddened roar the French soldiers charged from cover and headed for the pier. From individual uniformed blobs they converged into a solid force, and as they surged on to the pier itself they merged into a single enemy.

McIntosh crouched in the bows and looked along the swivel gun. He ignored the sporadic musket fire, and waited until the soldiers were packed into a yelling, tangled throng before he jerked back the lanyard. 'There, my beauties!' He stood up wildly in the pitching boat as the canister shot cut through the screaming soldiers like a scythe. 'That's fer the cap'n! An' all the others!'

Before the second wave of soldiers had reached the bloody, threshing carnage on the pier the lugger had gone about and headed out to sea. Aboard there was silence now, and even when the *Phalarope*'s raked masts rounded the headland and bore down on the small boat like a protective parent, the exhausted men could not even muster a cheer.

Okes looked back at the island, at the smoke, and the vague outline of the headland battery. It was over.

The lugger was to be abandoned after the raid, so Okes had it laid alongside the *Phalarope*, where many hands reached down for the wounded and the silent victors.

Captain Rennie stood aside to allow Okes to climb up the frigate's side. He said, 'After *you*, Mr. Okes. I'd not want to spoil your entrance this morning!'

Okes stared at him, his mouth hanging open to reply. Then he saw the cold hostility in Rennie's eyes and decided against it. He must expect jealousy, he told himself firmly. He must be prepared to deal with it.

He reached for the main chains and swung himself up and over the frigate's side. For a moment longer he stared around the familiar deck. He had survived.

9

Defeat

Bolitho did not actually remember hearing the exploding magazine. It was more like a sensation, or the end of a nightmarish dream when a man awakes even more afraid of the waiting reality. He recalled sitting in the stern of the crowded and half-swamped boat, staring back at the hissing, writhing water where the transport had made her last dive to the bottom. His eyes ached from the blaze, and were now dulled by the ship's sudden disappearance and the shadow which reached across the high-sided anchorage to hide the pain and terror beneath.

His men were laughing and chattering with relief and excitement, but as Bolitho turned back to search for the treacherous rockfalls at the foot of the cliff the whole world seemed to explode in one gigantic tremor. Rocks rained down into the water, and as the men pulled desperately at the oars one large piece of splintered stone struck the stem like a hammer, and Bolitho staggered to his feet as the sea surged jubilantly into the listing boat.

It seemed as if the bombardment from above would never cease. He saw one man swept underwater by a complete section of cliff even as he tried to scramble up on to the rocks. Belsey, the master's mate, fell cursing into deep water, and when Stockdale heaved him bodily up on to the rocks he yelled in anguish, 'Me arm! God, me arm's broken!'

Bolitho's dazed thoughts were slowly returning to normal, and as he called encouragement to his half-drowned men his mind rebelled against what he knew to be true. Someone had fired the magazine without waiting for him and his party. He could find only small gratitude for the fact that had his boat returned minutes earlier they would have all been blasted skyward with the magazine and the battery.

He called, 'Follow me, lads! We'll climb along the water's edge on these rocks. The tide's dropping, so we should be able to reach the steps well enough.' He groped his way forward, knowing that they would follow. There was no choice. At the far end of the anchorage he could hear the frantic cries and the urgent notes of a trumpet. The French were too busy saving their own to care about the raiding party. But it would not last. Then the vengeance would be swift and final.

He staggered to a halt and blinked through the haze of acrid smoke. In the pale morning light which filtered down the steep ravine he could clearly see the remains of the bridge. There was no point in climbing the steps now. There was no way back to the beach.

A seaman ran dazedly past him and stared open mouthed at the wreckage. 'You bastards!' His voice shook with despair. 'You damn, cowardly *bastards*!'

'Silence!' Bolitho pushed the man back with the others. 'No doubt there was a good reason for blowing the bridge this early.' But he saw the look on Stockdale's face and knew that he had seen the lie in his eyes.

Belsey moaned and leaned against Stockdale for support. 'They left us to die! Ran to save their precious skins!'

Bolitho held up his hand. 'Quiet!' He cocked his head. 'Listen!'

A seaman said sharply, 'Over there, sir. I heard somethin' too.'

They scrambled over the smoking, splintered timbers until the first seaman fell back with a gasp of horror. Midshipman Farquhar was sitting propped against the ravine's rough wall, his body pinned in position by a great baulk of timber, and lying close by his side was a neatly severed leg.

Farquhar opened his eyes and croaked, 'Thank God, sir! I thought I was going to die alone!' He saw their expressions and managed a painful grin. 'It's not *my* leg, sir! It belongs to our Spanish prisoner!'

Bolitho glanced around him and then up at the brightening sky. 'Right. Lift that timber off him, and be very careful!' He knelt beside the midshipman and ran his hands swiftly beneath the massive beam, keeping his eyes on Farquhar's taut features as his fingers probed at his trapped body.

Farquhar said between his teeth, 'Nothing broken it seems!' He lay back and closed his eyes as the beam quivered and began to move. 'I was looking for you, sir. Then I returned to the magazine and saw that the fuse was almost burned through!' He sounded near breaking. 'I seized our Spaniard and ran for the bridge, but just as we reached it the whole thing blew up and dropped into the ravine.' He winced. 'And us with it!'

The beam was dragged clear, and Bolitho tightened his jaw as he saw the smashed remains of their prisoner. He asked harshly, 'How did it happen?'

Farquhar allowed himself to be lifted to his feet. Immediately his legs buckled, and Stockdale said gruffly, ' 'Ere, I'll take the young gentleman, sir!'

Farquhar clung to Stockdale's shoulder and said, 'Sorry about all this, sir. I'll be all right in a while.' He remembered Bolitho's question and said vaguely, 'I can't understand it, sir. I still can't believe it happened.'

Bolitho pulled the dirk from Farquhar's belt and handed it to one of the seamen. 'Here, make a good splint with this for Mr. Belsey's arm. It will suffice until we get back to the *Phalarope*.'

Belsey watched the men's awkward fingers and groaned. 'Watch what yer doin'! You're like a pair of blind whores!'

Bolitho walked slowly along the weed-encrusted stonework. Fourteen men including himself. One with a broken arm, and one already half delirious from a ball in his shoulder. Farquhar looked as if he might fall unconscious, too.

He tried to push the bitterness and suspicion to the back of his mind.

That would keep. Right now he had to get these men to safety. No doubt the rest of the raiding party was already embarked in the lugger. He suddenly felt calmer. Whatever else happened, he had succeeded in his work. Two transports destroyed and a valuable sloop with them. And without a battery Mola Island would be useless to the French and their allies for a long while to come.

Stockdale called throatily, 'The second longboat, sir! It'll still be tied to the jetty where we left it!'

Bolitho scrambled across the wet stones and stared down at the remaining boat. It was not much of a craft. Patched and well used, and with only four oars and a mere scrap of canvas furled around the mast for every purpose. But no doubt the garrison had only used it for visiting the ships in harbour.

He said grimly, 'Get them aboard, Stockdale. We'll have to make the best of it.'

A ray of yellow sunlight lanced suddenly across the headland and glittered in the deep water. Without effort Bolitho could see the gleaming barrel of one of the battery's cannon almost below the swinging boat. A few feet this way and there would be no way out at all!

'Four of you man the oars! The rest of you take turns in baling and keeping a sharp lookout!'

Belsey struggled into a sitting position and peered at his splinted arm. The limb was tightly wrapped in an assortment of rags and strips of clothing, and stuck out in front of him like a club. He shook his head. 'Gawd! If I ever use this flipper again I'll be surprised!'

'Shove off! Give way together!' Bolitho squatted on the gunwale and pushed the tiller hard over. As the boat moved swiftly with the current he stared up at the blackened crest of the headland and wondered what had happened in those last minutes before Farquhar had been flung to almost certain death.

Farquhar moved weakly against the boat's side and snapped, 'Pull lively, Robinson! I'll flay you alive if you don't do your share!'

In spite of his misery Bolitho smiled to himself. Farquhar's experiences had not softened his attitude to duty.

The oars rose and fell steadily, and the boat moved further and further from the jutting headland with its attendant pall of drifting smoke.

A man in the bows spoke Bolitho's thoughts for him, and for once he could find no words to rebuke him. The sailor stared back along the labouring men and snarled, 'Gone! Look round, lads! The bloody ship's gone without us!'

Farquhar said bitterly, 'She must have gone around the island, sir. We'll never catch her now.'

'I know.' Bolitho shaded his eyes against the glare and looked thoughtfully at the stumpy mast. 'Get that sail broken out, lads. We'll get clear of Mola Island and make for the nearest friendly one.' His crisp tone hid the doubt and the anger.

Stockdale wiped the wounded seaman's forehead with a wet rag and muttered, 'A miracle would come in 'andy, sir!'

Bolitho stripped off his tattered coat and regarded him calmly. 'I'm afraid that is not my province, Stockdale, but I will bear it in mind.'

He settled against the tiller bar and steered towards the rising sun.

Lieutenant Thomas Herrick listened to the bell as it announced the end of the first Dog Watch and then resumed his pacing back and forth across the quarterdeck.

With a warm but fresh breeze from her quarter the *Phalarope* had made good time back to her patrol area, yet Herrick could find nothing but apprehension and a sense of loss at the speedy passage. He still could not accept what had happened, and felt the same inner anguish he had experienced when the weary raiding party had clambered up the frigate's side.

Even then he had been unwilling to accept that Bolitho was missing. Then he had seen Rennie's grim features and had felt the nervous uncertainty of the other returning sailors and marines. Only Okes had appeared unmoved by the disaster. No, Herrick frowned as he tried to relive exactly the moment Okes had stepped aboard, unmoved was not the proper description. There had been a sort of guarded jauntiness about him which was totally out of character. Herrick had gone to question him, but Vibart had summoned Okes to the quarterdeck where he had been brooding in silence since the landing party had left for the shore.

Rennie had been unusually reticent. But when Herrick had persisted, the marine had said shortly, 'It was a dangerous mission, Thomas. We must always expect such things to happen!' He had been watching Okes speaking jerkily to the first lieutenant and he had added bitterly, 'I was sent to this ship with my detachment to reinforce the discipline. To protect the officers from any new threat of mutiny.' His eyes had blazed with sudden anger. 'It now appears that the *Phalarope*'s officers must be protected from each other!' Rennie had ended, 'I must attend to my wounded. They at least have nothing of which to be ashamed!'

Herrick had then cornered McIntosh, the gunner's mate. The latter had looked nervously at the quarterdeck before replying, 'How can I tell, sir? I just did my duty. Mr. Farquhar was the only one who must have seen what happened.' He had gestured wearily astern. 'And he's back there, dead with the rest!'

'But you think something went wrong, don't you?' Herrick's voice had been harsh.

'You know I can't afford to answer that, Mr. Herrick?' The man had looked back at the wounded and exhausted seamen from the lugger. 'It took a lot of pain and sweat to get where I am now. You know what would happen to me if I made accusations.'

Herrick had let him go, his eyes contemptuous, yet knowing in his heart that McIntosh was speaking the truth.

He stiffened as he heard Vibart's heavy step beside him.

'Pipe the hands aft, Mr. Herrick. I will tell them what is to be done.' Vibart looked composed and calm. Only his eyes betrayed a certain glitter which could be either excitement or triumph.

Herrick said, 'Are you sure there is nothing more we can do?'

Vibart stared past him at the ruffled water. 'I told you this morning, Mr.

Herrick, just as I voiced my fears to the captain. The venture was dangerous and foolhardy. That it was a success is fortunate for all of us. But Bolitho knew the risk he was taking. There is nothing more to be said.'

Herrick persisted. 'But is Lieutenant Okes *sure?*'

'I am satisfied with his report.' There was a new edge to Vibart's tone. 'So that is enough!' He walked ponderously to the weather rail and sniffed loudly. 'At least we are back in our proper area. Now we can contact the flagship.'

Herrick spoke swiftly to Midshipman Neale and watched him scamper forward. Then he heard the boatswain's mates shouting, 'All hands! All hands! Lay aft!'

As the men poured up from below he crossed to Vibart and said slowly, 'He was a good officer. I still think he could have escaped.'

'Then I will trouble you to keep your opinions to yourself, Mr. Herrick!' The deepset eyes were flecked with anger. 'You may have considered yourself one of his favourites, but I will have no such behaviour now.'

He turned away from Herrick's taut features as Quintal, the boatswain, touched his hat and rumbled, 'All present, sir.'

Vibart strode to the quarterdeck rail and stared down at the upturned faces. Herrick stayed by the helmsmen watching Vibart closely.

Vibart said, 'We are back on our patrol. We will shortly make contact with the admiral, and I will in due course tell him of our great success!'

Herrick felt himself tremble with anger. So it was a great success now, was it? When Bolitho was alive it had been foolhardy and dangerous, but now that Vibart stood to reap the full credit it was already a different picture.

'I am not satisfied with the recent slackness of discipline aboard, and I intend that this ship will return to a proper state of efficiency as of now!'

Vibart was staring round the assembled crew, his face flushed. Herrick felt sick. He is enjoying it, he thought. He is actually glad Bolitho is dead!

Herrick turned as Okes stepped through the cabin hatch and walked uncertainly towards him. Herrick took his sleeve and whispered fiercely, 'What did you tell Vibart, Matthew? For God's sake, what is the matter with you?'

Okes drew back. 'I told him nothing but the truth! Am I to be blamed for Bolitho's misfortunes?'

'And what of young Farquhar? Did you *see* him die?'

Okes looked away. 'Of course I did. What the devil are you trying to imply?' But there was a shake in his voice, and Herrick was suddenly reminded of Okes's behaviour during the battle with the privateer. His fear, his complete terror. A man could not change overnight.

'I want to know, Matthew. You had better tell me now.'

Okes seemed to have recovered himself, and when he looked at Herrick his eyes were opaque and expressionless. 'I told the truth, damn you!' He tried to smile. 'But you should not worry too much. You'll be moving up to second lieutenant!'

Herrick stepped back and looked at him with disgust. 'And *you* will be first, no doubt! And both you and Vibart will be the heroes of the day!'

Okes's face drained of colour. 'How dare you! You were not there, so it is easy to be jealous and insulting! Bolitho was *only* a man!'

'And *you* are not fit to polish his shoes!' Herrick swung round as Vibart stepped between them.

'I will have no quarrelling aboard my ship, Mr. Herrick. Any more of it and I will make an entry in the log!' He looked hard at Okes. 'Come to the cabin. I have a few things to say to you.'

Herrick watched them go, sickened and helpless.

Little Neale asked quietly, 'What does it all mean, sir?'

Herrick looked down at him, his face grave. 'It means that we must watch our step in the weeks ahead, my boy. With the captain gone I feel no security here.'

He stiffened as he saw Evans, the purser, hurrying aft, an aggrieved expression on his ferret face. Behind him Thain, the master-at-arms, ushered two frightened-looking seamen, his face leaving Herrick in no doubt as to what would happen next. Floggings, and more floggings. All the old scores kept hidden while Bolitho had been in command would break into the open like festering sores.

He faced Evans and said sharply, 'Well? What is it now?'

Evans smiled nervously. 'Caught these men red-handed! Stealing rum they were!'

Herrick's heart sank and he called the men forward. 'Is that right?' He realised that both seamen had taken part in the raiding party.

One of the men said sullenly, 'Aye, sir. The rum was for one of our mates. 'E was wounded. We reckoned it would 'elp 'im.' His companion nodded in agreement.

Herrick took Evans aside. 'It could be true.'

'Of course it is true!' Evans stared at him in amazement. 'But that is hardly the point! Stealing is stealing. There is no excuse, and you know it.' He eyed Herrick with little disguised glee. 'So you had better inform Mr. Vibart.' He drew himself up importantly. 'Or I will, Mr. Herrick!'

'Don't you get stroppy with me, Evans!' Herrick's face was a mask of fury. 'Or I'll have you broken, believe me!' But it was only anger. There was nothing else he could do but inform Vibart.

He handed over the watch to Neale and went wearily below. The sentry opened the cabin door for him before he had reached it, and Herrick guessed that the marine had correctly foreseen his surprise. Vibart had moved into Bolitho's quarters already. It only added to Herrick's sense of nightmarish unreality.

Vibart looked up from the desk and stared at him.

'Two men for punishment.' Herrick saw Okes leaning against the stern windows, his face lost in thought.

Vibart leaned back in the chair. 'Say "sir" when you address me, Mr. Herrick'. He frowned. 'I can't imagine why you make such a point of worsening your position?' He continued coldly, 'Make a report in the log, Mr. Herrick. Punishment at eight bells tomorrow morning. Two dozen lashes apiece.'

Herrick swallowed. 'But I have not told you their offence yet, sir!'

'No need.' Vibart gestured towards the open skylight. 'I happened to overhear your nonsensical conversation with Mr. Evans just now. And I must warn you I do not approve of your apparent wish to toady with men who lie and steal!'

Herrick felt the cabin closing in around him. 'Is that all?' He swallowed again. '*Sir?*'

'For the present.' Vibart looked almost relaxed. 'We will alter course to the south'rd in one hour. Try and make sure that the men do not slacken off during your watch.'

'Aye, aye, sir.' Herrick contracted his stomach muscles into a tight knot.

Outside the cabin he turned momentarily and looked back. The door was shut again and the marine sentry stared blankly in front of him beneath the swinging lantern. It was just as if Pomfret had returned and now sat back there in the big cabin. Herrick shook his head and mounted the ladder to the quarterdeck. It was all moving so much to a pattern again that he found himself wondering if Pomfret *had* been the controlling influence which had made the *Phalarope* into a living hell!

When he returned to the deck he saw that the sun had already moved closer to the horizon. The sea was empty, a great desert of silver and purple hues, with an horizon like a knife edge.

Out here a ship's captain was God indeed, he thought bitterly. Only under Bolitho had he felt the meaning of purpose and understanding, and after Pomfret it had seemed like a new chance of life.

He looked aft to the taffrail as if expecting to see Bolitho's tall shape watching the trim of the sails or just waiting for the sun to reach the horizon. Herrick had never disturbed Bolitho at those moments, but had drawn on each occasion to better his own understanding of the man. In his mind's eye he could still see the strong profile, the firm mouth which could be amused and sad almost at the same instant. It did not seem possible that such a man could be wiped out like something from a slate.

He resumed his slow pacing, his chin low on his chest. In this world, he thought, you could never depend on anything.

To the tired men in the longboat the night seemed cold and cheerless, and even those who had cursed the blazing sunlight and bemoaned their urgent thirst found no comfort from the darkness.

Bolitho groped his way aft to where Farquhar was sitting beside the tiller. With Stockdale's assistance he had just dropped a dead seaman over the side while the other men had watched in silence. The sailor in question had been spared the worst of his wound and the suffering of pain and thirst by remaining almost unconscious from the moment he had been shot down by the sloop's deck watch. The longboat was moving so slowly under her small sail that it seemed to take an age for the corpse to bob astern. There was not even an anchor to weight the man's body. In fact there was not much of anything. Just a cask of rancid water and little more than a day's ration of a cup per man.

Bolitho sank into the sternsheets and stared up at the glittering ceiling of stars. 'Keep her due south if you can.' He felt dry and aching with fatigue. 'I wish we could get a bit more wind in this wretched sail.'

Farquhar said, 'I think the boat would sink, sir! It feels rotten and worm-eaten!'

Bolitho eased his legs and thought back over the long, slow passage of time. If that was only the first day, he pondered, what would happen in the next? And the next after that?

The men were quiet enough, but that too could be dangerous. The first relief at escaping from the French could soon give way to mistrust and recriminations. The misery of being a prisoner of war might soon appear comfort itself compared with a living death without food or water.

Farquhar said absently, 'In Hampshire there will be snow on the hills now, I expect. All the sheep will be brought down to their feed, and the farm workers will be drinking good ale by their firesides.' He licked his lips. 'A few will be thinking of us maybe.'

Bolitho nodded, feeling his eyelids droop. 'A few.' He thought of his father in the big house and the row of watchful portraits. After this there would be no heir to carry on the family's name, he thought dully. Maybe some rich merchant would buy the house when his father died, and would find time to wonder at the portraits and the other relics of deeds and men soon forgotten. He said, 'I am going to try and sleep for an hour. Call me if you need anything.'

He closed his eyes and did not even hear Farquhar's reply.

Then he was aware of his arm being tugged and of the boat swaying and rolling as the listless seamen came to life and crowded excitedly in the bows. For a moment longer he imagined that he was dreaming. Then he heard Farquhar shout, 'Look, sir! She came to look for us after all!'

Bolitho staggered to his feet, his sore eyes probing over the heads of his men as he tried to pierce the darkness. Then he saw it. It was more an absence of familiar stars than an actual outline, but as he stared he began to see the contours of something darker and sharper. A ship.

He snapped, 'Make a light, Stockdale! Fire some of those rags!'

The sliver of moon struck silver from the distant sails, and against the night's dark backcloth Bolitho could see the darker tracery of raked masts and rigging. It was a frigate right enough.

The makeshift flare sizzled and then burst into flames, so that once more the eyes were blinded and limited to the small confines of the boat. Some men were cheering, others merely hugged each other and grinned like children.

'Now we shall get an answer to the mystery, Mr. Farquhar.' Bolitho pushed the tiller over as the ship changed shape and moved silently above them. He could hear the creak of yards, the sudden flurry of canvas as the frigate started to back her sails and heave to. He thought he heard a distant hail and the sound of running feet.

He said, 'Lower the sail, Stockdale! You men forrard, get ready to catch a line!' But nobody needed any encouragement from him.

The bowsprit swung dizzily barely feet away, and as Stockdale lit another crude flare Bolitho felt the grip of ice around his heart. The frigate's figurehead danced and flickered in the light as if it was alive. A gilt-painted demon wielding a pair of furnace irons like weapons of war.

Stockdale threw the flare into the water and turned to stare at Bolitho. 'Did you see, sir? Did you *see*?'

Bolitho let his arm go limp. 'Yes, Stockdale. It is the *Andiron*!'

The cheers and jubilation in the longboat died as suddenly as the flare, and the men stood or sat like stricken beings as lanterns shone down from the frigate deck and a grapnel bit into the boat's gunwale.

His men stood aside to let Bolitho pass as he made his way to the bows and reached out for the dangling ladder which had suddenly appeared. He was still too fatigued and too stunned by the change of events to mark a clear sequence of what was happening. His mind would only record brief, unreal images, magnified and distorted by patches of light from the circle of lanterns. Glittering bayonets, and pressing, curious faces.

As he stepped into the lamplight he heard a mixture of gasps and comments. An Irish voice called, 'It's an English officer!' Another with a twangy colonial accent broke in. 'Hell it is! It's a *captain*!'

One by one the *Phalarope*'s men climbed up the side and were pushed into line against the ship's gangway. An officer in a dark coat and cocked hat pushed through the packed crowd and regarded Bolitho with amusement.

'Welcome aboard, Cap'n! A real pleasure!' He turned and shouted, 'Put the men under guard and drop a round shot through that coffin of a boat!' To a massive Negro he added, 'Separate any officers amongst them and take 'em aft!' Then to Bolitho he made a mock bow. 'Now you will come with me, I am sure the captain will be glad to make your acquaintance.'

Even in the uncertain light of the lanterns Bolitho was able to distinguish the old, familiar details of the privateer's maindeck. He recalled with sudden clarity the last time he had visited the ship to see his friend Captain Masterman, a grave but friendly officer, who unlike many of his contemporaries had always been willing to share his knowledge and experience, and pleased to answer Bolitho's constant stream of questions.

The memory helped to drive back some of the gnawing despair, so that he automatically straightened his shoulders and was able to feel some bitter satisfaction at the scars and crudely repaired damage left from the *Phalarope*'s broadsides. The *Andiron*'s captain must have been heading for Mola Island to complete the repairs, he thought. Maybe the captured lugger's contents of spars and canvas had been earmarked for the *Andiron* alone.

He ducked his head as the officer led the way below the wide quarterdeck. At each step of the way he saw curious groups of the frigate's crew as they gathered to watch him pass. They were a mixed crew sure enough, he decided. Some were openly hostile and called insultingly as he strode by. Others dropped their eyes or hid their faces, and Bolitho guessed that they were probably English deserters, some even members of the *Andiron*'s original crew. There were Negroes and olive-skinned Mexicans. Loud-mouthed Irishmen and dark faced sailors who must have breathed their first breaths by the Mediterranean. But it was obviously a close-knit company, if only because of their mutual danger and the hazards of their chosen trade.

The officer opened a heavy door and stood aside to let Bolitho enter a small, sparsely furnished cabin.

'You can wait here. We have to get under way now, but I guess the captain'll want to see you soon.' He held out his hand. 'I'll take the sword.' He saw Bolitho's look of resentment and added, 'And in case you start getting ideas of glory, there is a guard right outside the door.' He took the sword and turned it over in his hands. 'A pretty ancient blade for an English captain?' He grinned. 'But then I imagine things are getting a bit difficult for you all round?'

Bolitho ignored him. The officer was goading him. There was no point in pleading or asking favours. He watched the lamplight shining dully on his father's sword and then deliberately turned his back.

He was a prisoner. He must save his energy for later. The door slammed and he heard the officer's feet moving away.

Wearily Bolitho slumped down on a sea chest and stared at the deck. Farquhar and Belsey would be kept apart like himself. No doubt the *Andiron*'s commander would wish to question each one separately. As he himself would have done. It was strange to realise that it was only two days since he had been questioning the terrified Spaniard aboard his own ship. And in the following period so much had happened that it was almost impossible to trace the pattern of time and events.

One thing was sure. He had lost his ship, and for him the future was an empty ruin.

The stuffy air in the cabin aided by the heavy fatigue in his body eventually took effect. As the deck canted slightly and the ship once more gathered way, Richard Bolitho leaned back against the cabin bulkhead and fell instantly asleep.

He was awakened by someone shaking his arm, and for a few more moments he found himself hoping it was all part of a terrible dream. Perhaps he could go back and take up reality again, even in the cramped uncertainty of the longboat. But it was the same officer who had escorted him to the cabin, and as Bolitho sat up on the chest he said, 'I thought you were dead!'

Bolitho realised with a further start that there was daylight in the passage outside the door, and as his mind accepted the reality of his position he heard the busy sounds of holystones and the sluice of water across the upperdeck.

'What time is it?'

The officer shrugged. 'Seven bells. You've been asleep for nearly seven hours at that!' He beckoned to a seaman in the passageway. 'There is some water for shaving and a razor.' He eyed Bolitho coldly. 'My man here will stay with you to make sure you don't cut your throat!'

'You are very considerate.' Bolitho took the bowl of hot water and ignored the seaman's look of fascinated interest. 'I would hate to die and miss seeing you hang, Lieutenant!'

The officer grinned calmly. 'You sure are a little firebrand, I'll say that for you.' He spoke sharply to the seaman. 'Just watch him, Jorgens! One false move and I'll expect you to deal with him, got it?'

The door slammed and the sailor said, 'The cap'n wants to see you when you's ready.' He licked his lips. 'He's havin' your breakfast got ready.' He sounded amazed at such treatment.

Bolitho continued with his shaving, but his mind was as busy as his razor. Perhaps it would be better to do as the officer had implied, he thought bitterly. One slash with the razor and his captors would be left with neither a ready victim nor a possible source of information.

He remembered Herrick's face when he had told him, 'Information. Out here the lack of it could lose a war.' Now his own words were coming back to mock him.

Then he thought of Farquhar and the others, and the look on Stockdale's battered face when the privateer's men had pulled them apart. It had an expression of trust and quiet confidence. At that terrible moment it had done more to hold back Bolitho's final despair than any words or deeds imaginable.

He wiped the razor and laid it on the chest. No, there was more to living than a man's own private hopes, he decided.

He pulled his torn uniform into shape and brushed the dark hair back from his forehead. 'I'm ready,' he said coolly. 'Perhaps you will lead the way?'

He followed the seaman along the passageway, and in the filtered daylight he saw more evidence of the brief battle. Smashed timbers shored up with makeshift beams, and telltale red blotches which so far had defied weeks of scrubbing.

An armed sailor stood aside and opened the main cabin door, and as Bolitho entered the once familiar place he was momentarily blinded by the dazzling reflections from sea and sky as the morning sunlight blazed across the wide stern windows.

The *Andiron's* captain was leaning out over the stern bench, his body a dark silhouette against the glittering water, but Bolitho's eyes fastened instead on his own sword which lay in the centre of the polished table.

He waited, standing quite still, his feet automatically braced against the ship's easy plunge and roll. Even this cabin was not spared from the *Phalarope's* wounded anger. More scars, and deeply gouged gaps left by flying splinters. *Andiron* must have spent little time in harbour, he thought.

The officer at the window turned very slowly, so that the light played across his face for a few moments before becoming once more a dark silhouette. For the second time in twenty-four hours Bolitho's reserve almost broke. It took all his strength to keep him from crying out in disbelief, but when the other man spoke he knew that this too was no fantasy.

'Welcome aboard the *Andiron*, Richard! When my second lieutenant brought me this sword I knew it had to be you!'

Bolitho stared at his brother, feeling the years dropping away, his brain reeling with a thousand memories. Hugh Bolitho, the son about whom his father had spoken so bitterly, yet with so much anxiety. Now commanding an enemy privateer! It was the culmination of every worst possible belief.

His brother said slowly, 'It had to happen of course. But I hoped it might be otherwise. At some other place perhaps.'

Bolitho heard himself say, 'Do you know what you have done? What this will do to . . .?' He faltered, even unable to accept that they were both sons of the same man. He added quietly, 'So you were in command when we fought your ship last month?'

Hugh Bolitho seemed to relax slightly, as if he considered the worst was now over. 'Yes. And that was a real surprise, I can tell you! We were just closing for the kill when I caught sight of you through my glass!' His face crinkled as he relived the moment. 'So I hauled off. You were lucky that day, my lad!'

Bolitho tried to hide the pain in his eyes and said shortly, 'Are you saying that my being there made a difference?'

'Did you think you had won the day, Richard?' For a moment longer Hugh Bolitho studied his brother with something like amusement. 'Believe me, in spite of your chain shot I could still have taken the *Phalarope*!' He shrugged and walked to the table and stared at the sword. 'I was taken off guard. I had no idea you were returning to the Indies.'

Bolitho watched his brother closely, noting the grey streaks in his dark hair, the lines of strain about his mouth. He was only four years older than himself, but there could have been ten years between them.

He said, 'Well, I am your prisoner now. What do you intend to do with me?'

The other man did not answer directly but picked up the sword and held it against the sun. 'So he gave it to *you*!' He shook his head, the gesture both familiar and painful. 'Poor Father. I imagine he believes the worst of me?'

'Are you surprised?'

Hugh Bolitho placed the sword on the table and thrust his hands deeply into his plain blue coat. 'I neither asked for nor expected this encounter, Richard. You may think as you please, but you know as well as I do that events out here are moving too quickly for a display of sentiment.' He watched his brother narrowly. 'When I saw you standing on your deck with that wretched crew of yours going to pieces around you, I could not bring myself to close the combat.' He waved one hand vaguely. 'Just like the old days, Richard. I could never find it easy to take what you thought was yours.'

Bolitho replied evenly, 'But you always did, didn't you?'

'Those days are past.' He pointed at a chart spread across another table. 'We are sailing for St. Kitts. We will make a landfall before night.' He watched the doubt in Bolitho's eyes. 'I know you so well, Richard. I can see the same old look of mistrust there!' He laughed. 'St. Kitts has already fallen to our ally. Sir Samuel Hood has pulled out to lick his wounds!' He waved across the chart. 'It will soon be over. Whether your government believes it or not, America will be an independent nation, perhaps sooner than they think!'

Bolitho felt his fingers locking together behind his back. While he was here being confronted with his past, his own world was falling apart. St. Kitts gone. Perhaps the French were already massing for an attack elsewhere. But where? They had the whole Caribbean to choose from.

His brother said quietly, 'If you are trying to make some scheme to foil my own plans you can forget it, Richard! For you the war is over.' He tapped the table with his fingertips. 'Unless?'

'Unless what?'

Hugh Bolitho walked round the table and stared him in the face. 'Unless you come in with us, Richard! I am well considered by the French. I am sure they would give you a ship of sorts! After what you did at Mola Island I am sure they would not deny your tenacity!' He smiled at some secret thought. 'It might even be the *Phalarope*.'

He studied Bolitho's unsmiling face and then walked back to the window. 'These are *our* waters now. We get our intelligence from many sources. Fishermen, trading boats, even slavers when we get the chance. With St. Kitts fallen your ships will draw further south to Antigua and beyond. There are not many patrols in this area now. It is too wasteful for your admiral, am I right?' He smiled sadly. 'Just one ship perhaps. Just one.'

Bolitho thought of the *Phalarope* and tried to imagine what Vibart would do.

'Your ship, Richard. The *Phalarope*! We need every frigate we can get. It is the same in all navies. And I have made sure that your admiral, that pompous fool, Sir Robert Napier, will be *informed* of our movements. I am quite sure that he will be so drunk with your success at Mola Island that he will soon despatch the *Phalarope* to find us! The admiral will surely be eager to avenge the loss of the *Andiron* from his command, eh?'

'You must be mad!' Bolitho watched his brother coldly.

'Mad? I think not, Richard. I have interrogated your men. They have told me how their ship was punished by Admiral Napier for letting *Andiron* escape. They told me also of the trouble there was aboard before you took command.' He spread his hands. 'I am afraid that most of your men have thrown in their lot with me. But do not distress yourself, it was wise of them. There is a whole new world opening up out here, and they will be part of it. When the war is over I will sail for England just to claim my inheritance, Richard. Then I will return to America. I have proved my worth out here. The past holds nothing for me.'

Bolitho said calmly, 'Then I pity your new nation! If it depends on traitors for existence it has a difficult course to steer.'

His brother remained unmoved. 'Traitors or patriots? It depends on a point of view! In any case, the *Andiron* will anchor off St. Kitts tonight. Not in the main harbour, but in a quiet little bay which I think would be considered quite ideal for recapturing her!' He threw back his head and laughed. 'Except that the *Phalarope* will be the one to step into the net, my brother!'

Bolitho stared at him without expression. 'As far as you are concerned I am a prisoner. I do not wish to tarnish either the name of my family or my country by being called a *brother*!'

Just for an instant he saw the barb go home. Then his brother recovered himself and said flatly, 'Then you will go below.' He picked up the sword again. 'I will wear this in future. It is mine by right!'

He banged the table and a sentry appeared in the doorway. Then he added, 'I am glad you are aboard my ship, Richard. This time, when the *Phalarope* comes creeping under my guns, I will have nothing to forestall me!'

'We will see.'

'We shall indeed.' Hugh Bolitho walked across to his chart. 'If I have the temper of your crew rightly, Richard, I think they will soon be eager to follow *Andiron*'s orders!'

Bolitho turned on his heel and walked back past the guard.

Behind him the *Andiron*'s captain stayed watching the door, his hand still holding the tarnished sword like a talisman.

10

The Red Baize Bag

For Richard Bolitho each day of captivity seemed longer than the one before, and the daily routine aboard the *Andiron* dragged into a slow torture. He was allowed the comparative freedom of the frigate's poop, from where he could watch the regular comings and goings of shore boats, the casual routine of a ship at anchor. At night he was returned to the solitude of a small cabin, and only joined Farquhar and Belsey for meals. Even then it was difficult to talk freely, because one of the privateer's warrant officers always waited close at hand.

It was a week since the *Andiron* had dropped her anchor, but to Bolitho it felt like an eternity. As each day passed he seemed to withdraw more and more into himself, going over his predicament again and again until his mind felt as if it was bursting.

From his small piece of deck he could see Belsey sitting gloomily on a hatch cover beside Farquhar, both apparently engaged in staring at the empty sea. Like everyone else aboard they were waiting, he thought bitterly. Waiting and wondering when *Phalarope* would approach the island and fall into the trap. He noticed that Belsey had a fresh bandage on his arm, and thought back to that first and only petty triumph when he had been allowed to join the other two after his meeting with his brother.

It was obvious at the time that both Farquhar and Belsey had already been told who the *Andiron*'s captain really was, just as it was equally plain to see their pitiful relief at his reappearance. Did they really believe that he would desert them and give his allegiance to the enemy? Even now he was surprised and faintly pleased to find that he was angry at the idea.

Belsey had been moving his bandaged arm painfully and had said, 'The ship's surgeon is goin' to have a look at it, sir.'

It had been then, and only then that Bolitho had remembered Farquhar's dirk which still lay hidden and used as a splint beneath the crude bandages. Hardly daring to speak, and watched by the others, he had broken a piece of wood from the cabin chair, and with Farquhar's help had replaced the dirk with a piece of polished mahogany. Once Belsey had yelped aloud and Bolitho had snapped, 'Keep quiet, you fool! We may have use for this later on!'

The dirk now lay hidden in his own bedding below decks, but after the agonising passing of days he could no longer view the possession of such a puny weapon with much hope.

He had seen little of his brother, and for that he was thankful. Once he had caught sight of him being rowed ashore in his gig. And on other occasions he had watched him staring at the tall mass of headland which towered above the anchored ship.

Bolitho had examined and thought over that one conversation in the stern cabin until he could see meanings where there were none. But he was sure of one thing. Hugh Bolitho was not bluffing. He had no need to.

The *Andiron* was anchored off the southern tip of the Island of Nevis, a smaller subsidiary of the main island, St. Kitts. Bolitho knew from experience that this small, oval-shaped island was separated by The Narrows a mere two miles or so from St. Kitts itself and a full fifteen miles from the main town of Basseterre where Hood had successfully stood siege until forced to cut his cables and retire to Antigua.

Nevis had been a good choice, Bolitho conceded grimly. During his endless walks up and down the poop he had watched the rapid preparations, the careful cunning which had gone into laying a perfect trap for any ship attempting to seize the *Andiron*.

The sheltered piece of water was commanded by the jutting promontory of Dogwood Point, while inland and towering like a miniature volcano was the bare outline of Saddle Hill. From either position even a wall-eyed lookout could quickly spot any unusual or suspicious approach and send a report down to both ship and shoreline.

It was so simple that Bolitho had to admit he would have used the same method himself. Perhaps it was because it was his own flesh and blood which was working out the plan, and a mind like his own was laying the snare.

If Sir Robert Napier had been informed of *Andiron*'s presence here, it was not unreasonable to expect him to take some sort of offensive action. A swift frigate attack would not match up to the smarting loss of St. Kitts, but it would do much for the morale of the embattled British fleet. It did not have to be the *Phalarope*, of course.

Bolitho discounted the idea immediately. His brother had been right about that, too. Admiral Napier would have few ships at his disposal now that Hood was back in the saddle. In addition, he would see *Phalarope*'s success as an act of justice to purge her name and avenge the memory of his own son.

He tried again to put himself into the position of an attacking captain. He would make a slow approach, just to make sure that the information about the *Andiron* was not suspect, and in order that the lookouts ashore should not see any sign of a masthead before sunset. Then under cover of darkness he would close the shore and drop a full boarding party of perhaps three or four boats. It would not be easy, but a ship foolish enough to anchor away from the defended base might be expected to fall after a swift struggle. He closed his eyes tightly and tried to blot out the picture of the attacking ship at the moment of truth and realisation.

There was a hidden battery of artillery already sighted and ranged across the whole area below the headland. And although to all outward appearances the *Andiron* was resting confidently below a friendly island, Bolitho had seen the preparations and the care his brother had gone to, to make sure of a victory.

Guns were loaded with grape and depressed behind their closed ports. Boarding nets were already slung, suitably slack to prevent a quick inrush of any who lived through the first holocaust of fire. The *Andiron's* men slept at their stations, each one armed to the teeth and eager to complete his captain's strategy.

Rockets were rigged on the quarterdeck, and as soon as the boarders were engaged the rockets would be fired. From further inshore the signal would be passed to a waiting French frigate and the battle would be all but over. The attacking ship would stand no chance if caught without the best part of her crew. And if she closed to give the boarding party support the shore artillery would pound her to fragments before she realised her mistake.

And if it was the *Phalarope* there was one further despairing thought. Vibart would be in command. It was hard to see his mind working fast enough to deal with such a situation.

Bolitho gritted his teeth and walked slowly to the side. The island looked at peace. The defenders had settled down now and were waiting like himself. Except that when the time came *he* would be battened below, helpless and wretched as he listened to the death of his own ship. Or worse, her capture, he thought for the hundredth time.

He felt a fresh pang of inner pain as he saw one of the *Andiron's* cutters unloading fruit alongside. There was no mistaking the bulky shape of Stockdale straddle-legged on the gunwale tossing up the nets of fruit as if they were weightless.

Strangely, that had been almost the hardest thing to bear. Stockdale of all people. Whether he had been eager or reluctant, Bolitho did not know, but he had gone over with the privateer's crew, and like sheep the other men from his raiding party had followed suit. He knew he could not blame them. If Stockdale, the captain's trusted coxswain, could change colours, why not they?

Stockdale looked up, squinting against the sun. Then he threw a mock salute, and some of the men laughed delightedly.

The American officer of the watch said dryly: 'Sometimes I think there's no such thing as loyalty, Capain! Just a *price*!'

Bolitho shrugged. 'Perhaps.'

The officer seemed glad of a chance to break Bolitho's brooding silence. 'I can't get over your being our captain's kin. It makes it kind of unnerving. But then I guess it's that way with you?'

Bolitho glanced quickly at the officer's tanned features. It was a friendly face. And that of a man lonely and tired by war, he thought. He said evenly, 'Have you been with him long?'

'A year or so.' The man frowned. 'It seems longer now. He came aboard as first lieutenant, but soon got command when the skipper was killed in a fight with one of your ships off Cape Cod.' He grinned. 'But I hope I'll be able to go home soon. I've a wife and two boys waiting for me. I should be tending my farm, not fighting King George!'

Bolitho recalled his brother's firm promise that he was returning to Cornwall to claim his rightful inheritance, and felt the same savage bitterness as when he had heard the words the first time.

He controlled his rising emotion and asked quietly, 'Do you really think it will be that simple?'

The man stared at him. 'What could happen now? I don't mean to add insult to injury, Captain, but I don't really think the British stand much of a chance to regain America.'

Bolitho smiled. 'I was thinking more of the French. If as you say American independence will be ratified by all those concerned, do you imagine the French will be prepared to sail away and leave you alone? They have done most of the fighting remember. Without their fleet and supplies do you think you would have succeeded thus far?'

The American scratched his head. 'War makes strange allies, Captain.'

'I know. I have seen some of them.' Bolitho looked away. 'I think the French will want to stay out here, as they tried to do in Canada.' He shook his head. 'You could easily exchange one master for another!'

The officer yawned and said wearily, 'Well, it's not for me to decide, thank the Lord!' He shaded his eyes and peered towards the dark shadow below Saddle Hill. A white and blue dot was moving rapidly down the rough track from the summit in a cloud of dust.

The officer looked meaningly at Bolitho and said briefly, 'Horse and rider! That means one thing, Captain. The bait has been accepted. It will be tonight, or not at all!'

There was a shout from the forecastle as a blinding needle of light stabbed out from the bleak headland. Someone was using a heliograph, and from further inland Bolitho heard the eager beating of drums.

He asked, 'How did they get a signal?'

The officer closed his mouth and then said not unkindly, 'There is a chain of fishing boats out there, Captain. They pass the sighting reports from boat to boat. The nearest one is well in sight of the hill lookouts.' He looked embarrassed. 'Why not try and forget it? There's nothing you can do now. Any more than *I* could do if the situation were reversed!'

Bolitho looked at him thoughtfully. 'Thank you. I will try to remember that.' Then he resumed his pacing, and with a shrug the officer returned to the opposite side of the poop.

The short truce was over. They were no longer fellow sailors. The flashing heliograph had made them enemies once more.

'It'll be sunset in one hour!' Daniel Proby, the *Phalarope's* master, scribbled slowly on his slate and then ambled across to join Herrick by the weather rail. 'But in all my experience I've not seen one like this!'

Herrick brought his mind back to the present and followed Proby's mournful gaze across the vast glittering waste of open sea.

For most of the afternoon and early evening the frigate had pushed her way steadily north-east, and now as she lay close-hauled on the port tack, every mast and spar, every inch of straining canvas shone with the hue of burnished copper. The sky, which for days had remained bright blue and empty, was streaked with long cruising clouds, streaming like trails of glowing smoke towards the far horizon. It was an angry sky, and the sea was reacting to the change in its own way. Instead of short, choppy white-caps the surface had altered to advancing lines of hump-backed rollers, one behind the other in neatly matched ranks which made the ship heave and groan as her figurehead lifted to the sky and then plunged forward and down in drawnout, sickening swoops.

Herrick said, 'Maybe a storm is coming through from the Atlantic?'

The master shook his head, unconvinced. 'You don't get much in the way of storms at this time of year.' He glanced aloft as the sails thundered as if to mock his words. 'All the same, we will have to take in another reef if it don't improve a bit.'

In spite of his gloom Herrick was able to smile to himself. He could not see Vibart being happy about that. For two days, since he had received his new orders, he had been driving the ship like a madman. He thought back again to the moment a lookout had sighted the distant sail. For an instant they had all imagined it was a patrolling frigate or the *Cassius* herself. But it had been a fast-moving brig, her low hull smothered in spray as she had gone about and run down towards the *Phalarope*.

Her arrival had been an unexpected but welcome diversion as far as Herrick was concerned. The tension aboard the frigate was getting bad enough to *feel*, like something with a soul of its own. In a matter of days there had been seven floggings, but instead of settling the crew into dumb servility it had only helped to drive a firm wedge between quarterdeck and forecastle. There was little chatter or laughter any more between decks, and when an officer passed close by a group of seamen, the latter would lapse into sullen silence and turn their faces away.

Midshipman Maynard had reported, 'The brig is *Witch of Looe*, sir! She has despatches for us!'

Vibart had waited importantly on the quarterdeck, alone and aloof, saying nothing and watching everything.

A boat had skipped across the choppy water, and soon a young lieutenant had climbed aboard carrying the inevitable canvas envelope.

Herrick had been standing nearby, straining his ears and trying to imagine what was happening. He had heard Vibart asking about the flagship and the lieutenant's brief reply.

'These orders are from the admiral, sir. I have nothing to add.'

The reply had been too brief, almost insolent, and Herrick had guessed that the young lieutenant was high enough on the admiral's list of favourites to afford such rudeness.

Vibart had started to tell the brig's messenger about the raid on Mola Island and had then clamped his jaw tightly shut. He had turned on his heel, merely adding for Herrick's benefit, 'Get the ship under way again, Mr. Herrick. I have work to do!'

He was always the same now, Herrick pondered. Fluctuating between ponderous self-importance and fits of blind rage. From one hour to the next you could never be sure of his reactions, and it was doubly bad because he was always in evidence. Watching and criticising and bawling out fresh orders to overrule those of his subordinates.

Herrick had stopped the lieutenant at the entry port and had tried to get more information.

The officer had regarded him thoughtfully. 'St. Kitts has fallen. The fleet is falling back and regrouping. I am on my way to Antigua now.' He had stared across at his own ship. 'But Rodney is said to be on his way back from England with twelve ships of the line. I hope to God he will be in time.' Then he added quickly, 'Where is your captain?'

'Dead.' Herrick's tongue had lingered on the word. 'We lost him at Mola Island.'

'Well, I don't care much for your new commander, my friend.' The lieutenant had paused above his swaying boat. 'We have been searching for the *Phalarope* for two days! The admiral will not be pleased that you were off your station, Mola Island or not!' He had rolled his eyes. 'Sir Robert is a stickler for routine.'

Herrick's mind shifted to the next part in the sequence of events which had sent the *Phalarope* on her new course towards the islands. Vibart had called a meeting in the stern cabin. Every officer and warrant officer had been present, and it was somehow typical of Vibart that while he sat comfortably in his chair, all the others were kept standing.

'Sir Robert Napier has received information that the *Andiron* is lying off Nevis.' He had plunged into what sounded very like a carefully rehearsed speech. 'She is apparently carrying out repairs and awaiting fresh orders, but there is no saying how long she will remain there.' He had looked slowly around their faces. 'Sir Robert requires that we make our way to Nevis forthwith to sink or cut-out the *Andiron*.' His words had dropped in the cabin like stones in a pool. 'We will make as quick a passage as possible.' He had glared meaningly. 'So make sure there are no mistakes, Mr. Proby!'

Herrick had been studying Vibart during his announcement, and had been surprised by his apparent eagerness to begin the operation. It might be a false piece of intelligence, but if not, it would not be an easy matter to cut-out an anchored ship close inshore to a hostile island.

Then, as Vibart had droned on about details and timing, he had realised that Vibart's demeanour owed much to his own uncertainty. So far, although he had been in command since Bolitho's loss, Okes stood in the best position to gain full credit for past successes against the enemy. He still had to ensure the firmness of his own control, and this new operation was the obvious opportunity.

It was odd that he had sent no despatches across to the *Witch of Looe*, Herrick thought. It was just as if he wanted to save the whole record for the admiral's ear alone. Sir Robert might be angry about *Phalarope* being off station, but the destruction of the Mola Island battery and transports, and a victory over the privateer *Andiron* would do much to placate anyone but the devil himself.

But now that Vibart had had time to consider the full implications of his orders he had changed yet again. As the ship drove towards the chosen rendezvous he had grown nervous and edgy, and more than once had let his impatience get the upper hand. Only that morning he had had a man flogged for letting a marline-spike fall from the foreyard. It had struck quivering in the deck within feet of Packwood, a boatswain's mate. Vibart had been brooding on the quarterdeck, watching the boats being checked and moved ready for instant lowering. Packwood's startled shout had given him yet one more outlet for his unpredictable temper.

'Get that man down here!' His voice had stopped all work on the maindeck. 'I saw what he did! That was meant to fall on Packwood!'

Even the boatswain's mate had voiced a protest. 'It's lively aloft today, sir. It was an accident.'

Vibart's face had gone scarlet. 'Silence! Or I'll see your backbones, too!'

Again the dread pipe. 'All hands lay aft to witness punishment!'

Again the agonising passage of time while the grating was rigged and the marines had made a scarlet rectangle on the quarterdeck.

The seaman in question was a man called Kirk. He was a thin, hollow-eyed sailor who had gone almost deaf after the encounter with the *Andiron*, his ears apparently permanently damaged by the thundering crash of broadsides.

Mr. Quintal, the boatswain, had walked slowly aft, the familiar red baize bag swinging from his wrist as the silent company parted to allow him through.

Up to the last moment, even as Vibart closed the Articles of War and announced harshly, 'Four dozen, Mr. Quintal!', Herrick doubted if Kirk had heard a single word.

Only when the boatswain's mates seized him and stripped his thin body and spread-eagled him across the grating like a writhing crucifix did he start to scream and protest.

Most men took their punishment in silence. The tremendous force of a single blow from the cat-o'-nine-tails was enough to drive the wind from the lungs and left little to cry on.

Kirk's cries continued as his wrists were tied in position so that his feet were only just touching the deck, and the boatswain's mates exchanged quick glances, momentarily unnerved by the man's terror.

Quintal drew the lash from the red bag and handed it to Packwood. Gruffly he had said, 'Two dozen. Josling can do the other two.' Under his breath he had added, 'If he lives that long!'

Vibart had replaced his hat and nodded curtly. 'Carry on!'

Herrick had seen plenty of floggings, and had steeled himself to accept what was part of naval life. But this one had seemed different, and unfair because of Vibart's obvious eagerness.

The marine drummer had struck into a quick roll, and Packwood had drawn back his thick arm.

'One!' The lash came down with a swishing crack.

As usual Herrick had been sickly fascinated by the time it took to show its mark. For a moment there was nothing on the man's naked back, not even a bruise, but even as the lash swung back for the second stroke the whole area of taut skin from the shoulder to the waist opened and shone in a criss-cross mass of fine cuts.

'Two!' Kirk screamed and wriggled helplessly on the grating, and Herrick saw blood on his chin and knew that he had bitten through his tongue.

'Three!' Packwood faltered and hit again, his eyes glassy as Kirk's back began to shred into a tangle of bloody flesh.

Vibart's voice had cut through the roll of the drum. 'Harder, Packwood! Don't go easy on the scum, unless you wish to change places with him!'

And so it had continued. Stroke by stroke, to the inhuman rattle of the drum. Kirk had fallen silent and limp after the first dozen, but when Ellice, the surgeon, had pronounced grimly, ' 'E's still alive, sir, but not takin' it well!', Vibart had snapped, 'Carry on with punishment!'

Herrick had seen Midshipman Neale holding Maynard's sleeve as if for support as the grisly flogging had continued.

Kirk had little flesh to begin with, and after eighteen strokes Herrick thought he could see the gleam of bone and muscle through the man's butchered skin.

Josling had taken the lash from his fellow boatswain's mate and had run it through his fingers to clear it of flesh and gristle. With a quick glance upwards at Vibart's expressionless face he had carried on with the second two dozen.

At the twentieth stroke Mr. Quintal had knocked up Josling's arm and had said firmly, 'That's enough, sir! He's dyin'!'

Kirk's bloodied body had been cut down and carried below, but only after Ellice had backed up the boatswain's quick intervention. He had muttered vaguely, 'Might live. Can't say. I think his kidneys have burst.'

Herrick had looked for some sign of pity or even triumph on Vibart's heavy features. But there had been nothing but stony indifference. Captain Pomfret had watched floggings like a man will watch a spectacle of sport, and at each bloody conclusion he was almost elated, as if he had just experienced some perverted sexual act. But not Vibart. There was nothing at all which Herrick could recognise as feeling of any sort.

He turned away swiftly as Vibart appeared at the cabin hatch and sniffed at the wind. Vibart studied the strange copper sky and remarked slowly, 'Wind's freshened. We'll shorten sail in ten minutes.' He glanced at Proby. 'Now, are you sure of our position? Our *exact* position?'

Proby nodded gloomily. 'Aye, sir. Nevis bears nor'-east, near on fifteen miles.'

Vibart regarded him searchingly. 'I hope for your sake that is so, Mr. Proby.' He contented himself with another quick bark at the helmsman, 'Watch her head, you fool! Keep her close to the wind!'

Herrick glanced aloft and knew that the ship was running perfectly. Vibart was obviously getting more and more on edge as they drew nearer the island. Not afraid. He had never shown a sign of fear at any time. No, it went far deeper, to the lurking possibility of failure.

Vibart saw Herrick watching him and snapped. 'Have you detailed the cutting-out parties?'

'Aye, sir. All the boats except the gig are prepared. The gig is unsuitable for this work.'

'I know that, Mr. Herrick!' Vibart's eyes were flecked with red. 'You will take over-all charge of the boarders with Maynard, Packwood and Parker in charge of the other three boats.' He looked darkly at the men working on deck. 'As a master's mate, Parker will be ideal for getting sail on the *Andiron* if you succeed in your attack.'

'Yes, sir.' Herrick knew all this. He had detailed each man personally, and had already decided on his set plan. He asked, 'Do you expect much opposition, sir?'

'We are committed now. It doesn't matter what I think!'

Proby consulted his massive watch and said, 'Call all hands! Prepare to shorten sail!'

Herrick wondered why Vibart had left it so long. Several times he had seen fishing boats in the far distance. There was no point in advertising the *Phalarope*'s haste by her obvious press of sail.

The seamen were already climbing the shrouds and pulling themselves out along the swaying yards. With the ship's uncomfortable motion the business of taking in sails was all the more dangerous to the unwary.

Vibart growled, 'This will make us harder to see. And with the wind rising all the time it will save us the trouble of shortening later on.' He seemed to be thinking aloud.

Proby cupped his hands and yelled hoarsely, 'Tops'ls and jib's all we need! Lively there!'

Followed by Vibart's eyes and the urgent shouts of their petty officers the men aloft fought at the thrashing canvas, cursing the wind and the treacherous sails which tried their utmost to hurl the men from the yards to the deck beneath.

Herrick felt the ship's motion ease slightly as topgallants and courses contracted and finally submitted to the struggling seamen. He watched the long cruising rollers and gauged the distance between them. It would be more sheltered below Nevis's lee, he thought, but even so it would not be easy to keep the raiding boats together. He caught sight of Okes standing at the lee rail, and found himself wondering why Vibart had not chosen him for the cutting-out expedition. If Okes was so changed and reliable, he was the obvious choice.

Captain Rennie sauntered across the quarterdeck and remarked quietly, 'Congratulations, Herrick. I hope you do well tonight. I wish I could come with you, but marines are hardly suitable for falling about in boats!' Herrick smiled. 'Thank you.'

Rennie gestured towards Okes. 'It would seem that our commanding officer knows more than we thought, eh? He will not trust this attack to a man who is as weak as water!'

Herrick glanced quickly at the open skylight. 'Keep your voice down! Your remarks might be taken seriously!'

Rennie shrugged but dropped his voice. 'I feel past caring. Like a man walking on ice. It can only take so much!'

He walked away, and Herrick stood watching the seamen shinning down from the work aloft. If only Bolitho were here to inspire and carry them all, he thought heavily. He could imagine the *Phalarope* sailing into Antigua with Vibart expanding with pleasure as cheers and congratulations marked their return to the fleet and to glory. It would make victory all the more bitter, he thought. But for Bolitho the *Phalarope* would never have got this far, and if Vibart retained his command the future was bleak indeed.

Tobias Ellice rolled aft and mounted the quarterdeck ladder, touching his shabby hat and belching simultaneously. 'Kirk's dead,' he grunted abruptly. 'I'm having him sewn up nice and neat like!'

Herrick replied, 'Very well. I'll put it in the log.' He could smell the rum on the surgeon's breath and wondered how the man was able to perform his duties.

Ellice said, 'You can also put in the log that I'm sick of this ship and the whole bloody lot of you!' He swayed tipsily and would have fallen but for Herrick's arm. He muttered, 'Treat 'em like dogs!' He shook his head vaguely. 'No, not dogs, they live like kings by comparison.'

Herrick regarded him wearily. 'Have you finished?'

Ellice took a giant red handkerchief from the tail of his coat and blew his nose loudly. 'You can sneer, Mr. Herrick! You're off to gain glory tonight and to test your steel against the enemy.' He bared his teeth and tried to focus Herrick in his rheumy eyes. 'But you'll change yer tune when you're down below waiting for the saw to lop off your pretty arm or take away a leg or two!'

'Only two?' Herrick eyed him with sad amusement.

Ellice became suddenly serious as his rum-sodden mind grappled with Herrick's question. 'You can live without 'em, boy! I've seen it many a time.' He dropped his voice. 'But watch out for your wedding-tackle! A woman'll forgive much, but lose that lot and you might as well be food for the fish!'

Herrick watched him go and then strode aft to the taffrail. Another man dead. Whose turn would it be next?

Bryan Ferguson took another cutlass from the deep chest and handed it to old Ben Strachan. The latter peered quickly along the heavy blade and then bent over the grindstone and began to run the cutlass back and forth across the spinning stone, his eyes gleaming brightly in the flying sparks.

Ferguson looked at the berth deck and at the leaping shadows cast by the madly swinging lanterns as the ship rolled and staggered beneath his feet. It was strange how he was now able to retain his balance, and even his stomach seemed able to resist the lurking agony of seasickness.

The low-beamed berth deck was strangely deserted by comparison with its usual appearance of crowded humanity, he thought. Apart from the men selected for the boarding parties, all other available hands were on deck preparing the ship for action. As he watched Strachan concentrating on his sharpening he could hear the menacing rumble of gun trucks as the main armament was carefully loaded and then lashed once more behind sealed ports. The decks were already sanded, and he could hear Mr. Brock, the gunner, yelling some last-minute instructions to his magazine party.

There was a strong smell of neat rum pervading the berth deck, and he turned to stare at the huddled groups of seamen who remained below enjoying a small moment of rest before taking to the boats.

He said quietly to Strachan, 'What will happen, do you think?'

Strachan tested the blade and laid it carefully on the pile beside him. 'Hard to tell, mate. I've been on a few cuttin' out raids meself. Sometimes it was all over with a few prayers and a few "Oh my Gods" an' afore you knew what 'ad 'appened you was back aboard none the worse! An' other times you was shocked to be still alive!'

Ferguson nodded, unable to picture the nerve-wrenching horror of a raid in total darkness. His new duties as clerk kept him away from that sort of danger and had somehow thrown him further apart from his companions.

It was all he could do to stay clear of trouble with the first lieutenant. Vibart read every order and account at least twice, and he never failed to follow up a complaint with a threat of punishment.

Ferguson thought back to the floggings and the last one in particular. He had wanted to hide his face, yet was stricken and mesmerised by the relentless punishment so that he had watched it to the end. Kirk had died in the sickbay, but his sobbing cries still seemed to hover in the space which had once been his home.

Strachan remarked, 'It's gettin' pretty rough up top. I wouldn't like to be takin' part!' He shook his grey head. 'It was as black as a pig's belly when I last took a look!'

Onslow, the big seaman from the *Cassius*, sauntered across and stared thoughtfully at Ferguson for several seconds. In his checked shirt and tight canvas trousers he looked even taller and more formidable than usual, and his thick hair was tied to the nape of his neck with a piece of red ribbon.

He said. 'You'll be staying aboard then?' He smiled. 'And quite right, too.' He rested his hand on Ferguson's thin shoulder. 'You save your energy, my lad. I'll want to be knowing what is happening down aft in the cabin.'

Ferguson stared at him. 'I – I don't understand?'

Onslow yawned and spread his arms. 'It's always just as well to know what the officers are planning next, y'see. That's what stops men like us staying rabble. With knowledge,' he tapped his forehead meaningly, 'we are equal to them, and *ready*!'

Lugg, a gunner's mate, ran down a ladder and squinted through the gloom. 'Right, you lot! On deck and lively about it! Each man take a cutlass and muster aft!'

Onslow eyed him calmly. 'What, no pistols?'

Lugg replied coldly, 'I'll pistol you if you don't learn some manners!'

There was a rasp of steel as each hurrying figure took a cutlass, and once or twice Ferguson spoke to a passing familiar face, but each time he received no answer.

Strachan wiped his hands and muttered, 'Save yer breath, mate. They're thinkin' of what lies ahead. There'll be talk enough later. I shouldn't wonder!'

John Allday hung back to the last. Then he picked up a cutlass and swung it slowly in the lamplight. Quietly he said, 'Be careful of Onslow, Bryan. He is a born troublemaker. I don't trust him an inch!'

Ferguson studied his friend with surprise and something like guilt. Since his unexpected change of jobs to captain's clerk he had seemingly drifted away from Allday's quiet protection, and whenever he had returned to the berth deck it had always been Onslow or his friend Pook who had dragged him into a tight circle of chatter and speculation.

Allday saw the uncertainty on Ferguson's face and added, 'You saw the flogging, Bryan. Be warned!'

'But Onslow is on our side, surely?' Ferguson wanted to understand. 'You heard him talking today. He was as sickened as the rest of us!'

'I heard him.' Allday's mouth twisted in a grim smile. 'But he only talks. He is never the one who goes to the gratings!'

Old Strachan mumbled, 'I seen a lad like 'im in the old *Gorgon*. Stirred up the men till they never knew which way ter jump. They 'anged 'im in the end!'

'And they'll hang all of us if he keeps up this mutinous talk!' Allday's eyes flashed. 'We are here, and we must make the best of it!'

Lugg peered down the ladder and bellowed, 'Come up on deck, you idle bugger! You're the last as usual!' There was no real anger in his voice. He was as tense and jumpy as everyone else aboard.

Ferguson called, 'Good luck!' but Allday was already running on deck, his eyes momentarily blinded in the darkness which enclosed the pitching hull like a cloak.

Overhead there were few stars, and then only occasionally visible between the low scudding clouds.

Petty officers were bawling names, and slapping and cursing the seamen pushed into separate parties near the boats which were already clear of their chocks and ready to be swayed outboard.

Allday saw the white lapels of Lieutenant Herrick's coat gleaming faintly against the dark sky and was strangely glad he was going with his boat. Midshipman Maynard seemed a likeable enough youngster, but he lacked both experience and confidence. He could see him now whispering furtively to his small friend Neale below the quarterdeck.

Herrick said sharply, 'Now listen to me, lads! I will lead in the launch. The cutter will follow close astern and then the pinnace. Mr. Parker will stay last in the jolly boat.' He had to shout above the moaning wind, and Allday glanced uneasily at the screaming water alongside and the rising spectres of blown spray. It would be a hard pull, he thought, and automatically spat on his hands.

He pricked up his ears as Parker, the master's mate, reported, 'All present, Mr. Herrick. Sixty-six men all told!'

'Very good. I will inform the . . .' He faltered and added harshly, 'I will tell Mr. Vibart!'

Allday bit his lip. There was no love lost between Herrick and the new captain, he thought.

He saw Onslow leaning negligently against a pike rack and remembered Ferguson's uneasiness. It was odd how eager Onslow had been to see Ferguson appointed as clerk, he decided. And how convenient it had been that Mathias, Bolitho's original clerk, had died in the hold.

'Sway out the cutter!' Mr. Quintal groped his way towards the tackle. 'Hoist away there!'

Allday faltered, his mind suddenly filled with one, stark picture. He had been masthead lookout the morning Mathias had fallen to his death. It was strange how he had not thought of the connection before. He had seen the clerk climbing through the small inspection hatch shortly before he had been found unconscious and dying. But there had already been someone else in the hold *before* that! He looked quickly at Onslow, remembering the exact moment and the fact that it had been Onslow who had reported the clerk's fall.

He felt Quintal's hard hand on his shoulder and threw his weight against the tackle with the others. All at once the sea seemed to become rougher and the *Phalarope* seemed to shrink by comparison.

Through his racing thoughts he heard Onslow say casually, 'We'll give the buggers a taste of steel!'

But who did he mean? Allday wondered.

11

Fortunes of War

The *Phalarope's* heavy launch, packed as she was with additional men for the cutting-out raid, began to ship water within minutes of leaving the security of the frigate's side.

Herrick wedged himself in one corner of the stern and peered over the heads of the straining oarsmen, his vision hampered by both darkness and a continuous stream of bursting spray. He tried to concentrate on the set plan of attack, but as time dragged by and the boat's swooping motion became more pronounced he found that half of his mind dwelt on the realisation that things were already moving against him. The wind had gained in force, and he didn't need to consult his small compass to know that it had also veered more to the east, so that what cover there might have been from the island was lost in an angry welter of tossing whitecaps and great swirling patterns of backwash from partially hidden rocks.

Every so often he looked astern and was thankful to see the cutter riding in his wake, her banks of oars slashing one moment at wave crests and then buried to the rowlocks as the boat dropped into another sickening trough.

Ryan, a seasoned quartermaster, swung the tiller bar and yelled, 'She'm takin' it poorly, sir! The lads are all but wore out!'

Herrick nodded but did not reply. It was obvious from the slow, laboured stroke that the men were already exhausted and in no shape for carrying out any sort of attack. More and more Herrick was nagged by the thought that Vibart had dropped the boats too soon. Nevis Island was still only a darker patch in the night's angry backcloth, and there was no sign at all of the chosen landmarks.

He felt a surge of anger when he remembered Vibart's brusqueness when he had last seen him. All he had wanted was to get the boats away. No second plan, no arrangements for possible discovery had even been discussed.

The *Andiron* was supposed to be anchored below Dogwood Point, but even allowing for better shelter inshore, it was still likely that her captain had called extra hands to watch for possible dangers in the rising wind. Herrick had a sudden picture of his exhausted boats' crews arriving at the ship's side to be met with a murderous fire from the awakened and eager gunners.

Ryan was shouting again. 'There's a strong drift, y'see! It'll carry us clear of the 'eadland, sir!' He sounded bitter. 'It'll be a long pull to clear the point at this rate.'

As if to back his words there was an anonymous rumble of voices from the darkened boat. Someone muttered, 'We should turn back. There's no chance now!'

Herrick glared down the boat. 'Silence! Do you want the whole island to hear us?'

Ryan whispered, 'Could we not lie beneath the point, sir?' He sounded slightly ashamed. 'We could rest the men a bit an' then try again.'

Herrick nodded, another plan forming in his brain. 'Good idea. Signal the cutter, Ryan.' He took the tiller as the quartermaster opened the shutter of his lantern and blinked it twice astern. To the oarsmen he snapped, 'Keep the stroke! *Together,* now!' There was no muttering, but he could sense them all watching him in the darkness. He added, 'The rest of you keep baling, and watch the oars. I want 'em muffled at every pull!'

Ryan said, 'Cutter's turnin', sir. I can see the pinnace back there, too.'

'Well, thank God for that!' Herrick forgot the grumbling seamen as the skyline hardened into a jagged overhanging cliff. It was Dogwood Point well enough, but they had drifted further than he had feared. They were not below it, but on the wrong side altogether. As he stared wretchedly at the land's hostile outline he felt the boat's motion begin to ease and heard the oars pick up a steadier time as the launch thrust into more sheltered water.

He said quietly, 'Oars! Easy with those blades now! You sound like a lot of damn cattle!'

The boat rode uneasily in the inshore swell while the weary sailors fell across their oars and sucked gratefully at the damp air. The pinnace moved out of the gloom and lay close by, and then the cutter crossed to the other side and paddled nearer so that Midshipman Maynard could make himself heard.

'What shall we do, Mr. Herrick?'

'Lie here for a bit!' Herrick spoke slowly to give himself time to sort out his hazy ideas. He wished Maynard would not sound so lost and bewildered in front of his men. Things were already bad enough. He added, 'Where is Mr. Parker and the jolly boat?'

Maynard shrugged, and Packwood, the boatswain's mate, called quickly from the pinnace, 'We've lost sight of him long since, Mr. Herrick!'

Herrick controlled his reply with an effort. 'Maybe he turned back?'

A seaman murmured, 'Sunk more likely!'

Herrick made up his mind. 'Come alongside! But get some fenders out!'

He waited, holding his breath as the two boats sidled against the launch. At each creak and thud he expected to hear shouts from ashore, or the ominous rattle of musket fire. But only the wind and the hissing spray interrupted his words as Maynard and Packwood craned to hear him.

'If we pull around the point we shall be too late to make an attack.'

Maynard muttered petulantly, 'We were given too far to row in my opinion. It was impossible from the start!'

Herrick snarled, 'No one is asking for your opinion, so just listen to me will you?' Herrick was surprised at the savagery in his own voice but hurried on, 'There should be a bit of foreshore below the point, so we'll head for it now. Mr. Packwood will wait with half a crew per boat and lie as close as possible to the rocks.' He waited, feeling the tension dragging at his patience. 'Understand?'

They nodded doubtfully and he continued, 'Mr. Maynard will accompany me ashore with thirty men. If we scale the point we should be able to see down the other side. If the *Andiron* is still there we might try an attack even now, especially if she looks peaceful enough and is close to the headland. Otherwise we will head back to the picking-up area.' He had a brief picture of Vibart's scorn and rage when he returned to announce the failure of the attack. He again felt the same unreasonable anger at the mission. The admiral should have sent a heavier force. Even the *Cassius* would have helped just by adding her strength and availability for the final withdrawal.

Perhaps it was his own fault after all. If he had not trusted Vibart's complacency and had checked the distance from the shore more carefully. If only he had allowed for the change of wind and the savage offshore drift. He shook himself angrily. It was too late now. The present was all that counted.

But he still found time to imagine Bolitho in these circumstances. The mental picture of that impassive face helped to steady him and he said in a level voice, 'Bear off and head for the rocks. But not a sound, *any* of you!'

One by one the boats moved inshore, and when almost hemmed in by dark-fanged rocks the first men leapt slipping and cursing into shallow water.

There was no point in trying to split the party into groups now, Herrick decided. It would take too long, and they had taken enough chances already. He watched the three boats move clear and then snapped, 'Mr. Maynard, come with me. McIntosh will take charge down here.' He groped through his mind to remember the carefully listed names. 'Allday and Martin follow me!'

Allday seemed a capable man, and Martin, who had once earned a rare living as a Dorset poacher, was as nimble and quiet as a rabbit.

As they climbed in silence up the steeply sloping cliff Herrick again thought of Bolitho and his dashing attack on Mola Island. There he had had to deal with every sort of danger, yet he had succeeded at the cost of his own life. Compared with Mola Island this escapade was nothing, he thought grimly.

And why had he made a point of suggesting an alternative to the attack? Was he perhaps already preparing to slip away to the waiting *Phalarope* without even attempting to complete the mission?

He stumbled and almost fell to the rocks below, but a hand seized his wrist and he heard Allday say, 'You must watch this sort of cliff, sir! It feels secure, but the stones are only caked in soil. There's no real grip in them.'

Herrick stared at him. Of course, Allday had been a shepherd as well as a sailor. After Cornwall's rocky cliffs and hills this was probably child's play to him.

As if reading his thoughts Allday murmured, 'Many's the time I've been down this sort of thing after a wandering lamb.'

They both froze into silence as Martin hissed, 'Sir! There's a sentry up yonder!'

Herrick stared. 'Where? Are you sure, man?'

Martin nodded vehemently. 'Thirty yards or so over there! I heard his boots. *There*!' His eyes gleamed excitedly. 'Did you hear 'em?'

'Yes, I did.' Herrick sank down on a ledge of wet grass. A sentry up here. What was the point of it? No man could see much beyond the edge of the cliff at night-time. He said, 'We'll crawl closer and take a look!'

Holding their weapons clear of the treacherous stones they wriggled across the side of the headland, their eyes smarting from straining and watching.

Herrick said at length, 'Martin, get away to the left. Allday, take the seaward side.' He watched them crawl away. 'We'll push on up this slope, Mr. Maynard. I feel that something is not quite right here.'

Allday came back first, his body bent double as he ran quickly from bush to bush. 'The *Andiron*'s there right enough, sir! She's just on the other side of the point. She's in complete darkness. Not a light or a sound from her!'

Maynard muttered, 'They must be damn confident!'

Allday said, 'The crew could be ashore, sir.'

'Unlikely.' Herrick tried to find the cause of his uncertainty. 'Their anchorage must be a good one.' He stiffened and then relaxed as Martin slithered down the slope on his scrawny buttocks.

Martin waited to regain his breath. 'Them's soldiers up there, sir!'

'What are they doing?' Herrick forced himself to remain calm.

'Sleepin' by the looks of it, sir!' Martin picked a thorn from his bare foot. 'They'm got a sentry at each end, but the rest is just lyin' about.' He shrugged. 'Sleepin' like I said!' He sounded scornful.

Herrick asked sharply, 'What did you mean, Martin, "at each end"?'

'Oh, I forgot, sir.' Martin grinned. 'They've got six pieces of artillery along the side of the cliff.'

Herrick felt strangely relaxed. Not knowing the odds was always worse than actually facing them. Almost to himself he said, 'Just two sentries, you say?'

Martin nodded. 'Aye, sir. An' about thirty men lyin' beside the guns.' He chuckled. 'I could'a cut their throats easily!'

Herrick said, 'You may have to.' Suddenly it was quite clear what he had to do. The *Andiron* slept at anchor because she was well protected by firmly mounted field pieces. No doubt each gun was already loaded and ranged to cover the whole anchorage. It was not an uncommon arrangement where no proper harbour was available.

He felt suddenly cold at the thought of what would have happened if his boats had made their planned attack. The casualties and the noise would have killed any chance of success.

He said flatly, 'Get to the beach, Mr. Maynard. Send every available man up here as fast as you can. Anchor the boats and let the remaining men swim ashore. Tell McIntosh and the others that I intend to rush the guns and put 'em out of action. Then we'll take to the boats and go for the *Andiron* as planned!'

They all watched him in silence. Then Maynard said, 'And you, sir?'

Herrick patted Martin's shoulder. 'Our poacher is going to earn his keep tonight, Mr. Maynard!'

Martin pulled a knife from his belt and handed his heavy cutlass to Allday. He said cheerfully, 'Easy, sir! It don't seen fair, do it?'

When Martin and Maynard had slithered back into the darkness Herrick said quietly, 'Those soldiers must be silenced as they sleep. Killed or clubbed, I don't care. But they must be kept from raising the alarm!'

Allday winced as Maynard's dirk clattered on a rock below and then said, 'It's them or us, isn't it, sir?'

'How is your arm, Mr. Belsey?' Bolitho heard the master's mate move somewhere in the pitch darkness and knew he had asked the question merely to break the nerve-jarring silence. With Belsey and Farquhar he had been hustled below and locked unceremoniously in a tiny unused storeroom somewhere beneath the *Andiron*'s forecastle, and after a short attempt at conversation each man had lapsed into silence and the apprehension of his own thoughts.

Belsey said, 'Fair enough, sir. But this motion is makin' me sweat!'

The ship's uneasy movement had certainly increased even during the last hour. The storeroom was below the *Andiron*'s water-line, and the savage jarring of the anchored hull was all the more apparent. The crew had already paid out more hawse to compensate for the sudden change of wind which now swept across the once protected anchorage with mounting ferocity.

Belsey added, 'Maybe the *Phalarope* will stand out to sea agin, sir? Surely they'll not send boats out in this lot?'

Bolitho was glad the others could not see his face. A change of weather would make little difference to Vibart's determination to produce a victory, he thought. From the moment the signal had been flashed down the hillside to the hidden defenders he had felt a growing despair, the fretting certainty of calamity and destruction for the *Phalarope* and her company. And he was powerless to help a single man.

He felt a sudden pressure at his shoulders as the ship heeled in a deep swell. She was snubbing at her cable at regular intervals now, and he could feel the deck lifting and then sliding back with each shuddering jerk.

He found himself thinking again of his brother, and wondered what he was doing at this moment. His earlier eagerness at the proposed massacre of *Phalarope*'s boarding party must have given way a little to the anxiety for his own ship's safety. At any other time he would have made sail and headed for the more sheltered side of the island. It was strange how the unexpected change of weather had taken a part in the game. Not that it could have any final effect. It merely prolonged the misery of waiting.

Farquhar said absently, 'I wish something would happen! This waiting is getting on my nerves!'

Bolitho shifted his position to stare at the brightly lit crack in the storeroom door. Occasionally a shadow blotted out the tiny sliver of light as a sentry moved his position in the narrow passageway beyond. As he rearranged his cramped limbs Bolitho felt the warm touch of steel against his leg and remembered the hidden dirk. For all the use it was now he could have left it in the cabin, he thought wearily.

It was strange that the guards had not bothered to search him. But they were so openly confident, and with such good reason, that it was only to be expected. Even his brother had found time to see him just as he was being led below to the storeroom.

Hugh Bolitho had been wearing their father's sword, as well as a brace of pistols, and seemed to have gained new life and excitement from the impending battle.

'Well, Richard. This is your last chance.' He had stood easily on the swaying deck, his head on one side as he had watched his brother with something like amusement. 'Just one decision, and it is yours to make!'

'I have nothing to say to you. Not now. Not ever!' Bolitho had tried not to stare at the sword. It had been like a final insult.

'Very well. After this I may see little of you. I will have much to do.' He had stared up at the angry sky. 'The wind is rising, but I expect to have visitors none the less!' He had added in a harder tone, 'You will have to take your chances with the French authorities. I must take *Andiron* to join the combined fleets.'

He had seen his brother's immediate caution and had continued calmly, 'I can tell you now, Richard. For you will be unable to take part. The French admiral, de Grasse, will join with a Spanish squadron. Together with our ships they will attack Jamaica.' He had made a curt gesture as if to demonstrate the finality of the campaign. 'I am afraid King George will have to find fresh fields to conquer elsewhere!'

Bolitho had said to his guard, 'I wish to go below.'

His brother had called after him, 'You are foolish, Richard. And what is worse, you are *wrong*!'

As he sat in the swaying storeroom Bolitho found plenty of time to relive the bitterness and the sense of defeat.

There was a scraping of metal as the bolts were drawn from the door, and Belsey groaned. 'Comin' to gloat again! God rot their bloody souls!'

But as the lamplight flooded the storeroom and seared their eyes Bolitho could only stare with surprise. Stockdale stood blinking in the doorway, a heavy boarding axe swinging from his hand.

Bolitho struggled to his feet and then caught sight of the sentry sprawled below the swinging lantern, the back of his head smashed in like an eggshell.

Stockdale said humbly, 'I am sorry it took me so long, Captain! But I had to win their confidence.' He grinned sheepishly. 'Even now I'm not sure I done as you expected.'

Bolitho could hardly speak. He gripped the man's massive arm and muttered, 'You did rightly, Stockdale. Have no fear of that!' To the others he said, 'Are you with me?'

Farquhar replied dazedly, 'Just tell me what to do, sir!'

'Quick, Stockdale!' Bolitho stepped into the passageway and peered into the darkness beyond the lantern. 'Tell me what is happening!'

The ex-prizefighter answered thickly, 'They're getting worried up top, sir. No sign of an attack, an' the ship's taking the wind badly.' He thought for a moment. 'Maybe we could swim for the beach, sir?' He nodded with rare excitement. 'Yes, we could do it with luck!'

Bolitho shook his head. 'Not yet. They will be watching like hawks. We must not think of ourselves. We must try to save the *Phalarope* before it is too late!'

Stockdale glanced at the corpse by his feet. 'They change the guard in half an hour, sir. There's not much time!'

'I see.' Bolitho tried to stifle the excitement and urgency in his mind and think more clearly. 'We cannot fight the whole crew, but with luck we might still surprise them!'

Belsey said, 'I'd like to take a few of the buggers with me!'

Bolitho drew the dirk from his breeches and held it glinting in the lamplight. 'Lead the way, Stockdale. If we can get to the forecastle there is something which we can do to provide a diversion!'

Farquhar picked up the dead guard's cutlass and murmured bleakly, 'Are you thinking of the cable, sir?'

Bolitho shot him a swift glance of approval. 'The ship is already dragging hard at her anchor. If we could cut the cable she would be in serious danger. Our men are out there somewhere, and they will soon pull clear when they see *Andiron* drifting towards the point!'

Belsey broke in excitedly, 'The *Andiron*'ll have to make sail, sir! Even then she might not be in time! She'll run hard aground with the wind in this quarter.'

'Begging your pardon, sir.' Stockdale looked at Bolitho sadly. 'They've already got a strong anchor party in the bows looking out for trouble!'

Bolitho smiled coldly. 'I'm not surprised.' He gestured to the others. 'Come, we have little time.' As they crept along the passageway he added, 'Remember that nine-pounder on the forecastle, Mr. Farquhar?'

Farquhar nodded, his eyes gleaming. 'Yes, sir. One of the bow-chasers!'

Bolitho paused below a narrow ladder, straining his eyes towards the hatch above. It might just work. They would all die for their efforts, but he knew that each man now understood that well enough.

He said quietly, 'The gun was lashed there while the rail was being repaired from *Phalarope*'s mauling. If it were cut loose now, in this gale, it would run amuck like a maddened bullock!'

Belsey sucked his teeth. 'My God! A nine-pounder weighs well over a ton! It'd take a bit of holding down!'

Bolitho said, 'If I cut the lashings, Stockdale, could you . . .?'

The man grinned down at him. 'Say no more, Captain!' He swung the heavy axe. 'Just a few minutes is all I'd need!'

'A few minutes are all you'll get, my lad!' Bolitho eased himself up the ladder and peered through the hatch. Again the whole deck area was deserted. He stared up the next and final ladder and then said. 'You can stay behind, Belsey. You can't fight with one arm.'

'Nor can I sit an' do nothin', sir!' Belsey eyed him stubbornly. 'Never mind me, sir. I can still do a bit.'

Any sound made by their stealthy footsteps was drowned by the creak of spars and the thrumming rattle of shrouds and rigging. Bolitho peered quickly at the nearest line of lashed guns and the shadowed shapes of their crews. Most of the men were lying on the deck or resting against the bulwark, and only a few were still on their feet. And they were watching outboard, their eyes only just raised above the hammock nettings.

Bolitho saw the solitary nine-pounder, its long outline jutting aft towards the maindeck. He could hear it creaking gently, as if angered by the lashings which held it tethered and impotent beside the capstan.

Bolitho brushed the sweat from his eyes and cursed the painful beating of his heart against his ribs. It was now or never. At any moment they would be seen for what they were and the gesture would have been in vain. While the others watched him with fixed fascination he stood up and sauntered openly towards the gun. Then he seated himself noisily on the deck and folded his arms across his chest as if trying to sleep.

Farquhar said between his teeth, 'God, look at him! Surely one of those men will realise who he is?'

But the very openness of Bolitho's movements seemed to have killed any immediate interest, and while the *Andiron* rolled from one sickening arc to another the ship's forecastle remined quiet and undisturbed.

Belsey turned on his side by the hatch coaming and croaked, 'Look! There's an officer coming!'

They watched in stricken silence as the blue and white shape of a ship's lieutenant made its way slowly forward from the maindeck towards the forecastle ladder. The officer had to pause half-way up the ladder as a heavier squall than usual struck the ship's side with a crash of spray which made the foremast vibrate like a young tree.

Then Stockdale who had turned his gaze back to Bolitho said, 'He's done it!'

As the frigate's bows lifted and yawed against her anchor cable the nine-pounder began to move. At first the movement was hardly noticeable, then with its small chocks squealing it thundered down the full length of the forecastle to smash with shivering force against the foot of the foremast.

Everyone was yelling and shouting at once. Some of the shouts changed to cries of fear as the gun swung malevolently as if controlled by invisible hands and then charged crazily back across the sloping deck.

The lieutenant called, 'You men! Get handspikes and fresh lashing! Lively there, or it'll smash through the side!'

The anchor watch rose from their concealed positions and ran back from the bows to join the stampede of men at the break of the forecastle. In the centre of the confusion, jubilant and deadly, the long nine-pounder turned its muzzle as if to sniff out new havoc, and then careered squeaking and rumbling towards the opposite side. It crashed against another gun and scattered a shot rack like loose pebbles. The rolling cannon balls added to the pandemonium, and some could be heard thudding on to the deck below.

A braver seaman than some leapt across the gun's breech, his hands already fastening a rope's eye around the muzzle. But as the gun trundled back again he screamed and fell against the bulwark to receive the twenty-six hundredweight of wood and metal full on his chest.

Bolitho seized Farquhar's arm and snapped, 'Look! They've got a wedge under the carriage! We've not long now.'

Even as he spoke some of the seamen around the gun turned and stared, their expressions of shock and disbelief changing to cold fury. Bolitho and his two companions slowly retreated towards the bows, the wind and sea at their backs, a converging mass of men driving towards them, all the more terrible because of their complete silence.

Then, to break the spell, a man bellowed, 'Kill them! Cut the bastards down!'

Pressed on by the men behind, the whole mob swept forward, only to sway to an uncertain halt as something like a gunshot echoed around the deck, followed instantly by Stockdale's great shout of triumph.

'It's parted! The cable's cut!'

For a moment longer the *Andiron*'s seamen stared at one another, and then as the realisation of their unexpected peril dawned on their minds they hesitated no longer. An officer was yelling from the maindeck, and the cry was carried forward by men who had still managed to keep their heads.

'Hands aloft! Hands aloft! Loose tops'ls!'

From aft Bolitho heard his brother's voice magnified and hardened by his speaking trumpet. 'Man the wheel there!' And then as the ship trembled from stem to stern like a released animal he shouted, 'Mr. Faulkner! Drive those men to the braces!'

Bolitho leaned against the rail, the dirk still held across his body as the frigate heeled still further and began to fall away. Men were running wildly up the shrouds, and already a small patch of canvas was billowing and flapping against the dark sky.

The speaking trumpet called again. 'Cover those men on the fo'c's'le! Shoot them down if they try to escape!'

Belsey wiped his forehead and muttered, 'If our lads *is* out there they'll not want to try an' board!' He peered at Bolitho's tense face. 'I can die in peace now, sir! I reckon we did right well tonight!'

Bolitho saw his face light up with a bright orange glow, and as he turned in surprise the air around him seemed to come alive with the searing whine of gunshot. Stays and halyards parted, and beyond his feet the deck planking splintered and cracked as a thousand balls swept across the forepart of the ship.

Farquhar pointed. 'Look! The battery has fired on us!' He waved his hat. 'The stupid fools have fired on their own men!'

Bolitho pulled him down. 'And us! So keep your head lowered, Mr. Farquhar. You may have use for it still!'

There was no further gunfire, but the one, carefully loaded salvo was sufficient. The prompt action by the *Andiron*'s officers and the quick response of her more level-headed sailors might have taken her clear of danger. But as the whining barrage of grapeshot swept her shrouds and yards free of men and cut down some of the hands still cramming her maindeck, the last opportunity was lost. The black outline of Dogwood Point appeared to grow double in size until the ship was dwarfed beneath it. Even then it looked as if the wind and tide would carry her clear, but as Bolitho pulled his gaping companions to the deck the *Andiron* gave a long-drawn-out shudder, followed instantly by a tremendous crash which threw the remaining seamen from their feet.

Belsey stared up at the sky and crossed himself. 'The main-mast is fallin'! My God, so is the mizzen!'

Fascinated, Bolitho watched the two great masts shiver and then bow very slowly towards the starboard side. Then as stays parted and the angle became more acute the masts thundered down in a flapping tangle of spars and torn sails to plunge eventually into the white-crested water alongside.

Another crash and yet another shook the hull, and while the deck tilted more and more towards the sea Bolitho dragged himself to his feet and shouted, 'She's hard on the sandbar! She'll break her back and capsize in minutes!'

He could hear guns tearing themselves from their lashings and charging across the deck to carve through the screaming, struggling remnants of their late masters. There was no hope of lowering a boat, and nobody even attempted it. Already some were leaping overboard, to be swept away instantly in the strong current. Others ran below as if to find safety in the darkness, and all around voices cried and pleaded, threatened and cursed as their ship broke up beneath them.

The foremast splintered some four feet from the deck and followed the rest into the sea. From a trim frigate the *Andiron* was changed into a lolling, dismasted hulk, already a thing of ugliness and horror.

Belsy shouted above the din, 'There's a hatch cover, sir! Look, floating by the bowsprit!' He watched Bolitho wildly. 'We could jump for it!'

Bolitho turned to watch as the deck shivered yet again and another released gun charged through a group of crawling seamen. Then he saw his brother standing alone by the quarterdeck rail, his body appearing to be at a forty-five-degree angle on the heeling deck. He was not calling any more, but was standing quite motionless, as if to share the agony of his ship to the last.

For a moment longer Bolitho stared towards him, separated from the other man by far more than a length of deck. He could feel a sudden surge of understanding, even pity, knowing full well how he himself would have felt at such a time.

Then he said sharply, 'Over you go, lads! Jump well clear!'

Belsey and Farquhar leaped together, and he saw them struggling towards the listing square of timber. Stockdale said hoarsely, 'Here, Captain, I'll jump with you!'

As he gripped the rail Bolitho heard a cry behind him and got a vague glimpse of an officer dragging himself up the canting deck towards him. He saw blood on the man's face and recognised him as the lieutenant who had shared his lonely captivity on the poop. The man who had spoken of his farm and the impossible freedom of peace.

Then he saw the pistol in the lieutenant's hand, and even as he tried to pull himself over the rail the deck lit up with a blinding flash, and something like a white-hot iron exploded across his ribs.

Stockdale tore his eyes from Bolitho and gave a short, animal cry. It was as if it had been torn from his very soul. With all his strength he cleaved outwards with his axe, the force of the blow almost decapitating the American officer, so that the man seemed to bow forward in a grisly salute.

Bolitho was vaguely aware of being gathered bodily in Stockdale's arms and then falling through the air. His lungs were bursting and his throat was filled with salt water, and when he tried to open his eyes there was only stinging darkness.

Then he was being hauled up and across the little raft, and he heard Belsey gasp, 'Oh the bloody bastards! They've done for the captain!'

Then Farquhar's voice, shaking but determined. 'For God's sake watch out! There's a boat! Keep down and stay silent!'

Bolitho tried to speak, but could only stare up at Stockdale's misty face framed against the low, scudding clouds. He could hear oars, the swish of a boat cutting through water. But captivity or death were not in vain. Not this time! He listened to the distant boom of surf across the wrecked frigate, the small cries of those who still clung to the shattered hull.

Then, as if from right overhead he heard a sharp cry followed instantly by the click of a flintlock. It was still a dream, and nothing seemed to affect him personally. Only when a loud, English voice called, 'Them's some of the devils down in th' water, sir!' did the slow realisation begin to break through the mist and the pain.

Farquhar stood up yelling, 'Don't shoot! Don't shoot, we're English!'

Then everyone seemed to be shouting at once, and as another boat pulled nearby Bolitho heard one familiar voice as if from far away.

'Who have you got there, Mr. Farquhar?' Herrick's question was shaking with emotion, as if he still mistrusted what he saw.

Farquhar replied, 'It's the captain!'

Bolitho felt hands lifting him up over the gunwale, and saw distorted faces swooping above him in vague, unreal patterns. Hands moved across his ribs, and there was the stabbing fire of fresh pain. Then the muffling comfort of a bandage, and all the time the excited chatter of the men around him. . . . His men.

Herrick had his face very close, so that Bolitho could see the brightness in his eyes. Somehow he wanted to say something, to reassure Herrick, to make him understand.

But he could no longer find the strength even for that. Instead he squeezed Herrick's hand, and then allowed the waiting darkness to gather him in like a cloak.

12

'Confusion to Our Enemies!'

The high afternoon sun blazed down on the sheltered water and threw a dancing pattern of reflections across the deckhead above Bolitho's small desk. Just by turning his head he could see the lush green hillsides of Antigua and a few scattered dwellings around the smooth stretch of St. John's harbour. He had to force himself back to his task of completing his report in readiness for the admiral's scrutiny.

He leaned his forehead against the palm of his hand, feeling the weakness moving through his veins, willing him to rest, to do anything but attend to the waiting duties and orders. Beneath his shirt he could feel the stiff embrace of the bandage, and allowed his mind to move back in time, as he had done so often since his unexpected return to the *Phalarope*.

Like everything else which had happened, it was difficult to separate fact from vague delirious pictures which had come and gone with the stabbing agony of his wound. By the merest chance the pistol ball had passed cleanly between his ribs, leaving a deep and ragged scar which made him wince with every sudden movement.

From the moment he had been dragged aboard the frigate and the boats had been hastily hoisted on deck his memory was blurred and disjointed. The savage and unheralded storm had only helped to add to the nightmare quality of his recollections, and for two weeks the ship had driven south-west ahead of the screaming wind, unable to do other than run before it under all but bare spars. Then as he had struggled to avoid the surgeon's clumsy care and the vague comings and goings of his officers, the wind had moderated and *Phalarope* had at last gone about to beat her way back to Antigua and make her report.

He stared down at the carefully listed descriptions and the mentions of individual names. Nothing must be left out. There was never time for second thoughts.

Each name brought back a different memory and gave him the strange sensation of being an onlooker.

Midshipman Charles Farquhar, who had behaved in a manner far exceeding his actual experience and authority and in the best interests of the Service. A sea-officer who would one day merit senior command.

Arthur Belsey, master's mate, who in spite of his injured arm did everything possible to assist the final destruction of the *Andiron*.

Bolitho tapped his pen thoughtfully against Belsey's name. That last wild leap to safety from the *Andiron*'s shattered hull had finished any hope he might have had for return to proper duty. His broken arm was now beyond repair, and he would be a weakened cripple for the rest of his life. With luck, a good mention in the report, plus Bolitho's commendation, might ensure his quick discharge with some suitable recognition for his long service. He would probably return to Plymouth and open a small inn there, Bolitho thought sadly. Every seaport was full of such men, broken and forgotten, but still clinging to the fringe of the sea which had discarded them.

Of Lieutenant Herrick's assault on the artillery there was little to add to the bare facts. If he had tried to embroider the truth, to give Herrick more of the praise which he so richly deserved, the admiral would be quick to see the other side of the coin. That it was largely luck, added to a goodly portion of impudence.

There were so many 'ifs', Bolitho thought moodily.

If the cutting-out party had been dropped closer inshore every man would be either dead or imprisoned. If the tide had not been too strong for Herrick's oarsmen he would have pressed on with his impossible mission, instead of taking the secondary path of his own making.

And what of Stockdale? Without his aid and unshaken loyalty none of these things would have come about at all. In his fight-dulled brain he had worked out each careful move, unaided and without guidance of anyone. And again his last action had been to save Bolitho's life.

But what could he do for him? There was no promotion open to him, no reward which made any sense. Once when he had pattered into the cabin to tend to Bolitho's wound he had asked the giant seaman what he would most cherish as payment for his bravery and his devotion.

Stockdale had not even hesitated. 'I'd like to go on serving you, Captain. I don't have no other wish!'

Bolitho had been considering the idea of getting Stockdale discharged ashore as soon as the ship returned to an English port. There with a little help he might be able to settle down to live his life in peace and security. But as what? Stockdale's prompt and simple reply had driven the suggestion from his mind. It would only have hurt the man.

He wrote: 'And of my coxswain, Mark Stockdale, I can only add that without his prompt action the entire mission might have ended in failure. By cutting the *Andiron*'s cable and thereby allowing her to drift beneath Lieutenant Herrick's fire he ensured the total and complete destruction of the ship with a minimum loss to our own side.' He signed his name wearily across the bottom and stood up. Pages of writing. It was to be hoped that they would be read by those unbiased against the *Phalarope*'s name.

At least Farquhar's uncle, Vice-Admiral Sir Henry Langford, would be pleased. His faith would be sustained, and given time his hopes for his nephew would certainly materialise.

Bolitho leaned out of the stern window and let the warm air caress his face. He could hear the creak of tackles and the steady splash of oars as boats plied back and forth to the shore. The ship had dropped anchor in the early morning, and all day the boats had been busy gathering fresh stores and taking the wounded to more comfortable quarters in the town.

He watched the impressive line of anchored ships, the growing might of the West Indies fleet. Perhaps their presence had dwarfed what might have otherwise been a triumphant return for the *Phalarope*. He frowned at his recurring thought. Maybe the *Phalarope* was still to be treated with shame and mistrust?

Bolitho let his eyes move slowly along the great ships with their towering masts and lines of open gunports. There was the *Formidable*, ninety-eight, fresh out of England with Sir George Rodney's flag at her truck. There were others too, their names already well known in the face of war. *Ajax* and *Resolution*, *Agamemnon* and *Royal Oak*, and Sir Samuel Hood's flagship *Barfleur*. And there were some he did not recognise at all, no doubt reinforcements brought by Rodney from the Channel Fleet. And they were all gathering for one purpose. To seek out and destroy the great French and Spanish fleet before it in turn drove the British from the Caribbean for good.

He turned his head to look towards his own small squadron on the other side of the anchorage. The elderly *Cassius* dwarfing the little *Witch of Looe*. And one other frigate, the *Volcano*, a vessel very similar to the *Phalarope*.

There was still no summons from the admiral. Just a brief message brought by a pink-faced midshipman to state that Bolitho's report was required before sunset. The frigate was to complete reprovisioning and await further orders. Nothing more.

Nothing more until something even stranger had happened.

Half-way through the forenoon a boat had put off from the *Cassius* and within minutes a dapper lieutenant had reported himself to Bolitho. He had said, 'Rear-Admiral Sir Robert Napier sends his compliments, sir. He wishes to inform you that he will be willing to accept an invitation for dinner tonight aboard your ship. He will be bringing our captain as an additional guest.' The officer had watched the consternation on Bolitho's features and had added helpfully, 'Is there anything I can do to help, sir?'

Bolitho had been stunned by the wording of the message. It was unusual for flag officers to dine aboard their less impressive ships. It was *unknown* for them actually to word their own invitations!

Bolitho had thought of his dwindling provisions and the crude results produced from the galley.

The lieutenant from the *Cassius* had obviously been well briefed. 'If I may make a suggestion, sir?'

Bolitho stared at him. 'Anything you can say would be a great help at this moment.'

'My captain is sending some stores from his own pantry, sir. In addition there will be some quite drinkable wine arriving within the hour.' He had ticked off the items on his fingers, his face wrapped in thought. Bolitho had guessed that the young man was not unused to the strange behaviour of his admiral. 'If I may suggest some lean pork, sir? It is in goodly supply in St. John's, and the cheese is newly arrived with Admiral Rodney's ships from England.'

Bolitho had sent for Vibart and the purser, Evans, and explained what was due to happen. For once Vibart seemed too surprised to make any comment, and Bolitho had said curtly, 'See to it, Mr. Vibart. And tell my servant to clean out the cabin and lay a full table.' He had felt suddenly reckless. 'Sir Robert Napier must not expect a flagship's fare aboard a mere frigate!'

Now, looking back, he knew that the momentary recklessness was more likely to have been a result of too much sun on the open quarterdeck and the weakening pain of his wound.

Well, it could not be helped. It was more than obvious what the admiral intended. With Rodney back at the reins he would not wish to lambast *Phalarope* in public. He would not even risk an open argument aboard his own flagship. No, he would come to the *Phalarope* in person, like God coming down to smite a sinner, Bolitho thought bitterly. No success would wipe away his first displeasure or recompense his son's death. If the *Andiron* lay under guard beneath the guns of his own flagship the admiral might have felt differently. But the privateer was now less than nothing. A mere pencilled mark on a chart.

Bolitho sat down heavily on the stern bench, suddenly tired and irritable. He stared at the waiting report and then called, 'Sentry! Pass the word for Mr. Herrick!'

The report could go across to *Cassius* now, he thought angrily. Whatever else happened, he wanted to make sure that his men received recognition and had their efforts properly recorded.

Herrick entered the cabin and stood alertly beside the desk. 'Take this envelope over to the flagship.' Bolitho saw the immediate concern on Herrick's open face and became more irritated. Try as he might he could not keep the dullness from his voice, and knew that in spite of all his efforts his fatigue was wearing him down, so that every word seemed to drag from his lips.

Herrick said carefully, 'May I suggest that you take a rest, sir? I think you have been doing too much.'

'Kindly attend to your duties, damn you!' Bolitho looked away, angry with Herrick but more so with himself for the unfairness of his attack.

'Aye, aye, sir.' Herrick seemed unmoved and said, 'May I ask if this is the full report about the *Andiron*, sir?'

Bolitho turned coldly. 'Of course it is! Were you afraid I'd not included your efforts in this escapade?'

Herrick eyed him steadily. 'I am sorry, sir. It's just that—' He swallowed hard. 'Well, we feel, those of us who took part,' he began to stammer. 'You are the one who should take all the credit, sir!'

Bolitho looked at the deck, the blood singing in his ears. 'You have a happy knack of making me feel ashamed, Mr. Herrick. I would be obliged if you would refrain from doing so in the future!' He looked up sharply, remembering with sudden clarity the sound of Herrick's voice in the darkness, the touch of his hands on his wound. 'But thank you.' He walked slowly to the desk. 'The attack on the *Andiron* was a series of lucky occurrences, Mr. Herrick. The end result may seem to some to justify this. But I must admit that I am still dissatisfied. I believe in luck, but I know that no man can *depend* upon it!'

'Yes, sir.' Herrick watched him closely. 'I just wanted you to know how we all feel.' His jaw jutted stubbornly. 'Whatever lies in store for us, we'll feel all the better for your being in command, sir.'

Bolitho ruffled the papers on his desk. 'Thank you. Now for God's sake go to the *Cassius*, Mr. Herrick.' He watched Herrick duck through the door and heard his voice calling for the quarter boat.

It was odd how easy it was to tell his fears to Herrick. Stranger too that Herrick was able to listen without taking advantage of this confidence.

His eye fell on the punishment book, and again he felt the tired glow of anger. While he had been a prisoner of his own brother the old disease had broken out again. Floggings and more floggings, with one man dying of his agony under the lash. Maybe there would be time to heal the damage, he thought grimly. He must accept Vibart's sullen explanations, just as he had had to recognise Okes' report on the attack on Mola Island. He must back up his own officers. And if they were weak and stupid, then *he* must take the blame for that also.

He thought too of Vibart's attitude since his return to command. Due to his wound and the swirling darkness of pain and sickness he had not seen his face at the actual moment of return. But in the days which had followed, the days and nights of creaking timbers and thundering seas against the hull, he had seen him several times. Once when he had been delirious and sweating in his swaying cot he had seen Vibart standing over him and had heard him ask, 'Will he live? Tell me, Mr. Ellice, will he *live?*'

Perhaps he had only imagined it. It was hard to tell now. But for a brief moment he was sure he had heard the true resentment in Vibart's voice. He wanted him to die. Just as his return from the dead was still leaving him resentful and bitter.

The door opened and Stockdale said throatily, 'I've told Atwell to lay out your best uniform, sir. And he'll be in here shortly to prepare the table.' He stared at Bolitho's worn features and then said flatly, 'You'll be taking a rest now, I expect?'

Bolitho glared at him. 'I have *work* to do, damn you!'

Stockdale said, 'I'll just turn your cot down. A couple of hours until the Dog Watches will do you a power of good.' He ignored Bolitho's expression and added cheerfully, 'I see the *Formidable*'s here, sir! She's a fine big ship an' no mistake! But then you'd need a big ship to hold an admiral like Rodney!' He stood a moment longer, one hand resting on the cot. 'Are you ready now, sir?'

Bolitho gave in. 'Well, just two hours. No more.'

He allowed Stockdale to help him into the cot and felt the tiredness closing in on him once more. Stockdale picked up his shoes and said to himself, 'You rest there. We'll need a good captain tonight to meet the bloody admiral!'

As he turned Stockdale's eye fell on Bolitho's empty rack above the cot, and for a moment he felt strangely unnerved. The sword was back there somewhere in the wrecked *Andiron*. If only he could have got it back. If only . . .

He stared down at Bolitho's face relaxed in sleep. And he wanted to do something for *me*! He pulled the curtain to shade Bolitho's face from the reflected sunlight and then ambled slowly towards the door.

The tall stone jetty threw a welcome rectangle of dark shade across the *Phalarope's* cutter as it rested easily alongside the steps. Packwood, the boatswain's mate, paused at the top of the steps and looked down at the lolling seamen in the boat. 'You can take a break. But nobody leaves the cutter, got it?'

Onslow squatted comfortably on the gunwale and pulled a short clay pipe from his shirt. Under his breath he murmured, 'Right, Mr. bloody Packwood! We do all the work, and you go off an' fill your belly with rum!'

Most of the other men were too weary to comment. All day they had pulled the cutter back and forth to the anchored frigate, the first excitement of seeing a friendly port again soon giving way to grumbling complaint.

Packwood was in charge of their party, and although a capable man and considered to be fair in his allocation of work, was plagued by a complete lack of imagination. If he had told the men that the work was essential, not only to the *Phalarope*'s efficiency, but more important, to the welfare of the crew once she returned to sea, some of the bitterness might have been dulled. As it was, Packwood had been too long in the Navy to seek for unnecessary explanations to anything. Work was work. Orders would be carried out at all times without question.

Pook, Onslow's constant companion, raised himself on his scrawny legs and peered towards the distant houses. He breathed out slowly. 'Mother of God! I kin see women!'

Onslow grimaced. 'What did you expect? Bloody clergymen?' He watched the men from beneath lowered lids. 'The officers will be doing themselves well enough. You see if I'm not right, lads!' He spat over the side. 'But just one of you try an' lay a little foot on the shore an' see what happens!' He gestured towards a red-coated marine who was leaning contentedly on his grounded musket. 'That bloody bullock'll place a ball between your eyes!'

John Allday lay across the oars and watched Onslow thoughtfully. Every word the man spoke seemed to be carefully weighted and fashioned before it was uttered. He turned as another seaman named Ritchie spoke up from the bow.

Ritchie was a slow-thinking Devon man, with an equally slow manner of speech. 'When we was at Nevis Oi didn't see yew runnin' off, Onslow!' He blinked his mild eyes against the glittering water. 'Yew had plenty of time to go an' join your rebel friends!'

Allday watched Onslow, expecting a flash of anger. But the tall seaman merely eyed Ritchie with something like pity. 'An' what good would that do? If I went over to the rebels or to the Frogs, do you think we'd be any better off?' He had their full attention now. 'No, lads. We'd be exchanging one master for another. A fresh flag, but make no mistake, the lash feels the same in any navy!'

Ritchie scratched his head. 'Oi still don't see what yew'm gettin' at!'

Pook sneered, 'That's because you're stupid, you great ox!'

'Easy, lads.' Onslow dropped his voice. 'I meant what I said. Out here or in the Americas a man can live well. A new life, with a chance to make something for himself!' He gave a small smile. 'But to start off right a man needs more than hope. He needs money, too!'

Nick Pochin stirred himself and said uneasily, 'If the war ends an' we gets paid off, we can go back to our homes.'

'And who'll want to remember you there?' Onslow looked down at him coldly. 'You've been away too long, like all the rest of us. There'll be nothing for you but begging on the streets!'

Pochin persisted. 'I was a good ploughman once. I could do it again!'

'Aye, maybe you could.' Onslow watched him closely, his eyes full of contempt. 'You can push your furrow for the rest of your stupid life. Until the furrow is deep enough for some fat squire to bury you in!'

Another voice asked cautiously, 'Well then? What's the point of arguing about it?'

'I'll tell you the point!' Onslow slid from the gunwale like a cat. 'Soon we'll be at sea again. You've seen the fleet mustering here. There'll be no rest for the likes of us. The buggers always need an extra frigate!' He pointed at the *Phalarope* as she swung gently at her anchor. 'There is our chance, lads! The price of our future!' He lowered his voice again. 'We could take the ship.' He spoke very slowly to allow each word to sink in. 'Then we could use her to bargain for our own price!' He looked around their grim faces. 'Just think of it! We could parley with the other side and name our own amount! Then with the money and a free passage we could split up and go our own ways, every one of us richer than he ever thought possible!'

Pochin sat up with a jerk. 'That's mutiny! You mad bugger, we'd all be caught and hanged!'

Onslow grinned. 'Never! After the war is over, who will have time to care about us?'

Pook added gleefully, 'He's right! We'd be rich!'

Allday said, 'And we'd never see England again!'

'And who cares about that?' Onslow threw back his head. 'Do you think we have any chance at present? You saw what they did to Kirk? You've seen men die week by week from disease or the lash. From battle or falling from aloft! And if you escape all that, it's more than likely that you'll get shipped off in some other ship, as *I* was!'

Allday felt a chill at his spine as the uneasiness and resentment moved through the boat like a threat. He said quickly, 'Do you think Captain Bolitho would stand for your ideas?' He looked at the others. 'I've been through the mill, but I trust the captain. He's a brave and fair man. He'll not let us down!'

Onslow shrugged. 'Suit yourself.' He added tightly, 'Just so long as you keep your thoughts *to* yourself, mate! If what I said gets out, we'll know where to come a'hunting!'

There was a scattered murmur of assent from the boat, and Allday realised with sudden shock that Onslow's little speech had already gone deep. It was strange that nobody had noticed before how Onslow had persisted in his efforts to rouse the men to mutiny. Perhaps because his words were carefully chosen and without the blind malice of a wronged sailor. The latter was too common to rouse much more than jeers.

He thought too of Mathias's death in the hold and Onslow's careful manoeuvring to get Ferguson the job as captain's clerk. The pattern was like a slow but deadly disease. When the symptoms came to light the victim was already beyond hope.

He said, 'You'll find me ready enough, Onslow! Just you keep out of *my* way!'

Pochin muttered, 'Watch out! 'E's comin' back!'

Packwood stood at the top of the steps, his face sweating profusely from a hasty tankard of rum. 'Right, my babies! Stand by to take on some more casks!' He swung his rattan casually. 'After this trip you can go to your sty and get cleaned up. The admiral is coming to see you all this evening!'

Pook nudged his friend. 'That Allday! Is he safe?'

Onslow ran his fingers around the loom of his oar. 'The men like him. It must be handled carefully. It needs thinking about.' He watched Allday's naked back rippling in the sunlight. 'But *handled* it must be!'

Punctual to the minute, Rear-Admiral Sir Robert Napier stepped through the *Phalarope's* entry port and removed his hat to receive his due respects. As the shrill pipes faded into silence and the marine guard presented arms the frigate's small drummer, accompanied by two reedy fifes, broke into a frail but jaunty march, and with a final glance around the upperdeck Bolitho stepped forward to meet his admiral.

Sir Robert nodded curtly to the assembled officers, and as the marines banged their muskets to the deck he carried out a brief but searching inspection of the guard, followed at a discreet distance by Rennie and Captain Cope of the *Cassius*.

Bolitho tried to gauge the admiral's mood or his real reason for his visit from the man's profile, but Sir Robert's pinched face remained sphinxlike and unchanging, even when he fired the occasional question or comment to Rennie about the bearing of the marines.

At the end of the double line of men he paused to survey the maindeck. 'You keep a smart ship, Bolitho.' There was nothing in his dry tone to suggest either praise or suspicion.

'Thank you, sir.' Bolitho wished that he was alone aboard the flagship in the great stern cabin. There he could face and deal with anything Sir Robert chose to say. These circumstances kept every comment on a formal and controlled level which made his nerves raw with uncertainty.

Whatever the admiral really thought of the ship, Bolitho was certainly satisfied with her appearance. Long before a frantic messenger had reported a flurry of activity aboard the flagship and the smartly crewed barge had pulled swiftly towards the *Phalarope's* side, Bolitho had been round his ship to make absolutely sure that Sir Robert would find no fault with her at least.

The ship's company had manned the side, every eye on the small-gold-laced figure in the stern of the barge, and now as the admiral stood in silent contemplation there was an atmosphere of nervous expectancy which defied even the fifes and drum on the quarterdeck.

The admiral said, 'You may dismiss the hands, Bolitho.'

At the prearranged signal the men poured from the maindeck, and with a clash of weapons the marines wheeled and followed suit.

Then he said, 'I have read the report, Bolitho. It had a great deal to say.' His wintry eyes drifted across Bolitho's set features. 'I was particularly interested in the part about the *Andiron*'s captain.' He saw Bolitho stiffen and continued calmly, 'As a matter of fact I had received information as to his identity, but I thought it best to let you carry out your task.' He shrugged, the movement painful beneath his heavy uniform. 'Of course, what I did not know was that you were in fact already a prisoner at his hands.'

'And if you had known, sir?' Bolitho tried to keep his tone relaxed.

'I am not sure. Your first lieutenant is apparently capable in many ways, but I fear he will always be a man who takes orders. A *born* subordinate!'

From the corner of his eye Bolitho saw Captain Cope being ushered below by his own officers, and waited for the admiral to continue. He did not have long to wait.

'*Andiron* is finished. Her very existence was a challenge and an insult to every man in our fleet. I have already passed my views on the matter to the Commander in Chief, and I have no doubt you will receive due recognition.' He faced Bolitho squarely. 'However, the fact that your own brother once commanded her and is obviously still alive may in some quarters be taken as some sort of connivance on your part.' He walked to the side and stared at the *Cassius*. 'I do not happen to take that view myself, Bolitho. I gave you the task, not in spite of the *Andiron*'s captain but because of him! You and your ship behaved very well indeed. I have told Sir George Rodney as much.' He added slowly, 'But had your brother been killed it might have been better all round.'

'I think I understand, sir.'

'Of course you do!' The admiral's old testiness was breaking through. 'To be killed is to be forgotten. But if he is taken in the future, he will have no defence. A public trial and hanging will follow. And I think you realise that such disgrace can smear a whole family!'

'Yes, sir.'

Sir Robert rubbed his hands. 'Well, enough of that. You carried out your orders as best you could. That will have to suffice for the present. You did in fact find out about the enemy's intentions. If it is true, it will weigh heavily in your favour.'

He looked up at the gently moving flag and murmured, 'We could do with a little good fortune at the moment!'

Sir Robert lapsed into silence until Bolitho had guided him below to his cabin where the other officers were already seated. With the table fully extended and ten officers already crammed round it, the cabin seemed to be full to capacity, and Bolitho found time to wonder why the admiral had bothered to make this journey away from the comparative luxury of his own quarters.

The officers rose to their feet and then sank expectantly into their seats again as Bolitho and the admiral squeezed around the head of the table.

Bolitho also realised for the first time that this was the only occasion he had sat down to dine with all his officers. As Atwell and two hastily recruited messmen began to serve dinner he glanced round the table marking the strange difference which seemed to have come over the familiar faces. They were like embarrassed strangers, he thought vaguely.

Apart from his lieutenants and Captain Rennie he had arranged for the three midshipmen to be present also. As representatives of the ship's warrant officers Proby, the master, and Tobias Ellice, the surgeon, sat in stiff discomfort, their eyes on their plates.

Still the admiral gave no sign of relaxing. In almost complete silence the dinner went on. But with it came the wine, this time brought by the admiral's personal steward, a tall, disdainful man in a scarlet jacket. It was then that Bolitho began to realise what Sir Robert was doing. Coupled with the tension and the unaccustomed richness of the excellent dinner, the wine began to take effect. When Bolitho noticed that the admiral had hardly eaten more than a bird's share of the food and made a point of keeping the same glass of wine at his elbow, he fully understood.

Voices grew louder, and while Sir Robert sat calmly at Bolitho's side the officers began to talk more freely. Bolitho did not know which he felt more. Annoyance or admiration. Not content with a bald report, no matter how concise, Sir Robert was here to hear for himself. From the men who until now had been mere names from Bolitho's pen.

Some of the strain seemed to drain out of him. Right or wrong, the admiral's sly methods were now beyond his control.

Slowly the story began to unfold. Each phase being taken up and polished by a different officer. The attack on Mola Island and the taking of the battery. The more eloquent elaborated on the plan as a whole, the less capable ones contenting themselves on painting the smaller parts to the overall picture.

There was humour too in some of the recollections. Like the story of Parker, the master's mate, who had commanded the jolly boat during the attack on the *Andiron*. Separated from the other boats by the rising sea, he had returned to the *Phalarope* only to have his discomfort further increased by a volley of musket fire from some vigilant marines. And the story of Captain Rennie conducting the retreat from Mola Island with his sword in one hand and half a chicken pie in the other. But this sort of reminiscence did not last.

Sir Robert snapped suddenly, 'And you, Mr. Farquhar, were left behind with the Spanish prisoner?'

Farquhar eyed him carefully, and for a moment Bolitho felt the tension returning to the crowded table. But Farquhar kept his head. Even the fact that it was well known that Sir Robert normally made a point of never addressing anyone below the rank of lieutenant failed to ruffle him.

'Yes, sir. I joined the captain and together we went into captivity.'

The admiral swung round in his chair and peered at Okes, who until now had remained almost silent. 'Your part in this business seems to have kept you very busy, Mr. Okes?'

The lieutenant looked up startled. 'Er, yes, sir. I did what I had to do. There was no other way!'

Sir Robert sipped his wine and eyed him coolly. 'For an officer who has gained nothing but glory you sound remarkably guarded, Mr. Okes. A modicum of modesty is welcome these days, but not when it sounds remarkably like guilt!' For a second longer he held Okes's pale face with his cold eyes, and then he laughed. It was a humourless sound, but it helped to break the sudden and unhappy silence.

'And you, Mr. Herrick?' Sir Robert craned round his own captain to stare along the table. 'Your exploits at Nevis seem a trifle haphazard? But against that you obtained the result you intended no doubt?'

Herrick gave a broad grin. 'Captain Bolitho has already pointed out to me the pitfalls of too much luck, sir!'

'Did he indeed?' The admiral's eyebrows rose slightly. 'I am gratified to hear it.'

And on it went in the same vein. The admiral would question and listen, or when that failed would openly provoke the luckless officer into some excited and unguarded reply.

The loyal toast was called for by the junior officer present. Midshipman Neale, dwarfed on either side by Proby and Ellice, squeaked, 'Gentlemen, the King!' and then sank into a blushing silence.

Bolitho noticed that the admiral's right hand was curled like a claw around his goblet, and when the latter saw him looking at it the admiral snapped petulantly, 'Damned rheumatism! Had it for years!'

For a few moments Bolitho took time to appreciate the man sitting by his side. Not the admiral, with all his petty foibles, his unfair uses of privilege and rank, but the actual man.

He was old, probably in his sixties, and to Bolitho's knowledge had not set foot ashore for more than a few days at a time in the last ten years. He had shifted his flag from ship to ship, dealing with problems and strategy which Bolitho could only half imagine.

The admiral was looking at him unwinkingly. 'Are you still wondering why I came, Bolitho?' He did not wait for an answer. 'I commanded a frigate myself many years ago. The happiest time in the Navy for me. Life was easier in many ways then. But the stakes were not so high.' The shutter dropped again. 'I came because I wanted to see what you have *made* of this ship.' He tugged at his chin as if to seek some way of avoiding a compliment. 'What I find does not displease me entirely.' He dropped his voice, so that it was almost lost in the newly awakened conversation around the table. 'Most of your officers appear to have great respect for you. I know from experience that it is very hard to come by!'

Bolitho gave a small smile. 'Thank you, sir.'

'And you can remove that stupid smile from your face!' The admiral shifted beneath his coat. 'I like to know the men whom I command! When I see a sail on the horizon I don't wish to know the size of her guns or the state of her paintwork. I want to know the mind of the man in control, see?' He stared over the heads of the lolling officers. 'England is fighting for her life. It is a war of defence now. The attack will come later, perhaps years later, after I am dead and buried! But until that time England depends on her ships, maybe only a couple of hundred ships which are in a position to act to full advantage!' He tapped on the table, so that the others fell silent and turned to listen. 'And those ships depend on their captains and no one else!'

Bolitho opened his mouth to speak but the admiral said testily, 'Hear me out! I know your reputation now. You are an idealist in many ways. You have hopes for better conditions for your men, so that they can make the sea an honourable career again.' He waved a finger. 'When I was younger I wanted all those things and more beside. But a good captain is the one who accepts all these difficulties as they stand and still manages to run an efficient ship, one worthy of honour and praise!'

He glared round the table. 'Well, gentlemen, did I make myself understood?'

Bolitho followed his gaze. Vibart, flushed and unsmiling. Herrick, still grinning and unquenched by the admiral's earlier sarcasm. Rennie, stiff-backed but with eyes so glassy that they were beyond focus. Old Daniel Proby, humbled by being with such illustrious company, yet whose face was stiff with sudden pride, as if he had heard a deeper meaning in the admiral's words. And Ellice, the bucolic surgeon, who had been drinking without pause since they had arrived at table. Bolitho could find time to pity Ellice. Poorly paid, like all ships' surgeons, it was no wonder he was more of a butcher than a doctor. It was a race which none would win. Drink or a fatal mistake, it was merely a matter of time.

Okes, still smarting from the admiral's keen appraisal of the half-remembered attack on Mola Island. Bolitho noticed how he kept darting quick, desperate glances towards Farquhar, who by comparison was calm and impassive, his thoughts perhaps far away. Maybe still back there below the shattered bridge where he had been left to die by the man who now sat watching him. The fact that Farquhar had made neither comment nor complaint must be all the more worrying for Okes, Bolitho thought grimly.

And the two other midshipmen, Maynard and Neale. Excited and untouched by the deeper channels of comment and thought around them. Bolitho was suddenly very aware of his responsibility to all of them.

The admiral stood up and lifted his glass. 'A toast!' His pale eyes flashed below the low beams. 'Death to the French!'

The glasses came up as one and the voices rumbled the reply, 'And confusion to our enemies!'

The admiral called to his captain, 'Time we were going, Cope!'

Bolitho followed him to the upperdeck, only half listening to the scamper of feet and the hurried creak of oars alongside. It was over. The admiral would never admit a mistake, but Bolitho knew that the worst was behind him. *Phalarope* was free of disgrace at last.

He lifted his hat as the admiral crossed to the port and waited until he had vanished to the waiting barge. Then he clamped on his hat and began to pace the deserted quarterdeck, his hands clasped behind him.

The admiral had also made it plain in his own way that if the ship was free of disgrace it was up to her captain to keep her so.

He looked at the riding lights dancing across the water and listened to the plaintive scrape of a violin and the accompanying sadness of an old shanty. If the men could still sing there was hope for all of them, he thought.

13

Danger from Within

The pipes shrilled in salute as Richard Bolitho stepped through the ornate entry port and on to the *Formidable's* wide deck. Automatically he doffed his hat to the quarterdeck, and as he returned the greeting of the flagship's officer of the watch he allowed his eyes to move swiftly up and around him, taking in the busy activity, the seemingly endless deck space and the long lines of gleaming guns.

An impeccable midshipman in white gloves crossed the deck at a trot, and under the beady eye of the duty officer led Bolitho aft towards the great stern cabin, to which every available captain had been summoned at an hour's notice.

Bolitho had been toying with his lonely breakfast, pondering on the previous night's strange dinner party and Sir Robert Napier's persistent questions, when Maynard had hurried into his cabin with news of the signal. As he had hurriedly changed into his best uniform Bolitho had wondered why Sir Robert had not mentioned this meeting with the Commander-in-Chief. He must have known about it. As Bolitho had stared unseeingly at his reflection in the bulkhead mirror he had wondered if Sir Robert was making just one more private test. He probably kept his glass trained on the *Phalarope*'s deck from the moment *Formidable* had hoisted her general signal.

He almost cannoned into the midshipman and realised that they had reached the great cabin. The youngster called, 'Captain Richard Bolitho of the *Phalarope*!'

But only those officers standing near the door took any notice, and soon returned to their own busy conversation. For that Bolitho was grateful. He made his way to one corner of the cabin, and as one messman took his hat another placed a tall glass of sherry in his hand. Neither spoke a word, and Bolitho guessed that it was no easy matter to remain calm and unruffled when serving the Commander-in-Chief.

He sipped at his glass and carefully studied the other officers. There must be about thirty captains present, he decided. Captains of every size and shape, of every age and seniority. After the first scrutiny Bolitho decided that he must be the most junior, but just as he had reached this conclusion he felt a movement at his elbow and turned to meet the gaze of a tall, gangling lieutenant whom he vaguely remembered as the commander of the little brig, *Witch of Looe*.

The latter raised his glass and said quietly, 'Your health, sir! I was coming across to see you and tell you how glad I am of your safe return.'

Bolitho smiled. 'Thank you.' He shrugged. 'I am afraid your name has escaped me.'

'Philip Dancer, sir.'

'I will remember it in future.' Bolitho saw the lieutenant loosening his neckcloth with one finger and suddenly realised that he was actually nervous. It was not easy to be so junior in such an illustrious gathering. He said quickly, 'I expect this seems a bit luxurious after your little brig?'

Dancer grimaced. 'Just a bit!'

They both looked at the great stern windows with the wide gallery beyond where the admiral could take an undisturbed walk above the ship's own wake. There were long boxes of potted plants too, and on the handsome sideboard Bolitho caught a glimpse of gleaming silver and cut glass below a fine painting of Hampton Court Palace.

Then the buzz of conversation died away, and every man turned to face a side door as the small procession entered the cabin.

Bolitho was shocked to see the change which had come over Sir George Rodney since he had last seen him some two years earlier. Beneath the resplendent uniform with its bright ribbon and decorations the admiral's once upright figure appeared bent and drooping, and his mouth, now set in a tight line, betrayed the illness which had plagued him for so many months. It was hard to picture him as the same man who had overwhelmed a powerful enemy force only two years ago to break through and relieve the besieged fortress of Gibraltar, or who had attacked and sacked St. Eustatius and taken over three million sterling back to England as a prize.

But the eyes were the same. Hard and steady, as if they drew and contained all the energy of his being.

At his side his second in command, Sir Samuel Hood, made a sharp contrast. He looked calm and composed as he studied the assembled officers, his features dominated by his large, arrogant nose and high forehead.

Behind his two superiors Sir Robert Napier looked almost insignificant, Bolitho thought.

Sir George Rodney lowered himself into a tall chair and folded his hands in his lap. Then he said curtly, 'I wanted you all here to tell you that it now seems likely the French and their allies will attempt a final overthrow of English forces in this area.' He coughed shortly and dabbed his mouth with a handkerchief. 'Comte de Grasse has assembled a strong force of ships of the line, the most powerful vessels ever gathered under one flag, and were I in his fortunate position I would have no hesitation in preparing to do battle.'

He coughed again, and Bolitho felt a tremor of uneasiness transmit itself through the watching officers. The strain of years of planning and fighting were paring Rodney away like a knife blade. When he had sailed for England there was not an officer in his fleet who did not believe it was his last journey and that another would return to take his place. But somewhere within that tired body was a soul of steel. Rodney intended to see no replacement in the West Indies to take either the fruits of his hard and unsparing work or the shame and misery of possible defeat.

Sir Samuel Hood said evenly, 'Intelligence has reached us that there is more to de Grasse's intentions than a mere sea victory. He has been gathering seasoned French troops, as well as supplying arms and assistance to the American colonials. He is a shrewd and dedicated strategist, and I believe he intends to exploit whatever successes he has already made.' He looked suddenly across the nearest heads and fixed his heavy lidded eyes on Bolitho.

'The captain of the frigate *Phalarope* has added to this information in no little amount, gentlemen!'

For a few seconds every head in the cabin turned to stare at him, and caught off guard by this turn of events Bolitho felt a tinge of confusion.

In those few seconds he got a vague impression of faces and the reactions of their owners. Some nodded approvingly, and some merely eyed him with barely masked envy. Others studied his face as if to search out some deeper meaning from the admiral's comment. A small item of praise from Hood, and therefore condoned by the great Rodney himself, could immediately mark Bolitho as a firm rival in the ladder of promotion and reward.

Hood added dryly. 'Now that you all know each other, we will continue! From this day forward our vigilance must be stepped up. Our patrols must make every effort to watch each enemy port and spare no efforts to pass information back to me. When de Grasse breaks out it will be swift and final. If we cannot call his challenge and close him in battle we are done for, and make no mistake about it!'

His deep, booming voice filled the crowded cabin, so that Bolitho could almost feel the import of his words like a physical force.

The admiral went on tirelessly and methodically to outline the known whereabouts of supply ships and enemy forces. He showed neither strain nor impatience, and there was nothing at all in his manner to betray the fact that he had only recently returned to Antigua after holding St. Kitts against the whole French military force and their attendant fleet.

Sir George Rodney interrupted, 'I want every one of you to study and familiarise yourselves with my signal requirements.' He looked sharply around the cabin. 'I will not tolerate any officer misunderstanding my signals, any more than I will accept excuses for failing to execute same!'

Several captains exchanged quick glances. It was well known that when Rodney had tried to close the French admiral de Guichen off Martinique, and had not succeeded because some of his captains had failed either to understand or react to his signals, he had been quite ruthless. More than one captain now lived on miserly half-pay in England with nothing but disgrace and bad memories for comfort.

Rodney continued in a calmer tone, 'Watch for my signals. Wherever, and on whatever ship my flag flies, *watch for my signals*!' He leaned back and stared at the deckhead. 'This time there will be no second chance. We will win a great victory, or we will lose everything.'

He nodded to Hood, who added briefly, 'Orders will be issued immediately to senior officers of squadrons. From the moment you leave here the fleet will be in all respects ready for sea. It is up to our patrolling frigates and sloops to watch the enemy's lairs like hounds.' He pounded the table with his fist. 'Give the Commander-in-Chief the scent and the kill is assured!'

There was a murmur of approval, and Bolitho realised that the meeting was over.

Lieutenant Dancer said quietly, 'I wonder where our squadron will be sent? I would hate to miss the final scene when it comes!'

Bolitho nodded, mentally smiling at the picture of the tiny *Witch of Looe* engaging de Grasse's three-deckers. Aloud he said, 'There are never enough frigates. In every war it is the same story. Too little too late,' But he could say it without bitterness. *Phalarope* would be needed more than ever now. With the vast sea areas, the complex hiding places amongst the lines of scattered islands, every frigate would have more than enough to do.

He realised with a start that a sharp-faced flag-lieutenant had crossed the cabin to stop him leaving with the others.

'Sir George Rodney wishes to speak to you.'

Bolitho hitched up his sword and walked across the thick carpet. By the table he halted, half listening to the retreating scrape of footsteps. He heard the door close and the distant shrill of pipes speeding the exit of the fleet's captains, and for a terrible moment he thought he had misunderstood the flag-lieutenant's words.

Rodney was still sitting in his chair, his eyes half closed as he stared at the deckhead. Hood and Sir Robert Napier were completely engrossed in a chart on a nearby desk, and even the messmen seemed busy and oblivious to the young captain by the table.

Then Rodney lowered his eyes and said wearily, 'I know your father, Bolitho. We sailed together, of course. A very gallant officer, and a good friend.' He let his gaze move slowly across Bolitho's tanned face and down the length of his body. 'You have a lot of him in you.' He nodded. 'I am glad to have you under my command.'

Bolitho thought of his father alone in the big house, watching the ships in the bay. He said, 'Thank you, sir. My father wished to be remembered to you.'

Rodney did not seem to hear. 'There is so much to do. So few ships for the task.' He signed deeply. 'I am sorry you had to meet your only brother in such a fashion.' His eyes were suddenly fixed and unwavering.

Bolitho saw Sir Robert Napier stiffen beside the chart and heard himself reply, 'He believes what he is doing is right, sir.'

The eyes were still hard on his face. 'And what do *you* believe?'

'He is my brother, sir. But if we meet again I will not betray my cause.' He hesitated. 'Or your trust, sir.'

Rodney nodded. 'I never doubted it, my boy.'

Sir Samuel Hood coughed politely, and Rodney said with sudden briskness, 'Return to your ship, Bolitho. I hope that both you and your father will be spared further hurt.' His eyes were cold as he added, 'It is easy to do your duty when there is no alternative. Yours was not an easy choice. Nor will it be if your brother is taken!'

He lapsed into silence, and the flag-lieutenant said impatiently, 'Your hat, sir! And I have just called for your boat!'

Bolitho followed the harassed officer into the sunlight, his mind still dwelling on the admiral's words. So the whole fleet would now know about his brother. In the confined, monastic world of ships permanently at sea he would be discussed and measured against past exploits and future events.

He ran down the gangway to the waiting boat and stared across at the anchored *Phalarope*. Once she had been on trial. Now it was the turn of her captain.

On the evening of the same day that Bolitho had attended the conference aboard the *Formidable*, and with a minimum of fuss or ceremony the *Phalarope* weighed and headed for the open sea.

The following morning found her a bare fifty miles to the south-west, her full set of sails drawing on the gentle breeze which did little to ease the growing power of the sun.

But this time she was not completely alone. Even from the deck it was possible to see the *Cassius*, her tall pyramids of canvas golden in the early sunlight as she moved on a ponderous and slow parallel course. Somewhere beyond her, hidden below the lip the horizon, was the frigate *Volcano*. Invisible, and ahead of the slow-moving formation, Lieutenant Dancer's tiny *Witch of Looe* alone enjoyed a certain freedom of movement beyond the scrutiny of her admiral.

Lieutenant Herrick had just taken over the forenoon watch and stood relaxed by the quarterdeck rail as he idly watched the men at work on the maindeck. Earlier the swabs and holystones had made the planking wet and pliable, but now as the heat slowly mounted above the gently swaying hull the decks shone in shimmering whiteness while the normal business of splicing and running repairs was carried out.

It was a peaceful scene, and the combination of warmth and a good breakfast left Herrick drowsy and at ease. Occasionally he cast an eye towards Midshipman Neale to make sure he had his glass trained on the distant flagship, and *Phalarope* was keeping as good a station as the wind allowed.

He could see Lieutenant Okes inspecting the starboard battery of twelve-pounders with Brock, the gunner, and wondered, not for the first time, what was going on behind his strained features. Ever since the raid on Mola Island Okes had been a changed man. And the admiral's casual comments across the dinner table had made him withdraw even more into himself.

As for Farquhar, it was quite impossible to tell what he was thinking. Herrick was not sure if he envied the midshipman's aloof reserve or admired him for it. It was strange how Farquhar's manner had always made him feel on the defensive. Perhaps it was because of his own humble beginnings, he decided. Even here, cooped up in a small frigate, Farquhar retained his distance and individuality.

Herrick tried to imagine what he would have felt if, as Rennie had suggested, Okes had retreated from the raid without care or interest, and had left *him* to die. He pictured himself reacting as Farquhar had done, but instantly in his heart he knew he was deceiving himself. More than likely it would have ended in an open conflict, with a court martial to round it off.

The helmsman coughed warningly, and Herrick turned quickly as Bolitho came up the cabin hatch. He touched his hat and waited as Bolitho walked first to the compass and then stood looking up at the masthead pendant. Then he relaxed slightly as Bolitho crossed to his side and looked down at the busy seamen on deck.

'Another fifty miles to our patrolling station, Mr. Herrick. At this speed we will need another day!' There was impatience in his tone, and a touch of irritation which Herrick was now able to recognise immediately.

Herrick said, 'But still it is comforting to see the *Cassius* abeam, sir. If de Grasse ventures out this way we will not be alone!'

Bolitho stared at the distant gleam of sails, but there was no response to Herrick's forced cheerfulness. 'Ah yes, the flagship.' He gave a bitter smile. 'Forty years old, and so much weed on her bottom that she crawls even in a strong gale!'

Herrick looked quickly at the *Cassius*. Up until this moment size and seniority had represented safety and a ready shield. He replied, 'I did not know, sir.'

'She was a Dutch prize, Mr. Herrick. Look at the rake of her beakhead!' Then as if realising that he was speaking from memory of things which were of no importance he added harshly, 'My God, this crawling makes me sick!'

Herrick tried another tack. 'Our orders, sir. May I ask what is expected of us?'

He immediately regretted his impulse and checked himself as Bolitho turned his head away to watch a slowly circling gull. But from the set of the captain's shoulders and the way his hands were locked on the rail he knew that he had struck on something uppermost in Bolitho's mind.

But Bolitho's voice was calm as he answered, 'We will take up our station fifty miles to the west'rd of Guadeloupe and keep contact with our' – he waved his hand towards the open sea – 'with our squadron!'

Herrick digested this information slowly. The excitement and frantic preparations at Antigua had left him in little doubt of an impending battle, and he knew that even now most of those proud ships he had watched with an undiminished fascination would have weighed and set sail to complete Rodney's plan to seek out and confront the Comte de Grasse.

Bolitho continued absently, 'There is a chain of ships up and down the Caribbean. One good sighting and the chase will be on.' But there was no excitement in his voice. 'Unfortunately, Martinique is another hundred miles to the south of our patrol area, Mr. Herrick. De Grasse will be there with the bulk of his ships. He will bide his time and then make a dash for Jamaica.' He turned swiftly and stared at Herrick's frowning face. 'And when Rodney's frigates report that the French have sailed, the fleet will attack him!' He shrugged, the gesture both angry and despairing. 'And we shall still be on our station, as useless as a signpost in a desert!'

'But the French may come this way, sir.' Herrick felt Bolitho's bitterness changing his own eagerness to gloom. As he spoke he realised the reason for Bolitho's earlier scorn of the elderly *Cassius*. It was obvious that Rodney was using Admiral Napier's small squadron for the least important part of his overall plan.

'And pigs may lay eggs, Mr. Herrick!' said Bolitho evenly. 'But not in our day!'

'I see, sir.' Herrick was at a loss for words.

Bolitho studied him gravely and then touched his arm. 'Cheer up, Mr. Herrick. I am bad company this morning.' He winced and fingered his side. 'I am thankful that ball missed anything vital. But I could well do without its reminder.'

Herrick watched him thoughtfully. 'You should take more rest, sir.'

'I find it hard even to sit down, Mr. Herrick.' Bolitho shaded his eyes to watch the set of the sails. 'There is so much happening. History is being made all around us!' He suddenly began to pace, so that Herrick had to fall in step to keep up with him. 'De Grasse will come out, I'm sure of it!' He was speaking quickly in time with his steps. 'You saw that freak gale which gave you your chance to rake the *Andiron*? Well, it was rare indeed for this time of year. But later,' he smiled grimly at some hidden memory, 'later in the year the hurricanes hit the West Indies in profusion. From August to September they follow one another like messengers from hell itself!' He shook his head firmly. 'No, Mr. Herrick, de Grasse will come out soon. He has much to accomplish before that time.'

Herrick said, 'But which way will he go?'

'Maybe through the Martinique Passage. But either way he will head straight for the central Caribbean. There are a thousand miles between him and Jamaica. You could lose a whole fleet in such an area. If we fail to make contact when he sails we will never catch him again until it is too late!'

Herrick nodded, at last understanding the full reason for Bolitho's apprehension. 'He has troops and guns. He can occupy any territory he chooses to take.'

'Quite so. The men and stores we dealt with at Mola Island were just a part of his strength. He had hoped to tie down the fleet while he drove on to Jamaica unimpeded. Now he knows we are alerted. His urgency will be all the keener.'

He stopped in his tracks and stared fixedly at the naked horizon. 'If only we knew! If only we could go and find out for ourselves!' Then he seemed to realise that he was showing his own despair and he added briefly, 'You may return to your watch, Mr. Herrick. I have some thinking to do.'

Herrick walked back to the rail, but as the sun beat down on the tinder-dry decks, he was constantly aware of Bolitho's shadow. Back and forth, up and down.

When Herrick had been a midshipman he had dreamed of the time when he might attain the impossible heights of a lieutenant. From then on he had watched the slow path to promotion, gauging his own progress by the experience or the incompetence of his superiors. And all the time, nursed in the back of his mind like some precious jewel, was the idea that one day he might at last hold a command of his own.

But now, as he watched Bolitho's restless shadow and imagined the fretting thoughts which kept it company, he was not so sure.

Half-way through the forenoon the pipes shrilled, 'Stand easy!' With varying degrees of relief the frigate's seamen threw themselves into patches of shade to make the most of the short break in routine.

John Allday stayed where he had been working, with his legs astride the larboard cathead, his bronzed body sheltered from the sun by the jibsail. In the foremost part of the ship he had been engaged in cleaning and scraping one of the great anchors, and as he squatted comfortably above the small bow wave he rested one foot on the anchor's massive stock, feeling its warmth against the bare skin. At his back the other members of the working party loungd in various stages of abandon, while above their heads the air was tinged with a slow-moving vapour of smoke from their long pipes.

Old Ben Strachan picked up a new rope and examined the eye-splice which one of the ship's boys had just completed. 'Not bad, youngster. Not bad at all.' He sucked noisily at his pipe and peered aft the length of the *Phalarope*'s deck. 'Is that the cap'n pacin' up an' down?'

Pochin, who was lying with his head cradled on his thick arms, muttered, 'Course it is! Must be mad to be in this 'eat when 'e could be down in 'is cabin!'

Allday swung one leg and stared thoughtfully at the clear water below him. Pochin was still worried about Onslow's words in the cutter. He was edgy, as if he realised his own guilt. Just listening to such talk made a man liable to be labelled a conspirator.

He turned slightly to look aft, and across the length of the ship he saw Herrick, watching him from the quarterdeck. The lieutenant gave him a brief nod of recognition before returning to his own contemplation, and Allday suddenly remembered that moment on the crumbling cliff when he had stopped Herrick from falling to the rocks below. In spite of his original intention to stay apart from internal affairs in the *Phalarope,* and to keep clear of loyalty to either faction, Allday was beginning to realise that such neutrality was impossible, even dangerous.

Allday liked Herrick, and recognised what he was trying to do. He was always ready to listen to complaints from his division, and was never quick to award punishment. But he was no fool, and few took advantage of his humane manner a second time.

Allday could see the captain still pacing the quarterdeck at the weather rail, coatless with his shirt open to his chest and his dark hair pulled back to the nape of his neck. He was a harder man to know, Allday thought, but it was strangely reassuring to see him back at his familiar place on the poop, Allday, perhaps better than most, knew the reputation of the Bolitho family. On his visits to Falmouth he had often heard them discussed in the taverns, and had even seen the house which was the captain's home. It was strange to realise that he had a brother fighting on the other side. Allday wondered how he would have felt. Not only that, but Bolitho's brother was said to have deserted from the Navy, a crime which could only be wiped out at the end of a rope.

He came back from his thoughts as Ferguson climbed up from the maindeck and walked across to the rail. He looked strained and self-conscious in his clean clothes, a marked contrast to the tired and sweating seamen who had once been his companions.

Ferguson fidgeted for a few moments and then said, 'Do you think we will see any more fighting?'

Pochin turned his head and growled, 'You should know! Aren't you in the captain's pocket?'

Allday grinned. 'Don't pay any attention to Nick.' He dropped his voice. 'Has Onslow been after you again?' He saw Ferguson's pale eyes flicker.

'Not much. He just passes the time with me sometimes.'

'Well, remember my warning, Bryan!' Allday studied him closely. 'I've not told a living soul aboard, but I believe he had a lot to do with Mathias's death.' He saw the disbelief on Ferguson's face and added sharply, 'In fact, I'm sure he had!'

'Why should he do a thing like that?' Ferguson tried to smile, but his mouth remained slack.

'He's a bad one. He knows no other life but this. He came to the fleet as a child. His world is bounded by the sides of a wooden hull.' He ran his hands along the carved cathead. 'I've met a few of his kind before, Bryan. They're as dangerous as wolves!'

Ferguson said, 'He'll not make trouble. He wouldn't dare!'

'No? And why do you think he keeps asking about the cabin? He's biding his time. His sort have a lot of patience.'

'The captain'd not stand for any more trouble!' Ferguson showed his agitation in the quick movements of his hands. 'I've heard him telling Mr. Vibart about taking care of the men. About how he wants them treated.'

Allday sighed. 'You see? You're even telling me what you've heard. If you want to stay safe you'd better keep what you know to yourself.'

Ferguson stared at him. 'You don't have to tell me!' He tightened his mouth with sudden anger. 'You're just like the others. You're jealous because of my job!'

Allday turned away. 'Suit yourself.'

He waited until he heard Ferguson moving aft again. Then he turned to watch as Onslow stepped from beside the mainmast to stop his passing. He saw Onslow grinning and patting Ferguson on the shoulder.

Pochin's hard voice interrupted his thoughts. 'What d'you reckon? D'you think Onslow is right?' He sounded worried. 'If there is more trouble aboard this ship we'll all be in it. We'll have to take sides!'

Allday replied flatly, 'You'd be a fool to pay heed to that one!' He tried to put some value to his words. 'Anyway, the captain'll make short work of him if he tries anything!'

Pochin nodded doubtfully. 'Maybe. Dyin' under a French broadside is one thing, but I'll not cough out blood for 'im or the buggers like Onslow!'

The pipes shrilled again, and the men stirred themselves back to work.

Allday kept his eyes down to his task as Quintal, the boatswain, and Josling, one of his mates, walked forward to inspect the forecastle. He heard Josling say, 'I see that the old *Cassius* was signalling just now, Mr. Quintal?'

Quintal replied in his deep voice, 'Aye, lad. We'll be hauling off shortly to our own little patrol area. It'll be a long job, I wouldn't wonder, so see that you keep the hands busy. There's nothing worse for discipline than too much free time.' The rest of his comments were lost to Allday as the two men moved up towards the bowsprit, but he had heard enough.

Phalarope was to be alone again, and out of sight of the flagship. The boatswain was right. With the heat and the dull monotony of an empty patrol, Onslow would find a good breeding ground for more trouble if he could.

He looked sideways at his silent companions, each man apparently engrossed in his own task, yet each no doubt thinking of that green patch of land which they had just left behind.

No ordinary seaman had set foot ashore. Some of the crew had not left a deck for years. It was hardly surprising that men like Onslow could find a ready audience.

He shaded his eyes and stared towards the horizon. Already the distant two-decker seemed smaller, her hull lost in the heat haze below the clear sky. Her sails had merged into one shining pyramid, and as he watched she appeared to sink lower in the glittering sea. Another hour and she would have vanished altogether.

After that, he thought coldly, you could trust no man.

Deep below the forecastle deck where Allday sat immersed in his own thoughts was the *Phalarope*'s cable tier. In harbour it was a spacious, empty place, but now, as the frigate moved listlessly on the calm water, it was packed to the deckhead with the massive anchor cables. Coil upon coil, the great, salt-hardened ropes added to the sour stench of the bilges and the richer smells of tar and hemp. Stout upright pillars on either side of the shelving hull held the cables clear of the timbers to allow easy access to the ship's fabric at all times. These 'carpenter's walks' as they were named ran the full length of the hull below the water-line to afford inspection and if necessary, repairs in time of battle. Little wider than a man's body, they were usually in total darkness.

But now, as the bow wave swished dully against the timbers and furtive rats continued their endless search for food, a small, shaded lantern cast an eerie light against the piled cable and threw a distorted reflection back to the faces of the men squeezed in the narrow passageway.

Onslow held the lantern higher and peered at the waiting men. He only had to count them to be sure. He knew each man's face and name without need for further examination.

'We must be quick, lads! We'll be missed if we stay too long!'

Like an echo he heard Pook's voice. 'Just pay heed to wot 'e says!'

Onslow's teeth gleamed in the darkness. He could feel his legs shaking with wild excitement, like the effect of rum on an empty stomach. 'We're pulling away from the other ships. I think the time has almost come to carry out our plan.'

He heard a dull murmur of agreement and grinned even broader. Just by saying *our* instead of *my* acted on these men like the crack of a whip.

'From what Ferguson has told me Bolitho intends to run to the south'rd. The *Phalarope*'ll be on the end of the patrol line. No chance of meeting any of the others, y'see?'

A voice asked from the darkness, ' 'Ow can we take the ship on our own?' He broke off with a yelp as Pook drove his elbow into his ribs.

Onslow said calmly, 'Leave that part to me. I'll tell you how and when.' He looked at the crouching line of dark figures. All the ones who had come with him from the *Cassius*, and several more recruited in the *Phalarope*. It was far more than he had dared to hope.

'We must get rid of the bloody bullocks. Without their red coats athwart the quarterdeck it'll be easy.'

Pook asked, 'Wot about Allday an' the like?'

'Ah yes.' Onslow smiled crookedly. 'Master John Allday.'

Pook added gloomily, 'The lads *listen* to 'im!'

'And if anything happened to Allday we'd get a lot more on our side, eh?' Onslow's brain was moving ahead of his words. 'But it has to be clever. If it looks like our doing we might as well hang ourselves!'

They all froze as heavy footsteps sounded overhead. Then as they died away Onslow continued easily, 'I think Allday guesses what happened to Mathias. He's too clever to live, is that one!' He reached out and gripped Pook's arm. 'So we'll make him a bloody martyr, shall we?' He gave a rumbling laugh. 'Now we can't do fairer than that!'

The same uncertain voice tried again. 'We'll be cut down afore we can raise a finger, I say!'

'*I'll* cut you down, you bugger!' For a moment Onslow's good humour retreated. Then he added more calmly. 'Now listen to me, all of you! We must wait a bit longer to get the lads more worried. Then when the time's ripe I'll tell you what I want. That fool Ferguson can keep an eye on the captain's log for me, just so that I know where we are. When we get a bit nearer some land, I'll be ready.'

He snapped his fingers. 'Those weapons we brought off from Mola Island. Have you got 'em safely stowed?'

Pook nodded. 'Aye, they'll not be discovered!'

'Right then. Get back to your work now, lads. And stay out of trouble. You're all marked men anyway, so don't give the bastards a chance to nail you!'

He watched them creeping away into the darkness beyond the dim lantern and felt satisfied. Now, just as he had told those poor sheep, it was just a matter of time.

14

Blood and Fresh Water

Tobias Ellice, the *Phalarope's* surgeon, arose wheezing from his uncomfortable stooping position and threw the sweat-stained bandage out of the open stern window. 'Right, sir. You kin stand up now if you like.' He stepped away from the bench seat as Bolitho threw his legs over the side and lifted himself to his feet.

Ellice mopped his streaming face and peered closely at the rough scar across Bolitho's ribs. 'Not a bad job of work, if I says so meself!' He beamed and licked his lips. 'It's thirsty work, an' no mistake!'

Bolitho touched the scar with his fingertips and then stood facing the open windows to allow the tiny breeze to play across his bare skin. It was good to be rid of the bandage, he thought. Its very embrace was a constant reminder of the *Andiron* and all that had gone before. It was well to leave it all in the past. There were troubles enough to deal with today and the next day after that.

It was a full fourteen days since they had sailed with the squadron from Antigua, and almost every one of them had been like this one. Hardly a lick of air which could seriously be called a breeze to fill the hungry sails or even to ventilate the ship. And all the time a broiling sun which seemed to bleach the colour from the sky itself. The nights brought little respite. Between decks the air remained humid and heavy with damp, and the seamen were further wearied by the constant calls to trim sails, only to be dismissed cursing and despairing as the wind died before a single sheet could be handled.

It was enough to break even the sturdiest heart, Bolitho thought heavily. And coupled with the fact that they had not sighted a single sail, and knew nothing of events beyond the mocking horizon, he found it was all he could do to restrain his own mounting impatience.

'How are the men?' He reached for a clean shirt and then relented. The old one would have to do. There was little point in badgering his servant to wash more clothes than necessary.

Ellice shrugged. 'Not happy, sir. 'Tis bad enough as it is without hungering after a drink all the time.'

'Water is precious, Mr. Ellice.' It was now reduced to a pint a day per man, which was less than adequate. But there was no telling how long it would be before their senseless vigil was broken. He had increased the daily ration of *Miss Taylor*, as the rough white wine from the victualling yard was named, but its satisfaction was only temporary. Within a few hours the drinker would be left as dry as before. He added as an afterthought, 'They must get as much fresh fruit as we can spare. It is the only thing to keep down disease out here.'

It was odd how much clamour and argument there had been in Antigua when he had insisted on a full cargo of fruit to be shipped for his crew. Maybe that was what the admiral had meant when he had said, 'You are an idealist in many ways!' But to Bolitho's practical mind it was only being sensible. Even though he had paid for the fruit from his own pocket he knew it was more of a good investment than a method of arousing favouritism with his men. A fit and healthy sailor was worth far more than a basket of fruit. In fact, the normal wastage did not stop there. Other men were used to care for their sick comrades, and their work had to be taken on by still more men. And so it went on, yet there were still plenty of captains who could see no further than their prize money as a measure of success.

He tucked his shirt into his breeches and said, 'Take a glass if you will, Mr. Ellice.' He looked away ashamed as the big, untidy man shambled quickly to the sideboard and slopped a generous portion of brandy into his goblet. Ellice's hand shook as he poured and downed a second glass before mumbling, 'Thankee, sir. That's the first today!'

Bolitho glanced at the shadow of the stern, close to the barely moving wake. The sun was high in the sky. It was more than likely that Ellice had already consumed a goodly portion from his private store.

'I did not see you go ashore in Antigua, Mr. Ellice? You had only to ask.'

Ellice licked his lips and shot a quick glance at the decanter. 'I never go on land now, sir, thankee all the same. At first I used to wander like a lovesick girl amongst the grass and weep when the shoreline dropped over the sea's edge.' He saw Bolitho nod towards the decanter and hurriedly poured another drink. 'Now when the ship sails I hardly looks up.' He shook his head as if to restore some broken memory. 'Anyway, I've seen it all!'

There was a tap at the door, but before Bolitho could call it burst open and Lieutenant Vibart stamped into the cabin. He looked strained and angry, and wasted no time in breaking his news.

'I have to report that we are almost out of fresh water, sir.'

Bolitho studied him for a few seconds. 'What do you mean?'

Vibart glanced round the cabin. 'I have the cooper outside, sir. It might save time if *he* told you!'

Bolitho ignored Vibart's insolent manner. 'Send him in.' He was glad that the sea's reflected glare kept his face in deep shadow. At every turn events seemed to twist and mock at his efforts. Now this, the one predominant worry, had been fanned alight even as he had been openly discussing it with Ellice.

Mr. Trevenen, the *Phalarope's* cooper, was an undersized warrant officer who was known for his extremely bad eyesight. Too long in too many darkened holds had left him half blind, like some creature of the night.

Now, as he stood blinking and shifting uneasily under Bolitho's stare he looked small and defenceless.

Bolitho stifled his usual feeling of pity which inevitably arose on the rare occasions of meeting the cooper. 'Well, spit it out, man! What the hell have you discovered?'

Trevenen gulped miserably. 'I've been doin' my rounds, sir. You see I always does 'em on a Thursday. If you build up a system of inspections you can . . .'

Vibart bellowed, '*Tell* him, you old fool!'

The cooper said in a small voice, 'Two thirds of me casks are foul with salt water, sir.' He peered at his feet. 'I don't understand it, sir. In all my years afloat I never seen nothin' like it.'

'Hold your damned tongue!' Vibart looked as if he would strike the wretched man. 'Admit that you made a mistake at Antigua. You're so bloody blind you don't know the difference! If I had my way I'd . . .'

Bolitho made himself speak slowly to give his mind time to recover from the shock. 'If you please, Mr. Vibart! I think *I* can evaluate the extent of this information!' He turned again to Trevenen. 'Are you sure now?'

The wrinkled head nodded violently. 'No mistake about it, sir!' He looked up, his faded eyes filling his face. 'In all my years, sir, I never . . .'

'I know, Mr. Trevenen, you just told us.' Bolitho added to Vibart sharply, 'Have the casks checked for yourself, Mr. Vibart. Separate the fresh ones from the others, and see that the salt water is drained away and the wood cleaned off.'

He strode to the chart and leaned across it, his face set in a deep frown. 'We are here.' He tapped the chart with the heavy dividers. 'Fifty miles south-west of Guadeloupe, give or take a mile.' He picked up his ruler and ran it across the thick parchment. 'There are some small islands to the south of us. Uninhabited and useless except for wrecking the unwary sailor.' He made a small cross on the chart and stood up. 'Call the hands and prepare to wear ship, Mr. Vibart. This breeze, slight though it is, will suit our purpose.'

He looked across at Trevenen. 'Whatever the reason for this, be it seepage or sheer carelessness, we must have water, and quickly! So prepare your party to take on a fresh supply.'

Trevenen blinked at him. He looked like a man who had just heard of a miracle at first hand.

Bolitho continued, 'We should make a landfall within two days, sooner if the wind finds us again. I have visited these islands before.' He touched the scar beneath the dark forelock of hair. 'There are streams and quite reliable pools on some of them.'

Vibart said heavily, 'The admiral gave no orders about leaving our station, sir.'

'Would you have the men die of thirst, Mr. Vibart?' Bolitho stared down at the chart again. 'But if you are worried I will have my clerk make an entry in the patrol report today.' He smiled wryly. 'Should I vanish again, you will have the necessary shield from Sir Robert's anger!'

Ellice said dreamily, 'I was in a ship once when this 'appened. Two of the seamen ran amuck for want of water!'

Vibart snarled, 'Well you at least will be untroubled by *that*, I imagine!'

Bolitho smiled in spite of his troubled thoughts. 'Carry on, Mr. Vibart. Have the hands mustered to their stations. I will be up directly.' He watched the door quiver in its frame and then said to Ellice, 'You asked for that, Mr. Ellice!'

The surgeon was unmoved. 'With all due respect to the first lieutenant, sir, but he was too long aboard a slaver, if you ask me. To 'im men is just bloody extra cargo!'

'That will do, Mr. Ellice.' Bolitho glanced at the decanter. As if by magic it had emptied during his talk with Trevenen. 'I suggest you take a turn around the maindeck.'

Ellice peered at him uncertainly. Then he grinned. 'Aye, sir. So I will. It'll give me a fair appetite!' He ambled away, his shabby coat hanging around him like a sack. Rain or fine, sun or sheeting squalls, Ellice was never dressed differently. Some had even suggested he slept in his clothes.

Bolitho dismissed him from his mind as the pipes shrilled and the decks thudded with bare feet as the men ran to their stations for wearing ship.

Within an hour the *Phalarope* had gone about, her sails flat and listless in the relentless glare. But in spite of the outward stillness there was enough power in the breeze to cause a small ripple beneath her gilt figure-head, and at the mainmast truck the commissioning pendant flapped and whipped with lonely agitation, as if it commanded the only strength the wind had to offer.

Lieutenant Herrick walked slowly aft along the maindeck, his eyes moving from side to side as he watched the men flaking down ropes and putting a last tautness in sheets and braces. He knew that they were discussing the news about the contaminated water, and other things beside, but as he passed even the usually friendly ones fell silent. The past two weeks of heat and dull discomfort were showing their teeth now, he decided. No one complained or grumbled any more. That was the worst sign of all.

He halted as Midshipman Maynard appeared below the quarterdeck and leaned heavily on a twelve-pounder. Beneath his tan his thin features were as pale as death, and his legs looked as if they were near collapse.

Herrick crossed to his side. 'What is it, lad? Are you ill?'

Maynard turned and stared at him, his eyes opaque with fear. For a moment he could not speak, then the words poured from his dry lips in a flood.

'I've just come from below, sir.' He screwed up his face. 'I was sent down to the orlop to fetch Mr. Evans.' He swallowed hard and tried to speak coherently. 'I found him in his cabin, sir.' He retched and swayed against the gun.

Herrick gripped his arm and whispered fiercely, 'Go on, lad! What the hell is wrong?'

'Dead!' The word was wrung from his lips. 'My God, sir! He's been cut to pieces!' He stared at Herrick's grim features, reliving the nightmare of his discovery. He repeated faintly, 'Cut to pieces.'

'Keep your voice down!' Herrick struggled to control his shocked thoughts. In a calmer tone he called, 'Mr. Quintal! Take Mr. Maynard aft and see that he is kept alone!'

The boatswain, caught in the act of reprimanding a seaman, stared from one to the other. He touched his forehead and said gruffly, 'Aye, aye, sir.' Then he asked quietly, 'Is somethin' up, sir?'

Herrick looked at Quintal's broad, competent face and answered flatly, 'It seems that the purser is dead, Mr. Quintal!' He saw the quick start of alarm in the man's eyes and added, 'Show no sign! This ship is like a tinderbox as it is.'

Herrick watched the boatswain leading the young midshipman into the shadow of the quarterdeck and then glanced quickly around him. Everything looked as it had two minutes earlier.

Lieutenant Okes had the watch and was standing at the quarterdeck rail, his eyes up at the topsails. Further aft Herrick could just see the captain in conversation with Vibart and Rennie, while at the wheel the two helmsmen looked as if they had been at their posts since time began.

Herrick walked slowly towards the lower cabin hatch. He made himself move calmly, but his heart felt as if it was in his throat.

With all hands employed trimming sails the lower deck was deserted and strangely alien. A few lanterns swung on their hooks, and as he began to climb down the second and last ladder Herrick could sense an air of menace and danger. Even so, he was totally unprepared for the sight in the purser's tiny cabin.

Deep in the hull of the ship the stillness was all the more apparent, and the solitary lantern on the low deckhead cast a steady circle of light on a scene which made Herrick's throat choke with bile. Evans, the purser, must have been secreting a bag of flour for his own private uses when his assailant had struck him down. He lay spread-eagled on the upended sack, his eyes bright in the lamplight, while from his severed throat a great torrent of dark blood seeped and congealed in the scattered flour. There was blood everywhere, and as Herrick stared with fixed horror at the corpse at his feet he saw that Evans had been stabbed and slashed as if by some crazed beast.

He leaned against the door and touched his face with his hand. His palm felt cold and clammy, and he thought of young Maynard alone with this appalling spectacle. No one could have blamed him if he had rushed screaming to the upperdeck.

'My God!' Herrick's voice hung in the gloom in a mocking echo. He almost cried out again as a foot rasped on the ladder behind him, but as he groped blindly for his pistol he saw that it was Captain Rennie, his scarlet coat like a reflection of the blood on the cabin deck.

Rennie brushed past him and stared fixedly at the corpse. Then he said coldly, 'I'll put two of my best men on guard here. The cabin must be sealed until there has been an investigation.' He eyed Herrick meaningly. 'You know what this means, don't you?'

Herrick felt himself nod. 'I do.' He pulled himself together. 'I'll go and tell the captain.'

As he climbed up the ladder Rennie called quietly, 'Easy, Thomas. There will be at least one guilty man watching your face on deck!'

Herrick glanced back at the open cabin door, making himself form a final picture of the murdered man. 'I suppose I was expecting something like this.' He bit his lip. 'But when it comes, it's still a shock.'

Rennie watched him go and then stepped carefully over the glaring corpse. Ignoring the thing by his polished boots he began to search methodically amongst the scattered souvenirs of the purser's life.

Herrick's face was like stone as he crossed to the weather side of the quarterdeck to where Bolitho was still speaking with Vibart. He touched his hat and waited until Bolitho turned to face him.

'Well, Mr. Herrick?' Bolitho's smile of welcome faded. 'Is it more trouble?'

Herrick looked quickly around him, 'Mr. Evans has been murdered, sir.' He spoke in a tight, clipped voice which he no longer recognised. 'Maynard found him a few minutes ago.' He ran his hand across his face. It was still cold, like the mark of death.

Bolitho said slowly, 'What have you done so far, Mr. Herrick?' There was nothing in his question to betray what he must be feeling, and his features were composed in an impassive mask. 'Take your time. Just tell me what you saw.'

Herrick moved closer to the rail, his eyes on the glittering water. In a slow, flat voice he described the events from the moment Maynard had appeared on deck to the actual second of realisation.

Bolitho listened in complete silence, and at Herrick's side Vibart stood swaying with the ship, his hands opening and closing from either anger or shock at Maynard's discovery.

Herrick concluded heavily. 'He had not been dead long, sir.' He found himself repeating the midshipman's words. 'He had been cut to pieces!'

Captain Rennie marched across the deck and said crisply, 'I have put some men on guard, sir.' He saw Bolitho looking at his boots, and bent quickly to wipe a bright stain from the polished leather. He added calmly, 'I've had a good look round, sir. Evans' pistols are missing. Stolen most likely.'

Bolitho eyed him thoughtfully. 'Thank you, gentlemen. You have both behaved very well.'

Vibart said vehemently, 'What did I tell you, sir? Softness with these scum is no use! They only understand a hard hand!'

Bolitho said, 'His pistols, you say?'

Rennie nodded. 'He had two small weapons. He was very proud of them. Gold-mounted and quite valuable, I believe. He said he got them in Spain.' He fell silent, as if he, like the others, was thinking of the dead man as he had once been. One of the most disliked men in the ship. A man with grudges and hates more than most. It was not difficult to understand that he would have an equal number of enemies.

Proby climbed the ladder and touched his hat. 'May I dismiss the watch below, sir?' He seemed to realise that he was intruding and muttered, 'Beggin' your pardon, sir!'

Bolitho said, 'Have the hands stay at their stations, Mr. Proby.' They all looked at him. There was a new coldness in Bolitho's voice and an unfamiliar hardness in his eyes. To Rennie he continued, 'Post sentries at every hatch. Nobody will go below.'

Vibart murmured, 'So you'll see it *my* way, sir?'

Bolitho swung round. 'Someone is guilty, Mr. Vibart. But not the whole ship! I don't want this man to escape, or his actions to contaminate the rest of our people!' In a calmer tone he said, 'Mr. Herrick, you will take the berth deck with Mr. Farquhar and the boatswain. Captain Rennie will search the rest of the ship with his own men.' He looked down at the waiting seamen on the decks and gangways. 'Mr. Vibart, you will take the upperdeck yourself with Mr. Brock. Look in every locker and beneath each gun, and be as quick as you can!'

He watched them troop down the ladder and then returned his attention to the crowded maindecks. Every sailor was now fully aware that something was wrong. He saw one nudge his companion, and another fell back fearfully as Vibart and the gunner pushed through the watching men.

Perhaps Vibart was right after all? He gripped his hands together behind him with such force that the pain helped to control his whirling mind. No, he must not think like that. Without faith there was nothing. Nothing at all.

As the minutes dragged on a growing wave of apprehension moved across the crowded maindeck like smoke from an uncontrollable fire. The seamen at the foot of the mainmast parted to allow Vibart and the gunner to move through and then shuffled together as if for mutual support.

Pochin rubbed his tarry hands on his trousers and glared angrily after Vibart's bulky figure. 'What the hell's happenin'?' He reached out as a boatswain's mate made to pass him. 'Do *you* know, Mr. Josling?'

Josling darted a quick glance at the quarterdeck. 'The purser. 'E's dead!'

A new ripple of uneasiness broke over the waiting men, and Pochin stared across at Allday who was leaning watchfully against the mast. 'Did you hear that, man?'

Allday nodded and then slowly turned his head to look at Onslow. He was standing a bit apart from the others, his legs relaxed, his brown arms hanging loosely at his sides. But there was an air of animal watchfulness about the man, betrayed in the flat hardness of his eyes and the excited dilation of his nostrils. Allday released his breath very slowly. In his own mind he had no doubt as to where the finger of accusation would point.

Old Strachan muttered, 'Looks bad, don't it? I got a feelin' that we're in for another squall!'

There was a sudden burst of activity from the quarterdeck, and as every head turned aft Captain Rennie's marines trooped up the ladders and formed a solid scarlet barrier athwart the deck. Sergeant Garwood dressed the ranks and then took his place beside the small drummer. Captain Rennie stood coolly ahead of his men, one hand resting on his sword hilt, his face empty of expression.

From the side of his mouth the sergeant rasped, 'Fix bayonets!' Every hand moved as one, the blades rippling along the swaying front rank before clicking into place on the long muskets.

On deck the tension was almost unbearable. Every man watched transfixed, afraid to speak or turn his head for fear of missing some part of this new drama. Here and there a hand moved to dash away the sweat, and somewhere in the packed throng a man began to cough nervously.

Allday saw the captain speaking with Lieutenant Herrick and the boatswain, and watched as Bolitho shook his head at something one of them had said. It might have been anger or disbelief. It was impossible to tell.

Vibart had realised that the search was over, and moved slowly aft, his hands pushing the silent men aside like reeds, his red-rimmed eyes fixed on the little group behind the marines.

Pochin whispered, 'We'll soon know now!'

Allday darted another glance at Onslow. For a moment he felt something like pity for him. He had been so long penned up in a ship he had known no other life but the ceaseless battle of the lower deck.

Captain Bolitho's voice broke into his thoughts, and when he looked aft again he saw him at the quarterdeck rail, his hands resting on the starboard carronade as he stared down at the assembled seamen.

'As most of you know by now, Mr. Evans the purser is dead. He was killed in his cabin a short while ago, without pity, and without reason.' He broke off as Herrick descended one of the ladders to speak to the first lieutenant. Then he continued in the same even tone, 'Every man will stand fast until the culprit has been taken!'

Pochin's scarred face was streaming with sweat. He said in a hoarse voice, ' 'E's got some 'opes! Every bastard in the ship 'ated the bloody purser!'

But no one responded or even gave him a glance. Every eye was on Vibart as he moved purposefully along the maindeck with Brock at his back.

Even the sound of sea and canvas seemed stilled, and as Vibart halted below the mainyard Allday could hear his heavy breathing and the squeak of his sword belt.

For a few seconds longer the awful suspense continued. Then, as Vibart ran his eye slowly around the watching faces, Brock stepped forward and lifted his cane.

'That's him, sir! That's the murderous cur!'

The cane fell in a tight arc, and Allday reeled back, half stunned from the blow.

The weeks and months dropped away, and he was back on the cliff road with Brock lashing out at his face with the same cane while the other members of the press gang crowded round to watch. He could feel the blood stinging the corner of his mouth, and there seemed to be a great roaring in his ears. Voices were calling and shouting all around him, yet he felt unable to move or defend himself as Brock struck him once more across the neck with his cane. Vibart was staring at him, his eyes almost hidden by his brows as he watched Brock pull him from the mast and away from the other men.

Old Strachen croaked, ' 'E was with me! 'E never done it, Mr. Vibart!'

At last Vibart seemed to find his voice. But his words were strangled, as if his body was so taut with insane anger that he could hardly get himself to speak. 'Silence, you stupid old fool!' He thrust the man aside. 'Or I will take you, too!'

Some of the men had recovered from the first shock and now surged forward, pressed on by those at the rear. Instantly there was a barked command from the quarterdeck, and a line of muskets rose above the rail. There was no doubting their intent, or the gleam in Sergeant Garwood's eyes.

Bolitho was still at one side of the rail, his figure dark against the pale sky. 'Bring that man aft, Mr. Vibart!'

Old Strachan was muttering vaguely, ' 'E was with me, I swear it!'

Brock pushed Allday towards the quarterdeck and snapped, 'Were you Strachan? *All* the time?'

Strachan was confused. 'Well, all but a minute, Mr. Brock!'

Brock's voice was harsh. 'It only takes a minute to kill a man!'

Allday made another effort to clear his dazed mind as he was pushed up a ladder and past the grim-faced marines. He felt like another person, someone on the outside untouched by the cruel reality of events. Even his limbs felt numb and beyond his control, and the cuts from Brock's cane had neither pain nor meaning. He saw Lieutenant Herrick watching him like a stranger, and beyond him Proby, the master, looked away, as if he could not bear to meet his eye.

Captain Bolitho seemed to appear from nowhere, and as they faced each other across three feet of deck Allday heard him say, 'John Allday, do you have anything to say?'

He had to move his numb lips several times before the words would come. 'No, sir.' An insane voice seemed to cry from the depths of his soul. Tell him! Tell him! He tried again. 'It wasn't me, sir.'

He tried to see beyond the shadow which hid the captain's face. He could see the lines at the corners of his mouth, a bead of sweat running from beneath the dark hair. But there was no reality. It was all part of the same nightmare.

Bolitho said, 'Do you recognise these?'

Someone held out a pair of small pistols, bright and evil looking in the sunlight.

Allday shook his head. 'No, sir.'

'Or this?' Bolitho's voice was quite empty of emotion.

This time it was a knife, the tip broken off by the force of savage blows, its worn handle dark with congealed blood.

Allday stared. 'It's mine, sir!' He clapped his hand to his belt, his fingers brushing against an empty sheath.

Bolitho said. 'The pistols were found amongst your possessions below. Your knife was discovered beneath Mr. Evans' locker.' He paused to let the words sink in. 'Where it was dropped after the struggle.'

Allday swayed. 'I didn't do it, sir.' The words seemed to hang in his throat. 'Why would I do such a thing?'

As if from a long way off he heard Vibart's harsh voice. 'Let me run him up to the yard now, sir! It will give others of his sort something to think about with him dancing from a halter!'

Bolitho snapped, 'I think you have said enough, Mr. Vibart!' He turned back to Allday. 'After your behaviour since you first came aboard, I had high hopes for you, Allday. Mr. Herrick has already spoken on your behalf, but on this occasion I can find no reason for leniency.' He paused. 'Under the Articles of War I could have you hanged forthwith. As it is, I intend that you should be tried by court martial as soon as the opportunity arises.'

There was a low murmur of despair from the maindeck, and Allday knew that in everyone's eyes he was already a dead man.

Bolitho turned away. 'Place him in irons, Mr. Vibart. But any unneccessary brutality will be answerable to me!'

Dazed, and stumbling like a drunken man, Allday allowed himself to be led below.

Deep below the maindeck there were two tiny cells, each just large enough to contain one man. Allday watched dumbly as the rough manacles were snapped around his wrists and ankles, but only when the door was slammed and bolted behind him and he was left in total darkness did the true realisation close on him like a vice.

By the time the *Phalarope* returned to port, and a necessary number of officers was available for a court martial, no one would remember or even care if he was guilty or not. He would be used as an example to others. A dancing, kicking puppet on the end of a rope as he was hauled slowly to the mainyard to the accompaniment of a drum's mournful beat.

He smashed his fists against the door, and heard the sound echo and vibrate in the stillness of the hull. Again and again, until he could feel the blood running across his fingers and taste the angry tears on his lips.

But when he fell exhausted and gasping behind the door, there was nothing but silence.

The deep, empty silence of a tomb.

Lieutenant Herrick rested his shoulder against an empty hammock netting and stared moodily along the frigate's deserted decks. An hour of the middle watch had passed, and in the bright moonlight the sails and rigging gave off an eerie glow, like those of some phantom vessel.

Try as he might, he could not put the thought of Allday and the murdered purser from his mind. He should have been able to tell himself that it was over and done with. Just one more item in the log to be talked over for a time and then forgotten. Evans was dead, and his killer was penned below in irons. That at least should be some small satisfaction to everybody. An undetected murderer, at large to terrorise the lower deck or to strike again, would have been far more to worry about.

He tried to picture Allday standing over that hideous corpse crazed enough to rip at the man's body until it was hardly human, yet calmly able to steal a pair of pistols and secrete them in his own quarters. It did not make any sense at all, but Herrick knew that had it been anyone else but Allday he would never have questioned such evidence.

Just before coming on watch Herrick had made his way below to the darkened cells, and after sending the marine sentry to the top of the ladder, had opened the door and held a lantern inside.

Allday had crouched against the opposite side, his hands shading his eyes from the light, his feet skidding in his own filth. Any disgust or anger Herrick may have felt faded in that instant. He had expected loud denials of guilt, or dumb insolence. Instead there was only a pathetic attempt at pride.

He had asked quietly, 'Have you anything more to tell me, Allday? I have not forgotten that you saved my life on the cliff. Perhaps if you tell me the full circumstances I will be able to do something to attract clemency on your behalf?'

Allday had made as if to brush his long hair from his eyes, and then looked down at the heavy manacles. In a barely controlled voice he had replied, 'I did not do it, Mr. Herrick. I cannot find a defence for something I *did not do*!'

'I see.' In the silence Herrick had heard the scampering rats, the strange, unknown creaks of a ship at sea. 'If you change your mind, I . . .'

Allday had tried to step towards him and had fallen forward on Herrick's arm. For a few seconds Herrick had felt the touch of his bare skin, damp with fear, had smelt his despair, like the odour of death.

Allday had said thickly, 'You don't believe me either! So what's the point?' His voice had gained some small inner strength. 'Just leave me alone! For God's sake leave me *alone*!'

But as Herrick had been about to rebolt the door Allday had asked quietly, 'D'you think they'll send me home for court martial, sir?'

Herrick knew that the Navy would have other ideas. Justice was swift and final. But as he had stared at the heavy studded door he had heard himself reply, 'Maybe they will. Why do you ask?'

The answer had been muffled, as if Allday had turned his face away. 'I would like to see the green hills again. Just once. Even for a few minutes!'

The sadness and despair of those last words had dogged Herrick for the rest of the day, and now during his watch they were with him still.

'Damn!' He spoke aloud with sudden anger, and the two helmsmen jerked upright by the wheel as if he had struck them.

The senior man watched anxiously as Herrick walked towards the wheel and said quickly, 'Full an' bye, sir! Course south by east!'

Herrick stared at him and then at the gently swinging compass card. Poor devils, he thought vaguely. Scared sick because I swore aloud.

A dark figure moved from the lee rail and walked slowly towards him. It was Proby, his heavy jowls glowing faintly from his short clay pipe.

Herrick said, 'Can't you sleep, Mr. Proby? The breeze is slight but steady now. There'll be nothing for you to attend to tonight.'

The master sucked noisily at the stem. 'It's the best time of the night, Mr Herrick. You can look into the wind's eye and think about what you've done with your life!'

Herrick looked sideways at Proby's crumpled features. In the pipe glow his face looked like a piece of weatherworn sculpture, but there was something reassuring about him all the same. Timeless, like the sea itself.

He said at length, 'Do you think we have heard the last of Evan's death?'

'Who can say?' Proby shifted on his flat feet. 'It takes time to clean such a deed from a man's memory. Aye, it takes a long time.'

The pipe glow suddenly vanished in the palm of Proby's beefy hand, and he said tersely, 'The captain is on deck, Mr. Herrick!' Then in a louder, matter-of-fact tone he said, 'We should make a good landfall tomorrow if this wind holds. So I'll bid you good night, Mr. Herrick!'

Then he was gone, and Herrick moved towards the lee rail. From the corner of his eye he could see Bolitho standing straight against the weather rail, the moonlight sharp across his white shirt as he stared at the glittering reflections beyond the ship.

Bolitho had not left the quarterdeck for more than an hour at a time, and ever since Allday's arrest he had been seen by the taffrail, either pacing the deck or just staring out to sea, as he was now.

Earlier Herrick had overhead the master speaking to Quintal, the boatswain, and now as he watched Bolitho's motionless figure the words came back to him. Quintal had said in a hoarse whisper, 'I didn't know he felt like that about Evans. He seems fair troubled by it all!'

Old Proby had weighed his words before replying. 'It's the deed which bothers the captain, Mr. Quintal. He feels betrayed, that's what is wrong with *him*!'

Herrick saw Bolitho touch the scar on his forehead and then rub the tiredness from his eyes. Proby was right, he thought. He feels it more than we realise. Whatever any of us does, he shares it like his own burden.

Before he realised what he was doing, Herrick had crossed the deck to Bolitho's side. Instantly he regretted his action. He half expected Bolitho to turn and reprimand him, and even that might have been better than the complete silence. He said, 'The wind is holding well, sir. The master has prophesied a quick landfall.'

'I think I heard him.' Bolitho seemed to be deep in his own thoughts.

Herrick saw that the captain's shirt was dark with thrown spray and clung close to his body like another skin. There were deep shadows beneath his eyes, and Herrick could almost feel the inner torment which was keeping Bolitho on deck instead of the privacy of the cabin.

He said. 'Would you like me to call your servant, sir? Perhaps a hot drink before you turn in for the night?'

Bolitho twisted round at the rail, his eyes bright in the moonlight. 'Spare me this small talk, Mr. Herrick! What is it which bothers you?'

Herrick swallowed hard and then blurted out, 'I have been speaking with Allday, sir. I know it was wrong, but I feel partly responsible for him.'

Bolitho was watching him closely. 'Go on.'

'He is one of my men, sir, and I think there may be more to what happened than we think.' He finished lamely, 'I know him better than most. He is not the sort to change.'

Bolitho sighed. 'Only the stars never change, Mr. Herrick.'

Herrick said stubbornly, 'Even so, he may be innocent!'

'And you think this is important?' Bolitho sounded tired. 'You believe that the life of one man, a man almost certain to be found guilty, is worth consideration?'

'Well, as a matter of fact, I do, sir.' Herrick felt Bolitho's eyes fixed on his face in a cold stare. 'The authorities will not listen to half a story . . .'

Bolitho shifted with sudden impatience. '*We* are the authority out here, Mr. Herrick! And I will decide what is to be done!'

Herrick looked away. 'Yes, sir.'

'As it happens, I entirely agree with you.' Bolitho pushed the lock of hair back from his forehead, ignoring Herrick's open astonishment. 'But I just wanted to hear it from one other person!'

He became suddenly brisk. 'I think I will go below now, Mr. Herrick, *without* a hot drink. Tomorrow we will search for fresh water and attend to the matter of fighting a war.' He paused momentarily by the rail. 'I will also think about what you have said tonight. It may be important for all of us.'

Without another word he turned on his heel and descended the cabin stairway. Herrick stared after him, his jaw hanging open.

'Well, I'll be damned!' He shook his head and grinned. 'Well, I'll be *double*-damned!'

15

The Storm Breaks

Surprisingly the wind did hold, and twenty hours after Proby's prophecy the *Phalarope*'s anchor splashed down into deep, clear water amidst a huddle of low, desolate islets.

Apart from lowering boats and filling them with water casks in readiness for the following morning, it was pointless to attempt a landing with night so close at hand, but at the first hint of daylight, long before the sun was able to burnish an edge to the horizon, the first boatloads of men grated up the narrow shelving beach of the nearest islet.

Bolitho climbed through the tangle of dark scrub at the top of the beach and stared round at the busy preparations behind him. The boats had already shoved off to collect more men, and the ones already landed were standing huddled together, as if conscious of the island's bleak inhospitality. One or two of the sailors were staggering like drunken revellers, their legs so used to the pitch and toss of a ship's deck that the unfamiliar land destroyed their sense of balance.

Petty officers bawled orders, and checked their lists of names, and as the next batch of men arrived to join the swelling mass of sailors at the water's edge the first parties picked up their casks and tools and began to stumble inland.

Lieutenant Okes appeared on the ridge and touched his hat. 'All working parties ready, sir.' He looked harassed.

Bolitho nodded. 'You have your orders, Mr. Okes. Just follow the rough map I made for you and you should find fresh water without difficulty. Keep the men moving fast before the sun comes up. You'll need every available man to carry the full casks down to the beach, so see they don't wander off.'

He saw Trevenen, the cooper, scurrying ahead of another party accompanied by Ledward, the carpenter, the latter ever hopeful of replenishing his stock of spare timber. He'd not find much here, Bolitho thought grimly. These islets were useless and left well alone, but for occasional fresh-water parties. Underfoot the ground was hidden by layer upon layer of rotten vegetation, its heavy stench well mixed with seagull droppings and small bright patches of fungus. Further inland there were a few hump-backed hills, from the top of which a man could see the sea in every direction.

Okes walked off after his men, and Bolitho caught sight of Farquhar's slim figure outlined against the green scrub, before he too vanished over the far side of the ridge. Bolitho had deliberately ordered the midshipman to join Okes in command of the main party. It would do them both good to work together if only to break down the strange air of watchful tension between them. It seemed as if Farquhar was playing some sort of game with Okes. Ever since his escape from the *Andiron* Farquhar had made a point of not speaking to Okes, but his presence alone seemed more than enough to reduce the lieutenant to a state of permanent agitation.

Okes had acted hastily during the retreat from Mola Island, but unless he made an open admission there was little point in pursuing the matter, Bolitho thought. He could sympathise with Farquhar, and wondered what he himself might have done under the same set of circumstances. Farquhar's built-in sense of caution had obviously taught him that there was more to a career than gaining petty triumphs. Also his breeding, the security of a powerful family, as well as his own self-confidence, gave him the ability to bide his time.

Herrick strode up the slope and said, 'Shall we return to the ship, sir!'

Bolitho shook his head. 'We'll walk a little further, Mr. Herrick.'

He pushed through a line of sun-scarred bushes and headed away from the beach. Herrick walked beside him in silence, no doubt thinking of the strangeness of the land around him. The sea's gentle hiss was gone and the air was heavy with alien smells and a thick, clinging humidity.

Bolitho said at length, 'I hope Okes can get the men working quickly. Every hour may be precious.'

'You are thinking of the French, sir?'

Bolitho wiped the sweat from his face and nodded. 'De Grasse may have sailed by now. If he behaves as Sir George Rodney believes he will, his fleet will already be striking west for Jamaica.' He looked up fretfully at the limp leaves and cloudless sky. 'Not a breath of wind. Nothing. We were lucky it held long enough for us to reach here!'

Herrick was breathing heavily. 'My God, sir, I'm feeling this!' He mopped his face. 'I have not set foot properly ashore since Falmouth. I had almost forgotten what it was like.'

Falmouth. Again the name brought back a flood of memories to Bolitho as he strode unseeingly through the thick scrub. His father would still be waiting and wondering, nursing the hurt which Hugh had left with him. Bolitho wondered momentarily what would have happened if he had seen and recognised his brother on the *Andiron*'s poop on that first savage encounter. Would he have pressed home his attack with such fervour? If he had caused Hugh's death it might have eased the minds of the Navy, but in his heart Bolitho knew that it would only have added to his father's grief and sense of loss.

Perhaps Hugh already had another ship. He dismissed the idea at once. The French would not trust another prize to a man who had allowed *Andiron* to fall into her own snare. And the American rebel government had few ships to spare. No, Hugh would have his own problems in plenty at this moment.

He thought too of Vibart, left behind in charge of the frigate. It was strange how Evans' murder had affected him. Bolitho had always thought Evans to be more of a toady than a friend of the first lieutenant. Yet his death seemed in some way to have deprived Vibart of something familiar and reliable, the last outlet from his own isolation. Bolitho knew that Vibart blamed him for Evans's death, as much as he hated Allday for the deed. Vibart viewed humanity like sentiment. To him both were useless hindrances to duty.

He also knew that he would never see eye to eye with Vibart whatever happened. To Bolitho the humane treatment of his men, the understanding of their problems, and the earning of their loyalty, were as precious as gold. Equally he knew he must uphold this difficult and bitter man, for commanding a ship of war left little room for personal animosity amongst officers.

Bolitho halted with a jerk and pointed. 'Is that a marine?'

Herrick stood beside him breathing deeply. A red coat flashed between the dull foliage and then another, and as Bolitho started forward, Sergeant Garwood appeared at the head of a file of sweating marines.

Bolitho asked sharply, 'What are you doing ashore, Sergeant?'

Garwood stared fixedly over Bolitho's shoulder. 'Mr. Vibart 'as sent all the marines across, sir.' He swallowed hard. 'The prisoner Allday 'as escaped, sir. We've been sent to catch 'im again!'

Bolitho heard Herrick catch his breath and glanced quickly at his streaming face. He could see the shock and disappointment plain on the lieulieutenant's features, as if he was personally involved.

'I see.' Bolitho controlled the sudden rise of anger and added calmly. 'Where is Captain Rennie?'

'T'other side of the island, sir.' Garwood looked unhappy. 'The relief sentry found the cell guard clubbed senseless an' the prisoner gone, sir. 'Is manacles 'ad been struck off too, sir.'

'So someone else was involved?' Bolitho stared hard at the sergeant's bronzed features. 'Who else is missing?'

The marine gulped. 'Yer clerk, Ferguson, sir!'

Bolitho turned away. 'Very well, I suppose you had better carry on now that you are here.' He watched the man clump gratefully away and then said tightly, 'Mr. Vibart was over hasty to send all the marines ashore. If the ship was surprised at her anchor by another vessel, there would be insufficient men to repel an attack.' He turned abruptly. 'Come, we will go back to the beach.'

Herrick said wretchedly, 'I am sorry, sir. I feel to blame more than ever. I trusted Allday, and I was the one who chose Ferguson as your clerk.'

Bolitho replied flatly, 'It has proved that we were both wrong, Mr. Herrick. An innocent man does not run!' He added, 'Mr. Vibart should not have allowed his anger to blind his judgement in this matter. Allday will surely die if he is left here. He will go mad on this island once the ship has sailed, and will not thank Ferguson for his rescue from a cell!'

They hurried across the beach, and the drowsing gig's crew jerked into life as the two officers climbed aboard.

Bolitho shaded his eyes to look at the anchored frigate as the gig moved slowly across the placid water. The sun was only just showing above the nearest hump of land, and the *Phalarope*'s yards and topmasts were shining as if coated with gilt.

Herrick asked quietly, 'If the marines catch Allday, sir. What will you do?'

'I will hang him this time, Mr. Herrick. For the sake of discipline I have no choice now.' He glanced back at the land. 'For that reason I hope they do not find him.'

The bowman hooked on to the chains, and Bolitho pulled himself through the entry port.

At his elbow Herrick snapped, 'Why did you not hail the gig, man?' His own unhappy thoughts put an unusual edge to his voice.

The seaman at the entry port blinked and stammered, 'I'm sorry, sir. I – I ...' His voice trailed away as he stared up at the quarterdeck

There was a tight group of seamen beneath the quarterdeck, and as the cold realisation seeped into Bolitho's brain, they pushed out into the growing sunlight which shone and reflected on their raised muskets.

Herrick thrust Bolitho aside and reached for his sword, but a giant sailor with a pistol snapped, 'Stay where you are, Mr. Herrick!' He pointed up at the quarterdeck rail. 'Otherwise it will go hard with that one!'

Two more men appeared from behind the cabin hatch, between them carrying the small, struggling figure of Midshipman Neale. One man drew a knife from his belt and laid it across Neale's throat, grinning down at the two officers as he did so.

The tall seaman, whom Bolitho now recognised as Onslow, stepped slowly across the maindeck, his pistol trained on Herrick. 'Well, Mr. Herrick? Do you drop your sword?' He grinned lazily. 'It's all the same to me!'

Bolitho said, 'Do as he says, Mr. Herrick.' He had seen the brightness in Onslow's eyes, and knew that the man was eager, desperately eager to kill. He was only just keeping his pent up madness in check. One false move and there would be no more time left to act.

The sword clattered on the deck. Onslow kicked it aside and called sharply, 'Take the gig's crew forrard and batten 'em down with the other pretty boys!' He tapped his nose with his pistol. 'They'll all join us later, or feed the fish!'

Some of the men laughed. It was a wild, explosive sound. Brittle with tension.

Bolitho studied Onslow, the first shock giving way to sudden caution. Every captain dreaded such a moment. Some had earned it, others had fallen foul of uncontrollable circumstances. Now it had happened to him. To the *Phalarope*.

It was mutiny.

Onslow watched as the gig's crew was bundled below deck and then said, 'We'll up anchor as soon as a likely wind blows. We have the master below, and either he or you will take the ship to open waters.'

Herrick said hoarsely, 'You're mad! You'll swing for this!'

The pistol barrel came down sharply, and Herrick dropped to his knees, his hands across his forehead.

Bolitho saw the blood bright across Herrick's fingers and said coldly, 'And if the wind fails to arrive, Onslow? What will you do?'

Onslow nodded, his eyes searching Bolitho's face. 'A good question. Well, we have a good little ship beneath us. We can sink any boat which tries to board us, do you not agree?'

Bolitho kept his face impassive, but realised that Onslow had good reasons for confidence. Outnumbered by the rest of the crew and Rennie's marines, Onslow was still in the position of king. Even a handful of men could keep boats at bay with the frigate's guns loaded with grape. He glanced at the sun. It would be hours yet before Okes started on the long march back to the beach.

He said slowly. 'So it was you all the time.'

Another man, small and stinking of rum, capered round the two officers. 'He done it all! Just as 'e said 'e would!'

Onslow snarled, 'Stow it, Pook!' Then more calmly, 'Your clerk told me when the ship was nearing land. All I had to do was foul the fresh-water casks with salt.' He laughed, amused by the very simplicity of his plan. 'Then, when you headed this way, I killed that rat Evans.'

Bolitho said, 'You must have been very afraid of Allday to incriminate him with murder!'

Onslow glanced along the deck and then said calmly, 'It was necessary. I knew if the bullocks were still aboard some of my white-livered friends might not be so willing to seize the ship!' He shrugged. 'So I had Allday released, and the bullocks went charging off after him. Just as I *knew* they would!'

'You've damned yourself, Onslow!' Bolitho kept his voice level. 'But think of these other men with you. Will you see them hanged?'

Onslow shouted, 'Shut your mouth! And think yourself lucky I've not had you strung up at the mainyard! I'm going to barter the ship for our freedom! No bloody navy'll catch us after that!'

Bolitho hardened his tone to hide his rising despair. 'You are a fool if you believe that!'

His head jerked back as Onslow struck him across the face with the back of his hand. '*Silence!*' Onslow's shout brought more men pressing around. Herrick was dragged to his feet and his hands were pinioned behind him. He was still dazed, and his face was streaming with blood.

Bolitho said, 'You can send the officers ashore. They are nothing to you, Onslow.'

'Ah now, Captain, you're wrong there!' Onslow's good humour was returning. 'Hostages. You may fetch a good price, too!' He laughed. 'But then you must be getting used to that!'

Pook yelled, 'Why not kill 'em now?' He waved a cutlass. 'Let me have 'em!'

Onslow looked at Bolitho. 'You see? Only I can save you.'

'What have you done with the first lieutenant?' Bolitho saw Pook nudge another seaman. 'Have you killed him, too?'

Pook sniggered. 'Not likely! We're savin' 'im for a bit o' sport later on!'

Onslow flexed his arms. 'He's flogged enough of us, Captain. I'll see how he likes the cat across *his* fat hide!'

Herrick muttered between his clenched teeth, 'Think of what you're doing! You are selling this ship to the enemy!'

'You're my enemy!' Onslow's nostrils flared as if he had been touched with a hot iron. 'I'll do what I like with her, and with you, too!'

Bolitho said quietly, 'Easy, Mr. Herrick. There is nothing you can do.'

'Spoken like a true gentleman!' Onslow gave a slow grin. 'It's best to know when you're beaten!' Then sharply he called, 'Lock them below, lads! And kill the first bugger who tries anything!'

Some of the men growled with obvious disapproval. Their lust was high. They were all committed. Bolitho knew that Onslow's careful plan was only half clear in their rum-sodden minds.

Onslow added, 'As soon as the wind gets up, we're off, lads! You can leave the rest to Harry Onslow!'

Herrick and Bolitho were pushed along the deck and down into the dark confines of a small storeroom. A moment later Midshipman Neale and Proby, the master, were thrust in with them and the door slammed shut.

High up the side of the cabin was a small circular port, used to ventilate the compartment and the stores it normally contained. Bolitho guessed that the mutineers had already dragged the contents elsewhere for their own uses.

In the darkness Neale sobbed, 'I – I'm sorry, sir! I let you down! I was on watch when it all happened!'

Bolitho said quietly, 'It was not your fault, boy. The odds were against you this time. It was just ironic that Onslow stayed aboard because he could not be trusted *off* the ship!'

Neale said brokenly, 'Mr. Vibart was in his cabin. They seized him and nearly killed him! Onslow stopped them just in time!'

Herrick said bleakly, 'Not for long!' Then with sudden fury, 'The fools! The French or the Spanish will never bargain with Onslow! They won't have to. They'll seize the *Phalarope* and take the whole lot prisoners!'

Bolitho said. 'I know that, Herrick. But if the mutineers began to think as you do, they'd have no reason for sparing our lives!'

'I see, sir.' Herrick was peering at him in the gloom. 'And I thought . . .'

'You imagined that I had given up hope?' Bolitho breathed out slowly. 'Not yet. Not without a fight!'

He stood up on an empty box and peered through the small vent hole. The ship had swung slightly at her cable and he could see the far end of the little beach and a low hill beyond. There was no sign of life. Nor had he expected any.

Proby muttered, 'Two of the mutineers I know well. Good men, with no cause to follow scum like Onslow and Pook!' He added thickly, 'It'll do 'em no good. They'll be caught and hanged with the rest!'

Herrick slipped and cursed in the darkness. 'Damn!' He groped with his fingers. 'Some old butter! Rancid as bilge water!'

Bolitho cocked his head to listen to the sudden stamp of feet and a wave of laughter. 'They've taken more than butter, Mr. Herrick. They'll be too drunk to control soon!' He thought of the knife's glitter across Neale's throat. Soon the second phase world be enacted. The mutineers would get bored with merely drinking. They would have to prove themselves. To kill.

He said, 'Can you come up here beside me, Neale?' He felt the midshipman struggling on to the box 'Now, do you think you could get through that vent?'

Neale's eyes flickered in the shaft of sunlight. He replied doubtfully, 'It's very small, sir.' Then more firmly, 'I'll try!'

Proby asked. 'What do you have in mind, sir?'

Bolitho ran his hands around the circular hole. It was barely ten inches across. He controlled the rising excitement in his heart. It *had* to be tried.

He said, 'If Neale could slip through . . .' He broke off. 'The butter! Quick, Neale, strip off your clothes!' He reached out for Herrick. 'We'll rub him with butter, Herrick, and ease him through, like a sponge in a gun barrel!'

Neale pulled off his clothes and stood uncertainly in the centre of the storeroom. In the faint glow from the vent hole his small body shone like some discarded statue. Bolitho took a double handful of stinking butter from the deck and ignoring Neale's cry of alarm slapped it across his shoulders. As Herrick followed suit Bolitho said quickly, 'The loyal men, Neale, where are they?'

Neale's teeth were beginning to chatter uncontrollably but he replied, 'In the cable tier, sir. The surgeon and some of the older hands as well.'

'Just as I thought.' Bolitho stood back and wiped his palms on his breeches. 'Now listen. If we get you through this hole, could you climb along the forechains?'

Neale nodded. 'I'll try, sir.'

'The others will be locked in the tier by staple. If I can distract the guards you open the door and release them.' He rested his hand on the boy's shoulder. 'But if anyone sees you, forget what I said and jump for it. You could swim ashore before anyone could catch you.'

He turned to the others. 'Right, lend a hand here!'

Neale felt like a greasy fish, and at the first attempt they nearly dropped him.

Herrick suggested, 'One arm first, Neale, then your head.'

They tried again, with the room plunged into total darkness as the struggling, wriggling midshipman was forced into the vent hole.

The boy was gasping with pain, and Proby said, 'Lucky he ain't no fatter.'

Then, with a sudden rush he was through, and after a few agonising seconds, while they all waited for a shouted challenge from the deck, his eyes appeared outside the vent hole. He was scarlet in the face and his shoulder was bleeding from the rough passage.

But he was strangely determined, and Bolitho said softly, 'Take your time, boy. And no chances!'

Neale vanished, and Herrick said heavily, 'Well, at least he's out of it if the worst happens.'

Bolitho looked at him sharply. It was almost as if Herrick had read his own thoughts. But he replied calmly, 'I'll blow this ship to hell before I let it fall to the enemy, Mr. Herrick! Make no mistake about it!'

Then, in silence, he settled down to wait.

John Allday leaned against a tall slab of rock, his chest heaving from exertion as he fought to regain his breath. A few paces away, lying like a corpse with his head and shoulders in a small pool, Bryan Ferguson drank deeply, pausing every so often to give a great gasp for air.

Allday turned to look back through the tangled mass of small trees through which they had just come. There was still no sign of pursuit, but he had no doubt that the alarm was now under way.

He said, 'I've not had time to thank you, Bryan. That was a rash thing you did!'

Ferguson rolled on to his side and stared at him with glazed eyes. 'Had to do it. Had to.'

'It's your neck as well as mine now, Bryan.' Allday studied him sadly. 'But at least we're free. There's always hope when you have your freedom!'

He had been lying in his darkened cell listening to the familiar sounds of boats filling with men and pushing off from the frigate's hull. Then, as the emptied ship had fallen into silence, there had been a cry of alarm and the thud of a body falling against the door.

Ferguson had wrenched it open, his mouth slack with fear, his fingers trembling as he had unlocked the shackles and gabbled out some vague ideas of escape.

The dawn was still a dull smudge in the sky as they had slipped quietly over the side into the cool water. Like many sailors Allday could hardly swim a stroke, but Ferguson, driven by the desperation of fear, had helped him, until choking and gasping they had both staggered on to the safety of the beach.

Hardly speaking they had run or crawled through dense brush, had climbed over fallen rocks, never pausing to either look back or listen. Now they were between two low hills, and exhaustion had pulled them both to a halt.

Allday said, 'Come on, we'd better get ourselves moving again. Up this hill. We'll be safe there. You should be able to see miles from the top.'

Ferguson was still staring at him. 'You were right about Onslow. He is a bad man!' He shuddered. 'I thought he was just trying to be friendly to me. I told him things about the captain's log. About what the ship was doing!' He staggered to his feet and followed Allday slowly up the side of the hill. 'No one will believe me now. I'm as guilty as he is!'

'At least you know I didn't kill the purser!' Allday squinted up at the sun. It would soon be time to stop and hide.

'Onslow boasted about it!' Ferguson gave another shudder. 'After you had been taken to the cells I overheard him talking with some of the others, Pook and Pochin. He boasted how he had killed Evans!'

Allday pulled him into a bush. 'Look!' He pointed across to a distant hillside at a slow-moving line of red dots. 'The bullocks are out looking for us already.'

Ferguson gave a low cry. 'I'll never get back home! I'll never see Grace again!'

Allday looked at him gravely. 'Hold on, Bryan! We're not finished yet. Maybe another ship will call here one day, and we'll pretend we're shipwrecked.'

He turned to watch the distant marines as they moved away to the right.

Marines in their heavy boots and equipment were no match for this sort of game, he thought. Even on a bare Cornish hillside he could have evaded them. Here it was easier, because of the heavy tangle of scrub all around them.

He said, 'It's all right. They're over the other side now. Come on, Bryan!'

They continued up the hillside until Allday found a sheltered clump of bushes which jutted from a great fallen slide of rock. He threw himself down and stared out at the great empty waste of water.

'We'll be safe here, Bryan. When the ship puts to sea we'll build a shelter like I had outside Falmouth. Don't worry about it.'

Ferguson was still standing, his eyes wide as he peered down at his friend. 'Onslow intends to take the ship!' His mouth quivered. 'He told me. He knew I couldn't do anything. He said that I was as guilty as the rest of them!'

Allday tried to grin. 'You're tired!' He tried again. 'Look, how can Onslow seize a frigate?' His grin faded into a look of shocked horror as the true implication dawned on him. He jumped to his feet and seized Ferguson's arm. 'Do you mean Onslow planned all of this? The fresh water, the murder, and my escape?' He did not wait for a reply. The expression on the other man's face was enough.

He gave a hollow groan. 'My God, Bryan! What are we going to do?'

Ferguson said weakly, 'I wanted to tell you. But there was no time! They'd have killed you anyway.'

Allday nodded heavily. 'I know, Bryan. I know.' He stared at the ground. 'I warned them about this.' He ran his fingers through his hair. 'Mutiny! I'll have no part of it!' He looked at Ferguson with sudden determination. 'We must go back and warn them.'

'It'll be too late!' Ferguson clasped his hands together. 'Anyway, I couldn't go! Don't you see? I'm one of them now!' Tears began to pour down his face. 'I couldn't take the lash, John! Please, I *couldn't*!'

Allday turned his back to hide his face from the other man. He stared out to sea, at the hard horizon line which seemed to represent the impossibility of distance. You poor little bugger, he thought. It must have cost a lot of pluck to knock down the sentry and open the cell. Over his shoulder he said calmly, 'I know, Bryan. But give me time to think things out.'

So it was all wasted after all. The determination to take life as it came, to accept danger and hardship in order that he should one day return home, had all come to nothing. It was curious that Ferguson, the one man aboard who had the most to lose, had been the one to spring off the disaster of mutiny.

And disaster it would be, he told himslf grimly. They never gave up a search for a mutineer. No matter how long it took. He remembered seeing some of them hanging in chains at Plymouth. Rotting, eyeless remnants left to the gulls as a warning to others.

Far out on the flat, glittering water something moved to break the calm emptiness of the horizon. Allday dropped on one knee and shaded his eyes with both hands. He blinked to clear the moisture and then looked again. Months at sea as a masthead lookout had given him the sailor's instinct to interpret more than was merely visible to the naked eye. He turned his head very slightly. There was another one. Much smaller. Probably a mile beyond the first.

Ferguson seemed to realise something was happening. 'What is it?'

Allday sat down on the rock at his side and stared at him thoughtfully. 'There are two frigates out yonder, Bryan. Big ones, probably Frogs by the look of 'em.' He let the words sink in and then asked quietly, 'Tell me about your wife back at Falmouth. Grace, isn't that her name?'

Ferguson nodded dumbly, still not understanding.

Allday reached out and took his hand firmly in his own. 'She'll not want to remember you as a mutineer, Bryan?' He saw the quick shake of the head, the unheeded tears on his sunburned cheeks. Then he continued, 'Nor will she want to remember you as the man who let his ship fall to the enemy without lifting a finger to help her.' He stood up slowly and pulled Ferguson to his feet. 'Take a look at those ships, Bryan, and then tell me what to do. You saved my life. I owe you that at least!'

Ferguson stared at the dancing reflections, too blinded with tears to see beyond Allday's quiet words. 'You want me to go back with you?' He spoke in a small voice, yet unable to stop himself. '*To go back?*'

Allday nodded, still keeping his eye on Ferguson's agonised face. 'We have to, Bryan. You can see that, can't you?'

He touched Ferguson's arm, and after a momentary hesitation began to walk down the side of the hill. He did not have to look back to know that Ferguson was following him.

Bolitho felt the hair stirring against the nape of his neck, and stood up to face the small vent hole. After a moment he said, 'Do you feel it? The wind is returning!'

Herrick replied uneasily, 'Okes will never be back in time. And even if he is ...'

Bolitho touched his lips. 'Quiet! Someone's coming!' He bent down and with a quick jerk thrust Neale's clothes out through the vent hole.

The door grated back and Pook peered in at them. He gestured with a heavy pistol. 'On deck! All of you!' His eyes were very bright, and his shirt was well stained with neat rum. Then he stared past Bolitho and shouted, 'Where's that brat gone, for Christ's sake?'

Bolitho said calmly, 'Out through the port. He swam ashore.'

Pook muttered, 'It'll do 'im no good! 'E can stay with the others to starve!'

Cursing and muttering to himself he drove the three officers on deck, where Onslow and some of his trusted men were assembled beside the wheel.

Bolitho whispered to Herrick, 'Don't provoke him. He looks too dangerous to trifle with!'

Onslow was certainly showing signs of strain, and as Bolitho and the others reached the quarterdeck rail he snapped, 'Right then! You can get the ship under way!' He levelled his pistol at Herrick's stomach and added meaningly, 'I shall shoot him if you try and trick me!'

Bolitho glanced along the maindeck, feeling his spirits sinking. There were some twenty men staring up at him. All the ones who had been sent from the *Cassius* and some others he recognised as old and trusted men of the original *Phalarope* crew. As he had remarked to the unhappy Neale, it was just bad luck that all these men had stayed together aboard the frigate while other, more reliable elements had been sent ashore with the water casks. Normally it would not have mattered. He bit his lip and stared beyond the bowsprit where a small islet seemed to be swinging on its own momentum as the wind tugged at the anchored ship. Now it made the difference between life and death to all of them.

He nodded to Proby. 'Tops'ls and jib, Mr. Proby.' To Onslow he said, 'We will need more men to break out the anchor.'

Onslow showed his teeth. 'A good try, but not good enough. I will cut the cable!' He waved the pistol. 'I have enough men here for the sails!' He hardened his jaw. 'Try that sort of trick again and I will kill the lieutenant!' He cocked the pistol and pointed it again at Herrick. 'Carry on, *sir*!'

Bolitho felt the sun beating down on his face and tried to shut out the overwhelming sensation of defeat. There was nothing he could do. He had even put young Neale's life in danger now.

Quietly he said, 'Very well, Onslow. But I hope you live long enough to regret this.'

A man yelled from forward, 'Look! There are some men on the beach!'

Onslow swung round, his eyes glinting. 'By God, there's a boat shoving off!'

Bolitho turned to watch as the *Phalarope's* jolly boat idled clear of the sand and began to move across the water. There were only two men in it, and he guessed that the landing party must have broken into panic at the sight of the frigate preparing to sail without them. Several mutineers were already aloft, and a jibsail flapped impatiently in the rising breeze. He could see many more men further along the green ridge and the glint of metal on a drawn sword.

Onslow said slowly, 'Let the boat get near enough to rake with a nine-pounder!' He was grinning. 'And fetch up Mr. bloody Vibart! We'll give those bastards something to remember us by!' To Bolitho he said, 'It will be a hanging after all, and who better?'

It took four men to drag the first lieutenant from the cabin hatch. His clothes were in ribbons, and his face was scarred and battered almost beyond recognition. For several seconds he stared up at the running noose which was already being passed down from the mainyard to eager hands on deck. Then he turned and looked up towards the quarterdeck, seeing Bolitho and the others for the first time. One of his eyes was closed, but the other stared straight at Onslow with neither fear nor hope.

Onslow called, 'Now, Mr. Vibart! Let us see you dance to our tune!' Some of the men laughed as he added, 'You'll get a good view from up there.'

Bolitho said, 'Leave him! You have *me*, Onslow, isn't that enough?'

But Vibart shouted, 'Save your pleadings for yourself! I don't want your damn pity!'

Suddenly a voice shouted, 'Look! In the jolly boat! It's Allday and Ferguson!'

Several men ran to the side, and one even started to cheer.

Onslow rasped, 'Stand by that gun! We don't need them here!'

Bolitho watched narrowly as another big seaman, the one called Pochin, pushed past the wheel and growled, ' 'Old on! It's Allday! 'E's a good mate, an' always 'as bin.' He looked down at the maindeck. 'What d'you say, lads?'

There was a rumble of agreement from some of the watching men, and Pochin added, 'Call the boat alongside.'

Bolitho could feel his heart pounding against his ribs as the boat bumped against the hull, and in sudden silence Allday and Ferguson climbed up through the entry port.

Pochin leaned over the rail and shouted, 'Welcome back, John! We'll sail together after all!'

But Allday stayed where he was below the starboard gangway, the sunlight bright across his upturned face. Then he said, 'I'll not sail with him!' He pointed straight at Onslow. 'He killed Evans and put the blame on me! I would have ended on a gallows but for Bryan here!'

Onslow replied calmly, 'But now you're free. I never intended you to die.' There was sweat on his forehead, and the knuckles around the pistol were white. 'You can stay with us, and welcome.'

Allday ignored him and turned to the men on deck. 'There are two French frigates out yonder, lads! Will you let the *Phalarope* fall to them because of the word of that murdering swine?' His voice grew louder. 'You, Pochin? Are you such a fool that you cannot see your own death?' He seized another seaman by the arm. 'And you, Ted! Can you live with this for the rest of your life?'

A babble of voices broke out, and even the men from aloft swarmed down to join the others in noisy argument.

Bolitho shot a glance at Herrick. It was now or never. He had seen two armed seamen walk aft to see what was happening. They had to be the sentries guarding the rest of the prisoners.

But it was Vibart who acted first. Broken and bleeding, his head sunk dejectedly in his shoulders, he was momentarily forgotten by the men around him.

With a sudden roar he lashed out and knocked his guards sprawling.

Bolitho yelled, 'Neale! Now, for God's sake!'

As he shouted he threw himself bodily sideways into Onslow, and together they rolled kicking and fighting across the deck.

Pook screamed with fury and had his feet kicked from under him by Herrick, who scooped up his pistol, cocked it and fired in a matter of seconds. The force of the shot lifted Pook from his knees and smashed him back against a carronade, his jaw and half his face blown to bloody fragments.

Somehow Onslow managed to fight himself free, and with one great bound cleared the rail to land amidst the other seamen. The sudden pistol shot had left the men standing like statues, but as Onslow hit the deck he snatched up a cutlass and yelled, 'To me, lads! Kill the bastards!'

Bolitho seized Onslow's pistol and fired point-blank at a man by the wheel, and then gasped, 'Go aft, Mr. Proby! Get weapons!'

There was a ragged volley from the forecastle, and the stunned mutineers reeled back across the maindeck as another handful of seamen surged up from below led by Belsey, the master's mate, his injured arm strapped across his body, but wielding a boarding axe with his good hand.

Herrick shouted, 'The boats are coming, sir!' He hurled his empty pistol at another shadowy figure and grabbed a cutlass from Proby. 'My God, the boats are coming at last!'

Bolitho snapped, 'Follow me!' Swinging the unfamiliar cutlass like a scythe he dashed down the ladder, hitting out with all his strength as a man charged across the deck with a long pike. He felt the hot blood spurt across his face as the massive blade sliced through the man's bulging neck artery as if it had been thread.

Faces loomed up, ugly and distorted, but faded into screams as he slashed his way across the deck to where Vibart was fighting with his bare hands against three mutineers. As he drove his cutlass into the nearest man's shoulder he saw the sun gleam on a knife, and heard Vibart's great bellow of agony. Then he was down, and as the released men from the cable tier charged into the fray, some of the remaining mutineers dropped their weapons and held up their hands.

Bolitho slipped in some blood and felt someone lifting him to his feet. It was Allday.

He managed to gasp, 'Thank you, Allday!'

But Allday was staring past him, to the far side, where encircled by levelled weapons and abandoned by his fellow conspirators, Onslow stood with his back against a gun, his cutlass still held in front of him.

Allday said, 'He is *mine*, sir!'

Bolitho was about to answer when he heard Vibart calling his name. In three strides he reached the man's side and knelt on the stained planking where Ellice and Belsey were holding Vibart's shoulders clear of the deck. There was a thin ribbon of blood running from the corner of Vibart's mouth, and as he lay staring up at Bolitho's grave features he looked suddenly old and frail.

Bolitho said quietly, 'Rest easy, Mr. Vibart. We'll soon have you comfortable.'

Vibart coughed, and the blood dribbled down his chin in a growing flood. 'Not this time. They've done for me this time!' He made as if to move his hand, but the effort was too much. From behind his shoulders the surgeon gave a quick shake of his head.

Bolitho said, 'It was a brave thing you did.'

There was a clash of steel across the deck, and Bolitho turned to see Allday and Onslow circling each other with bared cutlasses. The other men stood watching in silence. This was no court martial. This was the justice of the lower deck.

Bolitho looked again at Vibart. 'Is there anything I can do for you?'

The dying man grimaced as a fresh agony ran through his body. 'Nothing. Not from you. Not from anybody!' He coughed again, but this time the torrent did not stop.

As the returning boats ground alongside and the gangways became alive with breathless men, Vibart died.

Bolitho stood up slowly and stared at the dead man. It was somehow typical and right that Vibart had remained unflinching and unshaken to the end.

He saw Captain Rennie and Midshipman Farquhar stepping over some wounded seamen, their faces drawn and ashen by what they saw. He clasped his hands behind him to hide his emotion from them.

'Put these men under guard, Mr. Farquhar. Then carry on at once with loading the fresh water. We sail as soon as it is completed.' He walked slowly across to the opposite side, and as the men parted to let him through he saw Onslow staring up at him, his eyes already glazed in death.

All at once Bolitho felt sick and unclean, as if the mutiny had left him with another, deeper scar.

He said harshly, 'I hope we can match the French as well as we can fight each other!' Then he turned and strode aft.

16

A Special Sort of Man

Midshipman Maynard tapped on the door of Bolitho's cabin and reported breathlessly, 'Mr. Herrick's respects, sir, and we have just sighted two sail on the starboard bow.' He darted a quick glance at the other officers who were standing beside Bolitho's desk. 'It's the flagship, and the frigate *Volcano.*'

Bolitho nodded, his face thoughtful. 'Thank you. My compliments to Mr. Herrick. Tell him to tack the ship to intercept.' He paused. 'And have the prisoners ready to be sent across to *Cassius.*'

He listened to Maynard's feet scurrying up the cabin ladder and then turned back to the other officers. 'Well, gentlemen, at last we have found the flagship.'

It had been two days since the *Phalarope* had crept away from the small islets. Two long days in which to think back on mutiny and murder. Bolitho had broken his normal practice of appearing regularly on the quarterdeck, and had spent long, brooding hours in his cabin, reliving each moment, torturing himself with regrets and recriminations.

He looked down at the chart and said slowly, 'From what Allday described, I would say that the French are out in force. The two frigates were probably feelers from de Grasse's main fleet. If so, they have changed their plans.' He tapped the chart with one finger. 'De Grasse would never waste frigates at a time like this. It looks to me as if he intends to avoid all the main channels and will use the Dominica Passage. That way he might well bypass our patrols.' He stopped thinking aloud, and with sudden briskness rolled up the chart and laid it to one side.

He said, 'I shall go over to the *Cassius* and speak to the admiral.' He glanced at the neat pile of reports on the desk. 'There is much that Sir Robert will wish to know.' How trite it sounded, he thought bitterly. Like items in the ship's log, bald of feeling or humanity. How could he describe the atmosphere on the maindeck when he had spoken a prayer before the shrouded corpses had slid over the side?

Lieutenant Vibart's body, alongside those of the dead mutineers. The rest of the crew had gathered round in silence. Not just a silence of respect or sadness, but something much deeper. It was like an air of shame, a combined feeling of guilt.

He stared at the watching officers beside him. Okes and Rennie. Farquhar and Proby.

Bolitho continued in the same curt tone, 'You all showed great resource and courage. I have made a full report and I trust it will receive proper attention.' He did not add that without such a report from the ship's captain the story of the brief, savage mutiny would overshadow all else with the admiral and his superiors. As it was it might still be insufficient to save the ship's name from further harm.

He looked hard at Okes. 'You will take over as first lieutenant of course, and Mr. Herrick will assume your duties forthwith.' He switched his gaze to Farquhar. 'I do not have to add to what I have put in my report about you. You're appointed acting lieutenant immediately. I have no doubt whatever that it will be confirmed with equal speed.'

Farquhar said, 'Thank you, sir.' He looked round as if expecting to see an immediate change in his surroundings. 'I am very grateful.'

Okes said nervously, 'I still can't believe that Mr. Vibart is dead.'

Bolitho eyed him impassively. 'Death is the only thing which is inevitable, Mr. Okes. Yet it is the one thing we can never take for granted!'

There was a tap at the door and Stockdale peered in. 'Flagship is signalling, Captain. For you to report on board as soon as possible.'

'Very well, Stockdale. Call away my boat's crew.' He added to the others, 'Remember this, gentlemen. The *Phalarope* was nearly lost by mutiny.' He allowed his tongue to linger on the word. 'What we have to decide now is whether we have gained anything by a reprieve.' He saw their quick exchange of glances and continued, 'The ship is either cleansed of evil or smeared by shame. The choice is ours. Yours and mine!' He looked around their grave faces. 'That is all. You may go.'

Stockdale reappeared as the officers filed out, and busied himself getting Bolitho's hat and sword. He said, 'Allday is waiting to see you, Captain.' He sounded disapproving.

'Yes, I sent for him.' He listened to the squeal of blocks as the gig was hoisted out, and remembered Stockdale's stricken face as he had returned with the rest of the shore party. He had stared round the stained deck at the corpses and then at his captain. He had said brokenly, 'I should never have left you, Captain! Not for an instant!' It was as if he believed he had failed Bolitho. He seemed to think that if he had stayed aboard the mutiny could never have happened.

Bolitho said quietly, 'Send him in. He is a good seaman, Stockdale. I wronged *him*, not the other way about!'

Stockdale shook his head, but shambled away to fetch the man who had broken the mutiny.

And what a risk he had taken, Bolitho thought. He had walked back towards the searching marines, knowing full well that they were unaware of his innocence, and that any man might shoot him down without waiting for an explanation. Allday had found Okes and Farquhar, and together it seemed they had decided it best for Allday to try to reach the ship unsupported by anyone but Ferguson. It was a right decision, and a brave one.

If Onslow had seen a boatload of men approaching the ship the balance would have tipped in his favour.

There was a tap at the door and Allday stepped into the cabin. Dressed in white trousers and checked shirt, his long hair tied back with a length of codline, he looked every inch the landsman's idea of a sailor. On his cheek and neck there were two diagonal scars where Brock had struck with his cane.

Bolitho faced him for several seconds. Then he said, 'I called you here to thank you properly for what you did, Allday. I wish I could say something which would help clean away the wrong which was done you.' He shrugged. 'But I know of no such reward.'

Allday relaxed slightly. 'I understand, sir. As it was, it all turned out for the best.' He grinned self-consciously. 'I was a bit scared, I can tell you, sir.' His eyes hardened. 'But when I saw Onslow, that was enough! I'm glad I was able to kill him!'

Bolitho studied Allday with new interest. He had a clean-cut, intelligent face, and but for his total lack of education might have gone far and done well by himself.

'Onslow should be a lesson to all of us, Allday.' Bolitho walked to the stern windows, his mind going back over the thought which had nagged him most since the mutiny. 'He was doomed by his life and circumstances. It is up to us not to make any more Onslows through cruelty or lack of understanding.' He swung round. 'No, Allday, I failed with Onslow. He was just a man like the rest of us. He never stood a real chance from the day he was born!'

Allday stared at him with surprise. 'There was nothing *you* could have done for him, if you'll excuse me saying so.' He spread his hands. 'He was a bad one, and I've seen a few in my time!'

Maynard peered in the door. 'Closing the flagship now, sir. Ready to lower the gig.'

'Very good.' Bolitho looked at Allday. 'Is there anything I can do for you?'

Allday shifted uncomfortably. 'There is one thing, sir.' Then he lifted his chin, his eyes suddenly clear and determined. 'It's about Ferguson, your clerk, sir. Are you sending him over with the other mutineers?'

Bolitho spread his arms to allow Stockdale to buckle on his sword. 'That was the intention, Allday.' He frowned. 'I know he came back with you, and did much to repair the damage he had done by his complicity with Onslow. But,' he shrugged, 'there are several charges against him. He aided the mutineers with confidential information, without which any sort of uprising might have been impossible. He attacked a sentry and released a prisoner, the guilt or innocence of whom had not been decided.' He picked up his hat and stared at it. 'Do you think he should warrant complete pardon?'

Allday said quietly, 'Remember what you said about Onslow, sir? Ferguson's no real sailor, and never will be.' He smiled sadly. 'I've looked after him since we were pressed together. If you do this to him I shall feel I've let him down. I shall feel as you do now over Onslow!'

Bolitho nodded. 'I will have to think about it.' He walked to the ladder, ducking below the beams. Then he said, 'Thank you, Allday. You put a forceful argument.'

He ran up into the sunlight and looked quickly across at the *Cassius*. She looked big and reliable against the blue water, and he could see the other frigate hove to beyond her.

Herrick touched his hat. 'Gig ready, sir.' He glanced questioningly at the silent group of manacled men by the entry port. 'Shall I send 'em over while you're with the admiral?'

'If you please, Mr. Herrick.' Bolitho caught sight of Allday's tall figure beside the cabin hatch and added sharply, 'But have Ferguson kept aboard. I will deal with him myself.'

Herrick looked mystified. 'Ferguson, sir?'

Bolitho eyed him coldly. 'He *is* my clerk, Mr. Herrick! Have you forgotten so soon that you chose him for me?' He gave a brief smile and saw the relief flooding across the other man's face.

'Aye, aye, sir!' Herrick strode to the rail. 'Man the side there! Stand by for the captain!'

The pipes trilled and Bolitho vanished down into the boat.

Herrick looked round as old Proby mumbled, 'How old is he? Twenty-five or six?' He gave a deep sigh. 'I'm twice his age and more beside, and there are others like me aboard the *Phalarope*.' He watched the little gig skimming through the whitecaps towards the swaying ship of the line. 'Yet he's like a father to all of us!' He shook his head. 'Have you seen the way the crew look at him now, Mr. Herrick? Like children caught out doing wrong. They know how he *feels* what has happened, how their shame is more'n doubled for him!'

Herrick stared at him. It was rare for the master to say so much all at once. 'I never realised that you admired him, too!'

Proby pouted his pendulous lip. 'I'm too old for admiration, Mr. Herrick. It's deeper'n that. Our captain is a special sort of man.' He frowned and then added, 'I'd die for him, and willingly. I can't say more'n that!' He turned with sudden anger. 'Blast me, Mr. Herrick! How can you let me go on like that?' He shuffled noisily across the quarterdeck like an untidy spider.

Herrick crossed to the rail, his mind still dwelling on Proby's words. Below, watched by armed marines, the remnants of Onslow's conspirators stood awaiting passage to the *Cassius*. Herrick did not share Bolitho's shame on their behalf. He would willingly have hanged each one of them single-handed, if only to lift the despair from Bolitho's shoulders.

He remembered his own exultation when Okes and Rennie had boarded the frigate and he had realised that the mutiny's sudden fire had been quenched. It was then that he had seen through Bolitho's careful mask and had penetrated to the man within. Yes, Proby was right. He was a very special sort of man.

Midshipman Neale crossed to his side and trained his glass on the flagship. Herrick glanced down at the small midshipman and remembered his frantic struggles as they thrust his greased body through the vent hole. Neale's sudden appearance had made quite a sensation when he had flung open the doors of the cable tier. As Ellice, the surgeon, had said later, 'There we all was, Mr. 'Errick, thinkin' of death or worse, an' suddenly the doors come flyin' open like the gates of 'eaven itself!' The surgeon's crimson face had crinkled into a grin. 'When I saw this little naked cherub with the sun behind 'im I thought I was already dead without knowin' it 'ad 'appened!'

Herrick smiled to himself. Neale seemed to have grown in stature since that dreadful day. He said, 'In a few years you'll be getting promoted like Mr. Farquhar if you go on like this.'

Neale considered the suggestion and then replied, 'I never doubted it, sir.' He flushed and added quickly, 'Well, not often!'

Sir Robert Napier walked stiffly to a small gilt chair and sat down. For several seconds he stared at Bolitho's tense features and then said dryly, 'You are a very erratic and unpredictable young man, Bolitho.' He tapped his fingertips together. 'But there is one thing to be said in your favour. You are never dull!'

Bolitho did not trust himself to smile. It was still far too early to know exactly how his ideas had been received. With fretting impatience he had waited in an adjoining cabin while the admiral read his reports, and after what seemed like an hour he was ushered into the great man's presence. There were two other captains already present. Cope of the *Cassius*, and a thickset, unsmiling man Bolitho recognised as Fox of the frigate *Volcano*.

The admiral said, 'It seems to me that you are getting unnecessarily excited about the French frigates which one of your men sighted.' He waved one hand across his big coloured chart. 'Look for yourself, Bolitho. The Leeward and Windward Islands are like a broken chain running from north to south. If the French fleet is out in force, and I say *if*, Sir George Rodney's frigates will have reported the fact, and both sides will have engaged already. That being so, what further can I do in the matter?' He leaned back, his eyes fixed on Bolitho's face.

Bolitho glanced quickly at the other officers. Cope, being Sir Robert's flag captain, would naturally stay non-committal until he knew his master's intentions. Fox was the man to convince. He was said to be a hard man, and as he was somewhat old for his rank, inclined to be over-cautious.

Bolitho took his own chart and laid it carefully across the admiral's. He started quietly. 'The whole plan to contain and engage the French fleet is based on one main theme, sir. We know that de Grasse has his strongest force at Martinique to the south. To meet with his Spanish ally and to reach Jamaica, his first necessity is to *avoid* any damaging action with us.'

The admiral said irritably, 'I know that, dammit!'

Bolitho continued, 'I believe that the two frigates were part of a scouting force, ahead of the main fleet.' He ran his finger along the chart. 'He could sail north from Martinique, and if necessary deploy his ships amongst the scattered islands on route. Then, at his most suitable moment he could swing west to Jamaica as planned.' He looked at Fox who met his eyes without expression. He added urgently, 'Sir George Rodney is depending on a quick engagement, sir. But suppose de Grasse avoids that first contact, or, even worse, he makes a feint attack on our ships and *then* heads north?' He waited, watching the admiral's pale eyes moving across the chart.

Sir Robert said grudgingly, 'It could happen, I suppose. De Grasse could skirt any hostile land and then keep close inshore of more friendly territory, Guadeloupe for instance.' He puckered his lower lip. 'He would thereby avoid a running battle in open water, like the Martinique Passage.' He nodded, his face suddenly grave. 'Yours is a dangerous supposition, Bolitho.'

Captain Cope said uneasily, 'If the French can get ahead of Rodney we're done for!'

Bolitho asked, 'Could I suggest something, sir?' He tried to gauge the extent of his own forcefulness. 'If I am wrong, there can be no real harm in my idea.'

The admiral shrugged. 'I cannot find it in my heart to dampen such rare enthusiasm, Bolitho.' He wagged one finger. 'But I do not promise to abide by it!'

Bolitho leaned across the chart. 'My ship was down here in search of fresh water . . .'

The admiral interrupted, 'And well off her allotted station incidentally!'

'Yes, sir.' Bolitho hurried on. 'Allowing for perhaps a day without wind, and a further two days to regain contact with their admiral, the two French frigates would have had ample time to examine the full extent of *this* Channel.' He stood back slightly as the other two captains craned over to look. 'There is a whole cluster of small islands to the north of the Dominica Passage.' He paused. 'The Isles des Saintes. If I were de Grasse, that is where I would make for. From that point he could swing west to Jamaica, or run for safety at Guadeloupe if Rodney's fleet is too close on his heels.' He swallowed and added, 'If our squadron moved south-east we might be in a better position to observe, and if necessary to report to Sir George Rodney what is happening!'

Sir Robert rubbed his chin. 'What do you think, Cope?'

The flag captain shifted uncomfortably on his feet. 'It's hard to say, sir. If Bolitho is right, and I am sure he has considered the matter most carefully, then de Grasse will have chosen the most unlikely route to slip past our blockade.' He added unhelpfully, 'But of course, if he is wrong, then we will have left our allotted station without good cause!'

The admiral glared at him. 'You do not have to remind me!' He turned his gaze on Fox, who was still leaning over the chart. 'Well?'

Fox straightened his back. 'I think I agree with Bolitho.' He paused. 'However, there is one point which he seems to have overlooked.' He jabbed at the pencilled lines with his finger. 'If Sir George Rodney flushes de Grasse away from the Dominica Passage the Frogs will certainly have the advantage. The wind is too poor to allow our fleet time to re-engage before de Grasse dashes for open water.' He drew his finger slowly across the chart in a straight line. 'But our squadron might be right across their line of escape!'

The admiral stirred in his chair. 'Do you think I had not considered this?' He glared at Bolitho. 'Well, who do *you* say?'

Bolitho answered stubbornly, 'I still say we shall be in a better position to report and if necessary, shadow the enemy, sir.'

The admiral stood up and began to pace with sudden agitation. 'If only I could get some real news! I sent the brig *Witch of Looe* away days ago to try and gain intelligence, but with this damn climate what can you expect?'

He stared through the open stern windows. 'Sometimes we are becalmed for days on end. The war could be over for all I know!'

Bolitho said, 'I could take the *Phalarope* to the south'rd, sir.'

'No!' The admiral's voice was like a whipcrack. 'I will have no captain of mine taking what should be my responsibility!'

He gave a frosty smile. 'Or was it your intention to force me into this decision?' He did not wait for a reply. 'Very well, gentlemen. We will make sail and proceed south-east immediately.' He stared at each of them in turn. 'But I want nothing foolhardy! If we sight the enemy we will retire and report our findings to Sir George Rodney.'

Bolitho masked his disappointment. He must be content. He had not even expected Sir Robert Napier to agree to leaving the present area, let alone to commit himself to what might well be a pointless and time-wasting venture.

As he turned to follow Fox the admiral added sharply, 'And as to that other matter, Bolitho.' He rested his hand on the open envelope. 'I will deal with that in my own way. I do not wish the reputation of my ships to be tarnished by mutiny. I intend that it should stay within the squadron.' He was looking impatient again. 'As for Lieutenant Vibart, well, I suppose it cannot be helped now. A dead officer is no use to me, no matter how he died!'

Bolitho tried to think of a suitable reply. 'He died bravely, sir.'

The admiral grunted. 'So did the Christians in Rome! And damn little good it did anybody!'

Bolitho backed from the cabin and then hurried on deck to summon his boat. The sea was still speckled with small white-caps, and the admiral's flag was streaming bravely in the freshening breeze. It was good sailing weather, he thought. And that was too rare to waste at any time.

With the ponderous two-decker between them, the frigates spread their sails and hauled off on either beam. By nightfall the wind had fallen slightly, but was still sufficient to make the sails boom with unaccustomed vigour as the yards were braced round to keep all three ships on a slow starboard tack.

Before the night fell completely to hide one vessel from another there was a final unhappy incident. Bolitho had been striding up and down the weather side of the quarterdeck when he heard Okes snap, 'Mr. Maynard! Lively there! Train your glass on the flagship. She seems to be hoisting a signal.' Bolitho had crossed the deck to watch the midshipman fumbling with his long telescope. It was strange for the admiral to be sending signals in such poor visibility. A flare would have been more effective.

Maynard had lowered his glass and looked round at the two officers. He had looked sick, as he had on the day he had discovered Evans's body. 'It's no signal, sir!'

Bolitho had taken the glass from the youth's hands and trained it across the hammock netting. Coldly he had watched the small black dot rising towards the *Cassius's* mainyard. It had twisted as it made its slow journey. Twisted and kicked, so that in his imagination Bolitho had thought he could hear the drum's staccato roll and the steady tramp of bare feet as the selected men had hauled the choking mutineer slowly up to the yard.

Maynard was wrong about one thing. It *was* a signal to every man who saw it.

Bolitho had returned the glass and said, 'I'm going below, Mr. Okes. See that you have the best lookouts aloft, and call me if you sight *anything.*' He had glanced quickly at Maynard and added quietly, 'That man, whoever he was, knew the price of his folly. Discipline demands that it be paid in full!'

He turned on his heel and walked below, despising himself for the cold unreality of his words. In his mind he seemed to hear Vibart's thick, accusing voice, still jeering at him for his weakness. What did one more death matter? Fever and unaccountable accident, the cannon's harvest or the end of a rope, it was all the same in the end.

He threw himself across his cot and stared at the deckhead. A captain had to be above such things, to be able to play God without thought for those who served him. Then he remembered Allday's words and the blind trust of men like Herrick and Stockdale. Such men deserved his attention, even his love, he thought vaguely. To use power as a tyrant was to be without honour. To be without honour was to be less than a man.

With that thought uppermost in his mind he fell into a deep sleep.

'Captain, sir!' Midshipman Neale rested his hand anxiously on Bolitho's arm and then jumped back in alarm as the cot swayed violently to one side.

Bolitho swung his legs to the deck and stared for a long moment while his mind sought to recover from the nightmare. He had been surrounded by screaming, faceless men, and his arms had been pinioned while he felt a noose being tightened around his neck. Neale's hand had only added to the nightmare's reality, and he could still feel the sweat running across his spine.

He said harshly, 'What is it?' The cabin was still in darkness, and it took him several more seconds to recover his composure.

Neale said, 'Mr. Herrick's respects, sir. He thinks you should know we've heard something.' He fell back another pace as Bolitho lurched to his feet. 'It sounded like gunfire, sir!'

Bolitho did not pause to find his coat but ran quickly to the quarterdeck. It was almost dawn, and already the sky was painted in a pale blue strip beyond the gently corkscrewing bows.

'What is it, Mr. Herrick?' He moved to the rail and cupped his hands to his ears.

Herrick stared at him uncertainly. 'I could be mistaken, sir. It might have been thunder.'

'Most unlikely,' Bolitho shivered slightly in the cool dawn breeze. 'Can you see the *Cassius* yet?'

'No, sir.' Herrick pointed vaguely. 'There's a mist coming up. It'll be another hot day, I'm thinking.'

Bolitho stiffened as a low rumble echoed sullenly across the open water. 'Maybe hotter than you think, Mr. Herrick.' He glanced up at the jerking canvas. 'The wind seems to be holding.' He was suddenly aware that there were several figures already standing on the maindeck. Everyone faced forward, listening and wondering.

Bolitho said, 'Call the hands.' He peered upwards again. In the dim light he could just see the masthead pendant whipping out like a pointing finger. 'Take out the second reef, Mr. Herrick. And set the fores'l and spanker.'

Herrick called for a boatswain's mate, and seconds later the ship came alive to the call of pipes and the stamp of running feet.

Then Herrick said, 'I still can't see the flagship, sir.'

'We won't wait for her!' Bolitho watched the men swarming aloft and listened to the harsh bark of commands. 'That is gunfire ahead. Make no mistake about it!'

Proby came on deck buttoning his heavy coat. He seemed half asleep, but as the big spanker filled with wind and the deck canted obediently to the wind's eager thrust he contained any comment he might have felt and crossed to the wheel.

Bolitho said calmly, 'Alter course two points to larboard, Mr. Proby.' The ship's sudden response to wind and sail had swept away the strain and sleep from his mind. He had been right. The waiting was almost over.

He looked sideways at Herrick and saw that his face was clearer in the growing light. He looked worried and not a little startled by the swift chain of events.

Bolitho said quietly. 'We will investigate, Mr. Herrick.' He pointed at the men swarming back along the yards. 'I want chain slings fitted on every yard. If we are called to action our people have enough to contend with at the guns. I don't want them crushed by falling spars.' He halted the lieutenant in his tracks. 'And have nets spread above the maindeck, too.' He made himself stand quite still by the rail, his hands resting on the worn and polished wood. He could feel the ship trembling beneath his palms, as if his thoughts were being transformed into new life, and the life was flowing through the *Phalarope* even as he watched.

From newly awakened chaos the ship had already settled down into a purposeful rhythm. All the weeks of training, the hours of persistent instruction were giving their rewards.

Stockdale joined him by the rail. 'I'll get your coat, sir.'

'Not yet, Stockdale. That can keep for a moment longer.' He turned as Okes appeared at the ladder, his face still crumpled from sleep. 'I want the hands to eat well this morning, Mr. Okes. I have a feeling that the galley fire will be out for some time to come.' He saw the understanding spreading across the officer's face. '*This* time we will be ready!'

Like a living creature the *Phalarope* lifted her bows and smashed jubilantly into each succeeding rank of low waves, the spray bursting back over her forecastle in long white streamers.

Herrick reported, 'Chain slings rigged, sir.'

'Very well.' It was an effort to speak calmly. 'Have the boats swung out for towing astern. If we fight today there will be enough splinters flying without the boats adding to them!'

Okes managed to ask, 'The gunfire, sir? What do you make of it?'

Bolitho saw several men pausing to listen to his reply. He said slowly, 'Two ships. One much smaller than the other by the sound of the firing.

We can be sure of one thing, Mr. Okes. They cannot both be enemies!'

Herrick was back again. 'What now, sir?'

'I am going down to shave and wash. When I return I will expect to hear that the men have been fed.' He smiled. 'After that, we shall have to see!'

But once back in his cabin it was almost more than he could bear to take time to shave and change his clothes. The breakfast which Stockdale hurriedly laid on the cabin table he could not even face. By tonight, or perhaps within the next few hours, he might be dead. Or even worse, screaming for mercy under the surgeon's knife. He shuddered. It was pointless even to think of it. More, it was harmful.

Stockdale said, 'I have laid out a fresh shirt, sir.' He looked searchingly at Bolitho. 'I think you should wear your best uniform, too.'

'For heaven's sake why, man?' He stared at the coxswain's battered face in surprise.

Stockdale replied gravely, 'This is the day, sir. I have the same feeling I had with you once before.' He added stubbornly, 'And the men will be looking to you, sir. They'll want to *see* you.' He nodded as if to settle the matter. 'After all that's happened they'll need to know you're with them.'

Bolitho stared at him, suddenly moved by the man's halting, broken voice. 'If you say so, Stockdale.'

Ten minutes later a voice echoed faintly above the sounds of sea and canvas. 'Deck there! Sail on the starboard bow!'

Bolitho made himself wait just a few more seconds as Stockdale buckled on his sword, and then walked to the cabin ladder. The quarterdeck seemed crammed with figures, all pointing and speaking at once. Every voice fell silent as Bolitho walked to the rail to take a telescope from Maynard.

Through the frigate's criss-cross of rigging he could see the distorted patterns of tossing whitecaps beyond her bows. The sky was already clear, but the water seemed to writhe in the grip of a slow-moving sea mist, and for once the new day felt drained of warmth.

Then he saw them. Two ships close together, their hulls hidden in a dense cloud of smoke and mist, their tattered sails hanging disembodied above the hidden battle below.

But the flags were easily visible. One blood red, like that which flew above him. The other clear and white. The flag of France.

He closed the telescope with a snap. 'Very well, Mr. Okes. Beat to quarters and clear for action!'

His eyes held them a moment longer. 'We must give well of ourselves today, gentlemen. If our people see us doing our best, they will be willing enough to do *their* duty!'

He half listened to the distant thunder of gunfire. 'Carry on, Mr. Okes!'

They all touched their hats and then looked at one another, as if each man realised that for some, maybe for all of them, it would be the last time.

Then the drum began to rattle, and the small moment was past.

17

Form Line of Battle!

Within ten minutes of the drum's urgent tattoo the *Phalarope* was cleared for action. Decks were sanded and buckets of water stood within reach of every gun. Over the whole ship there had fallen a strange, gripping stillness, broken only by the uneasy slap of canvas and the steady sluice of water around the stem.

Bolitho shaded his eyes and watched the sun's unearthly orange glow as it tried to filter through the unending wall of sea mist. The bang and clatter of gunfire had become more uneven and sporadic with each dragging minute, and now as the distance fell away between the *Phalarope* and the other ships there came new sounds, more vicious, and somehow more personal. Bolitho could hear the sharp cracks of muskets and pistols, the jarring scrape of steel against steel, and above all the mingling cries of men fighting for their lives.

Okes wiped his face with the back of his hand and said quickly, 'This damn mist! I can't see what's happening!'

Bolitho glanced at him briefly. 'It is a godsend, Mr. Okes. They are too busy to see us!' He lifted his hand to the quartermaster. 'Starboard a point!' Then he walked to the rail and looked down at Herrick's upturned face.

'Have the guns loaded, but do not run out until I tell you.'

He saw the gunners push the fresh charges down the gaping muzzles, followed by the round, gleaming shot. The more experienced gun captains took time to fondle each ball, weighing it almost lovingly to make sure that the first salvo would be a perfect one.

He heard Herrick shout, 'Double-shotted and grape, lads! Let 'em *feel* it this time!'

A stronger breath of wind rolled aside the mist around the entangled ships, and Bolitho tightened his lips into a thin line. Almost stern on to the *Phalarope's* swift approach was a French frigate, and alongside, listing and battered almost beyond recognition, was the little brig, *Witch of Looe*. One mast was already gone, and the other seemed to be held upright only by the remaining stays. He thought of her commander, the young Lieutenant Dancer he had met aboard the flagship, and marvelled at the man's pluck or wasted courage which had made him match his ship against this powerful opponent. His little pop-guns against the still-smoking twelve-pounders.

Okes said, 'They've seen us, sir!' He swallowed hard as something like an animal growl floated across the water. 'My God, look at them!'

The *Witch of Looe*'s shattered deck seemed to be swamped in French sailors, and as the drifting gunsmoke parted momentarily to allow the sunlight to play across the carnage, Bolitho saw the small knot of defenders, still fighting back from the brig's small quarterdeck. In a few more minutes they would be swamped completely.

The gunports along the French frigate's disengaged side suddenly opened, and to the steady rumble of trucks the guns appeared like a line of bared teeth.

Bolitho shut his ears and mind to the victorious shouts from the French frigate and concentrated his thoughts on the narrowing strip of water between them. Less than a cable's length to go, with neither ship able to fire. *Phalarope* was almost dead in line with the other ship's stern, so that if she held her course her bowsprit would drive straight through the stern windows. On one side of the enemy frigate lay the listing, riddled brig, and on the other the guns waited to claim another victim.

Bolitho called sharply, 'Run out the starboard battery!'

He watched as his men threw themselves against the tackle falls, and in a squealing, protesting line the guns trundled up the slight slope of the deck and out through the open ports.

There was a great bellow of noise from the French ship, wild and inhuman. The sound gained from killing and madness. *Phalarope*'s own men remained tense and cold, their eyes unblinking as the enemy's pockmarked sails grew higher and higher above the bows.

Bolitho placed his hands on the rail and said slowly, 'Now send your men across to the larboard battery, Mr. Herrick!' He saw the quick, mystified glances and added harshly, 'In another minute I am going to turn to starboard and go alongside the *Witch of Looe*. She is low in the water, our broadside should pass right above her!'

Herrick's frown gave way to a look of open admiration. 'Aye, aye, sir!'

Bolitho's voice stopped him in his tracks. 'Quietly there! I don't want the Frogs to see what we're doing!'

Crouching almost on their knees the gunners scuttled across to the opposite side, their excitement instantly quelled by hoarse threats from the gun captains.

Nearer and nearer. A few musket balls whined harmlessly overhead, but for the most part the French captain was prepared to wait. He could match gun for gun, and as *Phalarope*'s bows and foremast would take the first punishment he could afford to feel confident. His own ship was drifting slowly downwind and his gunners could thank the *Witch of Looe*'s weight alongside for a steadier platform beneath their feet. There was a faint ripple of cheering, drowned instantly by a fresh outburst of musket fire.

Proby muttered, 'The brig's people are cheering us, sir!'

Bolitho ignored him. One error now and his ship would change into a shambles. Fifty yards, thirty yards. Bolitho lifted his hand. He saw Quintal crouching like a runner, one beefy hand resting on the nearest seaman at the braces.

Bolitho shouted, '*Now!*'

At his side Proby added his weight to the wheel, as with a scream of blocks the yards began to swing, the sails flapping in protest, but answering the challenge of wind and rudder.

'Run out!' Bolitho felt ice cold as the larboard battery squealed across the sanded planks. 'Fire as your guns bear!'

He pounded the rail, counting each frantic second. For a moment he thought that he had mistimed the change of course, but even as he waited, holding his breath and hardly daring to watch, the bowsprit swung lazily across the French ship's high stern, almost brushing away a small group of sailors which had gathered above the hammock nettings.

Herrick ran from gun to gun, making sure that each successive shot went home. Not that he need have troubled. As the French gunners ran dazedly from the opposite side the first shots went crashing home. The *Phalarope* shuddered as she ground against the little brig, but maintained her way steadily down the ship's side, her guns belching fire and death above the heads of the stunned boarders and the remaining members of the brig's crew.

Bolitho winced as the quarterdeck nine-pounders joined in the din. But still there was no answer from the French ship. Bolitho had guessed correctly that the guns which stared impotently at the *Phalarope*'s smashing attack would have been in action right up to the moment of grappling and boarding the little brig.

He watched as great pieces of the frigate's bulwark caved in and fragments of torn planking rose above the smoke as if thrown from an invisible hand. An axe flashed dully, and Bolitho yelled, 'He's trying to free himself!' He drew his sword. 'Over you go, lads! Boarders away!'

As the *Phalarope* ground to a sluggish halt, her bows locked into the brig's fallen rigging and spars, Bolitho ran down the port gangway and clambered on to the *Witch of Looe*'s tilting deck. For a moment nobody followed him, and then with a great roar, half cheer and half scream, the waiting seamen swept over the bulwark behind him.

Most of the French sailors, caught between the *Phalarope's* savage gunfire and the revived members of the brig's crew, threw up their hands in surrender, but Bolitho thrust them aside, his sword raised high towards his own men. 'Come on, lads! We'll take the frigate!' There would be time enough for the boarders later, he thought vaguely.

Once up the frigate's shot-pitted side the resistance became fierce and deadly. Wild, crazed faces floated around Bolitho as he hacked his way aft towards the poop, and his feet barely supported him in the heel-thick layer of blood which seemed to cover the deck like fresh paint. The enemy's upperdeck had been crammed with men. Some were boarders recalled from the *Witch of Looe*, and others were gunners caught off guard by the *Phalarope's* sudden change of course. This tangled, momentarily disorganised mass of men had received the full force of the broadside. All the *Phalarope*'s larboard twelve-pounders and the quarterdeck battery as well, every one double-shotted and loaded with grape for good measure. It looked as if a maniac had been throwing buckets of blood everywhere. Even the lower edges of the sails were speckled in scarlet, and fragments of men hung from upended guns and splintered bulwarks alike.

A French officer, hatless and bleeding from a scalp wound, leapt in front of Bolitho, his thin sword red almost to its hilt. Bolitho lifted his own sword, but felt it parried aside, and saw the French officer's expression change from anxiety to sudden exultation. Bolitho tried to draw back, but the struggling press of figures prevented it. He could not lift his sword in time. He saw the man's arm come round, heard the swish of steel, and waited for the shock of the thrust.

Instead the Frenchman's face twisted with alarm as a battle-crazed marine burst through the throng, his fixed bayonet held in front of him like a spear. The sword swung round yet again, but it was too late. The momentum of the marine's charge impaled the officer on the bayonet and threw them both against the poop ladder. The marine screamed with wild delight and stamped his boot on the Frenchman's stomach, at the same moment wrenching out the dripping bayonet. The French officer sank slowly to his knees, his mouth opening and shutting like a dying fish. The marine stared at him as if for the first time and then thrust the bayonet home again.

Bolitho caught his arm. 'That's enough! For God's sake, man!' The marine did not seem to hear him, but after a brief startled look at his captain's face he charged off into the battle once more, his expression one of concentration and hatred.

The frigate's captain lay on the poop, his shoulders supported by a young lieutenant. Someone was tying a crude tourniquet around the shattered stump of one leg, and the captain was only just hanging on to his senses as fighting, stabbing seamen reeled and staggered across his body.

Bolitho shouted, 'Strike! *Strike*, Captain! While you still have some men left!' He did not recognise his own voice, and his hand around the hilt of his sword was wet with sweat. He thought of the crazed marine and knew that he too was in danger of giving way to the lust of the battle.

The French captain gestured faintly, and the lieutenant gasped, 'We strike! M'sieu, we strike!'

But even after the white flag had fluttered to the deck and men had been hauled bodily from the work of killing, it took time to make the *Phalarope*'s men realise they had won.

The first to congratulate Bolitho was Dancer of the *Witch of Looe*. Bleeding from several wounds, his arm tied across his chest with a piece of codline, he limped over the splintered, bloodstained deck and held out his good hand. 'Thank you, sir! I was never more pleased to see any man!'

Bolitho sheathed his sword. 'Your own ship is sinking, I fear.' He looked up at the frigate's tattered sails. 'But you sold her dearly.'

Dancer swayed and then gripped Bolitho's arm. 'I was trying to warn Sir Robert! The French are out, sir!' He squinted his eyes as if to restore his dazed thoughts. 'Three days ago de Grasse met up with Rodney's fleet, but after a quick clash at long range, broke off the battle.' He pointed vaguely through the smoke. 'I have been trying to shadow the Frogs, and this morning I saw the whole fleet nor'-west of Dominica!' He shook his head. 'I think Sir Gorge Rodney has managed to engage them again, but I cannot be sure. I was caught by this frigate before I could get back to the squadron.' He smiled ruefully. 'Now I have no ship at all!'

Bolitho frowned. 'Have you enough men to take this frigate as prize?'

Dancer stared. 'But she is *your* prize, sir!'

'We can discuss the share of financial reward at a later and more convenient time, Lieutenant!' Bolitho smiled. 'In the meantime I suggest you herd these prisoners below and make as much speed as you can with these rags for some port of safety.' He peered up through the smoke. 'The wind has veered slightly to the south-east. It should carry you clear of any impending battle!'

Herrick blundered through the mess and tangle of corpses, his sword dangling from his wrist. He touched his hat. 'We have just sighted the *Cassius*, sir!'

'Very well,' Bolitho held Dancer's hand. 'Thank you for your news. At least it will justify Sir Robert's leaving his proper station!' He turned on his heel and climbed back across the sinking brig towards his own ship.

Still deep in thought he clambered over the bulwark and walked along the gangway. The gunners were standing below him, their faces upturned as he passed. The marine marksmen high in the tops and the little powder monkeys by the magazine hatch, all stood and stared at the slim solitary figure framed against the torn sails of the vanquished Frenchman.

It had been a swift and incredible victory. Not a man injured let alone killed in the attack, and no damage to the *Phalarope* at all. Some good men had died in the fight aboard the enemy ship, but the success far outweighed any such loss. A frigate taken as a prize, the *Witch of Looe* revenged if not saved, and all within an hour.

Yet Bolitho thought of none of these things. In his mind's eye he could see his well-worn chart, and the enemy's fleet moving in an irresistible tide towards the open sea, and Jamaica the prize.

Then a voice yelled out from the maindeck and Bolitho turned startled and caught off guard.

'Three cheers, lads! Three cheers for our Dick!'

Bolitho stared round at the quarterdeck as the air was split with wild, uncontrollable cheering, Herrick and Rennie were openly grinning at him. Neale and Maynard waving their hats to the men on deck below. Bolitho felt confused and entirely unprepared, and as the three cheers extended to a frenzied shouting Herrick crossed to his side and said, 'Well done, sir! Well *done*!'

Bolitho said, 'What is the matter with everyone today?'

Herrick replied firmly, 'You've given them more than a *victory*, sir! You've given 'em back their self-respect!'

The cheering died away as if from a signal, and Herrick said quietly, 'They want you to tell them, sir.' He dropped his eyes.

Bolitho moved to the rail and stared slowly around the familiar faces. These men. His men. The thoughts chased one another through his mind like shadows. Starve them, beat them. Let them face scurvy and disease, and death a hundred different ways. But still they could cheer. He gripped the rail hard and stared above their heads. When he spoke his voice was quiet, and those men furthest away leaned forward to hear it better.

'This morning we fought and beat a French frigate!' He saw some of the men nudging each other and grinning like children. 'But more important to me is the fact that we fought as a single unit, as a King's ship should, and must fight!' A few of the older seamen nodded soberly, and Bolitho tried to steel himself for what he had to tell them.

It was no use just telling men to fight. They had to be led. It was an act of mutual trust. He cleared his throat. 'When you see an enemy ship abeam and the balls begin to fly overhead, you all fight for many reasons.' He looked around their tanned and expectant faces. 'You fight out of comradeship, to protect each other and avenge well-loved friends who have already laid down their lives. Or you fight out of fear, a fear which breeds a power of hatred for the enemy who is always faceless yet ever present. And above all we fight for our ship!' He waved his arm around him. 'This is our ship, and will remain so, as long as we have the will to live and die for what is right!'

Some of the men started to cheer again, but he held up his hand, his eyes suddenly sad. 'But this short fight today was only a beginning. I cannot tell you how our small deeds will fit into the great pattern of battle, for I do not know. I only know that it is our common duty to fight today, and to fight as we have never done before!'

He had their full attention now, and he hated himself for the truth which had to be told. 'This morning we had luck on our side. But before this day dies we will need much more than that.'

As he paused the air seemed to give a sullen shudder, which as every man turned to stare across the captured ship alongside extended into a low, menacing rumble, like thunder across distant hills.

Bolitho continued steadily, 'Over there, lads, lies the enemy!'

He watched each man in turn, his heart suddenly dreading what was to come. He had brought them all to this. For no matter what reason, or how justified his efforts might be seen by others, he had committed his ship and his men to the inevitable.

He felt a sudden gust of warm wind at his neck, and as he watched the low, writhing bank of morning mist began to move clear. One minute the two frigates with the sinking wreck of the *Witch of Looe* between them made up their own small world. To one beam lay the sun-tinted mist, and to the other the open sea, where night had already crossed the hard horizon, and the topsails of the labouring *Cassius* showed above its edge, gleaming in the sunlight like a pink shell. Then, as the mist rolled away that small world broke up for ever.

Shrouded in haze to the south-east Bolitho could see the low wedge of Dominica, while away to the north the scattered islands which were called the Saintes. But between these two there was no horizon. It was a sight so vast and so terrible that nobody said a word. From side to side, as far as the eye could reach, the blue water was topped with an unbroken line of ships. There seemed to be no gap between each towering crop of sails, and as the growing sunlight reflected across the apparently motionless panorama of armed might, Bolitho was reminded of an old painting he had seen as a child. The armoured knights at Agincourt, their great horses bedecked in standards and glittering mail, the proud pennants and banners streaming from lances as they gathered to charge the flimsy line of English archers.

Almost desperately he looked down at his spellbound men. 'Well, lads, what do you say?' He pointed towards the great shimmering line of ships.

'Beyond that fleet lies England, across five thousand miles of open sea. At our back is Jamaica.' He pointed down between his feet. 'And below us is a thousand fathoms to the bottom!' He leaned forward, his eyes flashing with sudden urgency. 'So which is it to be, lads?'

The new sound of distant gunfire was drowned in the sudden wave of wild and uncontrolled cheering which swept across the *Phalarope*'s main-deck, to be caught and carried by those aboard the captured frigate. Even wounded men who were being carried below shouted with the rest, some not knowing why, or even having heard Bolitho's words. It was as if all the bitterness and pent-up frustrations were being swept away by their great chorus of voices.

Bolitho turned away, and Herrick who was nearest saw the strange sadness and disbelief in his eyes. He said quickly, 'There's your answer, sir!' He was excited like the others, even jubilant.

When Bolitho turned to look at him he studied the lieutenant as if he was a stranger. 'Tell me, Mr. Herrick, have you ever seen a sea battle?' He waved towards the horizon. 'Like this one will be?' He did not wait for a reply. '*I* have. There is no dash and madcap victory. No hit-and-run when the game gets too rough.' He gripped his hands behind him and stared unseeingly past the other officers. 'The sky is so dark with smoke that it is like hell. Even the ships cry out, did you know that?' His voice became harsher. 'They cry because they are being torn apart, like the fools who man them!'

He swung round as Midshipman Maynard said hoarsely, 'Flagship's signalling, sir.'

Bolitho walked to the weather side and stared down at the listing brig. The water was already lapping over her bulwark, and only discarded corpses lolled on her battle-torn deck. He snapped, 'Do not acknowledge, Mr. Maynard!' To Herrick he added, 'Cast off from the brig and get under way.' He looked up at the masthead. 'We will steer due east!'

Herrick asked, 'What of the flagship, sir?'

'Sir Robert is a gallant gentleman, Mr. Herrick. But his seniority will have made him more careful than I.' He gave a short smile. 'And *his* men may not be so keen to die on this fine day!' His smile vanished. 'Now get those men to their stations, and stop this damn cheering!'

The *Phalarope* idled clear from the wreckage, and as the captured frigate cast off her grappling irons the little brig rolled slowly on to her beam, the bursting air bubbles tinged with scarlet as the creeping water surged triumphantly across her battered hull.

Bolitho lifted his glass as the yards went round and the deck canted slightly to the wind. He could see the frigate *Volcano*'s topmasts beyond the *Cassius*, and wondered how her captain would react to this awesome sight. Sir Robert Napier still had time to retire. One definite signal would take them all out of danger, mute witnesses as the French burst from the battle and headed for their goal.

Bolitho made up his mind. 'Mr. Maynard, make a signal to the *Flag*.' He saw Herrick look at Rennie and shrug, as if his captain's actions were now quite beyond his ability to keep up. 'Enemy in sight!'

He did not watch the flags soaring up the yards, but made himself walk back and forth across the quarterdeck, followed by the eyes of Rennie's square of marines. This was the decisive moment. Sir Robert was an old man, and past his best. To try to delay the French ships would give him nothing but glory he would never see. It might even be so futile that his action would be remembered with a scorn which could overshadow and despoil his whole career.

Maynard called, '*Flag* has acknowledged, sir!'

Bolitho bit his lip and continued his pacing. He could imagine the admiral's rasping voice as he dictated his signals, the uncertainty of the flag-captain, and the cautious confidence of Fox in the *Volcano*.

Maynard said suddenly, 'I can just make out her hoist, sir!' His eye was pressed to the end of the big telescope. '*Flag* to *Volcano*. Prepare for battle!'

The word flashed along the quarterdeck and down to the men waiting by the guns. Again the cheering, and again the cheer taken up across the water aboard the French ship. Bolitho waved absently as he saw Lieutenant Dancer's limping figure by the taffrail as the captured ship braced her yards and spread her tattered sails abreast the low wind.

Herrick said excitedly, '*Cassius* is making all sail, sir! My God, what a sight!' He seemed more impressed by the flagship's sudden activity than the fleet at his back.

Bolitho said, 'Have every man armed, Mr. Herrick. Put cutlasses and tomahawks at each gun. There will be plenty of fighting before long!'

Maynard lowered his glass, his voice shaking as he stared across at his captain. 'From *Flag*, sir! General signal.' He sounded as if he was trying to feel each word. '*Form line of battle!*'

Bolitho nodded slowly. 'Shorten sail, Mr. Herrick. We will bide here and allow the *Cassius* to meet up with us.' He sniffed the air. 'I feel we will lose the wind very soon. Dominica will act as a lee, I am afraid.'

He moved to the weather side and raised his glass across the nettings. Very slowly he moved the lens from side to side. In the small magnified picture he could see the dull flash of cannon fire, the brave flags and the gleam of sails as ship after mighty ship wheeled ponderously into line. He could feel the sweat at his spine, as he had after his nightmare. But this was real, yet harder to comprehend. God, there were three-deckers in plenty, perhaps sixty sail of the line, British and French, gliding together for a first, inexorable embrace.

He said sharply, 'Pass the word for Mr. Brock!' He did not lower his glass until the gunner reached the quarterdeck.

'Mr. Brock, I want both carronades taken to the forecastle. Put your best hands in charge of them, and see that their slides are freshly smeared with tallow.' He closed the glass and studied the gunner's dour face. 'The carronades are the only weapons we possess which the French lack.' He stared down at the nearest weapon, snub-nosed and ugly, and lacking either the grace or the proportion of a proper deck gun. Yet a carronade could throw a massive sixty-eight pound shot at short range, the power of which was devastating. Each circular shot burst on impact to deluge everything nearby with murderous cast-iron balls. One shot had the lethal quality of grape, added to which was the weight of a much heavier weapon.

He walked slowly to the rail and looked down at the neat decks. Had he forgotten anything? He ignored Brock and his stripped working party struggling and cursing the heavy carronades. He had to concentrate his full being on the task ahead. He must trust each officer and man. If they failed now, it was his fault for some earlier lapse in judgement.

Suddenly the restless, crowded figures below each gangway took on another meaning. Bolitho felt the pain of loss, as if he was looking at faces already dead. Quintal, the boatswain, spitting on his hands and pointing aloft for the benefit of the men who waited to sail the ship into action. Farquhar, slim and self-contained, walking abreast his battery of guns, his eyes moving over each weapon and every man in its crew. And the seamen themselves. Tanned and healthy in spite of their discomforts. Some faces standing out more than others. Here a man who had done well at Mola Island. There another who had fled from his station when they had met the *Andiron*.

He let his eyes move up the shrouds, to the men like Allday still at work aloft, and the marines kneeling in the tops with their long muskets loaded and ready.

Then aft, here to the quarterdeck. With its nine-pounders, and Neale's tiny figure dwarfed by that of a pigtailed gunner's mate. And Proby, old Proby, waving his arms like some fat scarecrow as he gave his instructions to the helmsmen. One of the men at the wheel Bolitho recognised as Strachan, the oldest sailor in the company. Too old to work a gun to Brock's satisfaction, he was still keen enough to stand his trick at the helm, and when the hell of battle swept this very deck, Bolitho knew a man like Strachan would never falter. Not because he was brave or stupid, but because it was part of his life. The only life he had known, and had been trained for.

Bolitho saw Okes watching him, his fingers playing nervously with the scabbard of his sword. Inwardly he wished it was Herrick at his side, but the latter would have his work cut out handling the ship's firepower. And anyway, Bolitho thought with sudden irritation, Okes was now first lieutenant. Vibart was dead. Not even a memory any more.

By the cabin hatch Stockdale saw Bolitho's grave face and gave a slight nod. He saw the captain's eyes catch the gesture and then move. But Stockdale was satisfied. Bolitho knew he was there. And that was enough.

Close-hauled, and making heavy weather of the faltering breeze, the three ships tacked into line. Just as they had rehearsed it so many frustrating times under the pitiless sun and beneath the eye of this same querulous admiral.

Bolitho raised his hat as the *Volcano's* sails billowed with sudden power and the lean frigate took her station in the lead. *Cassius* followed heavily in her wake, and as more flags soared aloft, Bolitho said sharply, 'Take station astern the *Flag*, Mr. Okes!'

He watched the men scampering to the braces, and then looked at the two-decker, as like an elderly but experienced warrior she opened her double line of ports and ran out her guns.

A voice pealed out suddenly, 'Deck there! Ships on the starboard bow!' A pause while every eye peered up at the tiny figure in the main crosstrees. 'Two ship o' the line! An' two frigates!'

Bolitho tried to control his impatience. At the rear of the small line *Phalarope* would engage last. By then, it might all be decided, he thought bitterly.

The sails flapped dejectedly, and he heard the helmsmen curse as the wheel went slack. 'Wind is backing to the east, sir!' Proby looked mournful.

'Very well.' Bolitho lifted his glass and tried to see the nearest enemy ships. The gunfire was louder and unending, but the main battle fleets seemed stationary as before. It was of course an illusion.

Beyond the *Cassius*'s flapping main course he saw a brief picture of the ships indicated by the lookout. Two big ones, very close in line. With two smaller sails, one on either beam. But the falling wind was playing havoc with his own men, he thought angrily. They had cheered, expecting to fight or die in glory. But this waiting, this agonising waiting, while all the time that slowly advancing fleet grew and grew, until the once exuberant seamen seemed too stunned to move, or drag their eyes from the smoke-shrouded ships.

Bolitho said, 'I am going aloft, Mr. Okes.' Without a glance at the sweating lieutenant he strode to the starboard gangway and made his way to the main shrouds. Even as a young midshipman Bolitho had never achieved a good head for heights, but after a quick look at the listless sails he started on the long climb to the main topmast.

As he swung through the lubber's hole of the maintop the waiting marines stared at him without speaking, and then turned their eyes back to the embattled fleets. The air was dinning with noise, and Bolitho's nostrils seemed full of the smell of powder and burned wood.

He found a solitary seaman perched in the crosstrees, and waited to regain his breath before opening his glass to stare over and beyond the slow-moving *Cassius*.

It was impossible to tell one line of battle from the other. The main British and French squadrons were practically ship to ship, yardarm to yardarm, their masts and sails enveloped in a dense pall of trapped gun-smoke.

He shifted the glass and tried not to look at the deck far below his dangling legs. Then he stiffened. The ships which this lookout had reported minutes earlier were breaking away from the main battle. The two ships of the line were in fact linked by a stout cable, and as he peered through the forerigging he realised that the furthest vessel, a big three-decker, was partially disabled and without either bowsprit or foremast.

The towing ship, hampered by her massive consort, yawed from side to side, her sails puffing and then falling slack in the sluggish wind. As she swung the sunlight threw strange shadows on her tall side, and on the gleaming rows of guns already run out and prepared to fight.

Bolitho nodded to the lookout. 'Keep a good eye on them.'

The man grinned. 'Got nothin' else to do, zur!' He leaned over to watch Bolitho's careful descent and then settled down at his post. As Bolitho made his way down the rough, vibrating ratlines he heard the man humming.

He found Okes and Rennie waiting for him beside the wheel. Bolitho said flatly, 'Two big ships right enough. But one of them is disabled. Probably in a collision during the night.' He rubbed his chin. 'The towing ship is flying a command flag. White over blue.' He forced a smile and called to Maynard, 'What do you make of that, my lad?'

The midshipman lowered his glass for a moment. 'Part of the French van, sir.' He looked uneasy.

'Right.' Bolitho walked to the rail. 'De Grasse will be worried about his transports. To mount an attack on Jamaica he will need more than fighting ships. He'll have troops and supplies in other craft, like the ones we burned at Mola Island.'

Okes said, 'While the fleet is engaged, de Grasse will try and force his transports this way!'

Bolitho nodded grimly. 'Right again.' He snapped his fingers. 'Part of the French van has been detached to clear the way for them!' He looked up at the listless sails. 'And three ships only bar their way.' He turned to Rennie who was swinging his sword idly against his polished boots. 'If we can turn the enemy's van, gentlemen, Sir George Rodney will do the rest!' He slapped his palms together. 'Like rabbits in a trap!'

Okes stared at the slow-moving ships ahead of the *Cassius*. 'In this case the rabbits are bigger than the hunters, sir!'

But Bolitho had already moved away. He paused beside the minute drummer boy and asked calmly, 'Give us a tune on your fife, boy.' He spoke loudly, so that the men at the nine-pounders could hear him.

The boy peered up from beneath his shako and swallowed hard. His lips were pale, and Bolitho could see his hands shaking against his tunic. 'Wh-what shall I play, sir?'

Bolitho looked around at the strained, watchful faces. 'What about "Hearts of Oak"? We all know that, eh, lads?'

And so with the overwhelming roar of battle drumming in their ears, the *Phalarope*'s sailors picked up the fife's feeble lilt.

Bolitho walked back to the weather side and lifted his glass. Even aboard the *Cassius* the men might hear the *Phalarope's* sailors singing the well-used words and gain some slight confidence.

'Come cheer up my lads,
'Tis to Glory we steer . . .'

Bolitho watched the great rolling bank of black smoke as it moved steadily towards the three British ships. It was like a living thing, he thought coldly. Writhing, and alight with angry red and orange flashes. Yet he was grateful for its presence. At least it hid the horror and the gruesome scenes beyond.

He looked down at his men, their faces momentarily engrossed in their singing. *They* would not have much longer to wait.

18

A Tradition of Victory

John Allday tied his neckerchief tightly around his head and ears and then dashed the sweat from his face with one forearm. Right forward on the frigate's tapered forecastle he had an uninterrupted view of the *Cassius*, and ahead of her he could just see part of the *Volcano*'s upper rigging. Deliberately he turned his back on them and on the smoke-shrouded tangle of ships beyond. He looked down at McIntosh, the gunner's mate, who was on his knees beside one of the carronades as if in prayer.

As Allday had slithered to the deck from the mainyard, Brock, the gunner, had halted him with a sharp, 'Here you!' For a moment they had faced each other once again. Allday, the pressed seaman, whose skin still bore the scars of Brock's cane, and who had nearly hanged because of another's treachery and cunning. And the gunner, hard-faced and expressionless, who rarely showed any trace of his inner feelings, if he had any.

Brock had gestured with his cane. 'Up forrard, you! Join the crews on the carronades!'

Allday had made to run off but Brock had added harshly, 'I was wrong about you it seems!' It was not an apology. Just a statement of fact. 'So get up there and do your best!' His thin mouth had moved in what might have been a smile. 'My God, Allday, your sheep would be proud of you today!'

He smiled at the recollection and then looked round with surprise as Ferguson scrambled up beside him. His eyes were bright with fear, and he clung to the hammock nettings as if he would fall without their support.

McIntosh grunted, 'What do *you* want here?'

'I-I was sent, sir.' Ferguson licked his lips. 'I'm no use for anything else.'

McIntosh turned back to his inspection of the training tackles. 'Christ Almighty!' was his only comment.

'Don't look at the ships, Bryan.' Allday picked up his cutlass and ran it through his belt. The hilt felt warm against his naked back. 'Just don't think about 'em. Keep down behind the nettings and do as I do.' He forced a grin. 'We have a fine view from here!'

Ritchie, the stolid Devon seaman, ran his fingers over the shot rack and asked vaguely, 'Wot are we to shoot at, Mr. McIntosh?'

The gunner's mate was edgy. 'The captain hasn't told me yet! When he does, I'll tell *you!*'

Ritchie shrugged. 'Us'll roast they devils!' He peered at the *Cassius*. 'The Frogs'll turn an' run!'

Kemp, one of the loaders, grimaced. 'When they sees *you* they will!'

Ferguson lowered his head against his arm. 'It's madness! We'll all be killed!'

Allday studied him sadly. He is right, he thought. Nothing can live against such a force. He said kindly, 'It's April, Bryan. Just think how it looks in Cornwall, eh? The hedgerows and the green fields . . .'

Ferguson stared at him. 'For God's sake, what are you talking about?'

Allday replied calmly, 'Have you forgotten already what nearly happened to us, Bryan?' He hardened his voice, knowing that Ferguson was at breaking point. 'Remember Nick Pochin?' He saw Ferguson flinch, but carried on. 'Well, he's dead, hanged aboard the *Cassius* with the other fools!'

Ferguson hung his head. 'I-I'm sorry.'

Allday said, 'I know you're afraid. And so am I. And so is the captain, I shouldn't wonder.'

At that moment Lieutenant Herrick stepped on to the forecastle and walked briskly to the carronades. 'Everything well, Mr. McIntosh?'

The gunner's mate stood up and wiped his palms on his trousers. 'Aye, sir.' He studied the lieutenant and then added, 'Mola Island seems a long time ago now, Mr. Herrick.'

Herrick stared aft along the maindeck to the raised quarterdeck where Okes stood stiffly beside the captain. Would Okes crack this time? He wondered. Which way would his private shame make him react? He replied, 'It does indeed.'

Okes's voice distorted by his speaking trumpet, echoed above the rumble of gunfire. 'Another pull on the weather forebrace there! Mr. Packwood, take that man's name!'

Herrick hid his dismay from McIntosh. Okes was so much on edge that he had to say something. Anything.

McIntosh said dryly. 'Promotion does not seem to solve *everything*, Mr. Herrick!'

Herrick swung round as flags broke from the *Cassius*'s yards. A moment later he heard Maynard yell, 'Engage the enemy, sir!' Then, in a slightly steadier voice, 'Tack in succession!'

The pipes trilled. 'Lee braces. Jump to it!'

Keeping time with the ponderous two-decker the frigates tacked slowly to the south-east. Herrick shaded his eyes as the sun lanced down between the sails, and saw the nearest enemy ships less than a quarter of a mile away. They were in no apparent order, but with their yards braced round were tacking on a converging course with the British squadron. The big three-decker hid her gaping ranks of guns in deep shadow as she swung slightly up wind. The tow had been cast off, and the leading ship of the line, unhampered by her massive consort, heeled easily in the breeze, her command flag pointing directly at the *Cassius*.

Herrick tried to clear the dryness from his throat. 'Carry on, Mr. McIntosh. I must attend my duties!'

He had to force himself to walk slowly down to the maindeck. As he passed an open hatch where a marine sentry leaned on his musket he saw the surgeon's scarlet face grinning up at him.

'Yer 'ealth, Mr. 'Errick!' He waved a tankard.

Herrick felt slightly mad. 'Damn you, Tobias! You'll not have my body today!'

Some of the men at the nearest guns chuckled. 'That's right, sir! You tell 'im!'

Herrick strode on to take up his position in the centre of the deck. Farquhar was below the quarterdeck, his haughty features slightly pale but determined. Herrick gave him a nod, but Farquhar did not seem to see him.

There was a crashing boom, all the more startling because every man had been expecting it. It was followed instantly by a ragged salvo, and another.

Bolitho's voice broke through Herrick's stricken thoughts. 'Note it in the log, Mr. Proby! We have engaged the enemy!' His voice was muffled as he turned away. 'Cut those boats adrift, Mr. Neale! They'll act like a damn sea anchor in this poor wind!'

Herrick looked at his hands. They were quite steady, yet he felt as if every bone and muscle was quivering uncontrollably. He could imagine the *Phalarope*'s boats drifting astern, and thought of Bolitho's earlier words to the crew.

'... below us it is a thousand fathoms to the bottom!' Herrick winced as another thunderous broadside sent a dull vibration through the planks at his feet. A thousand fathoms, and now not even a boat to save the survivors!

He looked up and saw that Bolitho had returned to the quarterdeck rail and was staring at him. He did not speak, but gave a strange, lingering smile, as if he was trying to convey some personal message to him.

Then Bolitho called sharply, 'Mr. Neale, do not run like that! Remember our people are watching you today!'

Herrick turned away. The message could have been for him, he thought. He felt strangely calmed by this realisation and walked to the larboard battery and looked down the line of guns. In a few minutes every one of them would be firing. In a few minutes. He studied the faces of the men beside them and felt suddenly humble.

'Well, lads, this is better than practice, eh?'

Surprisingly they laughed at his stupid joke, and in spite of the cold fingers around his stomach Herrick was able to join them.

Bolitho blinked in the reflected sunlight and peered across the weather rail. Ahead of the *Phalarope* the flagship was holding her course, but the frigate *Volcano* which had been leading the line was pulling away to larboard, breaking the pattern as two French frigates drove down towards her.

Rennie gasped, 'He's done for! We cannot give him any help!'

The sea's surface shimmered as another crashing broadside rippled along the *Volcano*'s gunports. Gun by gun, each one carefully aimed and fired in rapid succession.

Undeterred the two frigates, with the wind in their favour, swept down on either beam.

Proby said sharply, '*Volcano*'s luffing!'

Bolitho breathed out painfully. Fox was no fool, and as wily as his name. As the two enemy frigates swept downwind for a quick kill the *Volcano* swung lazily into the wind, her sails flapping in violent protest. The nearest French ship realised her mistake just too late. As her yards started to swing, the *Volcano* presented her opposite side and fired a full salvo. The French ship seemed to stagger as if dealt a body blow. Across the water Bolitho could hear the crash of falling spars and the sliding thunder of overturned cannon. All else was hidden in the billowing clouds of smoke, but above it he could see *Volcano*'s ensign and all three masts still standing.

'Flagship signalling! "Close on *Flag*!"' Maynard ran to hoist an acknowledgement.

Bolitho tore his eyes from Captain Fox's lithe frigate as it went about to take the wind's advantage from the two Frenchmen. *Cassius* was heading straight for the powerful two-decker with the command flag. She would need all the help she could get. Fox would have to manage for himself for a while.

'Starboard a point!' Bolitho ran to the rail and leaned out as far as he could. Then he saw the towering sails of the ship of the line as it drove down on a converging course with the flagship. They should pass port to port, he thought. He shouted to the maindeck, 'Stand by, Mr. Herrick!'

Okes yelled, 'The Frenchman's changing his tack, sir!' He was jumping with agitation. 'God in hell, sir! He's turning across the *Cassius*'s bows!'

Either the French captain was unwilling to face a gun for gun contest, or he hoped to rake the *Cassius*'s bows and masts as he crossed her course, Bolitho was not quite sure which. But either way he had not allowed for the extra sail carried by Admiral Napier's elderly flagship.

Instead, the two ships crossed their bowsprits and then met at right-angles with a sickening crash. As they locked together both ships opened fire, the arrowhead of water between them erupting in a great sheet of flame and black smoke.

Bolitho watched in chilled silence as *Cassius*'s foremast and main topgallant leaned drunkenly and then smashed down into the all-enveloping smoke. He could see rigging and spars ripping away the sails and scattering men from the tops like dead fruit.

Another broadside split the air apart, and Bolitho knew that the *Cassius*'s forward guns were within feet of the enemy's. Yet still they stayed locked together, their splintered bowsprits and jib-booms entangled like the tusks of two crazed beasts from a nightmare.

Bolitho cupped his hands. 'Both carronades to starboard!' He waved his hand at Proby. 'We will put her across the enemy's stern, if we can!' He half ducked as a ball screamed overhead and slapped through the driver leaving a ragged tear. A stray shot from the giants, but just as deadly, he thought grimly.

All around him men were coughing and wiping their eyes as the smoke reached out and over the frigate's decks.

The helmsman cursed as the *Cassius*'s torn sails loomed over the fog like some great spectre. But Bolitho gauged the set of the flagship's masts and knew he was on the right course. The fog closed in again, and he saw the double lines of flashes as both fired salvo after salvo at pointblank range.

He could hear the two hulls grinding together, the screams and cries of the wounded and dying, mingled with the unbelievable sound of the admiral's drum and fife band. It was impossible to tell what they were playing, or how a man could live, let alone think of an empty tune in that holocaust.

But Bolitho shouted, 'A cheer, lads! Give a cheer to the *Flag!*'

Muskets banged through the smoke, and Bolitho heard the balls thudding into the bulwarks and whining against the nine-pounders.

Rennie bellowed, 'Marksmen! Shoot down those bastards!' And from aloft came an answering volley.

The wind seemed to have gone altogether, although in the dense smoke it was impossible to gauge either speed or distance. Then out of the flickering, choking fog Bolitho saw the stern of the two-decker. It seemed to hang above the *Phalarope*'s starboard bow like an ornate cliff, and he could see the flash of musket fire from her stern windows as marksmen directed their attention to the frigate's forecastle.

Bolitho banged the rail with his hands, ignoring the whining balls and the cries from forward. In his mind he was picturing the enemy ship's lower gundeck. Cleared for action it was one long battery which ran from one end of the ship to the other. Bolitho had been a midshipman in a ship of the line, and he knew that there must be upwards of three hundred men in there, stooping in semi-darkness, choking in the acrid fumes, and firing their guns more from familiarity than accuracy.

He shouted, 'The carronades, Mr. McIntosh! Fire as we cross her stern!'

Rennie grinned and wiped his face with his sleeve. 'That'll kill a few, sir!'

Bolitho bit his lip as the sound of a mast thundering across smashed and broken rigging broke through the roar of combat. *Cassius* was a very old ship. Much more of this punishment and she would either break up or sink as she fought!

He wondered what had happened to the *Volcano*, and worse, the crippled three-decker. If the latter was able to engage, it would be over in minutes. Her lower gundeck was crammed with thirty-two-pounders. One of those could smash through two and a half feet of solid oak at maximum range. Bolitho tried not to picture what would happen to the *Phalarope*'s frail timbers.

'Ready, sir!' McIntosh was yelling like a madman.

Bolitho drew his sword. 'Larboard a point, Mr. Proby!' He watched the jib flapping and dropped his sword.

'Fire!'

Herrick felt the deck shudder beneath him as both carronades fired almost together. As the thick muzzle smoke eddied clear he stared up at the French ship's stern, momentarily forgetting the battle which raged around him. A few seconds earlier he had watched the tall stern emerge from the fog of gunfire and had seen the great cabin windows with their life-sized figures on either quarter, full breasted nymphs carrying tridents with the vessel's name, *Ondine*, in scarlet and gilt across the wide counter between them, and had marvelled at the ship's overpowering appearance of grandeur and indestructibility. As the smoke moved clear he gaped at the black jagged holes which left the stern like the entrance of a fire-scarred cave. At the horror and chaos beyond he could only briefly imagine, for as a fresh gust of wind moved busily through the *Phalarope's* sails the deck tilted, and with her helm hard over she swung in a tight arc around the enemy ship's larboard quarter.

He shouted hoarsely above the din, 'Ready, lads!' He peered along the crouching line of gun captains. 'Fire as you bear!'

The first guns of the starboard battery fired as one, and in ragged succession the others followed as lanyard after lanyard was pulled taut, and the double-shotted charges crashed into the trapped smoke alongside.

A few men were cheering, their cries broken by coughs and curses as the smoke swirled back through the open ports.

Herrick yelled, 'Reload! Reload and run out!' He watched narrowly as the frigate moved down the other ship's beam, barely twenty yards clear. He could see the crowded heads on the high bulwark, the stabbing yellow flashes of muskets from her tops, but from the lower gundeck with its line of powerful guns there was not a single shot in reply. The carronades' lethal attack must have swept through the crowded gundeck like a scythe through a field of standing corn.

But as he watched he saw the first guns on the upperdeck lurch back at their ports, and then in the twinkling of an eye the whole upper battery erupted in one deafening broadside.

Herrick fell back, half stunned by the volume of the combined sounds of exploding guns, followed instantly by the demoniac scream of balls above his head. The nets which Bolitho had ordered to be placed over the maindeck jumped and vibrated to falling wreckage, blocks, severed rigging and whole strips of blackened canvas. But Herrick stared up with amazement as he realised that the ill-aimed broadside had missed everything vital to *Phalarope's* movements. Not a mast or spar had fallen. Had it been the lower battery, he knew that the frigate's starboard side and gunports would now be a shattered ruin.

He heard the gun captains shouting like demons. 'Run out! Heave on the tackles! Stand clear!' Then with the jerk of trigger lines the guns rumbled back to the full extent of their tackles.

A musket clattered by Herrick's feet, and as he stared upwards he looked into the dead eyes of a spreadeagled marine who had pitched down from the maintop on to the net below.

But he forgot the marine immediately as something more terrible took his attention. Through the smoke, falling like a giant tree, he saw the *Ondine's* mizzenmast. It was impossible, but it was happening. Mast, top and topgallant, with all the attendant weight of sails, rigging and yards, hung in the air as if caught in a strong wind. Then, amid the screams and desperate cries of those men caught like flies in the shrouds, it crashed down across the *Phalarope's* quarterdeck. The hull quivered as if the frigate had hit a reef, and as Herrick ran aft to the ladder he felt the *Phalarope* shake from truck to keel and then begin to swing slowly to starboard. Like an unyielding bridge the *Ondine's* severed mast held both ships together, and as a fresh burst of musket fire struck foot-long splinters from the deck, Herrick fought his way up the ladder and stared with dismay at the destruction around him.

A complete yard had fallen amongst Rennie's marines, and he turned away from the smashed, writhing remains as Sergeant Garwood roared, 'Stand to! Leave those men alone!' He was glaring at the remainder of his marines. 'Rapid fire on her poop, my lads!' He vanished in a fresh cloud of smoke as the frigate's guns fired again, the shots crashing into the *Ondine*'s hull, which at the nearest point was ten feet clear.

Herrick pushed past the struggling seamen who were trying to hack away the French rigging and dropped on one knee beside Bolitho. For a moment he thought the captain had been hit by a musket ball, but as he slid his arm beneath his shoulders Bolitho opened his eyes and struggled into a sitting position. He blinked at Herrick's anxious face and said, 'Keep the guns firing, Herrick!' He peered up at the enemy ship alongside and pulled himself to his feet. 'We must stop them boarding us!' He groped for his sword and shouted harshly, 'Cut that wreckage away!'

Okes staggered through the smoke, his breeches and coat splashed with blood and torn flesh. His eyes seemed to fill his face, and although he appeared to be shouting, Herrick could hear nothing.

Bolitho pointed with his sword. 'Mr. Okes, clear the larboard battery and prepare to repel boarders!' He reached out and shook the lieutenant like a dog. 'Do you hear me, damn you?'

Okes nodded violently, and a long thread of spittle ran down his chin.

Bolitho pushed him to the ladder, but Herrick said quickly, 'I'll do it, sir!'

'No you won't!' Bolitho looked wild. 'Get your guns firing! It is our only chance!'

At that moment the *Ondine*'s guns banged out once again, and Herrick flinched as the salvo seared his face like a hot wind. He saw a party of sailors hacking away a length of broken shrouds. In the next instant there was nothing but a squirming mass of pulped flesh and bones, with a gaping gash in the lee bulwark beyond.

Bolitho shouted in his ear, 'We'll not be so lucky next time!'

Herrick ran down the ladder, closing his eyes and ears to the horror beside him as more great blows shook the frigate's hull like hammers on an anvil. He walked through the smoke, his eyes streaming, his throat like sand, as he shouted wild and unheeded encouragement to the powder-blackened gunners.

Farquhar caught his arm and shouted, 'They'll never cut that mast away in time!' He pointed towards the *Ondine*'s lower gundeck. 'They'll not be silent for ever!'

Herrick did not reply. With the wind at her beam, and held aft by the broken mast, the *Phalarope*'s bows were starting to swing inwards towards the *Ondine*'s hull. Through the smoke he could see men running along the two-decker's side towards the point of contact, the filtered sunlight playing on raised weapons.

He saw Okes groping towards the forecastle, his sword still in its sheath. He snapped, 'Go with him, Mr. Farquhar! He looks in a bad condition!'

Farquhar's eyes gleamed coldly. 'It will be a pleasure!'

Herrick flinched as a complete section of the starboard gangway splintered skyward and one of the twelve-pounders lurched on to its side. A seaman screamed as a severed head landed at his feet, and another ran from the gun, his eyes blinded by flying splinters.

Herrick called, 'Take those men below!' But as he shouted he heard the sudden clank of pumps and knew that it was probably just as safe on deck.

He tried to shut it all from his mind and made himself walk back along the line of guns. Men were falling all around him but he knew he must not falter, and shouted, 'Keep hitting 'em, lads!' He waved his hat. 'If you want to see England again, keep those guns firing!'

On the forecastle the men from the unemployed guns gathered below the nettings, their hands gripping cutlasses and boarding axes as the bowsprit quivered against the enemy's forerigging. Okes croaked, 'Over you go, lads! Keep those swine off our bows!'

Some of the men cheered and began to scramble out along the bowsprit, others fell back as a flurry of musket shots cut through the eager sailors and sent their corpses spinning into the water below.

Farquhar said urgently. 'You must lead them! My God, you're asking the impossible!'

Okes swung round, his mouth slack. 'Hold your tongue! *I'll* give the orders!'

Farquhar eyed him coolly. 'I have said nothing in the past, *Mr.* Okes! But I will say it now as it seems we will all die today!' His hat was plucked away by a musket ball but he did not drop his eyes. 'You are a cheat, a coward and a liar! If I thought you were worth it, I would discredit you here and now in front of these men, whom you are too squeamish to lead!' He turned his back on Okes's stricken face and shouted, 'Follow me, you ragged heroes!' He waved his sword. 'Make way for a younger man!'

They laughed like lunatics and slapped his shoulders as he crawled over the nettings and clambered on to the smooth bowsprit. Shots whined all around him, but he was breathless with a mixture of relief and madness. All this was worth it, if only for telling Okes what he thought of him for his cowardice at Mola Island.

Okes stared back at the quarterdeck and whimpered as a seaman crawled past him, half disembowelled by a great sliver of torn planking. Bolitho was still at the quarterdeck rail, a speaking trumpet in one hand, his sword in the other. His uniform seemed to shine in the frail sunlight, and Okes could see the hammock nettings jumping as hidden marksmen tried to find the *Phalarope*'s captain.

Okes cried, 'I hope they kill you! I hope they kill all of you!'

He sobbed and groped for his sword. Nobody listened to his wild words, or even heeded his presence on the blood-spattered forecastle. He thought of the stinging words and the contempt in Farquhar's eyes.

'*Never!*' He pulled himself towards the bowsprit where already some of the men were clashing steel with the enemy seamen. 'I'll show the lot of you!' Heedless of the curses and screams he pulled himself over the clinging sailors and hacked at a French petty officer with his sword. He saw the man's shocked surprise as a great gash opened across his neck and he fell between the grinding hulls. Then he was up and over, pushing Farquhar aside in his frenzied efforts to reach and strike at the enemy.

Farquhar saw the madness on Okes's face and tried to pull him back. But it was useless. Encouraged by the apparent bravery of their officers the British sailors swarmed on to the *Ondine*'s bulwark.

Okes snarled, 'Are you afraid, Mr. Farquhar?' He threw back his head and emitted a shrill laugh. 'Your uncle won't like that!'

Farquhar parried a thrusting pike and followed Okes down on to the wide deck. It was every man for himself now.

Bolitho strained his eyes through the smoke and watched his men changing from defenders to boarders. Whoever had decided to board the *Ondine* had made the right guess, he thought grimly. He heard the axes ringing on the tangle of wreckage behind him and knew it was impossible to free *Phalarope* from its embrace before the *Ondine*'s heavy guns were brought back into action.

He crossed the deck and said to Rennie, 'We must board her from aft, too!' He saw the marine nod. 'Get some men together immediately!'

He heard someone sobbing and saw Neale on his knees below the lee rail. Midshipman Maynard was lying on his back, one hand held upright entangled in a signal lanyard, his eyes wide and unseeing and strangely peaceful. Neale was holding his hand and rocking back and forth, oblivious to the crash of gunfire and the slapping musket balls which had already claimed his friend.

Bolitho reached down and pulled Neale to his feet. The boy's last reserve seemed to collapse, and with a frantic cry he buried his face in Bolitho's coat, his body shaking with convulsions of grief. Bolitho prised him away and lifted his chin with the hilt of his sword. For a moment he stared down at him, then he said gravely, 'Take a grip on yourself, Mr. Neale!' He saw the stunned look in Neale's eyes and shut his mind to the fact that he was talking with a terrified thirteen-year-old child who had just lost his best friend. 'You are a King's officer, Neale!' He softened his voice. 'I said earlier, our people are watching you today. Do you think you can help me now?'

Neale brushed his eyes with his sleeve and looked back at Maynard's body by the bulwark. As the halyard jerked in the breeze his arm moved as if he still held on to life. Then Neale turned back to Bolitho and said brokenly, 'I'm all right now, sir!'

Bolitho watched him walk back to the shouting gunners, a small figure half hidden in the smoke and flame of this savage battle.

Rennie reappeared, a cut above one eye. 'Ready, sir!' He swung his curved sword. 'Shall I take 'em across?'

Bolitho looked around the battered quarterdeck. There seemed to be more corpses than live men, he thought wearily. He faltered as a shot crashed against the quarterdeck ladder and tore into the planking like a plough. With disbelief he saw Proby put his hands to his face and watched his fingers clawing at the sudden torrent of blood. The master staggered against the wheel, but as Strachan left the spokes to hold him he fell moaning on to his side and lay still. His hands thudded on the planking, and Bolitho saw that his face had been torn away.

'We must take the *Ondine*!' The words were wrung from his lips. 'If the

French see their command ship strike, they'll ...' He faltered and stared again at Proby's body. I've done for the lot of them! He felt the anguish changing to helpless anger. I have sacrificed the ship and every man aboard just for *this*!

But Rennie eyed him evenly and said, 'It is the right decision, sir!' He straightened his hat and said to his sergeant, 'Right, Garwood, do you feel like a little walk?'

Bolitho stared at him. It was as if the marine had been reading his mind. He said, 'The *Cassius* will support us.' He looked at the waiting marines. They crouched like animals, wild and beyond fear or even anger. 'It's us or them, lads!'

Then, as the men shouted and cheered he jumped on to the *Ondine*'s broken mast and began to claw his way across. Once he looked down at the water below him. It was littered with broken woodwork and sodden corpses, French and British alike.

As he reached the *Ondine*'s poop he felt the balls whining past him and heard screams at his back as men fell to join the waiting corpses below. Then as he reached the scarred bulwark he hacked away the remains of the French boarding nets and leapt down on to the deck. Dead and dying lay everywhere, but when he glanced quickly across the far side he felt a further sense of shock as he saw the *Cassius*. She was not alongside any more, but drifting away in the smoke of her own wounds, a mastless hulk, battered beyond recognition. From every scupper he could see long, glistening streams of blood, which poured down the ship's side to colour the water in one unbroken stain. It was as if the ship herself was bleeding to death. But from the stump of her mizzen the ensign, pitted and torn with shot holes, still flapped in defiance, and as Rennie's yelling marines swept across the *Ondine*'s poop there was a burst of cheering from the *Cassius*'s deck. It was not much of a cheer, for there could not be many left to raise it, but to Bolitho it acted like the stab of a spur.

He ran across the littered deck, cutting down two seamen with hardly a pause, propelled on by the cheering and the battle-crazed men at his back. He could see his men on the *Ondine*'s forecastle, almost encircled by an overwhelming mass of French seamen, their stubborn resistance faltering as they were forced back towards the rail.

Bolitho yelled, 'Hold on *Phalarope*'s!' He saw the Frenchmen falter and turn to face this new threat. 'To me, lads! Cut your way through 'em!'

More men were swarming from the frigate now, and he saw Herrick's uniform through the smoke as he waved his men forward.

He turned as Okes slashed a path for himself in the press of figures, his sword gleaming red as he cut down a screaming midshipman and went on towards a man who was reloading a swivel gun beside the quarterdeck. Okes was bleeding from a dozen wounds, and as he reached the ladder the swivel gun exploded with a dull roar. The packed grapeshot lifted Okes like a rag doll and flung him lifeless into the fighting men below the ladder. The gunner fell a second later, cut down by a swinging cutlass.

Then, all at once, it was over. The deck clattered with the weapons thrown down by the *Ondine*'s seamen, and Bolitho realised that their cries of defiance had changed to pleas for quarter. He knew he could not hold his men back if they wanted to complete the slaughter. It fell to some unknown sailor to break the spell of destruction and killing.

'A cheer for the *Phalarope*!' The voice cracked with relief and jubilation. 'An' a cheer for Mad Dick!'

Bolitho climbed down the ladder, past the dazed Frenchmen and the mangled litter of entwined corpses.

'Captain Rennie!' He paused beside the remains of Lieutenant Okes. 'Hoist our flag above the French ensign!' He felt his hands shaking. 'Let them all see what you have done today.'

Sergeant Garwood said gruffly, 'The cap'n is dead, sir!' He unrolled the flag carefully. 'But I will do it!'

'Dead?' Bolitho stared after him. 'Rennie, too?' He felt Herrick pulling his arm and asked heavily, 'What is it?'

'The ship is ours, sir!' Herrick was shaking with excitement. 'The gun-deck is like a slaughterhouse! Our carronades did more than . . .' He broke off as he saw Bolitho's face.

'Very well, Mr. Herrick. Thank you.' His voice shook. 'Thank *all* of you!' He turned away as more cheering echoed round the bloody decks.

Herrick shook his head as if he was beyond understanding. 'A two-decker, sir! What a victory!'

Bolitho replied quietly, 'We have a tradition of victory, Mr. Herrick.' He seemed to be speaking to himself. 'Now gather our people and send them back to the ship. They have cut the wreckage away.' He stared dully at the *Phalarope* and let his eyes move slowly along her length. There were great gaping holes in her once-trim hull, and she was well down by the head. It sounded as if the pumps were only just containing the inrush of water. All three topmasts had gone, and the sails flapped in the breeze in long canvas streamers. He could see bodies hanging in the tops, the great patches of scarlet across the smashed and buckled planking below. Intruding for the first time since their battle had begun came the distant thunder of that other great fight. Still far away and impersonal.

Bolitho made another effort to pull himself together. 'Lively, Mr. Herrick! The battle is still not over!'

If only his men would stop cheering. If only he could get away and be with himself.

Herrick waved his arm. 'Clear the ship, lads! We can take this wreck later in our own good time!'

Bolitho walked to the bulwark. Across the gap he could see Neale standing just where he had left him beside the wheel. He said, 'Tell my coxswain to take Mr. Okes and Captain Rennie over to the ship.' He saw Herrick's sudden anxiety and felt despair closing in again. 'Not Stockdale, Mr. Herrick?'

Herrick nodded. 'He fell as you were fighting on the poop, sir. He was defending your back from the marksmen.' He tried to smile. 'I am sure that was what he would have wished!'

Bolitho stared at him. Stockdale dead. And he had not even seen him fall.

Farquhar pushed forward, his features wildly excited. 'Captain, sir! The lookouts report that our fleet has broken the enemy's line in two places!' He stared round the stained, watching faces. 'Rodney has broken the French line, do you hear?'

Bolitho felt the breeze across his cheek, feeling its way through the battle's stench like an awed stranger. So de Grasse was beaten. He stared at the listing frigate below him, feeling the prick of emotion behind his eyes. Was all this sacrifice for nothing after all?

Herrick took his arm and said thickly, '*Look*, sir! Over yonder!'

As the freshening wind pushed away the curtain of smoke from the embattled and shattered ship, Bolitho saw the tall outline of the big three-decker. Her guns were still run out, and her paintwork was gleaming and unscarred by any cannon. Throughout the fighting she had lain impotent or unwilling to face the holocaust of close combat, and no British blood had been given to her massive armament.

Yet in spite of all these things there was another flag flying above her own. The same that flew on the dismasted *Cassius* and aboard the *Ondine*. The same as the *Phalarope*'s own ensign and the victorious *Volcano* which now pushed her way through the last rolling bank of smoke.

Herrick asked soberly, 'Do you need more than that, sir? She's struck to *you*!'

Bolitho nodded and then climbed over the bulwark. 'We will get the ship under way, Mr. Herrick. Though I fear she may never fight again!'

Herrick said quietly, 'There'll be other ships, sir.'

Bolitho stepped down on to the *Phalarope*'s gangway and walked slowly above the spent and sweating gunners.

'Other ships?' He touched the splintered rail and smiled sadly. 'Not like this one, Mr. Herrick.' He tilted his head and looked up at the flag.

'Not like the *Phalarope*!'

Epilogue

Lieutenant Thomas Herrick pulled his boat cloak closer around his shoulders and picked up his small travelling bag. The houses around the cobbled square were thickly covered in snow, and the wind which blew strongly inland from Falmouth Bay and seemed to pierce his bones to the marrow, told him that there was more to come. For a moment longer he watched the ostlers guiding the steaming horses into the inn yard, leaving the slush-stained coach which Herrick had just vacated isolated and empty. Through the inn windows he could see a cheerful fire and hear voices raised in laughter and busy conversation.

He was suddenly tempted to go inside and join these unknown people. After the long journey from Plymouth, and four days on the road before that, he felt drained and weary, but as he looked up at the mist-shrouded hump of Pendennis Castle and the bleak hillside beyond he knew he was only deluding himself. He turned his back on the inn and started up the narrow lane from the square. Everything seemed smaller than he remembered it. Even the church with its low wall and the leaning stones within the graveyard appeared to have shrunk since that last and only visit. He stepped sideways into a mound of muddy snow as two shouting children dashed past him dragging a homemade sledge. Neither gave Herrick a glance. That too was different from the last time.

Herrick ducked his head as a strong gust whipped the snow from a low hedgerow and across his face, and when he looked up again he saw the old house, square and grey, facing him like a picture from all those past memories. He quickened his pace, suddenly nervous and unsure of himself.

He heard the bell jangling within the house, and even as he released the heavy iron handle the door swung open, and a neat fair-haired woman in a dark dress and white cap stood aside to greet him.

Herrick said uncertainly, 'Good day, ma'am. My name is Herrick. I have just driven from the other side of England.'

She took his cloak and hat and stared at him with a strange, secret smile. 'That's a long journey, sir. The master is expecting you.'

At that moment the door at the far side of the hall swung open and Bolitho stepped forward to meet him. For a long moment they both stood quite still, their hands clasped in an embrace which neither wanted to break.

Then Bolitho said, 'Come into the study, Thomas. There is a good fire waiting!'

Herrick allowed himself to be placed in a deep leather chair, and let his eyes stray over the old portraits which lined the panelled walls.

Bolitho watched him gravely. 'I am glad you came, Thomas. More glad than I can say.' He seemed nervous and ill at ease.

Herrick said, 'How it all comes back to me as I sit here. It is a year and a month since we weighed anchor from Falmouth and sailed for the West Indies together.' He shook his head sadly. 'Now it is all finished. The peace is signed at Versailles. It is over.'

Bolitho was staring into the fire, the dancing reflections playing across his dark hair and his grey, steady eyes. He said suddenly, 'My father is dead, Thomas.' He paused as Herrick jerked upright in his chair. 'And so is Hugh, my brother!'

Herrick did not know what to say. He wanted to find some word of comfort, something to ease the pain from Bolitho's voice. Without effort he could throw his mind back over the months, to the aftermath of the battle when the listing, battered *Phalarope* had limped painfully to Antigua for repairs. Herrick had known that Bolitho was offered an immediate passage home to England, for a better and bigger command. But he had stayed with the frigate. Nursing her through every indignity of the dockyard, and watching over the care and treatment of her sick and wounded men.

October had arrived, and with her refit only half completed the *Phalarope* was ordered home to England. The Battle of the Saintes, as it was soon to be known, was the last great struggle of that unfortunate war. As the frigate dropped her anchor at Spithead, England rejoiced to the sounds of peace. It was an unsatisfactory agreement, but for England the war had been too long on the defensive. And as Pitt had remarked to the House of Commons, 'A defensive war can only end in inevitable defeat.'

Bolitho had left the ship at Portsmouth, but only after every man had been properly paid off and letters of credit had been sent to the dependants of her many dead. Then with hardly a word he had left for Falmouth.

As first lieutenant, Herrick had stayed to hand over the ship to the dockyard, then he too had gone to his home in Kent.

Bolitho's letter had arrived within a few days, and Herrick had set off for Cornwall, hardly knowing if the invitation was genuine or just common courtesy.

But as he looked at the big, shadowed room and Bolitho's slim figure before the fire, he began to understand for the first time. Bolitho was now completely alone.

He said quietly, 'I am sorry. I had no idea.'

Bolitho said, 'My father died three months ago.' He gave a short, bitter smile. 'Hugh went a few months after the Saintes battle. He was killed by accident. A runaway horse, I believe.'

Herrick stared at him. 'How do you know all this?'

Bolitho opened a cupboard and then laid a sword on the table. In the firelight it gleamed with sudden brightness which hid the tarnished gilt and well-worn scabbard.

Bolitho said quietly, 'Hugh sent this to my father. To give it back to me.' He turned back to the fire. 'He wrote that he considered it to be mine by right.'

The door opened, and the fair-haired woman entered with a tray of hot punch.

Bolitho smiled. 'Thank you, Mrs. Ferguson. We will dine directly.'

As the door closed again Bolitho saw the question on Herrick's face. 'Yes, that is the wife of Ferguson, my clerk. He works for me, too.'

Herrick nodded and took one of the goblets. 'He lost an arm at the Saintes. I remember.'

Bolitho poured himself a drink and held it to the firelight. 'His wife did not die after all. And Ferguson is quite a hero in the town!' It seemed to amuse him, and Herrick saw the old smile playing at the corners of his mouth. Bolitho added, 'Now the war is done, Thomas. You and I are on the beach. I wonder what lies ahead for those like us?'

Herrick replied thoughtfully, 'This peace will not last.' He lifted his goblet. 'To old friends, sir!' He paused, seeing the memories all over again. 'To the ship, bless her!'

Bolitho drained his drink and gripped his hands behind him. Even that unconscious gesture stabbed Herrick's memory like a knife. The screaming shot, the crash and thunder of battle, with Bolitho pacing the quarterdeck like a man deep in thought.

'And you, sir? What will you do now?'

Bolitho shrugged. 'I have the chance to become a landowner, I suppose. And a magistrate like my father.' He looked up at the portraits. 'But I can wait. For another ship.'

The door opened, and a man in a green apron asked, 'Will you be requiring any more wine from the cellar, Captain?'

Herrick jumped to his feet. 'My God! Allday!'

Allday grinned self-consciously. 'Aye, Mr. Herrick. 'Tis me right enough!'

Bolitho looked from one to the other. 'After Stockdale died, Allday here said he wanted to change his mind about leaving the Service.' He smiled sadly. 'So if the chance comes we will go back to sea together.'

Bolitho picked up the sword and held it in both hands. Over his shoulder he added quietly, 'When that time comes I will want a good first lieutenant, Thomas.' He turned and looked straight into Herrick's eyes.

Herrick felt the warmth flooding back through his body, sweeping away the doubt and the sense of loss. He raised his goblet. 'It is not far to Kent, sir. I'll be ready when you give me the word!'

Bolitho turned his face away and watched the snow whipping across the windows. For a while longer he looked at the grey sky and scudding clouds, and imagined he could hear the wind whining through shrouds and taut rigging, with the hiss of thrown spray rising above the lee bulwark.

Then he faced his friend and said firmly, 'Come, Thomas, there is much to talk about!'

Allday watched them go into the dining-room, and then with a quiet smile he placed the sword carefully back in the cupboard.

Command a King's Ship

To the Contessa with love

Contents

1	The Admiral's Choice	463
2	Free of the Land	474
3	A Mixed Gathering	486
4	Death of a Ship	498
5	The Work of a Demon	510
6	Attack Overland	524
7	Herrick's Decision	537
8	Madras	550
9	Gift from a Lady	563
10	Another Flag	571
11	Luck of the Game	582
12	In for a Blow	596
13	No Quarter	610
14	The Bristol Sailmaker	624
15	Face to Face	635
16	No Better, No Worse than Most	648
17	Close Action	660
18	In the King's Name	676
	Epilogue	688

Danger and Death dance to the wild music of the gale, and when it is night they dance with a fiercer abandon, as if to allay the fears that beset the sailormen who feel their touch but see them not.

GEORGE H. GRANT

1

The Admiral's Choice

An Admiralty messenger opened the door of a small anteroom and said politely, 'If you would be so good as to wait, sir.' He stood aside to allow Captain Richard Bolitho to pass and added, 'Sir John knows you are here.'

Bolitho waited until the door had closed and then walked to a bright fire which was crackling below a tall mantel. He was thankful that the messenger had brought him to this small room and not to one of the larger ones. As he had hurried into the Admiralty from the bitter March wind which was sweeping down Whitehall he had been dreading a confrontation in one of those crowded waiting-rooms, crammed with unemployed officers who watched the comings and goings of more fortunate visitors with something like hatred.

Bolitho had known the feeling, too, even though he had told himself often enough that he was better off than most. For he had come back to England a year ago, to find the country at peace, and the towns and villages already filling with unwanted soldiers and seamen. With his home in Falmouth, an established estate, and all the hard-earned prize money he had brought with him, he knew he should have been grateful.

He moved away from the fire and stared down at the broad roadway below the window. It had been raining for most of the morning, but now the sky had completely cleared, so that the many puddles and ruts glittered in the harsh light like patches of pale blue silk. Only the steaming nostrils of countless horses which passed this way and that, the hurrying figures bowed into the wind, made a lie of the momentary colour.

He sighed. It was March 1784, only just over a year since his return home from the West Indies, yet it seemed like a century.

Whenever possible he had quit Falmouth to make the long journey to London, to this seat of Admiralty, to try and discover why his letters had gone unanswered, why his pleas for a ship, *any* ship, had been ignored. And always the waiting-rooms had seemed to get more and more crowded. The familiar voices and tales of ships and campaigns had become forced, less confident, as day by day they were turned away. Ships were laid up by the score, and every seaport had its full quota of a war's flotsam. Cripples, and men made deaf and blind by cannon fire, others half mad from what they had seen and endured. With the signing of peace the previous year such sights had become too common to mention, too despairing even for hope.

He stiffened as two figures turned a corner below the window. Even without the facings on their tattered red coats he knew they had been soldiers. A carriage was standing by the roadside, the horses nodding their heads together as they explored the contents of their feeding bags. The coachman was chatting to a smartly dressed servant from a nearby house, and neither took a scrap of notice of the two tattered veterans.

One of them pushed his companion against a stone balustrade and then walked towards the coach. Bolitho realized that the man left clinging to the stonework was blind, his head turned towards the roadway as if trying to hear where his friend had gone. It needed no words.

The soldier faced the coachman and his companion and held out his hand. It was neither arrogant nor servile, and strangely moving. The coachman hesitated and then fumbled inside his heavy coat.

At that moment another figure ran lightly down some steps and wrenched open the coach door. He was well attired against the cold, and the buckles on his shoes held the watery sunlight like diamonds. He stared at the soldier and then snapped angrily at his coachman. The servant ran to the horses' heads, and within seconds the coach was clattering away into the busy press of carriages and carts. The soldier stood staring after it and then gave a weary shrug. He returned to his companion, and with linked arms they moved slowly around the next corner.

Bolitho struggled with the window catch, but it was stuck fast, his mind reeling with anger and shame at what he had just seen.

A voice asked, 'May I help, sir?' It was the messenger again.

Bolitho replied, 'I was going to throw some coins to two crippled soldiers.' He broke off, seeing the mild astonishment in the messenger's eyes.

The man said, 'Bless you, sir, you'd get used to such sights in London.'

'Not me.'

'I was going to tell you, sir, that Sir John will see you now.'

Bolitho followed him into the passageway again, conscious of the sudden dryness in his throat. He remembered so clearly his last visit here, a month ago almost to the day. And that time he had been summoned by letter, and not left fretting and fuming in a waiting-room. It had seemed like a dream, an incredible stroke of good fortune. It still did, despite all the difficulties which had been crammed into so short a time.

He was to assume command immediately of His Britannic Majesty's Ship *Undine*, of thirty-two guns, then lying in the dockyard at Portsmouth completing a refit.

As he had hurried from the Admiralty on that occasion he had felt the excitement on his face like guilt, aware of the other watching eyes, the envy and resentment.

The task of taking command, of gathering the dockyard's resources to his aid to prepare *Undine* for sea, had cost him dearly. With the Navy being cut down to a quarter of its wartime strength, he had been surprised to discover that it was harder to obtain spare cordage and spars rather than the reverse. A weary shipwright had confided in him that dockyard officials were more intent on making a profit with private dealers than they were on aiding one small frigate.

He had bribed, threatened and driven almost every man in the yard until he had obtained more or less what he needed. It seemed they saw his departure as the only way of returning to their own affairs.

He had walked around his new command in her dock with mixed feelings. Above all, the excitement and the challenge she represented. Gone were the pangs he had felt in Falmouth whenever he had seen a man-of-war weathering the headland below the castle. But also he had discovered something more. His last command had been *Phalarope*, a frigate very similar to *Undine*, if slightly longer by a few feet. To Bolitho she had been everything, perhaps because they had come through so much together. In the West Indies, at the battle of the Saintes he had felt his precious *Phalarope* battered almost to a hulk beneath him. There would never, *could* never, be another like her. But as he had walked up and down the stone wall of the dock he had sensed a new elation.

Halfway through the hurried overhaul he had received an unheralded visit from Rear Admiral Sir John Winslade, the man who had greeted him at the Admiralty. He had given little away, but after a cursory inspection of the ship and Bolitho's preparations he had said, 'I can tell you now. I'm sending you to India. That's all I can reveal for the moment.' He had run his eye over the few riggers working on yards and shrouds and had added dryly, 'I only hope for your sake you'll be ready on time.'

There was a lot in what Winslade had hinted. Officers on half-pay were easy to obtain. To crew a King's ship without the urgency of a war or the pressgang was something else entirely. Had *Undine* been sailing in better-known waters things might have been different. And had Bolitho been a man other than himself, he might have been tempted to keep her destination a secret until he had signed on sufficient hands and it was too late for them to escape.

He had had the usual flowery-worded handbills distributed around the port and nearby villages. He had sent recruiting parties as far inland as Guildford on the Portsmouth Road, but with small success. And now, as he followed the messenger towards some high gilded doors he knew *Undine* was still fifty short of her complement.

In one thing Bolitho had been more fortunate. *Undine*'s previous captain had kept a shrewd eye on his ship's professional men. Bolitho had taken charge to discover that *Undine* still carried the hard core of senior men, the warrant officers, a first class sailmaker, and one of the most economical carpenters he had ever watched at work. His predecessor had quit the Navy for good to seek a career in Parliament. Or as he had put it, 'I've had a bellyful of fighting with iron. From now on, my young friend, I'll do it with slander!'

Rear Admiral Sir John Winslade was standing with his back to a fire, his coat-tails parted to allow the maximum warmth to reach him. Few people knew much about him. He had distinguished himself vaguely in some single-ship action off Brest, and had then been neatly placed inside the Admiralty. There was nothing about his pale, austere features to distinguish him in any way. In fact, he was so ordinary that his gold-laced coat seemed to be wearing him rather than the other way round.

Bolitho was twenty-seven and a half years old, but had already held two commands, and knew enough about senior officers not to take them at face value.

Winslade let his coat-tails drop and waited for Bolitho to reach him. He held out his hand and said, 'You are punctual. It is just as well. We have much to discuss.' He moved to a small lacquered table. 'Some claret, I think.' He smiled for the first time. It was like the sunlight in Whitehall. Frail, and easily removed.

He pulled up a chair for Bolitho. 'Your health, Captain.' He added, 'I suppose you know why I asked for you to be given this command?'

Bolitho cleared his throat. 'I assumed, sir, that as Captain Stewart was entering politics that you required another for . . .'

Winslade gave a wry smile. '*Please*, Bolitho. Modesty at the expense of sincerity is just so much top-hamper. I trust you will bear that in mind?'

He sipped at his claret and continued in the same dry voice, 'For this particular commission I have to be sure of *Undine*'s captain. You will be on the other side of the globe. I have to know what you are thinking so that I can act on such despatches as I might receive in due course.'

Bolitho tried to relax. 'Thank you.' He smiled awkwardly. 'I mean, for your trust, sir.'

'Quite so.' Winslade reached for the decanter. 'I know your background, your record, especially in the recent war with France and her Allies. Your behaviour when you were on the American station reads favourably. A full scale war and a bloody rebellion in America must have been a good schoolroom for so young a commander. But that war is done with. It is up to us,' he smiled slightly, '*some* of us, to ensure that we are never forced into such a helpless stalemate again.'

Bolitho exclaimed, 'We did not lose the war, sir.'

'We did not win it either. That is more to the point.'

Bolitho thought suddenly of the last battle. The screams and yells on every side, the crash of gunfire and falling spars. So many had died that day. So many familiar faces just swept away. Others had been left, like the two ragged soldiers, to fend as best they could.

He said quietly, 'We did our best, sir.'

The admiral was watching him thoughtfully. 'I agree. You may not have won a war, but you did win a respite of sorts. A time to draw breath and face facts.'

'You think the peace will not last, sir?'

'An enemy is always an enemy, Bolitho. Only the vanquished know peace of mind. Oh yes, we will fight again, be sure of it.'

He put down his glass and added sharply, 'Now, about your ship. Are you prepared?'

Bolitho met his gaze. 'I am still short of hands, but the ship is as ready as she will ever be, sir. I had her warped out of the dockyard two days ago, and she is now anchored at Spithead awaiting final provisioning.'

'How short?'

Two words, but they left no room for manoeuvre.

'Fifty, sir. But my lieutenants are still trying to gather more.'

The admiral did not blink. 'I see. Well, it's up to you. In the meantime I will obtain a warrant for you to take some "volunteers" from the prison hulks in Portsmouth harbour.'

Bolitho said, 'It's a sad thing that we must rely on convicts.'

'They are men. That is all you require at the moment. As it is, you will probably be doing some of the wretches a favour. Most of 'em were to be transported to the penal colonies in America. Now, with America gone, we will have to look elsewhere for new settlements. There is some talk of Botany Bay, in New Holland, but it may be rumour, of course.'

He stood up and walked to a window. 'I knew your father. I was saddened to hear of his death. While you were in the West Indies, I believe?' He did not wait for a reply. 'This mission would have been well cut for him. Something to get his teeth into. Self-dependence, decisions to be made on the spot which could make or break the man in command. Everything a young frigate captain dreams of, right?'

'Yes, sir.'

He pictured his father as he had last seen him. The very day he had sailed for the Indies in *Phalarope*. A tired, broken man. Made bitter by his other son's betrayal. Hugh Bolitho had been the apple of his eye. Four years older than Richard, he had been a born gambler, and had ended in killing a brother officer in a duel. Worse, he had fled to America, to join the Revolutionary forces and later to command a privateer against the British. It had been that knowledge which had really killed Bolitho's father, no matter what the doctor had said.

He tightened his grip on his glass. Much of his prize money had gone into buying back land which his father had sold to pay Hugh's debts. But nothing could buy back his honour. It was fortunate that Hugh had died. If they had ever met again Bolitho imagined he might kill him for what he had done.

'More claret?' Winslade seemed absorbed with his own thoughts. 'I'm sending you to Madras. There you will report to . . . , well, it will be in your final orders. No sense in idle gossip.' He added, 'Just in case you cannot get your ship manned, eh?'

'I'll get them, sir. If I have to go to Cornwall.'

'I hope that will not be necessary.'

Winslade changed tack again. 'During the American campaign you probably noticed that there was little co-operation between military and civilian government. The forces on the ground fought the battles and confided in neither. That must not happen again. The task I am giving you would be better handled by a squadron, with an admiral's flag for good measure. But it would invite attention, and *that* Parliament will not tolerate in this uneasy peace.'

He asked suddenly, 'Where are you staying in London?'

'The George at Southwark.'

'I will give you an address. A friend's residence in St. James's Square.' He smiled at Bolitho's grave features. 'Come, don't look so gloomy. It is time you made your way in affairs and put the line of battle behind you. Your mission may bring you to eyes other than those of jaded flag officers. Get to know people. It can do nothing but good. I will send a courier with instructions for your first lieutenant.' He darted him a quick glance. 'Herrick, I gather. From your last ship.'

'Yes, sir.' It sounded like 'of course'. There had never been any doubt whom he would ask for if he got another ship.

'Well then, Mr. Herrick it is. He can take charge of local matters. I'll need you in London for four days.' He hardened his tone as Bolitho looked about to protest. 'At *least!*'

The admiral regarded Bolitho for several seconds. Craving to get back to his ship, uncertain of himself in these overwhelming surroundings. It was all there and more besides. As Bolitho had entered the room it had been like seeing his father all those long years ago. Tall, slim, with that black hair tied at the nape of his neck. The loose lock which hung above his right eye told another story. Once as he had raised his glass it had fallen aside to display a livid scar which ran high into the hairline. Winslade was glad about his choice. There was intelligence on Bolitho's grave features, and compassion too, which even his service in seven years of war had not displaced. He could have picked from a hundred captains, but he had wanted one who needed a ship and the sea and not merely the security such things represented. He also required a man who could think and act accordingly. Not one who would rest content on the weight of his broadsides. Bolitho's record had shown plainly enough that he was rarely content to use written orders as a substitute for initiative. Several admirals had growled as much when Winslade had put his name forward for command. But he had got his way, for Winslade had the weight of Parliament behind him, which was another rarity.

He sighed and picked up a small bell from the table.

'You go and arrange to move to the address I will give you. I have much to do, so you may as well enjoy yourself while you can.'

He shook the bell and a servant entered with Bolitho's cocked hat and sword. Winslade watched as the man buckled the sword deftly around his waist.

'Same old blade, eh?' He touched it with his fingers. It was very smooth and worn, and a good deal lighter than more modern swords.

Bolitho smiled. 'Aye, sir. My father gave it to me after . . .'

'I know. Forget about your brother, Bolitho.' He touched the hilt again. 'Your family have brought too much honour for many generations to be brought down by one man.'

He thrust out his hand. 'Take care. I daresay there are quite a few tongues wagging about your visit here today.'

Bolitho followed the servant into the corridor, his mind moving restlessly from one aspect of his visit to another. Madras, another continent, and that sounded like a mere beginning to whatever it was he was supposed to do.

Every mile sailed would have its separate challenge. He smiled quietly. And reward. He paused in the doorway and stared at the bustling people and carriages. Open sea instead of noise and dirt. A ship, a living, vital being instead of dull, pretentious buildings.

A hand touched his arm, and he turned to see a young man in a shabby blue coat studying him anxiously.

'What is it?'

The man said quickly, 'I'm Chatterton, Captain. I was once second lieutenant in the *Warrior*, seventy-four.' He hesitated, watching Bolitho's grave face. 'I heard you were commissioning, sir, I was wondering...'

'I'm sorry, Mr. Chatterton. I have a full wardroom.'

'Yes, sir, I had guessed as much.' He swallowed. 'I could sign as master's mate perhaps?'

Bolitho shook his head. 'It is only seamen I lack, I'm afraid.'

He saw the disappointment clouding the man's face. The old *Warrior* had been in the thick of it. She was rarely absent from any battle, and men had spoken her name with pride. Now her second lieutenant was waiting like a beggar.

He said quietly, 'If I can help.' He thrust his hand into his pocket. 'Tide you over awhile.'

'Thank you, no, sir.' He forced a grin. 'Not yet anyway.' He pulled up his coat collar. As he walked away he called, 'Good luck, Captain!'

Bolitho watched him until he was out of sight. It might have been Herrick, he thought. Any of us.

His Majesty's frigate *Undine* tugged resentfully at her cable as a stiffening south-easterly wind ripped the Solent into a mass of vicious whitecaps.

Lieutenant Thomas Herrick turned up the collar of his heavy watchcoat and took another stroll across the quarterdeck, his eyes slitted against a mixture of rain and spray which made the taut rigging shine in the poor light like black glass.

Despite the weather there was still plenty of activity on deck and alongside in the pitching store boats and water lighters. Here and there on the gangways and right forward in the eyes of the ship the red coats of watchful marines made a pleasant change from the mixtures of dull grey elsewhere. The marines were supposed to ensure that the traffic in provisions and last-moment equipment was one way, and none was escaping through an open port as barter for cheap drink or other favours with friends ashore.

Herrick grinned and stamped his feet on the wet planking. They had done a lot of work in the month since he had joined the ship. Others might curse the weather, the uncertainties offered by a long voyage, the prospect of hardship from sea and wind, but not he. The past year had been far more of a burden for him, and he was glad, no thankful, to be back aboard a King's ship. He had entered the Navy when he was still a few weeks short of twelve years old, and these last long months following the signing of peace with France and the recognition of American independence had been his first experience of being away from the one life he understood and trusted.

Unlike many of his contemporaries, Herrick had nothing but his own resources to sustain him. He came of a poor family, his father being a clerk in their home town of Rochester in Kent. When he had gone there after paying off the *Phalarope* and saying his farewell to Bolitho, he had discovered things to be even worse than he had expected. His father's health had deteriorated, and he seemed to be coughing his life away, day in, day out. Herrick's only sister was a cripple and incapable of doing much but help her mother about the house, so his homecoming was seen in rather different ways from his own sense of rejection. A friend of his father's employer had gained him an appointment as mate in a small brig which earned a living carrying general cargo up and down the east coast and occasionally across the channel to Holland. The owner was a miserly man who kept the brig so shorthanded that there were barely enough men to work ship, let along handle cargo, load lighters and keep the vessel in good repair.

When he had received Bolitho's letter, accompanied by his commission from the Admiralty charging him to report on board *Undine*, he had been almost too stunned to realise his good fortune. He had not seen Bolitho since that one last visit to his home in Falmouth, and perhaps deep inside he had believed that their friendship, which had strengthened in storm and under bloody broadsides, would be no match for peace.

Their worlds were, after all, too far apart. Bolitho's great stone house, had seemed like a palace to Herrick. His background, his ancestry of seafaring officers, put him in a different sphere entirely. Herrick was the first in his family to go to sea, and that was the least of their differences.

But Bolitho had not changed. When they had met on this same quarter-deck a month ago he had known it with that first glance. It was still there, the quiet sadness, which could give way to something like boyish excitement in the twinkling of an eye.

Above all, Bolitho too was pleased to be back, keen to test himself and his new ship whenever a chance offered itself.

A midshipman scuttled over the deck and touched his hat.

'Cutter's returning, sir.'

He was small, pinched with cold. He had been aboard just three weeks.

'Thank you, Mr. Penn. That'll be some new hands, I hope.' He eyed the boy unsympathetically. 'Now smarten yourself, the captain may be returning today.'

He continued his pacing.

Bolitho had been in London for five days. It would be good to hear his news, to get the order to sail from this bitter Solent.

He watched the cutter lifting and plunging across the whitecaps, the oars moving sluggishly despite the efforts of the boat's coxswain. He saw the cocked hat of John Soames, the third lieutenant, in the sternsheets, and wondered if he had had any luck with recruits.

In the *Phalarope* Herrick had begun his commission as third lieutenant, rising to Bolitho's second-in-command as those above him died in combat. He wondered briefly if Soames was already thinking of his own prospects in the months ahead. He was a giant of a man and in his thirtieth year, three years older than Herrick. He had got his commission as lieutenant very late in life, and by a roundabout route, mostly, as far as Herrick could gather, in the merchant service and later as master's mate in a King's ship. Tough, self-taught, he was hard to know. A suspicious man.

Quite different from Villiers Davy, the second lieutenant. As his name suggested, he was of good family, with the money and proud looks to back up his quicksilver wit. Herrick was not sure of him either, but told himself that any dislike he might harbour was because Davy reminded him of an arrogant midshipman they had carried in *Phalarope*.

Feet thumped on deck and he turned to see Triphook, the purser, crouching through the drizzle, a bulky ledger under his coat.

The purser grimaced. 'Evil day, Mr. Herrick.' He gestured to the boats alongside. 'God damn those thieves. They'd rob a blind man, so they would.'

Herrick chuckled. 'Not like you pursers, eh?'

Triphook eyed him severely. He was stooped and very thin, with large yellow teeth like a mournful horse.

'I hope that was not seriously meant, *sir*?'

Herrick craned over the dripping nettings to watch the cutter hooking on to the chains. God, their oarsmanship was bad. Bolitho would expect far better, and before too long.

He snapped, 'Easy, Mr. Triphook. But I was merely *reminding* you. I recall we had a purser in my last ship. A man called Evans. He lined his pockets at the people's expense. Gave them foul food when they had much to trouble them in other directions.'

Triphook watched him doubtfully.

'What happened?'

'Captain Bolitho made him pay for fresh meat from his own purse. Cask for cask with each that was rotten.' He grinned. 'So be warned, my friend!'

'He'll have no cause to fault *me*, Mr. Herrick.' He walked away his voice lacking conviction as he added, 'You can be certain of that.'

Lieutenant Soames came aft, touching his hat and scowling at the deck as he reported, 'Five hands, sir. I've been on the road all day, I'm fair hoarse from calling the tune of those handbills.'

Herrick nodded. He could sympathise. He had done it often enough himself. Five hands. They still needed thirty. Even then it would not allow for death and injury to be expected on any long voyage.

Soames asked thickly, 'Any more news?'

'None. Just that we are to sail for Madras. But I think it will be soon now.'

Soames said, 'Good riddance to the land, I say. Streets full of drunken men, prime hands we could well do with.' He hesitated. 'With your permission I might take a boat away tonight and catch a few as they reel from their damn ale houses, eh?'

They turned as a shriek of laughter echoed up from the gun deck, and a woman, her breasts bare to the rain, ran from beneath the larboard gangway. She was pursued by two seamen, both obviously the worse for drink, who left little to the imagination as to their intentions.

Herrick barked, 'Tell that slut to get below! Or I'll have her thrown over the side!' He saw the astonished midshipman watching the spectacle with wide-eyed wonder and added harshly, 'Mr. Penn! *Jump to it*, I say!'

Soames showed a rare grin. 'Offend your feelings, Mr. Herrick?'

Herrick shrugged. 'I know it is supposed to be the proper thing to allow our people women and drink in harbour.' He thought of his sister. Anchored in that damned chair. What he would give to see her running free like that Portsmouth trollop. 'But it never fails to sicken me.'

Soames sighed. 'Half the bastards would desert otherwise, signed on or not. The romance of Madras soon wears off when the rum goes short.'

Herrick said, 'What you asked earlier. I cannot agree. It would be a bad beginning. Men taken in such a way would harbour plenty of grievances. One rotten apple can sour a full barrel.'

Soames eyed him calmly. 'It seems to me that this ship is almost *full* of bad apples. The volunteers are probably on the run from debt, or the hangman himself. Some are aboard just to see what they can lay their fingers on when we are many miles from proper authority.'

Herrick replied, 'Captain Bolitho will have sufficient authority, Mr. Soames.'

'I forgot. You were in the same ship. There was a mutiny.' It sounded like an accusation.

'Not of his making.' He turned on him angrily. 'Be so good as to have the new men fed and issued with slop clothing.'

He waited, watching the resentment in the big man's eyes.

He added, 'Another of our captain's requirements. I suggest you acquaint yourself with his demands. Life will be easier for you.'

Soames strode away and Herrick relaxed. He must not let him get into his skin so easily. But any criticism, or even hint of it, always affected him. To Herrick, Bolitho represented all the things he would like to be. The fact he also knew some of his secret faults as well made him doubly sure of his loyalty. He shook his head. It was stronger even than that.

He peered over the nettings towards the shore, seeing the walls of the harbour battery glinting like lead in the rain. Beyond Portsmouth Point the land was almost hidden in murk. It would be good to get away. His pay would mount up, and go towards helping out at home. With his share of prize money which he gained under Bolitho in the West Indies he had been able to buy several small luxuries to make their lot easier until his next return. And when might that be? Two years? It was better never to contemplate such matters.

He saw a ship's boy duck into the rain to turn the hour-glass beside the deserted wheel, and waited for him to chime the hour on the bell. Time to send the working part of the watch below. He grimaced. The wardroom might be little better. Soames under a cloud of inner thought. Davy probing his guard with some new, smart jest or other. Giles Bellairs, the captain of marines, well on the way to intoxication by this time, knowing his hefty sergeant could deal with the affairs of his small detachment. Triphook probably brooding over the issue of clothing to the new men. Typical of the purser. He could face the prospect of a great sea voyage, with each league measured in salt pork and beef, iron-hard-biscuit, juice to prevent scurvy, beer and spirits to supplement fresh water which would soon be alive in its casks, and all the thousand other items under his control, with equanimity. But one small issue of clothing, while they still wore what they had come aboard in, was too much for his sense of values. He would learn. He grinned into the cold wind. They all would, once Bolitho brought the ship alive.

More shouts from alongside, and Penn, the midshipman, called anxiously, 'Beg pardon, sir, but I fear the surgeon is in difficulties.'

Herrick frowned. The surgeon's name was Charles Whitmarsh. A man of culture, but one with something troubling him. Most ship's surgeons, in

Herrick's experience, had been butchers. Nobody else would go to sea and face the horrors of mangled men screaming and dying after a savage battle with the enemy. In peacetime he had expected it might be different.

Whitmarsh was a drunkard. As Herrick peered down at the jolly boat as it bobbed and curtsied at the chains, he saw a boatswain's mate and two seamen struggling to fit the surgeon into a bowline to assist his passage up the side. He was a big man, almost as large as Soames, and in the grey light his features shone with all the brightness of a marine's coat.

Herrick snapped, 'Have a cargo net lowered, Mr. Penn. It is not dignified, but neither is this, by God!'

Whitmarsh landed eventually on the gun deck, his hair awry, his face set in a great beaming smile. One of his assistants and two marines lifted him bodily and took him aft below the quarterdeck. He would sleep in his small sickbay for a few hours, and then begin again.

Penn asked nervously, 'Is he unwell, sir?'

Herrick looked at the youth gravely. 'A thought tipsy, lad, but well enough to remove a limb or two, I daresay.' He relented and touched his shoulder. 'Go below. Your relief will be up soon.'

He watched him hurry away and grinned. It was hard to recall that he had been like Penn. Unsure, frightened, with each hour presenting some new sight and sound to break his boy's illusions.

A marine yelled, 'Guardboat shovin' off from the sallyport, sir!'

Herrick nodded. 'Very well.'

That would mean orders for the *Undine*. He let his gaze move forward between the tall, spiralling masts with their taut maze of shrouds and rigging, the neatly furled canvas and to the bowsprit, below which *Undine*'s beautiful, full-breasted figurehead of a water-nymph stared impassively to every horizon. It also meant that Bolitho would be returning. *Today*.

And for Thomas Herrick that was more than enough.

2

Free of the Land

Captain Richard Bolitho stood in the shelter of the stone wall beside the sallyport and peered through the chilling drizzle. It was afternoon, but with the sky so overcast by low cloud it could have been much later.

He was tired and stiff from the long coach ride, and the journey had been made especially irritating by his two jovial companions. Businessmen from the City of London, they had become more loud-voiced after each stop for change of horses and refreshment at the many inns down the Portsmouth road. They were off to France in a packet ship, to contact new agencies there, and so, with luck, expand their trade. To Bolitho it was still hard to accept. Just a year back the Channel had been the only barrier between this country and their common enemy. The moat. The last ditch, as some news-sheet had described it. Now it seemed as if it was all forgotten by such men as his travelling companions. It had become merely an irritating delay which made their journey just so much longer.

He shrugged his shoulders deeper inside his boat-cloak, suddenly impatient for the last moments to pass, so that he could get back to the ship. The cloak was new, from a good London tailor. Rear Admiral Winslade's friend had taken him there, and managed to do so without making Bolitho feel the complete ignoramus. He smiled to himself despite his other uncertainties. He would never get used to London. Too large, too busy, where nobody had time to draw breath. And noisy. No wonder the rich houses around St. James's Square had sent servants out every few hours to spread fresh straw on the roadway. The grinding roar of carriage wheels was enough to wake the dead. It had been a beautiful house, his hosts charming, if slightly amused by his questions. Even now, he was still unsure of their strange ways. It was not just enough to live in that fine, fashionable residence, with its splendid spiral staircase and huge chandeliers. To be *right*, you had to live on the best side of the square, the east side. Winslade's friends lived there. Bolitho smiled again. They would.

Bolitho had met several very influential people, and his hosts had given two dinner parties with that in mind. He knew well enough from past experience that without their help it would have been impossible. Aboard ship a captain was next only to God. In London society he hardly registered at all.

But that was behind him now. He was back. His orders would be waiting, and only the actual time of weighing anchor was left to conjecture.

He peered round the wall once more, feeling the wind on his face like a whip. The signal tower had informed *Undine* of his arrival, and very soon now a boat would arrive at the wooden pier below the wall. He wondered how his coxswain, Allday, was managing. His first ship as captain's coxswain, but Bolitho understood him well enough to know there was little to fear on his behalf. It would be good to see him, too. Something familiar. A face to hold on to.

He glanced up the narrow street to where some servants from the George Inn, where the coach had finally come to rest, were guarding his pile of luggage. He thought of the personal purchases he had made. Maybe London had got some hold on him after all.

When Bolitho had got his first command of the sloop *Sparrow* during the American Revolution, he had had little time to acquaint himself with luxuries. But in London, with the remains of his prize money, he had made up for it. Now shirts, and some comfortable shoes. This great boat-cloak, which the tailor had assured him would keep out even the heaviest downpour. It had been partly Winslade's doing, he was certain of that. His host had casually mentioned that Bolitho's mission in *Undine* required not merely a competent captain, but one who would look the part, no matter what sort of government official he might meet. There was, he had added gently, a matter of wine.

Together they had gone to a low-beamed shop in St. James's Street. It was not a bit what Bolitho might have imagined. It had the sign of a coffee mill outside its door, and the owner's names, Pickering and Clarke, painted in gold leaf above. It was a friendly place, even intimate. It could almost have been Falmouth.

It was to be hoped the wine had already arrived aboard *Undine*. Otherwise, it was likely he would have to sail without it, and leave a large hole in his purse as well.

It would be a strange and exciting sensation to sit in his cabin, hundreds of miles from England, and sample some of that beautiful madeira. It would bring back all those pictures of London again. The buildings, the clever talk, the way women looked at you. Once or twice he had felt uneasy about that. It had reminded him bitterly of New York during the war. The boldness in their faces. The confident arrogance which had seemed like second nature to them.

An idler called, 'Yer boat's a-comin', Cap'n! He touched his hat. 'I'll give 'ee a 'and!' He hurried away to call the inn servants, his mind dwelling on what he might expect from a frigate's captain.

Bolitho stepped out into the wind, his hat jammed well down over his forehead. It was the *Undine*'s launch, her largest boat, the oars rising and falling like gulls' wings as she headed straight for the pier. It must be a hard pull, he thought. Otherwise Allday would have brought the gig.

He found he was trembling, and it was all he could do to prevent a grin from splitting his face in two. The dark green launch, the oarsmen in their checked shirts and white trousers, it was all there. Like a homecoming.

The oars rose in the air and stood like twin lines of swaying white bones, while the bowman made fast to the jetty and aided a smart midshipman to step ashore.

The latter removed his hat with a flourish and said, 'At your service, sir.'

It was Midshipman Valentine Keen, a very elegant young man who was being appointed to the *Undine* more to get him away from England than to further his naval advancement, Bolitho suspected. He was the senior midshipman, and if he survived the round voyage would probably return as a lieutenant. At any rate, as a man.

'My boxes are yonder, Mr. Keen.'

He saw Allday standing motionless in the sternsheets, his blue coat and white trousers flapping in the wind, his tanned features barely able to remain impassive.

Theirs was a strange relationship. Allday had come aboard Bolitho's last ship as a pressed man. Yet when the ship had paid off at the end of the war Allday had stayed with him at Falmouth. Servant; guardian. Trusted friend. Now as his coxswain he would be ever nearby. Sometimes an only contact with that other, remote world beyond the cabin bulkhead.

Allday had been a seaman all his life, but for a period when he had been a shepherd in Cornwall, where Bolitho's pressgang had found him. An odd beginning. Bolitho thought of his previous coxswain, Mark Stockdale. A battered ex-prizefighter who could hardly speak because of his maimed vocal cords. He had died protecting Bolitho's back at the Saintes. Poor Stockdale. Bolitho had not even seen him fall.

Allday clambered ashore.

'Everything's ready, Captain. A good meal in the cabin.' He snarled at one of the seamen, 'Grab that chest, you oaf, or I'll have your liver!'

The seaman nodded and grinned.

Bolitho was satisfied. Allday's strange charm seemed to be working already. He could curse and fight like a madman if required. But Bolitho had seen him caring for wounded men and knew his other side. It was no wonder that the girls in farms and villages around Falmouth would miss him. Better though for Allday, Bolitho decided. There had been rumours enough lately about his conquests.

Then at last it was all done. The boat loaded, the idler and servants paid. The oars sending the long launch purposefully through the tossing water.

Bolitho sat in silence, huddled in his cloak, his eyes on the distant frigate. She was beautiful. In some ways more so than *Phalarope*, if that were possible. Only four years old, she had been built in a yard at Frindsbury on the River Medway. Not far from Herrick's home. One hundred and thirty feet long on her gun deck, and built of good English oak, she was the picture of a shipbuilder's art. No wonder the Admiralty had been loath to lay her up in ordinary like so many of her consorts at the end of the war. She had cost nearly fourteen thousand pounds, as Bolitho had been told more than once. Not that he needed to be reminded. He was lucky to get her.

There was a brief break in the scudding clouds, and the watery light played down along *Undine*'s gun ports to her clean sheathing as she rolled uneasily in the swell. Best Anglesey copper. Stout enough for anything. Bolitho recalled what her previous captain, Stewart, had confided. In a fierce skirmish off Ushant he had been raked by heavy guns from a French seventy-four. *Undine* had taken four balls right on her waterline. She had been fortunate to reach England afloat. Frigates were meant for speed and hit-and-run fighting, not for matching metal with a line of battleship. Bolitho knew from his own grim experience what that could do to so graceful a hull.

Stewart had added that despite careful supervision he was still unsure as to the perfection of the repairs. With the copper replaced, it took more than internal inspection to discover the true value of a dockyard's overhaul. Copper protected the hull from many sorts of weed and clinging growth which could slow a ship to a painful crawl. But behind it could lurk every captain's real enemy, rot. Rot which could change a perfect hull into a ripe, treacherous trap for the unwary. Admiral Kempenfelt's own flagship, the *Royal George*, had heeled over and sunk right here in Portsmouth just two years ago, with the loss of hundreds of lives. It was said that her bottom had fallen clean away with rot. If it could happen to a lofty first-rate at anchor, it would do worse to a frigate.

Bolitho came out of his thoughts as he heard the shrill of boatswain's calls above the wind, the stamp of feet as the marines prepared to receive him. He stared up at the towering masts, the movement of figures around the entry port and above in the shrouds. They had had a month to get used to seeing him about the ship, except for the unknown quantity, the newly recruited part of the company. They might be wondering about him now. What he was like. Too harsh, or too easy-going. To them, once the anchor was catted, he was everything, good or bad, skilful or incompetent. There was no other ear to listen to their complaints, no other voice to reward or punish.

'Easy all!' Allday stood half poised, the tiller bar in his fist. 'Toss your oars!'

The boat thrust forward and the bowman hooked on to the main chains at the first attempt. Bolitho guessed that Allday had been busy during his stay in London.

He stood up and waited for the right moment, knowing Allday was watching like a cat in case he should slip between launch and ship, or worse, tumble backwards in a welter of flailing arms and legs. Bolitho had seen it happen, and recalled his own cruel amusement at the spectacle of his new captain arriving aboard in a dripping heap.

Then, with the spray barely finding time to catch his legs, he was up and on board, his ears ringing to the shrill of calls and to the slap of marines' muskets while they presented arms. He doffed his hat to the quarterdeck, and nodded to Herrick and the others.

'Good to be back, Mr. Herrick.' His tone was curt.

'Welcome aboard, sir.' Herrick was equally so. But their eyes shone with something more than routine formality. Something which none of the others saw, or shared.

Bolitho removed his cloak and handed it to Midshipman Penn. He turned to allow the fading light to play across the broad white lapels of his dress coat. They would all know he was here. He saw the few hands working aloft on last minute splicing, others crowded on gangways and down on the main deck between the twin lines of black twelve-pounder guns.

He smiled, amused at his own gesture. 'I will go below now.'

'I have placed the orders in your cabin, sir.'

Herrick was bursting with questions. It was obvious from his flat, formal voice. But his eyes, those eyes which were so blue, and which could look so hurt, made a lie of his rigidity.

'Very well, I will call you directly.'

He made to walk aft to the cabin hatchway when he saw some figures gathered just below the quarterdeck rail. In mixed garments, they were in the process of being checked against a list by Lieutenant Davy.

He called, 'New hands, Mr. Davy?'

Herrick said quietly, 'We are still thirty under strength, sir.'

'Aye, sir.' Davy squinted up through the light drizzle, his handsome face set in a confident smile. 'I am about to get them to make their marks.'

Bolitho crossed to the ladder and ran down to the gun deck. God, how wretched they all looked. Half-starved, ragged, beaten. Even the demanding life aboard ship could surely be no worse than what had made them thus.

He watched Davy's neat, elegant hands as he arranged the book on top of a twelve-pounder's breech.

'Come along now, make your marks.'

They shuffled forward, self-conscious, awkward, and very aware that their new captain was nearby.

Bolitho's eye stopped on the one at the end of the line. A sturdy man, well-muscled, and with a pigtail protruding from beneath his battered hat. One prime seaman at least.

He realised Bolitho was watching him and hurried forward to the gun.

Davy snapped, 'Here now, hold your damn eagerness!'

Bolitho asked, 'Your name?'

He hesitated. 'Turpin, sir.'

Davy was getting angry. 'Stand still and remove your hat to the captain, damn your eyes! If you know anything, you should know respect!'

But the man stood stockstill, his face a mixture of despair and shame.

Bolitho reached out and removed an old coat which Turpin had been carrying across his right forearm.

He asked gently, 'Where did you lose your right hand, Turpin?'

The man lowered his eyes. 'I was in the *Barfleur*, sir. I lost it at the Chesapeake in '81.' He looked up, his eyes showing pride, but only briefly. 'Gun captain, I was, sir.'

Davy interjected, 'I am *most* sorry, sir. I did not realise the fellow was crippled. I will have him sent ashore.'

Bolitho said, 'You intended to sign the articles with your left hand. Is it *that* important?'

Turpin nodded. 'I'm a seaman, sir.' He looked round angrily as one of the recruited men nudged his companion. 'Not like *some*!' He turned back to Bolitho, his voice falling away. 'I can do anything, sir.'

Bolitho hardly heard him. He was thinking back to the Chesapeake. The smoke and din. The columns of wheeling ships, like armoured knights at

Agincourt. You never got away from it. This man Turpin had been nearby, like hundreds of others. Cheering and dying, cursing and working their guns like souls possessed. He thought of the two fat merchants on the coach. So men like that could grow richer.

He said harshly, 'Sign him on, Mr. Davy. One hand from the old *Barfleur* will be more use to me than many others.'

He strode aft beneath the quarterdeck, angry with himself, and with Davy for not having the compassion to understand. It was a stupid thing to do. Pointless.

Allday was carrying one of the chests aft to the cabin, where a marine stood like a toy soldier beneath the spiralling deckhead lantern.

He said cheerfully, 'That was a good thing you just did, Captain.'

'Don't talk like a fool, Allday!' He strode past him and winced as his head grazed an overhead beam. When he glared back at Allday his coxswain's homely features were quite expressionless. 'He could probably do *your* work.'

Allday nodded gravely. 'Aye, sir, it is true that I am over-taxed!'

'Damn your impertinence!' It was useless with Allday. 'I don't know why I tolerate you!'

Allday took his sword and walked with it to the cabin bulkhead.

'I once knew a man in Bodmin, Captain.' He stood back and studied the sword critically. 'Used to hammer a block of wood with a blunt axe, he did. I asked him why he didn't use a sharper blade and finish the job properly.' Allday turned and smiled calmly. 'He said that when the wood was broken he'd have nothing to work his temper on.'

Bolitho sat down at the table. 'Thank you. I must remember to get a better axe.'

Allday grinned. 'My pleasure, Captain.' He strode out to fetch another chest.

Bolitho pulled the heavy sealed envelope towards him. With some education behind him Allday might have become almost anything. He slit open the envelope and smiled to himself. Without it he was quite bad enough.

Herrick stepped into the cabin, his hat tucked under one arm.

'You sent for me, sir?'

Bolitho was standing by the great stern windows, his body moving easily with the ship's motion. *Undine* had swung her stern to the change of tide, and through the thick glass Herrick could see the distant lights of Portsmouth Point, glimmering and changing shape through the droplets of rain and spray. In the pitching deckhead lanterns the cabin looked snug and inviting. The bench seat around the stern was covered with fine green leather, and Bolitho's desk and chairs stood out against the deck covering of black and white checked canvas like ripe chestnut.

'Sit down, Thomas.'

Bolitho turned slowly and looked at him. He had been back aboard for over an hour, reading and re-reading his orders to ensure he would miss nothing.

He added, 'We will weigh tomorrow afternoon. I have a warrant in my orders which entitles me to accept "volunteers" from the convict hulks in

Portsmouth. I would be obliged if you would attend to that as soon after first light as is convenient.'

Herrick nodded, watching Bolitho's grave features, noting the restless movements of his hands, the fact that his carefully prepared meal lay untouched in the adjoining dining space. He was troubled. Uncertain about something.

Bolitho said, 'We are to sail for Teneriffe.' He saw Herrick stiffen and added quietly, 'I know, Thomas. You are like me. It comes hard to tack freely into a port where months back we could have expected a somewhat different welcome.'

Herrick grinned. 'Heated shot, no doubt.'

'There we will embark two, maybe three passengers. After replenishing whatever stores we lack, we will proceed without further delay to our destination, Madras.' He seemed to be musing aloud. 'Over twelve thousand miles. Long enough to get to know one another. And our ship. The orders state that we will proceed with all haste. For that reason we must ensure our people learn their work well. I want no delays because of carelessness or unnecessary damage to canvas and rigging.'

Herrick rubbed his chin. 'A long haul.'

'Aye, Thomas. A hundred days. That is what I intend.' He smiled, the gravity fading instantly. 'With your help, of course.'

Herrick nodded. 'May I ask what we are expected to accomplish?'

Bolitho looked down at the folded sheets of his orders. 'I still know very little. But I have read quite a lot between the lines.'

He began to pace from side to side, his shadow moving unevenly with the roll of the hull.

'When the war ended, Thomas, it was necessary to make concessions. To restore a balance. We had captured Trincomalee in Ceylon from the Dutch. The finest naval harbour and the best placed in the Indian Ocean. The French admiral, Suffren, captured it from us, and when war ended gave it back to Holland. We have returned many West Indian islands to France, as well as her Indian stations. And Spain, well, she has been given back Minorca.' He shrugged. 'Many men on both sides died for nothing, it seems.'

Herrick sounded confused. 'But what of us, sir? Did we get nothing out of all this?'

Bolitho smiled. 'I believe we are about to do so. Hence the extreme secrecy and our vague orders concerning Teneriffe.'

He paused and looked down at the stocky lieutenant.

'Without Trincomalee we are in the same position as before the war. We still need a good harbour for our ships. A base to control a wide area. A stepping-stone to expand the East Indies trade.'

Herrick grunted. 'I'd have thought the East India Company had got all it wanted.'

Bolitho's mind returned to the men on the coach. Others he had met in London.

'There are those in authority who see power as the essential foundation of national superiority. Commercial wealth as a means to such power.' He glanced at a twelve-pounder gun at the forward end of his cabin, its squat outline masked by a chintz cover. 'And war as the means to all three.'

Herrick bit his lip. 'And we are to be the "probe", so to speak?'

'I may be quite wrong, Thomas. But you must know my thinking. Just in case things go against us.'

He remembered Winslade's words at the Admiralty. *The task I am giving you would be better handled by a squadron.* He wanted someone he could trust. Or did he merely need a scapegoat should things go wrong? Bolitho had always complained bitterly about being tied to too strict orders. His new ones were so vague that he felt even more restricted. Only one thing was clear. He would take on board a Mr. James Raymond at Teneriffe, and place the ship at his disposal. Raymond was a trusted government courier, and would be carrying the latest despatches to Madras.

Herrick remarked, 'It will take some getting used to. But being at sea again in a ship such as *Undine* will make a world of difference.'

Bolitho nodded. 'We must ensure that our people are prepared for anything peace or no peace. Where we are going they may be less inclined to accept our views without argument.'

He sat down on the bench and stared through the spattered glass.

'I will speak with the other officers at eight bells tomorrow while you are in the hulks.' He smiled at Herrick's reflection. 'I am sending you because *you* will understand. You'll not frighten them all to death!'

He stood up quickly.

'Now, Thomas, we will take a glass of claret.'

Herrick leaned forward. 'That was a goodly selection you had sent from London, sir.'

Bolitho shook his head. 'We will save *that* for more trying times.' He lifted a decanter from its rack. 'This is more usual to our tastes!'

They drank their claret in comfortable silence. Bolitho was thinking how strange it was to be sitting quietly when the voyage which lay ahead demanded so much of all of them. But it was useless to prowl about the decks or poke into stores and spirit rooms. *Undine* was ready for sea. As ready as she could ever be. He thought of his officers, the extensions of his ideas and authority. He knew little of any of them. Soames was a competent seaman, but was inclined to harshness when things did not go right immediately. His superior, Davy, was harder to know. Outwardly cool and unruffled, he had a ruthless streak like many of his kind. The sailing master was called Ezekiel Mudge, a broad lump of a man who looked old enough to be his grandfather. In fact he was sixty, and certainly the oldest master Bolitho had met. Old Mudge would prove to be one of the most important when they reached the Indian Ocean. He had originally served in the East India Company, and had endured more storms, shipwrecks, pirates and a dozen other hazards than any man alive, if his record was to be believed. He had a huge beaked nose, with the eyes perched on either side of it like tiny, bright stones. A formidable person, and one who would be watching his captain's seamanship for flaws, Bolitho was certain of that.

The three midshipmen seemed fairly average. Penn was the youngest, and had come aboard three days after his twelfth birthday. Keen and Armitage were both seventeen, but whereas the former showed the same elegant carelessness as Lieutenant Davy, Armitage appeared to be forever looking over his shoulder. A mother's boy. Four days after he had reported aboard with his gleaming new uniform and polished dirk his mother had in fact come to Portsmouth to visit him. Her husband was a man of some influence, and she had swept into the dockyard in a beautiful carriage like some visiting duchess.

Bolitho had greeted her briefly and allowed her to meet Armitage in the seclusion of the wardroom. If she had seen the actual quarters where her child was to serve his months at sea she would probably have collapsed.

He had had to send Herrick in the end to interrupt the embraces and the mother's plaintive sobs with a feeble excuse about Armitage being required for duty. Duty; he could hardly move about the ship without falling headlong over a block or a ringbolt.

Giles Bellairs, the debonair captain of marines, was more like a caricature than a real person. Incredibly smart, shoulders always rigidly squared, he looked as if he had had his uniforms moulded around his limbs like wax. He spoke in short, clipped sentences, and barely extended much beyond matters of hunting, wildfowling and, of course, drill. His marines were his whole life, although he hardly ever seemed to utter much in the way of orders. His massive sergeant, Coaker, took care of the close contact with the marines and Bellairs contended himself with an occasional 'Carry on, Sar'nt Coaker!' or 'I say, Sar'nt, that fellah's like a bundle of old rags, what?' He was one of the few people in Bolitho's experience who could get completely drunk without any outward change of expression.

Triphook, the purser, appeared very competent, if grudging with his rations. He had taken a lot of care to ensure that the victualling yard had not filled the lower hold with rotten casks, to be discovered too late to take action. That in itself was rare.

Bolitho's thoughts came back to the surgeon. He had been aboard for two weeks. Had he been able to get a replacement he would have done so. Whitmarsh was a drunkard in the worst sense. Sober he had a quiet, even gentle manner. Drunk, which was often, he seemed to come apart like an old sail in a sudden squall.

He tightened his jaw. Whitmarsh would mend his ways. Or else....

Feet scraped across the planks overhead and Herrick said, 'There's a few below decks tonight who'll be wondering if they've done a'right by signing on.' He chuckled. 'Too late now.'

Bolitho stared astern at the black, swirling water, hearing the urgent tide banging and squeaking around the rudder.

'Aye. It's a long step from land to sea. Far more so than most people realise.' He returned his glass to the rack. 'I think I shall turn in now. It will be a long day tomorrow.'

Herrick stood up and nodded. 'I'll bid you good night, sir.'

He knew full well that Bolitho would stay awake for hours yet. Pacing and planning, searching for last-minute faults, possible mistakes in the arrangement of watch-bills and delegation of duties. Bolitho would know he was aware of this fact, too.

The door closed and Bolitho walked right aft to lean his hands on the centre sill. He could feel the woodwork vibrating under his palms, the hull trembling all around him in time to the squeak of stays, the clatter and slap of halliards and blocks.

Who would watch them go? Would anyone care? One more ship slipping down channel like hundreds before her.

There was a nervous tap at the door, and Noddall, the cabin servant, pattered into the lantern light. A small man, with the pointed face of an anxious rodent. He even held his hands in front of him like two nervous paws.

'Yer supper, sir. You've not touched it.' He started to gather up the plates. 'Won't do, sir. It won't *do*.'

Bolitho smiled as Noddall scampered away to his pantry. He was so absorbed in his own little world it seemed as if he had not even noticed there was a change of command.

He threw his new cloak across his shoulders and left the cabin. On the pitch-dark quarterdeck he groped his way aft to the taffrail and stared towards the land. Countless lights and hidden houses. He turned and looked along his ship, the wind blowing his hair across his face, the chill making him hold his breath. The riding light reflected on the taut shrouds like pale gold, and right forward he saw a smaller lantern, where the lonely anchor watch kept a wary eye on the cable.

It *felt* different, he decided. No sentries on each gangway to watch for a sneak attack or a mass attempt at desertion. No nets to delay a sudden rush of enemy boarders. He touched a quarterdeck six-pounder with one hand. It felt like wet ice. But for how long, he wondered?

The master's mate of the watch prowled past, and then sheered away as he saw his captain by the rail.

'All's well, zur!' he called.

'Thank you.'

Bolitho did not know the man's name. Not yet. In the next hundred days he would know more than their names, he thought. As they would about him.

With a sigh he returned to his cabin, his hair plastered to his head, his cheeks tingling from the cold. There was no sign of Noddall, but the cot was ready for him, and there was something hot in a mug nearby.

A minute after his head was on the pillow he was fast asleep.

The next day dawned as grey as the one before, but overnight the rain had stopped, and the wind held firm from the south-east.

All forenoon the work went on without relaxation, the petty officers checking and re-checking their lists of names, putting them to faces, making sure seasoned hands were spaced among the untried and untrained.

Bolitho dictated a final report to his clerk, a dried-up man named Pope, and then signed it in readiness for the last boat. He found time to speak with his officers, and seek out Mr. Tapril, the gunner, in his magazine to discuss moving some of the spare gun parts and tackle further aft and help adjust the vessel's trim until she had consumed some of her own stores to compensate for it.

He was changing into his seagoing coat, with its faded lace and dull buttons, when Herrick entered the cabin and reported he had brought fifteen new men from the hulks.

'What was it like?'

Herrick sighed. 'It was a sort of hell, sir. I could have got treble the number, a whole company of 'em, if I'd been able to bring their women and wives, too.'

Bolitho paused as he tied his neckcloth. '*Women*? In the hulks?'

'Aye, sir.' Herrick shuddered. 'I hope I never see the like again.'

'Very well. Sign them on, but don't give them anything to do just yet. I doubt they've the strength to lift a marlin spike after being penned up like that.'

A midshipman appeared in the open door.

'Mr. Davy's respects, sir.' His eyes darted around the cabin, missing nothing. 'And the anchor's hove short.'

'Thank you.' Bolitho smiled. 'Next time stay awhile, Mr. Penn, and have a better look.'

The boy vanished, and Bolitho looked steadily at Herrick.

'Well, Thomas?'

Herrick nodded firmly. 'Aye, sir. I'm ready. It's been a long wait.'

They climbed up to the quarterdeck together, and while Herrick moved to the forward rail with his speaking trumpet, Bolitho stood aft, a little apart from the others who were gathered restlessly at their stations.

Clink, clink, clink, the capstan was turning more slowly now, the men's backs bent almost double as the hull pulled heavily on the anchor.

Bolitho looked at the master's untidy shape beside the double wheel. He had four helmsmen. He was taking no chances, it seemed. With the helm, or his new captain's skill.

'Get the ship under way, if you please.' He saw Herrick's trumpet moving. 'Once clear of this local shipping we will lay her on the larboard tack and steer sou'-west by west.'

Old Mudge nodded heavily, one eye hidden beyond the headland of a nose.

'Aye, aye, sir.'

Herrick yelled, 'Stand by on the capstan!' He shaded his eyes to peer up at the masthead pendant. 'Loose heads'ls!'

The answering flap and clatter of released canvas made several new men peer round, confused and startled. A petty officer thrust a line into a man's hand and bellowed, ' 'Old it, you bugger! Don't stand there like a bloody woman!'

Bolitho saw a bosun's mate right forward astride the bowsprit, one arm circling above his head as the cable grew stiffer and more vertical beneath the gilded water-nymph.

'Hands aloft! Loose tops'ls!'

Bolitho relaxed slightly as the nimble-footed topmen swarmed up the ratlines on either beam. No sense in rushing it this first time. The watching eyes ashore could think what they liked. He'd get no thanks for letting her drive ashore.

'Man the braces!'

Herrick was hanging over the rail, his trumpet moving from side to side like a coachman's blunderbuss.

'Lively there! Mr. Shellabeer, get those damned idlers aft on the double, I say!'

Shellabeer was the boatswain, a swarthy, taciturn man who looked more like a Spaniard than a Devonian.

Bolitho leaned back, his hands on his hips, watching the swift figures dashing out on the vibrating yards like monkeys. It made him feel sick to watch their indifference to such heights.

First one, then the next great topsail billowed and banged loosely in confusion, while the seamen on the yards clung on, calling to each other, or jeering at their opposite numbers on the other masts.

'Anchor's aweigh, sir!'

Like a thing released from chains the frigate swung dizzily across the steep troughs, men falling and slithering at the braces as they fought to haul the great yards round, to cup the wind and master it.

'Lee braces there! Heave away!' Herrick was hoarse.

Bolitho gritted his teeth and forced himself to remain quite still as she plunged further and further astride the wind. Here and there a bosun's mate struck out with his rope starter or pushed a man bodily to brace or halliard.

Then with a booming roar like thunder the sails filled and hardened to the wind's steady thrust, the deck canting over and holding steady as the helmsmen threw themselves on their spokes.

He made himself take a glass from Midshipman Keen and trained it across the starboard quarter, keeping his face impassive, even though he was almost shaking with excitement and relief.

The sail drill was very bad, the placing of trained men too sketchy for comfort, but they were away! Free of the land.

He saw a few people on the Point watching them heel over on the larboard tack, the top of a shining carriage just below the wall. Perhaps it was Armitage's mother, weeping as she watched her offspring being taken from her.

The master shouted gruffly, 'Sou'-west by west, sir! Full an' bye!'

When Bolitho turned to answer him he saw that the master was nodding with something like approval.

'Thank you, Mr. Mudge. We will get the courses on her directly.'

He walked forward to join Herrick at the rail, his body angled steeply to the deck. Some of the confusion was being cleared, with men picking their way amidst loose coils of rope like survivors from a battle.

Herrick looked at him sadly. 'It was terrible, sir.'

'I agree, Mr. Herrick.' He could not restrain a smile. 'But it will improve, eh?'

By late afternoon *Undine* had beaten clear of the Isle of Wight and was standing well out in the Channel.

By evening only her reefed topsails were visible, and soon even they had disappeared.

3

A Mixed Gathering

On the morning of the fourteenth day after weighing anchor at Spithead Bolitho was in his cabin sipping a mug of coffee and pondering for the countless time on what he had achieved.

The previous evening they had sighted the dull hump of Teneriffe sprawled like a cloud across the horizon, and he had decided to heave-to and avoid the hazards of a night approach. *Fourteen days.* It felt an eternity. They had been plagued by foul weather for much of that time. Flicking over the pages of his personal log he could see the countless, frustrating entries. Headwinds, occasional but fierce gales, and the constant need to shorten sail, to reef down and ride it out as best they could. The dreaded Bay of Biscay had been kind to them, that at least was a mercy. Otherwise, with almost half the ship's company too seasick to venture aloft, or too terrified to scramble out along the dizzily pitching yards without physical violence being used on them, it was likely *Undine* might have reached no further.

Bolitho appreciated what it must be like for many of his men. Shrieking winds, overcrowded conditions in a creaking, rolling hull where their food, if they could face it, often ended up in a mess of bilge water and vomit. It produced a kind of numbness, like that given to a man left abandoned in the sea. For a while he strikes out bravely, swimming he knows not where, until he is too exhausted, too dazed to care. He is without authority or any sort of guidance. It is his turning point.

Bolitho recognised all the signs well enough, and knew it was the same sort of challenge for him. Give in to his own understanding and sympathy, listen too much to excuses from his hard-worked lieutenants and warrant officers, and he would never regain control, or be able to rally his company when the real pressure came.

He knew that many cursed him behind his back, prayed for him to fall dead or vanish overboard in the night. He saw their glances, sensed their resentment as he pushed them through each day, each hour of every one of those days. Sail drill, and more drill against Herrick's watch, while he himself made sure all engaged knew he was following their efforts. He made the men on *Undine*'s three masts race each other in their struggle to shorten or make more sail, until finally he drove them even harder to work not in competition but as a gasping, silently cursing team.

Now, as he sat with the mug in his hands he found some grudging satisfaction in what they had done. What they had achieved together, willingly or otherwise. When *Undine* dropped her anchor in the roads of Santa Cruz today, the watching Spaniards would see a semblance of order and discipline, of efficiency which they had come to know and fear in times of war.

But if he had driven his company to the limit he had not spared himself either. And he was feeling it, despite the inviting rays of early sunshine which made reflections dance across the low deckhead. Barely a watch had passed without his going on deck to lend his presence. Lieutenant Davy had little experience of handling a ship in foul weather, but would learn, given time. Soames was too prone to lose patience when faced with a disaster on deck. He would knock some luckless seaman aside and leap into his place yelling, 'You're useless! I'd rather do it myself!' Only Herrick rode out the storm of Bolitho's persistent demands, and Bolitho felt sorry that his friend had been made to carry the brunt of the work. It was too easy to punish men, when in fact it was an officer's fault for losing his own head, or not being able to find the right words in the teeth of a raging gale. Herrick stood firmly between wardroom and lower deck, and twixt captain and company.

There had even been two floggings, something which he had hoped to avoid. Each case had been within the private world of the lower deck. The first a simple one of stealing from another sailor's small hoard of money. The second, far more serious, had been a savage knife-fight which had ended in a man having his face opened from ear to jaw. It was still not certain if he would live.

A real grudge fight, a momentary spark of anger caused by fatigue and constant work, he did not really know. In a well-trained ship of war it was likely he would never have heard about either case. The justice of the lower deck was far more drastic and instant when their own world was threatened by a thief or one too fond of his knife.

Bolitho despised captains who used authority without consideration for the misery it might entail, who meted out savage punishment without getting to the root of the trouble and thereby avoiding it. Herrick knew how he felt. When Bolitho had first met him he had been the junior lieutenant in his ship. A ship where the previous captain had been so severe, so unthinkingly brutal with his punishments that the seeds of mutiny had been well and truly laid.

Herrick knew better than most about such things, and yet he had intervened personally to persuade Bolitho to avoid the floggings. It was their first real disagreement, and Bolitho had hated to see the sudden hurt in Herrick's eyes.

Bolitho had said, 'This is a new company. It takes time to weld people together so that each can rely on his companion under all circumstances. Many are entirely ignorant of the Navy's ways and its demands. They hate to see "others" getting away with crimes they themselves avoid. At this stage we cannot allow them to split into separate groups. Old hands and the new recruits, professional criminals and the weak ones who have no protection but to ally themselves with some other faction.'

Herrick had persisted, 'But in *peacetime*, sir, maybe it takes all the longer.'

'We can't afford the luxury of finding out.' He had hardened his voice. 'You know how I feel. It is not easy.'

The thief had taken his punishment without a whimper, a dozen lashes at the gratings while *Undine* had cruised along beneath a clearing sky, some guns throwing their shadows round and round across the tense drama below.

As he had read from the Articles of War, Bolitho had looked along his command at the watching men in shrouds and rigging, the sharp red lines of Bellairs' marines, Herrick and all the rest. The second culprit had been a brute of a man called Sullivan. He had volunteered to a recruiting party outside Portsmouth, and had all the looks of a hardened criminal. But he had served in a King's ship before and should have been an asset.

Three dozen lashes. Little enough in the Navy's view for half killing a fellow seaman. Had he laid a hand on an officer he would have faced death rather than a flogging.

The actual punishment was terrible. Sullivan had broken down completely at the first blow across his naked back, and as the boatswain's mates took turns to lay the lash over his shoulders and spine he had wriggled and screamed like a madman, his mouth frothing with foam, his eyes like marbles in his distorted face.

Mr. Midshipman Armitage had almost fainted, and some of those who had just recovered from their own sickness had vomited in unison, despite the harsh shouts from their petty officers.

Then it had ended, the watching men giving a kind of sigh as they were dismissed below.

Sullivan had been cut down and carried to Whitmarsh's sickbay, where no doubt he had been restored by a plentiful ration of rum.

Each day following the punishment, as he had paced the quarterdeck or supervised a change of tack, Bolitho had felt the eyes watching him. Seeing him perhaps as enemy rather than commander. He had told himself often enough that when you accepted the honour of command you carried all of it. Not just the authority and the pride of controlling a living, vital ship, but the knocks and kicks as well.

There was a tap on the door and Herrick stepped into the cabin.

'About another hour, sir. With your permission I will give the order to clew up all canvas except tops'ls and jib. It will make our entrance more easy to manage.'

'Have some coffee, Thomas.' He relaxed as Herrick seated himself across the table. 'I am burning to know what we are about.'

Herrick took a mug and tested the coffee with his tongue. 'Me, too.' He smiled over the rim. 'Once or twice back there I thought we might never reach land!'

'Yes. I can feel for many of our people. Some will never have seen the sea, let alone driven so far from England. Now, they know that Africa lies somewhere over the larboard bulwark. That we are going to the other side of the earth. Some are even beginning to feel like seamen, when just weeks back they had thumbs where their fingers should be.'

Herrick's smile widened. 'Due to you, sir. I am sometimes very thankful that I hold no command. Or chance of one either.'

Bolitho watched him thoughtfully. The rift was healed.

'I am afraid the choice may not be yours, Thomas.' He stood up. 'In fact, I shall see that you get command whenever the opportunity offers itself, if only to drive some of your wild idealism into the bilges!'

They grinned at each other like conspirators.

'Now be off with you while I change into a better coat.' He grimaced. 'To show our Spanish friends some respect, eh?'

A little over an hour later, gliding above her own reflection, *Undine* moved slowly towards the anchorage in the roads. In the bright sunlight the island of Teneriffe seemed to abound with colour, and Bolitho heard several of the watching seamen gasping with awe. The hills were no longer hidden in shadow, but danced on the glare with every shade and hue. And everything was brighter and larger, at least it appeared so to the new hands. Shimmering white buildings, brilliant blue sea, with beaches and surf to make a man catch his breath and stare.

Allday stood aft by the cabin hatch and remarked, 'I'll bet some Don'd like to rake us as we come by!'

Bolitho ran his eye quickly along his ship, trying to see her as those ashore would. She looked very smart, and gave little hint of the sweat and effort which had gone to make her so. The best ensign fluttered from the gaff, the scarlet matching that of the marines' swaying lines athwart the quarterdeck. On the larboard gangway Tapril, the gunner, was having a last hurried discussion with his mates in readiness to begin a salute to the Spanish flag which flew so proudly above the headland battery.

Old Mudge was beside the wheel, hands hidden in the folds of his watch-coat. He seemed to retain the same clothing no matter what the weather might do, hot or cold, rain or fine. He kept a variety of instruments and personal items in his capacious pockets, and Bolitho guessed that sometime, long past, he had been made to rush on deck and stay there with half of his things still scattered around his cabin.

He growled to the helmsman and they edged the wheel over a few spokes, the main topsail filling and then drooping again as the ship idled beneath the land's protection.

Herrick trained his glass on the land and then said, 'Passing the point now, sir!'

'Very well.' Bolitho waved his hand to Tapril. 'Begin the salute.'

And as the English frigate continued slowly towards her anchorage the frail morning air shook and trembled to the regular crash of cannon fire. Gun for gun the Spanish replied, the smoke hanging almost motionless above the shallowing water.

Bolitho gripped his hands together behind him, feeling the sweat exploring his spine under his heavy dress coat and making one of his new shirts cling like a wet towel.

It was strange to stand so impassively as the slow barrage went on around him. Like some trick or dream. At any moment he half-expected to see the bulwark blast apart, or a ball to come screaming amongst the rigid marines and cut them to a bloody gruel.

The last shot hammered his ears, and as the drifting smoke moved away from the decks he saw another frigate anchored at the head of the roads. Spanish, larger than *Undine*, her colours and pendants very bright against the green shore beyond. Her captain, too, had probably been remembering, he thought.

He glanced up at the masthead pendant as it whipped half-heartedly in the breeze. Soon now. More orders. A new piece to fit into the puzzle.

Mudge blew his great nose loudly, a thing he always did before carrying out some part of his duties.

'Ready, sir.'

'Very well. Man the braces. Hands wear ship, if you please.'

Bare feet padded across the newly-scrubbed decks in a steady rush to obey his repeated order, and Bolitho breathed out slowly as each man reached his station without mishap.

'Tops'l sheets!'

The flag above the battery dipped in the glare and then returned to its proper place. Some small boats were shoving off from the land, and Bolitho saw that many were loaded with fruit and other items for barter. With all their bread ruined in the first storm, and few fresh fruits to rival those in the boats, Triphook, the purser, would be busy indeed.

'Tops'l clew lines!'

A boatswain's mate shook his fist at some anonymous figure on the fore topsail yard. 'Yew clumsy bugger! You 'old on with one 'and or yew'll never see yer doxy again!'

Bolitho watched the narrowing strip of water, his eyes half-closed against the searing glare.

'Helm a'lee!'

He waited, as with dignity *Undine* turned quietly into the wind, her remaining canvas shivering violently.

'*Let go!*'

There was a yell from forward, followed by a splash as the anchor plunged down beneath the golden figurehead.

Herrick waited until the last of the canvas had vanished as if by magic along the yards and said, 'They did quite well, I thought, sir?'

Bolitho watched him, holding back the smile. Then, relenting, he replied, '*Quite* well, Mr. Herrick.'

Herrick grinned. 'You'll not need the gig today, sir. A boat's heading out to us in fine style.'

Allday strode forward and presented Bolitho's sword. He frowned and muttered, 'Not the gig, Captain?' He sounded aggrieved.

Bolitho held out his arms to allow the coxswain to buckle the belt around his waist.

'Not this time, Allday.'

It was terrible how both Herrick and Allday watched over his every move.

The marines were stamping and shuffling into a new formation by the entry port, Sergeant Coaker's face shining beneath his black shako like a great sweating fruit.

Bolitho turned to watch the approaching launch, a grand affair with a gilded and canopied cockpit. Beside it, Allday's poor gig would look like a Falmouth harbour boat. A resplendent officer stood watching the anchored frigate, a scroll under one arm. The usual welcoming words. The first link to whatever lay ahead.

He said quietly, 'You will remain aboard, Mr. Herrick. Mr. Davy will accompany me ashore.' He ignored the obvious disappointment. 'Take good care of matters here, and make certain our people are ready for anything.'

Herrick touched his hat. 'Aye, aye, sir.' He hurried away to tell Davy of his good fortune.

Bolitho smiled gravely. With shore boats and other temptations, it would need all of Herrick's skill to keep the ship from being swamped by traders and less respectable visitors.

He heard Herrick say, 'So *you* are to accompany the captain, Mr. Davy.'

Davy hesitated, gauging the moment and Herrick's mood. Then he said calmly, 'A wise choice, if I may say so, Mr. Herrick.'

Bolitho turned away, hiding his smile, as Herrick snapped, 'Well, you are damn little use here, are you?'

Then as the four minute drummer boys struck up with their flutes and drums *Hearts of Oak* and Bellairs' sweating guard presented muskets, Bolitho stepped forward to greet his visitor.

The Governor's Residence was well situated on a gently sloping road above the main anchorage. On his way from the ship by barge and carriage Bolitho was relieved to discover that his official escort, a major of artillery spoke very little English, and contented himself with occasional exclamations of pleasure whenever they passed anything unusual.

It was obvious that everything was well planned, and that from the moment *Undine's* topgallants had been sighted the previous evening things had begun to move.

Bolitho barely remembered meeting the Governor. A bearded, courteous man who shook his hand, received Bolitho's formal greetings on behalf of King George, and who then withdrew to allow an aide to conduct the two British officers to another room.

Davy, who was not easily impressed, whispered, 'By God, sir, the Dons live well. No wonder the treasure ships stop here en route for Spain. A ready market for 'em, I would think.'

The room into which they were ushered was spacious indeed. Long and cool, with a tiled floor and a plentiful selection of well-carved furniture and handsome rugs. There was one huge table in the centre, made entirely of marble. It would take seven gun crews to move it, Bolitho decided.

There were about a dozen people standing around the table, *arranged*, he thought, so that without wasting time he could distinguish those who counted from those who did not.

The man he guessed to be James Raymond stepped forward and said quickly, 'I am Raymond, Captain. Welcome. We had expected you earlier perhaps.' He spoke very abruptly. Afraid of wasting time? Unsure of himself? It was hard to tell.

He was in his early thirties, well dressed, and had features which could pass as handsome but for his petulant frown.

He said, 'And this is Don Luis Puigserver, His Most Catholic Majesty's personal emissary.'

Puigserver was a sturdy man, with biscuit-coloured features and a pair of black eyebrows which dominated the rest of his face. He had hard eyes, but there was charm, too, as he stepped forward and took Bolitho's hand.

'A pleasure, *Capitan*. You have a fine ship.' He gestured to a tall figure by the window. '*Capitan* Alfonso Triarte of the *Nervion* had much praise for the way she behaved.'

Bolitho looked at the other man. Very senior. He would be, to command the big frigate in the roads. He returned Bolitho's examination without much show of pleasure. Like two dogs who have fought once too often, perhaps.

He forgot all about Triarte as the emissary said smoothly, 'I will be brief. You will wish to return to your ship, to make last arrangements for sailing to our destination.'

Bolitho watched him curiously. There was something very compelling about the man. His stocky figure, his legs which looked so muscled, despite the fine silk stockings, even the rough handshake could not disguise his confident assurance. No wonder the Governor had been quick to pass Bolitho on to him. Puigserver obviously commanded respect.

He snapped his spatulate fingers and a nervous aide hurried forward to take Bolitho's hat and sword. Another beckoned to some servants, and in minutes everyone was seated around the altar-like table, a beautifully cut goblet at his elbow.

Only Puigserver remained standing. He watched the servants filling the goblets with sparkling wine, his face completely unruffled. But when Bolitho glanced down he saw one of his feet tapping very insistently on the tiled floor.

He raised his glass. 'Gentlemen. To our friendship.'

They stood up and swallowed the wine. It was excellent, and Bolitho had a mental picture of his own doubts and fumblings in the shop at St. James's Street.

Puigserver continued, 'Little came out of the war but a need to avoid further bloodshed. I will not waste our time by making empty promises which I cannot keep, but I can only hope that we may further our separate causes in peace.'

Bolitho glanced quickly at the others. Raymond leaning back in his chair, trying to appear relaxed, but as taut as a spring. The Spanish captain looking at his wine, eyes distant. Most of the others had the empty expressions of those who pretend to understand when in fact they do not. It seemed likely to Bolitho that they only understood one word in ten.

Davy sat stiffly on the opposite side of the table, his clean features glowing with heat, his face set in a mask of formality.

It all boiled down to the three of them. Don Luis Puigserver, Raymond and himself.

The former said, 'Thankfully, Spain has received back Minorca and certain other islands as concessions following the *unfortunate* war.' His eyes rested on Bolitho very briefly. Dark, almost black. They were like Spanish olives. 'In return, His Most Catholic Majesty has seen fit to bless this new venture between us.' He looked at Raymond. 'Perhaps you would be good enough to expand the details, yes?'

Raymond made to stand up and changed his mind.

'As you will know, Captain Bolitho, the French Admiral Suffren was responsible for many attacks on our ships and possessions in the East Indies and India itself. Holland and Spain' – he hesitated as *Capitan* Triarte coughed gently – 'were France's allies, but they had not the available squadrons and men to protect their possessions in that area. Suffren did it for them. He captured Trincomalee from us and restored it to the Dutch after the war. There were several other instances, but you will know of most of them, Captain. Now, in exchange for certain other considerations which need not concern you, Spain has agreed in principle to hand over to Britain one of her remaining possessions in, er, Borneo.' He eyed Bolitho flatly. 'Which is where you will eventually be going, of course.'

Of course. It sounded so simple. Another two or three thousand miles added to their present voyage. The way Raymond spoke it could have been Plymouth.

Bolitho said quietly, 'I am not certain I understand the purpose of all this.'

Puigserver interjected, 'Of that I am sure, *Capitan*.' He glanced coldly at Raymond. 'Let us be frank. To avoid further trouble in this uneasy truce, for that is what it is, we must move with caution. The French gained next to nothing in the Indies despite all their efforts, and they are, how you say? *Touchy* about any swift expansions around their dwindling influence there. Your final destination will be Teluk Pendang. A fine anchorage, a commanding position for any country with the will to expand elsewhere in that area. A bridge to empire, as some Greek once remarked.'

Bolitho nodded. 'I see, *Señor*.'

He did not, nor had he even heard of the place mentioned.

Raymond said sharply, 'When peace was signed last year, our Government despatched the frigate *Fortunate* to Madras with the bones of this present agreement in her care. On her way around the Cape of Good Hope she met with two of Suffren's frigates which were returning to France. Naturally enough they knew nothing of the peace, and *Fortunate*'s captain was given no time to explain the point. They fought, and *Fortunate* so battered one of the enemy that she took fire and sank. Unfortunately, she, too, was set ablaze and was lost with most of her company.'

Bolitho could picture the scene. Three ships on an open sea. Countries at peace at last, but their captains eager to fight, as they had been conditioned to do.

'However, one of the French captains, the surviving one, was a veteran called Le Chaumareys. One of France's best.'

Bolitho smiled. 'I have heard of him.'

Raymond seemed flustered. 'Yes. I am sure of it. Well, it is believed in some quarters that France, through Le Chaumareys, now knows about this arrangement we are making with Spain. If that is so, then France will be troubled at the prospect of our gaining another possession, one which *she* fought for on Spain's behalf.'

Bolitho did understand now. All the veiled remarks at the Admiralty. The secrecy. No wonder. One hint that England was about to push her way further into the East Indies, no matter for what outward reason, and a war might burst out again like an exploding magazine.

He asked, 'What are we to do?'

Raymond replied, 'You will sail in company with the *Nervion.*' He swallowed hard. '*She* will be the senior ship, and you will act accordingly. Upon arrival at Madras you will embark the new British Governor and convey him, with whatever forces he may have, to his new destination. Teluk Pendang. I will accompany you with despatches for him, and to advise in any way I can.'

Puigserver beamed at them, his black eyebrows arched like great bows. 'And *I* will be there to ensure that there is no nonsense from our people, eh?'

Raymond added wearily, 'The French have a forty-four-gun frigate in that area, the *Argus*. It is said that Le Chaumareys is with her. He knows the Sunda Isles and Borneo as well as any European can.

Bolitho breathed out slowly. It was a good plan as far as it went. A British squadron would invite an open battle sooner or later, but two frigates, one from each nation, would be more than a match for the heavily-armed *Argus* both verbally and in artillery.

Puigserver walked slowly to the broad window and stared down at the anchored ships.

'A long voyage, gentlemen, but I hope a rewarding one for us all.' He turned towards Bolitho, his square face in shadow. 'Are you ready to sail again?'

'Aye, *Señor*. My people are preparing to take in more water and fresh fruit, if that is possible.'

'It is being attended to, *Capitan.*' He showed his teeth. 'I am sorry I cannot entertain you now, but in any case, this island is a dismal place. If you come to Bilbao.' He kissed his fingertips. '*Then* I will show you how to live, eh?' He laughed at Raymond's grim features. 'And I suspect we will all know ourselves *much* better after this voyage is done!'

The Spanish aides bowed politely as Puigserver walked to the door, and he called, 'We will meet before we sail.' He turned away. 'But tomorrow we raise our anchors, come what may.'

Raymond walked round the table as the babble of conversation broke out again. He whispered fiercely, 'That damned fellow! One more day with him and I would have told him a thing or two!'

Bolitho asked, 'In which vessel will you be sailing? Mine is a fine ship, but smaller by far than the Spaniard.'

Raymond twisted round to watch the Spanish captain who was discussing something with his companions in a low voice.

'Sail in the *Nervion*? If your ship were a damned collier brig I'd take her in preference!'

Davy whispered, 'I think they expect us to leave, sir.'

Raymond scowled. 'I will come to our ship and arrange things there. Where no ears listen even to one's breathing!'

Bolitho saw his escort waiting outside the door and smiled to himself. Raymond seemed to have a very vital role in things. Tact, however, was beyond him.

They returned to the jetty with hardly a word, but Bolitho was very conscious of the tension within the man Raymond. On a knife edge. Tortured by something. His work was overreaching him perhaps.

As the scarlet-coated oarsmen propelled the Governor's barge towards *Undine* Bolitho felt a sense of relief. A ship he could understand. Raymond's life was as alien as the moon.

Raymond clambered up from the barge and stared vaguely at the assembled side-party, at the comings and goings of *Undine's* seamen as they worked the tackles on the opposite side. Casks and nets of fruit, and straw hats to protect the unwary from sunburn.

Bolitho nodded to Herrick. 'All well?' He touched Raymond's arm. 'Mr. Raymond will be a passenger with us.' He turned sharply as he heard a shrill of laughter from the cabin hatch. 'Who let that woman on board? In God's name, Mr. Herrick, this is not the Nore or Portsmouth Point!'

Then he saw the girl. Small and dark, in a bright red dress, she was talking to Allday, who was obviously enjoying himself.

Raymond said heavily, 'I had hoped to explain earlier, Captain. That girl is a maid-servant. My *wife's* maid.' He looked as if he was going to be sick.

Herrick tried to dispel Bolitho's sudden anger. 'She came out with her lady just an hour back, sir. She had authority.' He looked worried 'I had little choice in the matter.'

'I see.'

Bolitho strode aft. All those thousands of miles in a small crowded ship-of-war. Raymond was bad enough, but his wife and a maid were too much. He saw some seamen nudging each other. They had probably been waiting just to see his reactions.

Very calmly he said, 'Perhaps you would, er, introduce me, Mr. Raymond?'

They went aft together, and Davy whispered, 'God's teeth, Mr. Herrick, what a mixed gathering we are fast becoming!'

Herrick glared at him. 'And I suppose you have been out there damn well enjoying yourself!'

'A little wine. Some fair company.' He chuckled. 'But I thought, too, of you, *sir*.'

Herrick grinned. 'To hell with you! Get into your working clothes and help with this loading. You need a million eyes today!'

In the meantime Bolitho had reached his cabin, and stared at it in dismay. There were boxes everywhere, and clothing spilled across furniture and guns, as if there had been a violent robbery aboard.

Mrs. Raymond was tall, unsmiling, and almost beside herself with anger.

Her husband exclaimed, 'You should have *waited*, Viola. This is our captain.'

Bolitho bowed slightly. 'Richard Bolitho, ma'am. I had just mentioned that a thirty-two-gun frigate has barely the room for luxury. However, since you have chosen to sail with us, I will do all that I can to—' He got no further.

'*Chosen?*' Her voice was husky with scorn. 'Please do not delude yourself, Captain. *He* does not wish me to travel in the *Nervion.*' Her mouth twisted in contempt. 'He fears for my safety when I am with Spanish *gentlemen!*'

Bolitho noticed Noddall hovering anxiously by the dining compartment and snapped, 'Help Mrs. Raymond's maid to stow all this ' – he looked round helplessly – 'gear.' He saw Raymond slump down on the bench seat like a dying man. No wonder he looked troubled. 'And pass the word for the first lieutenant.' He glanced around the cabin, speaking his thoughts aloud. 'We will have these twelve-pounders removed temporarily and put quakers in their place. That will allow a little more room.'

Raymond looked up dully. 'Quakers?'

'Wooden muzzles. They give an appearance that we are still fully armed.' He forced a smile. 'Quakers having an opposition to war.'

Herrick appeared by the door. 'Sir?'

'We will rig extra screens here, Mr. Herrick. A larger sleeping compartment for our passengers. To larboard, I think.'

Mrs. Raymond said calmly, 'For me and my maid, if you please.' She looked at her husband. 'He will bed elsewhere on *this* ship.'

Herrick studied her curiously but said, 'Mr. Raymond to starboard then. And what about you, sir?'

Bolitho sighed. 'Chart space.' He looked at the others. 'We will dine together here, if you agree.'

Nobody answered.

Midshipman Keen hovered by the door, his eyes on the woman.

'Mr. Soames's respects, sir, and the captain of *Nervion* is about to board us.'

Bolitho swung round and then gasped as his chin cracked against a heavy chest.

He said between his teeth, 'I will endeavour to be hospitable, Mr. Herrick!'

Herrick kept his face blank. 'I am certain of it, sir.'

It was early morning by the time Bolitho had pulled himself wearily into his cot, his mind still reeling from entertaining *Capitan* Triarte and some of his officers. He had been made to go across to the *Nervion* where the captain had again made a point of comparing the spacious comfort with *Undine's* overcrowded quarters. It had not helped at all. Now the ship lay quiet again, and he tried to picture Mrs. Raymond who was sleeping beyond the newly-rigged screen. He had seen her in the cabin when the Spanish officers had come aboard. Aloof yet tempting, with little to reveal her true feelings for her husband. A dangerous woman to cross, he thought.

How still the ship felt. Perhaps, like himself, everyone was too weary to move. Guns had been trundled away and lowered with difficulty into the holds. More stores and heavy gear had had to be swayed aft to readjust the trim once again. It was surprising how much larger the cabin looked without the guns there.

He groaned as his head found some new ache to offer him. He would not see much of it though. He turned his face to the pillow, the sweat running across his chest with the effort. One thing was certain. He had rarely had better incentive for a fast passage.

He was up and about at first light, eager to get his work done before the heat of the day made thinking more difficult. In the afternoon, to the distant strains of a military band and the cheers of a crowd along the waterfront, *Undine* weighed anchor, and with *Nervion* in the lead, her great foresail displaying a resplendent cross of scarlet and gold, worked clear of the roads before setting more canvas to the wind.

Some small craft followed them across the glittering water, but were soon outpaced by the graceful frigates. By dusk they had the sea to themselves, with only the stars for company.

4

Death of a Ship

Ezekiel Mudge, *Undine*'s sailing master, sat comfortably in one of Bolitho's chairs and peered at the chart which was laid across the desk. Without his hat he looked even older, but there was assurance in his voice as he said, 'This wind'll freshen in the next day or so, sir. You mark my words.' He tapped the chart with his own brass dividers which he had just fished from one of his pockets. 'For now, the nor'-east trades will suit us, and we'll be up to the Cape Verde Islands in a week, with any luck.' He sat back and studied Bolitho's reactions.

'Much as I thought.'

Bolitho walked to the stern windows and leaned his hands on the sill. It was hot, like wood from a fire, and beyond the frigate's small, frothing wake the sea was blinding in the glare. His shirt was open to the waist, and he could feel the sweat running down his shoulders, a dryness in his throat like dust.

It was almost noon, and Herrick would be waiting for the midshipmen to report to him on the quarterdeck to shoot the sun for their present position. A full week, but for a few hours, since they had sailed from Santa Cruz, and daily the sun had pinned them down, had defied the light airs which had tried to give them comfort. Today the wind had strengthened slightly, and *Undine* was ghosting along on the starboard tack with all sails drawing well.

There was little satisfaction in Bolitho's thoughts. For *Undine* had suffered her first casualty, a young seaman who had fallen overboard just as darkness had been closing in the previous day. Signalling his intention to the Spanish captain, Bolitho had gone about to begin a search for the luckless man. He had been working aloft on the main topsail yard, framed against the dying sunlight like a bronze statue. Had he been a raw recruit, or some heavy-handed landsman, it was likely he would still be alive. But he had been too confident, too careless perhaps for those last vital seconds as he had changed his position. One cry as he had fallen, and then his head had broken surface almost level with the mizzen, his arms beating at the sea as he tried to keep pace with the ship.

Davy had told him that the seaman was a good swimmer, and that fact had given some hope they might pick him up. They had lowered two boats, and for most of the night had searched in vain. Dawn had found them on course again, but to Bolitho's anger he had discovered that the *Nervion* had made no attempt to shorten sail or stay in company, and only in the last half-hour had the masthead reported sighting her topgallant sails once again.

The seaman's death had been an additional thorn to prod at his determination to weld the ship together. He had seen the Spanish officers watching their first attempts at gun drill through their telescopes, slapping their thighs with amusement whenever something went wrong, which was often. They themselves never drilled anything. They seemed to treat the voyage as a form of entertainment.

Even Raymond had remarked, 'Why bother with gun drill, Captain? I do not know much about such matters, but surely your men find it irksome in this damned heat?'

He had replied, 'It is my responsibility, Mr. Raymond. I daresay it may be unnecessary for this mission, but I'll take no chances.'

Raymond's wife had kept aloof from all of them, and during the day spent much of her time under a small awning which Herrick's men had rigged for her and the maid right aft by the taffrail. Whenever they met, usually at meal times, she spoke only briefly, and then touched on personal matters which Bolitho barely understood. She appeared to enjoy hinting to her husband that he was too backward, that he lacked assurance when it was most needed. Once he had heard her say hotly, 'They ride right over you, James! How can I hold up my head in London when you suffer so many insults! Why, Margaret's husband was knighted for his services, and he is five years your junior!' And so on.

Now, as he turned to look at Mudge, he wondered what he and the others were thinking of their captain. Driving them all too hard, and for no purpose. Making them turn to and work at those stubborn guns while aboard the Spaniard the offwatch hands sprawled about sleeping or drinking wine like passengers.

As if reading his thoughts, Mudge said, 'Don't mind what some o' the buggers are sayin', sir. You're young, but you've a mind for the right thing, if you'll pardon the liberty.' He plucked at his great nose. 'I've seen many a cap'n taken all aback 'cause he worn't ready when the time came.' He chuckled, his small eyes vanishing into his wrinkles. 'An' as you well knows, sir, when things *do* go wrong it's no blamed use slappin' yer hip an' blastin' yer eye, an' blamin' all else.' He tugged a watch the size of a turnip from an inner pocket. 'I must away on deck, if you can spare me, sir. Mr. 'Errick likes me to be there when we compares our reckonin'.' It seemed to amuse him. 'As I said, sir, you stand firm. You don't 'ave to *like* a cap'n, but by God you've got to trust 'un!' He lumbered from the cabin, his shoes making the deck creak as he passed.

Bolitho sat down and tugged at his open shirt. It was a beginning.

Allday peered into the cabin. 'Can I send your servant in now, Captain?' He darted a glance at the table. 'He'll be wanting to get your meal laid.'

Bolitho smiled. 'Very well.'

It was stupid to let small things prey on his mind. But with Mudge it was different. Important. He had probably sailed with more captains than Bolitho had met in his whole life.

They both looked round as Midshipman Keen stood in the doorway. Already he was well tanned, and looked as healthy and fresh as a veteran sailor.

'Mr. Herrick's respects, sir. Masthead has just reported sighting another vessel ahead of the Spaniard. On a converging tack. Small. Maybe a brig.'

'I will come up.' Bolitho smiled. 'The voyage appears to agree with you, Mr. Keen.'

The youth grinned. 'Aye, sir. Though I fear my father sent me away for other reasons but my health.'

As he hurried away Allday murmured, 'Young devil, that one! Got some poor girl into trouble, I'll wager!'

Bolitho kept his face impassive. 'Not like you, of course, Allday.'

He strode out past the sentry and climbed quickly to the quarterdeck. Even though he was expecting it, the heat came down on him like the mouth of an open furnace. He felt the decks seams sticking to his shoes, the searing touch on his face and neck as he crossed to the weather side and looked along his command.

With her pale, lightweight canvas bent on, and her deck tilting to the wind, *Undine* was moving well. Spray leapt up and round the jib boom at irregular intervals, and far above his head he saw the pendant streaming abeam like a thin whip.

Mudge and Herrick were muttering together, their sextants gleaming in the sunlight, like gold, while two midshipmen, Armitage and Penn, compared notes, their faces screwed in worried concentration.

Soames was by the quarterdeck rail and turned as Bolitho asked, 'About this newcomer. What is she, do you reckon?'

Soames looked crushed with heat, his hair matted to his forehead, as if he had been swimming.

'Some trader, I expect, sir.' He did not sound as if he cared. 'Maybe she intends to ask the Spaniard for her position.' He scowled. 'Not that they'll know much!'

Bolitho took a glass from the rack and climbed into the mizzen shrouds. Moving it gradually he soon found the *Nervion*, far ahead on the larboard bow, a picture of beauty under her great spread of canvas, her hull gleaming in the sun like metal. He trained the glass further to starboard and then held it steady on the other vessel. Almost hidden in heat haze, but he could see the tan-coloured sails well enough, the uneven outline of her rig. Square on the fore, fore-and-aft on the mainmast. He felt vaguely angry.

'A brigantine, Mr. Soames.'

'Aye, sir.'

Bolitho looked at him and then climbed back to the deck. 'In future, I want a full report of each sighting, no matter how trivial it might appear at the time.'

Soames tightened his jaw. 'Sir.'

Herrick called, 'It was my fault, sir. I should have told Mr. Keen to pass a full description to you.'

Bolitho walked aft. 'Mr. Soames has the watch, I believe.'

Herrick followed him. 'Well, yes, sir.'

Bolitho saw the two helmsmen stiffen as he moved to the compass. The card was steady enough. South by west, and with plenty of sea room. The African coast lay somewhere across the larboard beam, over thirty leagues distant. There was nothing on their ocean but the three ships. Coincidence? A need to make contact perhaps?

Soames's indifference pricked at his mind like a burr and he snapped, 'Make certain our watchkeepers know what they are about, Mr. Herrick.' He saw Keen leaning against the nettings. 'Send *him* aloft with a glass. An untried eye might tell us more.'

Mudge ambled towards him and said gruffly, 'Near as makes no difference, sir. Cape Blanco should be abeam now.' He rubbed his chin. 'The most westly point o' that savage continent. An' quite close enough, if you ask me!'

His chest went up and down to a small wheezing accompaniment. It was as near as he ever got to laughing.

Keen's voice came down from the masthead. 'Deck there! Brigantine is still closing the *Nervion*!'

Herrick cupped his hands. 'Does she show any colours?'

'None, sir!'

Herrick clambered into the shrouds with his own telescope. After a while he called, 'The Dons don't seem worried, sir.'

Mudge growled. ''Ardly likely to be bothered about that little pot o' paint, is they?'

Bolitho said, 'Bring her up a point, Mr. Mudge. It would be best if we regain company with our companion.'

He turned as a voice asked, 'Are you *troubled*, Captain?'

Mrs. Raymond was standing by the trunk of the mizzen mast, her face shadowed by a great straw hat which she had brought from Teneriffe.

He shook his head. 'Merely curious, ma'am.' In his crumpled shirt and breeches he felt suddenly clumsy. 'I'm sorry there is not more to amuse you during the day.'

She smiled. 'Things may yet improve.'

'Deck there!' Keen's voice made them all look up. 'The other vessel is going about, sir!'

Herrick called, 'He's right. The brigantine's going to cross clean over the Don's bows!' He turned, grinning broadly. 'That'll make 'em hop about!'

The grin vanished as a dull bang echoed and re-echoed over the water.

Keen yelled, 'She's fired on the *Nervion*!' A second bang reached the quarterdeck and he cried again, 'And another!' He was almost screaming with excitement. 'He's put a ball through her forecourse!'

Bolitho ran to the shrouds and joined Herrick.

'Let me see.'

He took the big glass and trained it on the two ships. The brigantine's shape had shortened, and she was presenting her stern to him even as she idled across the frigate's broader outline. Even at such a distance it was possible to see the confusion aboard the Spanish frigate, the glint of sunlight on weapons as her company ran to quarters.

Herrick said hoarsely, 'That brigantine's master must be mad. No one but a crazy man would cross swords with a frigate!'

Bolitho did not reply. He was straining his eye to watch the little drama framed in his lens. The brigantine had fired two shots, one of which, if not both, had scored a mark. Now she was tacking jauntily away, and it was evident, as the *Nervion* began to spread more sail, that *Capitan* Triarte intended to give chase.

He said, '*Nervion*'ll be up to her within the hour. They're both changing tack now.'

'Perhaps that fool imagined *Nervion* was a fat merchantman, eh?' Davy had arrived on deck. 'But no, it is not possible.'

Herrick followed Bolitho down from the shrouds and watched him dubiously.

'Shall we join in the chase, sir?'

Mudge almost pushed him aside as he barked, 'Chase be damned, I say!'

They looked at him.

'We must stop that mad Don, sir!' He waved his big hand across the nettings. 'Off Cape Blanco, sir, there's a powerful great reef, an' it runs near on a 'undred miles to seaward. *Nervion*'s in risk now, but if 'er master brings 'er up another point he'll be across that damned reef afore 'e knows it!'

Bolitho stared at him. 'Get the royals on her, Mr. Herrick! Lively now!' He walked quickly to the helm. 'We must make more speed.'

Soames called, 'The Don's come up another point by the look of her, sir!'

Mudge was already squinting at the compass bowl. 'Jesus! 'E's steerin' sou'sou'-east!' He looked at Bolitho imploringly. 'We'll never catch 'im in time!'

Bolitho paced to the quarterdeck rail and back again. Weariness, the scorching heat, all was forgotten but that distant pyramid of white sails, with the smaller, will-o'-the-wisp brigantine dancing ahead. Mad? A confused pirate? It made no difference now.

He snapped, 'Clear away a bow chaser, Mr. Herrick. We will endeavour to distract the *Nervion*.'

Herrick was peering aloft, shading his eyes with his speaking trumpet as the topmen set the additional sails.

'Aye, aye, sir!' He yelled, 'Fetch Mr. Tapril!'

But the gunner was already forward, supervising the crew of a long nine-pounder.

Bolitho said sharply, '*Nervion*'s pulled over still further, Mr. Mudge.' He could not hide the anguish in his voice.

How could it be happening? The sea so huge, so empty. And yet, the reef *was* there. He had heard of it before from men who had passed this way. Many good ships had foundered on its hard spine.

'Larboard gun ready, sir!'

'*Fire!*'

It crashed out, the brown smoke drifting downwind and dispersing long before the telltale waterspout lifted like a feather far astern of the other frigate.

'Another. Keep firing.' He looked at Mudge. 'Bring her up a point.'

Mudge protested, 'I'll not be responsible, sir.'

'No. *I will.*'

He strode forward to the rail again, his shirt flapping open across his chest, yet feeling no benefit from the wind. When he looked up he saw the sails drawing firmly, as would the Spaniard's. With such power to drive her, she would disembowel herself on the reef, unless Triarte acted, and at once.

The deck shook as another ball whined and ricocheted across the blue water.

Bolitho yelled, 'Masthead! What are they doing?'

The lookout replied, his rougher voice leaving no doubt in Bolitho's mind, 'Th' Dons is gainin', sir! They're runnin' out their guns right this moment!'

Maybe the Spaniards had heard the bow chaser, even observed a fall of shot, but imagined the stupid British were still exercising gunnery. Or perhaps they believed *Undine* was so furious at missing the chase that Bolitho was firing at this impossible range merely to take the edge off his temper.

He heard himself ask, 'How long, Mr. Mudge?'

Mudge replied thickly, 'She should 'ave struck, sir. That damned brigantine must 'ave crossed the reef in safety. She'll draw little enough, I'm thinkin'.'

Bolitho stared at him. 'But if *she* got through, then perhaps . . .'

The master shook his head. 'No chance, sir.'

A great yell came from the watching seamen in the bows. When Bolitho swung round he stared with horror as the Spanish frigate lifted, drove forward again and then slewed round on the hidden reef. Over and around her all her masts and yards, the flailing sails and rigging splashed and cascaded in a chaos which was terrible to see. So great was the impact that she had presented her larboard side to the reef, and through the open gunports the water must now be surging in a triumphant flood, while men trapped in the tangled rigging and broken spars floundered in terror, or were being crushed by the cannon as they tore from their lashings.

The brigantine had changed tack. She was not even pausing to watch the full extent of her work.

Bolitho said harshly, 'Shorten sail, Mr. Herrick. We will heave-to presently and get every boat in the water. We must do all we can to save them.'

He saw some of the men by the bow chasers pointing and chattering as *Nervion* yawed still further on her side, spilling more broken timber and shattered planking into the swell above the reef.

'And get those hands to *work*, Mr. Herrick!' He swung away. 'I'll not have them watch others drown, as if it was a day's amusement!'

He made himself cross the deck once more, and when he looked towards the reef he almost expected to see *Nervion*'s proud silhouette standing before the wind. That this was a bad dream. A nightmare.

But why? *Why?* The question seemed to mock him. To hammer at his brain. How could it have happened?

'I'd not venture any closer, sir.' Mudge was watching him grimly. 'If we gets a shift of wind we could still run foul of the reef.'

Bolitho nodded heavily. 'I agree.' He looked away. 'And thank you.'

Mudge said quietly, 'It worn't your fault. You done all you could.'

'Heave to, Mr. Herrick.' He could barely keep his voice level. 'Have the boats swayed out.'

Soames remarked, 'A long pull, sir. Near on three miles.'

Bolitho did not even hear him. He was seeing the little brigantine. It was no coincidence. No rash act of the moment.

Mudge said, 'There'll not be many, sir.' He fumbled in his pockets. 'There's sharks a'plenty in these waters.'

As *Undine* came up into the wind, her remaining sails thundering and flapping noisily in protest, the boats were lowered with surprisingly little delay. It was as if something had reached out across the three miles of smiling water to touch each and every one of them. A plea for help, a cry of warning, it was difficult to define. But as the first boat shoved off from the side, and the seamen at the oars picked up the stroke, Bolitho saw that their faces were grim and suddenly determined. As he had not seen them before.

Allday said, 'I'll take the gig, if I may, Captain.'

'Yes.' Their eyes met. 'Do what you can.'

'I will.'

Then he was gone, yelling for his men.

'Warn the surgeon to be prepared, Mr. Herrick.' He saw the quick exchange of glances and added coldly, 'And if he is the worse for drink I will have him flogged.'

All the boats were away now, while far beyond their busy oars he could see the remains of the other ship writhing on the invisible reef, the great foresail with its red and gold crucifix still floating around the wreckage like a beautiful shroud.

Bolitho began to pace up and down below the nettings, his hands behind him, his body swaying to the untidy motion as the ship rolled in each undulating trough.

He heard Raymond say, 'Captain Triarte was wrong. He made a stupid error of judgement.'

He paused and looked at him. 'He has paid for it, Mr. Raymond!'

Raymond saw the contempt in Bolitho's grey eyes and walked away. 'I was only saying . . .' But nobody looked at him.

Herrick watched Bolitho pacing back and forth and wished he could say something to ease his despair. But better than most, he knew that at such moments Bolitho was the only one who could help himself.

Hours later, as the boats pulled wearily back towards their ship, Bolitho was still on deck, his shirt dark with sweat, his mind aching from his deliberations.

Herrick reported, 'No more than forty survivors, sir. Some are in a bad way, I fear.' He saw the question in Bolitho's eyes and nodded. 'The surgeon's ready, sir. I saw to that.'

Bolitho walked slowly to the nettings and craned over to watch the first boat, the gig, as it hooked on to the chains. One man, cradled against Allday's legs, and held firmly by two seamen, was shrieking like a tortured woman. A shark had taken a piece from his shoulder big enough to thrust a round-shot through. He turned away sickened.

'In God's name, Thomas, send more hands to help those poor devils.'

Herrick said, 'It is being done, sir.'

Bolitho looked up at the flapping ensign at the gaff. 'By heaven, if this is how we behave in peace, then I would we were at war.'

He watched some of the oarsmen clambering aboard. Hands blistered, backs and faces raw from the sun, they said very little as they went below. Perhaps what they had seen at the reef had taught them more than drill, and would act as a warning to all of them.

He began to pace again. *And to me.*

Bolitho strode into the cabin and paused below the skylight. It was almost sunset, and the open stern windows shone in the dying glare like burnished copper. Within the cabin the shadows bobbed this way and that to the frigate's steady motion and the swinging deckhead lanterns, and he watched the little group by the windows with something like disbelief.

Don Luis Puigserver sat awkwardly on the bench seat, one arm in a sling, his chest and ribs encased in bandages. When he had been dragged aboard with the other survivors a few hours earlier he had passed unrecognised until a gasping Spanish lieutenant, the only one of *Nervion*'s officers to be rescued, had managed to explain the truth. Then, Bolitho had thought it was too late. The thickset Spaniard had been unconscious and covered with angry scars and bruises. The fact he had survived that long had been hard to accept when Bolitho had recalled the *Nervion*'s final destruction. Of the forty or so to reach *Undine*'s protection, ten had already died, and several of the remainder were in a bad state. Crushed under falling spars, half drowned by the inrush of water, the *Nervion*'s original complement of two hundred and seventy men had been totally unprepared for the horror which had awaited them on the reef. While their vessel had foundered and smashed herself to pieces, the surging water had suddenly erupted in a maelstrom of dashing shapes as the sharks had hurried to the attack. Terrified men had seen their companions torn to bloody remnants, when moments before they had been setting more sail and manning their guns to run down the impudent brigantine.

When *Undine*'s boats had arrived it had been nearly over. A few men had swam desperately back to the capsized frigate, only to be dragged down as she had slid from the reef for her last plunge. Others had clung to floating spars and upturned boats and had watched in terror as one by one their grey attackers had plucked them screaming into the churned, scarlet water.

And now, Puigserver was sitting here in the cabin, his face almost composed as he sipped steadily from a goblet of wine. He was naked to the waist, and Bolitho could see some extent of the bruising on his body, evidence of his will to survive.

He said quietly, 'I am grateful that you are in better spirits, *Señor*.'

The Spaniard made to grin, but winced at the effort. He waved the surgeon and one of his assistants aside and asked, 'My men? How many?'

Bolitho looked past him towards the horizon. A thread of copper, fading even as he watched.

'Thirty.' He shrugged. 'Many were badly mauled.'

Puigserver took another swallow. 'It was terrible to behold.' His dark eyes hardened. '*Capitan* Triarte was so enraged by that other ship's attack that he went after her like a man possessed. He was too hot-blooded. Not like you.'

Bolitho smiled gravely. *Not like you.* But suppose he had not had a sailing master like Mudge? One so experienced, so travelled as to *feel* the reef's danger like another of his stored memories. It was likely *Undine* might have shared the Spaniard's fate. It made him chill, despite the lifeless air in the cabin.

Somewhere beyond the bulkhead a man screamed. A thin, long-drawn sound which stopped abruptly as if a door had been slammed on it.

Whitmarsh wiped his hands on his apron and straightened his back, his head bowed beneath the beams.

He said, 'Don Puigserver will be comfortable for a while, sir. I would like to return to my other charges.' He was sweating very badly, and a muscle at one corner of his face twitched uncontrollably.

Bolitho nodded. 'Thank you. Please inform me of any help you might require.'

The surgeon touched the Spaniard's bandages vaguely. 'God's help perhaps.' He gave a wry smile. 'Out here, we have little else.'

As he left with his assistant Puigserver murmured, 'A man with an inner torment, *Capitan*.' He grimaced. 'But a gentle one for his trade.'

Allday was folding up a towel and some unused dressings and said, 'Mr. Raymond was asking to see you, Captain.' He frowned. 'I told him you had given orders that the cabin was to be kept for the surgeon until his work was done with Don Puig—' he coughed, '... the Spanish gentleman.'

'What did he want?'

Bolitho was so weary he hardly cared. He had seen little of Raymond since the survivors had been brought aboard, and had heard he had been in the wardroom.

Allday replied, 'He was wishing to make a complaint, Captain. His wife took a displeasure at you asking her to help tend the injured.' He frowned again. 'I told him you had more important work to do.' He picked up his things and walked to the door.

Puigserver leaned back and closed his eyes. Without the others present he seemed willing to reveal the pain he was really enduring.

He said, 'Your All-day is a remarkable fellow, eh? With a few hundred of his kind I might think again about a campaign in the South Americas.'

Bolitho sighed. 'He worries too much.'

Puigserver opened his eyes and smiled. 'He seems to think you are worth worrying about, *Capitan*.'

He leaned forward, his face suddenly intense. 'But before Raymond and the others come amongst us, I must speak. I want your opinion about the wreck. I *need* it.'

Bolitho walked to the bulkhead and touched the sword with his fingers.

He said, 'I have thought of little else, *Señor*. At first I believed the brigantine to be a pirate, her captain so confused or so in dread of his crew as to need a battle to keep them together. But I cannot believe it in my heart. Someone knew of our intenions.'

The Spaniard watched him intently. 'The French perhaps?'

'Maybe. If their government is so concerned at our movements it must mean that when they sank the *Fortunate* they did indeed capture her despatches intact. It would have to be something really vital to play such a dangerous game.'

Puigserver reached for the wine bottle. 'A game which *did* work.'

'Then you, too, are of the same mind, *Señor*?' He watched the man's outline, paler now against the darkened windows.

He did not reply directly. 'If, and I am only saying *if*, this someone intended such a course of action, he will have known we were two ships in company.' He paused and then said sharply, 'A reaction, *Capitan*! Quickly!'

Bolitho said, 'It would make no difference. He would realise that this is a combined mission. One ship without the other makes further progress impossible, and . . .'

Puigserver was banging his hip with the goblet, wine slopping over his leg like blood.

He shouted excitedly, '*And?* Go on, *Capitan! And what?*'

Bolitho looked away and replied firmly, 'I must return either to England or to Teneriffe and await further orders.'

When he looked again at the Spaniard he saw he was slumped back on the seat, his square features strained, his chest heaving as if from a fight.

Puigserver said thickly, 'When you came to Santa Cruz, I knew you were a man of thoughts and not merely of words.' He shook his head. 'Let me finish. This man, these creatures, whoever they are, who would let my people die so horribly, *want you to turn back*!'

Bolitho watched him, fascinated, awed by his strength.

'Without you being here, *Señor*.' He looked away. 'I would have had no option.'

'Exactly, *Capitan*.'

He peered at Bolitho over the rim of the goblet, his eyes shining in the lantern light like tawny stones.

Bolitho added, 'By the time I returned to England, new plans were made and agreed upon, something might have happened in the East Indies or elsewhere which we could not control.'

'Give me your hand, *Capitan*.' He groped forward, his breathing sharper. 'In a moment I will sleep. It has been a wretched day, but far worse for many others.'

Bolitho took his hand, suddenly moved by Puigserver's obvious sincerity.

The latter asked slowly, 'How many have you in this little ship?'

Bolitho pictured the riffraff brought aboard at Spithead. The ragged men from the prison hulks, the smartly-dressed ones fleeing from some crime or other in London. The gun captain with only one hand. All of them.

He said, 'They have the makings, *Señor*. Two hundred, all told, including my marines.' He smiled, if only to break the tension. 'And I will sign on those of your men who have survived, if I may?'

Puigserver did not seem to hear. But his grip was like iron as he said, 'Two hundred, eh?'

He nodded grimly. 'It will be sufficient.'

Bolitho watched him. 'We go on, *Señor*?'

'You are *my Capitan* now. What do *you* say?'

Bolitho smiled. 'But you know already, *Señor*.'

Puigserver gave a great sigh. 'If you will send that fool Raymond in to me, and your clerk, I will put my seal on this new undertaking.' His voice hardened. 'Today I saw and heard many men die in fear and horror. Whatever made that foul deed necessary, I intend to set the record right. And when I do, *Capitan*, I will make it a reckoning which our enemies will long remember.'

There was a tap at the door and Midshipman Armitage stood outlined by the swinging lantern in the passageway.

'Mr. Herrick's respects, sir. The wind's freshening from the nor'-east.' He faltered, like a child repeating a lesson to his tutor.

'I will come up directly.'

Bolitho thought suddenly of Mudge, how he had prophesied a better wind. He would be up there with Herrick, waiting for the night's orders. Armitage's message told him all that and more. Whatever was decided now might settle the fate of the ship and every man aboard.

He looked at Puigserver. 'It is settled then, *Señor*?'

'Yes, *Capitan*.' He was getting more drowsy. 'You can leave me now. And send Raymond before I sleep like some drunken goatherd.'

Bolitho followed the midshipman from his cabin, noting how stiffly the sentry at the door was holding his musket. He had probably been listening, and by tonight it would be all over the ship. Not merely a voyage to display the Navy's reach in foreign parts, but one with a real prospect of danger. He smiled grimly as he reached the quarterdeck ladder. It might make gun drill less irksome for them in future.

He found Herrick and Mudge near the helm, the master with a shaded lantern held over his slate, upon which he made his surprisingly neat calculations.

Bolitho walked up the weather side, looking aloft at the bulging canvas, hearing the sea creaming along the hull like water in a mill sluice.

Then he returned to where they were waiting and said, 'You may shorten sail for the night, Mr. Herrick. Tomorrow you can sign on any of the *Nervion*'s people you find suitable.' He paused as another frantic cry floated up from the orlop deck. 'Though I fear it may not be many.'

Herrick asked, 'We are not going about then, sir?'

Mudge exclaimed. 'An' a good thing, too, if I may say so, sir.' He rubbed his bulging rump with one hand. 'Me rheumatism will sheer off when we gets to a 'otter climate.'

Bolitho looked at Herrick. 'We go forward, Thomas. To finish what was begun back there on the reef.'

Herrick seemed satisfied. 'I'm for that.'

He made to walk to the rail where a bosun's mate awaited his orders, but Bolitho stopped him, saying, 'From this night on, Thomas, we must keep our wits about us. No unnecessary pauses for fresh water if prying eyes are nearby. We will ration every drop if necessary, and stand or fall by our own resources. But we must stay clear of the land where an enemy might betray our course or intentions. If, as I now believe, someone is working against us, we must use his methods against him. Gain ourselves time by every ruse we can invent.'

Herrick nodded. 'That makes good sense, sir.'

'Then I hope it may seem so to our people.' He walked to the weather side. 'You may carry on now.'

Herrick turned away. 'Call the hands. We will shorten sail.'

As the shouts echoed between decks and the seamen came dashing on to the gangways, Herrick said, 'I almost forgot, sir. Mrs. Raymond is worried about her accommodation.'

'It is arranged.' He paused and watched the hands scampering to the shrouds. 'Don Puigserver will sleep in the main cabin. Mrs. Raymond can retain her own cot with the maid.'

Herrick sounded cautious. 'I doubt she will like that, sir.'

Bolitho continued his pacing. 'Then she may say so, Mr. Herrick. And when she does I will explain what *I* think of a woman so pampered she will not lift a finger to help a dying man!'

A master's mate strode along the gangway. 'All mustered, sir!'

Herrick was still watching the pacing figure, the open white shirt clearly etched against the nettings and the sea beyond. In the next few weeks *Undine* would get much smaller, he thought.

'Very well, Mr. Fowlar. Get the to'gan's'ls off her. If the weather freshens up we may have to reef tops'ls before the night's done.'

Old Mudge rubbed his aching back. 'The weather is a fool!' But nobody heeded him.

Bolitho saw the topmen sliding down to the deck, with barely a word to each other as they were checked again by their petty officers. Around the vibrating bowsprit the spindrift rode in the wind like pale arrows, and high above the deck he saw the topsails hardening and puffing out their bellies to a combined chorus of creaking rigging and blocks.

'Dismiss the watch below.' Herrick's voice was as usual. He took Bolitho's word as he would a rope to save himself from drowning.

In the darkness Bolitho smiled. Perhaps it was better to be so.

In the cabin Don Puigserver sat at the desk and watched the clerk's quill scraping across his written orders. Raymond was leaning against the quarter windows, his face expressionless as he peered into the darkness.

Then across his shoulder he said, 'It is a great responsibility, Don Puigserver. I am not sure I can advise in its favour.'

The Spaniard leaned painfully against the chair-back and listened to the regular footsteps across the deck overhead. Up and down.

'It is not mine alone, *Señor* Raymond. I am in good company, believe me.'

Above and around them the *Undine* moved and murmured in time with sea and wind. Right forward below the bowsprit the golden nymph stared unwinkingly at the darkened horizon. Decision and destiny, triumph and disappointment meant nothing to her. She had the ocean, and that was life itself.

5

The Work of a Demon

Bolitho stood loosely by the quarterdeck rail, his body partly shaded from the harsh glare by the thick mainmast trunk, and watched the routine work around him. Eight bells chimed from the forecastle, and he could hear Herrick and Mudge comparing notes from their noon sights, while Soames, who was officer of the watch, prowled restlessly by the cabin hatch as he awaited his relief.

Just to watch the slow, lethargic movements of the men on the gangways and gun deck was enough. Thirty-four days since they had seen *Nervion's* destruction on the reef, and nearly two months since weighing anchor at Spithead. It had been hard work all the way, and from the moment the Spanish ship had foundered the atmosphere aboard had been compressed and strained to the limit.

The last few days had been the worst part, he thought. For a while his company had gained some excitement at crossing the Equator, with all its mysteries and myths. He had issued an extra ration of rum, and for a time he had observed some benefit from the change. The new hands had seen the line-crossing as a kind of test which they had somehow managed to pass. The old seamen had grown in stature as they had recounted or lied about the number of occasions they had sailed these waters in other ships. A fiddler had emerged, and after a self-conscious overture had brought some music and scratchy gaiety to their daily lives.

And then, the last of the badly injured Spaniards had begun to die. It had been like the final pressure on them all. Whitmarsh had done all he could. He had carried out several amputations, and as the pitiful cries had floated up from his sickbay Bolitho had felt the brief satisfaction of drawing his company together fading once again. The dying Spaniard had dragged it out for many days. Nearly a month he had ebbed and rallied, sobbing and groaning, or sleeping peacefully while Whitmarsh had stayed with him hour by hour. It had seemed as if the surgeon was testing his own resources, searching for some new cracking point. The last of his patients to die had been the ones mauled by sharks, those which because of their wounds could not be saved or despatched by amputations. Gangrene had set into their flesh, and the whole ship had been pervaded by a stench so revolting that even the most charitable had prayed for the sufferers to die.

He saw the afternoon watch mustering below the quarterdeck, while Lieutenant Davy strode aft and waited for Soames to sign his report in the log. Even Davy looked weary and bedraggled, his handsome face so tanned by hours on duty he could have been a Spaniard.

They all avoided Bolitho's eye. As if they were afraid of him, or that they needed all their energies merely to get through another day.

Davy reported, 'The watch is aft.'

Soames glared at him. 'A moment *late*, Mr. Davy.'

Davy regarded him disdainfully and then turned to his master's mate. 'Relieve the wheel.'

Soames stamped to the hatch and disappeared below.

Bolitho clenched his hands behind him and took a few steps away from the mast. The only satisfaction was the wind. The previous day, as they had changed tack towards the east and the masthead had reported sighting land far abeam, the westerlies had made themselves felt. As he shaded his eyes to peer aloft he could see the impatient thrust of power in every sail, the mainyard bending and trembling like one giant bow. That blur of land had been Cape Agulhas, the southernmost tip of the African continent. Now, stretching before the crisscross of rigging and shrouds lay the blue emptiness of the Indian Ocean, and like many of his new seamen who had contemplated their crossing the Equator, he was able to consider what together they had achieved to reach this far. The Cape of Good Hope was to all intents the half-way of their voyage, and to this day he had kept his word. Mile upon mile, day after scorching day, driving wildly in blustery squalls, or lying becalmed, with every sail hanging lifeless, he had used everything he knew to keep up their spirits. When that had faltered he had speeded up the daily routine. Gun and sail drill, and competitions between messes for the offwatch hands.

He saw the purser and his assistant waiting beside a puncheon of pork which had just been swayed up from the forward hold. Midshipman Keen stood nearby, trying to appear knowledgeable as Triphook had the new cask opened and proceeded to check through each four-pound piece of salt pork before he allowed it to be carried to the galley. Keen, whose junior authority as midshipman of the watch made him the captain's representative on such occasions, probably imagined it to be a waste of time. Bolitho knew otherwise from past experience. It was well known for dishonest victualling yards to give short measure, or to make up the contents of a cask with hunks of rotten meat, even pieces of old canvas, knowing as they did that by the time a ship's purser discovered the fault he would be well clear of the land and unable to complain. Pursers, too, were known to line their own pockets by sharp practice with their opposite numbers ashore.

Bolitho saw the gaunt purser nod mournfully and mark his ledger, apparently satisfied. Then he followed the little procession forward to the galley, his shoes squeaking as they clung to the sun-heated pitch between the deck seams.

The heat, the relentless, unbroken days were testing enough. But Bolitho knew it only needed a hint of corruption, some suggestion that the ship's company were being cheated by their officers, and the whole voyage might explode. He had asked himself over and over again if he was allowing his last experience to pray on his mind. Even the word itself, *mutiny*, had struck fear into the heart of many a captain, especially one far from friendly company and higher authority.

He took a few paces along the side and winced as his wrist brushed against the bulwark. The timbers were bone-dry, the paint cracking, despite regular attention.

He paused and shaded his eyes to watch some large fish jumping far abeam. *Water*. It was usually uppermost in his mind. With the new hands, and the need to use much of their precious water supply to help the sick and injured, even rationing might not be enough.

He saw two Negro seamen lounging by the larboard gangway. It was a mixed company indeed. When they had sailed from Spithead it had been varied enough. Now, with the small list of Spanish survivors, they were even more colourful. Apart from the sole Spanish officer, a sad-eyed lieutenant named Rojart, there were ten seamen, two boys who were little more than children, and five soldiers. The latter, at first grateful to have survived, were now openly resentful of their new status. Carried aboard *Nervion* as part of Puigserver's personal guard, they were now neither fish nor fowl, and while they tried to act as seamen, they were usually found watching *Undine*'s sweating marines with both envy and contempt.

Herrick stepped into his thoughts and reported, 'The master and I agree.' He held out the slate. 'If you would care to examine this, sir.' He sounded unusually guarded.

Mudge ambled into the shadow of the hammock nettings and said, 'If you are about to alter course, sir.' He dragged out his handkerchief. 'It is as good a time as any.' He blew his nose violently.

Herrick said quickly, 'I would like to make a suggestion, sir.'

Mudge moved away and stood patiently near the helmsman.

It was hard to tell if Herrick had just thought of his suggestion, or if he had discussed it with the others.

'Some were a mite surprised when you stood clear of Cape Town, sir.' His eyes were very blue in the glare. 'We could have landed our remaining sick people and taken in fresh water. I doubt that the Dutch government there would pay much heed to our movements.'

'Do you, Mr. Herrick?'

He saw a puff of dull smoke from the galley. Soon now the offwatch men would be having a meal in the sweltering heat of their messes. The remains of yesterday's salt beef. Skillygolee, as they named it. A mixture of oatmeal gruel, crushed biscuits and lumps of boiled meat. And all that washed down with a full ration of beer. It was likely the latter was stale and without life. But anything was better than the meagre ration of water.

He jerked himself back to Herrick, suddenly irritated. 'And who put you up to this remarkable assessment?' He saw Herrick's face cloud over but added, 'It has an unfamiliar ring to it.'

Herrick said, 'It's just that I do not wish to see you driving yourself, sir. I felt as you did about *Nervion*'s loss, but it is done, and there's an end to it. You did all you could for her people . . .'

Bolitho said, 'Thank you for your concern, but I am not driving myself or our people to no purpose. I believe we may be needed, even at this moment.'

'Perhaps, sir.'

Bolitho regarded him searchingly. 'Perhaps indeed, but then that is my responsibility. If I have acted wrongly, then you may receive promotion more quickly than you thought.' He turned away. 'When the hands have eaten we will lay her on the new course. Nor'-east by east.' He looked at the masthead pendant. 'See how it blows. We'll get the royals on her directly and run with the wind under our coat-tails while it lasts.'

Herrick bit his lip. 'I still believe we should touch land, sir, if only to collect water.'

'As I do, Mr. Herrick.' He faced him coldly. 'And that I will do whenever I can without arousing interest elsewhere. I have my orders. I intend to carry them out as best I can, do you understand?'

They watched each other, their eyes angry, troubled, and concerned by the sudden flare-up between them.

'Very good, sir.' Herrick stood back, his eyes squinting in the sun. 'You can rely on me.'

'I was beginning to wonder, Mr. Herrick.' Bolitho half stepped forward, one hand outstretched as Herrick swung away, his face taut with dismay.

He had not meant the words to form in that way. If he had ever doubted anything in his life, Herrick's loyalty was not one of them. He felt ashamed and angry. Perhaps the strain of this empty monotony, of carrying men who wanted to do nothing but crawl away from work and the sun, of torturing his mind with plans and doubts, had taken a far greater toll than he had imagined.

He turned on his heel and saw Davy watching him curiously.

'Mr. Davy, you have only just taken over your watch, and I would not wish to disrupt your thoughts. But examine the forecourse, if you please, and set some of your hands to put it to rights.' He saw the lieutenant fall back from his anger and added, 'It looks as slack as the watch on deck!'

As he strode to the cabin hatch he saw the lieutenant hurrying to the rail. The fact that the forecourse was not drawing as it should was no excuse for taking out his temper on Davy.

He strode past the sentry and slammed the cabin door behind him. But there was no escape here. Noddall was laying plates on the table, his face stiffly resentful as Mrs. Raymond's maid followed him around the cabin like an amused child.

Raymond was slumped in a chair by the stern windows, apparently dozing, and his wife sat on the bench seat, fanning herself, and watching Noddall's preparations, a look of complete boredom on her face.

Bolitho made to go but she called, 'Come *along*, Captain. We barely see you from day to day.' She patted the bench seat with the fan. 'Sit awhile. Your precious ship will survive, I think.'

Bolitho sat down and leaned one elbow on the sill. It was good to feel life in the wind again, to watch the lift and swirl of foam as it surged freely from the counter, or came up gurgling around the rudder.

Then he turned slightly and looked at her. She had been aboard all this time and yet he knew little of her. She was watching him now, her eyes partly amused, partly questioning. Probably two or three years older than himself, he thought. Not beautiful, but with the aristocratic presence which commanded instant attention. She had fine, even teeth, and her hair, which she had allowed to flow loosely across her shoulders, was the colour of autumn. While he and the rest of his officers had found difficulty in keeping cool, or finding a clean shirt after the sun's tyranny or some fierce squall in the South Atlantic, she had always managed to remain perfect. As she was now. Her gown was not merely worn, it was *arranged*, so that he and not she looked out of place against the stern windows. Her earrings were heavy, and he guessed their value would pay most of his marines for a year or more.

She smiled. 'Do you enjoy what you see, Captain?'

Bolitho started. 'I am sorry, ma'am. I am tired.'

She exclaimed, 'How gallant! I am sorry it is only weariness which makes you look at me.' She held up the fan and added, 'I am mocking you, Captain. Do not look so depressed.'

Bolitho smiled. 'Thank you.'

He thought suddenly of that other time. In New York, three years ago. Another ship his first command, and the world opening up just for him. A woman had shown him that life was not so kind, nor was it easy.

He admitted, 'I have had a lot on my mind. I have been used to action and sharp decisions for most of my life. Merely to make sail and face an empty sea day by day is something alien to me. Sometimes I feel more like a grocery-captain than that of a man-o'-war.'

She watched him thoughtfully. 'I can believe it. I should have realised earlier.' She gave a slow smile, her lashes hiding her eyes. 'Then maybe I would not have offended you.'

Bolitho shook his head. 'Much of it was my fault. I have been so long in ships of war that I have become used to expecting others to share my dedication. If there is a fire I expect all close by to quench it. If a man tries to overrun authority by mutiny or in an enemy's name I would call for others to strike him down, or do so myself.' He faced her gravely. 'That is why I expected you to aid the men injured in the wreck.' He shrugged. 'Again, I *expected* it. I did not ask.'

She nodded. 'That admission must have surprised you, as much as it did me, Captain.' She showed her teeth. 'It has cleared the air a little?'

'Yes.'

He touched his forehead unconsciously, plucking at the rebellious lock of black hair which clung to the skin with sweat.

He saw her eyes widen as she caught sight of the livid scar beneath and said quickly, 'Forgive me, ma'am. I must go and examine my charts before we dine.'

She watched him as he stood up and said, 'You wear your authority well, Captain.' She glanced at her sleeping husband. 'Unlike some.'

Bolitho did not know how to reply. 'I am afraid that is hardly for me to discuss, ma'am.'

He looked up as feet thudded across the deck and shadows flitted above the open skylight.

She asked, 'What is it?'

He did not see the annoyance in her eyes.

'I am not sure. A ship perhaps. I gave orders I was to be informed so that I can take avoiding action.'

Noddall paused, two forks in his hand. 'I 'eard no 'ail from th' mast'ead, sir.'

There was a rap at the door and Herrick stood in the entrance, his chest heaving from exertion.

'I am sorry to burst in.' He looked past Bolitho towards the woman. 'It would be better if you came with me, sir.'

Bolitho stepped from the cabin and pulled the door behind him. In the doorway which opened on to the ship's wardroom he saw a small group waiting for him. They looked confused. Stricken. Like strangers. There was Bellairs, accompanied by his towering sergeant, Triphook, his horse teeth bared as if to snap at an unseen attacker, and cowering just behind him was the ship's cooper, a small hunched petty officer named Joseph Duff. He was the second oldest man aboard, and wore steel-rimmed spectacles at his work, although he usually managed to hide them from his messmates for much of the time.

Herrick said quietly, 'Duff has reported that most of the fresh water is undrinkable, sir.' He swallowed under Bolitho's stare. 'He was doing his usual inspection and has just reported to the ship's corporal.'

Triphook was murmuring fervently, 'In all my days. Never, *never* have I seen the like!'

Bolitho beckoned to the cooper. 'Well, Duff, I am waiting. What is this find which you have discovered?'

Duff blinked at him through the oval glasses. He looked like a grey-haired mole.

'Me usual inspection, sir.'

He grew smaller as they crowded round him. Soames had come from his own cabin, and loomed over Bellairs's shoulder like a cliff.

Duff continued shakily, 'The casks was all good 'uns, I saw to that, sir. First thing I always looks for. I learned me work under a fine old cooper in the *Gladiator* when I first took on, sir, an'—'

'For God's sake, Duff!' Herrick sounded desperate. *'Tell the captain!'*

Duff lowered his head. 'Most of the casks is foul, sir. They *'as* to be.'

Sergeant Coaker stepped forward, his boots creaking as the ship tilted in a sudden trough. He was holding a small bundle, but keeping it away from his tunic as if it were alive.

'Open it.'

The sergeant unfolded the parcel very carefully, his face set like stone.

Bolitho felt the deck soaring violently, tasted the vomit clawing at his throat. Screwed up, as if at the instant shock of amputation, it was a human hand.

Soames choked, 'In the name of Christ!'

Duff said in a small voice, 'In all of 'em sir. 'Cept the last two casks by the bulk'ead.'

Triphook said heavily, 'He's right, sir. Bits of flesh.' He trembled violently, his face breaking out in sweat. 'The work of a demon!'

There was a sharp cry of horror, and Bolitho stepped in front of the cooper as Mrs. Raymond gasped, 'I'm going to be sick.' He saw her leaning against the marine sentry, her face like chalk as she stared fixedly at the group by the wardroom.

Bolitho snapped, 'Get rid of that object!' To Noddall's hovering shadow he added, 'Call that damned maid and attend to the lady!' His mind was reeling from Duff's gruesome discovery. What it meant, and what he now had to do. 'Fetch the surgeon.'

Bellairs dabbed his lips with a handkerchief. 'Carry on Sar'nt Coaker. Pass the word for Mr. Whitmarsh.' He glanced at the others. 'Though I doubt he will be able to assist, what?'

Herrick asked, 'Would you care to come in here, sir?' He stood aside to allow Bolitho to enter the wardroom.

It was small and compact, the table laid for a meal, and at odds with the twelve-pounders which were lashed at each open port. Bolitho sat down heavily on a seat chest and stared through the nearest gun port. The fair wind and dancing water held no more attraction. Danger was within the ship. His ship.

Herrick prompted, 'Some wine, sir.'

When he turned Bolitho saw the others watching him. Soames at the top of the table. Bellairs and Triphook seated on the opposite side. In those fleeting seconds he recalled his own life as a junior lieutenant in a frigate. The wardroom was the place you shared not merely your food and your life, you shared your doubts, and drew on your companions for help whenever it was needed. Aft, behind his bulkhead, the captain had been a remote, godly character beyond reach. At no time that he could recall had he imagined a captain required anything but obedience.

It even *felt* different here. Pistols in a rack. Some shirts hanging to air which the wardroom servant had just washed. The smell of something simmering in a pot.

He replied, 'Thank you. I would relish a glass just now.'

They relaxed slightly and Soames said, 'It will mean turning back, sir.' He thought about it. 'Or making for the African coast mebbee.'

Feet creaked outside the door and then Mudge pushed his way into the wardroom, his grey hair sprouting as he threw his hat into a corner.

'God blast me eyes, but what's this bloody deed I've bin told?' He saw Bolitho and muttered, 'Beggin' yer pardon, sir. I was not expecting to discover you in 'ere.'

Herrick held out a glass. 'Some Rhenish, sir.' He did not smile, but his eyes were calm. Almost pleading. 'Still fairly fresh, I think.'

Bolitho sipped it gratefully. 'Thank you.' He tasted the sourness in his throat. 'After what I have just witnessed . . .' He swung round as the surgeon lurched through the door, his shirt unbuttoned, his gaze bleary.

'You have been told the news, Mr. Whitmarsh?'

He watched the effort he was making to focus his eyes, the growth of stubble on his chin. Whitmarsh had been quietly making up for all the time he had stayed with his patients.

'*Well?*'

Whitmarsh groped his way to a gun and leaned on it with both hands, sucking air through the open port like a drowning man.

'I heard, sir.' He retched. 'I heard.'

Bolitho watched him impassively. 'As the water casks were fresh when stowed aboard at Spithead, it would seem likely that these human fragments came from your surgery.' He waited, feeling pity for the man, but knowing the need for haste. 'Would you agree?'

'I expect so.'

Whitmarsh lurched to the table and poured a large measure of wine.

Bolitho said sharply, 'If you drink that, Mr. Whitmarsh, I will see to it that you do not get another drop while you are under my command.' He stood up. 'Now, think, man! Who could have done this?'

Whitmarsh stared at the glass in his hand, his body swaying badly, despite the easy motion.

'I was kept busy. They were in a poor way, sir. I had my loblolly boys and my mate to assist me.' He screwed up his red face in an effort to remember, the sweat dripping off his chin like rain. 'It was Sullivan. I gave him him the job of clearing amputated limbs and the like from my sickbay. He was very helpful.' He nodded vaguely. 'It's all coming to me now. Sullivan.' He turned and stared fixedly at Bolitho. 'The man *you* had flogged, sir.'

Herrick said harshly, 'Don't be so bloody impertinent to the captain!'

Bolitho found he was suddenly very calm. 'In your opinion, Mr. Whitmarsh, will the casks be any further use after this?'

'None.' The surgeon was still glaring at him. 'They must be scoured at once. The contents thrown overboard. A mouthful of that water, after gangrenous flesh has been in it, and you'll have a raging fever aboard! I've known it happen. There's no cure.'

Bolitho placed his glass on the table very slowly. Giving his mind time to steady.

'It seems that you are not the only one who wishes to turn back, Mr. Herrick. Now take hold of Sullivan and guard him before he does some other mischief.' He turned to Whitmarsh. 'I have not finished with you yet!'

Feet clattered on the quarterdeck ladder and Herrick reappeared in the doorway.

'Sir! That fool Sullivan is aloft on the cro'jack yard! He's raving mad! Nobody can get near him!'

Then Bolitho heard men shouting, more feet pounding overhead.

He said, 'I will go up.'

He found the gangways crowded with seamen and marines, while Don Puigserver and his Spanish lieutenant had joined Davy by the quarterdeck rail to watch a bosun's mate who was clinging to the mizzen shrouds and trying to reach Sullivan. The seaman was perched on the yard, totally indifferent to the great billowing sail at his back and the hard sunlight which lanced across his body. He was completely naked, but for his belt, where he carried the broad bladed dirk which had brought about his flogging in the first place.

Davy said anxiously, 'I did not know what to do, sir. The man is obviously moonstruck or worse.'

The bosun's mate bellowed, 'Now yew get down on deck, or by the livin' Jesus I'll pitch you there meself!'

Sullivan threw back his head and laughed. It was a shrill, unnerving sound.

'Now, now, Mr. Roskilly! What would you do then? Lay your little rope's end on me?' He laughed again and then pulled out the knife. 'Come along then, matey! I'm awaitin' you, you goddamned lickspittle!'

Bolitho called, 'Come down, Roskilly! You'll do no good by getting killed!'

Sullivan craned under the vibrating yard. 'Well, blow me down, mates, an' who 'ave we 'ere? Our gallant captain, no less!' He rocked with laughter. 'An' 'e's all aback 'cause poor old Tom Sullivan's spoiled the water for him!'

Some of the watching seamen had been grinning at the spectacle on the quarterdeck. The mention of water soon altered that.

Bolitho looked at the upturned faces, feeling the spreading alarm like the edge of a fire.

He walked aft, his shoes loud in the sudden hush around him. Below the yard he stopped and looked up.

'Come along, Sullivan.' He was in the sunlight and with no shade from the bellying sail above. He felt the sweat pouring down his chest and thighs, just as he could sense the other man's hatred. 'You have done enough today!'

Sullivan cackled. 'Did you hear that, lads? Done enough!' He twisted on the yard, the glare playing across the scars on his back, pale against the tanned skin. 'You've done enough to me, Cap'n bloody Bolitho!'

Herrick snapped, 'Sergeant Coaker! Have one of your marksmen brought aft! That man is a damned danger up there!'

'Belay that!' Bolitho kept his eyes on the crossjack yard. 'He is past reason. I'll not have him shot down like some mad dog.'

He sensed Puigserver was watching him and not the man on the yard, and that Allday was close by, a cutlass in his hand. But they were all excluded. It was between him and Sullivan.

He called, 'I am *asking* you, Sullivan!' He recalled the woman's face in the cabin. *I did not ask.*

'You go to hell, Captain!' Sullivan was screaming now, his naked body twisting on the yard as if in torment. 'An' I'll take you there 'now!'

Bolitho hardly saw his hand move, just the brief flash of sunlight on the blade, and then gasped as the knife cut through his sleeve before embedding itself in the deck by his right shoe. So great was the force that nearly an inch of blade was driven into the planking.

Sullivan was transfixed, a long streamer of spittle trailing to the wind as he stared down at Bolitho at the foot of the mast.

Bolitho remained motionless, feeling the blood running down his elbow and forearm and on to the deck. He did not take his eyes off Sullivan, and the concentration helped to overcome the searing pain left by the blade.

Sullivan stood up wildly and began to scramble outboard along the yard. Everybody began to yell at once, and Bolitho felt Herrick gripping his arm, another wrapping a cloth around it, deadening the pain.

Whitmarsh had appeared below the nettings, and he, too, was shouting at the man framed against the clear sky.

Sullivan turned and spoke in a level voice for the first time. 'And you, too, *Doctor*! God damn you to *hell*!' Then he jumped out and down, his body hitting the water with a violent splash.

For a moment he floated past the quarter, and as the spanker's great shadow passed over him he clasped his hands above his head and vanished.

Herrick said, 'We could never pick him up. If we tried to heave-to under this canvas, we'd tear the sticks out of her.'

Bolitho did not know to whom he was speaking. Perhaps to himself.

He walked to the hatch, holding his torn and bloodied sleeve with one hand. He saw the bosun's mate, Roskilly, pulling the knife out of the deck. He was a strong man, but it took him two attempts to tug it clear.

Puigserver followed him below and then stepped in front of him.

'That was a brave thing you did, *Capitan*.' He sighed. 'But he could have killed you.'

Bolitho nodded. The pain was getting worse. 'We have some hard times ahead, *Señor*. We must find water, and soon.' He tightened his jaw. 'But I am not turning back.'

Puigserver eyed him sadly. 'You made a gesture. One which might have ended your life. And all for a madman.'

Bolitho walked to the cabin. 'Maybe we were both mad.'

Herrick hurried after him, and as they entered the cabin Bolitho saw there was a chair directly under the skylight. Raymond must have been standing on it to watch the drama overhead.

Mrs. Raymond was aft by the windows. She looked very pale, but came towards him saying, 'Your arm, Captain.' She shouted to her maid, 'Bandages!'

Bolitho realised that Herrick was in the cabin. 'Well?'

Herrick watched him worriedly. 'What you did—'

'It could have killed me. I know.' Bolitho forced a smile. 'I have already been told.'

Herrick breathed out slowly. 'And I believed I knew you, sir.'

'And now?' He looked at him steadily. 'Thomas?'

Herrick grinned. 'I only know that you never cease to surprise me. *And* others.' He gestured to the deckhead. 'A seaman who has been cursing and complaining for near on a month was just heard to damn Sullivan's soul for threatening the life of *his* captain.' His grin faded. 'But I'd rather you rallied our people in some other way, sir.'

Bolitho held out his arm as the maid carried a basin to the desk.

'If you *know* of any way to keep up their spirits, Thomas, I'd be obliged to hear it. In the meantime, call the hands and get the royals on her. I want every stitch she can carry.' He checked him as he made for the door. 'And pass the word. One pint of water per day.' He glanced around the cabin. 'Officers and passengers included.'

Herrick hesitated. 'And the surgeon, sir?'

Bolitho looked down at the maid as she cleaned the deep cut on his arm. She returned his glance boldly.

He said, 'I am in good hands, it seems. I will think about Mr. Whitmarsh when I have more time.' He added grimly, 'And at this moment, time is of the greatest value in the world.'

Bolitho waited by the open stern windows and watched the moon making a fine path across the water. The sea looked unusually choppy, but he knew it was from a steep undertow which explored the depths many miles from the African coast. At his back he heard the others moving into the cabin and finding somewhere to sit, the sounds of goblets and wine as Noddall went about his business. Despite the cool air after the day's blazing sunlight his body felt drained and stiff, and about him the ship creaked and groaned, her timbers so dried-out that it was a wonder she was not leaking like an old bucket.

A week since Sullivan had jumped to his death, Seven long days while he had taken his ship inshore time and time again, only to stand off at the report of some sail, or an unexplained sighting of a native craft.

Now, he could delay no longer. He had been visited by Whitmarsh that afternoon, a man so tormented by his own worries that it had been a difficult interview. Whitmarsh had made it quite definite that he could no longer be held responsible if Bolitho persisted in staying clear of land. The two remaining casks of water were almost empty, and what remained was little better than scum. More men were lying ill on the orlop deck, and those fit enough to work ship had to be watched by the minute. Tempers flared, and petty officers went about their duties with an eye on their backs for a knifethrust in a momentary display of madness.

Herrick reported, 'All ready, sir.' Like the others. Tense. Watchful.

Bolitho turned and looked around his officers. All but Soames, who was on duty, were present. Even the three midshipmen. He watched them gravely. It might teach them something, he thought.

'I intend to close the land again tomorrow.'

He saw Don Puigserver by the bulkhead with his lieutenant. Raymond a few feet away from him, rubbing his face in sharp, agitated movements.

Davy said, 'Makes fine sense, sir.' He swallowed some wine. 'If we give our people more rum to drink as we cut down the water, we'll be too tipsy to do anything!' He forced a smile. 'A fine situation it would be!'

Bolitho turned to Mudge. He was in the largest chair still wearing his thick coat, and staring up at the open skylight as a moth darted into the lantern's beam. He saw Bolitho's expression and sighed.

'I called at this place just the once, sir. When I was master's mate in the *Windsor*, Indiaman. We was in much the same trouble ourselves then. No water, becalmed for weeks on end, an' with 'alf the people goin' wild with thirst.'

Bolitho asked, 'But there *is* water available?'

Mudge moved his chair towards the desk in short, squeaky jerks. Then he jabbed the open chart with his thumb.

'We'm now in th' Mozambique Channel, as we all knows.' He glared at Midshipman Armitage. ''Cept for some too hignorant to *learn* aright!' He continued in a more unruffled tone, 'Th' African coast is fair wild 'ereabouts, an' not a lot be known about it. Ships put in, of course.' His eyes gleamed as he looked up at Bolitho. 'For water. To trade mebbee. An' to find theirselves some black ivory from time to time.'

Midshipman Keen was leaning over his shoulder, his face the only one present which showed little sign of strain.

'Black ivory, sir?'

Herrick said sharply, 'Slaves.'

Mudge leaned back comfortably. 'It follows that we must be careful. Land in force, get the water, if I can recall exactly where it is, and stand out to sea agin.'

Bellairs said, 'My marines will give a good account, thank you!'

Mudge regarded him scornfully. 'Just so, Cap'n Bellairs, sir. In their pretty coats, with their drums and fifes, I can picture it a fair treat!' He added harshly, 'They'd 'ave 'em for breakfast afore they could polish their bloody boots!'

'Well, *really*!' Bellairs was shocked.

Bolitho nodded. 'Very well then. The wind is staying with us, so we should be able to anchor by noon tomorrow.'

Mudge agreed. 'Aye. But not close inshore, sir. There's a fat bit o' reef just around the point. It'll mean every boat in th' water, an' a 'ard pull for all 'ands.'

'Yes.' Bolitho looked at Davy. 'You can arrange the arming of each boat with the gunner. Swivels for launch and cutter. Musketoons for the rest.' He glanced round at their intent faces. 'I'll want an officer with each party. Some of our people will need watching, if only for their own sakes.' He let his words sink in. 'Remember it well. Many of them are quite raw to this sort of work, although because we have been together for over two months, you may see them as veterans. They are not, so treat them accordingly. *Lead* them, do not be content to leave your work to others less qualified.'

He saw the midshipmen exchanging glances like boys about to take part in some private escapade. Keen, his eyes sparkling with excitement. Little Penn, openly impressed by being included. Poor Armitage, his forehead raw red from being on watch for a few moments without a hat. They were even less experienced than most of the men.

He looked at the chart. But for Sullivan they might have made the whole voyage to Madras without a pause, despite their shortages. Herrick had tried to help by saying it was bad luck. Puigserver had stated that he was behind him, whatever he decided was best for the ship. But it was still his decision, and nobody else could change that.

Some of those present in the cabin had stopped speaking with the surgeon altogether, and perhaps for that reason alone Bolitho had made no further comment about his choice of Sullivan as a helper, giving him the opportunity, crazy or not, of fouling the water supply. He saw him only on matters of sick reports, and each time was shocked by his appearance. The man was boiling inside, bitter, and yet unable to share his problems. He did not even want to.

He heard a woman's voice saw the others look up at the skylight as feet passed overhead. Mrs. Raymond and her maid taking their usual stroll under the stars. He hoped Soames would ensure they did not stray from the quarterdeck. He would not answer for their safety at the hands of some of the seamen. He could understand how many of them felt.

To the volunteers it must seem a far cry from the recruiting posters, and to the men from the prison hulks it might now appear to be a bad exchange of circumstances. Even those hiding from crimes committed ashore would find room for doubt and resentment. The crimes would have faded with the fear of arrest and trial. But the heat and thirst, and the daily grind of disciplined duty were only too real.

He saw Raymond biting his lip, his eyes following the footsteps as if he was seeing through the deckhead itself. If anything, he and his wife were moving further apart by being confined in the ship. It was a strange relationship.

He thought back over the past days and one particular incident. He had been in his small makeshift cabin in the chart space, and Allday had been changing the bandage on his arm for him. She had entered the cabin without knocking, in fact, neither of them had heard her approach. She had stood by the open port, quite relaxed, and had watched him without saying a word. Bolitho had been stripped to the waist, and as he reached for a fresh shirt she had said softly, 'I see you bear yet another scar, Captain.'

Bolitho's hand had gone to his side, suddenly conscious of the ragged mark where a pistol ball had missed his ribs by a thread. He had seen it exactly, as he was seeing it now. The privateer's tilting deck, the American lieutenant running towards him, taking aim. The crash of a shot. The sharp, stabbing agony. Oblivion.

Allday had said rudely, 'The captain's dressing! Ships' ways are different from those ashore, it seems!'

But she had stood firm, her lips slightly parted, while she watched him. But how could she have understood what he was thinking? That the ball had been fired by one of his own brother's officers. A traitor. A wanted renegade, now dead and forgotten by most.

But not by me.

He shook himself out of his brooding thoughts. Nothing mattered now but the work in hand. Water. All that he needed to take them to Madras. Beyond that was another challenge. It could wait.

He said, 'That is all, gentlemen.' He realised he had spoken more abruptly than intended and added, 'We have a fine ship. One of the most efficient and modern devices created by man. We can give a good account of ourselves to any vessel but a ship of the line.' He paused as Herrick smiled at him, bridging the gap between them as he, too, remembered. 'Except for rare, and not to be encouraged, occasions! But without water to drink we are like stumbling old men, with neither the means nor the will to face another day. Remember what I have said. Be vigilant. For the moment that is all I ask of you.'

They filed out of the cabin, leaving him with Puigserver and Raymond. Raymond looked hopefully at the Spaniard, but when he made no attempt to take his usual walk on deck he, too, left the cabin.

Bolitho sat down and watched the moonlight as it played across the *Undine*'s bubbling wake.

'What is the matter with him, *Señor?*' It was strange how easy it was to talk to him.

Just over a year back he had been an enemy. One Bolitho would have killed in battle had he not called for quarter. He smiled to himself. Or the other way round. He was a powerful man, that was certain, and much of his counsel he kept to himself. But Bolitho trusted him. The ship's company, for the most part, had also accepted him as their own. Like Allday, who had long given up trying to pronounce his name, they called him *Mister Pigsliver*. But they said it with something near to affection.

Puigserver regarded him with quiet amusement.

'My dear *Captain*, he is like a watchdog. He fears for his wife, what *she* will do, rather than what others will do to her!' He chuckled, the sound rising from his belly. 'She, I think, is beginning to enjoy the game, knowing that every man aboard sees her in a different eye. She stands proudly, a tigress in our midst.'

'You seem to know a great deal about her, *Señor*.'

The smile broadened. 'You know your ships, *Capitan*. Unlike me, I fear you still have much to learn about women, eh?'

Bolitho made to protest and then changed his mind. The memory was still too painful to leave room for a denial.

6

Attack Overland

'Well, Thomas, what d'you make of it at close quarters?' Bolitho's voice was hushed, as with the others around him he stared towards the shore.

They had made a careful approach since dawn, seeing the land gaining shape and substance, and then as the sun had found them again, they had watched the colour, the endless panorama of green.

With two experienced leadsmen in the chains, and under minimum canvas, *Undine* had felt her way towards the land. It had looked like an untouched world, with jungle so thick it seemed impossible for anything to move freely away from the sea.

Herrick replied quietly, 'The master seems satisfied, sir.' He trained his telescope over the hammock nettings. 'As he described it. A round headland to the north. And that strange-looking hill about a mile inland.'

Bolitho stepped on to a bollard and peered down over the nettings. *Undine* had finally dropped anchor some four cables offshore to give her sea-room and a safe depth at all times. Nevertheless, it looked very shallow, and he could even see the great shadow of *Undine*'s coppered hull on the bottom. Pale sand. Like that on the various small, crescent-shaped beaches they had seen on their cautious approach.

Long trailers of strange weed, writhing to the current far below the ship as if in a tired sort of dance. But to larboard, as the ship swung to her cable he saw other shapes, browns and greens, like stains in the water. Reefs. Mudge was right to be so careful. Not that anyone would need reminding after *Nervion*'s fate.

Alongside, the first boats had already been swayed out, and Shellabeer, the boatswain, was gesticulating with his fists at some Spanish seamen who were baling one of them. It would do the frail hulls good to be afloat again, Bolitho thought.

He said absently, 'I shall go with the boats, and you will keep a good watch in case of trouble.'

He could almost feel Herrick's unspoken protest, but added, 'If anything goes wrong ashore it might help some of our people if they see I'm sharing it with them.' He turned and clapped Herrick's shoulder. 'Besides which, I feel like stretching my legs. It is my prerogative.'

On the gun deck Davy was striding back and forth inspecting the men mustered for the boats, checking weapons and the tackle for hoisting and lowering water casks when the work was begun.

Overhead the sky was very pale, as if the sun had boiled the colour from it and had spread it instead across the glittering stretch of sea between ship and shore.

Bolitho marvelled at the stillness. Just an occasional necklace of white surf along the nearest beach and at the foot of the headland. It was as if it was holding its breath, and he could imagine a thousand eyes watching the anchored frigate from amongst the trees.

There were loud thumps as the swivel guns were lowered into the bows of launch and cutter, and more shouted orders while the bell-mouthed musketoons found their proper mountings in gig and pinnace. The jolly boat was to remain with the ship. It was too small for the great casks, and might be needed in an emergency.

He rubbed his chin and stared at the land. Emergency. It appeared safe enough. All the way along the coast, as they had slipped past one bay or inlet after another, and all of which had seemed identical to everyone but Mudge, he had waited for some sign, a hint of danger. But not a boat drawn up on the sand, not a wisp of smoke from a fire, not even a bird had broken the stillness.

'Boats ready, sir!' Shellabeer tilted his swarthy face in the glare.

Bolitho walked to the rail and looked down at the gun deck. The seamen seemed altered yet again. Perhaps because of their cutlasses, the way they glanced at each other, their torment of thirst momentarily put aside. Most of them were very different from the men who had first joined the ship. Their bared backs were well browned, with only an occasional scar of sunburn to mark the foolish or the unwary.

He called, 'Over yonder is Africa, lads.' He felt the rustle of excitement expanding like a wind over corn. 'You'll be seeing many more places before we are homeward bound again. Do as you are bid, stay with your parties, and no harm should come to you.' He hardened his tone. 'But it is a dangerous country, and the natives hereabouts have had little cause to like or trust the foreign sailorman. So keep a good watch, and work well with the casks.' He nodded. 'Man your boats.'

Mudge joined him at the gangway as the first men swung their way down the side.

'I should be a'goin' with you, sir. I've told me best master's mate, Fowlar, what to look for, an' 'e's a good man, that 'e be.'

Bolitho lifted his arms as Allday buckled on his sword.

'Then what troubles you, Mr. Mudge?'

Mudge scowled. 'Time was when I could swim 'alf a mile an' then march another with a full load on me back!'

Herrick, grinned. 'And still have the wind to bed a fine wench, I'll be bound!'

Mudge glared at him. 'Your time'll come, Mr. 'Errick. It ain't no pleasure, gettin' old!'

Bolitho smiled. 'Your value is here.'

To Herrick he said, 'Rig boarding nets during our stay. With only an anchor watch and the marines at your back, you might be in bother if someone tries to surprise you.' He touched his arm. 'I know. I am over-cautious. I can read your face like a chart. But better so than dead.' He glanced at the shore. 'Especially here.'

He walked to the entry port. 'The boats will return two by two. Send the rest of the men as soon as you can. They'll tire easily enough in this heat.'

He saw Puigserver wave to him from the gangway, and Raymond watching from right aft by his wife's little canopy. He touched his hat to the side party and climbed quickly down into the gig where Allday waited by the tiller.

'Shove off!'

One by one the boats idled clear of the frigate's shadow, and then with oars moving in unison turned towards the land. Bolitho remained standing to examine his little flotilla.

Lieutenant Soames with the launch, *Undine*'s largest boat, every inch of space filled with men and casks, while in the bows a gun captain crouched over the loaded swivel like some kind of figurehead. Then the cutter, also deeply laden, with Davy in control his figure very slim against that of Mr. Pryke, *Undine*'s portly carpenter. As was proper, Pryke was going ashore in the hopes of finding timber suitable for small repairs about the ship.

Midshipman Keen, accompanied by little Penn, had the pinnace, and Bolitho could see them bobbing about with obvious excitement as they pulled steadily across the water.

Bolitho glanced astern at his ship, seeing the figures on her deck already small and impersonal. Someone was in the cabin, and he guessed it was Mrs. Raymond, watching the boats, avoiding her husband, probably neither.

Then he looked down at the men in the gig, at the weapons between their straddled legs, at the way they avoided his scrutiny. Right forward he saw a man moving the musketoon from side to side to free the mount from caked salt, and realised it was Turpin, the one who had tried so desperately to deceive Davy at Spithead. He saw Bolitho watching him and held up his arm. In place of his hand he had a hook of bright steel. He called, 'The gunner had it fixed up for me, sir!' He was grinning. 'Better'n the real thing!'

Bolitho smiled at him. He at least seemed in good spirits.

He watched the slow moving hulls. About eighty officers and men with more to follow when he could spare the boats. He sat down and shaded his eyes with his hat. As he did so he touched the scar above his eye, remembering that other watering party he had been with so long ago. The sudden charge, screams all about him, that great towering savage brandishing a cutlass he had just seized from a dying sailor. He had seen it only for a second, and then fallen senseless, his face a mask of blood. It had been a close-run thing. But for his coxswain, it would have been the end.

Herrick probably resented his landing with this watering party. It was work normally given to a lieutenant. But that memory, like the scar, was a constant reminder of what could go wrong without any sort of warning.

'Cable to go, Captain!' Allday eased the tiller bar slightly.

Bolitho started. He must have been dreaming. *Undine* looked far away now. A graceful toy. While right across the bows and reaching out on either hand like huge green arms, was the land.

Once again Mudge's memory proved to be sure and reliable. Within two hours of beaching the boats and sorting the hands into working parties, the master's mate, Fowlar, reported finding a little stream, and that the water was the freshest thing he had tasted for years.

The work was begun immediately. Armed pickets were placed at carefully chosen vantage points, and lookouts sent to the top of the small hill, below which Mudge's stream gurgled away into the dense jungle. After the first uncertainty of stepping on to dry land, with all the usual unsteadiness to their sea-legs, the sailors soon settled down to the task. Pryke, the carpenter, and his mates quickly assembled some heavy sledges upon which the filled casks would be hauled down to the boats, and while the cooper stood watchfully at the stream the other men were busy with axes, clearing a path through the trees under Fowlar's personal supervision.

With Midshipman Penn trotting at his heels to act as messenger, Bolitho retained contact between beach and stream, making several journeys to ensure the operation was working smoothly. Lieutenant Soames was in charge of the beach, and of allocating more men to the work as they were ferried ashore. Davy had the inland part, while Keen was usually to be seen with some armed men at his back trudging around the labouring sailors to make sure there were no unwelcome visitors.

Fowlar had discovered two native fireplaces almost immediately. But they were decayed and scattered, and it seemed unlikely that anyone had been near them for months. Nevertheless, as he paused to watch over the progress of each party, Bolitho was conscious of a feeling of menace. Of hostility, which was hard to define.

On his way inland to the stream yet again he had to stand aside as a heavy sledge, hauled by some two dozen blaspheming seamen, careered past him, shaking the undergrowth, and making several great red birds flap between the trees, squawking discordantly. Bolitho watched the birds and then stepped back on to the crude trail. It was good to know something was alive here, he thought. Beneath the trees, where the sky was hidden from view, the air was heavy, and stank of rotting vegetation. Here and there, something clicked and rustled, or a small beady eye glittered momentarily in filtered sunlight before vanishing just as swiftly.

Penn gasped, 'Might be *snakes*, sir!' He was panting hard, his shirt plastered to his body from his exertions to keep up.

Bolitho found Davy beneath a wall of overhanging rock, marking his list as yet another cask was sealed by Duff for the bumpy ride to the beach.

The second lieutenant straightened his back and observed, 'Going well, sir.'

'Good.' Bolitho stooped and cupped his hands into the stream. It was like wine, despite the rotten looking roots which sprouted from either bank. 'We will finish before dark.'

He looked up at a patch of blue sky as the trees gave a stealthy rustle. It was unmoving air below the matted branches, but above and to seaward the wind was holding well.

'I am going up the hill, Mr. Davy.' He thought he heard Penn sigh with despair. 'I hope your lookouts are awake.'

It was a long hard walk, and when they moved clear of the trees for the final climb to the summit, Bolitho felt the sun searing down on his shoulders, the heat through his shoes from the rough stones, like coals off a grate.

But the two lookouts seemed contented enough. In their stained trousers and shirts, with their tanned faces almost hidden by straw hats, they looked more like castaways than British seamen.

They had rigged a small shelter with a scrap of canvas, behind which lay their weapons, water flasks and a large brass telescope.

One knuckled his forehead and said ' 'Orizon's clear, Cap'n!'

Bolitho tugged his hat over his eyes as he stared down the hill. The coastline was more uneven than he had imagined, water glittering between the thick layers of trees to reveal some inlet or cover not marked on any chart. Inland, and towards a distant barrier of tall hills, there was nothing but an undulating sea of trees. So close-knit, it looked possible to walk upright across the top of them.

He picked up the telescope and trained it on the ship. She was writhing and bending in a surface haze, but he saw the boats moving back and forth, very slowly, like tired water-beetles. He felt grit and dust under his fingers, and guessed the telescope had spent more time lying on the hillside than in use.

He heard Penn sucking noisily at a water flask, and could sense the lookouts willing him to leave them in peace. Theirs might be a thirsty job, but it was far easier than hauling casks through the forest. He moved the glass again. All those men, sledges and casks, yet from here he could see none of them. Even the beach was shielded. The boats, as they drew near the shore, appeared to vanish into the trees, as if swallowed whole.

Bolitho turned to his right, the movement making the men stir with alarm. In the telescope's lens the trees and slivers of trapped water grew and receded as he continued his search. Something had touched the corner of his eye, but what? The lookouts were watching him doubtfully, each caught in his own attitude as if mesmerised.

A trick of light. He blinked and rubbed his eye. Nothing.

He began another slow scrutiny. Thick, characterless forest. Or was that merely what he *expected* to see? And therefore . . . He stiffened and held his breath. When he lowered the glass the picture fell away into the distance. He waited, counting seconds, allowing his breathing to steady.

The lookouts had begun to whisper again, and Penn was drinking as before. They probably imagined he had been too long in the sun.

He lifted the glass very carefully. There, to the right, where he had already noticed a faint gleam of water, was something darker, at odds with the forest's greens and browns. He stared at it until his eye watered so painfully he could not continue.

Then he closed the glass with a snap and said, 'There is a ship yonder.' He saw Penn gaping at him, transfixed. 'To the south'rd. It must be some sort of inlet which we did not see earlier.'

He shaded his eyes, trying to estimate the distance, where it lay in relation to *Undine* and the beach where he had come ashore.

One of the lookouts exclaimed, 'Oi never saw nothin', sir.' He looked frightened, and worse.

Bolitho stared past him, trying to think.

'Take this glass and make sure you can see it 'now!'

He knew the seaman was more frightened of his captain, or what might become of him because of his negligence, than anything this discovery might mean.

Bolitho's mind recorded all these reactions as he said, 'Have you found it?'

'Aye, sir!' The man bobbed unhappily. ' 'Tis a mast, right enough.'

'Thank you.' Bolitho added dryly, 'Keep your eye on it. I do not want it to vanish again!'

Penn dropped the flask and scuttled after him as he strode down the hill.

'Wh-what might it mean, sir?'

'Several things.' He felt the trees, looming around him, a small relief from the sun's torment. 'They may have sighted us and are lying low until we weigh. Perhaps they are intent on some other mischief, I am not certain.'

He quickened his pace, ignoring creepers and fronds which plucked at his body. But for that brief flaw in the lens's picture he would have seen nothing, *known* nothing about the other vessel. Perhaps it would have been better that way. Maybe he was worrying to no purpose.

He found Davy as before, lounging in the shade of the hillside, his features relaxed as he watched his men filling the casks.

'Where is Mr. Fowlar?'

Davy came out of his torpor with a jerk. 'Er, on the beach, sir.'

'*Damn!*'

Another hard mile before he could examine Fowlar's chart and Mudge's notes. He looked up at the sky. Hours yet before sunset, but when it did come it would be quick. Shutting out the light like a curtain.

'I have discovered a ship, Mr. Davy. Well hidden, to the south'rd of us.' He saw the carpenter emerge from the undergrowth, a saw glinting in one fist. 'Take charge here, Mr. Pryke.' He beckoned to Davy. 'We are going to the beach.'

Pryke nodded, his fat face glowing like a ripe apple. 'Aye, sir.' He looked at Duff. 'There be only five more casks, by my reckonin'.'

'Well, speed the work. I want our people mustered as soon as the last one is filled.

Davy hurried along at his side, his handsome face puzzled.

'Do you think this ship may be an enemy, sir?'

'I intend to find out.'

They completed the journey in silence, and Bolitho knew that Davy, like the lookouts, thought he was making too much of it.

Fowlar listened to him calmly and then examined his chart.

'If it is where I believe, then it is not marked here. So it must lie somewhere 'twixt this beach and the next bay.' He made a mark. 'About there, I would suggest, sir.'

'Could we reach it before dark? Overland?'

Fowlar's eyes widened but he answered, 'It looks close enough, sir. No more'n three mile or so. But that is four times as much in the jungle.' He dropped his eyes from Bolitho's gaze. 'You *might* be able to do it, sir.'

Davy asked, 'But if we wait until tomorrow, sir? We could have *Undine* anchored nearer this vessel you have found.'

'It would take too long. She may have weighed and gone overnight. And if they are aware of our presence and purpose, a boat attack would be useless in daylight, and in a confined inlet. You should know that, Mr. Davy.'

Davy looked at his shoes. 'Yes, sir.'

Another heavy cask lurched down the beach, the men panting like animals running from the hounds.

Soames, who had trudged up the beach to listen, said suddenly, 'She might be a slaver. In which case she will be well armed.' He rubbed his chin and nodded. 'Yours is a good plan, sir.' His thick forefingers scratched over the chart. 'We could cross the bottom of the hill where it reaches for the sea and strike south. If we travel lightly we should be at the inlet before dark.' He looked at Davy, his eyes hard. 'I'll pick some good men. Ones who won't falter when the passage gets rough.'

Davy said nothing, he was obviously smarting because Soames had offered a course of action rather than an unthinking suggestion.

Bolitho looked towards the ship. 'Very well. We will rest the hands for half an hour. Then we will begin. Forty men should be sufficient if we are careful. It may be a complete waste of time.' He thought of the silent jungle. *Watching*. 'But to be anchored so dangerously inland? I doubt it.'

He beckoned to Penn. 'I will write my orders for the first lieutenant, and you will take them across directly. *Undine* will send her boats tomorrow morning and pick us up from seaward. By then we should know.' He glanced at Davy. 'One way or the other.'

He saw Keen coming out of the trees, a pistol hanging casually from his belt. As he turned towards the sea he halted and raised one arm to point. It was the jolly boat, darting across the water at full speed, the oars winking in the sunlight like silver.

Eventually it ground on to the beach, and without waiting for it to be made fast, Midshipman Armitage leapt over the gunwale and then fell face down on the sand.

Allday, who had been watching critically, exclaimed, 'God damn me, Captain! That young gentleman will stumble on an acorn!'

Armitage hurried up the beach, his cheeks scarlet as he dashed past the groups of grinning seamen.

He stammered, 'Mr. Herrick's respects, sir!' He paused to wipe sand from his chin. 'And we have sighted some small craft to the north of here.' He pointed haphazardly into the trees. 'A whole party of them. Mr. Herrick thinks they may come this way, although ...' he stopped, screwing up his face as he usually did when passing a message, '... although they have vanished for the present.' He nodded, relieved, as he recalled the last part 'Mr. Herrick suggests they have gone into another beach for some purpose.'

Bolitho gripped his hands behind him. The very thing he had been expecting had happened. It could not have come at a worse time.

'Thank you, Mr. Armitage.'

Davy said quietly, 'That has put paid to the venture, sir. We cannot be divided if hostile natives are about.'

Soames said scathingly, 'A plague on that, Mr. Davy! We have enough powder and shot to scatter a thousand bloody savages!'

'That will do!' Bolitho glared at them, his mind struggling with the problem. 'Mr. Herrick is probably correct. They may have gone ashore to hunt, or to make camp. Either way, it makes our mission all the more urgent.' He watched Soames thoughtfully, seeing the mixture of anger and triumph in his deepset eyes. 'Select your men at once.'

Davy asked stiffly, 'What will *I* do, sir?'

Bolitho turned away. In a hand-to-hand struggle Soames would be the better man. If things went against them, Herrick would need brains rather than brawn if he was to continue the voyage on his own resources.

'You will return to the ship with the last of the shore parties.' He scribbled a note on Fowlar's pad. 'And you will convey my . . .' he hesitated, not seeing the desperation which clouded Davy's face, '. . . my ideas to him as best you can.'

Davy said tightly, 'I am senior to Soames, sir. It is my right to take part in this!'

Bolitho looked at him calmly. 'I will decide where your duty lies. Your *loyalty* I take for granted.' He watched Soames marching up and down a double line of men. 'Your turn will come, be sure of that.'

A shadow fell across Fowlar's chart and Bolitho saw the Spanish lieutenant, Rojart, watching him, his face as sad as ever.

'Yes, *Teniente?*'

He must have come ashore in one of the other boats.

Rojart said, 'I arrive to offer my services, *Capitan.*' He looked at Davy and Allday, his face very proud. 'Don Luis 'as instructed me to do all I can to 'elp you.'

Bolitho sighed. Rojart had already shown himself to be somewhat of a dreamer. Or perhaps his cruel experiences in the shipwreck had made him as he was. But one more officer, Spanish or not, would be useful. He also provided an excuse.

He said to Davy, 'So you see, Mr. Herrick will need your services more than ever now?'

To Rojart he replied, 'I accept your offer, *Teniente*, thank you.'

The Spaniard gave a flashing smile and bowed. 'Your *servant, Capitan!*'

Allday grinned and murmured, 'God help us all!'

Another cask was being manhandled on to the beach, and Duff puffed out of the trees, folding his spectacles as he shouted, 'That be the last 'un, sir!' He beamed at the onlookers. 'A full load!'

Soames tightened his sword belt and said, 'Ready when you are, sir.' He pointed to the assembled seamen. 'All armed, but without any unnecessary gear to drag 'em back.' He ignored Davy.

Keen and his pickets were gathering at the end of the beach, and by the shallows Pryke stood guard over an odd pile of timber which his mates had collected for him.

Davy touched his hat formally. 'I wish you luck, sir.'

Bolitho smiled. 'Thank you. I hope we will not need it just yet.'

He glanced at Fowlar. 'Lead the way and make notes as we go. Who knows, we may come here again some day.'

Then he turned his back on the sea and strode up the beach towards the trees.

'We will rest now.'

Bolitho dragged his watch from his breeches pocket and peered at it. Its face was harder to see than the last occasion. When he looked up at a gap in the trees he thought the sky was already duller, the trees touched with purple instead of gold. Around him the seamen dropped wearily on their knees or leaned against the trees, trying to gain relief after their forced march. The first part had not been too difficult. With axes swinging to carve a trail, they had made good time, but as they drew closer to where Bolitho and Fowlar estimated the inlet lay, they had stopped using axes, and had fought their way through the brush and creeper with bare hands.

He looked at them thoughtfully. Their shirts were ripped and torn, faces and arms bloody from encounters with treacherous branches and thorns. At their backs the intertwined trees had grown blacker, and seemed to shiver in the vapour of dead vegetation as if in a wind which could not be felt.

Soames was wiping his face and neck with a rag. 'I've sent scouts ahead, sir.' He knocked a water bottle from a man's mouth. '*Easy*, damn you! That may have to last awhile yet!'

Bolitho saw him with different eyes. Like the men Soames had selected as scouts, for instance. Not the toughest or the most seasoned seamen as a lieutenant of his background might be expected to choose. Both scouts were from *Undine*'s newest recruits and had never been to sea before. One had worked on a farm, and the other had been a Norfolk wildfowler. Excellent choices both, he thought. They had gone off into the trees with hardly a sound.

Allday muttered, 'What d'you think, Captain?'

His sturdy figure, familiar and reassuring, made Bolitho relax slightly.

He replied, 'I think we are very near now.'

He wondered how Herrick was managing, and whether he had sighted any more native craft. He shivered. Like most of his men, he felt out of place here. Cut off.

Fowlar hissed, 'Stand to, lads! Someone's a'comin!'

Muskets moved blindly in the gloom, and a few men started to draw their cutlasses.

Soames snapped, 'A scout!' He strode towards the shadow. 'By God, Hodges, that was quickly done.'

The man stepped into the small clearing and looked at Bolitho.

'I found the ship, sir. She be about 'alf a mile away.' He stretched out one arm. 'If we veers a piece we should be able to reach 'er within the hour.'

'What else?'

Hodges shrugged. He was a lean man, and Bolitho could well picture him as a wildfowler, creeping about in the Norfolk marshes.

He said, 'I didn't stray too near, you'll understand, sir. But they're anchored close in. There's more on 'em ashore in a clearing. I 'eard someone,' he faltered, 'sort of moanin'.' He shuddered. 'It made me flesh tingle, I can tell you, sir.'

Soames said harshly, 'As I thought. Bloody slavers. They'll have a camp ashore. They collect the poor devils and sort 'em into groups. Girls in one party, men in t'other. They weigh 'em, then decide who will last the voyage to wherever the cargo is bound.'

Fowlar spat on the dead leaves and nodded. 'The rest they leave behind. Cut their throats to save powder and shot.'

Bolitho looked at the scout, trying to shut Fowlar's blunt comment from his thoughts. Everyone knew it happened. Nobody seemed to know how to deal with it. Especially when many influential persons reaped a rich profit from the trade.

'Are there guards about?'

'I saw two, sir. But they seem well content. The ship 'as two guns run out.'

Soames grunted. 'No doubt. A bellyful of grape or canister if anyone tries to free those bastards!'

The Spanish lieutenant moved amongst them. Despite the rough passage through the trees he managed to remain very elegant in his ruffled shirt and wide cuffs.

'Per'aps we should continue towards the shore, *Capitan*.' He shrugged eloquently. 'There is no sense in arousing this ship if she is a mere slaver, yes?'

Soames turned away, saying nothing. But Bolitho guessed that like most sailors he was disgusted that Rojart could accept slavery as a natural state of affairs.

'We go forward, *Teniente*. In any case, our boats will not come for us until tomorrow.'

He looked at Soames. 'Take charge. I am going to see for myself.' He beckoned to Midshipman Keen. 'You, too.' As he felt his way out of the clearing he added, 'The rest of you, be ready to follow. No talking, and hold on to each other if you fear getting separated. Any man who fires a musket by whatever means or accident will feel my anger!'

Hodges pushed ahead saying, 'My mate, Billy Norris, is keepin' a weather eye on 'em, sir. Follow close. I've marked the way.'

Bolitho took his word, although he could see no marks anywhere.

It was amazing how near they had been. It seemed no time at all before Hodges was tapping his arm and gesturing for him to take cover amidst some sharp-toothed scrub, and here, opening up like a theatre, was the inlet. And how much lighter it seemed, the sunlight still lingering on the trees, and painting the sluggishly moving water with rippling reflections.

He eased himself forward, trying to ignore the painful jabs in his hands and chest. Then he froze, forgetting all the discomfort and uncertainty as he saw the ship for the first time.

Behind him he heard Allday voicing his thoughts.

'By God, Captain, it's the one which lured the Dons on to that reef!'

Bolitho nodded. The brigantine appeared larger in the confined inlet, but there was no mistaking her. He knew he would not forget her for many a year to come.

He heard the same pitiful moaning Hodges had described, and then the sharp clatter of steel on the far side of the inlet.

Allday whispered, 'Putting manacles on the wretches.'

'Yes.'

He wriggled forward again, seeing the brigantine's anchor cable, a boat alongside, the glow of light from her poop. As before, no flag. But there was no doubting her watchfulness. Two guns already run out, muzzles depressed to rake any attacker.

A boat glided from the shore, very slowly, and Bolitho tensed as a woman cried out, the sound dragging at his nerves as it echoed around the trees.

'Taking slaves aboard.' Allday ground his teeth. 'They'll be off shortly. That's my guess.'

Bolitho agreed.

To Keen he said, 'Fetch the others. Tell them to take care.' He sought out the crouching shape of the second scout. 'You go with him.'

To Allday he said quietly, 'If we can seize her, we'll know for sure who was behind *Nervion*'s destruction.'

Allday had his cutlass in both hands. 'I'm for that, Captain!'

More thuds and sounds from alongside the brigantine, and another shrill cry rising to a scream until it was swiftly silenced by a blow.

Bolitho tried to estimate how far this point was from the sea. The slaver's master would need to be able to slip away as quietly as he had entered. He would require stealth. As little noise as possible until he was clear. It seemed incredible to be watching this same vessel. While *Undine* had waited to search for *Nervion*'s survivors, and had then taken wide detours to avoid land and other ships, the slaver had pushed on with his own affairs. As if nothing had happened. It took iron-hard nerves for that. There were more sharp cries. Like animals at slaughter. Slavers had no nerves. No pity.

He heard furtive noises behind him and Soames's voice, flat, unemotional. 'Young Keen was right then. It *is* the same vessel.' He squinted at the tree-tops beyond the brigantine. 'Not much time left, sir. It'll be as black as a boot in an hour. Maybe less.'

'What I believe, too.' Bolitho looked at the clearing where the slaves were being gathered. A few wisps of smoke from fires. Probably for a blacksmith to work on the manacles. But it was the weakest point. 'Take twenty men and move around the camp. At the first sign of alarm you open fire with everything you have. Create panic if nothing else.'

'Aye. Makes sense.'

Bolitho nodded, his mind chilling with excitement. A kind of madness which always came at such moments.

'I'll want ten men who can swim. If we can board her while the slaves are being loaded, we might be able to hold the poop until you rush the boats and join us.'

He heard Soames rubbing his chin.

'A wild plan, sir, but it's now or never, it seems to me.'

'It's settled then. Tell Rojart to keep a few hands here to protect our flank. For this is the way we must go if all fails.'

Soames started to crawl away, hissing his orders into the forest until he appeared satisfied.

Other figures rustled and grunted nearby, and Keen said, 'Our party is ready, sir.'

'*Our* party?'

Keen's teeth looked very white in the fading light. 'I am an excellent swimmer, sir.'

Allday muttered anxiously, 'I hope there are none of those damned serpents in the water.'

Bolitho looked around at their faces. How well he had got to know most of them. He saw it all in these last moments. Fear, anxiety, wildness to match his own. Even brutal eagerness.

He said shortly, 'We will slide into the water below the bushes. Leave your shoes and everything else but your weapons.' He sought out Allday. 'See that the pistols are well wrapped. It should keep them dry for a while.'

He studied the sky. It was darkening swiftly, and only the tree-tops still held the gentle glow of sunlight. In the inlet and around the anchored brigantine the water was dull. Like liquid mud.

'*Now!*'

He caught his breath as the water came up to his waist and then his neck. It was very warm. He waited a few more seconds, expecting to hear a shout or the sound of a musket. But the muffled cries from the camp told him he had chosen the time well. They were too busy to watch everywhere at once.

The others were in the water behind him, their weapons held high as they paddled slowly away from the bank.

Keen was overtaking him, his arms moving smoothly. He whispered, 'I'll make for the cable, sir.' He was actually grinning.

Further, and further still, until they had passed the half-way, and Bolitho knew if they were discovered now they would be lost. The masts and yards stood high overhead, the furled sails sharp against the sky, the lantern light shining more brightly in the descending gloom. Feet thudded on deck and a man laughed wildly. A drunkard's laugh. Perhaps you needed extra rum for such work, he thought.

And then, as if by magic, they were all together, clawing the rounded hull below the starboard cathead, the current dragging at their legs, folding them against the rough timbers as they fought to stay concealed.

Allday gasped, 'The boats'll never see us here. We're safe for a bit.'

At that very instant a terrible cry floated across the water, and for a moment Bolitho imagined someone had been killed.

But the seaman at his side was floundering and pointing towards the bank which they had just left.

Even in the dying light it was easy to recognise Rojart's ruffled shirt. He was standing in the open, his arms held out as if to seize the inlet and everything it contained. He yelled again and again, waving his fists, stamping his feet, as if he had gone raving mad.

Rojart's sudden appearance had brought a complete hush to the brigantine's deck, but now as voices babbled and shouted and more feet thudded along the planking, Bolitho knew any hope of surprise was gone.

Keen had been clinging to the bobstay below the bowsprit, but now allowed himself to drift down towards him.

He gasped wretchedly, 'Nobody told Rojart it was the ship which sank *Nervion*. He must have just discovered—'

The sound of the shot was deafening and seemed to come from almost overhead. The smoke gushed and eddied across the swirling water, making more than one man duck his face to avoid a fit of coughing.

Before it hid the bank Bolitho saw Rojart hurled away by a full charge of canister. A bloody rag. Not a man at all.

He clung to the line which Allday had bent on to the bobstay and tried to clear his mind. The unexpected and unforeseen.

He winced as another shot crashed out from further aft, the hull shivering under his fingers as if alive. A ball this time, he heard it smashing through the trees and then fading away completely.

And it was then, from beyond the hidden camp, that Soames's men opened fire.

7

Herrick's Decision

The sporadic bang of musket fire was almost drowned by the mingled cries and screams from the terrified slaves. Bolitho heard men tumbling into a boat on the opposite side of the brigantine, and confused yells which were probably to encourage their companions in the camp.

He gestured to Allday. 'Now! Over the bows!'

His limbs were like lead as he hauled himself up and across the small beakhead, his heart pounding his ribs, hearing the gasps and frantic whispers from the men below him.

As they climbed on to the forecastle he saw groups of manacled natives, their naked bodies crowded together while they watched what was happening on the land. Two armed seamen stood beside a swivel gun, but as the boat pulled away from the side they were unable to fire without hitting their comrades.

Allday bellowed, 'At 'em, lads!' Then he was flying along the deck, his heavy cutlass taking a man across the neck and felling him without even a cry.

The second guard dropped on one knee and aimed a musket as more and more of Bolitho's party scrambled aboard. Faces lit up in the flash, and Bolitho felt the ball whine past, the sickening sound as it smashed into flesh and bone.

More of the brigantine's crew were dashing wildly from the poop, firing as they came, regardless of the screaming slaves who fell dying in their path.

A naked girl, her body shining with sweat, was trying to reach one of the fallen slaves, her arms pinioned by a length of chain. Husband? Brother? Bolitho had no time even to guess as one of the crew hacked her down with his cutlass in order to bar the way aft.

Bolitho felt his sword jerk in his hand as he crossed blades with the girl's killer. He saw the hatred on the man's bearded face, the madness in his eyes as they pressed forward and apart, feet sliding in someone's blood, bodies balanced to withstand each parry.

All round the deck others were fighting and slashing in the shadows with only an occasional pistol shot to throw light on friend and enemy.

Bolitho pushed the man against the main mast, forcing him backwards over the spider-band while their hilts stayed locked below his throat. He could feel the other man's anger giving way to fear, saw the sudden anguish as he jerked the hilt free and struck him hard across the mouth with it. As he fell away, gasping for breath, Bolitho turned and thrust. The man gave one shriek, lifting an arm as the blade drove under his shoulder and deeper still.

Allday dashed to his side and gasped, 'Well done, Captain!' He rolled the man away with his foot. Then he snarled, 'And another, by God!'

The seaman had jumped from the shrouds. To take them by surprise from above, to escape the unexpected attack, Bolitho did not know. All he heard was Allday's quick breathing, the swish of his blade as he slashed the man down and then finished him with one more terrible blow.

'Two boats comin', sir!'

Bolitho ran to the bulwark, and then ducked as a ball slammed hard into the rail by his fingers.

He yelled, 'Train that swivel on them!'

Someone scuttled past him firing a pistol as he fled from Allday's cutlass. Bolitho spun round, sobbing as the pain lanced into his thigh. But when he felt his leg and the jagged tear in his breeches there was no blood, no agonising splinter of broken bone.

The man who had fired had inadvertently run too close to the yelling slaves. Chains swung like serpents, and he vanished beneath a struggling heap of screaming, shining bodies.

Allday threw his arm around Bolitho's waist. 'Where are you hit, Captain?' His anxiety was clear even amidst the din of shouting and screaming.

Bolitho pushed him aside, gasping between his teeth, 'Hit my watch, damn his eyes!'

Allday grinned and ducked after him. 'I think *his* time has stopped, too!'

Bolitho only glanced at the thing which had rolled away from the panting slaves. They had literally torn him to pieces.

He dragged Allday clear. 'Stray too close and you will follow him!'

'Ungrateful dogs!'

Bolitho reached the abandoned swivel and swung it towards the nearest long boat.

'Probably think we are a different lot of slavers.'

He jerked the lanyard, feeling the hot breath from the muzzle as the canister exploded across the crowded boat. Screams and curses, bodies splashing in the water, and others still firing from the sternsheets.

He twisted round, trying to see where Soames had reached on the shore. But it was impossible to be certain. Shots stabbed and whimpered over the inlet, and once he thought he heard, steel on steel.

Then he turned and looked inboard. 'How many?' He caught Keen's wrist as he lurched past, a dirk gleaming in one hand, an empty pistol held like a club in the other.

Keen stared at him dazedly. 'We seem to have lost five of our people, sir. But the slavers have either been killed or have jumped overboard.'

Bolitho strained his ears for the sounds of more oars, the one thing which would tell him Soames was coming to his aid.

There was a loud thud from aft, and he guessed that another boat was grappling in readiness for boarding. He peered at his little party. Five dead, one obviously wounded. It was not enough.

Allday shouted hoarsely, 'We can manhandle one of the guns to the hold and put a ball through her bottom! If we can hold 'em on the poop while—'

Bolitho shook his head, pointing at the slaves. 'They are held by more than one chain. They would go down with the ship.'

He could feel the fight dying in his surviving men, like fire under heavy rain. Most of them were staring aft, each unwilling to be the first to challenge this new attack.

They did not have long to wait. The poop doors burst open and a group of men charged along the littered deck, their voices yelling wildly in what seemed like a dozen different languages.

Bolitho balanced himself on the balls of his feet, the sword angled across his body.

'Cut the cable! We'll let her drift ashore in the shallows!'

A ball shrieked above his head, and he turned to see one of his men sprawled headlong, blood gushing from his thoat. He had been struck by a marksman somewhere in the shrouds.

Allday yelled, 'Stand fast, you bastards!'

But it was useless, the remaining seamen were clambering forward again, dropping their weapons in their frantic haste to get away.

Only Keen remained between him and the beakhead, his arms at his sides, his young body swaying with exhaustion.

Allday said, 'Come *on*, Captain! It's no use!' He fired a pistol into the advancing shadows, and grunted with satisfaction as a man screamed in agony.

The next seconds were too blurred to understand. One moment Bolitho was astride the bowsprit, and the next he was swimming towards the black wall of trees. He could not remember diving or regaining the surface, although his lungs were raw from shouting, from keeping alive.

Feathers of spray spurted nearby, and he heard feet stamping along the brigantine's deck as more men climbed from boats or swam out from the shore. Shots whimpered above his head, and there was one short cry as a seaman was hit and disappeared beneath the surface.

'Keep together!'

It was all he could do to speak, and the foul-tasting water was slopping again and again into his mouth.

He saw a white figure splashing down the beach, and when he groped for his sword he stumbled headlong, his feet stubbing against sand and stone beneath him.

But it was Soames, his chest heaving from exertion, his hair wild as he pulled Bolitho to dry land.

Bolitho gasped at the air. They had failed. They had lost several good men. For nothing.

Allday was hauling Keen from the water, and two more figures lay on the sand like corpses, only their fierce breathing telling otherwise. There were no others.

A gun banged out from the brigantine, but the ball went wide, splintering through the trees to a chorus of shrieks from birds and slaves alike.

Soames said harshly, 'I could only capture one boat, sir. The slaver had a large party ashore.' He sounded angry. Despairing. 'When they fired at that damn Spaniard my lads started to attack. It was too soon. I'm sorry, sir.'

'Not your fault.' Bolitho walked heavily along the water's edge, searching for one more swimmer. 'How many did you lose?'

Soames replied indifferently, 'Seven or eight.' He gestured to several dark shapes along the beach. 'But we took a dozen of the others!' He added with sudden fury, 'We could have taken that damn ship! I *know* we could!'

'Yes.' Bolitho gave up his search. 'Muster our people and lead me to the boat. We must pick up Mr. Fowlar and his party while it's dark. The slaver will be ready for us by dawn, I'm thinking.'

It was not much of a boat, and leaked badly from a couple of stray musket balls.

One by one the weary seamen clambered into it, hardly looking at each other, or even caring where they were. If they were called on to fight now they would fail completely.

Bolitho watched them anxiously. Vaguely he recalled Herrick's words all those weeks back. *Different in peacetime*. Perhaps they were.

The wounded men were sobbing quietly, and he pushed Keen towards them. 'See to them.' He saw the youth draw back, knew that he, too, was close to breaking. He reached out and squeezed his shoulder. 'Hold on, Mr. Keen.'

To Soames he said quietly, 'Mr. Fowlar's party can take the oars. They'll be in better shape.'

He turned as a new sound intruded from the trees. Like one huge beast stamping its feet, while a combined chorus of yells echoed and re-echoed around the inlet.

Allday muttered, 'What in the name of God is that?'

'The slaves at the camp.' Soames was standing beside Bolitho as the boat edged away from the land. 'They know something we don't.'

Bolitho swayed as the overloaded craft rocked dangerously in the current. The slaves must realise that, despite the brigantine's presence, and the power of her guns, they would not now be taken as captives to the other side of the world. Not this time anyway. He thought of the native craft Herrick had sighted. They might be here already.

He snapped, 'Easy there! I can see Mr. Fowlar!'

The master's mate peered into the boat with obvious dismay.

'I'll never get my party in, too, sir!'

Soames jerked his thumb towards the trees.

'You will if you wish to stay alive!'

Allday took the tiller and checked each man as he climbed into the boat. Somehow they all got in, barely leaving the oarsmen room to pull, and with the hull so low in the water there was hardly six inches of freeboard.

'Shove off!'

He winced as a gun banged out, the long orange flame of fire darting from the vessel's side like a vicious tongue. The ball hissed astern of the boat and pounded into the sand.

Bolitho called, 'Easy now! Watch the stroke, lads!'

Too many splashes and the gunners would have an aiming mark.

Keen whispered, 'One of them has just died, sir.' He added hoarsely, 'Hodges.'

'Heave him over the side. Watch the trim, lads. Keep her steady.'

Poor Hodges. He would not walk in the marshes again. Never feel the North Sea on his face, or see the ducks in flight. He shook himself angrily. What was the matter with him?

The corpse drifted clear, and another man shited along the thwart.

Soames observed, 'They've ceased firing. Probably licking their wounds, like us.'

'Most likely.'

Bolitho felt the bitterness rising again. The slaver had lost several men, but had still enough captives to make his visit profitable whether he retrieved the rest from the camp or not. Whereas . . . He tried not to face the fact that they had failed. His men had fallen back, probably because they had lost whatever faith they had held in him.

Nervion's attacker was as much a mystery as before. A slaver's crew was usually made up from the sweepings of many ports and many tongues. Perhaps Davy had been right after all, and he should never have attempted to capture the brigantine.

His head was aching to match the bruise on his thigh. He was barely able to think any more.

Fowlar said, 'Mr. Mudge has explained it to me, sir. The ship will have to stand well out tomorrow because of the shoals hereabouts. The slaver's master doubtless knows a better passage, but . . .' He left the rest unsaid.

'Very well.' Bolitho saw an overhanging clump of trees reaching out across the water like a partly demolished bridge. 'We will make fast here. Rest the men, and share out the last of our water and rations.'

Nobody replied, and some of them appeared to be sleeping where they sat or crouched like so many bundles.

He tried not to think about the brigantine. But for his action she would be in ignorance of *Undine*'s presence. It was obvious they had not seen her, nor had they understood who had attacked and tried to capture their ship. After all, it was not unknown for one slaver to prey upon another for extra profit.

But now, because of his persistence, her master would recognise *Undine* as soon as he stood out to sea. *Undine* would be unable to venture too close inshore, and a long chase would prove just as fruitless. So, if he had been involved in delaying Puigserver's mission, he would now know that *Undine* at least was on her way.

He clenched his fingers around his sword until the pain steadied him. But for Rojart they would have succeeded. How many battles had been lost by a single, stupid oversight? Poor Rojart. The ship which had destroyed his *Nervion* was the last thing he had seen on earth. Then she had murdered him just as brutally.

The bowman called, 'I can see a beach to larboard, Cap'n! Looks safe enough!'

Allday glanced at Bolitho's shoulders, feeling his despair as if it were his own.

Bolitho said, 'Take her there, Allday.' He pushed his other thoughts aside with something like physical force. 'We will work in three watches. Two hours at a time.' He tried again. 'Post sentries, and keep a good lookout.'

The bowman leapt over the stem and waded into the shallows, a line across his ragged shoulder like a halter. The boat nudged on to hard sand, tilting drunkenly to the current and the sudden shift of men as they staggered ashore.

Bolitho listened to Soames as he picked out his sentries for the first watch. Had he been in charge of the boarding party, would he have hesitated? He doubted it. Soames would have done what he saw as his duty, helpless slaves or not, and put a ball through the brigantine's bottom or touched off her magazine. In this climate she would have been gutted in minutes, leaving the slavers isolated and easy to capture at leisure.

Because he had not been able to destroy the slaves, Bolitho had gained nothing. And he had lost nearly a third of his original party as well.

Allday slumped down beside him and handed him a water flask.

'I've secured the boat, Captain.' He yawned hugely. 'I just hope we don't have to pull too far in it, that's all.' Then he said, 'Don't you fret, things aren't that bad.' When Bolitho remained silent he added, 'We've seen an' done much worse in our time. I know some of our people took to their heels instead of rallying when they were most needed, but times are different, or seem so to many of 'em.'

Bolitho looked at him dully, but could not see his expression.

'How so?'

Allday shrugged. 'They don't see the sense in getting killed for a few slaves, or a ship they know nothing about. In the old *Phalarope* it was different, y'see. A flag to follow, an enemy you could recognise.'

Bolitho laid back against a tree and closed his eyes, hearing the jungle coming alive for the night. Squeaks and roars, groans and rustling.

He said, 'You mean that they do not care?'

Allday grinned. 'If it was a *proper* war, Captain, a real one like the last, we'd soon make 'em into fighters.'

'So, unless they are threatened personally they will not fight for those less fortunate?' Bolitho opened his eyes and studied the stars overhead. 'Before this voyage is done, I fear that some of them may come to understand otherwise.'

But Allday had fallen asleep, his cutlass across his chest like a dead knight.

Bolitho stood up quietly and walked to the boat to see how the wounded man had settled down for the night. He saw the stars reflected on the sluggish water, and was surprised to discover he was feeling less despairing.

He looked back at the trees, but Allday's shape was lost in darkness. By accident or design he did not know, but it had often happened with Allday. He seemed to hit upon the very thing which was troubling him in his simple, open manner. Not dispel it completely, but stand back from it and keep it in its proper perspective.

When he reached the boat he found the seaman sleeping heavily, his rough bandage very white against the planking.

Keen looked up, startled. 'Sorry, I did not see you, sir.'

Bolitho replied, 'Rest, easy, Mr. Keen. We are snug here for the night.'

As he walked away, Fowlar, who had been washing his face and hands in the water, moved to the boat and said admiringly, 'What a man, eh? Never a one to weep an' wail when things go hard.'

Keen nodded. 'I know. I hope I'm like him one day.'

Fowlar laughed, the sound bringing more cries from the forest. 'Bless you, Mr. Keen, I'm sure he'd be flattered to know that!'

Keen turned back to watch the wounded seaman. Under his breath he said fervently, 'Well, I *do*, and that's an end to it!'

In the pale glow of morning both sea and sky were joined by a filtered, milky haze. As the overcrowded longboat moved ponderously away from the trees and tiny beaches which lined both sides of the inlet, Bolitho watched for some sign of life or movement which might betray an ambush. A few birds floated overhead, and far beyond the last jutting spit of land he saw open water, colourless in the strange light.

He turned his attention to the men in the boat. Their brief rest seemed to have had little effect. They looked tired and anxious, their clothes filthy with dirt and dried blood, faces dark with stubble. There was little to associate them with a King's ship.

Soames was standing upright beside Allday, peering ahead, watching the men who baled away the seeping water, keeping an eye on the remaining wounded sailor. His eyes were never still.

Keen was right forward, squatting on the stemhead, his bare legs and feet dangling in the water while he watched the nearest bank, his body sagging as if from a great weight.

The hull lifted and dipped as the first inshore swell rolled into the inlet. Some of the men croaked with alarm, but most merely stared listlessly in front of them, beyond caring.

Bolitho said, 'We will turn to larboard when we get into open water. It will make our meeting with *Undine*'s boats all the quicker.'

Soames glanced at him. 'Could be hours before they come. It'll be like a damned oven today, I'm thinking.'

Bolitho groped for his watch and winced as his fingers touched the bruise. When he lifted the watch from his pocket he stared at it for several seconds, seeing where the ball had lanced from it, smashing both shield and mechanism to fragments, but saving him from injury. But for it, he would probably be dying now, or at best a prisoner aboard the brigantine.

Soames said quietly, 'Made short work of that, sir.'

Bolitho nodded. He could remember exactly when his mother had given it to him. He had just been commissioned lieutenant. The watch had meant a lot to him, partly because it reminded him of her, of her gentleness and forebearance over losing her family to the sea.

The boat tilted, and several voices shouted in protest, and he saw Keen struggling back into the hull, his face shocked as he yelled, 'Ahead, sir! Larboard bow!'

Bolitho stood up, one hand on Allday's shoulder as he stared at the two low shapes which were emerging around the last spit of land. They were moving quite fast, the long paddles plunging and rising in perfect unison as they headed purposefully into the inlet.

Fowlar said harshly, 'War canoes. I seen plenty on 'em in my time. There'll be more close by, if I'm not mistaken.' He dragged out his pistol and fumbled with a powder horn.

Soames slitted his eyes to watch the two low canoes, his face like a mask. 'God's teeth, there must be thirty men in each of 'em!'

One of the seamen shouted wildly, 'It ain't fair! We got no reason to fear 'em, lads! We ain't no slavers!'

'Silence, that man!' Fowlar cocked the pistol and rested it on his forearm. 'To them we're all the bloody same, so hold your noise!'

Bolitho said, 'Speed the stroke. They may let us pass.'

Allday kept his eyes on the oars. 'If you say so, Captain.'

Another man called, 'Astern, sir! I can see the brigantine's tops'ls!'

Bolitho turned carefully to avoid unsettling the oarsmen. The man had not been mistaken. Far astern, and moving at a snail's pace above some low trees, was a limp square of sail. The slaver must have taken stock of his position and got under way before dawn. The lifeless canvas told Bolitho that the ship was being warped downstream with the aid of her boats. But once in open water she would be free and away. He glanced again at the advancing canoes. Whereas he and his men would stay here and die. If they were lucky.

Soames asked, 'What can we do, sir? We can't outpace those canoes, and they'll not let us get near enough to grapple.' He was fidgeting with his sword-hilt, showing anxiety for the first time.

Bolitho called, 'Check the powder and shot.'

There would not be much left. What with the confused battle ashore and his own boarding party leaving their weapons behind, he could hope for very little.

Fowlar reported, 'Bare enough for one shot per man, sir.'

'Very well. Send the two best marksmen aft. Give them all the powder you have.' To Soames he added softly, 'We might hold them off until our own boats come for us.'

The canoes had stopped, their paddles glinting as they backed at the water, holding the slim hulls motionless like a pair of pike.

Bolitho wished he had a telescope, but that too lay somewhere in the jungle. He could see the natives clearly enough, their skins very black, their bodies angled to the paddles in readiness to move at a second's notice. In the stern of each hull was a tall man waring a bright head-dress, his body hidden by an oval shield. He thought of the slaves in the clearing. The girl who had been killed on the brigantine's deck. These silent watchers would show no mercy for anyone. He saw the spears glinting in the growing sunlight. Only blood would satisfy them.

Nearer and nearer, until less than half a cable separated them from the poised canoes. Bolitho looked at the two muskets in the sternsheets. Fowlar had one, and a scar-faced seaman held the other. Between them the pile of powder and shot seemed even smaller now.

'Bear to starboard, Allday.' He was surprised how unemotional he sounded. 'They will have to move soon.'

As the longboat swung heavily towards the centre of the opening both canoes came alive, the paddles darting into the water at a great pace, the air suddenly filled with the beat of a drum and the animal cry of a single warrior in the prow of the leading craft.

Bolitho felt the boat thrusting ahead beneath this feet, saw the sweat on the oarsmen's faces, the eyes which turned to watch the oncoming canoes widening with fear.

He shouted, 'Take care! Keep the stroke! Eyes in the boat!'

Something hit the water alongside and threw spray over his legs. It must have been a heavy stone, for immediately a whole volley of them rained down on the heads and backs of the struggling seamen, knocking some of them unconscious. The stroke was failing, and one oar had drifted away as still more jagged stones plunged amongst them.

Bolitho said, 'Open fire!'

Fowlar squeezed his trigger, and cursed as the ball went astray. The other musket banged out, and one of the natives screamed and pitched from his canoe.

Soames yelled, 'Keep baling!'

He fired his pistol abeam, and swore with satisfaction as another black figure plunged into the water.

Both canoes were swinging round in a wide arc to follow astern, one on either quarter. They were cut off now from each side of the inlet, and ahead the sea was opening up to greet them, mocking them with its emptiness.

Fowlar fired again, and had better luck, bringing down a plumed figure who was apparently beating out the time for the paddles.

The seamen were all so busy at the oars, or peering fearfully astern, that hardly any of them saw the real threat until it was almost too late.

Bolitho yelled, 'Get forrard, Mr. Fowlar! Fire when you can!'

He stared fixedly at the canoes which had suddenly swept around the green hump of land, spreading out like a fan as they surged towards him. A dozen at least, all filled with whooping, screaming savages. The first shot made them falter, but only for minutes. Then they came on again, the canoes cutting through the inshore swell like sword-blades.

Some of the seamen were whimpering and pulling haphazardly at their oars, others tried to stand up, while a few began to gather fallen stones to defend themselves.

Fowlar yelled, 'That is my last ball, sir!' He cursed as a heavy stone, hurled at extreme range by a sling, glanced off the gunwale and cut open the back of his hand.

The leading canoe was drawing very near, the din of chanting and the drum almost deafening.

Bolitho drew his sword and shouted, 'Ready, lads!' He looked at his cowering men. 'Close quarters!'

But it was not to be. Instead, another volley of stones clattered over the boat, striking one seaman so badly that he fell overboard. The man with the musket fired and brought down two savages with one shot. The canoe swung away, some of the paddles being dropped so that the floundering seaman could be hauled up into their midst.

Bolitho watched, sickened, as they dragged the man to his feet, pinioning his arms and holding him so that he faced the slow-moving longboat. He could see the blood on his neck where the stone had hit him, imagine his screams which were drowned by the yelling figures who held him. One, with a high head-dress, waved a knife above his head, back and forth, back and forth, so that the captured seaman followed it with his eyes as if watching a snake, his mouth like a black hole as he continued to scream.

The knife came down very slowly, the blood shining in the sunlight and making several of the seamen retch and groan with horror.

Allday said tightly, 'Jesus Christ, they're skinning him alive!'

Bolitho seized the marksman's shoulder, feeling him jump as if he was dying with the man in the canoe.

'Do what you can.' He had to force the words out.

When he looked astern again he saw that the man was still alive, writhing like a soul in hell as the knife did its work.

The musket bucked against the sailor's shoulder, and Bolitho turned away, fighting back the nausea.

Soames said thickly, 'The only way, sir. I'd not let a dog suffer like that.'

Fowlar shouted, 'Brigantine's away, sir!'

The slaver had slipped into deeper water almost without anyone noticing her. Boats hoisted inboard, and already her foresail set and drawing well as she rode clear of the protecting land.

The canoes were forming into two arrowheads again, the drums getting wilder as they manoeuvred for the final attack.

Bolitho held his sword towards the hazy horizon. 'Pull, lads! We'll not go under without a fight!'

It was an empty speech, but it was better than merely standing and watching them overwhelmed, tortured and killed without lifting a finger.

Allday whispered, 'Here they come.' He held the tiller between his legs and drew his cutlass. 'Keep close, Captain. We'll show the bastards.'

Bolitho looked at him. They were outnumbered ten to one, and his men were already fit to drop, the fight gone out of them.

He said simply, 'We will, Allday.' He touched his thick forearm. 'And thank you.'

A great yell made him turn, and as the boat swayed dangerously to the sudden shift of bodies he saw the crisp topsails and jib, the figurehead shining in the milky glare like pure gold, as *Undine* tacked around the headland, her starboard battery run out in a line of black teeth.

Soames bellowed, 'Sit down! You'll have us in the sea otherwise!'

Allday said hoarsely, 'Now, there is a *sight*, Captain.'

Fowlar called, 'She's going about, sir! In God's name, she's a'comin' though the shoals!'

Bolitho could barely breathe as he watched *Undine*'s graceful outline shortening, her sails in momentary disarray until the yards had been trimmed again. If she struck now she would share *Nervion*'s fate, and worse, when the survivors were taken by the war canoes.

But she showed no hesitation, and he could see the blood-red coats of the marines along the quarterdeck nettings, and even imagined he could discern

Herrick and Mudge beside the wheel as the frigate heeled heavily to the wind, her gunports almost awash.

Keen was yelling, '*Huzza! Huzza*, lads!' He was cheering and weeping, waving his shirt above his head, the closeness of danger forgotten.

The brigantine had already changed tack, clawing clear of a dark smudge below the surface while she set more sail to carry her to the south.

Fowlar said with disbelief, 'She's goin' after the slaver! They must be mad!'

Bolitho did not speak. Just watching his ship was enough. It told him what Herrick was thinking and doing, as if he had shouted it aloud. Herrick knew he could not engage all the canoes in time to save Bolitho and his small party. He was going to stop the brigantine and so distract the war canoes in the only way he knew.

As the realisation came to him, *Undine* opened fire. It was a slow, carefully-aimed broadside, the guns belching smoke and flame at regulated intervals while the frigate swept further and further amongst the hidden shoals.

Someone gave a cracked cheer as the brigantine's foretopmast shuddered and then curtsied down into the sea alongside in a tangle of rigging and canvas. The effect was immediate, and within seconds she was paying off to the wind, her hull broadside on as another volley crashed and ricochetted all around her. One twelve-pound ball struck the sea near her quarter and shattered into fragments, so near was the shoal to the surface.

'*She's struck!*'

Everyone was yelling and screaming like a madman, hugging each other and sobbing with disbelief.

Bolitho dragged his gaze from the brigantine which had slewed round either on a shoal or a sandspit, her canvas in pandemonium while she continued to drive ashore.

He held his breath as *Undine* shortened sail, the tiny figures on her yards like ants, her copper glinting brightly as she thrust round again on the opposite tack. Another half a cable, and she would have been aground.

Allday shouted, 'She's hove-to, Captain, an' there's a boat being dropped!'

Bolitho nodded, unable to answer.

The canoes were paddling furiously towards the helpless brigantine, and more canoes had appeared around the headland, the latter very careful to stay clear of *Undine*'s bared guns. The frigate's big launch was speeding across the choppy water, and when one of the canoes turned towards it the crash of its swivel gun was enough to make the yelling natives join their companions elsewhere.

Davy stood in the sternsheets, very erect and proper. Even his oarsmen seemed totally unreal against the tattered, cheering remnants of Bolitho's landing party.

The captured longboat was already sinking, more planks having been stove open by stones, and Bolitho doubted if they could have lasted another half-hour even without the attacking canoes.

As the launch grappled alongside, and hands dragged the gasping survivors to safety, he turned to watch the listing brigantine. Even at this distance it was possible to hear the muskets, the baying chorus from the canoes as they surrounded her for the final attack. Revenge or justice, the slaver's end would be terrible indeed.

Davy took his wrist and helped him into the other boat.

'Good to see you again, sir.' He looked at Soames and grinned. 'And you, of course.'

Bolitho sat down and felt his limbs beginning to quiver uncontrollably. He kept his eyes on the ship as she grew and towered above him, very conscious of his own feelings for her, and those who had risked their lives for him.

Herrick was waiting to greet him, his anxiety matched only by his relief as he took Bolitho's hands and said, 'Thank God you're safe!'

Bolitho fought for time, looking at the loosely flapping sails, the watching marines, the gun crews who had paused in their swabbing to look at him and grin. Herrick had taken a terrible chance. It had been sheer lunacy. And he could tell from Mudge's expression, beaming and nodding by the compass, that his was an equal share.

But there was something new here, which had been lacking before. He tried to name it.

Herrick was saying, 'We heard the shooting, sir, and guessed you might be in trouble. Instead of sending boats, we came in strength, so to speak.' He let his glance move along the busy figures at the guns and waiting by the braces. 'They did well. They were glad to be here.'

Bolitho nodded, understanding. *Pride*. That was it. To find it had cost them dear, and it could have gone much worse.

He said, 'Get the ship under way, if you please. Let us stand away from this damnable coast.' He paused, searching for the words. 'And, Thomas, if you ever doubt your ability to command again, I will remind you of today. You handled her to perfection.'

Herrick looked at Mudge and almost winked. 'We have a good captain, sir, and are beginning to feel the benefit of his drills and exercises.'

Bolitho turned aft, suddenly spent. 'I shall not forget.'

Then he walked to the cabin hatch with Allday at his heels.

Mudge ambled to Herrick's side. 'A near thing, Mr. 'Errick. If you 'adn't given the order. I don't know if I'd 'ave 'ad the will to persist through them shoals.'

Herrick looked at him, remembering Bolitho's expression, the guard no longer hiding his thoughts.

'Well, Mr. Mudge, I reckon it was well worth it.'

He stared at the misty shore line and at a growing plume of smoke. The brigantine must have caught fire, he thought. For a while longer he held on to the picture of the battered, listing boat, with Bolitho upright in the sternsheets, that old tarnished sword in his hand. If he had not disobeyed Bolitho's order to put the ship's safety before all else, he would indeed be in command now, and Bolitho back there, dying in agony.

'Get the hands to the braces!' He walked to the rail with his speaking trumpet. 'And God bless lady luck!'

Below the cabin hatch Bolitho heard Herrick laugh, and then the clatter of blocks as the seamen went to their stations for getting under way again.

Allday asked quietly, 'Can I fetch you some wine, Captain? Or something a mite more powerful?'

Bolitho leaned against the mizzen mast trunk and felt it vibrating urgently to the pressure of wind and canvas high overhead.

'D'you know, Allday, I think that after all the trouble we went through to get it, I would like a glass of fresh water.'

8

Madras

Bolitho stood very still by the quarterdeck rail and watched the vast spread of land which reached away on either bow. In the morning sunlight the countless white buildings seemed to rise tier upon tier, the uneven skyline decorated at irregular intervals by tall minarets and plump golden domes. It was breathtaking, and he could tell from the quiet way the seamen were moving around the decks that they were equally impressed.

He turned and looked at Herrick. Very tanned, and strangely unreachable in his best uniform.

'We did it.'

Bolitho raised his telescope and watched some high-prowed dhows scudding abeam, their gaunt sails like wings. Even they were part of the magic.

Mudge said, 'Ease off a point.' Then he, too, fell silent as the wheel squeaked over.

Perhaps he was satisfied, and so he should be, Bolitho thought. Madras, the name itself was like one great milestone for what they had achieved together. Three months and two days after weighing anchor at Spithead. Back there, Bolitho had seen disbelief on Mudge's heavy face when he had suggested they might make the voyage in one hundred days.

Herrick said quietly, 'Aye, sir. Since we quit the African coast lady luck came with us for certain.' He grinned broadly.

'You and your lady luck.' But he smiled all the same.

It had seemed much as Herrick had described. Within a few days of leaving the land, the dead and dying far astern, the wind had risen from the south-west, the fringe of the monsoon which on this occasion had acted as a friend. Day after day, with all sail set, *Undine* had bounded along, freely, recklessly, her forecastle never clear of bursting spray, while dolphins and other strange fish had stayed close in company. It was just as if that terrible confrontation with the war canoes, seeing the seaman being flayed alive, and all else had been one last great challenge.

He glanced up at the gently flapping topsails and forward to the solitary jib, the power barely enough now to carry them into the wide anchorage and between that impressive spread of shipping.

Madras, the most important British station on the south-east coast of another continent. A stepping-stone to advancement elsewhere, to trade and further discovery. Even the names were like fresh challenges. Siam and Malacca, south-east to Java, and beyond to a million unknown islands.

He saw a towering merchantman spreading more sail as she tacked heavily into a pale bank of sea-haze. With her chequered gunports and impeccable sail drill she could have been a man-of-war. But she was one of the East India Company's ships, and three months back Bolitho would have given his right arm for just a few of her seamen. Well trained and disciplined, they were far superior to the Navy's companies in many respects. The Company could and did afford better pay and conditions for its people, while the Navy still had to depend on what it could get by other means, and in time of war that usually meant relying on the pressgangs.

Bolitho had often considered the unfairness of the system. One day, perhaps in his own life, he hoped to see the change come. When the Navy could offer the same fair inducements.

The big Indiaman's flag dipped from her peak, and Bolitho heard Keen calling to his signalling party to return the salute.

Then he looked again at his own company, knowing he would not willingly change them now, merely because it would make life easier. Browned by the sun, toughened by hard work and regular drills with sails and weapons, they were a far cry from that motley assortment at Spithead.

He glanced towards the Indiaman and smiled. Perfect or not, she had had to dip her flag to a King's ship. His *Undine*.

Mudge blew his nose and called, ' 'Bout five minutes now, sir.'

Bolitho raised his hand and saw the master's mate with the anchor party acknowledge. It was Fowlar. A man who had proved his worth, and his loyalty. Who had already earned promotion whenever an opportunity came.

Captain Bellairs was inspecting his marine drummers, and looking even more like a toy soldier in the blazing sunlight.

Davy and Soames were on the gun deck with their separate divisions, and the ship had never looked better.

He heard voices behind him and turned to see Don Puigserver and Raymond speaking together by the taffrail. Like him they were probably eager to discover what awaited them here in Madras. Puigserver was surprisingly elegant. His clothing consisted of a lieutenant's dress-coat which had been taken apart and re-fashioned by Mrs. Raymond's maid, aided willingly by Jonas Tait, *Undine*'s sailmaker. Tait had one eye, but was very skilful, even if he was the most villainous looking man aboard. The maid seemed to find him fascinating.

'Well, Captain, you must be pleased with yourself today?'

Mrs. Raymond stepped from the cabin hatch and crossed to his side. She walked easily, so used had she become to *Undine*'s motions and behaviour in every sort of sea. She, too, had altered. Still aloof for much of the time, yet lacking the old veil of disinterest in shipboard life which had first irritated Bolitho. Her large stock of personal delicacies which had come aboard at Santa Cruz had long been consumed, and yet she had taken to the cabin's simple fare with little complaint.

'I am, ma'am.' He pointed towards the bows. 'You will soon be able to shed the smells and sounds of a small frigate. I have no doubt that an English lady reigns like a queen out here.'

'Perhaps.' She turned her head as if to watch her husband. 'I hope to see you when you come ashore. Here, after all, you are king?' She laughed lightly. 'In many ways I am sorry to leave the ship.'

Bolitho watched her thoughtfully. He remembered when he had arrived aboard after the running battle with the canoes. Spent, almost asleep on his feet as weariness replaced the will to fight, and memory pushed aside his immediate relief at his own survival. She had guided him to a chair, rapping out orders to her maid, to a startled Noddall, and even to Allday as she had taken charge. She had told someone to fetch the surgeon, but when Bolitho had said harshly, 'I'm not hurt! The ball hit my damned watch!', she had thrown back her head and laughed. The unexpected reaction had angered him, then as she had gripped his hand, quite unable to stop her laugher, he had found himself joining in. Perhaps that, more than anything else, had steadied him, had released all the anxiety he had been forced to conceal until that moment.

Some of it must have shown on his face as he remembered, for she said softly, 'Can I share them?'

'My thoughts?' He smiled awkwardly. 'I was thinking of something. My watch.'

He saw her lip begin to tremble again, and wondered why he had not noticed the fine shape of her chin and throat. Until now. When it was too late. He felt himself flushing. For what?

She nodded. 'It was cruel to laugh so. But you looked so angry, when anyone but you would have been grateful.'

She turned her face away as Herrick called, 'Ready, sir!'

'Carry on, Mr. Herrick.'

'Aye, sir.' But his eyes were on the woman. Then he hurried to the rail yelling, 'Man the lee braces! Hands wear ship!'

Undine swung easily into the wind, her anchor splashing down into water so blue it looked like satin.

Puigserver pointed at a small procession of boats which were already moving towards the ship and said, 'A time for ceremony, *Capitan*. Poor Rojart would have enjoyed this part.'

He was a different man now. Steely eyes, impatient to move again. To get his plans into order.

Behind him, Raymond was watching the oncoming boats with a look of apprehension rather than excitement on his face.

With the anchor down, and all sails neatly furled, *Undine*'s decks were bustling with life as her company prepared to take on stores, visitors, or whatever they were ordered to do. Above all, to be ready to sail again within hours, should it be required.

Bolitho knew he would be needed for a dozen things at once. Even now he could see the purser hovering to catch his eye, and Mudge, waiting to suggest or ask something.

He said, 'Perhaps I will see you on land, Mrs. Raymond.' The others were listening, and he could feel their glances, their interest. 'It has not been an easy passage for you, and I would wish to thank you for your, er,' he faltered, seeing her lip quiver very slightly, 'forbearance.'

Equally gravely she replied, 'And may I thank you in turn, Captain, for your companionship.'

Bolitho made to bow to her, but she held up her hand and said, 'Until the next time, Captain.'

He took her hand and touched the back of it with his lips. He felt her fingers give his just the merest squeeze, and when he glanced at her face he knew it was no accident.

Then it was all over as he was caught up in the turmoil of receiving visitors from the governor and handing his despatches to the officer of the guardboat.

As a brightly-canopied launch pulled clear of *Undine*'s black shadow he saw his passengers looking astern towards him, growing smaller with each sweep of the bars.

Herrick said cheerfully, 'I expect you'll be glad to have the cabin to yourself, sir. You've waited long enough.'

'Yes, Thomas. Indeed I will.'

'Now, sir, concerning extra hands . . .'

Herrick had seen the lie in Bolitho's grey eyes, and decided it was prudent to change the subject immediately.

It was late afternoon when Bolitho received a summons to report in person to the governor. He had begun to think that his part of the mission had been cancelled, or that in Madras his status had shrunk so much he would merely stay at arm's length and do as he was bid whenever it might suit the proper authority.

Accompanied by Herrick and Midshipman Keen, he was carried ashore in *Undine*'s gig, despite a haughty equerry's insistence that a local boat would be more fitting and comfortable.

An open carriage was waiting to convey them to the governor's residence, and for the whole of the short journey they barely exchanged a word. The bright colours, the surrounding press of chattering people, the whole strangeness of the town took their complete attention. Bolitho found the people very interesting indeed. How different their skins were, ranging from pale brown, no darker than young Keen's tan, to those who were as black as the warriors he had seen in Africa. Turbans and flowing robes, cattle and dejected goats, all milled across the winding streets, in and around the curtained shops and bazaars in an unending panorama of noise and movement.

The governor's residence was more like a fort than a house, with slits in the walls for weapons, and well guarded by Indian troops. The latter were most impressive. Turbaned and bearded, yet they wore the familiar red coat of British infantry set off with baggy blue pantaloons and high white gaiters.

Herrick gestured to the flag which drooped, barely moving, from a high staff and murmured, 'That, at least, is familiar.'

Once through the gates and into the cool shadows of the house it was another world again. The noise of the streets was sealed off as if by a great door, and all around was an air of watchful elegance. Fine rugs and heavy brass ornaments, bare-armed servants who moved noiselessly like ghosts, and tiled passageways which led away in every direction as in a maze.

The equerry said smoothly, 'The governor will see you at once, Captain.' He eyed the others without enthusiasm. 'Alone.'

Bolitho looked at Herrick. 'Mr. Keen will remain here in case I need to pass a message to the ship. You can make good use of your time as you will.' He turned to hide his face from the equerry. 'Don't forget to keep an eye open for extra hands.'

Herrick grinned, relieved perhaps at being spared yet another set of questions and answers. The visitors to the ship had kept him on his feet since the anchor had been let go. The sight of an English frigate seemed to attract far more interest than the comings and goings of merchantmen. A link with home. Some word or hint of what these people had left behind in their search for empire.

He said, 'Good luck, sir. This is a far cry from Rochester!'

The equerry watched him leave and then glanced at Keen. To Bolitho he said, 'I'll send the young gentleman to the troops' quarters if you wish.'

Bolitho smiled. 'I am sure he will be happier here.'

Keen met the man's stare calmly and replied, 'Indeed I will, sir.' He could not resist adding, 'My father will be glad to learn of your hospitality when next I write.'

Bolitho turned away. 'His father owns quite a large portion of your trading agency here.'

The equerry said no more, but led the way down the grandest of the passages. He opened some double doors and announced with as much dignity as he still retained, 'Captain Richard Bolitho of His Britannic Majesty's Ship *Undine*.'

Bolitho already knew the governor's name, but little else about him. Sir Montagu Strang was almost hidden behind a great desk, the sides of which appeared to be made of ebony, with feet fashioned of massive silver claws. He was a frail, grey-haired man, with a pallid complexion which told its own story of some past fever. Hooded eyes, a thin, unsmiling mouth, he was studying Bolitho's approach along a strip of blue carpet as a hunter might examine a possible victim.

'Welcome, Bolitho.' The thin mouth turned upwards a fraction, as if it hurt him to make the effort.

It was then and only then Bolitho realised that Strang's attitude was not one of disdain, for as he moved around the desk he saw that the governor had been standing to receive him, and not in a chair as he had first thought.

'Thank you, sir.'

Bolitho tried not to show surprise, or worse, pity. Down to his waist Sir Montagu was a normal if slight figure. Beyond that his legs were tiny, those of a dwarf, and his neat hands hung seemingly to his knees.

Strang continued in the same crisp tone, 'Please select a chair. I have a few things to say before we join the *others*.' He let his gaze move over him before adding, 'I have read your report, and those of certain onlookers. You did well, and have made a fast passage. Your action in trying to save *Ner-*

vion's people, your attack on the slave-ship, if only partly successful, are the two better pieces of news today.'

Bolitho sat down on the edge of a throne-like chair and then realised for the first time that the great overhead fan was being worked by a tiny Indian who was squatting in a far corner, apparently asleep, his bare foot jerking a cord to keep it in regular motion.

Strang returned to his desk and sat down. Bolitho guessed he always behaved in this manner with a new visitor. To get it over with and avoid embarrassment. He had heard that Strang had spent many years in India, as a representative of government, as an adviser on trade and native affairs. A very important man. No wonder he had chosen power out here rather than suffer the constant humiliation of gaping eyes in London.

He said calmly, 'Now, Bolitho, to business. I have been waiting too long for despatches, wondering if my original suggestions have been accepted. *Nervion*'s loss was a serious blow, but your apparent determination to continue with the voyage without further advice cancels it out in some ways. You have Don Puigserver's admiration, it seems, although whether that is good or bad remains to be seen.' His hooded eyes flashed angrily. 'The Spaniards lost great opportunities in Teluk Pendang. As a race they are stealers rather than builders. The sword and the crucifix are about the most they can offer.'

Bolitho gripped his hands together and tried not to let his mind drift on Strang's words. So the mission was still in being. *Undine* would be going to Teluk Pendang.

Strang said sharply, 'I can see that you are ahead of me, Bolitho! Allow me to fill in a few small chinks, eh?' Then he smiled. 'But it is refreshing to find one still able to *think* at all.'

Beyond the cool room Bolitho heard the distant call of a bugle. It sounded strangely sad.

Strang saw his expression and said, 'We were hard put during the war. Hyder Ali, the ruler of Mysore, and one with a real hatred for us, had plenty of support from the French. But for the Navy, I fear the Fleur de Lys and not the Union Flag would fly above here today.' He continued in an almost matter-of-fact tone. 'But that is not your concern. The sooner we can install a British governor in Pendang Bay the better I will be pleased. Since the end of the war, the Spanish garrison there, which comprised mainly of native soldiers, has been in a state of confusion. Fever and some sort of mutiny made their work impossible. I am hardly surprised that the King of Spain is so willing to rid himself of the station.' His voice hardened.

'However, under our protection it will prosper. The local native ruler is harmless enough. He must be, to allow the Spanish garrison to be alive. But further to the west is a vast area, almost uncharted, and plundered by another, less charitable *prince*, Muljadi. If we are to extend our gains, he must be contained, is that understood?'

'I think so, sir.' Bolitho frowned. 'Yours is a great responsibility.'

'Quite. The wind always shakes the top of the tree, Bolitho.'

'I am not certain what I will be required to do, sir. I would have thought a fresh garrison of soldiers would be a better force than mine.'

'I know otherwise.' His voice was scathing as he added. 'Native troops for the most part, with British officers whose minds have become numbed by heat and other, er, local attractions. I must have mobility. Your ship, in fact. The French, as you are now aware, are very interested. They have a frigate somewhere in those waters, and that, too, you know. Which is why I cannot afford open conflict. If we are to succeed, we must be in the right.'

'And if this Muljadi opposes us, or those showing friendship, sir?'

Strang walked to a wall tapestry and touched it lightly. 'You will crush him.' He swung round with surprising agility. 'In the King's name.'

He picked up a small bell and shook it impatiently. 'I am arranging a transport for the troops, and all the stores required. The East India Company will provide a suitable vessel in due course. The rest will be up to you. Under the new governor's hand, that is. Rear Admiral Beves Conway has made many of the arrangements.' He darted a quick glance at him. 'You know him then?'

'Why, yes, sir.' Bolitho's mind grappled with a dozen memories at once. 'He commanded the *Gorgon*, seventy-four. My second ship.' He smiled, despite Strang's set features. 'I was sixteen.'

'It will be an interesting reunion, no doubt.' Strang glared at the open door where a servant stood watching him anxiously.

'Take the captain to the chamber. And next time I ring this bell I want you here *at once*!'

As Bolitho made to leave, Strang added, 'You saw a Company ship leaving harbour as you entered today?'

'Yes, sir.'

'Homeward bound. A rich cargo for England.' He smiled gently. 'No, I am not full of regrets or pining for the homeland, which in any case is Scotland. I merely wished you to know that the vessel's crew had a long night's celebration, too much to drink, a way sailors have.' He turned his back. 'Some twenty of her hands were too drunk to return on board. They are in the care of my officers. They have enough to do without the trouble of drunken oafs who, had they been in a naval vessel, would no doubt have been flogged for desertion. I do not wish to know about it further, but should your lieutenants care to take over the *responsibility*, I am certain you could make better use of some extra men.'

Bolitho smiled. 'Thank you, sir.'

'I will join you shortly. Now go and take wine with my staff.'

Bolitho found Keen in the entrance hall, and passed the news to him without delay.

The midshipman's eyes widened and he said, 'I'll tell Mr. Davy at once, sir. Though I doubt if "John Company" will thank you for taking hands from an Indiaman.' He chuckled. 'Nor will they, sir!'

Bolitho hurried along the passage where he had seen the servant waiting for him, his mind returning to Strang's other news. Beves Conway, then the captain of a two decker, had always been something of a hero to him. Cold and remote in many ways, but a superb seaman, and not one given to undue harshness, even with his midshipmen.

He had left the *Gorgon* before Bolitho, having held the command for several years. After that he had disappeared completely, which was unusual in the Navy. Faces, like ships, came and went repeatedly, like the sea and wind which governed their lives. With Conway in control of things there would be little tolerance for failure, he thought.

He was ushered into the vaulted room described as the chamber, and was surprised to find it filled with a variety of people, including a number of women.

He saw Puigserver, still dressed in his makeshift clothes, and Raymond in close conversation with a heavy-jowled major. Raymond left his companion immediately, and with barely a nod of recognition, guided Bolitho around the chamber, making introductions, hardly able to hide his impatience if someone asked about England, or what the latest fashion was at home. 'Home' was somewhat vague, but for the most part seemed to be London.

Raymond paused while Bolitho took a glass of wine from a bowing servant.

'Like a lot of damned farmers!' He smiled at a lady as she passed, but added savagely, 'But they live well enough here!'

Bolitho watched him curiously. Raymond had tried to show his contempt, but had sounded only envious.

Then he heard a familiar voice, and when he turned observed Mrs. Raymond talking with someone he had not so far met.

She saw him immediately and called, 'Come and join us!' Her smile faded slightly as she noticed her husband. 'We have been talking about local customs.'

Raymond said abruptly, 'Rear Admiral Conway, the new governor of Teluk Pendang.'

Conway had been standing with his back to Bolitho. He was dressed in a dull bottle-green coat, his shoulders sloping badly so that he seemed to be leaning forward. He turned to face Bolitho, his eyes moving rapidly, noting all that they saw.

Bolitho said, 'It is good to see you again, sir.'

He did not know how to continue. If he had met Conway in Plymouth or anywhere else he would have walked past him. Could anyone change so much in twelve years? He looked thin and very intense, with two deep lines running from his hooked nose to his jaw, so that the mouth appeared to be suspended between them. Only the eyes were familiar. Cool, calculating.

Conway held out his hand. 'Richard Bolitho, eh.' The handshake, like his tone, was dry. 'And a post captain, no less. Well, well.'

Bolitho tried to relax. It was like seeing someone looking through a mask. A rear admiral, but seniority apart, he was only one rank higher than himself. And no title, no proud knighthood to mark his climb to success.

He said quietly, 'I have been very fortunate, sir.'

Mrs. Raymond touched Conway's sleeve with her fan. 'He is too modest by far. I have had good opportunity to watch the captain at his duties, and listen to his past exploits.'

Conway's glance darted between them. 'Did he relate them *well*, ma'am?'

'I heard them from others.' Her eyes regarded him coldly. 'To drag self-praise from the captain is to try and open an oyster with a feather!'

Conway picked a thread from his waistcoat. 'I am relieved to hear it.'

Raymond said, 'It seems I am to accompany you to the new station, sir.'

He did not hide his haste to distract Conway's attention from his wife's sudden anger.

'That is so.' Conway looked at Bolitho. 'The captain will tell you I am not one to tolerate mistakes. I require everyone connected with the hand-over of governorship within reach.' He glanced at the chattering people around him. 'Not here, living in spoiled unreality.'

Behind his shoulder Mrs. Raymond looked at Bolitho and pouted.

Conway said, 'I must go and speak to the military.' He bobbed his head. 'If you will excuse me, ma'am.'

Raymond waited just a few seconds, then exploded. 'Do you *have* to make a scene, Viola? In God's name, Conway could be important to me. To us!'

She looked at Bolitho. 'He is a pompous . . .' she sought for a word, '. . . bore!' To her husband she added, 'And it makes me sick the way you grovel to his kind. You always seem to throw yourself after the failures.'

Raymond stared at her. 'He is the new governor! What are you suggesting?'

She flashed a smile to someone across the room. 'You do not know anything. He is a failure. You have only to look at him!'

Strangely enough, Raymond appeared relieved. 'Is that all? I thought you had heard something.' He stared after Conway. 'I had better go to him. Sir Montagu Strang has instructed me to give all my experience to aid him.'

She held her fan across her lips and whispered, 'That should take very little time.' She slipped one hand through Bolitho's arm. 'And now, Captain, you can escort me, if you will.'

Bolitho was still thinking of that rapid exchange between them. Most of all of Conway, and what he had become.

She squeezed his arm. 'I am waiting.'

'An honour.' He smiled at her impatience. 'And thank you for your defence just now.' He shook his head. 'Although I cannot imagine what has happened to Conway.'

Her fingers dug into his arm. 'One day, some stupid officer will say that about you.' She tossed her head. 'Anyway, it was true. The pompous old bore!'

Bolitho saw the heavy-jowled major watching him and then turning to murmur to a fellow soldier.

'There will be talk, ma'am, if we walk about like this.'

'Good.' She looked at him calmly. 'Do you care?'

'Well, no.'

She nodded. 'And my name is Viola. Please use it in future.'

True to his word, Sir Montagu Strang lost no time in putting his long-standing plan into operation. Two days after *Undine*'s arrival at Madras the *Bedford*, a heavy transport wearing the flag of the East India Company, dropped anchor nearby and began to take in stores and equipment for the new station.

After his first visit to the governor's residence, Bolitho had had no time for relaxation. So little was known of Teluk Pendang, except by those who had been engaged with local trade there, that it was some while before he was satisfied with his calculations. Mudge, who knew the waters well, gave his cautious approval, and when Bolitho had paid a visit to the *Bedford*'s captain, he had been quick to praise not merely his work, but also his readiness to consult an officer of the Company.

'Not like a King's officer!' He had been greatly amused. 'Most of 'em would rather drive aground than inquire from the likes of us!' Bolitho wondered what his attitude might have been had he known about the twenty extra seamen he had poached from the all-powerful E.I.C.

Before he had left the transport he had caught his first sight of the troops who were being sent to replace the Spanish garrison. They looked as if they intended to make their new station a permanent home, for they were accompanied by as many wives and children, varied livestock, and a great mass of pots and pans, which made him wonder where they could all be stowed. *Bedford*'s captain was unimpressed, so he guessed it was the normal way of doing things out here.

He was in his cabin writing his readiness report when Herrick arrived to announce that a launch was approaching. Its only passenger was Rear Admiral Beves Conway.

Bolitho hurried on deck, half wondering why Conway had stayed away from him since *Undine*'s arrival, and partly concerned at the lack of notice.

To his surprise he saw that Conway was still dressed in his green coat, devoid of decorations or sword. He was not even wearing his hat as he stepped through the entry port and bowed curtly to Bellairs's guard of honour and to the quarterdeck at large.

'Taut ship, Bolitho.'

The eyes flitted this way and that, and Bolitho tried to dispel his sudden resentment at Conway's attitude. Perhaps he had always been like this, even in the *Gorgon* when Bolitho had watched his regular appearances on the quarterdeck or poop with something like awe.

'Dismiss the side party. This is an informal visit.'

Conway walked to a six-pounder and ran his hand across the breech. Then he looked aloft where some hands were blacking down the rigging, making it shine like ebony.

He nodded. 'She looks well enough.'

He turned his attention to the *Bedford*, at the booms which swayed back and forth above the boats and lighters moored around her.

Bolitho was able to watch him less cautiously, and saw the thinness of his hair, which was completely grey.

Without turning Conway asked, 'What is your estimated time of arrival at our destination?'

'Given fair winds, sir, and in accordance with all I have discovered, I hope to make a landfall in eighteen days. Three weeks at the most. I have already been told that I am to sail ahead of the transport.'

'My idea.' Conway turned and looked at him searchingly. 'No sense in dragging our feet with that damned hulk.'

'Then you will be coming in *Undine*, sir?'

'Disappointed?' Conway shrugged. 'Of course I shall. I have made arrangements for my baggage to be sent out this afternoon.'

Bolitho's picture of his cabin faded. He had thought of it often since arriving at Madras. Somewhere he could examine his mistakes and assemble his advantages. Puigserver was one thing. Conway another entirely. It would be like being Conway's junior officer again.

He said, 'I will inform my first lieutenant at once, sir.'

'Herrick?' He sounded indifferent. 'No need.'

Bolitho stared at him. That was not like Conway.

He tried again. 'At least we shall have a rear admiral's flag at the mizzen when we reach Teluk Pendang, sir.'

The effect was startling. Conway spun round, his features working with sudden anger.

'Was that slur intended? Does it give you some twisted pleasure to sneer? If so, I will damn soon break you for your insolence!'

Bolitho kept his voice calm, aware of Herrick watching nearby with obvious concern. 'I am sorry, sir. I meant no disrespect.'

Conway took a deep breath. 'No flag, Bolitho. I am the governor-elect of Pendang Bay, a place neither you nor most of the world has ever heard of until now.' The bitterness had put a new edge to his voice. 'To all intents I am out of naval service. What respect I receive at your hands will be arranged accordingly.'

Bolitho stared at him. It was suddenly all too clear. Conway had been putting off this moment, not out of haughtiness or from any sort of envy at Bolitho's steady promotion since their first meeting, but because he was a broken man.

'Then it will be done well, sir. That I can promise you.' He looked away. 'I have been fortunate in the Navy, in many cases I have been aided by sheer chance, or luck, as my first lieutenant would say. But I have never forgotten where I first gained the value of experience, and the patience of my own captain.'

Conway fumbled with his waistcoat, apparently oblivious to the sun across his neck and shoulders.

'That was kindly said.' He looked at his hands and then thrust them behind his back. 'May we go below?'

In the cabin he moved about restlessly, touching the furniture, peering into corners without saying anything.

Then he looked at one of the wooden quakers and snapped, 'This was done for that woman, eh?'

'Yes, sir. But I will see that they remain until you are settled in your new command.' He had meant to say residence, but the word just slipped out.

Conway watched him, his thin face expressionless. Then he said, 'No. Have the guns replaced. I need no bloody pampering. I want this ship ready for anything. A few missing guns might make a world of difference.' He did not explain, but asked in the same abrasive tone, 'That woman? Mrs. Raymond. How did she stand up to three months in a fifth-rate, eh?'

'Better than I had expected.'

'Hmm.' He studied Bolitho grimly, his features in shadow. 'Watch yourself with her. She is three years older than you, but the gap in experience is immeasurably wider.'

Bolitho said hastily, 'Might I ask when sailing orders will arrive, sir?'

'Tomorrow probably, but I can tell you now. You will weigh the day after you receive your orders. No delays. Maximum haste. We will have company on the passage.'

'Sir?'

Bolitho was certain that Conway's thoughts were elsewhere, even though his ideas came out in perfect order.

'Brig. Don Puigserver has chartered her for his own use. Partly my suggestion. It is too close to the war for me to take a Don as a friend.'

'I see, sir.'

'You don't. But no matter.'

He walked to the stern windows and stared at the shoreline, at the countless tiny craft which jostled the waterfront like busy insects.

'I would like to stay aboard, Bolitho.'

'Until we weigh, sir?'

Bolitho looked around the cabin. Tiny compared with the residence ashore.

'Yes.' He swung away from the windows. 'D'you object?'

Just for a second it was there again. The same voice which Bolitho still remembered.

'No, sir.' He smiled. 'I have been waiting to broach some wine I have brought from London, I—'

'London?' Conway sighed. 'That cursed place. I've not set foot there for five years. A plague on it and its selfishness!'

'Perhaps it has changed since—'

'People do not change, Bolitho.' He touched his breast. 'Not here, inside. You, of all people, should know that. When I learned who commanded my *transport*, I knew you would be as you are. Not so merry-eyed and trusting perhaps, but you've not altered.'

Bolitho stayed silent, watching the emotions on the other man's face, each one perhaps representing a memory.

'*Gorgon* seems an eternity back in time. The best moments were with her, although I did not realise it was so.'

Bolitho said carefully, 'Your new post will probably make you believe otherwise, sir.'

'You think that?' Conway smiled, but no humour touched his eyes. 'It is given to me because I will succeed. I *must*. There is nothing else left. When you make a slip, Bolitho, you sometimes get one final chance to redeem yourself.' He pounded one hand against the other. 'And I intend to succeed!'

There was a tap at the door and Allday stepped into the cabin.

'Who is this fellow?'

'My coxswain, sir.' Bolitho had to smile at the incredulous look on Allday's face.

'I see.'

Allday said, 'Mr. Herrick's respects, and could you come on deck to receive *Bedford*'s captain.'

Bolitho excused himself to Conway and followed him from the cabin.

Allday muttered, '*Fellow*, Captain? He was a trifle hard, I thought.'

Bolitho grinned. 'I am sure that when he knows you better he will call you by your first name!'

Allday faced him guardedly and then chuckled. 'No doubt, Captain.' He lowered his voice. 'A message has been sent aboard.' He held out an engraved card, tiny in his broad palm.

She had written across the back. *Eight o'clock. Please come.*

Bolitho stared from it to Allday's masklike face.

'Who gave you this?'

'A servant, Captain.' His eyes did not even flicker. 'The lady knows she can trust me.'

Bolitho turned away to hide his expression. 'Thank you.'

Allday watched him hurry up the quarterdeck ladder and grinned. 'It will do him good.' He saw the marine sentry watching him and snapped, 'Who are you gaping at?' He grinned again. 'My good fellow?'

9

Gift from a Lady

One hour before the morning watch was relieved Bolitho came on deck to enjoy the most peaceful time of the day. With his shirt open to his waist he crossed to the weather side and studied the set of each individual sail before going aft to consult the compass. Madras lay twelve days astern, but the wind, which had begun so promisingly, had lulled to a gentle breeze, so that even with all sails set it was unlikely they could maintain more than four knots.

Fowlar was scribbling on the slate beside the wheel, but straightened his back as Bolitho approached.

He touched his forehead and reported, 'East by south, sir. Full an' bye.'

Bolitho nodded and shaded his eyes to watch the sails again. The wind, such as it was, came from the south-west, and *Undine*'s yards were braced well round, laying her over to the starboard tack. About a mile abeam the brig *Rosalind* had no difficulty in maintaining station on her heavier consort, and Bolitho found himself tempted to take a telescope and examine her more closely.

Fowlar seemed to think that he was expected to add something to his report and said, 'Might pick up before nightfall, sir. Mr. Mudge seems to think the wind'll freshen when once we enter the Malacca Strait.'

'Er, yes.'

Bolitho tried to compose himself. From *Rosalind*'s deck *Undine* must make a beautiful sight under full canvas. But for once this gave him little consolation. He wanted to drive his ship faster to become involved with his mission. Ghosting along like this, even if idyllic for poet or artist, gave too much time for other thoughts.

He saw Davy hurrying towards him, frowning as he said, 'I beg pardon for not seeing you come on deck, sir.' He gestured towards the main mast. 'I was dealing with a complaint from a marine.' He added swiftly, 'Nothing important.'

'You are officer of the watch, Mr. Davy. You should know by now I don't interfere in your affairs merely to excite attention.' He smiled. 'A fine day, is it not?'

'Yes, sir.'

Davy followed his gaze over the nettings. The sea was very blue, and apart from the low-hulled brig there was not a speck of land or another ship to break the emptiness, its sense of vastness.

Davy asked casually, 'Is it true this sort of mission often leads to permanent appointments in the realm of colonial government, sir?'

Bolitho nodded. 'Rear Admiral Conway's appointment is such.'

He watched Davy's tanned features gravely. He was worried about something. It was showing now, just like the time when he had selected Soames and not him for the raiding party.

'I was thinking . . .' Davy faltered. 'I am of course well content with life as a King's officer. It is what I want. I am the first in my family to follow the sea. My father was a city merchant and had no use for service life. He was loath to allow me to enter the Navy.'

Bolitho wished he would get on with it. He said encouragingly, 'Mr. Herrick is like you. The first sailor in his family.'

'Yes.' Davy looked suddenly desperate as Soames emerged from the cabin hatch, yawning and consulting his pocket watch. 'Well, it is not *exactly* what I meant, sir.'

Bolitho turned and faced him. 'Mr. Davy, I would be obliged if you would come to the point. In an hour it will be an oven again. I would like to take my walk before breakfast, and not wait until after dinner tonight.'

Davy bit his lip. 'I am sorry, sir.' He nodded firmly. 'Yes, I will try to explain.' He lowered his eyes. 'May I speak of your brother, sir?'

Bolitho tensed. 'My *late* brother?'

'I did not mean to offend.' Davy looked up and allowed the words to come out in a flood. 'I heard somewhere that he quit the Navy.'

Bolitho waited. Always it seemed to catch up with him. Now even his second lieutenant was risking a rebuke to satisfy his own curiosity. But he was wrong in Davy's case.

Davy said quietly, 'It was because of his gambling, I was told?'

He looked so strained, so pleading, that Bolitho forgot his own bitterness and asked, 'Is that what bothers you? Gambling?'

'Yes, sir. Like a fool I tried to win back my losses in London. With my father dead I am responsible for my mother's welfare, and that of the estate.' He looked away. 'In time of war I might have gained early promotion, and all the prize-money which went with it.'

'You could have just as easily been killed.' Bolitho added gently, 'Am I to be told how much you owe?'

'Twenty, sir.'

Bolitho stared at him. 'In God's name, you could pawn your dress-coat for more, man!'

Davy gritted his teeth. 'Twenty *thousand*, sir.'

Bolitho ran his fingers through his hair. '*Undine* and the brig yonder would cost about that sum. And I thought you had more sense.'

'Perhaps I should have kept my secret, sir.' Davy was shamefaced. Wretched.

'No. It is better shared. At least you are safe from your creditors out here.' He watched Davy grimly. 'But twenty thousand. It is a small fortune.'

Soames clumped past and beckoned to a bosun's mate. 'Have the watch piped aft, Kellock.' He was careful to keep to the lee side of the deck.

Davy hurried on, well aware that Soames was waiting to relieve him. 'You see, sir, I thought that on a voyage such as ours I might gain some new standing.'

'I see. However, this is a mission of protection, not of discovery, or the capture of Spanish gold.' He nodded to Soames and added softly, 'But I will keep it in mind.'

He began to pace the deck while the two lieutenants conversed over the compass.

Undine had gathered all sorts within her slender hull. It was not only the lower deck which sported its fortune-hunters, it seemed. He saw Midshipman Keen walking along the larboard gangway with Armitage, and prayed he would never be left in Davy's predicament, or in one such as his brother Hugh's.

In family background Davy and Keen were similar. Both had wealthy parents who had gained promotion in trade rather than in the King's service. Davy's father had died leaving his son and heir totally unprepared for the temptations which he himself had managed to overcome. Keen on the other hand had been sent to sea *because* of his father's riches and influence. Herrick had said that Keen had confided in him during a night watch in the Indian Ocean. *To make a man of me.* It had seemed to amuse him, Herrick had said. But Keen's father must be a remarkable man, Bolitho thought. There were not many who would risk a son's life or limb for such a goal.

He saw Noddall scurrying aft along the gun deck with a can of boiling water from the galley. Conway must be up and about, waiting to be shaved. It was surprising how little Conway's presence aboard had interfered with daily life. He had explained it himself. *Informal.* That did not mean he was disinterested. Quite the reverse. Whenever a ship had been sighted, or the hands had been called to reef or make sail, he had been there, watching. Once, when becalmed for half a day, the seamen had streamed a seine net in the hopes of getting some fresh fish. Just a few flounders, and some flat-headed fish which Mudge had knowingly described as 'foxes' were the entire result of their efforts, but Conway could not have been more pleased if they had caught a whale.

It was as if he was living out every hour, like a prisoner awaiting sentence. It was not pleasant to watch.

Bolitho was not quite twenty-eight years old, but as a post-captain with two previous commands behind him he had learned to accept, if not agree, with many of the Navy's judgements.

Conway's experience had come out at dinner, one evening in the cabin. It was the second day out of Madras, and Bolitho had told Noddall to fetch some of his special wine to make it an occasion. It was madeira, the most expensive he had ever purchased in his life. Conway hardly seemed to notice. Had he been offered cider, Bolitho doubted if he would have remarked on it. But he had become very drunk. Not slowly, or by accident, or even out of bravado. But with the firm determination of one who has been too often alone, and wishes to blur the realisation without delay.

It had all happened two years back in these same waters, when the French admiral, Suffren, had captured Trincomalee and very nearly toppled Britain's power in India for good. Conway had started to tell his story as if Bolitho had not been there. As if he just wanted to make sure he could still remember it.

He had been in command of an inshore squadron and employed on the protection of supply ships and military convoys. A sloop had brought news of a French squadron off the coast of Ceylon, and without ado he had set off to engage or cripple the enemy ships until help arrived to complete the victory.

Unbeknown to Conway, another sloop was already searching for him, sent by the Commander-in-Chief with new orders for the defence of Trincomalee. Conway reached the area where the French had been sighted, only to find them gone. Fishermen informed him they had sailed towards the very position he had just left, and with an anxiety which Bolitho could only imagine, he had put his ships about once again. He managed to find and bring the French rear to a brief but unsatisfactory action before losing contact in the night. When dawn united his small squadron again, Conway found the supply ships which he had been guarding had been captured or destroyed, and when the admiral's sloop contacted him, she, too, had fresh news to cancel all previous instructions. Trincomalee had been taken.

In the silence of the cabin Conway's voice had risen suddenly, like a dying man's cry.

'Another day and I've have brought them to grips! Not Suffren, nor any other admiral, could have got us out of Ceylon then!'

Bolitho looked up as the first working parties swarmed aloft for the constant round of repairs, splicing and stitching. It was all too plain. Conway could have emerged a hero. Instead he was seized upon as a scapegoat. He must still have influence somewhere, he thought. A governorship, no matter where it was, represented reward rather than a continuance of disgrace.

He halted in his stride, his mind suddenly very alert. But suppose there was a second, more devious reason? Another scapegoat perhaps?

He shook his head. What would be the point of that?

Bolitho turned as Allday walked along the quarterdeck towards him.

'Breakfast's ready, Captain.' He squinted his eyes towards the brig. 'Still with us then?' He smiled calmly at Bolitho's steady gaze. 'That's good.'

Bolitho watched him and wondered. It was the same look he had given when he had brought the gig for him at Madras.

'Thank you.' He added coldly, 'And *what* is amusing you now?'

Allday shrugged. 'Hard to put a name to it, Captain. It's a sort of glow I get inside sometimes.' He massaged his stomach. 'Comforting.'

Bolitho strode past him towards the hatch. His morning had been badly interrupted.

As he stepped into the cool shadows between decks he imagined Viola Raymond just a mile abeam in the brig. Her husband would be watching her. *Mister Pigsliver* would be watching both of them.

It was still hard to know what she really thought about him, or if she saw his attraction as some sort of game. There had been several visitors staying at the residence, soldiers, Company officials, but she had been determined to keep him to herself. It had not been anything she had actually said. It had been more of an excitement, a sense of recklessness. A dare which he found impossible to ignore.

She had no longer stayed at arms' length, and several times had allowed her hand to linger on his, even when Raymond had been close by.

When he had made to return to the ship she had followed him on to a shaded terrace below the inner wall, and had held out a small box.

'For you.'

She had made light of it, but he had seen the hot eagerness in her eyes, the thrust of her breasts beneath her gown as he had opened the box.

It was a gold watch.

While he had turned it over in his hands she had gripped his arm and had whispered, 'I will always remember your face that day . . .' But she had not laughed that time. 'Do not refuse my little gift, *please*.'

He had taken her hand and kissed it, his mind grappling with what he was doing, seeing all the dangers, and yet dismissing them.

'It is as well you are sailing in another ship, Captain!' She had laughed and then had pulled his hand below her breasts. 'See how my heart beats now! A week, a day even, and who can say what might occur!'

Bolitho walked past the sentry and into the cabin, his mind still hanging on to that moment.

Conway was spreading thick treacle on a biscuit, his wispy hair ruffling in the breeze from the stern windows.

'What time is it, Bolitho?'

'Time, sir?'

Conway eyed him wryly before taking a mouthful.

'I observed that you had your, er, new watch in your hand and assumed that time was of some importance?'

Bolitho stared at him, the midshipman in front of his captain again.

Then he grinned. 'It was a memory, sir, that was all.'

Conway sniffed. 'That I can well believe!'

'It makes a fine sight, Thomas.'

Bolitho lowered the telescope and wiped his forehead with the back of one hand. The noon sun was merciless, but like most of the men around him, or standing high in the shrouds, he was momentarily unaware of it. Fifteen days out of Madras, and in spite of the wind's perversity, *Undine* had done well. Bolitho had made many landfalls in his time, but the sight of any shore after the hazards and doubts of navigation never failed to move him.

And now, just visible through the glare of sea and sky, he could see a smudge of green across the larboard side, and felt a fresh excitement and satisfaction. The narrowest part of the Malacca Strait. To starboard, hidden even to the masthead lookout, was the great scimitar-shaped island of Sumatra, poised as if to squeeze the strait shut and leave them sailing in a wilderness forever.

Herrick said, 'It seems a mite too narrow for comfort, sir.'

Bolitho smiled at him. 'It is wider than the English Channel even here, Thomas. The master assures me it is the safest course to take.'

'Perhaps.' Herrick shaded his eyes again. 'So that is Malacca, eh? It is hard to believe we have reached this far.'

'And in five days or so, with God's good grace, we'll anchor in Pendang Bay.' He paused, seeing the doubt in Herrick's blue eyes. 'Well, come on, Thomas, let us see that smile again!'

'Yes, sir, I *know* it is a good and fast passage, and I am well satisfied, as you are.' He fidgeted with his belt buckle. 'But I am more concerned with something else.'

'I see.'

Bolitho waited, knowing what was coming. He had seen the worry mounting in Herrick's face over the past fifteen days. Having to spend much of his time with the admiral, Bolitho had had little chance of enjoying Herrick's company. A walk together before dusk, a pipe of tobacco and a glass of wine.

Herrick said bluntly, 'Everyone knows about it, sir. It's not my place to speak on your behaviour, but . . .'

'But that is exactly what you are about to do?' Bolitho smiled gravely. 'It is all right, Thomas, I am not going to snap your head off!'

Herrick would not relent. 'It is no joke, sir. The lady is the wife of an important government official. If this sort of tale ever reached England, you would be in real danger, and that's the truth.'

'Thank you for your concern.' He glanced ahead where far beyond the gently spiralling bowsprit he saw *Rosalind* leading the way through the shallows and sandspits as she had no doubt done many times before. 'But it is something I do not wish to discuss. Even with you, if you are to disagree with everything I say.'

'Yes, sir, I'm sorry.' But Herrick added stubbornly, 'I can't stand by and see you in irons because of others, sir, not without trying at least to help.'

Bolitho gripped his arm. 'Then we will say no more of the matter, Thomas. Agreed?'

'Aye, sir.' Herrick regarded him unhappily. 'If it is the way you want it.'

A seaman left the galley and darted down an open hatch below the forecastle. He was carrying a bucket and swab.

Herrick said wearily, 'The surgeon is sick again. That man must be going to clean out his quarters.'

Bolitho looked at him. 'Drunk, I suppose?'

'It would seem so. But there is little to occupy him, sir, and our people have been remarkably free of illness.'

'That is just as well.' Bolitho felt unreasonably angry. 'What in hell's name am I to do with him?'

'He has a lot on his mind, sir.'

'So have many others.'

Herrick kept his voice even. 'He saw his young brother hanged for a crime of which he was later proved innocent. Even if he had been guilty it would still have been a terrible thing to watch.'

Bolitho swung round from the rail. 'How did you discover this?'

'At Madras. He came aboard drunk. I was a mite harsh with him and he started to rave about it. It is destroying him.'

'Thank you for telling me, even if it is somewhat late.'

Herrick did not flinch. 'You have been rather *busy*, sir. I did not wish to trouble you.'

Bolitho sighed. 'I take your point. But in future I would like to hear everything. Most ship's surgeons are no more than butchers. Whitmarsh has been something more, but as a drunken sot he is a menace to everyone aboard. I am sorry for his brother, I for one can appreciate his feelings.' He looked steadily at Herrick. 'We will have to see what we can do to put things right for him, whether he likes it or not.'

Herrick nodded gravely. 'I agree, sir. The one afflicted is not always the best judge of his own malady.' He tried not to grin. 'If you see what I mean, sir.'

Bolitho slapped his shoulder. 'By God, Thomas, you go too far! I am not surprised your father sent *you to* sea!'

Then he walked up the tilting deck to the weather side and left Herrick to supervise his watch.

So they knew all about it, did they? He touched the bulge in his breeches pocket. What would Herrick say if he saw the inscription inside the watch-guard, he wondered?

'We will wear ship directly, Mr. Herrick.' Bolitho strode to the compass and peered over Mudge's untidy shoulder. 'Steer nor'nor'-east.'

Herrick touched his hat. 'Aye, aye, sir.' He was equally formal.

It was five days since they had discussed Viola Raymond and the doctor's personal problem, and in that time Bolitho had never felt better. The ship had settled down to a regular, unhurried routine, and even the drills had passed off without complaint. At gunnery *Undine*'s company still had a lot to learn, but at least they moved as a team and not a stumbling, confused rabble.

He raised his glass and studied the new shapes and patterns which parted sea from sky. Mudge had assured him that Pendang Bay lay some five miles distant, but it was difficult to accept that they had all but arrived at their destination. Over fifteen thousand miles. Another world. A different life.

'Hands wear ship! Man the braces there!'

Shoes scraped on the planking, and Bolitho turned to study Conway's reaction as he came on deck. It was early morning, and for a few seconds he thought he was imagining what he saw.

Conway was wearing his rear admiral's uniform, complete with laced cocked hat and sword. The latter he held like a pointer, as if unsure of his reception.

Bolitho said, 'Good morning, sir.'

He saw Herrick staring at them, his speaking trumpet in mid-air.

Conway joined him by the rail and raised his head to watch as the great yards creaked round in unison, while the straining seamen hauled and panted at the braces.

'Well?' His tone was wary. 'What do you think?'

'I think you look right for the occasion, sir.'

He saw the quick tightening of Conway's mouth, the lines on either side deepening still further. It was moving, if pathetic, to see Conway's gratitude, for that was what it was.

'It is a bit creased of course. I was merely trying it on to see if it required alteration.' He added sharply, 'If I am to be governor, I'll land as I intend to continue, damn their eyes!'

Midshipman Armitage was watching the brig as she trimmed her yards to take station off *Undine*'s lee.

He remarked nervously, 'Thunderstorm, sir.'

But Bolitho was already snatching a telescope.

'Not this time, Mr. Armitage.' He looked at Herrick. 'Shorten sail, if you please, and then beat to quarters.'

He saw them all gaping at him. Like total strangers.

'That *thunderstorm* is of a kind I have come to respect!'

10

Another Flag

'Ship cleared for action, sir.' Herrick watched Bolitho's face anxiously.

Bolitho moved the telescope slowly from bow to bow, trying to avoid the overlapping mesh of shrouds and stays as he stared fixedly at the shore. Because of the glare which filtered through the morning haze it was impossible to fix any proper mark or to take an accurate bearing.

He replied, 'Too long, Mr. Herrick. I want the time cut to twelve minutes.' He was speaking merely to give himself another moment to gather his thoughts.

The distant gunfire had stopped, but there had been at least a dozen shots. Sharp and loud, despite the range. Probably small pieces.

He swung the glass further to starboard, seeing the low-lying wedge of land reaching out to lie parallel with their slow approach. The eastern headland of Pendang Bay. There was no room for further doubt.

Something dark intruded into the lens, and he saw the brig tilting to the low breeze, her yards alive with tiny figures as she finished reefing. A huge Spanish flag had been hoisted to her peak, blinding white in the glare, and he found time to wonder how *Rosalind's* master was reacting to Puigserver's show of national pride.

Almost without intending to speak aloud he said, 'I wish the Don was here with us. I think combined thought and action may be called for.'

He heard Conway grunt. 'Unnecessary. Ours is the ship of war, Bolitho. I want no damned Spaniard under my feet today.'

Herrick asked quietly, 'What d'you make of it, sir?'

Bolitho shook his head. 'An attack on the settlement maybe. But I understand the place is well defended and—'

Conway interrupted harshly, 'All this fuss over a few bloody savages!'

Herrick was standing beside Mudge and whispered, 'I expect that is what poor Captain Cook said!'

Bolitho turned sharply. 'If you've all nothing better to do than make stupid remarks . . .' He swung away and added, 'Two good leadsmen in the chains immediately. Begin sounding.' To Mudge he snapped, 'Let her fall off a point.'

The edge in his tone was having the right effect. Men who seconds earlier had been chatting and gossiping about what might be happening ashore were now silent and alert, standing to their guns, or grouped at halliards and braces for the next command.

The wheel creaked, the sound very loud in the sudden stillness, and the helmsman called, 'Nor'-east by north, sir!'

'Very well.'

Bolitho glanced at Conway's profile, the glassy intentness in his eye.

From forward came the leadsman's cry, 'No bottom, sir!'

Bolitho looked at Mudge, but the master's heavy face was expressionless. He probably thought it was a waste of time to take soundings. The chart, and all available information, told them the water was deep until the last cable or so. Or maybe he thought his captain was so nervous that he was afraid to leave anything to chance.

Another, single crack echoed out from the mist-shrouded coast and died away very gradually.

Bolitho tugged out his new watch and stared at it. At this speed it would take near on an hour to close the land. But it could not be helped.

'No bottom, sir!'

He said, 'Pass the word for Captain Bellairs. I'll want a full landing party. Tell Mr. Davy to prepare the boats for lowering once we have anchored. He will take charge of them.'

Conway said briefly, 'Good beach, I'm told. The settlement and fort are on a slope to the western side of the bay.'

Herrick strode aft and touched his hat. 'Shall I order the guns to load, sir?' He sounded guarded.

'Not yet, Mr. Herrick.'

Bolitho trained his glass across the larboard bow. Settlement, fort, they could have been imagination. The blurred green outline of the land looked totally deserted.

He heard the marine sergeant bellowing orders, the stamp of boots as his men were divided and sub-divided in readiness to disembark. Bellairs was watching them from the starboard gangway, his face completely blank, but his eyes missing nothing.

'By the mark twenty!' The leadsman sounded triumphant.

Mudge nodded gloomily. 'About right. Twenty fathoms hereabouts.'

Some small birds darted across the sea's face and circled above the braced yards. Bolitho watched them, recalling the swifts flying about the grey stone house in Falmouth. It would be fine there today. Sunshine, bright colours. The hills dotted with sheep and cattle. The town itself busy with farmers and sailors, each depending on the other, as it had always been.

He saw Herrick nearby and said quietly, 'Forgive my anger just now.'

Herrick smiled. 'No matter, sir. You were right. We have been caught unawares already on this venture. Trouble will not fade away merely because we turn our backs on it.'

'*Rosalind*'s settin' 'er fores'l again, sir!'

They turned to watch as the brig dipped to the wind and gathered way.

Conway snarled. 'By God, the Don intends to lead us inshore, blast him!'

'It is his right, sir.' Bolitho trained his glass on the other vessel, seeing the busy figures above and below, the great slash of her ensign with its crowned shield bright in the sunlight. 'It is still the territory of the Spanish Royal Company until he says otherwise.'

Conway scowled. 'That is mere formality.' He stared hard at him. 'Fire a warning shot, Captain!'

Bolitho looked at Herrick. 'Pass the word forrard. One ball. But mind it drops well clear of the brig.'

The leadsman called again, 'Deep eighteen!'

Bolitho shut his ears to the squeak of gun trucks as the foremost twelve-pounder was run out. The gun captain was peering along the muzzle, and as the light touched him Bolitho saw that one hand was a metal hook. Turpin.

Herrick shouted, 'Ready, sir!'

'As you will then.'

The gun crashed out, and seconds later a thin waterspout rose like a feather far beyond the brig's bowsprit.

Bolitho said, 'Well, at least they will know we are coming, sir.'

Conway snapped, 'Savages. I'll soon get to the bottom of this little matter.'

Bolitho sighed as the brig fell off slightly, her foresail already being brailed up in response to his rough signal. The thought of having a poorly armed brig lying between an enemy and his own artillery was a worry he could not afford. And she was aboard *Rosalind*, too.

He turned round sharply, angry with himself for allowing his thoughts to drift. Right now he needed to be completely clear. His mind like steel.

'Mr. Mudge, d'you know much of this place, other than you have already told me?'

The master shrugged. 'Very few people 'ave seen inland, sir. 'Ead 'unters, warrin' tribes there are a'plenty, I'm told. But the natives are often sailors, pirates from the north of Borneo. Sea-Dyaks they calls 'em. Many a good ship 'as been overrun at anchor by them devils.' He shook his jowls. 'Then it's snip, snip with their long knives an' poor Jack is no more!'

At that moment a seaman beside a six-pounder pointed aloft as the mast-head pendant licked out with renewed energy.

Like a long, low curtain the sea mist began to move and shred itself, vanishing into the land, and laying bare endless stretches of beach, thick jungle, and finally the overlapping hills beyond.

Herrick lowered his telescope and exclaimed, 'And is *that* the settlement, sir?'

Bolitho steadied his own glass, not daring to look at Conway's face. What he had first taken to be a heap of lopped and piled trees was shaping itself into long, spiked palisades, supported and guarded at regular intervals by squat, timbered blockhouses. As the mist slipped away he saw what must be the governor's residence. It had to be, for it was the largest building in sight. Again, it was built entirely of timber, with an upper and lower rampart and one spindly watchtower in its centre, above which the Spanish flag lifted occasionally in the sea breeze.

Conway said thickly, 'In God's name!' The words were wrung from his throat.

Bolitho watched the distant fort for some sign of life other than the flag.

The place looked crude, but was well sited, easy to defend. There must be settlements like this all over the world, he thought. But what about *before?* Someone had first to wade ashore from a boat, or march through swamp and jungle to plant a flag. To claim the land for his own country. He had heard of islands in the Pacific which were regularly claimed and re-claimed by half a dozen nations, sometimes out of the genuine desire to colonise, but often merely because their ships paused there for no other reason than to find water and firewood.

'By the mark ten!'

He looked at Herrick. 'We will anchor in eight fathoms.' He saw Allday scrambling over the gig on its chocks. 'Then boats away as fast as you can.'

He turned his attention to the cruising wavelets which had risen to enjoy the freshening breeze. It was a large but well-sheltered bay. It was said that the Spanish Royal Company had claimed it years earlier almost by accident. They had intended to place their settlement further north, to gain access for trade with the Philippines. But fever, losses in ships and resources had found them here instead. It was easy to understand why the Spaniards had lost heart, easier still to realise how much more important it would be to the British. Within reach of both India and the vast, barely-tapped resources of the China Seas, it could be a vital link, given time and skilful handling. With the French and Spaniards gone from the area, only the power of the Dutch East Indiamen offered any sort of competition. He glanced quickly at Conway's stiff features. But was he the one to begin it, he wondered?

Fighting men rarely saw much further than the strategy and tactics of the moment. And one made bitter and desperate by past mistakes would be less inclined to compromise.

'People leaving the palisade, sir!'

Bolitho raised the glass again. Twos and threes, some carrying muskets, others limping down the sand towards the water's edge and a long, partly-constructed pier of rough timber and piles. Most of them were so dark-skinned they could be natives, but the uniforms were Spanish well enough.

Not one of them waved. They merely stood or sat dejectedly watching the frigate's careful approach.

Herrick said under his breath, 'God, they look like scarecrows!'

'What did you expect, Mr. Herrick, *sir?*' Unseen and unheard, the surgeon had appeared on the quarterdeck, his face and neck like raw meat.

Bolitho watched him impassively. 'You are recovered, it seems, Mr. Whitmarsh?'

The surgeon turned his gaze on him. His eyes were red-rimmed with strain, so that they looked too hot for their sockets.

He muttered vaguely, 'We have arrived, I see, sir.' He reached out for support and, finding none, almost fell headlong. He mumbled, 'Pattern never changes. First they hand over their power of protection to us. With ships and men if needed to give power to that *protection.* When all is safe the traders will come, and the Company's flag will be supreme.'

Bolitho asked coldly, 'And then what?'

Whitmarsh regarded him emptily. 'The place will become a colony, a possession. Or if we have cleaned it out like an empty shell, we will simply . . .' he retched, '. . . discard it. Cast it away!'

Conway seemed to hear him for the first time. 'Get off this deck, you drink-sodden creature!' His face was working with despair, a need to release his anger. 'Or by heaven you will be sorry!'

The surgeon gave an awkward bow. 'But I *am* sorry, believe me! Sorry for you, sir, at being given this wretched task.' He swayed towards Bolitho. 'For the good captain, who will eventually be made to stand between justice and tyranny. And more sorry perhaps ...' He pitched forward in an untidy heap and lay completely still.

'By the mark eight!'

The leadsman's call brought Bolitho back to reality.

He snapped, 'Have him taken to his quarters.'

As some seamen seized the inert surgeon and carried him to the ladder, he caught the sour odour of vomit and spilled wine. The stench of a man's decay.

Conway was still staring at the deck. 'Another second and I'd have had him in irons!' He glared at Bolitho. '*Well?*'

'There was something in what he said, sir. What is on a sober man's mind is often on a drunkard's tongue.'

Herrick called, 'Close enough, I think, sir.'

Bolitho hurried to the quarterdeck rail, glad to be free of Conway's mood. He studied the lie of the smaller headland to larboard, the great eastern one on the opposite beam, thrusting out to sea, and already a delicate green in the early sunlight.

'Signal our intention to *Rosalind*, and then wear ship, if you please.' He waited until the anchor party had assembled above the cathead. Then he added, 'Tell Davy to keep our people together once we are ashore. I want no plague raging through *Undine*.'

'D'you think there is fever here, sir?'

For just a moment there was fear in Herrick's eyes. Like most seamen he could accept blood and broadside, as well as the harsh discipline which guided his daily life. But the unknown, the terror of plague which could render a whole ship useless, turn her into a floating tomb, was entirely different.

'That we will discover directly.'

'*Rosalind*'s acknowledged, sir!'

Keen seemed his usual carefree self. Even Armitage was watching the land with something like expectancy.

'Wear ship!'

'Man the lee braces!'

Bolitho saw the helm going over, and moved to Conway's side to avoid the rush of seamen across the quarterdeck as the frigate turned slowly into the wind.

'Will you wait for Don Puigserver, sir?'

Conway looked at him, a nerve jumping in his throat, as the anchor plunged into the clear water in a mighty cascade of spray.

'I suppose so.' He peered towards the brig which was already swinging easily to her cable. 'I wish you to accompany me.'

'An honour, sir.'

'You think so?' Conway removed the gold-laced hat and ran his palm over his grey hair. He smiled bitterly. 'We shall see.'

Noddall came on deck with Bolitho's sword, but quailed as Allday rasped, 'Here, give me that!'

He hurried to Bolitho's side and carefully buckled the scabbard into place, muttering, 'The very idea!'

Then he straightened his back and stared at the boats which were being swayed up and over the nettings.

'A long way we've come together, Captain.' He turned to watch the brig's boats being lowered into the water. 'It's not a happy place, I'm thinking.'

Bolitho did not hear him. He watched the marines clambering out and down into the swaying boats, their coats very red, their boots slipping and clattering as they always did. Captain Bellairs was studying each and every one of them, especially the young corporal who carried the sheathed Union Flag which would soon be planted on foreign soil.

Like many sea officers, Bolitho had often thought about such moments, but the mental picture had always been grander and vaster. Endless lines of men, bands playing, cheering people, and the anchored ships looking splendid and secure at the sea's edge.

Now he understood differently. It was only a beginning. Small, but no less impressive because of that.

Conway said, 'Well, we had best begin. I see the Don is already on his way.'

The brig's boats were indeed moving inshore, one bearing the Spanish flag, the others that of the Company.

Bolitho was thankful Viola Raymond was remaining aboard the *Rosalind*.

Conway followed him into the gig, and with the armed and crowded boats fanning out on either beam they started towards the nearest beach.

Bolitho could smell the jungle long before they were within hail of the people by the frothing surf, like incense, heady and overpowering. He gripped his sword-hilt tighter and tried to compose himself. It was a moment he must always try to remember.

He glanced quickly at Conway for some sign of reaction. He looked remote and sadly stern.

The new governor of Teluk Pendang had arrived.

Lieutenant Thomas Herrick walked a few paces across the quarterdeck, his movements restless as he watched Bellairs's marines and some seamen below the nearest palisade. It was just past noon, with the sun blazing down on the anchored ships with savage intensity. Most of the unemployed hands were sheltering by the guns beneath the gangways, but Herrick felt unable to leave the deck, even though his head was swimming, his shirt plastered against his body like a wet rag.

Tugging at her cable, the *Undine* had swung her stern towards the long, pale beach, and with the visibility sharp and clear, it was easier to see the extent of Conway's new command. Larger than he had first imagined it had obviously been planned and constructed by a military engineer. Even the unfinished timber pier looked neat and strong, but like the rest of the place, was in a state of bad neglect.

As he had paced the quarterdeck, or peered across the taffrail, Herrick had seen Bolitho and some of the landing party moving along the wooden ramparts, or exploring the ground between the two separate palisades which guarded the approaches to the fort and its surrounding buildings. The boats lay like dead fish on the beach, exactly where they had ground ashore some four hours earlier. He had watched some marines hauling the swivel guns towards the fort, others, harried by the massive Sergeant Coaker, had manned the ramparts, or could now be seen patrolling near the pier. The handful of Spanish soldiers had withdrawn into the fort, and of the enemy, or whatever the garrison had been firing at, there was not a sign.

He turned as a heavy step fell on the tinder-dry planking and saw Soames shading his eyes with one hand, and munching a biscuit with the other.

'Any sign yet, sir?' Soames eyed the distant settlement without enthusiasm. 'What a place to end your years, eh?'

Herrick was worried. Something should have happened by now. There were supposed to be some three hundred Spanish soldiers and followers in the settlement, and God alone knew how many local natives. From what he had seen there were hardly any. The same old thought crossed his mind. Plague perhaps? Or something even more terrible.

He replied, 'They appear to be examining the inner defences. I am not surprised the Dons wish to be rid of it.' He shuddered. 'From here it looks as if the damned jungle is pushing the whole lot back into the sea.'

Soames shrugged and pointed his half-eaten biscuit at the gun deck. 'Shall I dismiss the gun crews? There seems to be little here to excite action.'

'No. There are only five of them manned. Change 'em round and send the others below for a spell.'

He was glad when Soames walked away. He needed to concentrate, to decide what to do if he was suddenly required to act without Bolitho at his elbow. It had been different the last time. A sort of wild recklessness had come over him, prompted as ever by the need to dash to Bolitho's aid in the only way he knew.

But here were no yelling savages, no darting canoes which a few bursts of canister could scatter. Silence, and depressing immobility.

Midshipman Penn called in his shrill voice, 'One of the boats is being launched, sir!'

Herrick felt his heart lift as the distant figure thrust *Undine*'s green-painted gig into the shallows. He saw Bolitho's tall figure striding down the beach, pausing to say something to Davy before swinging his legs over the gunwale.

At last. Soon they would know what was happening. Only four hours, but to Herrick it felt an age.

'Muster the side party. Stand by to receive the captain!'

Bolitho looked strained and thoughtful as he climbed up through the entry port, his coat covered with sandy dust, his face damp with sweat. He glanced at the motionless side party but did not seem to see them.

He said, 'Have the surgeon and his mates sent ashore to report to Mr. Davy. When the other boats arrive I want powder and shot, food and fresh fruit sent over, too.' He peered towards the anchored brig and at another boat which was pulling quickly towards her. 'I have sent word for *Rosalind* to assist in every way she can.' He looked at Herrick's round face and smiled for the first time. 'Easy, Thomas. It is not the end, though it was nearly so. Come to my cabin when you have dealt with my orders. Allday has a list of things required.'

When Herrick finally joined Bolitho in the stern cabin he found him stripped to the waist and drinking a large tankard of lemon juice.

'Sit down, Thomas.'

Herrick sat, aware that although Bolitho sounded controlled and level, there was something else, something familiar which told him his mind was busy along another tack.

'When the war ended there was a garrison of about three hundred here.' It was as if he was drawing a picture, just as it had been painted for him. 'The commandant, the King of Spain's trusted controller, was Colonel Don José Pastor, a dedicated soldier to all accounts, and one well used to building such settlements. He gained some trust from the natives, and by barter and other inducements, as well as the usual Spanish use of force, he was able to create a strong defence line, as well as clear much of the surrounding land. There is even a road of sorts, although that now is overgrown. A wilderness.'

Herrick ventured, 'Fever?'

'That, of course, but no more than you might expect in such a place.' He studied Herrick for several seconds, his eyes very grey in the reflected light. 'The settlement has been under almost constant attack for over a year. At first they thought it was only the work of marauding tribesmen, Dyak pirates maybe who were becoming worried by the spread of Spanish influence in their midst. Colonel Pastor had set up a Catholic mission above the settlement. The monks were found terribly mutilated and headless.' He did not see Herrick's expression of horror. 'Then others died when the fresh-water pools were poisoned. The garrison had to fall back upon its own little stream within the walls. But for it, the fight would have ended long ago. Think of it, Thomas, if you had been an officer here. Trying to hold up morale, fighting an unseen enemy, while day by day your strength is dwindling. Each dawn you would be watching the horizon, praying for a ship, any vessel which would bring relief. Only one came in the whole of that time, but would not land its people for fear of the plague. She merely dropped despatches and left. God knows, I can understand that. They are like living skeletons over yonder.' He looked round as a boat pulled clear of the hull. 'Let us hope our surgeon will find others to help and think less of himself.'

Herrick asked quietly, 'What will Admiral Conway do, sir?'

Bolitho closed his eyes, remembering the small gathering in the room at the top of the wooden fort, hearing Puigserver's emotional voice as he had translated the report of the settlement's one remaining officer, Captain Vega.

The attacks had gone on and on, and when once an armed picket had been ambushed, the fort's defenders had nearly been driven mad by the screams and pitiful cries as their comrades had been tortured to death within sight of the walls.

Bolitho said, 'To the west of us is a small cluster of islands. The Benua Group.'

Herrick nodded, unable to understand .'Yes. We passed them a day back.'

'They lie astride the strait between Borneo and the islands of Sumatra and Java.' His tone hardened. 'This self-styled prince, Muljadi, has his stronghold there. The Dutch built a fortress in one of the isles many years ago, but abandoned it when disease killed most of the garrison.' He looked through the stern windows, his eyes grave. 'Not like Conway's new domain, Thomas. It is built of stone.'

Herrick attempted to shift Bolitho from his mood of passive despair. 'But a few ships and men would soon destroy this damned Muljadi, surely?'

'Once, Perhaps.' Bolitho drained the glass and stared at it. 'This morning there was a final attempt to overthrow the defences here. I expect the attacker saw *Undine* pass through the strait yesterday and knew they must make haste. Now they are gone into the jungle. Captain Vega of the garrison says they will head west to the marsh district, where they will be taken by sea to Muljadi's stronghold.' He gave a great sigh. 'Of all the men at the settlement, there are but fifty survivors. Poisoned darts, musket balls, for they have our weapons, too, and fever have wrought a terrible price from them. There was even a mutiny, when Vega's men fought with their own native soldiers, most of them too crazed with drink and despair to know what they were about.'

Herrick stared at him. 'What of Colonel Pastor, sir? Is he also killed?'

Bolitho sat down and massaged the white scar above his ribs. 'I am coming to that part. Weeks back, a ship *did* finally arrive. Not to bring help, or to offer relief to people from their own part of the world. She was the *Argus*, Thomas.' He swung round, the weariness falling away like a cloak. 'Of forty-four guns, under the hand of *Capitaine* Le Chaumareys. He landed himself and met with Colonel Don Pastor. He brought a message from Muljadi. *Personally.*' He gripped the deck with both hands. 'And required him to lower the flag, to relinquish all claims on the settlement in the name of Spain.'

'My God.'

'Indeed. Apparently the colonel told of help which would soon arrive, but Le Chaumareys laughed at him. Said there would be no relief, no ships coming to his aid.'

'Then the French do have a hand in this, sir?'

'A big one.' His face lit up. 'Cannot you see it, Thomas? Le Chaumareys was instructed to force the Spanish to surrender their rights here. He knew better than most that *Nervion* or *Undine*, or both, would be delayed by any means available. With the settlement handed over to Muljadi, and a written agreement from Pastor, who after all is his King's representative here, there would be nothing we or anyone else could do. I have no doubt Le Chaumareys had further orders to recognise Muljadi's rule in the name of France, and to offer him whatever he needed to control his alliance.' He looked towards the beach, at the seamen who were unloading two of the boats. 'But we *did* come, Thomas. Too late for Colonel Pastor, for he left in the *Argus* to parley for his men with Muljadi. I pity him, even if I admire his courage.'

Herrick nodded slowly, his eyes clouded. 'And when he had gone, the last attack began. No governor, few defenders. Dead men have little to say.'

Herrick thought of their slow approach that morning, the mist on the water distorting the sounds of cannon fire. No wonder the remaining, ragged defenders had not been able to wave or greet them. *Undine* must have seemed like a miracle.

Bolitho said, 'Don Puigserver is our one real card. He can act in the name of Spain and assure Conway of his country's confidence.'

'How did *he* react to the news?'

Bolitho thought of the Spaniard's face as he had listened to Vega. Anguish, shame and then fury. He had seen it all. Only Conway's attitude still remained in shadow. He had said little, and not even argued with Raymond when he had started off on what Parliament would or would not support. Only one thing was certain. The affair had to be contained. No build-up of additional force, no acceptance that there had been a change in rulership, here or anywhere else. As Raymond had explained more than once, the Dutch were too busy recouping their losses caused by the war to want another conflict in their midst. If France thrust more naval might into the area, then Spain, too, might change her views about her untried allegiance with Britain. It could be war, all over again.

Only when Bolitho had made to leave for his ship had the rear admiral drawn him into a corner.

He had said very calmly, 'Politics, a need for furthering trade or colonial power, all are attitudes. Only one thing is properly clear to me, as it must be to you, Bolitho.' He had held his gaze, searching for a reaction before adding, 'Every puzzle must have a key. This one has two. *Undine* and *Argus*. Governments may try to use more power later on, but by then it will be too late for us all. If *Undine* is lost, so are we. Be sure that Le Chaumareys is already well aware of it!'

When Bolitho had made to question him further he had said, 'He is a good officer, make no mistake. Our squadrons had cause to damn his eyes in the war. France has loaned Muljadi their best, as I hope England has aided me in the same manner!'

Much of his thoughts Bolitho had spoken aloud, for Herrick exclaimed, 'But it is not war, sir! No Frenchman will cross swords for fear of starting one!'

Bolitho watched him and was glad he was here. 'Le Chaumareys will have a letter of marque. He is far from a fool. When he runs out those forty-four guns it will be Muljadi's flag at his peak, not the Fleur de Lys of France.' He stood up and moved vaguely about the cabin. 'But behind each breech will be an experienced crew, the cream of his navy. While we . . .' He half turned, his face suddenly drained again. 'But that is enough. Battles are not won or lost on daydreams.'

Herrick nodded. 'And what will we do now, sir?'

Bolitho tugged the shirt over his head, the same stained one as before.

'We will weigh when the tide is right. If Muljadi has vessels in the area we must close with them. Show him we mean to continue what we have begun.'

He pulled Herrick towards the stern windows as a bugle wailed sadly across the glittering water. Above the fort there was Conway's new flag, the little group of marines beneath it glowing like tiny red insects.

'See, Thomas, there is no drawing back. Not for Conway. Not for any of us.'

Herrick watched the little tableau doubtfully. 'Better to await the *Bedford* surely? With troops and more cannon we would stand a better chance.'

'That is what Le Chaumareys will be thinking.' He smiled, his face suddenly very young. 'At least, I *hope* that is so!'

Herrick groped for this hat, glad of something to occupy his mind and to hold back the apprehension Bolitho's news had brought.

'Will we leave Bellairs and his marines?'

'Half of them. There is much to be done. With corpses lying unburied, the place is a dunghill. The defences are stout, but in need of good men to patrol them. *Rosalind* will remain also under the protection of the battery, such as it is. I think her master is eager to get clear of this place, but Conway is more than a match for him.'

Herrick moved towards the door. 'It is not what I was expecting, sir.'

'Nor I. But like it or not, we have a duty. If Muljadi and his threat is to be overcome, then he must be seen as a common pirate.' He ran his hands along the desk top. '*Argus* or no!'

Herrick hurried out, his thoughts tugging in several directions at once. He found Mudge in the wardroom staring gloomily at a plate of salt beef.

The master asked, 'Are we off again, Mr. 'Errick?'

Herrick smiled. Fact soon grew from rumour in a small ship.

'Yes. The *Argus* is busy here, it seems. As a privateer, and not openly in the name of France.'

Mudge yawned. Unimpressed. 'Nothin' new. We used to do the same for the Company in India. A few ready muzzles always seemed to impress a doubtin' rajah if a little strength was called for.'

Herrick looked at him and sighed. 'So the Frogs will back an armed uprising, and we will support the protection of trade. But what of the people in between, Mr. Mudge?'

The master pushed his plate away with disgust. 'Never asked 'em!' was all he said.

11

Luck of the Game

Bolitho studied the masthead pendant and then walked aft to the compass. North-west by west. It was mid-afternoon, and despite the sky's unclouded, relentless glare there was sufficient wind to make it easier to endure. *Undine* had been made to lie at anchor in Pendang Bay almost until dusk the previous day, the set of the coastal currents and the wind's determination to remain from the south-west making a night passage too dangerous even to attempt. But in the last moments the wind had backed considerably, and with her sleek hull tilting to its pressure, *Undine* had beaten out of the bay, losing the settlement and its grim memories in purple shadow.

But if the wind had remained fresh it was still necessary to hold the ship close-hauled, the yards braced round to keep each sail drawing and steer *Undine* clear of the land. Should the wind veer without warning, and she lay too close to that undulating pattern of green coast, *Undine* could easily find herself hard upon a lee shore, and in real danger.

Herrick asked, 'How much longer will we continue, sir?'

Bolitho did not reply immediately. He was watching the tiny triangular sails of *Undine*'s cutter as it tacked daintily around a small clump of rocky islets.

Then he shifted his gaze to the maintop where Midshipman Keen sat with one bare leg dangling over the barricade, a telescope trained on the distant boat. Davy had the cutter, and would signal the moment he sighted anything. There was no sense in taking the ship too close when good visibility remained. He said, 'We are off the south-western cape, or as near as I can calculate. There are marshes and swamps a'plenty, according to Mr. Mudge and Fowlar. If Captain Vega's information is correct, the Muljadi's vessels may be close by.'

He turned his face into the wind, feeling the sweat drying on his forehead and neck.

'The Benua Islands are about a hundred miles to the west'rd of us. A goodly piece of open water, if we get the chance to run these pirates down.'

Herrick watched him doubtfully, but was comforted by Bolitho's apparent optimism.

'What do we *know* of Muljadi, sir?'

Bolitho walked up the slanting deck to the weather rail and tugged the sticky shirt clear of his ribs.

'Little or nothing. Originally he came from somewhere in North Africa, Morocco or the Barbary Coast, it is said. He was taken as a slave by the Dons and chained in one of their galleys. He escaped and was recaptured.'

Herrick whistled quietly. 'I imagine the Dons were hard with him.'

Bolitho thought suddenly of the elderly Colonel Pastor and his impossible mission.

'The Dons lopped off a hand and an ear and left him marooned on some desolate beach.'

Herrick shook his head. 'Yet somehow he reached the Indies, and can now strike fear into his old masters.'

Bolitho regarded him impassively. 'Or whoever stands between him and his final goal, whatever that may be.'

They both stared up as Keen yelled, 'Deck there! Cutter's signalled, sir! Mr. Davy points to the north'rd!'

Bolitho snatched a glass. 'Of course! I should have realised!'

He trained it on the cutter, and then beyond to the gently sloping cape. Tiny islets, crumbling ridges and rocks, and everywhere the unbroken backcloth of green. Any small vessel could work her way through there, as Davy's cutter was now doing.

Herrick slammed his fists together. 'Got 'em, by God!'

Bolitho said crisply, 'We will remain on this tack for the present. Hoist the recall signal for Mr. Davy and then beat to quarters.' He smiled, if only to ease the mounting excitement. 'In *ten* minutes maybe?'

Herrick waited until Keen had shinned down a backstay to rejoin his signal party and then yelled, 'Beat to quarters! Clear for action!'

A solitary drummer-boy did the best he could, his sticks blurring in double-time as the tattoo brought the hands tumbling from hatchways and gratings.

'That might frighten 'em off, sir.'

Mudge was by his helmsmen, his jowl working on some meat or a quid of tobacco. There was little to choose between them, Bolitho often thought.

'I believe otherwise.'

Bolitho watched the bare-backed seamen dashing to their guns, casting off the lashings and groping for the tools of their trade. A reduced detachment of marines, under the command of a solitary corporal, was parading across the quarterdeck, while a handful more clambered aloft to the foretop and its swivel gun.

The cutter had already turned bows-on, her sails lowered, and thrusting through the inshore swell under oars alone.

'They will not have met with many frigates, I'm thinking. Their leader will try to reach open sea and outreach us, rather than face a blockade or the risk of our landing marines at his back.' He touched Mudge's arm impetuously. 'He'll not know how unused we are to such affairs, eh?'
be taught a lesson, an' double quick, in my reckonin'!'

Mudge pouted. 'I only 'ope that bugger Muljadi is 'ere, too! 'E needs to

'Deck there!' The lookout at the masthead waited until the scamper on the gun deck stopped. 'Sail on th' lee bow!'

'By heaven, so there is!' Midshipman Keen gripped a seaman's arm and added excitedly, 'Schooner by the cut of her!'

The seaman, pigtailed, and with ten years in the Navy, glanced at him and grinned.

'By God, I envy you young gennlemen your learnin', sir!'

But his sarcasm was lost in the excitement of the moment.

Herrick held up his hand as the last gun captain faced aft towards him. From the break below the quarterdeck a bosun's mate shouted, 'All cleared aft, sir!' Herrick swung round and saw Bolitho examining his new watch.

'Cleared for action, sir.'

'Twelve minutes, *exactly*.' Bolitho glanced up at the masthead. 'But for the lookout's hail, I believe you may have done it in less.' He let the mock formality drop. 'Well done, Mr. Herrick and pass the word to all hands.'

He walked back down the angled deck and trained his glass across the nettings. Two raked masts with big dark sails. Like wings. They appeared motionless, the hull still hidden beyond one more probing spit of land. It was an illusion. She was edging around the last dangerous point. After that she would be up and away. But it would take her a good while yet.

He swung round. 'Where is that damned cutter?'

Mowll, the master-at-arms, and easily the most unpopular man aboard, called, 'Comin' up fast, sir!'

'Well, signal Mr. Davy to make haste. I'll have to leave him astern otherwise.'

'Deck there! 'Tis another sail on th' lee bow!'

Herrick watched in silence until he had discovered the second pair of sails in his glass.

'Another schooner. Probably Company ships taken by these pirates.'

'No doubt.'

Bolitho turned to watch the cutter swinging round to drive beneath the main chains with a shuddering thud. Curses and clattering oars, all were finally quenched by Davy's angry voice and the more patient tones of Shellabeer, the boatswain, who was studying the whole manoeuvre from the gangway with obvious disgust.

Allday had been standing behind Bolitho and whispered, 'Should have had young Mr. Armitage in charge, Captain. He'd have driven right through into the spirit store, cutter an' all'

Bolitho smiled and allowed Allday to buckle on his sword. He had not seen his coxswain since breakfast, just after dawn. Yet the moment of danger, a hint of action, and he was here. Without fuss, and hardly a word to betray his presence.

'Maybe.'

He saw Midshipman Armitage with Soames below the foremast, checking a list of gun crews which Soames had re-allotted on passage from India. He found a moment to wonder what Armitage's mother would think if she saw her adored boy now. Leaner and well tanned, his hair too long, and his shirt in need of a good wash. She would probably burst into tears all over again. But in one way he had not changed. He was still as clumsy and as lacking in confidence as his first day aboard.

Little Penn, on the other hand, who was strutting importantly beside the starboard battery of twelve-pounders and waiting to assist Lieutenant Davy, had no such handicap. If anything, he was prone to attempt tasks which were several spans of experience beyond his twelve years.

Davy came struggling aft, ducking beneath a swinging shadow as the cutter was hoisted inboard and on to its chocks above the gun deck. He was soaked in spray, but very pleased with himself.

Bolitho said, 'That was well done. By making a quick sighting-report, you have given us an edge on those two vessels.'

Davy beamed. 'Some prize-money perhaps, sir?'

Bolitho hid a smile. 'We will see.'

Herrick waited for Davy to join his gun crews and then said, 'Just the two schooners. Nothing else in sight.' He rubbed his hands noisily.

Bolitho lowered the telescope and nodded. 'Very well, Mr. Herrick. You may load and run out now.' He glanced at the masthead pendant for the hundredth time. 'We will make more sail directly, and show these pirates what they are against.'

'Both Schooners are keeping well inshore, sir.' Herrick lowered his telescope and turned to watch Bolitho's reactions. 'With that rig they can sail really close to the wind.'

Bolitho walked to the compass, the picture of the two other vessels sharp in his mind. For over half an hour they had worked slowly and methodically between a small crop of islets, and were now following the coastline towards a sloping spur of headland. Around that there was yet another bay, with more jutting spits of land, but the schooners would choose their moment most carefully. Go about and dash for the open sea, separate perhaps, and so lessen *Undine*'s chances of conquest.

They were both well-handled vessels, and through his glass he had seen an assortment of small cannon and swivels, and an equally varied selection of men.

Mudge watched him gloomily. 'Wind's backed a'piece, sir. *Might* 'old.'

Bolitho turned and stared along his ship, weighing the risks and the gains. The green headland was reaching down towards *Undine*'s starboard bow, or so it appeared. In fact, it was still some three miles distant. The two schooners, black against the lively wave crests, seemed to overlap into one ungainly craft, their great sails etched across the land.

He said firmly, 'Get the t'gallants on her, and alter course two points to starboard.'

Herrick stared at him. 'It'll be close, sir. If the wind veers we'll be hard put to beat off the shore.'

When Bolitho did not reply he sighed and lifted his speaking trumpet. 'Man the braces!'

From further aft the helmsmen spun their spokes, the senior one squinting at the flapping canvas and at the tilting compass bowl until even Mudge was satisfied.

'Nor'-west by north, sir!'

'Very well.'

Bolitho studied the headland again. A trap for the two schooners, or a last resting place for *Undine*, as Herrick seemed to think.

Herrick was watching the topmen, waiting until the topgallant sails were freed and then brought under control like bulging steel breastplates. *Undine* was moving swiftly now, for with the wind sweeping tightly across her larboard quarter, and with topsails and topgallants braced to best advantage, there was little doubt the range was falling away.

Mudge asked worriedly, 'D'you think they'll try to go about, sir?'

'Perhaps.' Bolitho shivered as a curtain of spray lifted and burst across the weather rail, soaking him to the skin, adding to his rising excitement. 'They'll try and weather the headland as close as they dare and use the next bay to change tack. Or, if one or both loses his head, we'll rake 'em as he goes about on this side of the headland.'

He peered at the gun deck, at the figures beside each twelve-pounder. One good broadside would be more than enough for any schooner. The second might strike without risking a similar fate. He shut it from his mind. The fight was not even begun yet.

He pictured Conway back there in his remote kingdom. He would know better than Puigserver or Raymond what was at stake. With any luck *Undine* might settle Conway's security long enough for him to demonstrate what he could do.

A faint crack echoed across the water and a white feather of spray showed itself for just a few seconds, well away from the starboard bow. It brought a chorus of jeers from the waiting gun crews.

'Run up the colours, Mr. Keen.'

Bolitho saw the handful of marines in the foretop adjusting their swivel gun. Some more were already cradling their long muskets along the hammock nettings, their faces stiff with concentration.

'One of 'em's making a run for it, sir!'

Bolitho caught his breath as the sternmost schooner tilted at a steep angle, her great mainsail sweeping above her deck like a huge wing while she altered course hard to larboard.

Somebody yelled, 'By Jesus, she's in irons! Look at th' bugger!'

The schooner's captain had mistimed it very badly, for as his command pounded round to cross the wind's eye and find sea-room elsewhere, the sails flapped and rippled in hopeless confusion.

Bolitho shouted, 'We'll take him first! Stand by, the larboard battery!'

He saw Soames hurrying down his line of guns, the captains crouching like athletes behind each breech, trigger lines taut as they peered through the open ports for a first sight of the target.

Bolitho straddled his legs and tried to hold his telescope on the nearest vessel. She was falling awkwardly down-wind, her narrow deck clearly visible as her crew fought to bring her back under control. *Undine* was overhauling her so rapidly that she was already lying some two cables from the larboard bow, and seemed to swell in size even as he watched. He saw the strange flag at her peak, black, with a red emblem in its centre. A prancing beast of some sort. He closed the glass with a snap and saw Keen flinch at the sound.

Allday grinned. 'Two minutes, Captain. Just right.' He nodded towards the opposite bow where the other schooner was holding steadily on course towards the headland. 'He seems content to let his mates go under.'

Soames was peering aft, his curved hanger glittering in the bright sunlight as he raised it slowly above his head. The glare was making him grimace so badly that he appeared to be grinning like a madman.

Bolitho looked at Mudge. 'Let her fall off another point.' He forced a smile. 'Not a moment longer than necessary, I promise.'

He pulled out his sword and held it casually across his shoulder. Through his crumpled shirt it felt like ice.

The helmsman yelled hoarsely, 'Nor', nor'-west it is, sir!'

There was no time to perfect the set of the yards, no time for anything now as with barely a stagger *Undine* turned even further towards the shore, the movement dragging the labouring schooner into the view of the eager gun captains.

Bolitho shouted, 'As you bear, Mr. Soames!'

Soames bellowed, 'Stand by!' He came loping aft, pausing at each gun to peer along its muzzle. Satisfied, he jumped aside and yelled, '*Fire!*'

Bolitho tensed as the uneven broadside belched and shuddered along his ship's side. Soames had done well. To an extra puff of wind which had pushed the frigate over to leeward, he had judged it perfectly, taking the enemy ship on the uproll, raking her savagely from end to end.

Bolitho grasped a stay, his eyes blinded with smoke as the wind funnelled it back through every port. Men were coughing and swearing in the thick brown fog, but urged on by shouts and threats they were still managing to sponge out and reload for another broadside when needed.

He stared with amazement at the schooner as the smoke cleared away from the quarterdeck. Dismasted, almost buried under a chaos of fallen spars and ripped canvas, she seemed a total wreck.

'Bring her back to nor'-west by north, Mr. Mudge.'

He did not see the master's face, his look of relief and admiration. His ears were still ringing to the thunder of cannon fire, the sharper, probing cracks of the quarterdeck six-pounders. He hoped the less experienced men had found time to tie their scarves over their ears. Caught at the wrong angle, it only took one shot to deafen a man. Often permanently.

'Run out!' Soames was peering at his crews as gun captain after captain raised a powder-blackened fist to show his weapon was loaded.

Herrick shouted, 'Now for t'other one!'

He waved to Davy at the starboard battery, the gesture impulsive, unnoticed by himself. Davy waved back, his movement jerky, like a puppet. As they swept after the second schooner Midshipman Penn moved slightly to place his lieutenant between him and any possible damage.

Herrick laughed aloud. 'By God, young Penn has the right idea, sir!' He peered up at the streaming pendant. 'The wind is still kind, and this is putting new heart into our people.'

Bolitho watched him gravely. Later they would talk about it. But when it was happening, to you, to those around you, it was pointless to discuss anything. You never really knew the man in action. Pride, anger, insanity, it was there, and more. Even on Herrick's homely face. His own, too, no doubt.

He said, 'We will run him as close as we can to the headland. After that it will be up to him. Strike or fight.'

He moved the sword-blade on his shoulder. The ice was gone. Now it was like a heated gun-barrel.

Mudge remarked. 'That master is a fool. 'E should 'ave gone about sooner. I would 'ave done so. Crossed *Undine*'s bows afore we could blast 'im.' He sighed. ' 'E'll not get a second chance, I'm thinkin'.'

Bolitho looked at him. Mudge was right of course. *Undine* was playing a dangerous game to drive so bravely towards a lee shore, but the schooners had taken even more of a chance.

Herrick was saying, 'Prize crew on one, and take the other in tow, eh, sir! We should get good recompense for two shooners, even if one of 'em is little more than a hulk.'

Bolitho watched the schooner without answering. Was Muljadi aboard her? Or in the other one, dying or already dead with some of his men? Better so, he thought, than fall into Puigserver's hands.

'Deck there!' The cry was almost lost above the chorus of spray and booming canvas. 'Ship on the larboard quarter!'

Bolitho swung round, imagining for a moment that the lookout had been too long in the sun. For an instant he could see nothing, and then as his vision cleared he saw the forecourse and topsail of another ship standing around the last headland, the one they had rounded so carefully in pursuit of the schooners.

Herrick gasped, 'What is she?' He stared at Bolitho. 'The *Argus*?'

Bolitho nodded grimly. 'I fear so, Mr. Herrick.'

He tried to keep his tone level when his whole being was screaming at him to act, to do the impossible. And how easy he had made it for them. He had allowed the schooners to draw him, like a fox after two rabbits. *Argus* must have been following them along the coast, waiting for the trap to be sprung, reading Bolitho's mind without even being able to see him.

Herrick exclaimed, 'Then, by God, we'll tell Mr. Frenchman to sheer off! This is none of his affair!'

Keen called, 'She's overhauling us, sir.'

Bolitho looked past him. The *Argus* was already beating well out on their larboard quarter, taking the wind-gage, doing exactly what he had attempted to do to the schooners. Now *Undine* was in the trap. Run aground, or try and claw to windward? He saw the sunlight flashing down the big frigate's exposed side, the small moving shadows above the creaming water as she ran out her whole broadside.

He thought of the man behind those guns. How did he feel at this moment?

Herrick said quietly, 'Eighteen-pounders, I'm told, sir?' He watched his face, as if hoping for a denial of *Argus*'s strength.

'Yes.'

He drew in a long breath as a flag broke from the Frenchman's peak. Black and red, like the ones which had flown above the schooners. *Letter of marque*. Hired by a foreign power, the flag merely to keep up a pretence of legality.

Keen lowered his telescope and said quickly, 'She's almost up to the dismasted schooner, sir.' He was managing to sound calm, but his hands were shaking badly. 'There are some men in the water. I think they were thrown outboard when the masts came down.'

Bolitho took the glass and watched, his mind cold as he saw the frigate ride through and over the men in the water. The captain had probably not even seen them. All he saw was *Undine*.

He raised his voice, hoping the others would not despair at its strangeness. 'We will alter course directly.' He ignored the unspoken protest on Mudge's heavy face .'Get the t'gallants off her, Mr. Herrick. The Frenchman will expect us to do so if we are about to fight.' He looked at Mudge again. 'Without so much canvas we may be able to gain a little room to give an account of ourselves.'

Mudge replied harshly, 'It'll mean crossin' 'er bows, sir! Even if we gets round without 'avin' the sticks torn out of us, what then? The *Argus* will overreach us and put a full broadside through our stern as she passes!'

Bolitho regarded him bleakly. 'I am relying on his desire to retain the wind-gage, for without it he might change places with us.' He saw no agreement in Mudge's tiny eyes. 'Or would you have me haul down our colours, eh?'

Mudge flushed angrily. 'That ain't fair, sir!'

Bolitho nodded. 'Neither is a battle.'

Mudge looked away. 'I'll do me best, sir. Lay 'er as close to th' wind as she's ever bin.' He tapped the compass bowl. 'If th' wind 'olds, we should be able to steer almost due west.' He strode to the wheel. 'God 'elp me.'

Bolitho turned and saw the topmen sliding down to the deck again, felt the more sluggish motion as *Undine* plunged ahead on topsails and fore-course. A glance at the other ship told him that her captain was doing likewise. He had no need to worry. *Undine* would have to stand and fight. There was no room left to run away. He walked slowly back and forth, stepping unseeingly over the six-pounder tackles, his knee brushing against a crouching seaman as he passed. *Argus*'s captain would be watching his every move. The advantage, if there was one, would last only seconds, a few minutes at best. He looked at the headland. It seemed very close now, extending far out beyond the larboard bow, like a great arm waiting to snatch them whole.

Then he strode to the quarterdeck rail and called, 'Mr. Soames! I will want a broadside as we put about. You have small chance of hitting him, but the sudden challenge may have an effect.' He let his gaze move slowly along the upturned faces. 'You will have to reload and run out quicker than ever before. The *Argus* is a powerful ship and will endeavour to use her heavier iron to full advantage. We must get to close quarters.' He felt the grin frozen to his lips like a clamp. 'Show him that our lads are better, no matter what damn flag he wears!'

A few raised a cheer, but it was not much of a rally.

Herrick said quietly, 'Ready when you are, sir.'

It seemed very quiet. Bolitho looked aloft yet again. The pendant flicked out as before. If the wind backed further it would be some small help. If it veered it would be disaster. Then he looked at Soames as he clumped heavily aft and disappeared below the quarterdeck. To supervise the sternmost twelve-pounders, which would bear first once they had altered course. Davy was by the foremast, sending some of his own gun crews across to assist the larboard battery. If *Argus*'s eighteen-pounders got to grips they would need plenty of replacements, he thought grimly.

He faced Herrick and smiled. 'Well, Thomas?'

Herrick shrugged. 'I'll tell you what I think when it's over and done with, sir.'

Bolitho nodded. It was an unnerving feeling. It always was, of course, and yet you imagined that each time was worse than the one before. In an hour, in minutes, he could be dead. Thomas Herrick, his friend, might be fighting a battle not of his choosing, or screaming out his life on the orlop deck.

And Mudge. Hand-picked because of his vast store of knowledge. But for this commission he would have been discharged now. Living with his children, and his grandchildren, too, in all probability.

He snapped, 'So be it then! Put the helm down!'

'Man the braces. Lively there!'

Shuddering and groaning in protest, *Undine* slewed round to the thunder of wind and wildly flapping canvas. Bolitho saw spray bursting through the open ports as she swayed further and further to the violent change of tack. From the corner of his eye he saw the *Argus*'s topsails lifting above the hammock nettings, her shape shortening as *Undine* swung round across her bows. A gun banged out, and the ball whimpered somewhere overhead. Someone must have fired too soon, or perhaps the French captain had already guessed what they were trying to do.

Soames was ready and waiting, and the first crash of gunfire shook the deck violently, the smoke swirling up and over the nettings in a writhing pall. Gun by gun down the side, from stern to bow, the six-pounders joining in as the *Argus* crossed each black muzzle. Bolitho saw her foresail jerk and throb to the onslaught, holes appearing like magic as Soames's gun crews fired, reloaded and fired again.

When he peered forward Bolitho saw that the headland had eased back to starboard, the schooner already tiny as she scuttled around it and into the next bay.

Mudge yelled, 'West by north, sir! Full an' bye!' He was mopping his eyes with his handkerchief, clinging to the mizzen mast pike rack to hold himself upright.

He gestured towards the gaff where the red ensign streamed almost abeam. 'Close as we can get, sir!'

Bolitho winced as the six-pounders barked out again, and saw the nearest one bounding inboard until caught and held by its tackle. Its crew was already sponging out and groping for fresh charges and another ball from the shot garland, eyes white and staring through the grime, voices lost in the crash and roar of cannon fire, the squeal of trucks as like angry hogs the heavy guns were run out towards the enemy.

The *Argus* had at last followed Bolitho's lead. She was swinging round, her yards braced almost fore and aft, to hold the wind and keep *Undine* under her lee.

Even as he watched Bolitho saw the long orange tongues flashing from her ports, the bombardment unhurried and carefully aimed as gun by gun she fired through the swirling curtain of smoke and spray.

A ball screamed above the quarterdeck and slapped through the maintopsail before dropping far abeam. Others were hitting the hull, above or below the waterline, Bolitho had no idea. He heard someone screaming through the choking smoke, saw men dashing hither and thither like prisoners in hell as they rammed home the new charges and threw their shining, blackened bodies to the tackles again and again.

Above the din he heard Soames's deep voice rallying and cursing as he kept his men at their guns. A swivel banged out from the top, and he imagined the marines were firing more to ease their own fears than with much hope of hitting anything.

A quarterdeck gun port seemed to explode in a great burst of flame, and Bolitho saw men, and pieces of men hurled in all directions at once as a ball tore splinters from the bulwark and transformed them into hideous darts.

One marine ran sobbing from the nettings, his hands clawing at what remained of his face. Others stood or knelt by their fallen companions, firing, reloading, firing, reloading, until it seemed life itself had stopped.

A down-draught of wind swirled the smoke away, and Bolitho saw the other frigate's yards and punctured sails barely fifty yards abeam. He saw the filtered sunlight touching pikes and cutlasses as the enemy prepared to board, or to fight off their attempt to do likewise. He gasped as another line of bright tongues darted through the smoke, felt the planks buck under his feet, the crash and clatter of a gun being overturned or smashed to fragments.

When he peered upwards he saw that the maintopsail was little better than a rag, but every spar was still intact. A wounded seaman clung to the mainyard, his blood running down one leg unheeded to the deck far below. Another seaman managed to reach him and drag him to safety, and together they crouched below the maintop, caught in the severed ratlines like two broken birds.

Herrick was yelling, 'He's trying to cripple us, sir! Take us as a prize!'

Bolitho nodded and stopped to drag an injured man clear of a six-pounder. He had already guessed *Argus*'s intentions. Another ship for Muljadi's use, or perhaps to replace *Argus* so that she could return to France.

The thought seemed to drive into his heart like a knife.

'We'll put the helm hard down! Swing the bows right into him!' He did not recognise his own voice. 'Tell Davy to get ready to grapple!' He seized Herrick's arm. 'We *must* grapple! He'll pound us to splinters at this rate!'

He felt the blast of a ball past his head, heard it strike the opposite bulwark and send a mass of wood splinters scything across the deck like arrows.

Herrick was yelling to Mudge and the men at the braces, and through the smoke Bolitho saw *Argus*'s shadowy outline loom above the forecastle, the sudden movement of figures in her bows as the two ships drove together.

Above the din of gunfire and shouting he heard the sails jerking and banging, the wind lost to them, the ship already falling sluggishly abeam.

Herrick staggered in some blood and gasped, 'No use! Can't grapple!'

Bolitho stared past him. The enemy was already edging ahead and across *Undine's* larboard bow, a few guns firing as she went, holding the wind and changing course very slightly while *Undine* floundered helplessly, her remaining sails almost aback.

She was going to rake *Undine* with every available gun, but give Bolitho time to haul down his colours before she reached his stern and finished what she had begun.

He felt Herrick tugging his arm.

'What now?'

Herrick pointed up through the smoke, where the sunlight was making a small path through the drifting smoke.

'The lookout, sir! He's reported a sail to the west'rd!' His eyes were shining with hope. 'The Frenchman's making off!'

Bolitho looked at him dully. It was true, and he had heard nothing. Deafened by gunfire, or fogged in his own despair, he did not know. But the *Argus* was already spreading her mainsail and was driving down-wind with gathering power towards the open strait.

Bolitho said, 'Hands to the braces, Mr. Herrick. Lay her on the larboard tack again. If we can signal this newcomer we may still be able to give chase.'

He heard a small cry, and when he turned he saw two seamen kneeling beside Keen's body. The midshipman was trying to reach down to his stomach, but one of the seamen was gripping his wrists while the other slit open his bloodstained breeches with a dirk and threw them aside. A few inches above the groin there was something like a broken bone, but Bolitho knew it was far worse. A wood splinter blasted from the deck, and probably held tight by its own barbs.

He knelt down and touched it with his fingers, seeing the blood pulsing across the youth's thigh, hearing his sobs as he tried not to scream.

Bolitho thought of Whitmarsh, far away in Pendang Bay, helping to heal the sick and wounded from the garrison.

One of the seamen said, ''E'll not last, sir, without 'elp. I'll fetch a surgeon's mate.'

Allday was kneeling beside him and said, 'No. I'll do it.'

Bolitho looked at him, seeing the determination on his face.

Then he turned and said, 'Easy, Mr. Keen. You'll be about again soon.'

He felt the rising anger and despair pricking his eyes. What had he brought them all to? He touched the midshipman's bare shoulder. It was smooth like a woman's. He had not even begun to live yet.

He snapped, 'Are you sure, Allday?'

The coxswain eyed him calmly. 'I'm as good as those other butchers.'

Davy came hurrying aft and touched his hat. 'Masthead has reported the other ship to be the *Bedford*, sir. The Frenchman must have thought her to be a man-of-war.'

He looked at Keen's wound and said hoarsely, 'My God.'

Bolitho stood up slowly, watching the midshipman's fingers opening and closing like trapped animals in the seaman's strong grip.

'Very well, Allday. Take him aft to the cabin. I'll be down myself as soon as I've attended to things here.'

Allday looked at him. 'Don't you fret, Captain. It's the luck of the game. Our turn will come.' He nodded to the two seamen. 'Pick him up.'

Keen gave a sharp cry as they moved him to the cabin hatch, and before he vanished below Bolitho saw that his eyes were fixed unwinkingly on the sky above the tattered sails. Trying to hold on to it? So that by keeping the picture in his mind he might retain his life itself.

Bolitho bent and picked up the midshipman's dirk from the stained deck. He handed it to Davy and said, 'We will make contact with the *Bedford*. There is nothing more we can do for the present but return to the settlement.'

Herrick said, 'The old *Bedford*.' He sounded bitter. 'A bloody storeship from Madras full of seasick soldiers and their womenfolk.'

Bolitho watched the helmsman bringing *Undine* carefully back on course, the skilful way they were allowing for the punctured sails' loss of power.

'If *Argus* had known that, she'd have done for both of us.' He saw the surprise and sudden concern and added simply, 'But not before we had rendered *her* equally useless.'

He glanced aloft at the masthead pendant. How many times had he done that? He took out his watch and flicked open the guard. Remembering. The whole sea-fight had taken less than two hours, and already *Argus* was almost lost in the offshore haze which marked the coming of evening. He shaded his eyes to look for the *Bedford*, and saw her topsails on the horizon like small yellow shells.

Then he looked around at the splintered planking, the small line of corpses which had been dragged below the weather gangway. There was much to do, and he must not give way for an instant if his men were to keep the will to fight again if the time came. He saw another corpse being carried up from the forehatch, and knew he would have to deal with the reports of damage, arrange for replacements and repairs. And burials.

He heard another sharp cry through the cabin skylight, and thought of Keen being spreadeagled there while Allday tried to extract the splinter.

He said, 'I am going below, Mr. Herrick. Deal with reports on damage and casualties.' He saw him nod. 'Thank you.'

As he hurried below Herrick said quietly, 'No. Thank *you*.'

Bolitho brushed past the sentry at his door and then stopped. It was very quiet in the cabin, and when he saw Keen's naked body lying on the deck he thought he was too late.

Allday said, 'All done, Captain.' He held up the jagged red lump in some pincers. 'I think he did very well, for a lad.'

Bolitho looked down at Keen's ashen face. There was blood on his lips where one of the seamen had held a strap between his teeth to prevent him from biting through his tongue. Noddall and the other seamen were finishing tying the dressing around the wound, and there was a thick smell of rum in the air.

Bolitho said quietly, 'Thank you, Allday. I never knew you understood such things.'

Allday shook his head. 'Did it to a sheep once. Poor thing fell down a cliff on to a broken sapling. Very much the same really.'

Bolitho walked to the stern windows and sucked in a lungful of air. 'You must tell Mr. Keen that when he is well again.' He turned and watched him gravely. 'Do you think he will fully recover?'

Allday nodded. 'Yes. Another inch or so and it might have been the end.' He forced a grin, seeing the strain on Bolitho's face. 'For the ladies, anyway!'

The door opened and Herrick said, 'We are within signalling distance of *Bedford*, sir.'

'I'll come up.' He paused and looked down at Keen. Even a glance told him his breathing was easier. 'Casualties?'

Herrick dropped his eyes. 'Ten killed, sir. Twenty wounded. It's a miracle we didn't lose far more. The carpenter and his mate are below, but it seems most of the holes are above the waterline. She's a *lucky* ship, sir.'

Bolitho looked from him to Allday. 'I'm the lucky one.' Then he walked from the cabin.

Allday shook his head and sighed, releasing more rum into the smoky air. 'My advice is to leave him be, Mr. Herrick, sir.'

Herrick nodded. 'I know. But he has taken this setback badly, though I know of no captain who could have done better.'

Allday dropped his voice. 'But one captain *did* do better today. And ours'll not rest until he's met with him again, I'm thinking.'

Keen gave a soft moan and Allday snapped, 'Come on, you idlers! Basin to his head! I've poured so much grog into his guts he'll spew all over the cabin when he comes to the surface again!'

Herrick smiled and walked out towards the ladder, seeing the men replacing the lashings on the guns, glancing at him and grinning as he passed.

One of them called, 'We showed the bastards, eh, sir?'

Herrick paused, 'That we did, lads. The captain was proud of you.'

The seaman grinned more broadly. 'Aye, sir. I seed 'im in the thick of it, walkin' about like 'e was on Plymouth 'Oe. I knew then that we was goin' to be all right.'

Herrick climbed towards the sunlight and stared up at the torn sails. If only you knew, he thought sadly.

He found the other lieutenants and warrant officers already assembled on the quarterdeck giving their various reports while Bolitho leaned against the mainmast trunk.

When he saw Herrick he said, 'There is still a good span of daylight left. We'll put the hands to replacing canvas and running-rigging while it lasts. I have ordered the galley fire to be lit, and we'll see that our people get a good meal.' He gestured towards the labouring storeship which was now less than a mile away. 'We might even poach a few extra hands from *her*, eh?'

Herrick saw the others watching Bolitho dully, their bodies almost limp with exhaustion and delayed shock. He guessed that this other Bolitho, cool, confident, filled with ideas again, was the one the seaman on the gun crew had pictured throughout the battle.

The fact that he knew the real Bolitho behind the shield made him feel suddenly privileged and restored.

12

In for a Blow

Rear Admiral Beves Conway made a dark silhouette against the window's colourful rectangle, but Bolitho could recognise his impatience even though his back was turned. Beyond him, still and peaceful above their own varying shadows, the anchored ships shone in the late sunlight.

Undine lay apart from the heavy transport and the little brig *Rosalind*, and it was impossible to see the damage she had received from the French frigate's eighteen-pounders. Occasionally, when there was a lull in the voices, Bolitho heard the echoes of thudding hammers, the rasp of saws to show that only distance made *Undine*'s trim appearance a lie.

The air in the big, timbered room was cool after the open bay, and although the various figures sitting around it looked as if they had barely moved since his last visit, Bolitho noticed that the place itself had changed considerably in so short a time. More furniture, some rugs, and a whole array of gleaming decanters and glasses made it look lived in, rather than a fortress under siege.

Don Luis Puigserver sat on a brass-bound chest, sipping wine, while James Raymond, tight-lipped and unsmiling, faced him across a littered table. The brig's master, Captain Vega of the original garrison and two red-coated soldiers from the *Bedford* made up the rest of the gathering. One of the latter, a heavy-faced man introduced briefly as Major Frederick Jardine, and who commanded the soldiers brought from Madras, Bolitho instantly recognised as the one he had seen there when he had been escorting Viola Raymond. He had a fat, belligerent face, and his small, piggy eyes had hardly left Bolitho since he had arrived. The other soldier, a Captain Strype, was his second-in-command, and a complete opposite. Tall and stick-thin, with a black moustache, he spoke with a lisp, and had a short, barking laugh. He was probably rather stupid, Bolitho thought, but was obviously much in awe of his superior.

Conway said sharply, 'Naturally I am very distressed to learn of *Argus*'s attack, Captain Bolitho.'

Raymond said, '*Unwarranted*, too.'

Conway turned lightly on his heels, his hair yellow in the sunlight. 'But not unexpected, Raymond. Not by *me*, that is. It was obvious from the beginning that the French were implicated. They have to be, for their own interest's sake. We are lucky that *Bedford*'s arrival put paid to their intention to take Captain Bolitho's ship from him.' He shifted his gaze, his tone incisive. 'And he would have done so, eh?'

Bolitho felt all their eyes on him. 'I believe so, sir.'

Conway bobbed his head. 'Good. Good, Bolitho. I wanted the truth and, believe me, I know what it cost you.'

Raymond tried again to put his point of view. 'I think, sir, that we should despatch the brig to Madras without delay. Sir Montagu Strang may consider that further operations here might be imprudent.' He ignored Conway's stiffening shoulders. 'Later, perhaps, some new plan may be conceived. Until then, we must take this affair as a warning.'

Conway rasped, 'A *warning*? Do you imagine that for one instant I will let some damned pirate work off his wrath on me and so imperil the very task I have just undertaken?' He stepped closer. 'Well, *do you*?'

Raymond paled but replied stubbornly, 'I am here on behalf of the government, sir. As an adviser. The French must realise that you are outmanoeuvred before you have begun. If this Muljadi is allowed to plunder and ravage these waters, then there is no chance of using Pendang Bay as a new and flourishing station for trade. No shipping master would risk it.' He turned towards the brig's captain. 'Is that not so?'

The man nodded glumly. 'We need more protection, sir.'

Raymond sounded triumphant. 'Exactly! That is what the French intend. If we ask for more men-of-war to patrol the area, they, too, will even the balance by sending additional consorts for *Argus*.'

Conway stared at him. 'Then so be it!'

'No, sir. It would mean war. *Argus* is protected by her letter of marque. Muljadi is protected by his own power and backed up by his French friends. There are a thousand Muljadis in the Indies, some who are genuine rulers, and some who reign over fewer people than Captain Bolitho does at present. We all want to extend our trade and influence, to China if need be, and beyond. There are riches we can only dream of, lands where people have never heard of King George, or Louis either, for that matter.'

Bolitho said quietly, 'You are advising the governor to admit defeat, sir. Do I understand correctly?'

Raymond smiled calmly. 'As you have done, eh?'

Bolitho walked to the window and stared down at his ship. It gave him time. Allowed the sudden blinding anger to depart. In the lower enclosure he saw Midshipman Keen sitting with one of the ship's boys rescued from the *Nervion*. He had been detailed to look after Keen, to assist him, if only by making him rest. It was still not possible to be sure he would recover from his wound. Was it really only the day before yesterday? The smoke and noise, the aftermath of hard, heavy work to put their ship to rights. The sea-burials, each corpse heavily weighted to ensure it went straight down to avoid the prowling sharks.

He said, 'I take it, Mr. Raymond, you have never borne arms for your country?' He did not wait for an answer. 'Had you ever worn the King's coat you would have known that one defeat, if admitted, is not the end of a battle.'

He heard Captain Strype say in his thin voice, 'By Gad, that's not much of an argument, what?'

Bolitho turned swiftly, his tone hard. 'I was addressing Mr. Raymond, sir, not some damned mercenary who because of his rank imagines himself to be a soldier!'

Don Puigserver brought his glass down to the table with a loud bang. 'Gentlemen! I know that Vega and I are no longer involved here. I also believe that both *Señor* Raymond and the governor,' he bowed slightly to Conway, 'are both right. With Muljadi free to use his ruthless power and so influence other *friendly* rulers in the Indies, you can make no advances. With more military strength you would only excite a hostile reaction and further French involvement.' He paused and gave an eloquent shrug. 'Which I doubt my own country could ignore.'

Bolitho nodded towards him, grateful for his interruption. Another second and he knew he would have said too much, and Conway, even had he wanted to, would have been unable to help him.

Major Jardine cleared his throat. 'Despite what the gallant captain has said,' he did not look at Bolitho, 'I believe my force will be sufficient. I have two hundred sepoys and a mule battery. All experienced.' He had a thick voice, and sweated badly, despite the room's comparative coolness.

Puigserver regarded him gravely. 'If *Nervion* had been here, none of this could have happened. An additional ship, the men, and the showing of our flag to the *Argus* would certainly have delayed, if not defeated, Muljadi's intentions.'

Conway said, 'But she is not here. Only the *Undine*.'

Jardine said thickly, 'And she does not seem to have acquitted herself too well.' He turned to Bolitho, his small eyes like steel. 'Even as a mere soldier, a *mercenary*, I can see that neither of the schooners lies at anchor, and as far as we know, the *Argus* still flies Muljadi's colours. What say *you*, Captain?'

Bolitho faced him. 'The first schooner turned turtle and sank. The other took advantage of *Argus*'s presence to escape.' He could feel little emotion now. Words and taunts were inevitable. It was better to get it over with. Clear the air.

'Indeed, yes.' Jardine leaned back in his chair, his polished boots squeaking. 'And then the *Bedford* arrived to give you help. The poor, much-maligned Company's own ship was the one to drive *Argus* away.'

'Had you been there, Major—'

Jardine spread his plump hands. 'But I was not, sir. I am a soldier. I am supposed to be able to leave such matters to our Navy, surely?'

Conway said coldly, 'I have heard enough. I will brook no more hostility here. Not from you, Bolitho,' he looked at Jardine, 'nor from anyone else!' He thrust his hands behind him, making his sloping shoulders droop even further. 'Had *Undine* been beaten in open combat I would have removed Captain Bolitho from command. He knows that well enough, and so should the rest of you. The Navy is too often expected to fight greater forces than itself possesses, and has been so successful in the past that victory against ridiculous odds is now taken for granted. By the empty-minded men of politics, and those who care more for quick profit than lasting security! As it is, Captain Bolitho will be required to sail without further delay, other than completing *necessary* repairs, for Muljadi's own territory in the strait.' He looked at Bolitho calmly. 'You will make contact with *Argus*'s captain under flag of truce, and convey a message which I will give you.'

Raymond said quickly, 'May I suggest, plead with you, sir, that you allow Don Puigserver to go with Captain Bolitho? He has the right to demand the freedom of Spain's last governor here, Colonel Pastor. He could explain his displeasure at such—'

Conway shouted, his voice bounding back from the timbered walls. 'I have been appointed governor, Raymond! I don't need your apron strings, nor do I need the help of the King of Spain, d'you understand?'

Raymond's defiance wilted under Conway's sudden anger. He said nothing.

Puigserver stood up and walked slowly towards the door, followed gratefully by *Capitan* Vega.

He paused and looked back at them, his eyes very dark. 'I would have accompanied *Capitan* Bolitho with pleasure, of course.' He smiled briefly. 'I have a great admiration for his courage, his . . .' he searched for the word, '. . . his integrity. But I have much to do. My task is to embark the remaining Spanish soldiers and their dependents on to the *Bedford*.' He glanced at Conway, his smile fading. 'As you remarked this morning, the flag of Spain no longer has authority here.'

Bolitho watched him stride out. He had sensed the tension as soon as he had arrived. It could not have been easy for Conway. Fretting over lack of news, waiting for supplies and troops to arrive. But he was wrong to antagonise Puigserver. If things went badly here, Conway would need all the references he could get, even in Spain.

Jardine remarked vaguely, 'I'd better be off then. Settle the sepoys in their company lines, and replace the marines as sentries and pickets.'

No thanks, no admiration for what Captain Bellairs and his marines had achieved in so short a time. Bolitho glanced through the window again. The encroaching brush and creeper cleared away, and corpses buried. The place used as a hospital had been cleaned and painted, and even Whitmarsh had been full of praise for their efforts.

Conway nodded. 'I will meet you here after sunset, Major.'

Bolitho waited until the two soldiers had left the room and then said, 'I am sorry about my outburst, sir. But I have had my bellyful of his kind.'

Conway grunted. 'Perhaps. But you will hold your tongue in future. If Jardine commanded only a handful of crippled beggars I would say the same. I need every man I can get.'

Raymond stood up and yawned. 'This damned heat. I think I'll take a nap before dinner.'

He, too, walked out. He did not look at Bolitho.

Conway said softly, 'He disliked your remark about bearing arms, you know.' He chuckled. 'His wife has been singing the praises of sea-officers in general during your absence, and you in particular.' He frowned. 'I seem to be plagued with those intent on disruption.'

'Is she well sir?' He could not face him. 'I have not seen her since my return.'

'She's been assisting that sot of a surgeon with the sick and wounded.' His eyebrows mounted. '*Surprised?* By God, Bolitho, you've much to learn about women!' He nodded sharply. 'But you'll see, all in good time.'

Bolitho recalled her refusal to help tend the injured aboard *Undine* after Puigserver had been carried aboard more dead than alive. And her reasons? He sighed. Perhaps Puigserver and Conway were both right. He had much to learn.

He replied, 'I will return to the ship, sir. There will be a lot to arrange.'

'Yes.' Conway watched him thoughtfully. 'And remember. When you meet *Argus*'s captain, keep your personal feelings to yourself. He is doing his own work as best he can. You would do the same if so ordered. If Le Chaumareys is still in command, and not killed by one of your guns, he will be eager to meet you also. He is older than you, but I think you may have something in common.' His lines deepened as he added dryly, 'A disrespect for your superiors, if nothing else!'

Bolitho picked up his hat. You could never be sure about Conway. Where the warmth ended and the steel began.

Conway said, 'Please come ashore tonight and dine with the rest of . . .' he waved one hand around the room, '. . . the castaways.'

Bolitho recognised the dismissal and walked from the room.

Beyond the palisades the jungle was as thick and as overpowering as ever, and yet already the place felt familiar, lasting.

He found Allday lounging in the shade below the main entrance. He was watching some native women who were washing clothes in a large wooden trough. They were small and olive-skinned, and although well covered, displayed supple charm which Allday apparently admired greatly.

He straightened his back and said, 'All done, Captain?' He saw Bolitho's glance and nodded. 'Fair little wenches. We will have to watch our people, Captain.'

'Only the people?'

Allday grinned. 'Ah, well now . . .'

At that moment Bolitho saw the surgeon emerge from the makeshift hospital, wiping his hands on a rag and squinting into the slanting sunlight.

He saw Bolitho and nodded. 'Two of the men wounded in your battle can return to work, sir. Two more died, as you know, but the rest stand a good chance of survival.' He looked away. 'Until the next time.'

Bolitho considered his words. A total of twelve had died because of *Argus*. Despite the luck at there being few in comparison to the fierceness of the battle, it was too many. He sighed. Perhaps Herrick had got some more 'volunteers' from the other ships.

Whitmarsh said, 'Your coxswain did a good job, by the way. The boy should have died by rights.' He looked at Allday. 'Wasted. You should make something of your life.'

Bolitho said quietly, 'I am glad you thanked him for his efforts on Mr. Keen's behalf. But I am sure he will decide his own future.'

Allday could have been stone-deaf for all the notice he paid to their comments.

Whitmarsh said, 'Well, anyway, sir, I've cleaned up a bit here. Most of them will heal, although a few more will die before they reach Spain. Disease mostly, of course.'

'Of course?'

Whitmarsh looked him full in the eyes. 'Rotten with it. Just as they have given it to these poor ignorant savages, too. If any one of your sailors comes to me with that damned pox, I'll make him wish he'd never touched a woman in his life!'

'They are your sailors, too, Mr. Whitmarsh.'

Bolitho regarded him searchingly. Despite his usual attitude where naval matters were concerned, he looked a great deal better. Or perhaps there was little to drink here? Either way, he was nothing like the drunken hulk who had tumbled aboard in England.

'So *there* you are, Captain!'

He turned and saw her watching him from the entrance. She was almost covered by a white smock, and wore the same straw hat she had brought from Santa Cruz. Her eyes were in shadow, but there was no doubting the warmth of her smile.

He replied, 'I am grateful for what you have done, ma'am.'

Whitmarsh nodded. 'She is the one who took charge here. Organised the whole hospital from top to bottom.' His admiration was genuine.

She smiled at Allday and then slipped her hand through Bolitho's arm. 'I'll walk with you to the beach, if I may. It is so refreshing to have you back again.'

Bolitho could feel Whitmarsh and Allday watching them.

He said, 'You are looking, er, very well.'

Her hand tightened very slightly. 'Say Viola.'

He smiled. 'Viola.'

'Better.'

When she spoke again her voice was different. 'I saw your ship dropping anchor and was half mad with anxiety. I wanted James to take me out to her by boat. He refused. He would. Then I saw you with a telescope. It was like being there with you. And today I have spent a little time with Valentine.'

'Valentine?' Bolitho looked at her profile. 'Who is that?'

She laughed. 'Of course, you would never remember a thing like a mere name. Why, I am speaking of your Mr. Keen.' The mood changed again. 'The poor boy. He looks so ill, yet can speak of no one but you.' She gripped his arm hard. 'I am almost jealous!'

Bolitho looked past her to where the gig lay beached on the sand, the small breakers hissing and receding around it. The boat's crew were engaged in noisy conversation with some seamen from the brig, and it was plain they were describing what they still saw as their victory over the *Argus* and the schooners.

He smiled, despite his earlier bitterness and disappointment. Perhaps they were right. To remain alive under such circumstances could well be seen as a victory.

She was looking at him, standing slightly apart as if searching for something.

'You smile, Captain? At me? At my boldness perhaps?'

He reached out and took her hand. 'Not that. Never.'

She tossed her head. 'That is better, Captain.'

He heard Allday's shoes on the sand, the sudden silence from the gig.

'The name is Richard,' he said gravely.

Allday heard their combined laughter and felt suddenly worried. This was a danger he could recognise well enough, far better than his captain, he thought.

He removed his hat as Bolitho walked down the beach towards the gig, and heard him say, 'I will be ashore later, ma'am.'

She held the hat brim to shade her eyes. 'Until then, Captain.'

But Allday had seen the look on her face before it was hidden in shadow. That, too, was something he could recognise. He glanced quickly at the tower above the fort and took a deep breath. Squalls ahead, he decided, and not too far away.

Bolitho looked at him. 'Well?'

Allday's face was rigid. 'So it would appear, Captain.'

Three days after returning to Teluk Pendang His Majesty's frigate *Undine* weighed anchor again and put to sea. By late afternoon of that day she stood well out in the glittering expanse of the Java Sea with not even a cormorant for company.

To any casual observer who might have watched her departure there was little to betray her mauling from *Argus*'s cannon, but as Bolitho came on deck he was well aware of it. Shrouds and stays which had been cut by grape and canister shone brightly in their fresh tar. Deck planking, hastily replaced, looked duller than the well-tried and holystoned wood which had been in the ship since she had been built. The sail-maker and his mates had been busier than most, and even now, as he walked slowly along the weather side, Bolitho saw Jonas Tait squatting with some helpers, his one eye gleaming watchfully as with needles and palms they continued with their patching.

Fowlar, who was master's mate of the watch, touched his forehead and reported, 'South-west by south, sir.' He gestured abeam. 'A bit of a swell, and Mr. Soames has gone forrard to check the gun lashings.'

Bolitho glanced at the compass and then the set of each sail by turn. He had already noticed the steep, sickening motion, but it was too early to gauge its importance. The barometer was unsteady, but that was usual in these latitudes, and when he had consulted Mudge he had chosen his words carefully.

'Could be in for a storm, sir. You never know in these waters.'

He nodded to Fowlar and walked to the quarterdeck rail, feeling the sun lingering on his shoulders and face. It was a fair wind, he thought, but sultry, and somehow depressing.

He saw Herrick speaking with Soames by the starboard twelve-pounders. The boatswain was there, too, pointing out various repairs yet to be done, and through the main hatch he heard the lively sounds of a jig from the ship's fiddler. Normal, everyday sights and noises. He shifted wearily and began to pace up and down the weather side.

From one corner of his eye he saw Soames climb from the gun deck, make as if to approach him, and then return to the opposite side of the deck. Bolitho was relieved. Soames had proved himself a tower of strength in a fight, but as a conversationalist he was heavy and limited.

And Bolitho needed to be left alone. To think. To examine the rights and the wrongs of what he had done. With the land left far astern, and once more abandoned to his own resources, he could view everything much more clearly. Now, as his shadow bobbed and swayed above the black six-pounders, he decided there were far more wrongs than rights.

Inevitable? Something which either of them could have stopped in a second merely by a word, a hint even? He recalled the way she had watched him across the table while the others had talked and chattered the night away. *Capitan* Vega had entertained them with a song so sad it had brought tears to his eyes. Puigserver had spoken of his adventures in the South Americas and the West Indies before the war. Raymond had become steadily drunk after getting into a fruitless argument with Major Jardine on the possibilities of a lasting peace with France.

Conway had remained terribly sober, or if not, Bolitho thought he must be a better actor than he had imagined.

When then, had the actual moment of decision arrived?

He had found himself on the upper rampart with her at his side, leaning over the rough timber to look at the anchored ships in the bay. They had made a fine picture. Tiny lights reflected on the uneasy water, the pale splash of oars as a guardboat patrolled monotonously around its heavier charges.

Without looking at him she had said, 'I want you to stay on shore tonight. Will you?'

Perhaps that had been the moment? He had felt reckless, dangerously so.

'I'll send a message to my first lieutenant.'

He turned to stare along the deck. Herrick was still talking to Shellabeer, and he wondered if he had guessed what had occurred.

He could remember the room exactly. More like a cell, with fewer luxuries than a lieutenant's cabin in a man-of-war. He had lain on the bed, his fingers locked behind his head, listening to the strange noises beyond the walls and the rapid beats of his own heart.

Cries from the jungle, the occasional call of a picket challenging one of the sergeants of the guard. Wind murmuring around the square tower without response from deck or rigging which was his normal life.

Then he had heard the sound of her footstep in the passageway, a quick whisper to her maid before she opened the door and shut it quickly behind her.

It was becoming harder to remember in perfect sequence. The continuity was confused. He could recall holding her tightly against his body, the warmth of her mouth on his, the sudden, overwhelming, desperate need which threw all last caution to the winds.

There had been no light in the tiny room, but that from the moon. He had seen her only briefly, her bare shoulder and thigh shining like silver before she had climbed on to the bed, pulling him down and down, until at last, spent and gasping with the extent of their desire they had lain together as one.

He could not remember sleeping at all. Just holding her, needing her, tortured by the realisation it could not last.

Once during the night and towards dawn she had whispered in his ear, 'Do not reproach yourself. It is not a question of honour. It is a part of life.' She had put her lips to his shoulder and had added softly, 'What a lovely smell you have. Of the ship. Salt and tar.' She had giggled quietly. 'I must have it, too.'

Then the nervous tap on the door, the quick scramble to pull on her gown as her faithful maid warned of the coming of another day.

But for Bolitho it had been different from all other days. He felt totally unlike anything he had been before. Alive, yet restless. Replete, but needing more.

He heard steps on the deck and saw Herrick watching him.

'Yes, Mr. Herrick?'

'Wind's freshening again, sir. Shall I call the hands to reef tops'ls?' He ran his eyes across the ship. 'Rigging's straining a'piece by the sound of it.'

'We'll give her her head a while longer. Until eight bells if possible, when we change tack and run to the west'rd. No sense in tiring the hands when one operation will suffice.' He leaned back, hands on hips as he stared at the main topgallant masthead, the long pendant undulating in the wind. 'She's a lot of power to offer us yet.'

'Aye, sir.' Herrick sounded tired.

'Is anything wrong?'

Bolitho walked to the weather rail and out of earshot of Soames and two seamen who were splicing halliards.

Herrick said quietly, 'You know already, sir. I've said my piece. What's done is done.'

Bolitho watched him gravely. 'Then let us leave it well alone.'

Herrick sighed. 'Very well, sir.' He looked at the helmsmen. 'I'm sorry I could only get four extra hands. Neither *Bedford* nor the *Rosalind* were eager to part with any more. And those I did obtain are troublemakers by the cut of them.' He gave a slow smile. 'Although Mr. Shellabeer assures me they will change their ways before another dawn.'

Midshipman Armitage ran up the ladder and touched his hat.

To Herrick he stammered, 'Mr. Tapril's respects, sir, and would you join him in the magazine.'

Herrick asked, 'Is that all?'

The boy looked uncomfortable. 'He said you'd *promised*, sir.'

'And so I did, Mr. Armitage.'

As the midshipman hurried away Herrick said, 'I was going to arrange to have the powder casks inspected and marked again. No sense in losing good powder.' He lowered his voice. 'Look, sir, are you *sure* you cannot see the folly of what you are doing? There is no telling what damage it might do to your career.'

Bolitho swung towards him and then saw the anxious concern on Herrick's face.

He replied, 'I am relying on your lady luck, Thomas!'

He walked towards the cabin hatch, adding for Soames's benefit, 'Call me the moment there is a change.'

Soames watched him go and then walked aft to the compass.

Fowlar watched him warily. Once back in England, he, too, would get the chance to obtain a commission as lieutenant. The captain had said as much, and that was good enough. But if he did make that first all-important step up the ladder, he hoped he would be happier about it than Lieutenant Soames appeared to be.

Soames rasped, 'Mr Fowlar, your helmsmen are wandering off a point or so! Damn my eyes, I don't expect that from you!'

Fowlar watched him move away and smiled to himself. There was nothing wrong with the helm, and Soames knew it. It was part of the game.

He said, 'Watch your helm, Mallard.'

Mallard transferred a plug of tobacco from one cheek to the other and nodded.

'Aye, Mr. Fowlar, sur.'

The watch continued.

Before the last dog watch had run its course it was obvious the rising wind made it necessary to reef topsails.

Bolitho gripped the hammock nettings and faced along his ship's length as he watched the petty officers checking their men in readiness for going aloft, while Shellabeer and his own hands were already busy scrambling about the boat-tier with further lashings.

Herrick shouted above the wind, 'A second reef within the hour, sir, if I'm any judge!'

Bolitho turned aft and felt the spray as it hissed freely above the weather quarter. The wind had backed rapidly and now blew lustily from the south-east, making the motion both violent and uncomfortable.

He replied, 'We will steer due west once we have reefed. On the larboard tack she will be steadier.'

He watched the great, steeply banked swell, like serried lines of angry glass hills. When the wind got up further, those rounded rollers would break into heavy waves.

Bolitho heard Mudge shout, 'We're in for a blow right enough, sir!' He was clinging to his misshapen hat, his small eyes watering in the wind. 'The barometer is poppin' about like a pea on a drum!'

Davy shouted, 'All mustered, sir!'

'Very well. Hands aloft.' Herrick held up his hand. 'Keep them from racing each other, and stop the bosun's mates from using their rope's-ends.' He glanced at Bolitho. 'One slip, and a man would go overboard without a chance of recovery.'

Bolitho agreed. Herrick always remembered things like that.

He said, 'I hope this doesn't last too long. If we have to ride it out it will upset Admiral Conway's other arrangements, I have no doubt.'

He looked up as faint shouts and curses told him of the struggle the topmen were having with the violent, unruly canvas. Fisting and kicking, pitching this way and that, with the deck far below, the very sight of their efforts made him feel queasy.

It took the best part of an hour to master the sails to Herrick's satisfaction, and by then it was time to take in yet another reef. Spray and spindrift whipped across the weather side, and every timber and stay seemed to be groaning in a protesting chorus.

Bolitho shouted, 'Lay her round another point, Mr. Herrick! We will steer west-by-south!'

Herrick nodded, his face running with spray. 'Afterguard to the mizzen braces!' He shook his speaking trumpet angrily. 'Keep together, damn you!'

A marine had slipped and fallen in a scarlet heap, knocking several of his comrades into confusion.

Bolitho pointed abeam, to the first glitter of white crests as the wind did its work.

'She's steadier, Mr. Herrick!' He relaxed as the experienced seamen rushed aft to help the marines and less skilled hands on seamen rushed aft to help the marines and less skilled hands on the mizzen braces. 'And not a man hurt, by the looks of it!'

Undine had paid off stiffly to the wind, her shrouds and ratlines shining jet-black against the rising swell. But with her yards comfortably braced, and canvas reduced to topsails and jibs, she was making the best of it.

Davy panted on to the quarterdeck, his shirt wringing and sodden.

'All secure, sir!' He lurched backwards, tottered and then reeled against the nettings, adding savagely, 'By the Lord, I'd forgotten what a real gale felt like!'

Bolitho smiled. 'Dismiss the watch below. But tell the boatswain to make regular inspections. We can't afford to lose precious gear for want of a good lashing.' He turned to Herrick. 'Come below with me.'

Despite the din of sea and strained timbers it seemed warm and inviting in the cabin. Bolitho watched the spray making diagonal patterns across the stern windows, heard the rudder grinding and squeaking while the helmsmen held the frigate on her new course.

Noddall pattered into the cabin, his small body steeply angled as he fetched goblets for the two officers.

Herrick wedged himself in a corner of the bench seat and regarded Bolitho questioningly.

'If we have to run before the wind, would it make so much difference, sir?'

Bolitho thought of his written orders, Conway's brief but lucid instructions.

'It might.' He waited until they both had goblets and said, 'To what we can achieve, Thomas!'

Herrick chuckled. 'I'll share *that* toast.'

Bolitho sat at the desk, feeling the desk tilting and then sliding into yet another trough.

He was glad he had insisted that Keen and some of the other wounded had been left at Pendang Bay. Too much of this sort of motion would burst open even the finest stitches.

He said, 'Admiral Conway intends to let *Bedford* put to sea as soon as we are on our way to the Benua Islands. I think he wishes to get rid of the Spanish troops and dependents as soon as possible.'

Herrick watched him. 'Bit risky, isn't it, sir? With the damned *Argus* still at large?'

Bolitho shook his head. 'I think not. I am certain the French or Muljadi will have agents watching Conway's settlement. They will have seen us weigh anchor. *Argus* will know we are coming well enough.'

Herrick looked glum. 'They are as clever as that, eh?'

'We must assume so. I think Conway is right. Better to get *Bedford* away with her passengers and despatches for Madras before things get any worse.'

'If there's a real storm, it'll put paid to everything.' Herrick cheered up somewhat. 'The Frogs don't like bad weather.'

Bolitho smiled at Herrick's confidence. 'This one may not care. He has been in these waters a long time, I believe. He is not one of the hit-and-run kind who used to dash out of Brest or Lorient and flee for home again at the sight of an English ship.' He rubbed his chin. 'This Le Chaumareys interests me. I would like to know more of him than his record in battle.'

Herrick nodded. 'He appears to know a lot about you, sir.'

'Too much.'

A steep roller cruised beneath the quarter, holding the ship up and tilting her forward at a steeper angle before freeing her again to sidle into the next rough. Beyond the closed door they heard the marine sentry slip and fall, his musket clattering away while he cursed and fought to regain his composure.

Bolitho said slowly, 'When we meet with *Argus*'s captain we must keep our eyes well opened. If he agrees to parley, we may learn something. If not, we must be ready to fight.'

Herrick frowned 'I'd rather fight, sir. It's the only way I know how to be at ease with a Frenchman.'

Bolitho thought suddenly of that room at the Admiralty, the calm features of Admiral Winslade as he had given a brief outline of *Undine*'s mission. Four months back. A time of peace, yet ships had foundered, and men had been killed or crippled for life.

But even the lordly power of admiralty, the guile and experience of politics were useless out here. A solitary, wind-swept frigate, minimum resources, and no guiding hand when one might be needed.

Herrick took Bolitho's quiet mood as a signal. He placed his goblet inside the table fiddles and rose carefully to his feet.

'Time to do my rounds, sir.' He cocked his head to listen as water gurgled and sluiced along the quarterdeck scuppers. 'I have the middle watch, and may snatch a cat-nap before I face the breeze.'

Bolitho pulled out his watch and felt Herrick looking at it.

'I will turn in now. I have a notion we may all be needed before long.'

In fact, it felt only minutes after his head had touched the pillow that someone was clinging to the cot and tapping his shoulder. It was Allday, his shadow rising and falling like a black spectre as the cabin lantern swung violently from the deckhead.

'Sorry to wake you, Captain, but it's getting far worse up top.' He paused to allow Bolitho's brain to clear. 'Mr. Herrick told me to pass the word.'

Bolitho stumbled out of the cot, instantly conscious of a new, more uneven motion. As he pulled on his breeches and shoes and held out his arms for a heavy tarpaulin coat he asked, 'What time is it?'

Allday had to shout as the sea thundered against the hull and surged angrily along the upper deck.

'Morning watch is about to be called, sir!'

'Tell Mr. Herrick! Call them *now*!' He gripped his arm and together they lurched half across the cabin like two tipsy sailors. 'I want all hands directly! I'm going to the chart space.'

He found Mudge already there, his lumpy figure sprawled across the table while he peered at the chart, blaspheming quietly as the lantern went mad above his head.

Bolitho snapped, 'How is it?'

He glanced up at him, his eyes red in the feeble glow.

'Bad, sir. We'll 'ave the canvas in shreds unless we lie to for a bit.'

Bolitho peered at the chart. Plenty of sea-room. That was the only consolation.

He hurried towards the quarterdeck ladder and almost fell as the ship swayed and corkscrewed in two separate motions. He fought his way to the wheel, where four helmsmen, their bodies lashed firmly to prevent their being caught unawares by an incoming wave, were fighting the spokes, their eyes glowing in the flickering compass light.

Herrick shouted, 'I've called all hands, sir! And I've put extra ones on the pumps!'

Bolitho peered at the jerking compass card. 'Very well. We will lie to under shortened maintops'l. Get Davy to put the best men aloft at once!'

He turned as a sound like gunshot echoed above the shriek of wind and sea, and saw the mizzen topsail rip itself apart, the fragments tearing yet again into ragged streamers, pale against the low, scudding clouds.

He could hear the dismal clank of pumps, hoarse cries as men blundered to their stations, dodging below the gangways as more frothing water flooded amongst them.

Fowlar shouted, 'The sailmaker has only just repaired that cro'jack, sir!' He was grinning, in spite of the confusion. 'He'll not be pleased!'

Bolitho was watching the black shapes of the topmen as they climbed cautiously up the vibrating ratlines. The wind flattened them occasionally against the shrouds, so that they hung motionless before starting up again for the topsail yards.

Mudge yelled, 'Th' quarter boat 'as carried away, sir!'

No one paid any heed, and Herrick spluttered in spray before saying, 'There goes the foretops'l, sir! Those lads are doing fine.'

Something dropped amongst the taut rigging before falling to the gun deck with a sickening thud.

Herrick shouted, 'Man from aloft! Take him to the surgeon!'

Bolitho bit his lip. It was unlikely he could live after such a fall.

Fighting every yard of the way, *Undine* came round into the wind, her hull awash from quarterdeck to beakhead, and with men clinging to tethered guns or stanchions as each wave surged and broke across her reeling deck.

Mudge bellowed hoarsely, 'She'll ride it out now, sir!'

Bolitho nodded, his mind cringing from the onslaught, the very vehemence of the storm.

'We'll set the spanker if the tops'l carries away. Tell the boatswain to have his hands ready, there'll not be time for regrets if that one goes!'

He felt a bowline being bent around his waist, and saw Allday's teeth bared in a grin.

'You look after us, Captain. This'll take care of you.'

Bolitho nodded, the breath knocked out of him. Then he clung to the dripping nettings, peering through the painful needles of spray as he watched over his command. A lucky ship? Perhaps he had spoken too soon. Tempted fate.

Herrick gasped, 'Could be over by first light, sir.'

But when dawn did come, and Bolitho saw the angry, copper-coloured clouds reflected upon the endless, jagged wavecrests, he knew it was not going to give up so willingly.

High above the deck, torn and broken cordage floated to the wind like dead creeper, and the solitary braced topsail looked so full-bellied that it could follow the fate of the other at any second.

He looked at Herrick, seeing the angry sores on his neck and hands where the blown salt had done its work. The other crouching, battered figures nearby were no better. He thought of the other frigate, probably snug in a protected anchorage, and felt the anger welling up inside him.

'Get some hands aloft, Mr. Herrick! There's work to be done!'

Herrick was already clawing his way along the nettings towards the rail.

Bolitho wiped his face and mouth with his arm. If they could weather this one, he thought, they would be ready for anything.

13

No Quarter

'Some more 'ot coffee, sir?' Noddall held his pot above Bolitho's mug without waiting for a reply.

Bolitho sipped it slowly, feeling the scalding liquid running through him. A taste of rum, too. Noddall was certainly doing his best.

He eased his shoulders and winced. Every bone and fibre seemed to ache. As if he had been in actual battle.

He studied the weary figures who were moving about the upper deck, made curiously ghostlike and unreal by the heavy vapour which rose from sodden planking and clothing alike.

It had been just that, he thought gravely. A battle, no less than if cannon had been employed. For three days and nights they had fought it out, their confined world made even smaller by the great roaring expanse of wave-crests, their minds blunted by the ceaseless shriek of the wind. Like him, the ship seemed to have had the breath knocked from her. Now, under barely drawing topsails, her littered decks steaming once more beneath an empty sky, she was thrusting only slowly above her reflection. In places paint had been pared away to display wood so bare it could have been the work of a carpenter. Everywhere men were at work, marlin spikes and needles, hammers and tackles, endeavouring to restore the ship which had carried them through such a frenzy that even Mudge had admitted it was one of the bitterest he had endured.

He came across the deck now, his coat steaming gently, his jowls almost hidden in white stubble.

'Accordin' to me reckonin', sir, we've overreached the Benua Group by a fair piece. When we checks the noon sights I'll be 'appier.' He squinted upwards towards the flapping pendant which had lost almost half its length in the storm. 'But the wind's veered as I thought it might. I suggest we 'old your new course, nor' nor-east, until we gets a better fix of our position.' He blew his nose loudly. 'An' I'd make so bold as to say 'ow well you 'andled 'er sir.' He puffed out his cheeks. 'A couple of times I thought we was done for.'

Bolitho looked away. 'Thank you.'

He was thinking of two men less fortunate. One had gone during the second night. Swept away without a sound. Nobody had seen him go. The other had slipped from the larboard cathead where he had been working feverishly to repair chafing lashings around the anchor stock. A solitary wavecrest had pulled him from his perch almost casually, so that for a while longer he had still imagined he would be saved. Willing hands had reached out for him, but another wave had flung him not outwards but high in the air like a kicking doll before hurling him against the massive anchor with savage force. Roskilly, a bosun's mate, had insisted he had heard the man's ribs cave in before he had been dragged screaming into the frothing water alongside.

Including the man who had fallen from aloft, that made three dead, with some seven others injured. Broken bones, fingers torn raw by bucking, sodden canvas, skin inflamed by salt, by wind, and by lines snaking through clutching hands in pitch darkness, made up most of the surgeon's list.

Herrick strode aft and said, 'I'm having a new jib bent on now, sir. The other's only fit for patching.' He took a mug from Noddall and cradled it gratefully to his mouth. 'Heaven help the poor sailorman!'

Bolitho looked at him. 'You'd not change it.'

Herrick grimaced. 'A few times back there I wondered if I'd get the choice!'

Davy, who had the watch, joined them by the rail.

'What are our chances of a landfall, sir?'

He looked older, less assured than he had before the action with the frigate. During the storm he had behaved well, so perhaps he still believed the only real menace came from a cannon's mouth.

Bolitho considered his question. 'That will depend on fixing our position. Allowing for our drift, and the shifting of the wind, I'd say we might sight the islands before nightfall.'

He smiled, the effort making him more conscious of the strain he had been under.

Herrick said dourly, 'The damned Frog will be laughing at us. Sitting in harbour under that bloody pirate's guns.'

Bolitho looked at him thoughtfully. The same idea had only left him occasionally, and that when he had needed all his thoughts elsewhere. To parley with the French captain was one thing. To accept that he was serving under Muljadi's flag meant far more. It would be an open admission of failure. An acceptance that Muljadi's sovereignty did exist. If Conway agreed to the latter, every other European power which had trading and protection rights in the Indies, especially the powerful Dutch East India Company, would see it as England's move to take all the advantages for herself. Which was exactly what the French would like.

What should he do if the French Captain refused to be moved by Conway's message? Patrol up and down outside the islands and draw *Argus* into combat? It would be a one-sided affair. Le Chaumareys was an old hand in these waters, knew every islet and cove where he had once hidden to avoid British frigates in time of war. Equally, he would be well advised to lie at anchor, living off the land, until *Undine* was made to withdraw.

He felt his tiredness putting an edge to his anger. If only the politicians were here to see what their ideas of world strategy actually represented in flesh and blood, in wood and canvas.

'Land ho! Fine on th' starboard bow!'

Davy rubbed his hands. 'Nearer than you thought, sir.'

Mudge said quickly, 'Never!' He fumbled with his slate and made some rapid calculations. 'There's a small islet, some forty miles to the south'rd of the Benuas, sir.' He peered round until he had discovered Midshipman Penn's diminutive shape by the taffrail. 'Aloft with ye, Mr. Penn, an' fetch the big glass for company.' He eyed him fiercely. 'Take a look, an' make me a sketch just like I taught you!'

He waited until the boy had scampered for the main shrouds and chuckled. 'Cap'n Cook 'ad the right idea, sir. Sketch an' describe every damn thing you see. Time'll come when every man-o'-war will 'ave a complete set o' pictures to study.' He watched Penn's progress. 'Not that some'll 'eed 'em, o' course.'

Bolitho smiled at Herrick. 'Better than I had expected. We'll have a man in the chains and begin soundings as we pass this islet of the master's. The chart describes some nineteen fathoms hereabouts, but I'd prefer to be certain.'

Twenty minutes later Penn returned to the deck, his brown features sprinkled with sweat. He held out his grubby pad and stood back to watch Mudge's reactions.

Over his shoulder Davy said, 'Looks like a whale to me.'

Mudge eyed him coldly. 'So it does.' To Penn he said, 'Fair work. It is 'ow I recalls it.' His small eyes returned to Davy. 'Exactly like a great rocky *whale*.' The merest pause. '*Sir*.'

'Anything there?'

Bolitho took a glass and trained it above the gun deck. As yet he could see nothing but the same, painful glare. He wondered momentarily where the storm had gone, how it could vanish after showing so much fury.

'Bless you, no, sir.' Mudge beamed at Davy's discomfort. 'Just a fistful o' rocks, like the tip of some undersea ridge, as no doubt it was one time. But I suppose it could be used as shelter in a full gale.'

Bolitho watched some seamen hauling a new length of hemp along the larboard gangway. Tired and unshaven perhaps, but there was something else, too. The way they worked together. Confidently.

He said, 'We will alter course a point, Mr. Davy, and take a look at your whale.'

Davy hurried to the rail. 'Mr. Penn! Pipe the hands to the braces!'

Herrick watched him, smiling easily. 'Any reason, sir?'

Bolitho shrugged. 'More of a feeling.'

He watched the men thronging along the decks, where the steamy vapour continued to drift amongst them. From forward he saw real smoke, as Bogle, the cook, got busy with the first hot meal they would have eaten since the storm had come and gone.

He saw the yards swinging to the pull of the braces, heard the helmsman cry, 'Nor'-east by north, sir!'

Davy hurried past to consult the binnacle and the set of the sails.

'Another pull on the weather mainbrace, Mr. Shellabeer!' He dabbed his streaming face. 'Now belay!'

Bolitho smiled. When Davy was irritated he always performed his duties better, for some reason.

He said, 'Put another good lookout aloft, if you please. I want that islet watched until we are up to it.'

He glanced at the sun's blinding patterns beyond the gently pitching bowsprit.

'I am going below to shave and to bribe Noddall into finding a clean shirt.'

Later, as he lay back in a chair while Allday busied himself with his razor, he found time to wonder what he would do if or when he met with *Argus*'s captain.

The hastily heated water, the skilful movement of the blade against his skin was making him relax, muscle by muscle, and he could feel the air from the open stern windows across his bare shoulders like a soothing embrace.

All around the world the King's captains were going about their affairs. Fighting scurvy and disease, carrying despatches for an admiral or some lonely outpost not marked on any schoolboy's map. Or pondering behind a cabin bulkhead in dread of mutiny, or planning some diversion to prevent one. Fighting maybe, with some dissident ruler who had attacked the King's subjects, defiled the flag, butchered men and women. He smiled. And some would be like himself. A tiny extension to a half-formed plan.

Through the open skylight he heard the lookout's cry, 'Deck there! Ship at anchor close inshore!'

He jumped to his feet, seizing the clean shirt and using it to dab away the soap from his chin.

Allday stood aside and grinned admiringly. 'By God, Captain, you must have more wiles than a farmyard cat! How did you know there was a ship?'

Bolitho was tucking the crumpled shirt inside his breeches. 'Magic, Allday!'

He hurried for the door, and then forced himself to wait until Midshipman Penn appeared in the entrance.

'A ship, sir! Mr. Davy's respects, and he believes it may be a schooner.'

'Thank you, Mr. Penn.' It was all he could do to appear calm. 'I will come up when I have completed dressing. My compliments to the first lieutenant, and please ask him to meet me on the quarterdeck.'

He turned and saw Allday hiding a smile.

'Is something amusing you?'

'Why, no, Captain.' Allday watched him gravely. 'But I am always ready to see my betters at their affairs.'

Bolitho smiled. 'Then I hope you learn from it.'

He walked into the passageway and made for the ladder.

Herrick greeted him excitedly. 'A schooner, sir! The man in the foremast crosstrees is my best lookout, and I had a glass sent aloft to him.' He stared at Bolitho with open astonishment. 'It is uncanny!'

Bolitho smiled shortly. 'A fair guess, if the truth be told. But it was a bad storm, and when the master suggested this small isle as a place for shelter I began a'thinking.'

He took Penn's telescope and trained it towards the bows. There was the islet now, an uneven blob of grey/blue. The masthead would be able to see much more.

'Where is the wind?'

Davy said, 'From the south-west, sir.'

Bolitho let his mind move accordingly. 'Alter course and lay her on the larboard tack.' He crossed to the binnacle, seeing the helmsmen watching him curiously. 'We will steer nor' nor'-west.'

He waited as a bosun's mate dashed to pipe the hands to the braces again. Then to Herrick and Davy he added slowly, 'This way we will keep the isle between us and the other vessel and hold our advantage to wind'rd. Get the courses on her, but keep the t'gallants furled for the present.'

Herrick understood at once. 'Aye, sir. The less canvas we display, the less likely they are to sight us.'

Bolitho glanced at Mudge, who had appeared with Fowlar beside the helm.

'You put the thought in my mind. I have always wondered why Muljadi has good warning of our movements. I think we shall soon know his methods.' He looked at the washed-out blue sky above the tapering masts. 'But for the storm we would have approached directly from the east'rd. Thanks to the weather's rough mood we have gained something for once.'

Herrick asked softly, 'What of the admiral's instructions, sir?' Then he grinned. 'I can see from your expression that you intend to choose your own moment, sir.'

Bolitho smiled. 'One cannot bargain if one is a beggar. I have learned that long since.'

He looked up as with sails cracking and shivering to the new tack *Undine* turned purposefully to larboard, the small, humped islet moving away from the weather bow as if released from an anchor.

'Nor' nor-west, sir! Full an' bye!'

Bolitho beckoned to Davy. 'Get the courses on her now.' To Mudge he called, 'How long, by your consideration?'

Mudge pouted. 'Two hours, sir.'

'Good. Then once the sails are drawing well we can send both watches for their meal.'

He watched the scurrying figures clawing along the yards, others standing below on deck ready to sheet home the great fore and main courses.

Herrick nodded approvingly. 'Bit different from when they came aboard, sir.'

Bolitho found he was desperately hungry. 'I think that applies to most of us.'

He strode to the cabin hatch, knowing that the unknown vessel might be harmless, or an old wreck long abandoned. Or one more trick to delay or deceive him.

Noddall watched him warily. 'It's salt beef again, sir.'

'That will be excellent.' He ignored the amazement on Noddall's rodent features. 'And I'll take some claret to wash it down.'

He leaned over the sill and stared at the frothing wake below the counter.

Chance, luck, call it what you will, he thought. It was all they had, and he intended to make good use of it.

'By th' mark seventeen!' The leadsman's cry rose easily above the sounds of flapping canvas as *Undine*, her courses again brailed up to the yards, glided steadily towards the islet.

Bolitho saw Shellabeer touch the leadsman's shoulder and reach out to feel the tallow arming in the bottom of the heavy weight before calling, 'Rocky bottom, sir!'

Bolitho nodded. As Mudge had described it, the small islet was more like an isolated rock pile than part of the sea-bed.

'Prepare to anchor, Mr. Herrick.'

He took a glass from Penn and moved it slowly over the ragged outline. They were five cables offshore, but it was close enough to see that the first smooth impression of a surfaced whale had changed severely. The rocks were blue/grey, like Cornish slate, and cut by wind and tide into massive steep gullies, as if some giant had hacked the islet into slices. Apart from a few clumps of gorse or rock flowers, it looked bare and unwelcoming, but there were plenty of sea-birds perched in little clefts, or circling busily above the highest point, which he estimated to be some three hundred feet above the water.

He heard Herrick shouting his orders, the creak of rigging as *Undine* dipped and rose again in a sudden swell. The water looked deep, but it was an illusion. He could see some narrow, stony beaches at the foot of the nearest cliff, and guessed that the safest anchorage was on the opposite side where the other vessel lay hidden. There was surf, too, steep and angry as it licked and spluttered around the one visible landing place.

'Helm a'lee!'

He moved his glass in time with the ship as she turned easily into the wind, watching for any sign of life, the merest movement to show their approach had been seen.

'Let go!'

The sound of the anchor hitting the water seemed unusually loud, and he imagined he could hear it echoing back from those desolate cliffs.

Herrick shouted, 'Lively, lads! Secure those lines!' To Davy he added, 'Lowering parties, man the tackles!'

Bolitho said, 'Have the leadsman watch his line now and see that the anchor is holding fast. If we begin to drag because of the rocky bottom we will veer more cable directly.'

'Aye, sir.'

Herrick hurried away, his face totally absorbed in his own duties.

With the ship swaying and pulling lazily to her cable, it was even quieter, and Bolitho saw some of the birds quitting their precarious perches to fly and circle above the mastheads.

Herrick returned, breathing heavily. 'We seem safe enough, sir. But I've told the anchor-watch to keep alert.' He squinted towards the shore. 'It looks like a graveyard.'

'We will need two boats.' Bolitho spoke his thoughts aloud. 'Gig and cutter will suffice. They will have to run smartly through that surf. The beach is steep by the look of it. So put a good cox'n in the cutter.'

He saw Allday signalling with his fist as the gig rose jerkily from its chocks, the guy-ropes tautening to swing it round and above the gangway.

He added with a smile, 'I think my boat is in safe hands.'

Herrick looked at him anxiously. 'Are *you* going, sir?'

'It is not for want of glory, Thomas.' He lowered his voice, watching the chosen hands as they mustered by the arms' chests. 'But I need to know what we are against, if anything.'

Herrick sounded unconvinced. 'But if the other craft is one of the pirates, sir, what then? Surely you'll want to sweep round and rake the devil as he slips his cable?'

'No.' He shook his head firmly. 'He will be safely anchored yonder. In shallower water than I'd dare enter close enough to rake him. Once clear he could lead us a merry maypole dance, and I fear we would never match his agility in these conditions.' His tone hardened. 'Besides which, I want to *take* him!'

'Boats lowered alongside, sir.' Davy came aft, a curved hanger dangling from his belt.

Bolitho touched his own sword-hilt and saw Captain Bellairs watching the boats with visible irritation at being left behind.

He called, 'Captain Bellairs, I would be obliged if I could have three of your very best sharpshooters in each boat!'

Bellairs brightened considerably and snapped at Sergeant Coaker, 'Well, lively, Sar'nt! Although they should *all* be excellent marksmen, what?'

Herrick grinned. 'That was thoughtful, sir.'

'Perhaps.' Bolitho shifted the glass again to watch some birds landing delicately along the clifftop. They would never do that if men were close by. 'But if seamen are better at scaling cliffs, there is no beating a well-aimed ball at the right moment!'

He nodded to Davy. 'Man your boats.' To Herrick he added casually, 'If things go wrong, you will find the admiral's orders in my cabin.'

'You can rely on me, sir.' Herrick was looking troubled again. 'But I'm certain that—'

Bolitho touched his arm and smiled. 'Yes. But just bear it in mind. If you have to, act upon them, as *you* see fit.'

He walked slowly towards the entry port, seeing the watching seamen and marines as he passed. Familiar now, he could put a name and a value on all of them.

Midshipman Armitage was looking confused and embarrassed. 'Sir! The sharpshooters will not remove their coats, sir!' He blushed as some of the oarsmen in the boats nudged each other and chuckled.

Bellairs snapped, 'Can't have my fellows tramping about like damn vagrants, what?' He saw Bolitho and added quickly, 'I mean, can we, sir?'

Bolitho slipped out of his blue coat and tossed it to Noddall who was hovering by the quarterdeck ladder.

'It is all right.' He nodded to the unsmiling marines. 'If I can shed a little authority, I am certain your men can.' He saw the sergeant gathering up the red coats and shakos, honour apparently restored. He added, 'And it will be a rough climb, with who knows what at the end of it.'

He paused above the swaying boats, trying to think of something he might have missed or forgotten.

Herrick said quietly, 'Good luck, sir.'

Bolitho ran his glance along the crowded gangway and up to the men in the shrouds.

'And you, Thomas. Have the people stand-to, watch and watch about. You know what to do.'

He saw Armitage staggering between the oarsmen in the gig. It was almost cruel to take him. A liability. But he had to begin somewhere. It was a marvel he had ever got to sea at all with a mother like his. If Keen had been here, he would have taken him. He saw Penn peering wistfully from the gun deck. He would have gone with the boats like a shot. He smiled to himself. No wonder the seamen called him 'The Tiger'.

Then he climbed down into the gig. No ceremony this time. As the boats shoved away from the side he was conscious of sudden tension.

'Take the lead, Allday.'

He watched the rocky cliffs rising higher and higher with each pull of the oars, and could feel the strong undertow as the inshore swell frothed and mounted into seething lines of breakers. When he glanced astern he saw the cutter's stem lifting and plunging through the flashing spray, Davy's head and shoulders swaying above the oarsmen while he, too, peered at the land. What was he thinking about? Being killed in this God-forsaken place? Taking a step nearer that badly needed prize-money? Bolitho wiped the spray from his face and concentrated on the swift approach. There was more chance of being drowned than of anything in the immediate future.

He glanced at Allday who was standing in a half crouch, one fist gripping the tiller bar, as he peered from bow to bow, gauging the set of the angry surf, the diagonal lines of breakers as they hurried noisily into the shadows below the cliffs. No need to warn him. Any suggestion at all might have the opposite effect and bring disaster.

Allday remarked, 'Very steep beach, Captain.' His sturdy figure swayed with the hull. 'Go in fast, put her bow round at the last moment t'wards the surf and beach her broadside-to.' He glanced down at him quickly, 'Does that sound fair, Captain?'

Bolitho smiled. 'Very fair.' It would also give them time to scramble ashore and help the cutter as she followed them in.

He felt a sudden chill and realised that the shadows had finally reached out to cover them, and he heard the slap of water, the creak of oars in rowlocks echoing back from the cliffs, as if there was a third and invisible boat nearby.

They almost planed across the last of the surf, the oars desperately keeping with the stroke until Allday yelled, '*Now!*' And as he slammed the tiller hard round he added, 'Back-water to larboard!'

Floundering and tilting dangerously the gig came to the beach almost broadside, the keel grinding across loose pebbles and weed in a violent, protesting shudder.

But men were already leaping into the spray, holding the gunwale, guiding the gig to safety with sheer brute-strength.

'Clear the boat!'

Allday steadied Bolitho's arm as with Armitage and the others he waded, reeled and finally walked on to firm beach.

Bolitho ran to the foot of the cliffs, leaving Allday to supervise the business of getting the gig safely secured.

He waved his arm towards the three marines. 'Spread out! See if you can find a way to the top!'

This, they understood, and with barely a glance towards the onrushing cutter they loped up the first crumbling rock-slide, their muskets primed and held ready.

Bolitho waited, staring up at the jagged clifftop, the pale blue sky above. No heads peering down. No sudden fusilade of musket balls.

He breathed more evenly and turned to watch the cutter as it edged round and plunged wildly before driving on to the beach and amongst the waiting seamen.

Davy staggered towards him, gasping for breath, but loading his pistol with remarkably steady fingers.

Bolitho said, 'Muster the men, and send your three marines after the others.'

He looked for Armitage, but he was nowhere to be seen.

'In God's name!'

Davy grinned as the midshipman came round a large boulder, buttoning his breeches.

Bolitho said harshly, 'If you must relieve yourself at such times, Mr. Armitage, I would be obliged if you would remain in sight!'

Armitage hung his head. 'S-sorry, sir.'

Bolitho relented. 'It would be safer for you, and I will try and hide any embarrassment you might cause me.'

Allday crunched over the loose shingle, chuckling as he, too, loaded a brace of pistols with fresh, dry powder.

'Bless me, Mr. Armitage, but I can understand how you feel!'

The youth stared at him unhappily. 'You can?'

'Why, once, I was hiding in a loft.' He winked at the cutter's coxswain. 'From the bloody pressgang, believe it or not, and all I could think of was pumping my bilges!'

Bolitho said to Davy, 'That seems to have helped his mind a little.'

He forgot Armitage's troubles and said, 'We'll leave four hands with the boats.'

He saw *Undine* swaying like a beautiful model, her stern windows flashing in the sunlight, and imagined Herrick watching their progress. He could send aid to the beached boats if trouble arrived. He looked up at the cliffs again. Damp, clammy, deceptively cool. That would change as soon as they reached the top and the waiting sun.

Bolitho waited for Davy to rejoin him. 'Best be moving off.'

He examined his landing party carefully as Allday waved them towards the cliffs. Thirty in all. Apart from Davy and Armitage, he had brought a master's mate named Carwithen, knowing the man would have resented being left behind after Fowlar's previous involvements. A dark, unsmiling man, he was, like Bolitho, a Cornishman, and hailed from the fishing village of Looe.

He waited while they checked their weapons. His chain of command. Ship or shore, it made no difference to them.

Carwithen said, 'I hope they've a drop to drink when we gets t'other side.'

Bolitho noticed that hardly anybody smiled at his remark. Carwithen was known as a hard man, given to physical violence if challenged. Good at his work, according to the master, but little beyond it. How different from Fowlar, Bolitho thought.

'Lead your party to the left, Mr. Davy, but allow the marines to set the pace.' He looked at Armitage. 'You keep with me.'

He saw a marine waving from a high ledge, indicating the path up the first section of cliff.

It was strange how sailors always hated the actual moment of leaving the sea behind. Like having a line attached to your belt, dragging you back. Bolitho eased the sword further around his hip and reached out for the nearest handhold. Smoothed away by timeless weather. Stained with droppings from a million sea-birds. No wonder ships avoided the place.

As he moved carefully up the fallen boulders he felt a small pressure against his thigh, the watch she had given him in Madras. He thought suddenly of that moment when she had offered him far more. And he had taken it without even a smallest hesitation. How soft, how alive she had felt in his arms.

He grimaced as his fingers slipped in a pile of fresh droppings. And how quickly circumstances could change, he thought grimly.

The passage across the small islet was to prove harder and more exhausting than anyone could have expected. From the moment they topped the first cliff and the sun engulfed them in its searing glare, they realised they must climb immediately into a treacherous gully before they could begin scaling the next part. And so it went on, until they were finally tramping across an almost circular depression which Bolitho guessed was the central part of the islet. It held the heat and shielded them from any sea-breeze, and their progress was further delayed by the clinging carpet of filth which covered the depression from side to side.

Allday gasped, 'Will we rest up once we get to the far side, Captain?' Like the others, his legs and arms were caked with muck, and his face masked in a fine film of dust. 'I am as dry as a hangman's eye!'

Bolitho refrained from looking at his watch again. He could tell from the sun's angle that it was late afternoon. It was taking too long.

He peered across to the other side of the unsheltered depression, seeing Davy's straggling line of men, the marine sharpshooters walking like hunters through a cloud of pale dust, their muskets over their shoulders.

He replied, 'Yes. But we must go carefully with the water ration.'

It was like being on top of the world, the curving sides of the depression hiding everything but the sun and open sky. One of the long, slanting shadows behind him faltered and then sprawled in the inches-deep bird droppings, and without turning he knew it was Armitage.

He heard a seaman say hoarsely, 'Give us yer 'and! Gawd, you do look a sight, beggin' yer pardon, sir!'

Poor Armitage. Bolitho kept his gaze fixed on the pale breeches of the marine directly ahead of him, his body smoking in haze and dust. There were rocks beyond the marine, probably marking the end of the depression. They could take a rest. Find brief shelter while they regained their senses.

He turned and sought out the seaman who had helped Armitage to his feet. 'Can you raise the breath to carry a message to the scouts ahead, Lincoln?'

The man bobbed his head. Small and wiry, his face was disfigured by a terrible scar from some past battle or a tavern brawl. A surgeon had made a bad job of it, and his mouth was drawn up at one side in a permanent, lopsided grin.

'Aye, sir.' The man shaded his eyes.

'Tell them to halt at those rocks.'

He saw Lincoln hurry ahead of the column, his tattered trousers flapping and stirring up more choking dust.

It took another hour to reach those rocks, and Bolitho had the impression he was taking two paces backwards for every one he advanced.

Davy's party arrived amongst the tall rocks almost at the same time, and while the men threw themselves down into the small patches of shade, gasping and wheezing like sick animals, Bolitho called the lieutenant aside and said, 'We will take a look.' He saw Davy nod wearily, his hair bleached so much that it was like corn in the sunlight.

They found a marine on the far side of the rocks, his eyes slitted with professional interest as he stared at the gently sloping hillside which continued without a break towards the sea. And there, cradled inside the narrowest sweep of the islet, the 'whale's tail', was the schooner.

She was so close inshore that for an instant longer Bolitho imagined she had been driven aground in the storm. Then he saw the drifting smoke from a fire on the beach, heard the muffled tap of hammers, and guessed her crew were carrying out repairs. They might even have had the schooner careened to put right some damage to her bilge or keel, but at first glance she looked well enough now.

Tiny figures moved about her deck, and there were several more on the beach and scattered amongst the rocks. The heaviest part of their work was apparently completed.

Davy said, 'They're looking in rock pools, sir. After shellfish or the like.'

Bolitho asked, 'How many, d'you reckon?'

Davy frowned. 'Two dozen, at a guess.'

Bolitho fell silent. It was a long way down the hillside, and no cover at all. His own men would be seen long before they could get to grips. He bit his lip, wondering if the schooner intended to wait another day, or longer.

Carwithen had joined them and said hoarsely, 'They'm not ready to quit yet, sir.' He was whispering, as if the schooner's crew were a few feet away. 'They've got their boats hauled well up the beach.'

Davy shrugged. 'I expect they feel very safe.'

Bolitho took a small glass and trained it carefully between the rocks. One false move, and the sunlight would throw a reflection from the telescope which would be seen for miles.

A lookout. There must be at least one on the shore. A man so placed that he could watch over the tiny cove and see everything but the far side of the island where *Undine* now lay at anchor. He smiled grimly. It was hardly surprising they had found no sentries when they had landed when he thought of their exhausting trek from the beach.

He stiffened, seeing a small movement on a ridge, almost in line with the motionless schooner. He adjusted the glass very slowly. A white, floppy hat, the darker blob of a face underneath.

'There's a lookout on that ridge. The one with the rock pools directly below it.'

Carwithen said, 'Easy. From the sea, no, but I could take him from behind with no trouble at all.' He sounded brutally eager.

The crash of a shot made them crouch lower, while from behind Bolitho heard the sudden clatter of weapons as his men dived for cover.

Something white and flapping fell from the sky and lay quite still on the beach. The searching sailors from the schooner paid very little attention as one of their number walked over to it and picked it up.

Carwithen, said, 'One of 'em's shot a booby. They make fair eatin' if you've nothin' better.'

The marine said. 'Then 'e must be a bloody good shot, sir.'

Bolitho looked at him. His own thought exactly. It would make a frontal assault virtually fatal for all of them.

He said, 'I'll send a message back to the ship. We must wait until dark.' To the marine he added, 'Take this glass, but keep it well shielded.' No need to add a warning or a threat. The marine had just proved he could think as well as shoot.

They found the others relaxed again amidst the rocks, and Allday said, 'Take a drink, Captain.' He held out a flask. 'Tastes like bilge water.'

Bolitho scribbled on his pad and handed it to one of the seamen. 'Take it back to the beach and give it to the petty officer there.' He saw the despair on his face and added gently, 'You need not return. You will have earned a rest by the time you reach *Undine*.'

He heard another shot, muffled this time by the rocks, but it was followed by a different sound, a soft thud.

Carwithen was on his feet in a second. ' 'Nother bird, sir!'

Bolitho followed him to where they had left the marine. He was staring with amazement at the big booby which had dropped almost at his feet, wings outspread, its breast clotted with bright blood.

Davy said harshly, 'Now, how in the name of hell did—'

But Bolitho held up his hand, freezing them all to silence.

Faintly at first, and then more insistently, he heard the scrape and clatter of loose stones as someone hurried up the hillside to collect the dead seabird.

He looked round swiftly. You could not hide thirty men amongst these few rocks. He saw Allday signalling everyone to remain quite still, saw the anxiety in Armitage's eyes as he stared transfixed at the last barrier where the sea's edge shone against the sky and rocks like the top of a great dam.

The sounds were much louder, and Bolitho could hear the man's heavy gasps as he struggled up the last part of the hill.

Nobody moved, and he saw the marine staring at his musket which was two feet away from his fingers. The slightest sound and they were done for.

It was then Carwithen acted. He was closest to the rock barrier, and with barely a sound he reached out and gathered up the dead bird, holding it just a few inches below the top of the nearest rock. His free hand he held under his short blue coat, and Bolitho could see his fingers moving beneath the cloth, trying to free something, while all the time his eyes were fixed unblinkingly on the bird.

It seemed to take an eternity before anything else happened. When it did, it was all too fast to follow.

The man's dark face gaping down at them, his eyes flicking from the bird to Carwithin even as he groped forward to retrieve his prize. The master's mate dropped the booby, the movement so swift that the man was thrown off balance, his hand groping at his belt and the gleaming butt of a pistol. Carwithin murmured, 'Not so, my pretty one!' It was said quietly, almost gently.

Then the other hand came out of his coat, a boarding axe twisting in his fingers as he brought the rearmost end, with its short, savage barb, hard down in the man's neck. With a great heave he gaffed him bodily over the rocks, withdrawing the axe, turning it again just as swiftly before hacking him full across the throat with its blade.

Armitage fell against the marine, whimpering and retching, blood spurting over his legs as the axe jerked free, hesitated and cut down again.

Bolitho seized Carwithen's arm, seeing the axe quivering above the bulging eyes and that great gaping wound. He could feel the pent-up hatred and madness in his biceps, the effort to shake him away and drive the axe again and again into the choking, bubbling thing at his feet.

'Easy! *Enough* damn you!'

There was another terrible silence while they stared at each other or at the corpse which was sprawled across the dead booby.

Carwithen whispered hoarsely, 'That bugger'll never raise hell again!'

Bolitho forced himself to examine the victim. Probably Javanese. Dressed in little better than rags, but the pistol was inscribed with the crest of the East India Company.

He heard Carwithen say, 'Took it off some poor sailor, the bastard!'

Nobody looked at him.

Bolitho knelt by the rocks and studied the beach with the glass. Carwithen had acted quickly and efficiently. But he had enjoyed it. Relished it.

He watched the distant lookout in his rocky ledge, the small figures still searching aimlessly amongst the pools.

He said quietly. 'They saw nothing.'

Davy looked at the sobbing midshipman and asked quietly, 'Will this change things for us, sir?'

Bolitho shook his head. 'Only when this man is missed by his companions.' He looked at the slanting shadows from the rocks. 'So we must bide our time and hope for darkness to come.'

He saw Carwithen wiping his boarding-axe on some cloth he had just cut from the dead man's smock. His face was devoid of anything but satisfaction.

Davy gestured to the others. 'Take this thing away and cover it with stones.' He swallowed hard. 'I'll not forget this day in a hurry.'

Bolitho gripped the midshipman's shoulder and pulled him away from the rocks. 'Listen, Mr. Armitage.' He shook him roughly, seeing the youth's eyes as he stared at the red smudge left by the corpse. 'Get a grip on yourself! I know it was a foul thing to witness, but you are not here today as a mere onlooker, d'you understand?' He shook him again, hating to see the pain and the revulsion in his eyes. 'You are one of my officers, and our people will have to look to you!'

Armitage nodded dazedly. 'Y-yes, sir. I'll try to—' He retched again.

Bolitho added gently, 'I'm sure you will.' He saw Allday watching him over the midshipman's quivering shoulders, the almost imperceptible shake of his head. 'Now be off with you, and check that my message has been sent.'

Allday said quietly, 'Poor lad. He'll never get used to this sort of thing.'

Bolitho looked at him gravely. 'Did you? Did I?'

Allday shrugged. 'We learned to hide what we thought, Captain. It's all a man *can* do.'

'Perhaps.' He saw Davy kicking dust across the drying blood. Then he looked at Carwithen's dark features as he examined the dead man's pistol. 'Although there are some who have no feelings at all, and I have always found them to be less than men.'

Allday followed him back into the shade. Bolitho's mood would soon change at a hint of action, and for the present it was best to leave him to his thoughts.

14

The Bristol Sailmaker

'Time to move, is it, sir?' Davey watched Bolitho as he craned over the rocks, his shirt pale against the darkening sky.

'I believe so. Tell Carwithen to muster the hands.'

He shivered as the sea-breeze explored his body. Once the sun had dipped over the hills at his back it grew cool, even cold, in minutes. They had been too long in the heat, plagued by sun and thirst, and a multitude of flies which had appeared as if by magic. He watched the anchored schooner's outline, the soft glow of lights from poop and forepeak. The fire on the beach had died to a blotch of red embers, and he could see nobody near it, but guessed the lookout was still in his refuge beyond the pools.

Allday whispered, 'All ready, Captain.' He held his cutlass clear of the rocks. 'Mr. Davy's making sure they all know what to do.'

Bolitho nodded without answering, trying to gauge the distance they must cover. Surprisingly, it seemed greater in the growing darkness, but he was reassured by the occasional snatches of voices from the vessel to show they had given no heed to their missing comrade.

Davy slithered down beside him. 'I've sent Carwithen's party away, sir.' He looked at the sky, the isolated puffs of light cloud. 'Wind's steady enough.'

'Yes.' Bolitho checked his pistol and tightened his belt. 'Follow me. Single file.'

Like ghosts they topped the last rock barrier, the sounds of loose stones and rubble seemingly very loud in the gloom. But as Davy had observed, the wind held steady, and was making a lively chop along the beach and narrow spur of headland. Noisy enough to drown any small sound they might be making.

Once, as they followed the curve of the hillside they all froze in their tracks as two dozing sea-birds rose flapping and screaming almost from under their feet.

Bolitho waited, listening to his heart, to the sharp breathing of the men at his back. Nothing. He lifted his arm and they began to move forward and downwards again.

When he looked across his shoulder he saw the rough edge of the rock barrier, where they had waited fretting for sunset, far above his slow-moving party. They were almost down to beach level now, and he heard a man curse quietly as he slipped in the first of the small pools. Davy's party were having to wade in the shallows to his right, and he hoped none of them would fall headlong into one of the rock pools there, now hidden by the rising tide.

He thought momentarily of the ship, anchored on the other side of the islet. The familiar sounds and smells. Herrick waiting anxiously for news of success or disaster. If it was to be the latter, he could do nothing to help this time. His would be the task of contacting the 'enemy' and making what he could of it. It was easier to think of them as the enemy. It never helped to picture them as men. Flesh and bone like himself.

Allday touched his arm urgently. 'Boat coming inshore, Captain!'

Bolitho held up his hand and brought both parties to a shuffling silence. The boat must have come around the schooner's hidden side. He could see the splash of oars, the lively froth of the stem as it bounced across the first leaping surf.

He thought of Carwithen and his handful of men who were creeping up and around the solitary lookout. They should have been there by now. He recalled Carwithen's brutal madness with the boarding axe, and wondered if he had been the one to strike the luckless lookout down.

A voice echoed suddenly in the darkness, and for an instant Bolitho imagined Carwithen had been delayed, or that the lookout was calling an alarm. But the voice came from the boat, louder this time, and despite the strange tongue, Bolitho knew the man was calling a question. Or a name perhaps.

Allday said, 'They've come a'looking for their mate, Captain.' He dropped to one knee to keep the grounding boat framed against the surf. 'Six of 'em.'

Bolitho said quietly, 'Stand fast, lads. Let them come to us.'

He heard a man clicking his jaws together. Tense, nervous. Probably terrified in these unfamiliar surroundings.

Allday said, 'One of 'em's going up the cliff to the lookout.'

Bolitho drew his sword very carefully. Of course. It would be the first place a searcher would go. Ask if the missing man had been seen.

He watched the other five strolling up the beach, swinging their weapons casually, chatting as they approached.

Bolitho glanced behind him. His men were barely visible as they crouched or knelt amongst fallen rocks, or squatted in the sea itself. He turned to study the oncoming shadows. Twenty yards, fifteen. Surely one would see them soon.

A terrible cry tore the stillness apart, hanging above the ridge long after the man had died.

Bolitho saw the five shadows turn in confusion, knew the dying scream must have been the man sent to the lookout.

He yelled, 'At 'em, lads!'

Without a shout or a cheer they were all up and rushing after the five figures who had turned back towards the surf.

One of them slipped and fell headlong, tried to rise, but was slashed into a sobbing heap by a seaman's cutlass as he dashed past.

The others had reached the boat, but deprived of two of their strength, were unable to shift it. Steel gleamed in the shadows, and as the seamen charged amongst them the fight became confused and deadly. A seaman caught his foot in the boat-rope and before he could recover his balance was pinned bodily to the shingle by a long sword. His killer died almost simultaneously. The remaining two threw down their weapons and were instantly clubbed into unmoving heaps by the maddened sailors.

Davy snapped tersely, 'One of ours is dead, sir.' He rolled the man over on to his back and dragged the cutlass from his fingers.

Bolitho eased the sword back into its scabbard. His legs felt shaky from running, from nervous tension. He looked at the anchored schooner. No shouts, no calls to arms. He thought he heard the same sing-song voice chanting above the seething surf, remote and vaguely sad.

Davy said hoarsely, 'Damned poor lookout, sir.'

Bolitho watched his men gathering around the two boats. The one which had been there all day was furthest up the shingle and would need the more men to move it.

He replied, 'Would *you* have expected trouble, in their place?'

Davy shrugged. 'I suppose not.'

Carwithen came hurrying down from the ridge, his helpers hard put to keep up with him.

He said savagely, 'That bloody fool Lincoln was too slow with his dirk!' He glared at the watching men around him. 'I'll see to him later!'

Bolitho said, 'Boats in the water.' He sought out the six marines. 'You take the second one. You know what to do.'

One, the man who had first sighted the schooner, grunted. 'We knows, sir. We holds the boat where we can see the poop, an' pin down anyone who tries to pass the lanterns there.'

Bolitho smiled. 'Captain Bellairs was right about you.'

Allday whispered, 'This way, Captain.'

He felt the surf engulfing his legs and waist, the boat's scarred planking as Allday reached down to drag him over the gunwale.

'Shove off!'

Bolitho restrained the urge to watch the frantic oars, the efforts to steer the boat clear of the surf. Just one blast of canister would be enough to nip his flimsy plan in the bud.

The boat lifted and then surged heavily forward, the blades taking control as the hull freed itself from the strong undertow. Bolitho saw the schooner's tall masts rising to greet him, the tracery of rigging and shrouds almost lost against the sky.

Allday stood straddle-legged and wary, the tiller bar held lightly in his fingertips.

'Easy all!' He craned forward as if to impress them more. 'Bow-man, ready!'

Astern Bolitho heard the regular splash of oars as the other boat pulled hastily towards the schooner's bows.

Allday said quickly, 'It's now or never, Captain!' His teeth were bared with concentration, so that some men in the forward part of the boat thought he was smiling.

Bolitho stood up beside him and reached out to fend off the overhanging quarter, as like a moving object it loomed right above the boat.

'*Now!*'

There was a yell and a quick clatter as the bow-man hurled his grapnel up and over the bulwark. With a jerking, grinding crash the boat came alongside, some men falling in confusion, while others climbed eagerly over their sprawled bodies and entangled oars as if using a living bridge to reach the vessel's main deck.

Figures were already dashing from the forecastle, but as a man ran wildly from aft there was a muffled bang, the well-aimed musket ball hurling him round like an insane dancer, his agony clearly silhouetted against the poop lanterns.

Bolitho felt rather than saw a figure coming at him from the scuppers. Something hissed above his head even as he ducked round and struck for his attacker with his sword. The swaying figure backed and came on again, and Bolitho realised he was holding a huge axe, swinging it from side to side as he advanced.

Carwithen exclaimed, 'A plague on that bastard!' and fired his pistol full in the man's face. To Bolitho he snarled, 'That'll teach him!'

Another of the crew had climbed frantically into the foremast shrouds and was being pursued by a yelling seaman. Once again a musket stabbed the darkness from the other boat, and with a faint cry the man fell headlong to the deck where he was promptly despatched by a waiting cutlass.

Allday yelled, 'Most of 'em have gone below, Captain!' He ran to a hatchway and fired his pistol into it. 'The fight's gone out of 'em now, I'm thinking!'

Bolitho peered aft at the poop lanterns. 'Call the other boat to give assistance!'

It was suddenly very quiet on the schooner's deck, and as Bolitho walked slowly towards the small cabin hatch just forward of the wheel he was conscious of his own footsteps and the feeling the fight was not yet over.

He moved warily around the outstretched corpse which had been the first to fall to a marine sharpshooter, its face shining in the lantern light, the lower jaw broken away as if by an axe stroke.

Allday said, 'Stand aside, Captain!'

But a seaman was already clambering over the hatch coaming, his face suddenly screwing up in terrible agony as a pistol exploded beneath him.

A shadow darted through the pluming smoke, and Bolitho saw it was the scarfaced seaman called Lincoln, his eyes like stones as he allowed his lean body to drop straight through the hatch, using his dead companion to cushion the fall. His feet thudded into the corpse, and as he turned he whipped a knife from between his teeth, hitting out twice in the darkness, the second blow bringing a scream of pain.

More men were swarming down after him, and Bolitho yelled, 'Bring a lantern! Drag those men clear!'

Feet pounded over the planking, and he heard Armitage calling anxiously from the boat alongside.

Carwithen was already down on the cabin deck, knocking a seaman aside even as he made to finish the wounded pirate with his dirk.

Bolitho paused on the ladder, searching for Davy, his mind still able to grapple with the realisation that Allday had saved his life. But for his warning, he and not that poor seaman would be lying there dead.

'Mr. Davy! Hoist both boats inboard once you have secured our prisoners!'

'Aye, aye, sir!' He sounded jubilant.

'And mount a guard on them. I want no fanatic opening the bilges to the sea before we can even make sail!'

He followed Allday down the ladder, the sea-noises suddenly muffled and lost.

A seaman kicked open the cabin door and darted inside with a levelled pistol.

'Nothin', zur!' He swung round as a shadow moved beyond an upended chair. 'Belay that, zur! There's another rascal 'ere! I'll get 'im for 'ee!'

Then he fell back in horror. 'By Jesus, zur! 'E's one of us!'

Bolitho stepped into the cabin, ducking low between the deckhead beams. He could appreciate the seaman's shocked surprise. It was a small, cringing wreck of a man. He was on his knees, fingers interlocked as in prayer while he swayed back and forth in time to the ship's motion.

Bolitho sheathed his sword, stepping between the quivering creature and his fierce-eyed seaman.

'Who are you?'

He made to move closer and the man threw himself bodily at his feet.

'Have mercy, Captain! I done nothin', sir! I'm just an honest sailorman, sir!'

He gripped Bolitho's shoes, and when he reached down to pull him to his feet Bolitho saw with horror that every nail had been torn from his fingers.

Allday said harshly, 'On your feet! You are speaking to a King's officer!'

'Easy.' Bolitho held up his hand. 'Look at him. He has suffered enough.'

A seaman dropped his cutlass and lifted the man into a chair. 'Oi'll get 'im a drink, Cap'n.'

He dragged open a cupboard and gaped as the little man screamed wildly, 'Don't touch! 'E'll flay you alive if you dare lay yer 'ooks on it!'

Bolitho asked, 'Who will?'

Then he seemed to realise what was happening. That it was not part of another in a whole procession of living nightmares. He stared at Bolitho's grave features, tears running unheeded down his sunken cheeks.

'*Muljadi!*'

Carwithen muttered, 'What, here?'

The creature peered around Bolitho, his terrified eyes searching the crowded passageway, the dead seaman below the hatch.

'There! 'Is *son*!'

Bolitho turned swiftly and stooped above the man brought down by Lincoln's knife. Of course, he should have seen it. Instead of congratulating himself on being spared a horrible death.

The man was still alive, although the seaman's blade had laid open his neck and shoulder in a great, gaping wound. Must have missed the artery by a whisker and no more.

He was naked to the waist, but his loose trousers, now blotchy with his own and the seaman's blood, were of the finest silk. His eyes were tightly shut, his chest moving in quick, uneven thrusts.

Carwithen said, 'Let me finish the bastard, sir!' He was almost pleading.

Bolitho ignored him. The man was not aged much more than twenty, and around his throat he wore a gold pendant in the form of a prancing beast. Like the one on Muljadi's flag. It was just possible.

He snapped, 'Bind his wound. I want him to live.'

He turned to the ragged figure in the cabin. 'My men will take care of you, but first I want—'

The figure edged nearer the door. 'Is it really over, sir?' He was shaking violently and close to collapse. 'It's not a cruel trick?'

Allday said quietly, 'This is Captain Bolitho, matey. Of His Majesty's Ship *Undine*.'

'Now tell us who *you* are?'

The little man sank down to the deck again. Like a cowed dog. 'I was sailmaker, sir. In the Portuguese barque *Alvares*. Took on in Lisbon when I lost me own ship. We was carryin' a mixed cargo from Java when we was attacked by pirates.'

'When was this?' Bolitho spoke carefully, very aware of the other man's confusion.

'A year back, sir. I think.' He closed his eyes with the effort. 'We was taken to Muljadi's anchorage, wot there was left of us. Muljadi's men killed most of 'em. Only kept me 'cause I was a sailmaker.'

'I tried to escape once. Didn't know I was bein' 'eld on an island, y'see. They caught me before I'd been free an hour. Put me to torture.' He was shaking more violently now. 'All of 'em sat there watchin'. Enjoyin' it. Laughin'.' He lurched to his feet and threw himself towards the door snatching up a cutlass as he screamed, 'Pulled out all my nails with pincers, an' worse, the *bloody bastards*!'

Lincoln caught his wrist and turned the cutlass away from the unconscious figure in the passageway.

'Easy, mate! You could cause a mischief with that, eh?'

The man's cheerful voice seemed to steady him in some way.

He turned and looked at Bolitho very steadily. 'Me name's Jonathan Potter, once of Bristol.'

Bolitho nodded gravely. 'Well, Jonathan Potter, you can be of great service to me. It will not bring back your friends, but it may prevent others suffering in the same manner.' He glanced at Allday. 'Look after him.'

He walked from the cabin, grateful for the clean air which greeted him on deck, the sense of purpose as Davy's men prepared to get under way. Potter had probably been the only Englishman aboard the Portuguese barque. For that, and no other reason, had his life been spared. Kept like a slave, a downtrodden creature less than a man. From what he had heard of Muljadi it seemed a far more truthful reason.

Davy crossed to his side, 'I am about ready to weigh, sir.' He paused, sensing Bolitho's mood. 'That poor devil must have suffered terribly, sir. He is scars and scabs from head to toe. Little more than bones.'

Bolitho studied his pale outline thoughtfully. 'Something kept him alive, Mr. Davy. Fear of death, a need for revenge, I know not which.' He grasped a stay as the deck swayed restlessly in the swell. 'But whatever it was, I intend to use it to good purpose.'

'And the schooner's master, sir?'

'If he is really Muljadi's son we have a catch indeed. But either way I want him kept alive, so pass the word to that effect.' He thought of Carwithen's eyes. 'To *all* hands.'

He peered abeam at the small islet where so much had happened. The craggy distortions were lost in deep shadow. It was a whale once again.

'We will run to the sou'-east directly and gain sea-room. I am not yet acquainted with these waters. By dawn we should be able to come about and make contact with *Undine*.' He looked at the men hurrying about the schooner's deck. 'She's a fine little prize.'

Davy stared at him and then at the vessel, the realisation coming to him apparently for the first time.

'I see, sir. A *prize*.' He nodded happily. 'Worth a good price, I'll be bound.'

Bolitho walked to the opposite side. 'I thought that might interest you, Mr. Davy.' He added, 'Now, have the capstan manned and break out the anchor while the wind holds.' He thought of Herrick. 'We are no longer beggars.'

Davy shook his head, not understanding. Then he looked at the helmsman and at the others gathering at the capstan bars and grinned broadly.

A prize at last. Perhaps the first of many.

Noddall hovered by the cabin table and bobbed his head with satisfaction as Bolitho pushed his empty plate aside.

'More like it, sir! A man works the fairer on a full belly!'

Bolitho leaned back in his chair and let his eyes move slowly around the cabin. It felt good to be back aboard *Undine* and with something to show for their efforts.

The lantern above the table seemed much dimmer, and when he glanced through the stern windows he saw that dawn had already given way to an empty sky, the horizon slanting across the thick, salt-stained glass like a thread of gold.

In the captured schooner he had rejoined *Undine* at almost the same hour as this, the previous day, the strain and tension of their short, bitter fight lost momentarily in the cheers from the watching seamen and marines.

Herrick had been almost beside himself with pleasure, and had insisted that Bolitho should go to his cabin without delay and rest.

The schooner had once been under the flag of the Dutch East India Company, although it was impossible to tell how long she had been in the pirates' hands. But from her filthy condition and disorder between decks it seemed likely it had been a considerable while since Dutch sailors had manned her.

He let his mind drift as he listened to bare feet padding overhead, the sluice of water and the clank of a pump as the decks were washed down for another day.

Noddall was right, he had eaten a good breakfast. Thinly sliced fat pork, fried pale brown with biscuit crumbs. Always his favourite. Helped down with strong coffee and some treacle.

Herrick tapped on the door and entered the cabin.

'Wind's holding steady from the sou'-west, sir.' He looked alert and cleareyed.

Bolitho smiled. 'Good, Thomas. Have some coffee.'

It was always strange how Herrick relaxed once there was a set plan to perform. If he really guessed how hazy it was in his captain's mind he gave no sign.

'Mr. Mudge informs me that we are logging some ten knots, sir.' Herrick took a mug from the servant and grinned. 'He's up there beaming away as if he's just won a fortune at the tables.'

Bolitho frowned. 'That means we should make a landfall at any time now. If yesterday's wind had been more than a snail's pace we could have been there now.' He spread his arms, feeling the touch of a clean shirt against his chest and back. 'But there was plenty to do.'

Herrick smiled. 'Mr. Davy's well on his way to Pendang Bay by now.'

Bolitho replied, 'Aye. He'll be feeling like a post-captain, if I'm not mistaken.'

When he had put Davy in charge of the schooner, and had sent him back to Conway, he had seen his face come alight, as if from within. He must have looked like that himself once, he thought. He had been put in charge of a prize when he had been a lieutenant, far younger than Davy. The first step to real command was said to be the greatest, so perhaps it would work for Davy, too.

He looked up at the open skylight as a voice pealed, 'Deck there! Land on the lee bow!'

Bolitho smiled, feeling the chill on his spine. 'If the *Argus* is elsewhere, I will have to think again.'

The door opened slightly and Midshipman Armitage reported, 'Mr. Soames's respects, sir. Masthead has sighted land on the lee bow.'

Bolitho said, 'Thank you, Mr. Armitage.'

He saw the deep hollows around his eyes, the nervous way his fingers twitched against his patched breeches. Unlike any of the others who had returned, he was unable to hide his real feelings. His fear. His knowledge that he could no longer contain it.

'My compliments to Mr. Soames. Tell him we will exercise both watches at gun drill in half an hour.' He hesitated and added, 'If there is anything troubling you, it would be as well to confide in the first lieutenant here, or myself, if you feel it might help.'

Armitage shook his head. 'N-no, sir. I am better now.' He hurried away.

Bolitho looked at his friend and asked quietly, 'What are we to do about that one?'

Herrick shrugged. 'You cannot carry them all, sir. He may get over it. We've all had to go through it at one time or another.'

'Now then, Thomas, that does not sound like you at all!' He smiled broadly. 'Admit you are concerned for the lad!'

Herrick looked embarrassed. 'Well, I was thinking of having a word with him.'

'I thought as much, Thomas. You haven't the right face for deceit!'

Another knock at the door announced the surgeon had arrived.

'Well, Mr. Whitmarsh?' Bolitho watched him framed in the doorway, the early sunlight from the cabin hatch making a halo around his huge head. 'Is our prisoner worse?'

Whitmarsh moved through the cabin like a man in a prison, ducking under each beam as if seeking a way of escape.

'He is well enough, sir. But I still believe, as I told you when you returned to the ship, that he should have been sent back to the settlement in the schooner.'

Bolitho saw Herrick's jaw tighten and knew he was about to silence the surgeon's aggressive outburst. Like the other officers, Herrick found it hard to cover his dislike for him. Whitmarsh was little help in the matter either.

Bolitho said calmly, 'I cannot answer for a prisoner if he is there and we are here, surely?'

He watched the beads of sweat trickling down the man's forehead and wondered if he had taken a drink this early. It was a wonder it had not killed him already.

Above his head he heard the regular stamp of boots, the click of metal, as the marines mustered for morning inspection.

He made himself say, 'You must trust my judgement, Mr. Whitmarsh, as I do yours in your own profession.'

The surgeon turned and glared at him. 'You are admitting that if you'd sent him back to Pendang Bay he would have been seized and hanged!'

Herrick retorted angrily, 'Damn your eyes, man, the fellow is a bloody pirate!'

Whitmarsh eyed him fiercely. 'In *your* opinion, no doubt!'

Bolitho stood up sharply and walked to the windows.

'You must live in reality, Mr. Whitmarsh. As a common pirate he would be tried and hanged, as well you know. But if he is the son of Muljadi he is something more than a cat's-paw, he could be used to bargain. There is more at stake here, more lives in peril than I feared. I'll not falter because of your personal feelings.'

Whitmarsh seized the edge of the table, his body hanging over it like a figurehead.

'If you'd suffered as I have—'

Bolitho turned on him, his voice harsh. 'I know about your brother, and I am deeply sorry for him! But how many felons and murderers have you seen hanging, rotting in chains, without even a thought?' He heard someone pause beside the open skylight and lowered his voice. 'Humanity, I admire. Hypocrisy, I totally reject!' He saw the fury giving way to pain on the surgeon's flushed features. 'So take care of the prisoner. If he is to be hanged, then so be it. But if I can use his life to advantage, and in doing so save it, then amen to *that*!'

Whitmarsh moved vaguely towards the door and then said thickly, 'And that man Potter you brought from the schooner, sir. You have put him to work already!'

Bolitho smiled 'Really, Mr. Whitmarsh, you do not give up easily. Potter is with the sailmaker as his assistant. He will not be worked to death, and I think that keeping busy will be a quicker cure than brooding over his recent sufferings.'

Whitmarsh stalked from the cabin, muttering under his breath.

Herrick exclaimed, 'What impertinence! In your shoes I'd have laid about him with a belaying-pin!'

'I doubt that.' Bolitho shook the coffee pot, but it was empty. 'But I feel that I'll never win his confidence, let alone his trust.'

Bolitho waited for Noddall to bring his dress coat and best cocked-hat, feeling rather ridiculous as the servant fussed and tugged at cuffs and lapels.

Herrick said bluntly, 'I think it's a bad risk, sir.'

'One I'll have to take, Thomas.' He saw Noddall pull a long strand of hair from one of the buttons. Her hair. He wondered if Herrick had noticed. He continued, 'We have to trust the French captain. All the rest is so much supposition.'

Noddall had taken the old sword from its rack on the bulkhead, but held it across his arm, knowing by now it was more than his life was worth to usurp Allday's ritual.

Bolitho thought of Whitmarsh's anger, and knew that much of it had good foundation. Had the prisoner been sent back in the schooner he would doubtlessly have been taken by Puigserver, if he was still at the settlement, or held in irons until he could be sent to the nearest Spanish authority. Then, if he was lucky, he would certainly be hanged. If not, his fate hardly bore thinking about. Like father, like son.

As it was, the schooner's surviving crewmen, a savage-looking collection of half-castes, Javanese and Indians, would meet a swift fate before much longer.

How many lives had they taken, he wondered? How many ships plundered, crews murdered, or broken into husks like Potter, the Bristol sailmaker? The bargain was probably one-sided.

He walked from the cabin, still pondering the rights and wrongs of instant justice.

On deck it was remaining fresh, the day's heat yet to come, and he took a few paces along the weather side while there was still time. In the heavy dress coat he would be dripping unless he held to the sails' curved shadows.

Fowlar touched his forehead and said awkwardly, 'May I thank you, sir?'

Bolitho smiled. 'You have earned it, Mr. Fowlar, have no fear.'

He had made the master's mate an acting-lieutenant to fill the gap left by Davy. Had young Keen been aboard, it would have been his chance. Another would be put in Fowlar's place. And so it went on, as in all ships.

Herrick took Fowlar aside and waited until Bolitho was pacing again.

'A word of warning. *Never* interrupt the captain when he is taking his walks.' He smiled at Fowlar's uncertainty. 'Unless in real emergency, of course, which does not include your promotion!' He touched his shirt. 'But congratulations, all the same.'

Bolitho had already forgotten them. He had seen the dark smudge of land which just topped the glittering horizon, and was wondering what he might find there. It looked at this distance like one great spread of land, but he knew it consisted of a crowded collection of islets, some even smaller than the one where they had captured Davy's schooner. The Dutch had originally occupied them because of their shape and position. Ships anchored amidst the surrounding islets would have the advantage of using any wind to put to sea, the use of several channels to avoid delay. The fortress had been built to protect the place from marauders, such as the one who now commanded it and challenged all authority and every flag. The Dutch still listed the Benuas as one of their possessions. But it was in name only, and they were no doubt glad to be rid of it and its unhappy history.

He saw the sailmaker speaking with Potter below the forecastle, and wondered if he would ever really recover from his suffering. It could not be easy for him to be drawing so near to Muljadi's stronghold again. But of all the people aboard, he was the only man, apart from the prisoner, who had seen what lay beyond the protective reefs and sandbars where he had endured so much.

He shivered slightly in spite of his heavy coat. Suppose he had misjudged his opponents? He, too, might become another Potter, a pitiful, broken thing which even his friends and his sisters in England might wish to think of as dead.

And Viola Raymond? How long would she take to forget him?

He shook himself out of his mood and said, 'Mr. Soames! You may beat to quarters and clear for action now!' He saw the ripple of excitement run through the men on the gun deck. 'Exercise the larboard battery first.'

Allday walked up the slanting deck and turned the sword over in his hands before buckling it to Bolitho's belt.

'You'll be taking me, of course, Captain.'

He spoke calmly, but Bolitho saw the anxiety in his eyes.

'Not this time.'

Calls shrilled along the berth deck, and the marine drummer boys ran breathlessly to the quarterdeck rail, pulling their sticks from their white crossbelts to begin their urgent tattoo.

Allday said stubbornly, 'But you'll be *needing* me, Captain!'

'Yes.' Bolitho looked at him gravely. 'I will always do that. . . .'

The rest of his words were lost in the rattle of drums, the stampede of feet as the *Undine*'s people ran to quarters once again.

15

Face to Face

Bolitho levelled his telescope across the hammock nettings and studied the overlapping islets in silence. All morning and into the forenoon watch, while *Undine* had cruised steadily towards them, he had noted each unusual feature, and had compared his findings with what he already knew. The main channel through the islets opened to the south, and almost in the centre of the approach was one stark hump of rock upon which stood the old stone fortress. Even now, with the nearest spurs of land less than two miles distant, it was impossible to see where the fortress began or the craggy hilltop ended.

'We will alter course again, Mr. Herrick.' He lowered the glass and dabbed his eye with his wrist. 'Steer east nor'-east.'

He saw the men by the larboard twelve-pounders peering through their open ports. The guns already shimmering in the sunlight as if they had just been fired.

Herrick shouted, 'Hands to the braces! Alter course two points to larboard, Mr. Mudge!'

Bolitho sought out the frail figure of Potter amongst the unemployed hands below the forecastle, and when he glanced up beckoned him aft.

He slipped out of his heavy coat and handed it with his hat to Allday, saying as calmly as he could, 'I will go aloft myself.'

Allday said nothing. He knew Bolitho well enough to understand what it was costing him.

Potter hurried on to the quarterdeck and knuckled his forehead.

'Sir?'

'D'you think you could climb to the maintop with me?'

Potter stared at him dully. 'If you says so, sir.'

Herrick called, 'East nor'-east, sir!'

He looked from Bolitho to the mainyard stretching athwartships and vibrating to the great press of canvas below it.

Bolitho unbuckled his sword and gave it to Allday. 'I may need your eyes today, Potter.'

Feeling every man watching him, he swung out on to the weather shrouds and began to climb, his fingers locking so tightly around each ratline that the pain helped to steady him. Up and up, with his gaze fixed on the futtock shrouds which leaned out and around the sturdy maintop where two marines were studying his progress with unblinking curiosity.

Bolitho gritted his teeth and fought the urge to look down. It was infuriating. Unfair. He had first gone to sea at the age of twelve. Year by year he had studied and matured, had replaced his child's infatuation for the Navy with a genuine understanding which had amounted almost to love. He had overcome sea-sickness, and had learned to hide his loneliness and grief from his companions when his mother had died while he had been at sea. So, too, his father was buried while Bolitho had been fighting Frenchman and American in and around the Caribbean. He had watched men suffer horribly in battle and his body bore enough scars to show the narrow margin between his own survival and death. Why then, should he be cursed with this hatred of heights?

He felt his shoes scrabbling on the ratlines as he hauled himself out and around the futtock shrouds, his body hanging in space and supported only by fingers and toes.

A marine said admiringly, 'By God, sir, that was a fair climb!'

Bolitho arrived beside him, his chest heaving painfully. He watched the marine to see if he was disguising his sarcasm, but saw it was the same sharpshooter who had discovered the anchored schooner just two days back.

He nodded and allowed himself a glance at the ship far below.

Foreshortened bodies moved about the quarterdeck, and when he looked forward he saw the leadsman in the chains, the blur of his arm as he hurled the heavy weight deftly beyond the bows.

He relaxed, and waited for Potter to scramble up beside him.

For a moment longer he toyed with the idea of forcing himself up the next length of quivering shrouds to the maintopsail yard, but rejected it. Apart from proving something to himself or showing his capability to those who might be watching from below, it would serve for little. Potter was exhausted by the climb, and if Herrick needed him urgently on deck he would look even more foolish if he fell headlong from his perch.

He unslung the telescope from his shoulder and trained it on the channel between the islets. In the time it had taken him to climb from the deck and regain his wind *Undine* had cruised over a cable, and it was possible to see the next overlapping islet behind the central hill with its forbidding fortress and steep, sunbaked cliff.

Potter said, 'I never bin to the east'rd side, sir. There's a good channel there, too, I'm told.' He shuddered. 'They used to bury the corpses in the sandbars at low water. What there was left of 'em.'

Bolitho stiffened and momentarily forgot the deck far beneath him. He saw the blacker silhouette of a ship's masts and yards almost hidden around the curve of the inner channel. A frigate.

Potter saw his interest and added dolefully, 'Best place to anchor, sir. The battery on the fortress can protect two channels at once, an' any craft wot chooses to lay there.'

Something pale flapped and broadened against the furthest islet. A small boat hoisting its sail.

Bolitho glanced quickly at the foretopmast where Herrick had run up a big white flag. One way or another they would soon know.

There was a hollow boom, and after what seemed like an age, a tall waterspout shot skywards about a cable off the larboard beam. He trained the glass quickly towards the fortress, but the smoke had already fanned away so it was impossible to gauge the angle of the shot.

He shifted the glass again and saw the boat moving more quickly around a litter of broken rocks, the sail braced back like the fin of a great shark.

He let out a long breath as he saw a white flag flapping from her masthead. His request to parley was accepted. The single shot from the battery was a warning.

Bolitho slung the telescope across his shoulder. 'You stay here, Potter. Keep an eye on everything, and try to remember any item which might be of use. It could well save lives one day.' He nodded casually to the two marine marksmen. 'I hope you'll not be needed.' He slung a leg over the low barricade and tried not to lower his eyes. '*Argus* intends us to do all the sweating!'

The men grinned and nudged each other, as if he had just given them access to some priceless and vital information.

Bolitho swallowed hard and began to make the journey to the deck. When he reached the point where he could see the nettings on the opposite side again he allowed himself to look at the group which awaited him by the bulwark. Herrick was smiling, although whether from relief or amusement it was hard to tell. Bolitho jumped down to the deck and glanced ruefully at his fresh shirt. It was dripping with sweat, and bore a black streak of tar across one shoulder.

He said, 'Never mind. The coat will hide that.' In a brisker tone he added, 'A boat is coming out, Mr. Herrick. Heave-to, if you please, and prepare to anchor.'

He glanced up at the great yards again. It had not been quite so bad as he had imagined that time. Then he thought of the ideal conditions as compared with a screaming gale, or making the same climb in pitch darkness, and changed his mind.

Bolitho allowed Herrick to shout his orders before asking Mudge, 'What did you make of that shot?'

The master regarded him dubiously. 'Old gun, I'd say, sir. From where I was standin' it sounded like a bronze piece.'

Bolitho nodded. 'As I thought, too. It would be likely that they'd still have the original cannon.' He rubbed his chin, thinking aloud. 'So they'd be loath to use heated shot for fear of splitting them.' He grinned at Mudge's mournful expression. 'Not that it matters much, I daresay. If they fired solid rock, they could scarcely fail to hit a ship trying to force the channel!'

Fowlar shouted, 'The boat has an officer aboard, sir.' He grinned. 'Most o' the hands are the colour of coffee, but he's a Frog if ever I saw one.'

Bolitho took a glass and watched the oncoming boat. Locally built, with the familiar high prow and lateen sail, it was moving fast and well on a converging tack. He saw the officer in question, standing easily below the mast, his cocked hat pulled down over his forehead to shade his eyes from the fierce glare. Fowlar was right. There was no mistaking this one.

He made himself walk a few paces away from the side, as with her courses brailed up and her topsails in booming confusion *Undine* turned noisily into the wind to await her visitors.

Bolitho gripped the rail and watched in silence as the boat surged round and under the main chains, where some of *Undine*'s seamen and Mr. Shellabeer waited to secure her lines and, if necessary, fend off any risk of collision.

He said, 'And now, Mr. Herrick, we shall see.'

He walked along the swaying gangway to the entry port and waited for the officer to scramble aboard. He stood quite alone framed against the cruising ranks of small whitecaps, his eyes exploring *Undine*'s gun deck, the watching seamen and marines above and below him. Seeing Bolitho, he removed his hat with a flourish and gave a small bow.

'Lieutenant Maurin, *m'sieu*. At your service.'

He bore no marks of rank, and his blue coat showed plenty of evidence of patching and repairs. He was tanned to the shade of old leather, and his eyes were those of a man who had been at sea for most of his life. Tough, self-assured, competent, it was all there on his face, Bolitho decided.

Bolitho nodded. 'And I am Captain Bolitho, of His Majesty's ship *Undine*.'

The lieutenant gave a wry smile. 'My *capitaine* 'as been expecting you.'

Bolitho glanced briefly at the cockade on Maurin's hat. It bore the small red beast instead of a French insignia.

He asked, 'And what is your nationality, Lieutenant?'

The man shrugged. 'I am employed in the service of Prince Muljadi.' He shrugged again. 'Naturally.'

Bolitho gave a wry smile. '*Naturally*.'

He added sharply, 'I wish to meet your captain, and without delay. I have certain matters to discuss.'

'But of course, *m'sieu*.' The lieutenant was looking at the men on deck. His eyes were always moving. Calculating. He continued, '*Capitaine* Le Chaumareys is prepared for me to remain aboard as 'ostage to ensure your, er, good 'ealth!'

Bolitho hid his relief. Had Le Chaumareys been killed or replaced he might have had to alter his tactics.

He said calmly, 'It will not be necessary. I have every faith in your captain's honour.'

Herrick exclaimed, 'But, sir, you cannot mean it! Keep him, I say! Your life is to valuable to risk on a Frenchman's word!'

Bolitho looked at him and smiled. 'If Le Chaumareys is the callous brute you describe, do you imagine he would care about losing a lieutenant if it were to gain him a better bargaining point?' He touched his arm. 'I have made some notes in my cabin. They may help you to pass the time in my absence.' He touched his hat to the quarterdeck and said to Maurin, 'I am ready.'

For a moment longer he stood in the port, looking down into the boat alongside. There were about a dozen men aboard, naked but for a few scraps of rags, but armed to the teeth, and with the looks of men prepared to kill without question.

Maurin said quietly, 'You will be safe with me, *m'sieu*.' He lowered himself swiftly on to the boat's gunwale, adding, 'For the moment.'

Bolitho jumped the last few feet and steadied himself against a crude backstay, very conscious of the acrid stench of sweat and filth which floated unheeded in the bilges.

'You choose strange allies, Lieutenant.'

Maurin signalled for the boat to be cast off, one hand resting casually on his pistol.

'Lie with a dog and you arise with fleas, *m'sieu*. It is quite common.'

Bolitho glanced at his profile. Another Herrick perhaps?

Then as the sail billowed and cracked to the wind, and the slim hull began to gather way, he forgot Maurin, even the anxious faces on *Undine*'s quarterdeck, as he considered what he was about to do.

Bolitho clung to the backstay as the boat scudded dangerously close to a line of black-toothed rocks and then went about to enter the main channel. He noticed that the current was strong and at odds with the incoming sea, and felt the hull leap and stagger as it straightened up for the final leg of the journey. When he looked astern he could see nothing of his own ship. She was already hidden by a wedge of land, the side of which lay deep in shadow.

Maurin asked suddenly, 'Why d'you take such risks, *m'sieu*?'

Bolitho looked at him impassively. 'Why do you?'

Maurin shrugged. 'I obey orders. But soon I will be going 'ome again. To Toulon. I 'ave not seen my family for . . .' He smiled sadly. 'Too long.'

Bolitho glanced across the lieutenant's shoulder and studied the grim fortress which was slipping past the port beam. It was still difficult to see the extent of its buildings. A high wall, undulating with the edge of the clifftop. The spaced windows were little more than black slits, like mournful eyes, while above, on the weatherworn battlements, he could see the muzzles of several large guns, just visible through their individual embrasures.

Maurin said, 'A foul place, is it not? But they are not like us. They live like crabs in the rocks.' He sounded contemptuous.

Bolitho saw several small boats bobbing at anchor, and a schooner similar to the one they had captured moored to a stone pier.

Maurin did not try to stop him looking at everything, to prevent his interest in the many figures which moved about the pier and up the sloping track to the fortress gates. Bolitho decided he was being brought by the main channel by careful design. So that he should see the growing strength of Muljadi's private army. And it was impressive. To think that a pirate, an alien to the Indies, could muster this force, and instil such discipline, was enough to impress anyone. Even a pompous fool like Major Jardine.

He turned as the boat's crew began to shorten sail, and saw the anchored frigate lying directly across the bows. Close to in a confined space she seemed even larger. Far bigger than *Undine*. Even his last command would have been reckless to match her deadly broadside of eighteen-pounders.

He remarked, 'A fine ship.'

Maurin nodded. 'The best. We 'ave been together for so long, we even think alike!'

Bolitho saw the activity around the entry port, the gleam of sunlight on fixed bayonets where a guard awaited his arrival. A very carefully staged performance, he thought. He noticed that boarding nets were furled along the gangways where they could be spread without delay. Fear of a cutting-out attack? More likely he was taking no chances with his new 'ally'. It was the only promising thing Bolitho had seen so far.

A small fishing dory drifted abeam, and he saw some natives standing in it shaking their fists at him and baring their teeth like wild beasts.

Maurin said simply 'They probably think you are a prisoner, eh?' It seemed to depress him.

Bolitho pushed him from his thoughts as the boat swung heavily towards the frigate's main chains. *Capitaine* Paul Le Chaumareys, a man about whom many tales had been told. Battles won, convoys harried and settlements destroyed. His record in the war had been formidable, just as Conway had described. But as an individual he was a mystery, mostly because he had spent much of his service far away from his own beloved France.

He ran his eyes the full length of the ship's side. *Argus*, the hundred-eyed messenger of Hera. Very appropriate for a man as elusive as Le Chaumareys, he thought. Sturdily built, and showing the scars and blemishes of hard service, she was a ship he would have been proud to command. She lacked *Undine*'s grace, but had a heavier toughness which could not be ignored.

The boat had made fast to the chains, and the crew stood grouped by the mast as Bolitho climbed up to the gunwale. Nobody attempted to assist him. Then, a young seaman jumped down from the chains and held out his hand.

'*M'sieu!*' He grinned broadly. '*A votre service!*'

Bolitho seized his wrist and levered himself towards the entry port. The French seaman could have been one of his own.

He removed his hat to the broad quarterdeck, and waited while the calls shrilled a salute and a guard presented muskets. Not crisply like Bellairs's marines would have done, but with a familiar jauntiness. Of long practice. Like the upper deck itself, he thought. Not dirty, but not gleaming and in perfect order either. Well used. Ready for anything.

'Ah, *Capitaine!*' Le Chaumareys stepped forward to greet him, his eyes fixed on Bolitho's face.

He was quite unlike anyone he had expected. Older. A good deal so. Perhaps in his middle forties. And one of the largest men he had ever met. Taller than six feet, with shoulders so broad that his bared head seemed tiny by comparison, especially as he wore his hair very short, like a convict.

'I welcome you to my ship.' He waved his hand around the deck. 'To my world, as it has been for so long.' He smiled, the effect lighting up his face in an instant. 'So come below to the cabin.' He nodded to Maurin. 'I will call for you when it is time.'

Bolitho followed him to the cabin hatch, seeing the eyes watching from both deck and gangways, the way they studied his every move, as if to discover something.

Le Chaumareys said casually, 'I hope Maurin took good care of you?'

'Very, thank you. His English is excellent.'

'Yes. One of the reasons I chose him for my ship. He is married to an Englishwoman.' He chuckled. 'You, of course, are *not* married. So why not a French bride for you, eh?'

He threw open the door and watched Bolitho's reactions. The cabin was large and well furnished, and like the rest of the ship, vaguely untidy. Lived in.

But Bolitho's attention was immediately drawn to a table which was laden with food.

Le Chaumareys remarked, 'Much of it is locally obtained.' He jabbed a large joint with his finger. 'Like this. It is very much the same as smoked ham. You must eat your fill, while you can, eh?' He chuckled, the sound rising from what Bolitho now saw to be a large belly.

He replied, 'I am here to present—'

The other captain wagged a finger. 'You are aboard a French ship, *m'sieu*. First we drink.'

He shouted a brief command and a servant hurried from the adjoining cabin with a tall crystal jug of wine. It was extremely good, as cool as spring water. Bolitho glanced from the jug to the table. Genuine? Or was it one more trick to show they were superior, even in their supplies and comforts?

A chair was brought for him, and when he was seated Le Chaumareys seemed to relax.

He said, 'I have heard of you, Bolitho. You had a fine record in the war for one so junior.' His eyes did not flicker as he added, 'It was difficult for you. The unfortunate affair of your brother.'

Bolitho watched him calmly. Le Chaumareys was a man he could understand. Like a duellist. Relaxed one moment, making a thrust the next.

He said, 'Thank you for your concern.'

The small head bobbed back and forth. 'You should have been in these waters during the war. Independence, an ability to work beyond the reach of some admiral, eh? I think it would have fitted you well.'

Bolitho felt the servant refilling his glass. 'I have come to speak with Muljadi.'

He tightened his grip on the glass. It had come out just like that, as if the words had been lying in his mind for months instead of seconds.

Le Chaumareys stared at him with amazement. 'Are you insane? He would have you screaming for death in a moment, and I could not help you. No, *m'sieu*, it would be a lunatic thing even to think of.'

Bolitho said, 'Then I will return to my ship.'

'But what of your Admiral Conway? His despatches? Is there nothing from him for me?'

'It would be pointless now.' Bolitho watched him warily. 'Besides which, you are not here as a French captain, but as a subordinate to Muljadi's authority.'

Le Chaumareys took a deep swallow from his glass, his eyes slitted against the reflected sunlight from the windows.

He said abruptly, 'Listen to me. Curb your impatience. As I have had to do, when I was your age, eh?' He looked around the cabin. 'I have my instructions. I obey them, as you must yours. But I have served France well, and I am near finished in the Indies. Perhaps I made my services too valuable to be allowed home earlier, but that is as may be. I *know* these seas like my own face. During the war I had to live off the islands for food and shelter, for repairs, and to glean intelligence about your patrols and convoys. When I was told to continue in these same waters I resented it, but I suppose I was flattered also. I am still needed, eh? Not like many who fought so bravely and are now without bread.' He looked at Bolitho sharply and added, 'As in your country, too, no doubt?'

Bolitho replied, 'Yes. It is much the same.'

Le Chaumareys smiled. 'Well then, my impetuous friend, we must not fight again! We are too much the same. Needed one minute, expendable the next!'

Bolitho said coldly, 'Many have died because of your actions. But for our arrival at Pendang Bay all the garrison would have been killed, and you must know it. A Spanish frigate was destroyed to delay our arrival, to allow this *Prince* Muljadi to give his piracy some sort of repute, to make him an ally of France, and a constant threat to peace.'

Le Chaumareys' eyes widened. 'Well said. But I had no part in *Nervion*'s destruction.' He held up one large fist. 'Of course, I *heard* about it. I hear many things I do not like. That is why I brought the Spanish commander here to parley for his garrison's safety. He was still the representative of his own King. He could agree to terms which but for your intervention would have given Muljadi certain rights in Pendang Bay.' He became very grave. 'I did not know an attack would be launched the very moment I had left the bay! You have my word, as a French officer!'

'And I accept it.'

Bolitho tried to remain calm, but could feel the blood tingling in his veins like ice water. It was exactly as he had imagined. A set, calculated plan which had begun perhaps in Europe, in Paris and London, even Madrid, and which had almost worked. But for his decision to take *Undine* and the *Nervion*'s few survivors to their destination, and Puigserver's arrival in Pendang Bay, the matter would be settled, and Le Chaumareys probably on his way home at last, his work done, and done well.

He heard himself say, 'I have come to take the commandant back to his own kind. Don Luis Puigserver, the King of Spain's representative, will be expecting his return.' He hardened his tone. 'Is Colonel Pastor still alive? Or is his death another thing you know of but did not approve?'

Le Chaumareys stood up and moved heavily to the quarter window.

'He is here. A prisoner of Muljadi. In that ruin on the hill. He will never allow you to take him, dead or alive. His presence can still give legality to his demands. Can show that England is unable to honour her word and protect the rights and citizens of Spain. A hard story to believe? But time and distance can make truth a mockery.'

'Then why would Muljadi fear to see *me*?' Bolitho watched him as he moved away from the window, his face lined and grim. 'I'd have thought he would have been eager to throw his power in my face.'

Le Chaumareys walked across the cabin, the deck creaking under his corpulent frame. He halted by Bolitho's chair and looked directly into his eyes.

'It is I who fear for *you*, Bolitho. Out here, in my *Argus*, I am Muljadi's arm, his reach. To him I am not merely a sea captain, but a symbol, a man who can spring his plans into reality. But beyond these timbers I cannot answer for your security, and that is the truth.' He hesitated, his eyes still on Bolitho's face. 'But I see I am wasting time. You are determined, no?'

Bolitho smiled gravely. 'Yes.'

Le Chaumareys added, 'I have met many Englishmen in war and peace. Some I liked, many I hated. Few did I respect.' He held out his hand. 'You I admire.' He smiled sadly. 'A fool, but a brave one. *That* I can admire.'

He rang a bell and then gestured to the table. 'And you eat nothing.'

Bolitho reached for his hat. 'If what you say is true, then it would be wasted, eh?' He smiled, despite his tumbling thoughts. 'And if not, I will have to content myself with salt pork in the future.'

A tall, lank-haired officer entered the cabin, and Le Chaumareys spoke to him swiftly in French. Then he picked up his own hat and said, 'My senior lieutenant, Bolitho. I have changed my mind. I am coming with you.' He shrugged. 'Curiosity, or to prove my orginal beliefs, I know not which. But without me you are a dead man.'

When they reached the quarterdeck Bolitho saw there was a boat already alongside, and that the gangways were filled with silent spectators. Having a good look, he thought grimly. A one-way journey, if he had miscalculated.

Le Chaumareys held his arm. 'Listen to me. I am older, and I expect, wiser than you. I can have you taken back to your ship. You will suffer no disgrace. In a year all this will be forgotten. Leave politics to those who daily dirty their hands without remorse.'

Bolitho shook his head. 'In my position, would *you?*' He forced a smile. 'Your face tells me what I need to know.'

Le Chaumareys nodded to his watching officers and then led the way to the entry port.

Bolitho glanced quickly along the gun deck, noting the fresh repairs to timbers and cordage. Where *Undine* had made her own challenge, and when he had felt the battle was nearly lost. It was an uncanny feeling to be walking with *Argus*'s captain. More like compatriots than men who had so recently tried to destroy each other. If they met again after this, there could be no more truces.

The boat pulled steadily across swirling water towards the pier below the fortress, the French seamen watching Bolitho the whole time. Curious? Or merely seeing the face of an enemy?

Le Chaumareys spoke only once on the short crossing.

'Do not lose your temper with Muljadi. One sign and he will have you seized. He is without pity.'

'And what about your position here?'

The Frenchman gave a bitter smile. 'He *needs* me, *m'sieu*.'

Once alongside the pier Bolitho gained a new understanding of the hatred he had seen earlier. With the French seamen surrounding him as an escort he was made to hurry up the steep slope towards the fortress, while on all sides voices rose in shouts and curses, and it was obvious that without Le Chaumareys' massive presence even the sailors would have been set upon.

The lower part of the fortress was little more than an empty shell, its courtyard littered with rushes and rags which the defenders and Muljadi's growing army of followers used for bedding. He looked up at the blue sky above the ramparts and saw the guns. Old but powerful, each with balls nearby, and long ropes which trailed carelessly to the courtyard, and some crude baskets which presumably were used to haul fresh powder and shot when required.

More rough steps, the sun probing across his shoulders, then sudden shadows making his body feel chilled and damp.

Le Chaumareys grunted, 'You will wait here.'

He led Bolitho into a roughly hewn room no bigger than a cable tier and strode towards an iron-studded door at one end. It was guarded by some heavily armed natives, who faced the French seamen as if hoping for a fight. Le Chaumareys seemed to sail right through them, like a three-decker breaking the line of battle. Supreme confidence, or a well-practised bluff. Bolitho did not know.

He did not have to wait long. The door was dragged open and he saw a large room, a chamber, which seemed to span the whole breadth of the upper fortress. Against the dull stone and smoky walls the dais at the far end made a fine splash of colour.

Muljadi was arranged on a pile of silk cushions, eyes fixed on the door, his body completely at ease.

He was naked to the waist, and wore only white baggy trousers and red leather boots underneath. He had no hair, so that in the sunlight from the slitted windows his head seemed pointed, and his single ear very prominent and grotesque.

Le Chaumareys was standing to one side of the dais, his face stern and alert. Around the walls were some of the dirtiest and cruellest-looking men Bolitho had ever seen in his life, although the quality of their weapons marked them as leaders or lieutenants in Muljadi's command.

He walked towards the dais, half expecting one of the onlookers to rush forward and cut him down, but nobody moved or spoke.

When he was within a few feet of the cushions Muljadi said flatly, 'That is close enough!'

He spoke good English, but with a strong accent which was probably Spanish.

He continued, 'Before I have you killed, *Captain*, is there anything you wish to say?'

Bolitho wanted to lick his parched lips. He heard the rustle of expectancy behind him, saw Le Chaumareys watching him with despair on his tanned face.

Bolitho said, 'On behalf of His Britannic Majesty, King George, I have come to demand the release of Colonel Don José Pastor, subject of Spain, and under my country's protection.'

Muljadi sat bolt upright, the stump of his severed wrist pointing like a gun.

'*Demand?* You insolent dog!'

Le Chaumareys stepped forward hastily. 'Let me explain, *m'sieu*.'

Muljadi screamed, 'You will address me *Highness*!' To Bolitho he added savagely, 'Call on your God for help! I will make you *plead* for death!'

Bolitho could feel his heart pumping against his ribs, the sweat pouring down his spine and gathering around his waist like ice-rime. Deliberately he reached into his pocket and pulled out his watch. As he flicked open the guard he heard Muljadi leap to his feet, the gasp of disbelief as he threw himself from the dais to seize Bolitho's wrist in a grip like a manacle.

He screamed into Bolitho's face, 'Where did you get *that*?'

He jerked up his wrist and the watch, upon which the prancing gold beast dangled like a fob.

Bolitho forced himself to keep his voice level. To stop his gaze from falling on the similar pendant which hung on Muljadi's chest.

'From a prisoner.' He added sharply, 'A pirate!'

Muljadi twisted his wrist slowly, his eyes like fires as he snarled, 'You lie! And you will suffer for it! *Now!*'

Le Chaumareys called, 'In God's name, do not *make* him kill you!'

Bolitho kept his eyes on Muljadi's, feeling his power, his hatred, but something more. Anxiety?

He said, 'If you take a telescope, you will be able to see my ship. You will also see there is a halter at the mainyard. If I do not return before dusk, your son will hang there, you have my word on it! I took this from his neck when I captured him and his schooner some forty miles to the south'rd of where we are standing.'

Muljadi's eyes seemed to be bulging right out of his head.

'*You lie!*'

Bolitho eased his wrist from Muljadi's grasp. The fingers had left marks like rope burns.

He said quietly, 'I will exchange him for your prisoner.' He looked at Le Chaumareys' astonished face. 'The *capitaine* can arrange it, I am certain.'

Muljadi ran to a window and snatched a telescope from one of his men.

Over his shoulder he said hoarsely, 'You will stay as hostage!'

Bolitho replied, 'No hostages. A fair bargain. You have my word, as a King's officer.'

Muljadi threw the telescope to the ground, shattering the lens in all directions. His chest was heaving violently, and his shaven head was glittering with tiny jewels of sweat.

'King's officer? Do you think I care for you?' He spat on the stones by Bolitho's shoes. 'You will suffer, that I promise you!'

Le Chaumareys called, 'Let it be done!' He hesitated. 'Highness!'

But Muljadi was almost beside himself. Like a madman. He suddenly grasped Bolitho's arm and propelled him to the opposite end of the chamber and thrust him against the window.

'Look down there, *Captain*!' He was spitting out each word like a pistol ball. 'I will give you your colonel, but it is too late to save you now!'

Bolitho stared down at the glittering water which snaked around and amongst the next cluster of islets. Anchored in a bend of the channel, her decks alive with hurrying figures, was a frigate.

He felt Muljadi's hatred turning to a wild jubilation as he shouted, 'Mine! All mine! Well, my *King's officer*, are you still so confident?'

Le Chaumareys said harshly, 'Why did you have to do that?'

Muljadi whirled round on him, his eyes wild. 'Do you think I have to be told what to do? That I am a child? I have waited long enough. The waiting is over now.'

A door grated open and Bolitho saw the Spanish commandant, supported on either side by an armed pirate, his eyes blinking in the light as if he was almost blind.

Bolitho strode past Muljadi and his men. 'I have come to take you home, *Señor*.' He saw the filth on his torn clothing, the shackle marks on his thin wrists. 'It was a brave thing you did.'

The old man peered blearily at him, his beard quivering as he said jerkily, 'I do not understand?'

Le Chaumareys said, 'Come. Now.' Under his breath he added, 'Or I will not answer for your safety!'

It was like a dream. Down the sloping track to the pier and into the boat, and for most of the way pursued by Muljadi's voice, which had lapsed into another language, although the threat was no less evident.

Bolitho said coldly, 'The frigate. She was English.'

Le Chaumareys nodded wearily. 'Yes. Damaged in battle in '82, she was beached near here and her company removed by another vessel. We have been working on her for two years almost. Putting her to rights. I was ordered to hand her to Muljadi ready for use, before I am allowed to return home.'

Bolitho did not look at him. He was supporting the Spanish commandant against his knees, feeling his sobs and his misery.

'Then I hope you are proud of your work, *m'sieu*. And what it may mean when Muljadi puts her to work.'

The French frigate's yards loomed above the boat, and Bolitho followed the other captain up to the entry port.

Le Chaumareys said abruptly, 'Maurin will attend to the transfer.'

He looked searchingly at Bolitho for several seconds.

'You are still young. One day you might have understood. Now that is past.' He thrust out his hand. 'When we meet again, as I fear we must, it will be for the last time.'

He turned on his heel and strode to the cabin hatch.

Bolitho pulled out his watch and examined the gold pendant. If he had been mistaken, or Potter had given him wrong information . . . He stopped his train of thought there and then. It did not bear even conjecture.

Then he thought of the captured frigate. But for Muljadi's flare of anger he would never have known of it. The knowledge was little help, but it was better than nothing, he decided.

Maurin said cheerfully, 'I will take a boat away to your ship, *m'sieu*. They will be surprised to learn of your safety, as I am.'

Bolitho smiled. 'I was well protected, thank you.' He glanced at the cabin hatch, but was uncertain what he meant.

16

No Better, No Worse than Most

Bolitho walked slowly along the upper rampart at the inland side of the settlement, watching the steamy haze rising from the jungle, the afternoon sunlight playing on the dripping leaves and fronds nearest the palisade. *Undine* had anchored shortly before noon below an empty blue sky, and yet during their slow approach towards Pendang Bay he had seen the land dark under the weather, and had almost envied the isolated downpour. He sighed, smelling the thick, heady scents from the jungle, the drowsy aromas of rotting leaves and roots hidden in deep shadow below the trees.

For the last two days *Undine* had been plagued with opposing wind, and when at last it had changed in their favour there had been little more than a breath to bring life to the sails.

He watched some red-coated sepoys working beyond the palisade, and two native women approaching the gateway with heavy bundles on their heads. At a glance it seemed nothing had changed, but now as he waited to confront Conway for the second time within the hour he knew everything was different.

He continued his walk to the next corner of the crude timber rampart and saw *Undine* riding easily to her cable, the captured schooner close abeam. As he looked towards the shallows where he had last seen the brig *Rosalind* when *Undine* had set sail for Muljadi's stronghold, it was all he could do to stop himself from cursing aloud. Like the transport *Bedford*, she had gone. Back to Madras, to carry despatches and Raymond's own appreciation of the situation to Sir Montagu Strang.

Bolitho had been shocked by Conway's appearance when he had reported ashore within thirty minutes of dropping anchor. Wild-eyed, more shrunken than ever, he had been almost beside himself with anger and despair.

He had shouted, 'You dare to stand here and tell me that you actually chose to ignore my orders? That despite the importance of my instructions you made no attempt to parley with Le Chaumareys?'

Bolitho had stood very still, his eyes on Conway's distorted features. An empty decanter lay on the table, and it was obvious he had been drinking heavily for some time.

'I could not parley, sir. To do so would have been to recognise Muljadi. Which is exactly what the French want.'

'Are you telling me something I do not already know?' Conway had gripped the table violently. 'I ordered you to tell Le Chaumareys to return Colonel Pastor unharmed! The Spanish government would have raised a savage argument against England if we had allowed him to remain a prisoner, and *right under my nose*.'

Bolitho recalled his own voice. Taut and flat. Not daring to arouse Conway's fury any more than it was.

'When I found I had captured Muljadi's son I knew I *could* bargain, sir. There was a good chance I would succeed. As it turned out, we arrived in time. I fear that Pastor would have died in a few more days.'

Conway had screamed, 'Pastor be damned! You took Muljadi's son, and you dared to release him! We could have had that bloody pirate crawling at our feet, pleading for his son's life!'

Bolitho had said abruptly, 'There was a frigate lost in these waters during the last months of the war.'

Conway had been taken off guard. 'Yes, yes. The *Imogene*, Captain Balfour.' He had squinted against the sun's glare from a window. 'Twenty-eight guns. Had been in battle with the French and then got caught by a gale. Drove aground, and her people were taken off by one of my sloops. What the *hell* does she have to do with it?'

'Everything, sir. But for my meeting with Muljadi I would never have known until we were totally unprepared. The frigate, the *Imogene*, is there, sir, in the Benuas, and from what I saw, about ready to weigh anchor.'

Conway had lurched against the table, as if Bolitho had actually struck him.

'If this is some trick, some ruse to deter my—'

'She is *there*, sir. Refitted and repaired, and I have no doubt well trained by Le Chaumareys' officers.' He could not conceal his bitterness. 'I had hoped the brig would still be here. You could have sent word. Demanded help. There is no choice in the matter now.'

The next part had been the worst. Conway walking unsteadily to the sideboard and fumbling with another decanter, and muttering, 'Betrayed, right from the start. Raymond insisted on sending the brig to Madras. She's a Company vessel, and I could hold her no longer. He had all the arguments. All the answers, too.' Claret had slopped over his shirt like blood as he had shouted, 'And me? Nothing but a cat's-paw! A tool for Strang and his friends to use as they please!'

He had smashed a goblet with the decanter and groped hurriedly for another, adding, 'And now you, the one man I trusted, tells me that Muljadi is ready to attack my settlement! Not merely content with showing me to be incompetent, Raymond will now tell his damned superiors that I cannot even hold this territory under the British flag!'

The door had opened noiselessly and Puigserver had moved into the room. He had glanced briefly at Conway and had said to Bolitho, 'I stayed until your return. My men have sailed in the *Bedford*, but I could not leave also without offering my gratitude for securing Don Pastor's release. You seem to make a habit of risking your life for others. I trust that this time it will not go unrewarded.' His black eyes had moved to Conway again. 'Eh, Admiral?'

Conway had stared at him vaguely. 'I must think.'

'We all must.' The Spaniard had settled in a chair, his eyes still on Conway. 'I heard some of it through the door.' He had shrugged. 'Not spying, you understand, but your voice was somewhat forceful.'

Conway had made a new effort to control himself. 'Conference. Immediately.' He had fixed Bolitho with a bleary stare. 'You wait outside. I must *think.*'

Now, as he looked emptily at the small figures below the palisade, Bolitho could feel his returning anger, a sense of urgency.

'*Richard!*'

He swung round and saw her at the corner of the square tower. She was well covered against the sun, and wore the same wide-brimmed hat as before. He hurried to her and seized her hands.

'Viola! I was wondering—'

She shook her head. 'Later. But listen.' She reached up and touched his cheek very gently, her eyes suddenly sad. 'It has been so long. Eleven days, but they were years. When the storm came I worried about you.'

He tried to speak, to break the pain in her voice, but she hurried on, 'I think James suspects. He has been very strange lately. Probably my maid let slip something. A good girl, but easily flattered into words.' She studied him searchingly. 'But no matter. He will do nothing. It is *you* I am concerned for.' She dropped her head. 'And it is all my fault. I wanted him to be something in this world, mostly, I suspect, for my own gain. I drove him too hard, too fast, wanting him to be the man he could never be.' She squeezed his hand. 'But you know all this.'

Voices echoed below the parapet and Bolitho thought he heard footsteps.

She said huskily, 'James will have sent his own report to Sir Montagu. He knows now that Conway is not the man for this appointment, and will use this knowledge to his own advantage. But you, my darling Richard, will be included in his report. I know him so well, you see. To get at you, to use his petty revenge, he will also blame you for the inability to destroy an ignorant pirate, French aid or no!'

He replied quietly, 'It is worse than that. Muljadi has many men at his back. When once he has overthrown this settlement the whole area will rise to support him. They have little choice. The pirates will become saviours, the protectors the invaders. It is not uncommon.'

She turned her head quickly and he saw a pulse jumping in her throat.

'Listen to me, Richard. Do not become further involved. You are valuable to your country and to all who look up to you. Do not, I implore you, continue to look up to those who are unfit even to lick your boots!' She cupped his face in her hands. 'Save your ship and yourself, and damn *their* eyes, I say!'

He held her wrists very gently. 'It is no longer so simple.' He thought of Le Chaumareys, encouraging him to quit, to get away and still retain his honour. 'And I wish to God you had sailed in the brig. Muljadi has more strength now, and when he comes . . .'

He let his gaze move outward and down towards the anchored frigate. How small she appeared in the harsh glare.

'There is only *Undine* between him and these walls.'

She stared at him, her eyes wide and suddenly understanding.

'And you intend to fight *all* of them?'

Bolitho prised her hands away as a sepoy corporal rounded the tower and said, 'Captain Bolitho, *sahib*, the governor will meet you, please.'

Bolitho looked at her and said, 'Now we will see, Viola.' He tried to smile. 'The battle's not done yet.'

He found Conway seated behind the table, his stained shirt covered by his heavy dress coat. Puigserver had not moved, and Raymond was standing with his back to a window, his face hidden in black shadow. Major Jardine and his second-in-command made up the conference.

Conway said sharply, 'I have told them, Bolitho. Word for word as you described it to me.'

'Thank you, sir.'

Bolitho looked at Raymond, knowing it would come from him.

'You took a great deal upon yourself, Captain. More, I suspect, than the governor intended?'

'Yes, sir. But I was taught to use initiative, especially when beyond the fleet's apron strings.' He saw Puigserver examining one shoe with sudden interest. 'The fact is, Muljadi intends to attack this settlement. It is all he can do now that he has lost his hostage, and understands that we are informed of his additional frigate. It has changed everything.'

Jardine said harshly, 'If he comes, my men can hold him off until help arrives. When the brig reaches Madras they'll soon send a force to finish this ruffian! Even when the Navy is apparently incapable of so doing, what?'

Bolitho waited, watching Raymond's hands on the window sill.

'Well, Mr. Raymond? Is the gallant major right?' He saw the hands take a firmer grip and added, 'Or did you suggest in your report to Sir Montagu Strang that Pendang Bay is, in your opinion, *no longer an asset?*'

Jardine bared his teeth. '*Rubbish!*' He hesitated and asked, 'Well, sir?'

Raymond sounded very calm. 'I told the truth. No ships will be sent, other than transports to remove the Company's soldiers and their dependents.'

Jardine exploded, 'But I can manage, sir! You should have told me first!'

Bolitho said, 'You cannot *manage*, Major. Muljadi will have more than a thousand men when he comes. His stronghold is crammed to capacity, that I *did* see. You may have been able to hold the walls until help was forthcoming from Madras. Without it, your only chance is a forced march through dense jungle to the east'rd to contact the Dutch East India Company base and find safety.' His tone hardened. 'But through dense jungle, and at this time of the year, I doubt if many would survive, even without attack from those who will want to impress Muljadi with their loyalty.'

Raymond said thickly, 'No blame can fall on my shoulders! I reported what I knew! I had no knowledge of this other frigate!' He tried to recover his original calm. 'Any more than you did!'

Conway stood up very deliberately, each movement an effort of will.

'But you could not wait, Mr. Raymond. You used your authority to seek your own ends and despatched the brig even after I requested she be held here until *Undine*'s return.'

He walked to the opposite side of the room and stared unseeingly at the close-knit jungle.

'So what can we do? How best can we prepare ourselves for slaughter?'

He turned with the speed of light and yelled, 'Well, Mr. Raymond? Will you explain, for indeed it is beyond me!'

Major Jardine stammered, 'Surely it cannot be that hopeless?'

Puigserver was watching Bolitho. 'Well, *Capitan*? You have been *inside* the lion's den, not us.'

Bolitho looked at Conway. 'May I suggest something, sir?'

The admiral nodded, his wispy hair in disorder. 'If there is anything left to say.'

Bolitho walked to the table and moved the heavy silver inkwells into a pattern.

'The Benuas are much as they appear on our charts, sir, although I suspect some of the smaller channels between the islets are silted and shallow. The fortress stands high on a central islet, a rock-pile, if you like.' His fingers made a sweeping gesture down the front of one inkwell. 'The seaward face of the islet is sheer, and what I first took to be reefs at its foot I now believe are fragments of cliff which have fallen away over many years of wear.'

He heard Captain Strype say gloomily, 'That rules out any hope of a scaling attempt. It *is* hopeless.'

Conway glared at him and then snapped, 'Continue. What about this cliff?'

Bolitho looked at him calmly. 'If we attack at once, sir.' He ignored the gasps. 'Before Muljadi is ready. We might nip his whole plan in the bud.'

Conway exclaimed, 'Attack? When you have just finished destroying our hopes even of staying alive!'

'The main gun battery is on the seaward rampart, sir. Bring it down and the ships at anchor will be without immediate protection.'

Conway was rubbing his chin in quick, nervous movements. 'Yes, I can see that. But how?'

Jardine sneered, 'An act of God maybe?'

'The schooner, sir.' Bolitho kept his gaze fixed on Conway's lined forehead, seeing all the doubts and apprehension gathering like a storm. 'We could use the prevailing wind, sail her straight on to the fallen rocks at the foot of the cliff, filled to the deck beams with powder and a goodly fuse. The explosion would, I believe, bring down more of the cliff.' He hesitated, feeling the sudden tension around him. 'And the battery.'

Captain Strype was staring at the inkwell as if seeing the actual explosion. 'It might well work, sir! A damn fine idea!'

Jardine growled, 'Hold your tongue! What sort of fool would do such a thing anyway?'

He fell back as Conway snapped, 'Be still!' To Bolitho he added, 'And you think this is a reasonable risk?'

'I do. The schooner would be lightly manned, and her crew could get clear in their boat once the final course was laid. A long fuse would allow them time enough.' He kept his eyes steady. 'The moment the charge explodes I will force the channel in *Undine* and take the anchored frigates before they can recover. After an explosion like that, they will not be expecting a further intrusion.'

Puigserver nodded grimly. 'Fair justice, too.'

Conway glared at him. 'It is the wildest plan I have ever discussed.'

Bolitho said quietly, 'I must argue that point, sir.'

'*What?*' Conway swung on him. 'Are you questioning me again?'

'I recall a certain captain, sir. Years back, when I was a stupid midshipman. He took a fair chance or so when he considered it necessary.'

Conway reached out and gripped his wrist. 'Thank you for that.' He looked away, patting his pockets as if searching for something. 'I'd forgotten.'

Bolitho said, 'The troops will have to remain here, of course.'

He thought he saw relief on Jardine's heavy face, resentment on his aide's. Strange, he thought, that the one who appeared the weaker was the stronger after all.

He added, 'If this plan fails, and we must face that possibility, it will be up to the sepoys to evacuate the settlement as best they can. But please take my word for this. No parley with Muljadi, for to him victory means only one thing. Extinction for all those who have represented his enemies throughout his entire life.' He pointed towards the window. 'And once through those palisades, there will be no time left for regrets.'

Conway returned to the table, his face very composed.

'I agree.' He glanced at Jardine. 'Set your men to work transferring powder to the schooner, every barrel and cask from our magazine, if that is what is needed.'

He looked at Bolitho. 'And who will command the schooner, have you thought of that?'

'I am not decided, sir.' He smiled gravely. 'Yet.'

He turned as Raymond walked around the table showing his face at last in the sunlight.

Raymond said, 'I acted as I thought fit.'

Conway nodded, his eyes contemptuous. 'If we survive this affair, you may yet share the advantages, if there are any.' His tone was like ice. 'If we fail, you will probably receive the knighthood you covet so dearly.' He paused as Raymond hurried to the door. 'Posthumously, of course!'

When he faced the table again Conway seemed about ten years younger. 'Now that I am decided, Bolitho, I cannot wait!'

Bolitho nodded. He could feel his muscles and bones aching as if from physical effort, and could barely realise what he had done, what he had committed himself and his ship to.

He said, 'I will return aboard now, sir. I need fresh water and fruit if there is any.'

Faces flashed across his thoughts. Carwithen with his axe embedded in the pirate's neck. Davy's pride at being given command of the schooner. Fowlar's genuine pleasure with his temporary promotion. And Herrick most of all. What would he say to this pathetic, desperate plan? Smile? Shake his head? Accept that at last his captain had made the one fatal mistake? For all of them.

Conway was saying, 'You are a sly-boots, Bolitho, more than I ever suspected.' He made as if to reach for the new decanter but changed his mind. 'If I am to lose my head, then it had better be a clear, one, eh?'

Puigserver was touching one of the silver inkwells with a spatulate finger.

'When will it be, *Capitan?*'

'Early.' Bolitho watched him thoughtfully. Puigserver, too. He had been in the story from the very beginning. 'Dawn attack.'

Conway nodded. 'And if ever you have prayed for the wind to set fair, then do it from now on.'

Bolitho smiled. 'Aye, sir. I will bear that in mind.'

He made to leave, but halted as the admiral added gruffly, 'Whatever the outcome, we will have tried. Done our best.'

When he turned towards the sunlight Bolitho was shocked to see the moisture in his eyes.

'Raymond was right, of course. I'm not the man for the appointment, nor do I suppose it was ever intended I should retain it once the settlement had been founded . . .' he hesitated, '. . . or lost. But we will show them.'

He strode to his private door and slammed it behind him.

Puigserver whistled. 'The old lion awakes, eh?'

Bolitho smiled sadly. 'If you have known him as I once did, *señor*. If you had seen the people cheering themselves hoarse, with the smoke of battle still thick between decks, then you would have understood.'

'Perhaps.' Puigserver grinned broadly. 'Now away with you. I think you have learned a great deal since we first met. About many things, eh?'

Bolitho walked out past a nodding servant, and then started as someone touched his sleeve. It was Viola Raymond's maid, her face screwed up with fright as she whispered, 'This way, sir! Just down here!'

Bolitho followed her quickly, and then saw the pale figure by a door at the far end of the passageway.

He asked, 'What is it? We should not meet like this.'

She stared at him, her eyes blazing. 'You are going to get killed! He just told me!' She threw her big hat on the floor and added angrily, 'And I don't care! I don't care what happens to you!' Then she threw herself against him, her voice breaking in sobs as she cried, 'It's a lie! I *do* care, my darling Richard! I'll die if anything happens to you! I didn't mean to say those things.'

He held her chin in his hand. 'Easy, Viola.' He pushed the hair from her forehead. It was hot and feverish. 'I had no choice.'

Her body shook uncontrollably and she gripped his arms even tighter, oblivious to her maid, and the real possibility that someone might walk into the passage at any second.

'And no chance! No chance at all!'

Bolitho held her away and waited until she was calmer.

'I must go now. And I *will* take care.' He saw her returning anguish and said quickly, 'I must not damage my new watch, now must I?'

She tried to return his smile, the tears flowing freely down her face as she said, 'I would never forgive you.'

He turned and walked towards the stairway, and then stopped again as she called his name. But she did not follow him. Instead she held up one hand, as if he was already a long way off. Beyond reach.

He found Allday waiting by the beached gig and said sharply, 'Back to the ship.'

Allday watched him curiously. 'They're taking powder casks to the schooner, Captain.'

'Is that a question?' He glared at him but Allday's face was unmoved.

'I was just thinking. Mr. Davy's not going to be happy about this.'

Bolitho clapped his arm. 'I know. And I have no excuse for taking out my temper on you.'

Allday squinted up at the timbered fort above the palisades, the white figure in one of the windows.

Under his breath he said, 'I know just how it feels, Captain.'

Bolitho twisted in the sternsheets to watch the boats busying themselves alongside the schooner. It had sounded so simple, so neat. To take two anchored frigates in a confined space was better than matching gun for gun in open waters. But many would curse his name as they died, nonetheless.

He sighed as the gig gathered speed towards the frigate. Puigserver had been right. He had learned a great deal since their meeting at Santa Cruz. Mostly about himself.

'All present, sir.' Herrick seated himself beside the cabin door and waited for Bolitho to speak.

Beyond the stern windows it was very dark, but it was possible to see the yellow lanterns moving back and forth between the settlement and the surf as the business of loading the schooner continued without pause.

Bolitho looked at the faces around the cabin. Everyone was here. He let his gaze rest briefly on Midshipman Keen. Even him, although the surgeon had told him he would not be responsible for his condition. Keen looked strained, and whenever he moved it was easy to see the pain on his mouth and eyes. But he had insisted on rejoining the ship.

Mudge and Soames, Fowlar, looking slightly self-conscious at his first important conference. Davy, whose handsome features were still showing some of the dismay remaining from Bolitho's news about the schooner. Captain Bellairs, debonair and bland-faced in the gently spiralling lantern light. The purser, as mournful as ever. Armitage and Penn, like ill-matched brothers, and lastly, below the skylight, Whitmarsh, the surgeon, his face glowing like a great beetroot.

Bolitho clasped his hands behind him. An average wardroom, he thought. No better, no worse than most, yet he was about to ask more of them than would be expected from a veteran company.

'You know me well enough by now to understand that I dislike speeches. Making or listening to them.'

He saw Herrick grin, and Mudge's tiny eyes vanish on either side of the great nose.

'At the beginning of this commission there were many aboard, wardroom included, who thought my methods too hard, my ideals too high for a ship on a peacetime mission. Now all of us know that things have changed, and our experience, our training is the only thing of value we have to protect us, and more to the point, those who are depending on our ability.'

He nodded to Herrick. 'Open the chart.'

As Mudge leaned forward to weigh down Herrick's chart with books and brass dividers he took another glance at their faces. Anxiety, trust? It was too early to know.

He continued, 'The schooner will sail directly into the main channel, using the easterly headland for cover until the last available moment. Once on course for the rocks at the foot of the cliff,' he paused to lay the dividers on the small cross, 'the helm will be lashed, and the crew will take to the boat. They will be recovered later.' He made himself smile, although his heart felt strangely heavy. 'After we have excised the two frigates while their people are still collecting their wits!'

Penn said, 'We'll show 'em, sir!' He quailed under Mudge's withering stare.

'And *we*,' Bolitho smiled at the scarlet-faced midshipman, 'driven on by Mr. Penn's enthusiasm, will move into the channel, rake both anchored ships, come about and rake 'em again.' He looked at Davy. 'So tell all gun crews to look alive. The first broadsides will be the telling ones.'

Bellairs drawled, 'Bit of a chance for the schooner, I'd say, sir. All that gunpowder aboard. One heated ball from the battery, and up she goes.' He blinked under Bolitho's level stare and added, 'No disrespect to the bold fellows aboard her, of course, but where would it leave *us*?'

Bolitho shook his head. 'The battery is old. I am almost certain that heated shot will not be available, for fear of splitting the guns. Normally they would not need it. With such an arc of fire, the battery can hit any vessel once it is within the two main channels.'

He smiled to hide the sudden doubt which Bellairs had laid in his mind. Suppose there was heated shot already simmering in furnaces? But he would have seen them, surely? No baskets could hoist glowing balls to that high rampart.

He said, 'And we will know that most of that battery is lying in the sea, where it should have been years ago.'

'We will weigh at first light tomorrow. The wind seems to be in our favour, and with luck it will serve our purposes. There remains just one matter . . .' He paused and saw Herrick watching him from across the cabin.

But he must not think of his friend. The best and firmest one he had ever had. He was his first lieutenant, the most competent officer in the ship. Nothing more counted. It must not.

He continued, 'Mr. Herrick will command the schooner.'

Herrick nodded, his face expressionless. 'Aye, sir. I'll take six good hands. Should be enough.'

Bolitho held his gaze, the rest of the officers fading around him as he said, 'I will leave it to you. If Potter wishes to join with you, then take him.' He saw Whitmarsh rising to protest and added harshly, 'He knows the channel. We need all the help we can get.'

The door opened slightly and Carwithen thrust his head into the lantern light.

'Beg pardon, sir, but the water casks 'ave been stowed, an' a message 'as been sent to say that the schooner is fully loaded.'

His gaze shifted to Fowlar, but there was no recognition. Fowlar's first step to promotion had already marked them apart, although it was possible they had never had much in common, Bolitho thought.

'Very well.' Bolitho waited for the door to close. 'Carry on, gentlemen. You all have your duties to attend.' He faltered, wondering why there were never the right words when you needed them most. 'We will have little time for discussion until this matter is settled.' *Or we are all dead.* 'Remember this, and remember it well. Our people will be looking to you, more than they, or you ever expected. Most of them have never been in a real sea fight, and when we last met with *Argus* many still believed we had won a battle rather than secured a retreat. This time there can be no retreat, for us, or the enemy. Le Chaumareys is a fine captain, probably the best ever produced by France. But he has one weakness.' He smiled gravely. 'One which we have not yet enjoyed. That of supreme confidence in his ship and himself. His belief, and your skill and determination will win the day for us if anything can.'

They stood up, silent and grim-faced, as if only just aware of their responsibilities. The finality of their position.

Then as they moved towards the door Bolitho said, 'A moment, Mr. Herrick.'

Alone together in the gently pitching cabin, Bolitho said, 'I had no choice.'

'I would have been dismayed, had you selected a junior, sir.' Herrick smiled. 'So there's an end to it.'

Bolitho held out his hand. 'May God protect you, Thomas. If I have misjudged this affair, or the enemy outwits us, then pull back at once. If I signal a recall, then abandon your attempt. If die we must, then I want you with me.'

Herrick gripped his hand tightly, his blue eyes suddenly concerned.

'Enough of this talk, sir! It is not like you. *Win* we must, and here's my hand on it!'

Bolitho followed him towards the door. Hating the moment. Conscious of the weight which he had caused to fall on his own shoulders. She had seen his danger, as had Le Chaumareys. Perhaps Herrick also.

On deck, in the noise and bustle of preparing for sea, the contact was at last broken.

Herrick said, 'I'll go and pick my hands, sir.'

Bolitho nodded, his heart aching. 'Carry on, Mr. Herrick. The second lieutenant will relieve you forthwith.'

As Herrick melted into the shadows Davy crossed the quarterdeck and touched his hat.

Bolitho said, 'I am sorry about your schooner. I seem to have little choice in anything at the moment.'

Davy shrugged. 'It does not seem to matter any more, sir. For once, I cannot see further than the next few days, nor care either.'

Bolitho seized his arm savagely and swung him round. 'Has nothing I said to you made any sense?'

Davy struggled in his fierce grip and blurted out, 'I – I am sorry, sir!'

'You will be if I hear you talking like that again! Your responsibility is to me, the ship and the people you command. Not to your own personal considerations. When a man starts to believe there are no more tomorrows, he is as good as sewn up in a hammock between two round-shot. Think of the tomorrows, believe in them, and the men who depend on your skill, or lack of it, will see their own survival on your face!' He relaxed his hold and added in a steadier tone, 'Now be off with you.'

He began to pace along the larboard side, his feet stepping automatically over ringbolts and gun tackles, although his eyes saw none of them. He had not been reprimanding Davy, but himself. It was no time for doubt or recrimination, but only for living the role he had adopted, had earned in a dozen battles or more.

'Boat ahoy!' The challenge rang out from the gangway where lanterns glinted on levelled muskets and bayonets.

From the bay itself came the reply. 'Don Luis Puigserver wishes to come aboard!'

Davy came hurrying aft. 'Is that in order, sir?'

Bolitho smiled, calm again. 'I was expecting him, I believe.'

The stocky figure rose through the port and hurried across the deck to greet him.

Puigserver said, 'I had to come, *Capitan*. *Nervion's* loss made me a part of this. I cannot withdraw until the matter is settled.' He patted the ornate pistols beneath his coat. 'And I am an excellent shot, no?'

'I could order you to leave, *señor*.'

'But?' Puigserver tilted his head to one side. 'But you will not. In any case, I have left written word to explain my deeds and my reasons. If we survive the battle, I will tear it to pieces. If not . . .' He left the rest unsaid.

'Then I accept your offer, *señor*. With gratitude.'

Puigserver walked to the nettings and stared across at a glittering riding-light. 'When will the schooner set sail?'

'Before dawn. She will need all the time available to work into her position to best advantage.'

Again the ache. The thought of Herrick sailing his floating magazine into the muzzles of Muljadi's battery.

'I see.' Puigserver yawned. 'Then I think I will join your offwatch officers for a glass in the wardroom. You will need your solitude tonight, I am thinking.'

Some hours later Bolitho was awakened by Allday's hand on his shoulder. He had fallen asleep in the cabin, his head on his forearm across the chart where he had been working.

Allday watched him anxiously. 'Schooner's weighed, Captain.'

Bolitho rubbed his eyes. Was it almost dawn? He felt suddenly chilled. Desperate for sleep.

Allday added quietly, 'Mister Pigsliver's gone, too.'

Bolitho stared at him, wondering if he had expected this. Had known it was what Puigserver had wanted from the moment he had outlined his plan.

'Is she well clear?'

'Aye, Captain.' Allday stretched and yawned. 'Stood round the headland half an hour back.' He added slowly, 'He'll be good company for Mr. Herrick, and that's no error.'

Bolitho looked at him. 'You *knew*, didn't you?'

'Aye, Captain.' Allday watched him sadly. 'I thought it for the best.'

Bolitho nodded. 'I expect it is.' He walked to the windows as if to see the riding-light still twinkling above the water. 'It is a bad thing to be alone.'

Allday glanced at the tarnished sword which hung from the bulkhead. For a moment he thought about Bolitho's other coxswain, who had died protecting his back from French marksmen at the Saintes. They had come a long way together since those times, he thought. Soon now, it might all end. He looked at Bolitho's shoulders as he peered through the stern windows.

But you will never be alone, Captain. Not while I've a breath left.

17

Close Action

Bolitho rested his hands on the quarterdeck rail and peered searchingly along his command. In the darkness the decks and gangways made a pale outline against the sea beyond the bows, and only the irregular drift of spray, the swirling white arrowhead from the stem gave any true hint of their progress.

He restrained himself from going aft again to examine his watch by the shaded compass light. Nothing had changed since his last inspection, and he was well aware of the danger of adding to the tension around him.

Three days since they had left the anchorage in Pendang Bay, making good speed with favourable winds for most of the time. They had stood well clear of the land, even the approaches to the little whale-shaped islet, in case Muljadi or Le Chaumareys had thought fit to place another craft there to warn of any unwelcome sail.

The previous evening, just before sunset, they had sighted Herrick's schooner, a tiny dark sliver on the copper-edged horizon, seemingly motionless as she idled to await *Undine*'s arrival at the arranged point of rendezvous. A brief dipping signal from a lantern before both vessels had lost each other again in darkness.

Bolitho shivered, feeling the cool, clammy air exploring his face and throat. The middle watch had only just run its course, and there was still an hour or so before any lightening of the sky could be expected. But overnight, while all hands had worked to prepare the ship for action, the clouds had gathered and thickened, brushing out the stars so that *Undine* seemed to be sailing remorselessly into a void.

He heard Mudge moving restlessly below the hammock nettings, rubbing his palms together to keep warm. The sailing master seemed unusually preoccupied. Perhaps his rheumatism was troubling him, or like Bolitho, he was thinking of Herrick, somewhere out there on *Undine*'s larboard bow.

Bolitho straightened his back and looked up at the blacker outlines of yards and rigging. The ship was sailing under topsails and jibs, and with only the great forecourse hiding the sea ahead of the bowsprit. It was strange to feel so chilled, when within hours the sun would be back to torment them, to add to whatever else lay in store.

He asked, 'How is the wind, Mr. Mudge?'

Mudge was glad to break the silence. 'Still sou'-west, sir. By an' large.' He coughed noisily. 'Under most occasions I'd be grateful for that.'

'What are you thinking?'

'Not sure, sir.' Mudge moved away from the seamen waiting by the quarterdeck six-pounders. 'It's too *uneven* for my tastes.'

Bolitho turned to peer forward again. The big forecourse seemed to echo Mudge's doubts. *Undine* was steering almost due north, and with the wind coming across her quarter she should have been making easy-going of it. But she was not. The forecourse would billow and harden, making the stays and shrouds hum and vibrate, holding the ship firm for several minutes. Then it would flap and bang in disorder before falling almost limp against the foremast for another frustrating period.

Mudge added doubtfully, 'You never knows in these waters. Not for sure.'

Bolitho looked at his untidy outline. If Mudge was worried, with all his experience, how much worse it would be for many of the others.

He called, 'Mr. Davy! I am going forrard directly.' He saw the lieutenant's shape detach itself from the rail. 'Tell Mr. Keen to keep me company.'

He slipped out of his tarpaulin coat and handed it to Allday. He had been so occupied with his own thoughts and doubts he had not fully realised how heavily these dragging hours must be affecting his company. He had ordered the ship to be prepared for action as soon as he was satisfied with the final leg of their course towards the Benua islands. Working in almost total darkness, the hands had completed the task almost as quickly as in broad daylight, so familiar had they become with their surroundings. Their home. It was a simple precaution. Sound travelled too easily at sea, and the clatter of screens being torn down, the scrape and squeak of nets being spread above the gun deck and chain slings being rigged to every yard seemed loud enough to wake the dead. But from then on they had nothing to do but wait. To fret on what daylight might bring, or take away.

Keen came out of the darkness, his shirt pale against a black six-pounder.

Bolitho asked, 'How is the wound?'

'Much better, thank you, sir.'

Bolitho smiled. He could almost feel the pain which was probably showing on Keen's face.

'Then take a stroll with me.'

Together they walked along the lee gangway, ducking below the taut nets which Shellabeer's men had rigged to catch falling cordage or worse, seeing the upturned faces of each gun crew, the restless shapes of the marine sentries at hatchways, or powder-monkeys huddled together while they waited to serve the silent cannon.

On to the forecastle, where the squat carronades pointed from either bow like tethered beasts, their crews shivering in the occasional dashes of spray.

Bolitho paused, one hand gripping the nettings as *Undine* sidled unsteadily into a deep trough. Most of the seamen were stripped to the waist, their bodies shining faintly above the dark water alongside.

'All ready, lads?'

He felt them crowd around him, their sudden interest at his arrival. Of necessity, the galley fire had been doused when the ship had gone to quarters. A hot drink now would be worth more than a dozen extra guns, he thought bitterly.

To Keen he said, 'Pass the word to Mr. Davy with my compliments. A double tot of rum for all hands.' He heard the instant response around him, the murmur of appreciation as it flowed aft along the gun deck. 'If the purser complains, tell him he'll have me to reckon with!'

'Thankee, sir! That was right thoughtful, sir!'

He strode to the ladder, turning away in case they could see his face through the darkness, or sense his mood. It was too easy to raise their spirits. So simple that it made him feel cheap, hypocritical. A double tot of rum. A few pence. Whereas within hours they might have given their lives, or their limbs.

Bolitho paced aft beside the main hatch, seeing Soames's great figure towering above that of Tapril, the gunner. He nodded to Fowlar nearby, and to the larboard crews of the twelve-pounders. All were his men, his responsibility.

He thought suddenly of Rear Admiral Sir John Winslade, all those weeks and months ago in his office at the Admiralty. He had needed a frigate captain he could know and trust. One whose mind he could follow even though it was on the other side of the globe.

He thought, too, of the ragged soldiers below the Admiralty window, one blind, the other begging for the both of them.

All the brave schemes and plans, the lofty preparations for a new world. Yet when it was boiled down, nothing was changed. *Undine* and *Argus* were but two ships, and yet their presence and their needs made them no less important than opposing fleets.

And if *Undine* failed, what would they say in those fine residences in Whitehall and St. James's Square, and in the busy coffee houses where mere rumour grew into fact in minutes? Would they care that men had fought and died for them in the King's name?

Someone gave a hoarse cheer in the gloom, and he guessed the rum had arrived on deck.

He continued aft, hardly aware that he had stopped short in his tracks as his bitterness had given way to anger. How spacious the deck seemed without the boats lying one upon the other across their tier. All were now towing astern, awaiting the moment to be cast adrift, mute spectators of the battle which might come. Which had to come.

It was always a bad moment, he thought. Boats were frail things, but in battle they made an additional menace with their splinters flying like savage darts. Despite the danger, most men would wish them kept aboard. A link, a hope for survival if things went badly.

Keen came back panting hard. 'All done, sir. Mr. Triphook *was* a trifle perturbed at the extra issue!' His teeth shone in the darkness. 'Would *you* care for a glass, sir?'

Bolitho disliked rum. But he saw the seamen and marines watching him and exclaimed, 'Indeed I would, Mr. Keen.'

He raised the glass to his mouth, the powerful stench of rum going straight to his empty stomach.

'To us, lads!'

He pictured Herrick and Puigserver aboard their floating bomb. *And to you, Thomas.*

Then he was glad he had accepted the rum and added, 'I can now understand what makes our Jacks so fearsome!' It brought more laughs, as he knew it would.

He glanced at the sky. Still without light, or sign of a star.

He said, 'I'll go below.' He touched the midshipman's arm. 'You remain here by the hatch. Call, if I am needed.'

Bolitho climbed down into the darkness, his feet less certain here. Anyone could call him when required, but he must spare Keen an unnecessary visit to the surgeon's domain. It might come soon enough. He recalled the great pulsating wound, Allday's gentleness as he had searched out that bloody splinter.

Another ladder. He paused, feeling the ship groaning around him. Different smells abounded on this deck. Tar and oakum, and that of tightly compressed humanity, even though the tiny messes were now deserted. And from forward the reek of the great anchor cables, of bilge water and damp clothing. Of a living, working ship.

A feeble lantern showed him the rest of the way to Whitmarsh's crude surgery. The sea-chests lashed together where terrified wounded would be saved or driven to despair. Leather straps to jam between teeth, dressings to contain the pain.

The surgeon's great shadow swayed across the tilting deck. Bolitho watched him narrowly. There was a stronger smell of brandy in the damp air. To quench pain, or to prepare Whitmarsh for his own private hell, he was not certain.

'All well, Mr. Whitmarsh?'

'Aye, sir.'

The surgeon lurched against the chests and braced his knee to the nearest one. He waved one hand around his silent assistants, the loblolly boys, the men who would hold their victims until the work was done. Brutalised by their trade. Without ears for the screams. Beyond pity.

'We are all awaiting what *you* send us, sir.'

Bolitho stared at him coldly. 'Will you never learn?'

The surgeon nodded heavily. 'I have learned well. Oh yes indeed, sir. As I have sawed away at a man's leg, or plugged carpenter's oakum into his empty eye-socket, with nothing to ease his torment but neat spirits, I have come closer to God than most!'

'If that be true, then I pray you get no closer.'

Bolitho nodded to the others and strode towards the ladder.

Whitmarsh called after him, 'Perhaps I shall be greeting *you*, sir!'

Bolitho did not reply. The surgeon was obviously going completely mad. His obsession with his brother's horrible death, his drinking, and the very way he earned his living were taking their toll. But he had to hang on to what remained of that other man. The one who had spoken of suffering with compassion, of serving others less fortunate.

He thought again of Herrick, and prayed he would get his boat away when the schooner was set upon her final course to destruction. Strange companions he had, too. Puigserver, and the frightened sailmaker from Bristol, finding courage from somewhere to sail back to that place which had broken his mind and body.

'Captain, sir!'

He quickened his pace as Keen's voice came down the next ladder.

'What is it?'

But as he gripped the ladder and turned his face towards the sky's faint rectangle he knew the answer. Slow, heavy drops of rain were falling across the hatchway, like small pebbles dropped from the yards as they tapped on planking or bounced across the gangways.

He dragged himself up the last few steps and hurried aft to the quarterdeck. He was within a few feet of it when the clouds opened and the rain came down in a great roaring, deafening torrent.

He yelled above the deluge, 'How is the wind now?'

Mudge was cringing by the binnacle, his hat awry in the fury of the downpour.

'Veerin', sir! Far as I can tell!'

Water hissed and gurgled down decks and scuppers, and the chilled gun crews pressed beneath the gangways and cowered behind the sealed ports to escape the torrential rain.

Bolitho felt Allday trying to throw the tarpaulin coat over his shoulders, but pushed him away. He was already soaked to the marrow, hair plastered over his forehead, his mind ringing to the din of rain and spray. Yet through it all he managed to keep contact with the ship and her affairs. The deck felt steady enough, despite the angry downpour, and above his head he managed to make out the maintopsail's shape flapping and shining wetly as the wind eased round still further.

He snapped, 'Hands to the braces, Mr. Davy! We will be full and bye directly!' He heard the men groping and cursing as they lurched to obey the orders, the protesting squeak of swollen cordage being hauled through blocks while yards were trimmed to hold the ship on her larboard tack. He called, 'Bring her up a point!'

Men slithered around the big double wheel, and he saw Carwithen punch one of the helmsmen as he bowed under the sheeting rain.

'Nor' by west, sir. Full an' bye she is!'

'Hold her so!'

Bolitho mopped his face with his sleeve. The probing downpour helped to clear his aching mind, to make him accept what was happening. If the wind continued to veer, even if it stayed where it was, Herrick would be unable to place his schooner in position where he could destroy Muljadi's battery. The disastrous change of wind made the rain feel like tears. Tears for all their hopes, their pathetic determination, which minutes ago had made even the impossible seem undaunting.

He lurched to Mudge's side and shouted, 'How far now, d'you reckon?'

'Four or five miles, no more, sir.' Mudge was staring at the rain with dismay. 'This lot'll pass over quick enough. But then . . .' He shrugged.

Bolitho looked away. He knew well enough. A rising wind was most likely once the sun appeared. A wind which would do no service to Herrick, and keep Le Chaumareys in the safety of his anchorage. *Undine* would be helpless. She would be made to stay offshore until the enemy's double strength was prepared and ready to fight on their terms. Or they could turn and run for Pendang Bay with nothing to offer but a final warning.

Davy shouted, 'By God, life is hard!'

Mudge glared at him. 'Life's a bloody rear-guard action Mr. Davy, from the day you're born!'

Bolitho swung round to silence both of them and then saw that the master's mate's face was clearer than before. He could even see Carwithen scowling at the same luckless helmsman. The dawn was forcing itself to be taken notice of.

He felt the blood racing in his head as he snapped, 'We will attack as before! Pass the word to all hands!'

Davy gaped at him. 'Without destroying the battery, sir?'

'It might not have worked anyway.' He tried to sound calm. 'The enemy will be listening to the rain and thanking God for being at anchor.' He added harshly, 'Are you deaf, man? Tell Mr. Soames to prepare for loading, once the rain is passed!'

Davy nodded jerkily and hurried to the rail.

Captain Bellairs strode to Bolitho's side and remarked coolly, 'Damn risky thing, sir, if you'll pardon my sayin' so.'

Bolitho felt his shoulders beginning to sag under the rain, the sudden spark deserting him.

'What would *you* have me do?'

Bellairs turned up his collar and pouted. 'Oh, I'd fight, sir, no choice in the matter, what? Pity though, all the same. Waste. Damn bloody waste.'

Bolitho nodded heavily. 'No argument there.'

'Deck there! Land ho!'

Bolitho walked stiffly to the lee side, his shoes squeaking on the puddled deck. A darker blur, reaching out on either bow, deceptively gentle in the feeble light.

A voice said, 'Rain's goin'.' He sounded surprised.

As if to mark its passing, the dripping forecourse lifted and boomed dully to receive a fresher gust of wind. It made Bolitho shiver and grit his teeth.

'Tell Mr. Soames. Load, and prepare to run out when I pass the word.'

He looked around for Keen. 'Run up the colours, if you please.'

Another voice muttered, 'No chance, mates. They'll do for the lot of us.'

Bolitho heard the halliards squeaking as the ensign dashed up to the peak and broke out to the wind, unseen as yet in the clinging darkness.

'As soon as it is light enough, Mr. Keen, have your party make a signal to the schooner. *Discontinue the action.* Mr. Herrick can stand off and retrieve our boats.'

Keen said, 'Aye, aye, sir, I'll see to it when—'

He turned angrily as a voice murmured from the shadows, 'Pick up our bloody corpses, more's the like!'

Keen shouted, 'Keep silence there! Master-at-arms, take that man's name!'

Bolitho said quietly, 'Easy. If it helps them to curse, then let it be so.'

Keen faced him, his fists doubled at his sides. 'But it's not *fair*, sir. It's not your doing.'

Bolitho smiled gravely. 'Thank you, Mr. Keen.'

He recalled with sudden clarity his lieutenant in his first command, the little sloop *Sparrow*. An American colonist, he had endured the worst of the war, serving his King, but fighting his own kind at the same time. What would he have replied? *I ain't so sure*. Bolitho could almost hear him, as if he was present at this very moment.

He turned quickly to starboard, seeing the glowing rim of sunlight as it probed above the bare horizon. Very soon now.

He discovered he was dreading the daylight, that which would lay them naked under the guns as they drove into the narrow channel where he had met Le Chaumareys.

Bolitho heard a step behind him and Allday's voice. Firm, unruffled. 'Better go below and get out of those wet things, Captain.'

He swung towards him, his voice cracking with strain. 'Do you think I have nothing else to do?'

The coxswain regarded him stubbornly. 'Not just yet, you haven't.' He added in the same flat tone, 'You remember the Saintes, Captain?' He did not wait for an answer. 'It was a bad time. All those Frogs, the sea abounding with their damned ships until it was nigh on bursting. I recalls it well. I was right forrard on one of the carronades. The lads were all quaking with fright at what was to come. Then I looked aft and saw you pacing the quarterdeck, like you were going to church instead of to hell.'

Bolitho stared at him, his mind suddenly steady. 'I remember.'

Allday nodded slowly. 'Aye. You wore your best uniform.'

Bolitho looked past him, recalling another voice. His coxswain who had died that day. *They'll want to see you*.

He replied quietly, 'Very well. But if I'm called . . .'

Allday gave a slow smile. '*Immediately*, Captain.'

Mudge said hoarsely, 'That was fool advice, man! The cap'n'll make a fine target for sharpshooters in 'is gold lace!'

Allday eyed him angrily. 'I know. He does, too. He also knows we are depending on him today, and that means *seeing* him.'

Mudge shook his head. 'Mad. You're all mad!'

'Deck there! Schooner fine on th' weather bow!'

Keen called, 'Hoist the signal to recall her!'

Allday was standing with his arms folded, his eyes on the spreading carpet of early light as it reached towards the islands.

'Mr. Herrick won't see it.'

Davy glared at him. 'It will be light enough very soon now.'

'I know, sir.' Allday looked at him sadly. 'But he'll not see it. Not Mr. Herrick.'

Without furniture or fittings the cabin felt strangely hostile, like an empty house which mourns a lost master and awaits another. Bolitho stood by the shuttered stern windows, his arms limp at his sides, while Noddall clucked around him and patted the heavy dress coat into position. Like the boat cloak, it had been made by a good London tailor with some of his prize-money.

Through the wide gap left by the screen, which had now been bolted to the deckhead, he could see straight out along the gun deck, the shapes and restless figures still only shadows in the frail light. Even here, in the cabin where he had found peace in solitude, or had sat with Viola Raymond, or shared a pipe with Herrick, there was no escape. The chintz covers had gone from the twelve-pounders and had followed the furniture to a safer stowage below the waterline, and by the guns on either beam the crews stood awkwardly, like unfinished statuary, conscious of his presence, wanting to watch him as he completed dressing, yet still held apart by the rigidity of their calling.

Bolitho cocked his head to listen to the rudder as it growled and pounded in response to the helm. The wind was fresher, heeling the ship over and holding it so. He saw the nearest gun captain checking his firing lanyard and noted how his body was angled to the deck.

Noddall was muttering, 'More like it, sir. Much more like it.' He said it fervently, as if repeating a prayer. 'Cap'n Stewart was always most particular, afore a fight.'

Bolitho wrenched his mind back from his doubts and misgivings. Stewart? Then he remembered. *Undine*'s last captain. Had he felt the same, too, he wondered?

Feet stamped over the deck above, and he heard someone shouting.

He snapped, 'That will have to suffice.'

He snatched up his hat and sword and then paused to pat Noddall's bony shoulder. He looked so small, with his hands held in front of him like paws, that he felt sudden compassion for him.

'Take care, Noddall. Stay down when the iron begins to fly. You're no fighting man, eh?'

He was shocked to see Noddall bobbing his head and tears running down his face.

In a small, broken voice he said, '*Thankee*, Cap'n!' He did not hide his gratitude. 'I couldn't face another battle. An' I'd not want to let you down, sir.'

Bolitho pushed past and hurried to the ladder. He had always taken him for granted. The little man who fussed over his table and darned his shirts. Content in his own small world. It had never occurred to him that he was terrified each time the ship cleared for action.

He ran up the last steps and saw Davy and Keen with telescopes trained towards the bows.

'What is the matter?'

Davy turned, and then stared at him. He swallowed hard, his eyes still on Bolitho's gold-laced coat.

'Schooner has not acknowledged, sir!'

Bolitho looked from him to the streaming flags, now bright against the dull topsails.

'Are you sure?'

Mudge growled, 'Yer cox'n seems to think she won't neither, sir.'

Bolitho ignored him, his eyes exploring the spread of land across the bows. Still lost in deep shadow, with only an occasional lip of light to betray the dawn. But the schooner was clear enough. In direct line with *Undine*'s plunging jib-boom, her canvas looked almost white against the cliffs and ragged hills.

Herrick must have seen the recall. He would have been anticipating it as soon as the wind veered. He peered up at the masthead pendant. God, how the wind had gone round. It must be west-south-west.

He shouted, 'Hands aloft, Mr. Davy! Get the t'gallants on her!'

He swung round, seeing them all in those brief seconds. Mudge's doubts. Carwithen behind him, his lips compressed into a thin line. The helmsman, the bare-backed gun crews, Keen with his signal party.

The calls shrilled, and shadows darted up the ratlines on either beam as the topmen hurried to set more canvas.

Davy shouted, 'Maybe Mr. Herrick intends to go ahead with the plan, sir!'

Bolitho looked at Allday, saw the way he was watching the schooner.

He said quietly, 'It would seem so, Mr. Davy.'

Under a heavier press of sail *Undine* thrust her shoulder into the creaming water with added urgency, the spray hurling itself above the forecastle and nettings in long spectres of foam. The hull shook and groaned to the pressure, and when he peered aloft Bolitho saw the upper yards bending forward to the wind. From the peak the ensign was clearly visible, like the marines' tunics as they stood in swaying lines by the hammock nettings, or knelt in the tops by their muskets and swivels. Like blood.

He heard himself say, 'Repeat the signal, Mr. Keen!' He barely recognised his own voice.

Soames stood on the breech of a twelve-pounder, gripping the gangway with both hands as he stared towards the land. Then he looked aft at Bolitho and gave a brief shrug. In his mind, Herrick was already dead.

Keen said huskily, 'It will not work! The wind'll carry the schooner clear! At best she'll explode in the centre of the channel!'

Penn shrilled from the gun deck. 'I heard a trumpet!'

Bolitho wiped his eyes, feeling the salt, raw and smarting. A trumpet. Some sentry on the fortress had left the protection of the wall to look seaward. He would see the schooner immediately, and *Undine* within the next few minutes.

The sea noises seemed louder than ever, with every piece of rigging and canvas banging and vibrating in chorus as the ship drove headlong towards the land, and the pale arrowhead which marked the entrance to the channel.

A dull bang echoed across the water, and a man yelled, 'They've opened fire, sir!'

Bolitho reached out for a telescope, seeing the grim faces of the seamen by the nearest guns. Waiting, behind closed ports. Hoping. Dreading.

He trained the glass with difficulty, his legs well braced on the swaying, slippery planking. He saw the schooner's masts swim past the lens, the patch of scarlet which had not been there before. He felt himself smiling, although he wanted to weep, to plead unheard words across those two miles of tossing white-horses. Herrick had hoisted his own ensign. To him, the schooner was not merely a floating bomb, she was a ship, *his* ship. Or perhaps he was trying, with that one simple gesture, to explain to Bolitho, too. To show he understood.

Another bang, and this time he saw the smoke from the battery before it was whisked away. A feather of spray lifted well out beyond the schooner to mark where the massive ball had fallen.

He kept his glass on the schooner. He saw the way the deck was leaning over, showing the bilges above the leaping spray, and knew Herrick could not lash the tiller for the final, and most dangerous, part of the journey.

Davy yelled, 'That ball was *over*, sir!'

Bolitho lowered the glass, Davy's words reaching through his anxiety. The fortress lookouts must have sighted *Undine* and not Herrick's little schooner. And by the time Muljadi's men had realised what was happening, Herrick had tacked too close inshore for the gunners to depress their muzzles sufficiently to hit him.

He looked again as a double explosion shuddered across the water. He saw the flashes only briefly, but watched the twin waterspouts burst skyward directly in line with the schooner, but on the seaward side of her.

Captain Bellairs forgot his usual calm and gripped the sergeant's arm and shouted, 'By God, Sar'nt Coaker, he's goin' to *sail her aground himself!*'

It took a few more seconds before the truth filtered the length and breadth of the frigate's decks.

Then, as the word moved gun by gun towards the bows, men stood and yelled like maniacs, waving their neckerchiefs, or capering the sanded decks like children. From the tops and the forecastle others joined, and even Midshipman Armitage, who moments earlier had been gripping a belaying pin rack as if to stop himself from falling, waved his hat in the air and yelled, 'Go on! You'll show them!'

Bolitho cleared his throat. 'Ask the masthead. Can he see the frigates?'

He tried not to think of the schooner's crammed holds. The fuse, perhaps already hissing quietly in the peace of the lower hull.

'Aye, sir! He can see the yards of the first one around the point!' Even Davy was wild-eyed, indifferent to the fight still to come, overwhelmed by Herrick's sacrifice.

There was more cannon fire now, and he could see splashes all around the schooner's hull. Probably from the nearest anchored frigate, or some smaller pieces on the spit of land which guarded the entrance. Bolitho found he was gritting his jaw so hard it was hurting badly.

The French were at last aware that something was happening, but they would not have guessed the full extent of the danger.

There was a combined groan from the watching hands. Bolitho raised the glass and saw the schooner's maintopmast buckle and then plunge down in a flailing mass of canvas and rigging.

Half to himself he whispered, 'Fall back, Thomas! In God's name, come about!'

Allday said, 'She's hit again, Captain. Badly this time.'

Bolitho dragged his mind away, knowing he must not think of Herrick. *Later*. But in minutes those guns would be ranging on *Undine* as she made that last desperate dash into the channel.

He drew his sword and held it above his head.

'See yonder, lads!' He only vaguely saw their faces turn towards him. It was like looking through a mist. 'Mr. Herrick has shown us the way!'

'She's struck!' Davy was almost beside himself. 'Hard and fast!'

The schooner had hit, lifted and then plunged firmly across the litter of broken rocks and stones. Exactly as they had pictured it. Had planned it with Conway's silver inkwells.

Even without a glass it was possible to see some small boats moving from the fortress's pier towards the stranded hull which now lay totally dismasted, the spray leaping over it like some old hulk. Occasional stabs of fire showed where marksmen were firing into the wreckage, and Bolitho prayed that the fuse was still alight, that Herrick would not be captured alive.

The explosion when it came was so sudden, so violent in colour and magnitude that it was hard to face, harder still to gauge. A solid wall of orange flame exploded from the rocks and spread out on either hand like huge fiery wings, engulfing the circling boats, searing away men and weapons and reducing them into ashes.

And then the sound came. When it reached the frigate it was with a steadily mounting roar which went on and on, until men stood clutching their ears, or staring stupefied at the miniature tidal wave which rolled past the frigate's hull, lifting it easily before dissipating itself astern in the last departing shadows.

Then it died away, as did the fires, leaving only tiny, glowing pinpricks of red and orange, like slow matches, to show where gorse and brush still smouldered on the hillside.

Once again, the sea and wind, the sounds of tackle and canvas returned, and Bolitho heard men talking, almost whispering, as if they had just witnessed an act of God.

He said harshly, 'Brail up the forecourse, Mr Davy!' He walked to the rail, each step like physical pain. 'Mr. Shellabeer! Cast all but the quarter boat adrift!' He must keep talking. Get them moving again. Clear that dreadful pyre from his own brain.

He saw Soames watching him and shouted, 'Load and run out, if you please!'

His words were almost lost in the flap and thunder of rebellious canvas as the big forecourse was brailed up to its yard. Like a curtain, he thought dully. Pulled away for the final scene. So that nothing should be missed.

He heard the port lids squeaking in unison, and then, as Soames barked his command, the gun crews threw themselves on their tackles, and with increasing haste the black muzzles rumbled towards the daylight, thrusting out above the creaming water on either beam.

Davy touched his hat. 'All guns run out, sir!' He looked strained.

'Thank you.'

Bolitho kept his eyes on the dark hump astride the channel. No flashes from those great muzzles. It had worked. Even if the garrison managed to manhandle some of the guns from the far side of the fortress it would be too late to fire on *Undine* as she surged into the drifting curtain of smoke.

He shaded his eyes and stared towards the spit of land, the dark lines which marked the masts and yards of the first anchored ship. *Soon. Soon.* He gripped the sword until his knuckles showed white. He could feel the hurt and the anger. The rising madness, which only revenge for Herrick would control.

And there was the sunlight, growing stronger every dragging minute. He climbed into the weather shrouds, heedless of the wind and leaping spray which dappled his coat like bright gems. Abeam he could see *Undine's* shadow reaching away across the broken water, his own blurred outline like part of the fabric itself.

He looked down at Mudge. 'Get ready to alter course once we are past that spit!'

He waited while those at the braces took the strain, each man an individual now as the sunlight found his naked back, or a tattoo, or some extra long pigtail to mark a seasoned sailor. He jumped down to the deck, tugging at his neckcloth, as if it were strangling him.

'Marines, stand to!' Bellairs had drawn his elegant hanger and was watching while his men nestled their long muskets on the closely packed hammock nettings.

At every open port a gun captain crouched with his lanyard almost taut as he watched for the first sign of a target.

The spit of land reached out as if to touch the bilges as the ship swept inshore, her bow wave causing a ripple amongst some jagged rocks which Bolitho remembered from his other visit.

'Braces there!'

Mudge shouted, 'Put the wheel to larboard! Lively now!'

Like a thoroughbred, *Undine* heeled round under pressure of canvas and rudder, the yards swinging together as she turned into the sunlight.

'Steer nor'-east by east!' Mudge heaved his ungainly bulk to assist the helmsmen. '*'Old 'er*, you buggers!'

There were several muffled bangs, and a ball cracked through the foretopsail with the sound of a whiplash.

But Bolitho barely noticed it. He was staring at the anchored frigate, the scrambling activity along her yards and deck where her company prepared for sea.

Davy echoed his dismay. 'She's not the *Argus*, sir!'

Bolitho nodded. It was the other frigate. The one which had been abandoned by her crew. He screwed up his eyes, trying to watch every movement, still attempting to accept what had happened.

Le Chaumareys had gone. By chance? Or had he once again proved his superiority, a cunning which had never been outmatched?

Almost savagely he lifted the old blade over his head and yelled, 'Starboard battery! As you bear!' The sword caught the glare as it cut down. '*Fire!*'

The broadside roared and flashed along *Undine's* starboard side, gun by gun, each captain taking his aim while Soames strode past every recoiling breech, yelling and peering towards the enemy. Bolitho watched the smoke spouting from the ports and rolling towards the other ship which seemed suspended in the fog, her hull lying almost diagonally across the starboard bow.

Here and there a gun flashed in reply, and he felt the deck planking jerk under his feet as at least one ball smashed into the side.

The quarterdeck gun crews were all shouting and cursing as they, too, joined in the battle. The stocky six-pounders hurled themselves inboard on the tackles, the wild-eyed seamen sponging out and ramming home fresh charges within seconds.

Overhead, and splashing violently into the channel on either beam, came a fusilade of smaller shot, from fortress or frigate Bolitho neither knew nor cared. As he paced briskly athwart the deck by the quarterdeck rail he saw nothing but the other ship's raked masts, the patch of colour from the prancing beast of her flag, the rising pall of smoke as again and again *Undine*'s broadside thundered into her.

Once he chilled as he saw some charred flotsam bobbing past the quarter, a headless corpse pirouetting in *Undine*'s crisp bow wave, tendrils of scarlet moving around it like obscene weed.

Herrick had known the *Argus* had gone. He must have seen the anchorage long before anyone in *Undine*. He would never have faltered. Bolitho felt his eyes stinging again, the hatred boiling inside him as the quarterdeck guns cracked out, their sharp detonations making his mind cringe even as their crews scrambled with handspikes to edge their weapons round for another salvo.

Herrick would have accepted it. As he had in the past. It was what he had lived for.

Bolitho shouted aloud, heedless of Mudge and Davy nearby. 'God damn them for their plans and their stupidity!'

Keen called, 'They've cut their cable, sir!'

Bolitho ran to the nettings, feeling a musket ball punch into the deck by his feet. It was true, Muljadi's frigate was yawing sluggishly in wind and current, her stern swinging like a gate across *Undine*'s path. Someone must have lost his nerve, or perhaps in the confusion of the exploding schooner and *Undine*'s savage attack an order had been misunderstood.

He yelled, 'We'll go alongside her! Stand by the tops'l halliards! Put the helm a'lee!'

As men dashed to the braces again, and topsails flapped and thundered wildly to their sudden freedom, *Undine* turned deliberately to larboard, her jib-boom sweeping round until it pointed to the distant pier and the litter of smouldering craft left by the explosion.

Soames bellowed, 'Point! Ready!' He was peering, red-eyed, along his panting gun crews, his sword held out like a staff. 'Drag that man away!' He ran forward to help pull a wounded seaman from a twelve-pounder. 'Now!' His sword flashed down '*Broadside!*'

This time, the whole battery exploded in a single wall of flames, the long tongues darting into the smoke, making it rise and twist, as if it, too, was dying in agony.

Someone gave a hoarse cheer. 'There goes th' bastard's fore!'

Bolitho ran to the gangway, marines and seamen pounding behind him.

High above the smoke the nimble topmen were already hurling their steel grapnels, jeering at one another as they raced even here to beat their opposite numbers on the other masts. Another cheer, as with a shuddering lurch *Undine* drove alongside the drifting frigate, her bowsprit rising above the poop. While the impetus carried them closer and closer together, the guns still bellowed, louder now as their fury matched across a bare thirty feet of tormented water.

'Boarders away!'

Bolitho waited, gripping the main shrouds, gauging the moment as Soames roared, 'Cease firing! At 'em, lads! Cut the bastards down!'

Then he was across, clinging to the enemy's boarding nets, which had been rent in great holes by the broadsides. Muljadi's own plans must have been ready, for there seemed to be hundreds of men surging to meet the cheering, cursing rush of boarders.

Muskets and pistols, while from somewhere overhead a swivel banged out, the packed canister tearing across the enemy's quarterdeck, hurling wood splinters and bodies in all directions.

A bearded face loomed out of the smoke, and Bolitho slashed at it, holding to the nets to keep from falling outboard and being crushed between the hulls. The man shrieked and dropped from view. A marine thrust Bolitho aside, screaming like a madman as he pinned a man with his bayonet before wrenching out the blade and ramming the musket's butt into a wounded pirate who was trying to crawl out of the fight.

Allday ducked under a cutlass and caught his attacker off-balance. He even pushed the man away with his left fist, giving himself room for a proper stroke with his own blade. It sounded like an axe on wood.

Bellairs was striding in the centre of a squad of marines, snapping unheard commands, his elegant hanger darting in and out like a silver tongue as he forced his way aft towards the enemy's quarterdeck.

Another wave of insane cheering, and Bolitho saw Soames leading his own boarding party up and over the frigate's main shrouds, muskets barking point-blank into the press below him, his sword crossing with that of a tall, lank-haired officer whom Bolitho remembered as Le Chaumareys' first lieutenant.

Soames slipped and sprawled across an upended cannon, and the Frenchman drew back his arm for the fatal thrust. But a marine was nearby, the musket ball taking away most of the lieutenant's skull and hurling him from the deck, like a rag doll.

Bolitho realised that Allday was shaking him by the arm, trying to make him understand something.

He yelled, 'The *hold*, Captain!' He jabbed at the wide hatchways with his cutlass. 'The bastards have set her afire!'

Bolitho stared at it, his brain and mind reeling from the screams and cheers, the grate of steel, the madness of close action. The smoke was already thicker. Perhaps Allday was right, or maybe a burning wad from one of *Undine*'s guns had found its way into the hull when Soames had sent his last broadside crashing home. Either way, both ships would be destroyed unless he acted, and at once.

He yelled, 'Captain Bellairs! *Fall back!*'

He saw Bellairs gaping at him, blood dripping unheeded from a gash on his forehead.

Then he, too, seemed to get a grip on his own lust of battle and shouted, 'Sound the retreat!' He sought out his sergeant whose massive frame had somehow avoided both steel and musket ball. 'Coaker! Take that fool's name if he don't do as I ask!'

Coaker gripped a small marine drummer boy, but he was dead, his eyes glazed and unseeing as Coaker wrenched the trumpet from his hands and blew it with all his might.

It was almost harder to discontinue the battle than to board the other frigate. Back and back, here and there a man falling, or being hauled bodily across the gap between the hulls to avoid capture. The pirates had at last seen their own danger, and without the French lieutenant in command they seemed intent only on abandoning their ship as quickly as they could.

The first tongue of flame licked through a hatch, bringing a chorus of shrieks from the abandoned wounded, and within seconds the gratings and surrounding boat tier were well ablaze.

Bolitho gripped the ratlines and took a last look as his men threw themselves on to *Undine's* gangway. Forward, Shellabeer's men were already cutting the lashing which held the hulls together, and with the topsails once more braced round, and the helm over, *Undine* began to sidle clear, the wind holding the smoke and sparks away from her own canvas and vulnerable rigging.

Mudge panted, 'What now, sir?'

Bolitho watched the frigate slipping past, a few crazed men still firing across the widening gap.

He shouted, 'A final broadside, Mr. Soames!'

But it was already too late. A great sheet of flame burst upwards through the vessel's gun deck, setting the broken foremast and sails alight and leaping to the mainyards like part of a forest fire.

Bolitho heard himself reply, 'Get the forecourse on her, and smartly with it. We'll not be able to beat back the way we came. That ship's magazine will go at any moment, so we will try the eastern channel.'

Mudge said, 'May be too shallow, sir.'

'Would you burn, Mr. Mudge?'

He strode to the taffrail to watch the frigate as the blaze engulfed the poop. An English ship. It were better this way, he thought vaguely.

He turned and added harshly, 'Mr. Davy, I want a full report of damage.' He waited, seeing the wildness draining from his eyes. 'And the bill for all this.'

Bolitho saw the yards edging round, the sails, pockmarked and blackened by the fight, hardening to the wind. The channel seemed wide enough. About a cable to starboard, more on the other side. He had managed worse.

'Boat in the water, sir!' Keen was standing in the shrouds with his telescope. 'Just two men in it.'

Mudge called, 'I'll 'old 'er steady, sir. We're steerin' almost nor'-east again, but I dunno—'

The rest of his words were lost as Keen yelled, 'Sir! *Sir!*' He stared down at Bolitho, his face shining with disbelief.

Davy snapped, 'Keep your head, Mr. Keen!'

But Keen did not seem to hear. 'It's Mr. Herrick!'

Bolitho stared at him and then clambered up beside him. The boat was a wreck, and the scrawny figure who was now standing to wave a scrap of rag above his head, looked like a scarecrow. Lying in the bottom of the boat, half-covered with water, was Herrick.

As he held the telescope Bolitho could feel his hands shaking violently, and saw Herrick's face, ashen beneath a rough bandage. Then he saw his eyes open, imagined the other man shouting the news to him, his words as plain as if he could hear them himself.

He said, 'Pass the word to the bosun. I want that boat grappled alongside.' He gripped the midshipman's wrist. 'And tell him to be careful. There'll be no second chance.'

Allday had gone below for something. Now he was back, his eyes everywhere, until Bolitho said quietly, 'The first lieutenant is coming aboard. Go forrard and bid him welcome for me, eh?'

As the frigate slipped past another shelving hump of land the sun came down to greet them, to warm their aching limbs, to hold the shock of battle at arm's length a while longer. A deep explosion came from the main channel, and more smoke spouted high above the nearest land to show the wind which awaited them in open water, and to sound the other vessel's final destruction.

Muljadi may or may not have been aboard, and the real fight was still ahead.

Bolitho heard shouts from forward, and then a cheer as some seamen clambered into the sinking boat to pluck Herrick and his companion back on board.

But whatever was waiting beyond the green humps of land, no matter how hopeless their gesture might be, they would be together.

18

In the King's Name

'Alter course two points.'

Bolitho tried to pace along the littered deck, but was unable to overcome his anxiety. It was an hour since they had edged into the eastern channel, under minimum canvas and with two leadsmen in the chains they had felt their way towards the sea.

An hour of answering demands and listening to reports. Ten killed, fifteen wounded, half of them seriously. Considering what they had done, it was a small enough bill, but as he watched the familiar bundles awaiting burial, or heard occasional cries from the main hatch, he found little comfort in it.

If only Allday would come on deck and tell him about Herrick. He had already questioned the surviving seaman. It had been the little man called Lincoln, the one with the permanent grin made by a grotesque scar.

Bolitho had watched him reliving it as he had stammered out his description, oblivious to his captain and officers crowding around him, and seemingly only half aware he was actually alive.

It had been much as Bolitho had imagined. Herrick had decided to destroy the battery, drive his schooner aground regardless of risk and the inevitability of death. At the last moment, with the fuse lit and the vessel being fired on from the hillside, Herrick had been struck by a falling block from the mainmast. The little seaman had said in a whisper, 'Then up comes Mister Pigsliver, as cool as you please. Take to th' boat, he shouts. I've an old score to settle, though 'e didn't say wot 'e meant like. By then there was only three 'ands left. So me an' Jethro lowers Mr. 'Errick into the dory, but t'other bloke, the little sailmaker named Potter, 'e decides to stay with the Don.' He had given a great shudder. 'So off we goes. Then the schooner blows up like the gates of 'ell, an' poor Jethro was lost overboard. I just kept paddlin', and prayin' that Mr. 'Errick would stir to 'is senses an' tell me wot to do.' He had paused, sobbing soundlessly. 'Then I looks up, an' *there she is*, large as life, th' old *Undine*. I shakes Mr. 'Errick and calls to 'im, look alive, sir, the ship's a' comin' for us, an' 'e – well – 'e just looks at me an' says, an' wot did you expect?'

Bolitho had said quietly, 'Thank you, Lincoln, I shall see you do not go unrewarded.'

The little man had added, 'An' you'll not forget to mention a piece about Mister Pigsliver, sir? I – I mean, 'e may be a Don, sir, but, but . . .' Then he had broken down completely.

Now, as he moved restlessly past the six-pounders where the gun captains knelt in the sunlight, checking their equipment, testing the tackles, their bodies stained with smoke and dried blood, Bolitho said to himself, 'No, I will not forget.'

'Deck there!'

He looked up, his eyes smarting in the glare.

'Open water ahead, sir!'

Shoes scraped by the cabin hatch and he swung round.

'Allday, where the *devil* have you been?'

But it was not Allday.

Bolitho strode across the deck and held out both hands. 'Thomas!' He gripped Herrick's hands in his, oblivious to the watching faces on every side. 'I don't know what to say!'

Herrick smiled sadly. 'I am the same, sir.'

'You should remain below until—'

'Deck there! Ship to the east'rd!'

Herrick withdrew his hands and replied quietly, 'I am the first lieutenant, sir.' He looked slowly around the quarterdeck, at the protruding splinters and the flapping edges of torn hammocks where musket balls had ripped home. 'My place is here.'

Davy crossed the deck and touched his hat. 'Beat to quarters again, sir?'

'Yes.'

Davy looked at Herrick and smiled. 'It seems you had no better luck in holding on to the schooner than I.' He added, 'I am relieved you are here, and that's the truth.'

Herrick touched the fresh bandage on his head and winced. 'If it had not been sworn otherwise, I would have said that Don Puigserver struck me down himself. He was that eager to finish what we had begun.'

He fell silent as the drums rattled out their tattoo and the lolling figures by guns and braces stirred themselves into life.

Bolitho was watching the last shoulder of land sliding away, the expanse of blue water and lively wavecrests growing and spreading to reveal an endless, dazzling horizon.

To larboard, her hull and spars black against the glare, lay the *Argus*. She appeared to be moving very slowly, her yards well braced to hold her on a converging tack.

Herrick muttered, 'Four miles, I'd say.'

'About that.'

Bolitho studied the other ship, unable to look away. She reminded him of a wild cat, the way she edged across the busy, white-capped waves. Stealthy, purposeful. Lethal.

He imagined he could hear the squeak of trucks as her smooth sides became barbed by gun muzzles. Le Chaumareys was taking his time. Waiting for Bolitho to make the first move.

He looked away at last, feeling the tension returning, but heavier than before. Perhaps Le Chaumareys had planned it this way, distrusting his ally Muljadi, guessing that Bolitho might bring off a stalemate, if not a victory, if he chose his own method of attack.

The *Undine*'s company had fought hard. He looked searchingly at the shot holes and punctured sails, heard the hammers as Pryke, the portly carpenter, and his mates got busy on repairs in the lower hull, and knew it was asking much of them to fight yet again, and to win against this great, black-hulled veteran of the French navy.

Then he glanced at those nearest him. He needed every bit of skill and experience they possessed, not least their courage.

'Well, Mr. Mudge, what of the wind now?'

'It'll get up, sir.' Mudge took out his handkerchief and blew his great nose violently. 'Might back a bit.' He gestured up at the masthead pendant. It was stiff, like a spear. 'I'd suggest, beggin' yer pardon, sir, that you fights under topsails only.'

Bolitho turned to Herrick. 'What do you say?'

Herrick was watching the other ship, his eyes like slits. 'Get to grips, sir. He'll pound us to pieces with those long guns otherwise.'

The deck lifted across the first true roller, and spray drifted high above the nettings.

'Let's be about it then.' Bolitho licked his parched lips. 'Get the forecourse off her.' He dropped his voice. 'And have those corpses buried directly. It does no good to see where some of us will end this morning.'

Herrick watched him calmly. 'I can think of better reasons for dying.' He glanced at the motionless seamen by the guns. 'But no better place for it.'

Bolitho walked to the rail and watched the *Argus* for several minutes. Le Chaumareys had a good position. He had probably considered it very carefully. He was over there now, watching him, expecting him to act. To try and take the wind-gage, or to alter course and attempt to cross his stern and cripple him with one good broadside as he passed.

The French frigate dipped to the swell, showing her copper for several seconds. The wind was tight across her exposed side, but Le Chaumareys was holding back, keeping on *Undine*'s larboard bow, barely making headway.

Bolitho bit his lip, his eyes running in the sun's fierce stare. His men would find it hard to shoot well into the blinding sunlight.

When he looked at the gun deck again he saw that the corpses were gone.

Herrick came aft and said, 'All done.'

He saw Bolitho's intent features and asked quietly, 'Is something wrong, sir?'

'I think I am starting to understand Le Chaumareys.' He could feel his heart beginning to pound again, the familiar chill at his neck and spine. 'I think he *wants* us to have the wind-gage.'

'But, sir . . .' Herrick's blue eyes darted to the *Argus* and back again. 'Is the sun in our eyes of greater value to him?' Understanding spread across his round face. 'It might well be. He can stand off and use his heavy artillery to better result.'

Bolitho turned, his eyes flashing. 'Well, it's not to be, Mr. Herrick! Get the t'gallants on her directly!' He added, 'I am sorry, Mr. Mudge, but if we lose the sticks out of her to your damned wind it may be better than losing them the other way!'

Herrick was already raising his speaking trumpet. 'Hands aloft! Loose t'ga'n's'ls!' When he looked at Bolitho again there was little to show what he had so recently endured. 'By God, sir, what we miss in weight we can show that bastard in agility today!'

Bolitho grinned at him, his lips painful. 'Alter course two points to starboard. We'll run for his bows.'

Allday folded his arms and watched Bolitho's shoulders, and then glanced up at the flag as it rippled in the freshening wind.

'And that is *all* the running you'll be doing, I'm thinking.'

'East nor'-east, sir!' Carwithen had one hand resting on the polished spokes as the helmsmen concentrated on the compass and the set of the sails overhead. 'Steady as she goes!'

Mudge rubbed his hands on his coat. 'She's movin' well, sir.'

Bolitho lowered his telescope and nodded thoughtfully. The extra power of the topgallants was laying *Undine* firmly in line across the other ship's path. *Argus* had not set any additional sail. Yet. He winced as the sunlight lanced down from the lens. Le Chaumareys still held the best position. He could alter course to lee'rd and present his broadside as *Undine* tried to pass him. Equally, he could allow her to cross his bows, and while she lost time in changing tack, he could take the wind-gage, sun's glare or not, and attack him from the other side.

Herrick said hoarsely, 'He's holding the same course. He may have let her fall off a point, but there's nothing in it.' He breathed out slowly. 'She makes a fair sight, God rot her!'

Bolitho smiled tightly. *Argus* had barely changed her bearing, but that was because *Undine* had altered course to starboard. She was much closer now, a bare two miles, so that he could see her red and yellow figurehead, the purposeful movement of figures about her sloping quarterdeck.

There was a sudden bang, and seconds later a thin waterspout rose lazily amongst the tossing wavecrests, slightly ahead of *Undine*'s path, and half a cable short. Ranging shot, or merely to unnerve *Undine*'s own gun crew. Another of Le Chaumareys' little ruses.

Herrick muttered fervently, 'If I know the Frogs, he'll try and dismast us with chain-shot and langridge. Another prize for his bloody ally!'

'You don't know *this* Frenchman, Mr. Herrick.' Bolitho recalled Le Chaumareys' face when he had spoken of home, his France which he had been denied for so long. 'My guess is he'll want a complete victory.'

The word made him feel uneasy. He could even picture *Undine* dismasted and wallowing amongst her own dead and dying before her final plunge. Like the one he himself had just destroyed. Like *Nervion*, and so many he had watched crumble and perish.

The stage was set. Two ships, with not even a seabird to watch their manoeuvres, their dedicated efforts to outwit each other.

'There, sir! He's setting his t'gallants!' Carwithen's voice jarred him from his thoughts.

Herrick exclaimed, 'He intends to outreach us after all.'

Bolitho watched intently as the *Argus*'s upper yards filled with freshly-set, bulging canvas. He could see the instant effect it had around her raked stem as she bit into the waves and thrust forward with sudden haste.

From his position behind the rail it looked to Bolitho as if the other ship's jib-boom was actually touching his own, although she was still over a mile away. Smoke wreathed above her hull, and he held his breath as the bright tongues of fire licked from her exposed ports.

The sea boiled and shot skywards as the heavy balls ploughed into the wind-ruffled water, or ricocheted away far abeam. One ball smashed hard down alongside, the shock transmitting itself to the very mastheads.

'Trying to rattle our wits!'

Herrick was grinning, but Bolitho saw the anxiety behind his eyes.

Le Chaumareys had not seemed the kind of man who wasted gestures on the wind. He was preparing his gun crews, showing them the range, probably telling them right now in his resonant voice exactly what he expected of them.

'By God, the devil's shortening sail again!'

Bolitho saw the topgallants vanishing along the *Argus*'s yards, and leaned across the rail.

'Stand by, the larboard battery!'

Perhaps he had found Le Chaumareys' one real weakness. That he *needed* to win and to survive. Bolitho knew that the two did not always walk hand in hand.

'Alter course three points to larboard!'

He heard the rush of feet, the confused shouts as his orders were relayed to the waiting seamen.

Mudge asked, 'Is that wise, sir?'

Bolitho waited as the helm went down, and then turned to watch the bowsprit swinging slowly and then more quickly to larboard, the other frigate suddenly enmeshed in the criss-cross of rigging and shrouds.

'Hold her so!'

He waited impatiently while Herrick bellowed through his trumpet, and the hands on the braces hauled feverishly to retrim the yards.

'Nor'-east by north, sir!' The helmsman sounded breathless.

With the wind sweeping tightly across the larboard quarter, *Undine* swept straight down towards the other ship, as if to cut her in halves. More flashes darted from the Frenchman's side, and Bolitho clenched his fists as metal shrieked overhead, parting rigging, slapping through sails and hurling spray in profusion on either beam.

'Now we shall see!'

Bolitho craned forward, gripping the rail, his eyes stinging painfully in the hazy glare. Another rippling line of flashes, the sounds of the broadside rolling across the water like the thunder of mighty drums. He felt the hull stagger violently, and saw some of the seamen below the quarterdeck exchanging quick, desperate glances.

Argus was still holding her course and speed, lying across *Undine*'s path and growing in size with every agonising minute.

More shots, and a savage jerk below his feet told Bolitho *Undine* was being hit again. But *Argus*'s broadsides were more ragged now, and fewer balls were falling near their target.

Herrick said fiercely, 'He'll have to do something!'

Bolitho did not reply, but stared fixedly through his telescope at the cluster of figures on *Argus*'s quarterdeck. He could see Le Chaumareys' powerful bulk, his small cropped head bobbing as he shouted commands to his subordinates. He would be missing his first lieutenant, Bolitho thought quickly. As he would have missed Herrick, but for their unlikely reunion.

He called, 'The *wind*, Mr. Mudge?' He dared not look at him.

'Backed a point, sir! From the pendant, I'd say it was near sou'-westerly!'

Herrick shouted, '*Argus* is standing away, sir!'

Somebody gave an isolated cheer, but Bolitho snapped, 'Keep the people quiet!' He added quickly, 'Stand by to alter course hard to larboard! I'll want her as close to the wind as you can lay her, Mr. Mudge!'

He watched, barely able to move, as *Argus*'s yards edged round, her outline shortening as she stood off, making a triangle between the two converging ships. She loosed another slow broadside, and Bolitho heard a scream from aloft, then saw a marine fall headlong on to the nets, blood gushing from his mouth and splashing on the gun crew immediately below him.

Le Chaumareys had mistaken Bolitho's headlong charge as an act of empty bravery. He had waited for the right moment before swinging clear to present his full broadside, to cripple *Undine* completely as she attempted to cross the bows.

Bolitho held up his hand, praying that those flashing guns would give him time to act.

'Larboard battery! Fire as you bear!'

Relieved, eager to hit back, the gun crews pounced on their weapons.

'Stand by!'

Davy watched as Soames hurried to the leading gun.

'*Fire!*'

Bolitho felt the hull quiver, and drew breath again as the smoke billowed away from the hull towards the enemy.

'Stand by to alter course!' He held Herrick's gaze. 'No, we are not going to embrace him just yet!' He felt the insane grin on his lips. 'We'll cross his stern. He has left the door open!'

A heavy ball smashed through the larboard bulwark, up-ending a twelve-pounder and painting the planking and gratings in bright, spreading scarlet.

Screams and curses were drowned as Soames bellowed, 'Stop your vents! Sponge out!' He glared wildly through the smoke. 'You, Manners! Take that handspike and *move yourself*, damn you!'

The man in question was gaping at his legs which had been spattered with blood and fragments from the neighbouring crew.

Bolitho dropped his hand. 'Now! Helm a'lee!'

To the mounting wind, and the sudden change of direction, *Undine* swayed over and down, the gun crews firing off another uneven salvo before *Argus* was plucked from their open ports.

Bolitho yelled, 'Mr. Davy! Starboard battery!'

Men dashed from the still-smoking guns and threw themselves to assist the opposite side. Overhead, spars and blocks strained and bucked in protest, and more than one seaman fell headlong as the ship came thundering up close to the wind, her yards almost fore and aft.

The fore topgallant sail split suddenly and violently, the fragments like streamers in the wind, but Bolitho ignored it. He was watching *Argus*'s black shape sliding out and away from the starboard bow while his own ship turned steeply towards her poop. Shots crashed into hull and rigging alike, and Bolitho watched sickened as two seamen were pulped into offal and broken weapons against the opposite side.

Davy's voice was almost a scream. 'Starboard battery! As you bear!'

The order to fire was lost in the first crash from the forward guns, followed instantly along the deck as the *Argus* loomed up and over the nettings like a black cliff.

'Sponge out! Reload! Run out!'

The crews had no trouble in running out, for the ship was heeling so steeply to the wind that each gun squealed down the deck like an enraged hog on the rampage.

Bolitho cupped his hands. 'Hold your fire!' He gestured to the men by the carronades on the forecastle. Several corpses lay near them, and he guessed Le Chaumarey's marksmen had realised his intention.

A musket ball clanged against a six-pounder, and one of the helmsmen fell kicking and spluttering, his chin shot away by the ricochet.

Bolitho shouted above the din, 'Let her fall off a point, Mr. Mudge, you know what I expect today!'

Shadows danced across the decks as pieces of broken rigging, blocks, a musket and other fragments bounced on the nets above.

And here was the *Argus*, plunging heavily to starboard, trying to follow *Undine* round, but losing the chance as the English frigate swept across her stern.

'Fire!'

A carronade banged loudly, biting fragments from *Argus*'s stern and smashing her small quarter-gallery to fragments. Gun by gun the twelve-pounders followed its example, the balls slamming into the stern, or scything through the gaping windows to create death and confusion within.

Men were cheering, despite threats and blows from their petty officers, and above the great writhing wall of smoke Bolitho saw the French frigate's masts moving slowly away and beyond the starboard quarter. But it was no time to falter now.

'We will wear ship, Mr. Herrick! Lay her on the starboard tack!'

'Aye, sir!' Herrick wiped his streaming face. Above the stains on his cheeks and mouth his bandage shone in the filtered sunlight like a turban. 'It's lively work today, sir!'

'Man the braces! Stand by to wear ship!'

A man screamed as he was dragged from a gun, bleeding badly. As Whitmarsh's mates lifted him he struggled and kicked to free himself, more terrified of what waited below than of dying on deck.

Sails thundering, and spilling wind from countless shotholes, *Undine* changed tack yet again, turning her bowsprit away from the islands and towards the sun.

The sea looked much wilder now, with short wavecrests crumbling to the wind, or throwing sheets of spray above the gangways with hardly a break.

Bolitho wiped his eyes and tried to restrain from coughing. Like his eyes, his lungs were raw with powder smoke, the stench of battle. He watched the other ship as she swam above the leaping spindrift. Willingly or not, Le Chaumareys had the wind-gage, and his ship now stood off *Undine*'s starboard bow, a bare cable's length away. If *Undine* continued to overhaul her, both ships would run parallel, a musket shot apart. *Argus* would get her revenge at such a murderous range.

He glanced quickly at Mudge. He, too, was watching the sea and the masthead pendant, but was it for the same reason?

But to ask him now, to show that he was in need of a miracle and had nothing to replace one, would take the fight out of his men no less than an instant defeat. He saw them at their guns, panting and gasping, tarred hands gripping tackles and rammers, sponges and handspikes. Their naked bodies were streaked with sweat which cut through the powder grime like the marks of a fine lash. Their eyes shone through their blackened faces as if trapped.

The marines were reloading their muskets, and Bellairs was strolling with his sergeant by the taffrail. At the helm another had taken the dead man's place, and Carwithen's coarse face was working on a plug of tobacco, his eyes cold, without expression. There were fewer men on the gun deck, although Bolitho had not seen many fall. Yet they had gone, had died or been maimed without a word from him to give reason for their sacrifice.

He reached out to steady himself as the deck tilted more steeply. When he peered over the riddled hammocks he saw the sea's face forming into short, steep ranks, ranging towards the two ships as if to push them away.

He yelled, 'Mr. Davy! *Are you ready?*'

Davy nodded dully. 'Every gun loaded with chain-shot, sir!'

'Good.' Bolitho looked at Herrick. 'I hope to God that the master knows his weather!' In a sharper tone he added, 'Get the forecourse on her!'

With the great foresail set and drawing, *Undine* began to overhaul the other ship at a remarkable pace.

Bolitho flinched as more balls crashed alongside from *Argus*'s sternchasers, one of them hurling the quarter-boat into spinning pieces.

A last challenge. That was what it had to look like. Gun to gun. No quarter until *Undine* was a sinking wreck.

He said, 'We will alter course when I give the word.'

He waited, aching in every muscle, his mind jumping to each gunshot from the Frenchman's poop. *Undine*'s jib-boom seemed to be prodding her larboard quarter like a lance. A few stabs of fire above her shattered stern showed where marksmen had taken fresh positions, and Bolitho saw two of his marines drop like red fruit from the foretop, their cries lost to the mounting wind.

Mudge said worriedly, 'We may lose our sticks when we comes round, sir!'

Bolitho ignored him.

'Ready lads!'

He watched the sea rising and breaking against *Argus*'s opposite quarter, the mounting pressure against her yards.

'Now!'

He gripped the rail as the helm went over and the bows started to pull towards the enemy. He saw *Argus* trimming her yards, the hull tilting steeply as she followed *Undine*'s turn.

Sunlight flashed on her quarterdeck, and then her side exploded in a line of great flashes, the air rent apart with the savagery of her broadside.

Bolitho almost fell as the massive weight of iron crashed into the hull or screamed and tore through the rigging overhead. He was choked by swirling smoke, his mind reeling from the combined noises of screams and yells, of musket fire from all angles.

Somehow he dragged himself up the angled deck and peered towards the *Argus*. Smoke was drifting from her last broadside so fast that *Undine* seemed to moving abeam to meet her. The illusion told him Mudge had been right, and as he watched *Argus*'s sails bellying out towards him, he also saw her gunports awash as the wind thrust her over. *Thank God for the wind.*

'Fire!' He had to repeat the order to make himself heard. *'Fire!'*

Undine's disengaged gunports were also awash, and her runout battery was pointing almost towards the sky as each captain jerked his lanyard.

Even above the roar of cannon fire and the wail of the wind Bolitho heard the chain-shot whimpering through the air and ripping into *Argus*'s fully exposed topsails and braced yards. He heard, too, the immediate clatter of severed rigging, the louder explosions of bursting stays and shrouds as foremast and maintopmast swayed together like great trees before booming and splintering into the smoke.

Bolitho waved his sword above his head. 'Hold her steady, Mr. Mudge! She'll be alongside directly!'

He ran to the gangway, and then stopped dead as the wind sucked the smoke downwind and away from the two drifting hulls. Dead and wounded lay everywhere, and as the marines ran to their places for boarding Bolitho saw Shellabeer mangled beneath a gun, and Pryke, the carpenter, pinned across a hatch coaming by a broken length of gangway, his blood linking with all the rest around him. And Fowlar, could that thing really be him?

But there was no more time to regret or to think. *Argus* was here, alongside, and as Soames led his men across the bows Bolitho shook his sword and yelled hoarsely, 'Over you go, lads!'

The French seamen were struggling to free themselves from the great tangle of spars and rigging, the broken cordage lying in heaps like giant serpents.

But the steel was ready enough. Bolitho crossed swords with a petty officer and then slipped in some blood, the breath driven from his body as the Frenchman pitched headlong across him. He felt the man jerk and kick, saw the awful agony in his eyes as Carwithen pulled him away, a boarding axe locked into his collar bone.

On every hand men were fighting and yelling, the pikes and bayonets waving above the more desperate work of sword and cutlass.

Davy was heading for the quarterdeck ladder, shouting to the men at his back, when a rally of French seamen left him momentarily isolated and alone. Bolitho watched his contorted face above the thrusting shoulders, saw his mouth shaping unheard screams as they cut him down, their weapons not still even after he had dropped from sight.

Midshipman Armitage stood shaking on the gangway, his skin like chalk as he shouted, 'Follow me!' Then he, too, was dead, pushed aside and trodden underfoot as the two opposing groups surged together again.

Bolitho saw it all as he fought his way aft towards the main quarterdeck ladder. Saw it, and recorded it in his mind. But without sequence, like a nightmare. As if he were a mere onlooker.

He reached the ladder and saw the French lieutenant facing him, the one named Maurin, who had an English wife. The rest seemed to fade into a swirling, embattled fog as the two swords reached out and circled each other.

Bolitho said harshly, 'Strike, Maurin! You have done enough!'

The Frenchman shook his head. 'It is not possible, *m'sieu*!'

Then he lunged forward, taking Bolitho's sword on the hilt, and deftly turning it towards the sea. Bolitho let himself fall back to the next step, seeing the desperation on Maurin's face, knowing, without understanding why, that this man alone stood between victory and senseless slaughter.

'Le Chaumareys is dead!' Bolitho tested the next step with his left foot. 'Am I not right?' He had to shout at the top of his voice as more of *Undine*'s men burst yelling on to the gun deck and attacked the French crew from behind. They must have climbed through the shattered stern, Bolitho realised dully. Again it was more of a reaction than anything. He added coldly, 'So for God's sake *strike*!'

Maurin hesitated, the uncertainty plain on his face, and then made up his mind. He sidestepped and raised his hilt almost level with his eyes before lunging towards Bolitho's chest.

Bolitho watched him with something like despair. Maurin had been too long in the one ship, had forgotten the need for change. It was easy. Too sickeningly easy.

Bolitho took his weight on his foot, parried the blade as it darted towards him, and struck. The lieutenant's weight was more than enough, and Bolitho almost had the sword wrenched from his grip as Maurin fell gasping to the deck below.

A pigtailed seaman raised his boarding pike, but Bolitho shouted, 'Touch him, and I'll kill you myself!'

He saw Herrick walking between the French seamen who were throwing their weapons on to the bloodied deck, the fight over. Their strength going at the sight of Maurin's last gesture.

He thrust the sword into its scabbard and walked heavily up the last few steps. He knew Allday was behind him, and Herrick took his place at his side as together they stood in silence looking at Le Chaumarey's body where it lay beside the abandoned wheel. He looked strangely peaceful, and amidst so much carnage and horror, almost unmarked. There was a dark stain below his shoulder, and a small trickle of blood from a corner of his mouth. Probably one of Bellairs' sharpshooters, Bolitho thought vaguely.

Bolitho said quietly, 'Well, we did meet, Captain. Just as you said we would.'

Lieutenant Soames knelt to unfasten Le Chaumareys' sword, but Bolitho said, 'Leave it. His was a bad cause, but he fought with honour.' He turned away, suddenly sick of the watching dead, their pathetic stillness. 'And cover him with his flag. His *proper* flag. He was no pirate!'

He saw Davy's body being carried to the gangway, and added, 'A moment longer and he would have seen *Argus* taken. Enough prize-money even for his debts perhaps.'

As they climbed across the trapped water between the drifting hulls Bolitho turned, startled, as some of the seamen gathered to cheer him. He looked at Herrick, but he shrugged and gave a sad smile.

'I know how you feel, sir, but they are glad to be alive. It is their way of thanking you.'

Bolitho touched his arm. 'Survival? I suppose it is a fair cause for battle.' He forced a smile. 'And for winning.'

Herrick picked up his hat and handed it to him. 'I'll set the people to work, sir. The pumps sound too busy for my liking.'

Bolitho nodded and walked slowly towards the stern, his shoes catching at splinters and broken cordage. By the taffrail he paused and looked wearily along his command, at the broken planking and stained decks, the figures which were picking their way amidst the debris, more like survivors than victors.

Then he leaned back and loosened his neckcloth, and shook open his best dress coat which was torn and slashed in a dozen places.

Above his head the flag was flapping more easily, the sudden squall having passed on as quickly as it had arrived to save them from *Argus*'s great guns. But for it . . .

He looked round, suddenly anxious, but saw Mudge in his place near the helm, cutting at a piece of cheese with a small knife which he had fished from one of his pockets. He looked very old in the dusty sunlight. Little Penn was squatting on a gun truck, having his wrist bandaged, and dabbing at his nose which had started to bleed when a charge had exploded prematurely nearby.

Bolitho watched them with something like love. Mudge and Penn. Age and innocence.

There was Keen, speaking with Soames, and looking very strained. But a man now.

Feet crunched on the debris, and he saw Noddall approaching him cautiously, a jug of wine clasped against his chest.

'I am afraid I can't yet find the glasses, sir.' He kept his eyes fixed on Bolitho's face, and had probably had them shut as he had groped past some of the horror below.

Bolitho held the jug to his lips and said, 'But this is some of my best wine.'

Noddall dabbed his eyes and smiled nervously. 'Aye, sir. All of it. The rest was destroyed by the battle.'

Bolitho let the wine fill his mouth, savouring it. Needing it. They had come a long way since that shop in St. James's Street, he thought.

And in a few weeks they would be ready again. The missing faces would still be remembered, but without the pain which even now was getting stronger. Terror would emerge as bravado, and courage be recalled as duty. He smiled bitterly, remembering the words from so long ago. *In the King's name.*

He heard Penn say in his squeaky voice, 'I was a bit frightened, Mr. Mudge.' An awkward pause. 'Just a *bit*.'

Old Mudge looked across the deck and held Bolitho's gaze. 'Frightened, boy? Gawd, 'e'll never make a cap'n, will 'e, sir?'

Bolitho smiled, sharing the moment with Mudge alone. For he knew, better than most, that the truth of battle was not for children.

Then he looked along his command again, at the gleaming shoulder of the proud figurehead below the bowsprit.

Undine was the real victor, he thought, and he was suddenly grateful to have her to himself.

Epilogue

Lieutenant Thomas Herrick stepped into the stern cabin and tucked his hat beneath his arm.

'You sent for me, sir?'

Bolitho was standing by the open windows, his hands on a sill, watching the weed on the sea-bed and tiny, bright fish darting around the motionless rudder.

It was afternoon, and along the shoreline of Pendang Bay the trees and green fronds waved and shone in a dozen hues to a steady breeze. Good sailing weather, he thought absently, but not for *Undine*. Not just yet.

He turned and gestured to a chair. 'Sit down, Thomas.'

He saw Herrick's gaze resting on the opened despatches which had been brought aboard that day. A brig from Madras. Orders and news.

'Another Indiaman will be arriving shortly, Thomas. This despatch is from the Admiral Commanding the Inshore Squadron. He is sending fresh hands to replace some of those we lost in battle.'

How easily said. *Lost in battle.* He glanced slowly around the cabin, knowing that Herrick was watching him, sharing his memories.

There was little to show of the mauling the ship had suffered under Le Chaumareys' guns. Fresh paint covered the repaired timbers, and the smell of tar and wood-shavings lingered throughout the hull. A month and two days since they had gone alongside *Argus*, but despite the back-breaking work, and the rewards of seeing the ship looking her old self again, the pictures of the fight hung in Bolitho's mind as if it were yesterday.

And how they had worked. Perhaps, like himself, the rest of the company had needed it, if only to hold the memories at bay a little longer.

Small moments stood out when you least expected them. Midshipman Penn crouching down as a gun recoiled inboard, wreathed in smoke, while its crew dashed forward again with sponge and rammer. A man had been hurled to the deck in a wave of flying splinters. Had lain there staring unwinkingly at the sky. Penn had reached out to touch him and had tried to jump away as the man had reached out to seize his wrist. He must have died at that very instant. Bolitho did not remember seeing the incident at the time, but it had lurked in wait within his mind. And Armitage leading his squad of boarders after Davy had fallen under those plunging blades. The clumsy, awkward midshipman, blind with terror, yet gathering his few reserves of strength only to find they were not enough.

And after the battle, the smells and the sounds, not least the surgeon fighting-drunk and being dragged bodily to his sickbay by three of his men.

When the wild cheering had given way to the realisation of victory, they had faced up to their own immediate situation. Wounded to be tended, the dead to be buried, and the work begun without delay.

Looking back, it was surprising they had reached Pendang Bay at all, Bolitho thought. Fore and main lower yards badly sprung, the mainmast itself so splintered and pitted that it was only quick work on stays and rigging which kept it upright, the tasks had seemed unending. More than a dozen holes below the waterline had kept the hands working at the pumps through every watch, as with the battered *Argus* in tow they had crawled painfully towards the land and safety. The captured frigate had already sailed under jury-rig for a yard in India where she would be quickly refitted and included in the Company's own private fleet.

Herrick asked, 'Any further instructions, sir?'

Bolitho reached for a bottle of wine. 'It is confirmed that Pendang Bay will be exchanged for another station now held by the Dutch East India Company.' He looked up, seeing the astonishment in Herrick's eyes. 'Now that we have established the settlement, the Dutch are more than willing to make the exchange, apparently.'

He recalled with sudden clarity Rear Admiral Conway's face when the first despatch had been opened. Brought from Madras by Raymond himself.

He had said hoarsely, 'So it was all for nothing?'

Raymond had looked away. 'No, sir. The other settlement in the north is far more suitable to our requirements. Sir Montagu Strang has explained. You will see that your part in all this is highly thought of.'

Later, when Raymond had left the room, Conway had said, 'Highly thought of. But a *new* governor will be appointed.'

Bolitho had replied, 'I am sorry, sir. It is a bitter victory.'

'Bitter?' Surprisingly, he had laughed. 'This sort of work is more for shopkeepers than sailors, Bolitho. Remember that well.'

He pushed a goblet across the table and realised that Herrick was still awaiting an answer.

'Once our replacements have been signed on, we will maintain a local patrol until ordered otherwise.' He smiled gravely. 'I am temporarily the senior officer in these waters. Not too surprising, since *Undine* is the only King's ship!'

Herrick grinned. 'And well earned, sir. When I realised how you had put yourself inside the French captain's mind, I—'

Bolitho looked away. 'If the wind had dropped, Thomas, you might think differently.'

'Lady Luck, sir?' The grin was broader.

There was a tap at the door and Penn stepped into the cabin.

'Mr. Davy's respects, sir. The Indiaman has just weighed. He said you wished to be told, sir.'

'Thank you.'

Bolitho waited for the door to close, his heart suddenly heavy. Even Penn had not helped. Keen now stood above as acting lieutenant, and Soames had replaced Davy. The same story. One dies, another profits.

Herrick said quietly, 'The Indiaman's sailing for Madras, sir. Our wounded will get better treatment there.'

Bolitho picked up his hat. 'We'll see her off.'

The sun across the quarterdeck was harsh enough, but in the steady offshore wind felt less severe as with Herrick he stood by the nettings to watch the deep-hulled Indiaman spreading her topsails, her paintwork and company flag very bright against the land.

Bolitho looked along *Undine*'s deck and saw the hands pausing in their work to watch the big ship as she tilted to the pressure, her hull shining while she continued to tack clear of the anchorage. Thinking of home perhaps, where the Indiaman would eventually make her landfall. Or of old friends lying bandaged within her fat hull, and of the others who were not here to see anything at all.

Bolitho beckoned to Penn. 'Your glass, if you please.'

Only once had he been able to see Viola Raymond alone since *Undine*'s return. Because of Raymond, or because she understood better than he that it was pointless to add to the pain of parting, Bolitho was still not certain.

'A fine ship, sir.' Herrick, too, had a glass. 'To think my old father wished me to go to sea in an Indiaman. Things would have been very different, I suppose.'

Bolitho tensed, seeing the pale green gown on the ornate poop, that same wide hat she had brought from Santa Cruz. He could hear her words to him, as if she had just spoken across the broad expanse of lively white-horses in the bay.

'If you come to London, please visit me. My husband has gained his promotion. What he wanted. What I thought *I* wanted, too.' She had squeezed his hand. 'I hope you got what you wanted from me?'

A gun boomed dully from the settlement, and another from the Indiaman's forecastle. Flags dipped in mutual respect.

Bolitho felt the ache returning. She was right. There must be no pain, only understanding. Peace, as after a great gale of wind. Something which they had seized, if only for a moment.

He thought of Raymond, going to a better appointment, while Conway returned to obscurity. It was impossible to fathom.

While he was much as before, except for that one moment. Or was he? By trying to mould him as she would have wished her husband, perhaps she had indeed changed him.

Penn called, 'Signal, sir! From *Wessex* to *Undine*.' He was straining his eye to a telescope to watch the flags breaking from the Indiaman's yards as she laboriously spelled out her message. *'Good luck go with you.'*

'Acknowledge.'

Bolitho kept his eye on the pale green figure. She was waving her hat slowly back and forth, her autumn hair blowing unrestricted to the wind.

Half to himself he said, 'And with you, my love.'

Some of the seamen were cheering and waving as the other vessel spread more canvas and heeled ponderously on a new tack.

Bolitho handed the telescope to a ship's boy and said, 'Well, Mr. Herrick?'

Herrick watched him and then nodded. 'Aye, sir. A glass of wine. I think we deserve it.'

Bolitho held on to the mood, keeping his eyes away from the Indiaman as she stood purposefully towards the headland.

'At least we have *earned* it.'

Allday watched them pass, seeing Bolitho's hand touch his side-pocket where he carried his watch. Just a brief gesture, but it told Allday a great deal. He walked to the nettings and stared after the departing Indiaman.

Sail away, my lady. You have left your mark, and for the better. But a closer embrace? He sighed. *Neither of them would have weathered it.*

Keen joined him by the bulwark.

'She makes a goodly sight, eh, Allday?'

Allday looked at him. 'Aye, sir.' *You don't know the half of it.* 'But a bit too good for a poor sailorman, sir.'

Keen walked away and began to pace the quarterdeck as he had watched Bolitho do a hundred times or more. He knew Allday was laughing at him, but did not care. He had been tested, and he had won through. That was more than he had dared to hope, and it was more than enough.

He paused by the skylight, hearing Bolitho's laugh and Herrick's quiet rejoinder.

And he had shared all of it with them.

When he looked again for the Indiaman she had slipped past the headland and gone from view.

He started to pace the deck once more. Acting-Lieutenant Valentine Keen, of His Majesty's frigate *Undine*, was content.

Richard

1756

Born Falmouth, son of James Bolitho

1768

Entered the King's service as a midshipman on 'MANXMAN' [80]

1772–73

Midshipman 'GORGON' [74]. (see 'Richard Bolitho-Midshipman' and 'Midshipman Bolitho and the Avenger')

1774

Promotion Lieutenant 'DESTINY' [28]

1775–77

Lieutenant 'TROJAN' [80] during the American Revolution. Later appointed prizemaster (see 'In Gallant Company')

1778

Promoted Commander 'SPARROW' [18] Battle of the Chesapeake (see 'Sloop of War')

1782

Promoted Captain 'PHALAROPE' [32]. West Indies. Battle of Saintes (see 'To Glory We Steer')

1784

Captain 'UNDINE' [32]. India and East Indies (see 'Command a King's Ship')